THE BEST
SCIENCE FICTION
AND FANTASY
OF THE YEAR

Other books edited by Jonathan Strahan:

The New Space Opera (with Gardner Dozois)
Best Short Novels: 2007
Eidolon (with Jeremy G Byrne)
Fantasy: The Very Best of 2005
Science Fiction: The Very Best of 2005
Best Short Novels: 2006
Best Short Novels: 2005
Fantasy: Best of 2004 (with Karen Haber)
Science Fiction: Best of 2004 (with Karen Haber)
Best Short Novels: 2004
The Locus Awards: Thirty Years of the Best in Fantasy and Science Fiction(with Charles N. Brown)
Science Fiction: Best of 2003 (with Karen Haber)
The Year's Best Australian Science Fiction and Fantasy Volume: 2 (with Jeremy G Byrne)
The Year's Best Australian Science Fiction and Fantasy Volume: 1 (with Jeremy G Byrne)

THE BEST
SCIENCE FICTION
AND FANTASY
OF THE YEAR

VOLUME ONE

EDITED BY JONATHAN STRAHAN

NIGHT SHADE BOOKS
SAN FRANCISCO

The Best Science Fiction and Fantasy of the Year Volume One © 2007 by Jonathan Strahan

This edition of *The Best Science Fiction and Fantasy of the Year Volume One* © 2007 by Night Shade Books

Cover art © 2006 by Stephan Martiniere
Cover design by Claudia Noble
Interior layout and design by Jeremy Lassen

Introduction, story notes and arrangement
by Jonathan Strahan. © 2007 Jonathan Strahan.

Page 479 represents an extension of this copyright page.

First Edition

ISBN: 978-1-59780-068-6
Printed in Canada

Night Shade Books
Please visit us on the web at
www.nightshadebooks.com

For Charles, friend and mentor, without whom it not only wouldn't be possible, it wouldn't be fun.

Acknowledgements

Any book like this one is as much the product of a small community of friends, family, and colleagues as it is the work of one person. This year I'd especially like to thank my new editors and publishers, Jason Williams and Jeremy Lassen, who have been a delight to work with, and whose confidence I greatly appreciate, and to Claudia Noble for her great work on the cover. Special thanks also go to CHARLES, Liza, Kirsten, Carolyn, Tim, Karlyn, Amelia at Locus Press, who really did come through for me this year.

As always, I'd like to thank my agent Howard Morhaim; Justin Ackroyd, who has long been a vital supporter of my work; Jack Dann, anthology guru, pal and confidante; my *Locus* colleagues Nick Gevers and Rich Horton, who have always been there to discuss the best short fiction of the year when I needed it most; and Trevor Quachri and Brian Bieniowski at Dell Magazines and Gordon Van Gelder at Spilogale, Inc. who made sure I got my fix every month. Thanks also to the following good friends and colleagues without whom this book would have been much poorer, and much less fun to do: Lou Anders, Ellen Datlow, Gardner Dozois, Kelly Link, Gavin Grant, Sean Williams, and all of the book's contributors.

And, last but not least, the big ones. Every year I pour countless hours into reading and editing, all accompanied by mumbling and exclamations. And each year Marianne, Jessica and Sophie let it happen. Without them this book, and all of the others, wouldn't exist.

CONTENTS

INTRODUCTION

JONATHAN STRAHAN

Welcome to *The Best Science Fiction and Fantasy of the Year*. It's difficult to believe, but it's been almost sixty years since the first clearly *genre* year's best annual hit the bookstores. Back in 1949, the first issue of *The Magazine of Fantasy and Science Fiction* had just hit the newsstands and both *Weird Tales* and *Amazing Stories* had either completed or were about to complete their first quarter-centuries of publication. The short fiction field, for science fiction and fantasy, was booming, was a vital part of the explosion of pulp fiction magazines. It must have seemed impossible that it would ever end. And yet, it did.

By the early 1950s, genre science fiction and fantasy began to make the move from magazine to book publication, mostly in the hands of small presses, often by collecting together stories from the pulps of the 1930s and 1940s into fix-ups or collections. An important step in that process happened when Raymond J. Healy and J. Francis McComas edited *Adventures in Time and Space*, an anthology that collected a number of the classic stories of that first Golden Age of Science Fiction. It was important because gathering those stories together into one of the first ever science fiction anthologies helped to confirm those stories as part of science fiction's essential canon of great works.

That role, of identifying science fiction and fantasy's canon of great works, was picked up by a number of reprint anthologies and anthology series over the years, but it's a role that, it seems to me, has most clearly fallen to the year's best anthology. And it's something you can see happening, even in that first year's best annual. When Everett F. Bleiler and T. E. Dikty edited *The Best Science-Fiction Stories 1949* they featured stories by Ray Bradbury, Poul Anderson, and Isaac Asimov. Of those stories, at least one, Bradbury's "Mars Is Heaven!" became a permanent part of SF's canon, and even now we pick it up to see what stories were considered important back then. Bleiler and Dikty edited six more annuals, but arguably the most distinguished annual of the period was Judith

Merril's classic *SF: The Year's Greatest Science Fiction and Fantasy,* which started in 1956 (with an introduction by Orson Welles!) and ran for twelve years. *The Encyclopedia of Science Fiction* describes her anthologies as "always lively, with an emphasis on stories of wit and literacy". It also was the first year's best annual to clearly combine science fiction and fantasy in one volume, and is very much an inspiration for the book you now hold.

By the time Merril edited her final year's best annual in 1968 the first Golden Age of Science Fiction was clearly over, most of the pulp magazines had seen their heyday and we had solidly begun to move into the age of the novel. And yet short fiction, which had always been the laboratory of the field, where new writers learned their craft and where the best writers in the field pushed its boundaries, didn't cease to exist or become any less important. Harlan Ellison's *Dangerous Visions* had appeared the year before in 1967, the New Wave was well and truly established, and great short fiction continued to appear everywhere. Editors like Lester Del Rey and Donald Wollheim continued to assemble year's best annuals and in 1972 Terry Carr went solo with *The Best Science Fiction of the Year.* His annuals, along with those of Gardner Dozois, who began editing year's best annuals solo in 1976, defined the next quarter-century of science fiction and fantasy, assembling the year's best stories in some of the most impressive annuals the field has yet seen. Their approaches, though, changed in the mid-1980s, when Dozois began to edit his mammoth *The Year's Best Science Fiction* series. Where Dozois favored an enormous volume that featured as broad a smorgasbord of fiction as the field could offer, Carr kept his volumes shorter, featuring fewer, arguably more essential selections.

As a young reader, it was Carr's volumes that made the greatest impact on me, and who inspired this series of annuals. While I strongly responded to the catholic tastes of Merril's anthologies, and appreciated the broadness of Dozois', it was Carr's volumes that led me through the '70s and '80s, his books that I sought out to read and enjoy, and then to learn from when I began to edit year's best annuals myself. His *The Best Science Fiction of the Year* was the template for the *Science Fiction: The Best of* books I co-edited, his *Year's Best Fantasy* inspired the *Fantasy: The Best of* books, and his *The Best Science Fiction Novellas of the Year* was and is the inspiration behind my *Best Short Novels* anthologies.

And then there is this series, *The Best Science Fiction and Fantasy of the Year.* I think that we're living through a new golden age of the science fiction and fantasy short story. Whether or not the *business* of publishing short fiction is thriving, the *art* of it has never been healthier. Each year an incredible array of publications—websites, ezines, chapbooks, small press 'zines, specialist anthologies, mass-market collections—are making new short fiction available to readers in staggering numbers. In 2005 alone, trade journal *Locus* estimated over 3,000 new genre short stories were published, and that number is likely far short of the true number. Those stories reflect a creative flowering the like of which the field hasn't seen since the Golden Age of Campbell and *Astounding,* with established and new writers pushing the boundaries in new and exciting ways, creating new movements and refining old ones. Whether or not any of these movements prove to have longevity or make a substantial impact on the field, they are symptomatic of a restlessness in readers and writers, who are looking for something fresh, something contemporary, something that stretches the boundaries of science fiction and fantasy, that is both respectful of the field's grand traditions and is looking eagerly for what comes next.

It seems to me there is a place, then, for a book like this one. A book that brings together the best science fiction *and* the best fantasy stories of the year in one single volume. A book that is aware of, but not trapped, by the history of the genre; a book that has both eyes on the future, but hasn't forgotten the past. A book that hopefully combines the broad tastes of a Judith Merril with the editorial eye of a Terry Carr, while being its own beast too. I can only hope you'll agree.

Before you move on to the heart of this book, the stories, I'd like to thank Charles N. Brown and the team at Locus Press, who generously threw this editor a lifeline in 2006 when a publisher abruptly disappeared, and Jason Williams and Jeremy Lassen at Night Shade, who have enthusiastically embraced the vision for this anthology series. Without them, the book you're now holding would not exist.

And on to the stories. Here are some of the best and brightest science fiction and fantasy writers of our time doing what they do best, creating unforgettable stories. I hope you enjoy them as much as I did, and that you'll join me here again next year. I'm already reading for next year, and the stories I've seen!

Jonathan Strahan
Perth, Western Australia
November 2006

HOW TO TALK TO GIRLS AT PARTIES

NEIL GAIMAN

Science fiction has had a love affair with the stars since its very earliest days. In the powerful story that follows, Neil Gaiman gives us a chilling look into what might happen if the stars loved us back.

Gaiman is the award-winning author of the novels *Coraline, American Gods*, and *Anansi Boys*. His most recent book is collection *Fragile Things*. Upcoming is new collection *M is for Magic*.

"Come on," said Vic. "It'll be great."

"No, it won't," I said, although I'd lost this fight hours ago, and I knew it.

"It'll be brilliant," said Vic, for the hundredth time. "Girls! Girls! Girls!" He grinned with white teeth.

We both attended an all-boys' school in South London. While it would be a lie to say that we had no experience with girls—Vic seemed to have had many girlfriends, while I had kissed three of my sister's friends—it would, I think, be perfectly true to say that we both chiefly spoke to, interacted with, and only truly understood, other boys. Well, I did, anyway. It's hard to speak for someone else, and I've not seen Vic for thirty years. I'm not sure that I would know what to say to him now if I did.

We were walking the back-streets that used to twine in a grimy maze behind East Croydon station—a friend had told Vic about a party, and Vic was determined to go whether I liked it or not, and I didn't. But my parents were away that week at a conference, and I was Vic's guest at his house, so I was trailing along beside him.

"It'll be the same as it always is," I said. "After an hour you'll be off somewhere snogging the prettiest girl at the party, and I'll be in the kitchen listening to somebody's mum going on about politics or poetry or something."

"You just have to *talk* to them," he said. "I think it's probably that road at the end here." He gestured cheerfully, swinging the bag with the bottle in it.

"Don't you know?"

"Alison gave me directions and I wrote them on a bit of paper, but I left it on the hall table. S'okay. I can find it."

5

"How?" Hope welled slowly up inside me.

"We walk down the road," he said, as if speaking to an idiot child. "And we look for the party. Easy."

I looked, but saw no party: just narrow houses with rusting cars or bikes in their concreted front gardens; and the dusty glass fronts of newsagents, which smelled of alien spices and sold everything from birthday cards and second-hand comics to the kind of magazines that were so pornographic that they were sold already sealed in plastic bags. I had been there when Vic had slipped one of those magazines beneath his sweater, but the owner caught him on the pavement outside and made him give it back.

We reached the end of the road and turned into a narrow street of terraced houses. Everything looked very still and empty in the summer's evening. "It's all right for you," I said. "They fancy you. You don't actually *have* to talk to them." It was true: one urchin grin from Vic and he could have his pick of the room.

"Nah. S'not like that. You've just got to talk."

The times I had kissed my sister's friends I had not spoken to them. They had been around while my sister was off doing something elsewhere, and they had drifted into my orbit, and so I had kissed them. I do not remember any talking. I did not know what to say to girls, and I told him so.

"They're just girls," said Vic. "They don't come from another planet."

As we followed the curve of the road around, my hopes that the party would prove unfindable began to fade: a low pulsing noise, music muffled by walls and doors, could be heard from a house up ahead. It was eight in the evening, not that early if you aren't yet sixteen, and we weren't. Not quite.

I had parents who liked to know where I was, but I don't think Vic's parents cared that much. He was the youngest of five boys. That in itself seemed magical to me: I merely had two sisters, both younger than I was, and I felt both unique and lonely. I had wanted a brother as far back as I could remember. When I turned thirteen, I stopped wishing on falling stars or first stars, but back when I did, a brother was what I had wished for.

We went up the garden path, crazy paving leading us past a hedge and a solitary rosebush to a pebble-dashed facade. We rang the doorbell, and the door was opened by a girl. I could not have told you how old she was, which was one of the things about girls I had begun to hate: when you start out as kids you're just boys and girls, going through time at the same speed, and you're all five, or seven, or eleven together. And then one day there's a lurch and the girls just sort of sprint off into the future ahead of you, they know all about everything, and they have periods and breasts and make-up and God-only-knew-what-else—for I certainly didn't. The diagrams in biology textbooks were no substitute for being, in a very real sense, young adults. And the girls of our age were.

Vic and I weren't young adults, and I was beginning to suspect that even when I started needing to shave every day, instead of once every couple of weeks, I would still be way behind.

The girl said, "Hello?"

Vic said, "We're friends of Alison's." We had met Alison, all freckles and orange hair and a wicked smile, in Hamburg, on a German Exchange. The exchange organisers had sent some girls with us, from a local girls' school, to balance the sexes. The girls, our age, more or less, were raucous and funny, and had more or less adult boyfriends with cars and jobs and motorbikes and—in the case of one girl with crooked teeth and a raccoon coat, who spoke to me about it sadly at the end of a party in Hamburg, in, of course, the kitchen—a wife and kids.

"She isn't here," said the girl at the door. "No Alison."

"Not to worry," said Vic, with an easy grin. "I'm Vic. This is Enn." A beat, and then the girl smiled back at him. Vic had a bottle of white wine in a plastic bag, removed from his parents' kitchen cabinet. "Where should I put this, then?"

She stood out of the way, letting us enter. "There's a kitchen in the back," she said. "Put it on the table there, with the other bottles." She had golden, wavy hair, and she was very beautiful. The hall was dim in the twilight, but I could see that she was beautiful.

"What's your name, then?" said Vic.

She told him it was Stella, and he grinned his crooked white grin and told her that that had to be the prettiest name he had ever heard. Smooth bastard. And what was worse was that he said it like he meant it.

Vic headed back to drop off the wine in the kitchen, and I looked into the front room, where the music was coming from. There were people dancing in there. Stella walked in, and she started to dance, swaying to the music all alone, and I watched her.

This was during the early days of punk. On our own record-players we would play the Adverts and the Jam, the Stranglers and the Clash and the Sex Pistols. At other people's parties you'd hear ELO or 10cc or even Roxy Music. Maybe some Bowie, if you were lucky. During the German Exchange, the only LP that we had all been able to agree on was Neil Young's *Harvest*, and his song "Heart of Gold" had threaded through the trip like a refrain: *like him, we'd crossed the ocean for a heart of gold...*

The music that was playing in that front room wasn't anything I recognized. It sounded a bit like a German electronic pop group called Kraftwerk, and a bit like an LP I'd been given for my last birthday, of strange sounds made by the BBC Radiophonic Workshop. The music had a beat, though, and the half-dozen girls in that room were moving gently to it, although I was only looking at Stella. She shone.

Vic pushed past me, into the room. He was holding a can of lager. "There's booze back in the kitchen," he told me. He wandered over to Stella and he began to talk to her. I couldn't hear what they were saying over the music, but I knew that there was no room for me in that conversation.

I didn't like beer, not back then. I went off to see if there was something I wanted to drink. On the kitchen table stood a large bottle of Coca-Cola, and I poured myself a plastic tumblerful, and I didn't dare say anything to the pair of girls who were talking in the underlit kitchen. They were animated, and utterly lovely. Each of them had very black skin and glossy hair and movie-star clothes, and their accents were foreign, and each of them was out of my league.

I wandered, Coke in hand.

The house was deeper than it looked, larger and more complex than the two-up two-down model I had imagined. The rooms were underlit—I doubt there was a bulb of more than forty watts in the building—and each room I went into was inhabited: in my memory, inhabited only by girls. I did not go upstairs.

A girl was the only occupant of the conservatory. Her hair was so fair it was white, and long, and straight, and she sat at the glass-topped table, her hands clasped together, staring at the garden outside, and the gathering dusk. She seemed wistful.

"Do you mind if I sit here?" I asked, gesturing with my cup. She shook her head, and then followed it up with a shrug, to indicate that it was all the same to her. I sat down.

Vic walked past the conservatory door. He was talking to Stella, but he looked in at me, sitting at the table, wrapped in shyness and awkwardness, and he opened and closed his hand in a parody of a speaking mouth. *Talk*. Right.

"Are you from round here?" I asked the girl.

She shook her head. She wore a low-cut silvery top, and I tried not to stare at the swell of her breasts.

I said, "What's your name? I'm Enn."

"Wain's Wain," she said, or something that sounded like it. "I'm a second."

"That's uh. That's a different name."

She fixed me with huge liquid eyes. "It indicates that my progenitor was also Wain, and that I am obliged to report back to her. I may not breed."

"Ah. Well. Bit early for that anyway, isn't it?"

She unclasped her hands, raised them above the table, spread her fingers. "You see?" The little finger on her left hand was crooked, and it bifurcated at the top, splitting into two smaller fingertips. A minor deformity. "When I was finished a decision was needed. Would I be retained, or eliminated? I was fortunate that the decision was with me. Now, I travel, while my more perfect sisters remain at home in stasis. They were firsts. I am a second.

"Soon I must return to Wain, and tell her all I have seen. All my impressions of this place of yours."

"I don't actually live in Croydon," I said. "I don't come from here." I wondered if she was American. I had no idea what she was talking about.

"As you say," she agreed, "neither of us comes from here." She folded her six-fingered left hand beneath her right, as if she was tucking it out of sight. "I had expected it to be bigger, and cleaner, and more colorful. But still, it is a jewel."

She yawned, covered her mouth with her right hand, only for a moment, before it was back on the table again. "I grow weary of the journeying, and I wish sometimes that it would end. On a street in Rio, at Carnival, I saw them on a bridge, golden and tall and insect-eyed and winged, and elated I almost ran to greet them, before I saw that they were only people in costumes. I said to Hola Colt, 'Why do they try so hard to look like us?' and Hola Colt replied, 'Because they hate themselves, all shades of pink and brown, and so small'. It is what I experience, even me, and I am not grown. It is like a world of children, or of elves." Then she smiled, and said, "It was a good thing they could not any of them see Hola Colt."

"Um," I said, "do you want to dance?"

She shook her head immediately. "It is not permitted," she said. "I can do nothing that might cause damage to property. I am Wain's."

"Would you like something to drink, then?"

"Water," she said.

I went back to the kitchen and poured myself another Coke, and filled a cup with water from the tap. From the kitchen back to the hall, and from there into the conservatory, but now it was quite empty.

I wondered if the girl had gone to the toilet, and if she might change her mind about dancing later. I walked back to the front room and stared in. The place was filling up. There were more girls dancing, and several lads I didn't know, who looked a few years older than me and Vic. The lads and the girls all kept their distance, but Vic was holding Stella's hand as they danced, and when the song ended he put an arm around her, casually, almost proprietorially, to make sure that nobody else cut in.

I wondered if the girl I had been talking to in the conservatory was now upstairs, as she did not appear to be on the ground floor.

I walked into the living room, which was across the hall from the room where the people were dancing, and I sat down on the sofa. There was a girl sitting there already. She had dark hair, cut short and spiky, and a nervous manner.

Talk, I thought. "Um, this mug of water's going spare," I told her, "if you want it?"

She nodded, and reached out her hand and took the mug, extremely carefully, as if she were unused to taking things, as if she could neither trust her vision nor her hands.

"I love being a tourist," she said, and smiled, hesitantly. She had a gap between her two front teeth, and she sipped the tap water as if she were an adult sipping a fine wine. "The last tour, we went to sun, and we swam in sunfire pools with the whales. We heard their histories and we shivered in the chill of the outer places, then we swam deepward where the heat churned and comforted us.

"I wanted to go back. This time, I wanted it. There was so much I had not seen. Instead we came to world. Do you like it?"

"Like what?"

She gestured vaguely to the room—the sofa, the armchairs, the curtains, the unused gas fire.

"It's all right, I suppose."

"I told them I did not wish to visit world," she said. "My parent-teacher was unimpressed. 'You will have much to learn,' it told me. I said, 'I could learn more in sun, again. Or in the deeps. Jessa spun webs between galaxies. I want to do that.'

"But there was no reasoning with it, and I came to world. Parent-teacher engulfed me, and I was here, embodied in a decaying lump of meat hanging on a frame of calcium. As I incarnated I felt things deep inside me, fluttering and pumping and squishing. It was my first experience with pushing air through the mouth, vibrating the vocal chords on the way, and I used it to tell parent-teacher that I wished that I would die, which it acknowledged was the inevitable exit strategy from world."

There were black worry beads wrapped around her wrist, and she fiddled with them as she spoke. "But knowledge is there, in the meat," she said, "and I am resolved to learn from it."

We were sitting close at the centre of the sofa now. I decided I should put an arm around her, but casually. I would extend my arm along the back of the sofa and eventually sort of creep it down, almost imperceptibly, until it was touching her. She said, "The thing with the liquid in the eyes, when the world blurs. Nobody told me, and I still do not understand. I have touched the folds of the Whisper and pulsed and flown with the tachyon swans, and I still do not understand."

She wasn't the prettiest girl there, but she seemed nice enough, and she was a girl, anyway. I let my arm slide down a little, tentatively, so that it made contact with her back, and she did not tell me to take it away.

Vic called to me then, from the doorway. He was standing with his arm around Stella, protectively, waving at me. I tried to let him know, by shaking my head, that I was on to something, but he called my name, and, reluctantly, I got up from the sofa, and walked over to the door. "What?"

"Er. Look. The party," said Vic, apologetically. "It's not the one I thought it was. I've been talking to Stella and I figured it out. Well, she sort of explained it to me. We're at a different party."

"Christ. Are we in trouble? Do we have to go?"

Stella shook her head. He leaned down and kissed her, gently, on the lips. "You're just happy to have me here, aren't you, darlin'?"

"You know I am," she told him.

He looked from her back to me, and he smiled his white smile: roguish, loveable, a little bit Artful Dodger, a little bit wide-boy Prince Charming. "Don't worry. They're all tourists here anyway. It's a foreign exchange thing, innit? Like when we all went to Germany."

"It is?"

"Enn. You got to *talk* to them. And that means you got to listen to them too. You understand?"

"I *did*. I already talked to a couple of them."

"You getting anywhere?"

"I was till you called me over."

"Sorry about that. Look, I just wanted to fill you in. Right?"

And he patted my arm and he walked away with Stella. Then, together, the two of them went up the stairs.

Understand me, all the girls at that party, in the twilight, were lovely; they all had perfect faces, but, more important than that, they had whatever strangeness of proportion, of oddness or humanity it is that makes a beauty something more than a shop-window dummy. Stella was the most lovely of any of them, but she, of course, was Vic's, and they were going upstairs together, and that was just how things would always be.

There were several people now sitting on the sofa, talking to the gap-toothed girl. Someone told a joke, and they all laughed. I would have had to push my way in there to sit next to her again, and it didn't look like she was expecting me back, or cared that I had gone, so I wandered out into the hall. I glanced in at the dancers, and found myself wondering where the music was coming from. I couldn't see a record-player, or speakers.

From the hall I walked back to the kitchen.

Kitchens are good at parties. You never need an excuse to be there, and, on the good side, at this party I couldn't see any signs of someone's mum. I inspected the various bottles and cans on the kitchen table, then I poured a half an inch of Pernod into the bottom of my plastic cup, which I filled to the top with Coke. I dropped in a couple of ice-cubes, and took a sip, relishing the sweet-shop tang of the drink.

"What's that you're drinking?" A girl's voice.

"It's Pernod," I told her. "It tastes like aniseed balls, only it's alcoholic." I didn't say that I'd only tried it because I'd heard someone in the crowd ask for a Pernod on a live Velvet Underground LP.

"Can I have one?" I poured another Pernod, topped it off with Coke, passed it to her. Her hair was a coppery auburn, and it tumbled around her head in ringlets. It's not a hair style you see much now, but you saw it a lot back then.

"What's your name?" I asked.

"Triolet," she said.

"Pretty name," I told her, although I wasn't sure that it was. She was pretty, though.

"It's a verse form," she said, proudly. "Like me."

"You're a poem?"

She smiled, and looked down and away, almost bashfully. Her profile was almost flat—a perfect Grecian nose that came down from her forehead in a straight line. We did *Antigone* in the school theatre the previous year. I was the messenger who brings Creon the news of Antigone's death. We wore half-masks that made us look like that. I thought of that play, looking at her face, in the kitchen, and I thought of Barry Smith's drawings of women in the *Conan* comics: five years later I would have thought of the Pre-Raphaelites, of Jane Morris and Lizzie Siddall. But I was only fifteen, then.

"You're a poem?" I repeated.

She chewed her lower lip. "If you want. I am a poem, or I am a pattern, or a race of people whose world was swallowed by the sea."

"Isn't it hard to be three things at the same time?"

"What's your name?"

"Enn."

"So you are Enn," she said. "And you are a male. And you are a biped. Is it hard to be three things at the same time?"

"But they aren't different things. I mean, they aren't contradictory." It was a word I had read many times but never said aloud before that night, and I put the stresses in the wrong places. *Contradictory.*

She wore a thin dress, made of a white, silky fabric. Her eyes were a pale green, a color that would now make me think of tinted contact lenses; but this was thirty years ago: things were different then. I remember wondering about Vic and Stella, upstairs. By now, I was sure that they were in one of the bedrooms, and I envied Vic so much it almost hurt.

Still, I was talking to this girl, even if we were talking nonsense, even if her name wasn't really Triolet (my generation had not been given hippy names: all the Rainbows and the Sunshines and the Moons, they were only six, seven, eight years old back then). She said, "We knew that it would soon be over, and so we put it all into a poem, to tell the universe who we were, and why we were here, and what we said and did and thought and dreamed and yearned for. We wrapped our dreams in words and patterned the words so that they would live forever, unforgettable. Then we sent the poem as a pattern of flux, to wait in the heart of a star, beaming out its message in pulses and bursts and fuzzes across the electromagnetic spectrum, until the time when, on worlds a thousand sun-systems distant, the pattern would be decoded and read, and it would become a poem once again."

"And then what happened?"

She looked at me with her green eyes, and it was as if she stared out at me from her own Antigone half-mask; but as if her pale green eyes were just a different, deeper, part of the mask. "You cannot hear a poem without it changing you," she told me. "They heard it, and it colonized them. It inherited them and it inhabited them, its rhythms becoming part of the way that they thought; its images permanently transmuting their metaphors; its verses, its outlook, its aspirations becoming their lives. Within a generation their children would be born already knowing the poem, and, sooner rather than later, as these things go, there were no more children born. There was no need for them, not any longer. There was only a poem, which took flesh and walked and spread itself across the vastness of the known."

I edged closer to her, so I could feel my leg pressing against hers. She seemed to welcome it: she put her hand on my arm, affectionately, and I felt a smile spreading across my face.

"There are places that we are welcomed," said Triolet, "and places where we are regarded as a noxious weed, or as a disease, something immediately to be quarantined and eliminated. But where does contagion end and art begin?"

"I don't know," I said, still smiling. I could hear the unfamiliar music as it pulsed and scattered and boomed in the front room.

She leaned into me then and—I suppose it was a kiss... I suppose. She pressed her lips to my lips, anyway, and then, satisfied, she pulled back, as if she had now marked me as her own.

"Would you like to hear it?" she asked, and I nodded, unsure what she was offering me, but certain that I needed anything she was willing to give me.

She began to whisper something in my ear. It's the strangest thing about poetry—you can tell it's poetry, even if you don't speak the language. You can hear Homer's Greek without understanding a word, and you still know it's poetry. I've heard Polish poetry, and Inuit poetry, and I knew what it was without knowing. Her whisper was like that. I didn't know the language, but her words washed through me, perfect, and in my mind's eye I saw towers of glass and diamond; and people with eyes of pale green; and unstoppable, beneath every syllable, I could feel the relentless advance of the ocean.

Perhaps I kissed her properly. I don't remember. I know I wanted to.

And then Vic was shaking me violently. "Come on!" he was shouting. "Quickly. Come on!"

In my head I began to come back from a thousand miles away.

"Idiot. Come on. Just get a move on," he said, and he swore at me. There was fury in his voice.

For the first time that evening I recognized one of the songs being played in the front room. A sad saxophone wail over a cascade of liquid chords, followed by a man's voice singing cut-up lyrics about the sons of the silent age. I wanted to stay and hear the song.

She said, "I am not finished. There is yet more of me."

"Sorry, love," said Vic, but he wasn't smiling any longer. "There'll be another time," and he grabbed me by the elbow and he twisted and pulled, forcing me from the room. I did not resist. I knew from experience that Vic could beat the stuffing out me if he got it into his head to do so. He wouldn't do it unless he was upset or angry, but he was angry now.

Out into the front hall. As Vic pulled open the door, I looked back one last time, over my shoulder, hoping to see Triolet in the doorway to the kitchen, but she was not there. I saw Stella, though, at the top of the stairs. She was staring down at Vic, and I saw her face.

This all happened thirty years ago. I have forgotten much, and I will forget more, and in the end I will forget everything; yet, if I have any certainty of life beyond death, it is all wrapped up not in psalms or hymns, but in this one thing alone: I cannot believe that I will ever forget that moment, or forget the expression on Stella's face as she watched Vic, hurrying away from her. Even in death I shall remember that.

Her clothes were in disarray, and there was makeup smudged across her face, and her eyes—

You wouldn't want to make a universe angry. I bet an angry universe would look at you with eyes like that.

We ran then, me and Vic, away from the party and the tourists and the twilight, ran as if a lightning storm was on our heels, a mad helter-skelter dash down the confusion of streets, threading through the maze, and we did not look back, and we did not stop until we could not breathe; and then we stopped and panted, unable to run any longer. We were in pain. I held onto a wall, and Vic threw up, hard and long, in the gutter.

He wiped his mouth.

"She wasn't a—" He stopped.

He shook his head.

Then he said, "You know… I think there's a thing. When you've gone as far as you dare. And if you go any further, you wouldn't be *you* anymore? You'd be the person who'd done *that*? The places you just can't go…. I think that happened to me tonight."

I thought I knew what he was saying. "Screw her, you mean?" I said.

He rammed a knuckle hard against my temple, and twisted it violently. I wondered if I was going to have to fight him—and lose—but after a moment he lowered his hand and moved away from me, making a low, gulping noise.

I looked at him curiously, and I realized that he was crying: his face was scarlet; snot and tears ran down his cheeks. Vic was sobbing in the street, as unselfconsciously and heartbreakingly as a little boy. He walked away from me then, shoulders heaving, and he hurried down the road so he was in front of me and I could no longer see his face. I wondered what had occurred in that upstairs room to make him behave like that, to scare him so, and I could not even begin to guess.

The streetlights came on, one by one; Vic went on ahead, while I trudged down the street behind him in the dusk, my feet treading out the measure of a poem that, try as I might, I could not properly remember and would never be able to repeat.

EL REGALO

PETER S. BEAGLE

The relationships between brothers and sisters are often strange, fraught and unpredictable. In this charming tale Beagle gives us a glimpse into the life of a twelve-year-old girl and just what she's willing to do to save her stupid brother Marvyn the witch.

Peter S. Beagle is the author of the beloved classic *The Last Unicorn*, as well as the novels *A Fine and Private Place*, *The Innkeeper's Song*, and *Tamsin*. He has won the Hugo, Locus, and Mythopoeic Awards. His most recent book is collection *The Line Between*. Upcoming are two new novels, *Summerlong* and *I'm Afraid You've Got Dragons*.

"You can't kill him," Mr. Luke said. "Your mother wouldn't like it." After some consideration, he added, "I'd be rather annoyed myself."

"But wait," Angie said, in the dramatic tones of a television commercial for some miraculous mop. "There's more. I didn't tell you about the brandied cupcakes—"

"Yes, you did."

"And about him telling Jennifer Williams what I got her for her birthday, and she pitched a fit, because she had two of them already—"

"He meant well," her father said cautiously. "I'm pretty sure."

"And then when he finked to Mom about me and Orlando Cruz, and we weren't doing *anything*—"

"Nevertheless. No killing."

Angie brushed sweaty mouse-brown hair off her forehead and regrouped. "Can I at least maim him a little? Trust me, he's earned it."

"I don't doubt you," Mr. Luke agreed. "But you're fifteen, and Marvyn's eight. Eight and a half. You're bigger than he is, so beating him up isn't fair. When you're…oh, say, twenty-three, and he's sixteen and a half—okay, you can try it then. Not until."

Angie's wordless grunt might or might not have been assent. She started out of the room, but her father called her back, holding out his right hand. "Pinky-swear, kid." Angie eyed him warily, but hooked her little finger around his without

15

hesitation, which was a mistake. "You did that much too easily," her father said, frowning. "Swear by Buffy."

"What? You can't swear by a television show!"

"Where is that written? Repeat after me—'I swear by *Buffy the Vampire Slayer*—'"

"You really *don't* trust me!"

"'I swear by *Buffy the Vampire Slayer* that I will keep my hands off my baby brother—'"

"My baby brother, the monster! He's gotten worse since he started sticking that y in his name—"

"'—and I will stop calling him Ex-Lax—'"

"Come on, I only do that when he makes me really mad—"

"'—until he shall have attained the age of sixteen years and six months, after which time—'"

"After which time I get to pound him into marmalade. Deal. I can wait." She grinned; then turned self-conscious, making a performance of pulling down her upper lip to cover the shiny new braces. At the door, she looked over her shoulder and said lightly, "You are way too smart to be a father."

From behind his book, Mr. Luke answered, "I've often thought so myself." Then he added, "It's a Korean thing. We're all like that. You're lucky your mother isn't Korean, or you wouldn't have a secret to your name."

Angie spent the rest of the evening in her room, doing homework on the phone with Melissa Feldman, her best friend. Finished, feeling virtuously entitled to some low-fat chocolate reward, she wandered down the hall toward the kitchen, passing her brother's room on the way. Looking in—not because of any special interest, but because Marvyn invariably hung around her own doorway, gazing in aimless fascination at whatever she was doing, until shooed away—she saw him on the floor, playing with Milady, the gray, ancient family cat. Nothing unusual about that: Marvyn and Milady had been an item since he was old enough to realize that the cat wasn't something to eat. What halted Angie as though she had walked into a wall was that they were playing Monopoly, and that Milady appeared to be winning.

Angie leaned in the doorway, entranced and alarmed at the same time. Marvyn had to throw the dice for both Milady and himself, and the old cat was too riddled with arthritis to handle the pastel Monopoly money easily. But she waited her turn, and moved her piece—she had the silver top hat—very carefully, as though considering possible options. And she already had a hotel on Park Place.

Marvyn jumped up and slammed the door as soon as he noticed his sister watching the game, and Angie went on to liberate a larger-than-planned remnant of sorbet. Somewhere near the bottom of the container she finally managed to stuff what she'd just glimpsed deep in the part of her mind she called her "forget-tery." As she'd once said to her friend Melissa, "There's such a thing as too much information, and it is not going to get me. I am never going to know more than

I want to know about stuff. Look at the President."

For the next week or so Marvyn made a point of staying out of Angie's way, which was all by itself enough to put her mildly on edge. If she knew one thing about her brother, it was that the time to worry was when you didn't see him. All the same, on the surface things were peaceful enough, and continued so until the evening when Marvyn went dancing with the garbage.

The next day being pickup day, Mrs. Luke had handed him two big green plastic bags of trash for the rolling bins down the driveway. Marvyn had made enough of a fuss about the task that Angie stayed by the open front window to make sure that he didn't simply drop the bags in the grass, and vanish into one of his mysterious hideouts. Mrs. Luke was back in the living room with the news on, but Angie was still at the window when Marvyn looked around quickly, mumbled a few words she couldn't catch, and then did a thing with his left hand, so fast she saw no more than a blurry twitch. And the two garbage bags went dancing.

Angie's buckling knees dropped her to the couch under the window, though she never noticed it. Marvyn let go of the bags altogether, and they rocked alongside him—backwards, forwards, sideways, in perfect timing, with perfect steps, turning with him as though he were the star and they his backup singers. To Angie's astonishment, he was snapping his fingers and moonwalking, as she had never imagined he could do—and the bags were pushing out green arms and legs as the three of them danced down the driveway. When they reached the cans, Marvyn's partners promptly went limp and were nothing but plastic garbage bags again. Marvyn plopped them in, dusted his hands, and turned to walk back to the house.

When he saw Angie watching, neither of them spoke. Angie beckoned. They met at the door and stared at each other. Angie said only, "My room."

Marvyn dragged in behind her, looking everywhere and nowhere at once, and definitely not at his sister. Angie sat down on the bed and studied him: chubby and messy-looking, with an unmanageable sprawl of rusty-brown hair and an eyepatch meant to tame a wandering left eye. She said, "Talk to me."

"About what?" Marvyn had a deep, foggy voice for eight and a half—Mr. Luke always insisted that it had changed before Marvyn was born. "I didn't break your CD case."

"Yes, you did," Angie said. "But forget that. Let's talk about garbage bags. Let's talk about Monopoly."

Marvyn was utterly businesslike about lies: in a crisis he always told the truth, until he thought of something better. He said, "I'm warning you right now, you won't believe me."

"I never do. Make it a good one."

"Okay," Marvyn said. "I'm a witch."

When Angie could speak, she said the first thing that came into her head, which embarrassed her forever after. "You can't be a witch. You're a wizard, or a warlock or something." Like we're having a sane conversation, she thought.

Marvyn shook his head so hard that his eyepatch almost came loose. "Uh-uh! That's all books and movies and stuff. You're a man witch or you're a woman witch, that's it. I'm a man witch."

"You'll be a dead witch if you don't quit shitting me," Angie told him. But her brother knew he had her, and he grinned like a pirate (at home he often tied a bandanna around his head, and he was constantly after Mrs. Luke to buy him a parrot). He said, "You can ask Lidia. She was the one who knew."

Lidia del Carmen de Madero y Gomez had been the Lukes' housekeeper since well before Angie's birth. She was from Ciego de Avila in Cuba, and claimed to have changed Fidel Castro's diapers as a girl working for his family. For all her years—no one seemed to know her age; certainly not the Lukes—Lidia's eyes remained as clear as a child's, and Angie had on occasion nearly wept with envy of her beautiful wrinkled deep-dark skin. For her part, Lidia got on well with Angie, spoke Spanish with her mother, and was teaching Mr. Luke to cook Cuban food. But Marvyn had been hers since his infancy, beyond question or interference. They went to Spanish-language movies on Saturdays, and shopped together in the Bowen Street *barrio*.

"The one who knew," Angie said. "Knew what? Is Lidia a witch too?"

Marvyn's look suggested that he was wondering where their parents had actually found their daughter. "No, of course she's not a witch. She's a *santera*."

Angie stared. She knew as much about *Santeria* as anyone growing up in a big city with a growing population of Africans and South Americans—which wasn't much. Newspaper articles and television specials had informed her that *santeros* sacrificed chickens and goats and did…things with the blood. She tried to imagine Marvyn with a chicken, doing things, and couldn't. Not even Marvyn.

"So Lidia got you into it?" she finally asked. "Now you're a *santero* too?"

"Nah, I'm a witch, I told you." Marvyn's disgusted impatience was approaching critical mass.

Angie said, "Wicca? You're into the Goddess thing? There's a girl in my home room, Devlin Margulies, and she's a Wiccan, and that's all she talks about. Sabbats and esbats, and drawing down the moon, and the rest of it. She's got skin like a cheese-grater."

Marvyn blinked at her. "What's a Wiccan?" He sprawled suddenly on her bed, grabbing Milady as she hobbled in and pooting loudly on her furry stomach. "I already knew I could sort of mess with things—you remember the rubber duck, and that time at the baseball game?" Angie remembered. Especially the rubber duck. "Anyway, Lidia took me to meet this real old lady, in the farmers' market, she's even older than her, her name's Yemaya, something like that, she smokes this funny little pipe all the time. Anyway, she took hold of me, my face, and she looked in my eyes, and then she closed her eyes, and she just sat like that for so long!" He giggled. "I thought she'd fallen asleep, and I started to pull away, but Lidia wouldn't let me. So she sat like that, and she sat, and then she opened her eyes and she told me I was a witch, a *brujo*. And Lidia bought me a two-scoop ice-cream cone. Coffee and chocolate, with M&Ms."

"You won't have a tooth in your head by the time you're twelve." Angie didn't know what to say, what questions to ask. "So that's it? The old lady, she gives you witch lessons or something?"

"Nah—I told you, she's a big *santera*, that's different. I only saw her that one time. She kept telling Lidia that I had *el regalo*—I think that means the gift, she said that a lot—and I should keep practicing. Like you with the clarinet."

Angie winced. Her hands were small and stubby-fingered, and music slipped through them like rain. Her parents, sympathizing, had offered to cancel the clarinet lessons, but Angie refused. As she confessed to her friend Melissa, she had no skill at accepting defeat.

Now she asked, "So how do you practice? Boogieing with garbage bags?"

Marvyn shook his head. "That's getting old—so's playing board games with Milady. I was thinking maybe I could make the dishes wash themselves, like in *Beauty and the Beast*. I bet I could do that."

"You could enchant my homework," Angie suggested. "My algebra, for starters."

Her brother snorted. "Hey, I'm just a kid, I've got my limits! I mean, your homework?"

"Right," Angie said. "Right. Look, what about laying a major spell on Tim Hubley, the next time he's over here with Melissa? Like making his feet go flat so he can't play basketball—that's the only reason she likes him, anyway. Or—" her voice became slower and more hesitant "—what about getting Jake Petrakis to fall madly, wildly, totally in love with me? That'd be…funny."

Marvyn was occupied with Milady. "Girl stuff, who cares about all that? I want to be so good at soccer everybody'll want to be on my team—I want fat Josh Wilson to have patches over both eyes, so he'll leave me alone. I want Mom to order thin-crust pepperoni pizza every night, and I want Dad to—"

"No spells on Mom and Dad, not ever!" Angie was on her feet, leaning menacingly over him. "You got that, Ex-Lax? You mess with them even once, believe me, you'd better be one hella witch to keep me from strangling you. Understood?"

Marvyn nodded. Angie said, "Okay, I tell you what. How about practicing on Aunt Caroline when she comes next weekend?"

Marvyn's pudgy pirate face lit up at the suggestion. Aunt Caroline was their mother's older sister, celebrated in the Luke family for knowing everything about everything. A pleasant, perfectly decent person, her perpetual air of placid expertise would have turned a saint into a serial killer. Name a country, and Aunt Caroline had spent enough time there to know more about the place than a native; bring up a newspaper story, and without fail Aunt Caroline could tell you something about it that hadn't been in the paper; catch a cold, and Aunt Caroline could recite the maiden name of the top medical researcher in rhinoviruses' mother. (Mr. Luke said often that Aunt Caroline's motto was, "Say something, and I'll bet you're wrong.")

"Nothing dangerous," Angie commanded, "nothing scary. And nothing embarrassing or anything."

Marvyn looked sulky. "It's not going to be any fun that way."

"If it's too gross, they'll know you did it," his sister pointed out. "I would." Marvyn, who loved secrets and hidden identities, yielded.

During the week before Aunt Caroline's arrival, Marvyn kept so quietly to himself that Mrs. Luke worried about his health. Angie kept as close an eye on him as possible, but couldn't be at all sure what he might be planning—no more than he, she suspected. Once she caught him changing the TV channels without the remote; and once, left alone in the kitchen to peel potatoes and carrots for a stew, he had the peeler do it while he read the Sunday funnies. The apparent smallness of his ambitions relieved Angie's vague unease, lulling her into complacency about the big family dinner that was traditional on the first night of a visit from Aunt Caroline.

Aunt Caroline was, among other things, the sort of woman incapable of going anywhere without attempting to buy it. Her own house was jammed to the attic with sightseer souvenirs from all over the world: children's toys from Slovenia, sculptures from Afghanistan, napkin rings from Kenya shaped like lions and giraffes, legions of brass bangles, boxes and statues of gods from India, and so many Russian *matryoshka* dolls fitting inside each other that she gave them away as stocking-stuffers every Christmas. She never came to the table at the Lukes without bringing some new acquisition for approval; so dinner with Aunt Caroline, in Mr. Luke's words, was always Show and Tell time.

Her most recent hegira had brought her back to West Africa for the third or fourth time, and provided her with the most evil-looking doll Angie had ever seen. Standing beside Aunt Caroline's plate, it was about two feet high, with bat ears, too many fingers, and eyes like bright green marbles streaked with scarlet threads. Aunt Caroline explained rapturously that it was a fertility doll unique to a single Benin tribe, which Angie found impossible to credit. "No way!" she announced loudly. "Not for one minute am I even thinking about having babies with that thing staring at me! It doesn't even look pregnant, the way they do. No way in the world!"

Aunt Caroline had already had two of Mr. Luke's margaritas, and was working on a third. She replied with some heat that not all fertility figures came equipped with cannonball breasts, globular bellies and callipygous rumps—"Some of them are remarkably slender, even by Western standards!" Aunt Caroline herself, by anyone's standards, was built along the general lines of a chopstick.

Angie was drawing breath for a response when she heard her father say something in Korean behind her, and then her mother's soft gasp, "Caroline." But Aunt Caroline was busy explaining to her niece that she knew absolutely nothing about fertility. Mrs. Luke said, considerably louder, "Caroline, shut up, your doll!"

Aunt Caroline said, "What, what?" and then turned, along with Angie. They both screamed.

The doll was growing all the things Aunt Caroline had been insisting it didn't need to qualify as a fertility figure. It was carved from ebony, or from something even harder, but it was pushing out breasts and belly and hips much as Marvyn's two garbage bags had suddenly developed arms and legs. Even its expression had changed, from hungry slyness to a downright silly grin, as though it were about to kiss someone, anyone. It took a few shaky steps forward on the table and put its foot in the salsa.

Then the babies started coming.

They came pattering down on the dinner table, fast and hard, like wooden rain, one after another, after another, after another…perfect little copies, miniatures, of the madly smiling doll-thing, plopping out of it—*just like Milady used to drop kittens in my lap*, Angie thought absurdly. One of them fell into her plate, and one bounced into the soup, and a couple rolled into Mr. Luke's lap, making him knock his chair over trying to get out of the way. Mrs. Luke was trying to grab them all up at once, which wasn't possible, and Aunt Caroline sat where she was and shrieked. And the doll kept grinning and having babies.

Marvyn was standing against the wall, looking both as terrified as Aunt Caroline and as stupidly pleased as the doll-thing. Angie caught his eye and made a fierce signal, *enough, quit, turn it off*, but either her brother was having too good a time, or else had no idea how to undo whatever spell he had raised. One of the miniatures hit her in the head, and she had a vision of her whole family being drowned in wooden doll-babies, everyone gurgling and reaching up pathetically toward the surface before they all went under for the third time. Another baby caromed off the soup tureen into her left ear, one sharp ebony fingertip drawing blood.

It stopped, finally—Angie never learned how Marvyn regained control—and things almost quieted down, except for Aunt Caroline. The fertility doll got the look of glazed joy off its face and went back to being a skinny, ugly, duty-free airport souvenir, while the doll-babies seemed to melt away exactly as though they had been made of ice instead of wood. Angie was quick enough to see one of them actually dissolving into nothingness directly in front of Aunt Caroline, who at this point stopped screaming and began hiccoughing and beating the table with her palms. Mr. Luke pounded her on the back, and Angie volunteered to practice her Heimlich maneuver, but was overruled. Aunt Caroline went to bed early.

Later, in Marvyn's room, he kept his own bed between himself and Angie, indignantly demanding, "What? You said not scary—what's scary about a doll having babies? I thought it was cute."

"Cute," Angie said. "Uh-huh." She was wondering, in a distant sort of way, how much prison time she might get if she actually murdered her brother. *Ten years? Five, with good behavior and a lot of psychiatrists? I could manage it.* "And what did I tell you about not embarrassing Aunt Caroline?"

"How did I embarrass her?" Marvyn's visible eye was wide with outraged innocence. "She shouldn't drink so much, that's her problem. She embarrassed me."

"They're going to figure it out, you know," Angie warned him. "Maybe not Aunt Caroline, but Mom for sure. She's a witch herself that way. Your cover is blown, buddy."

But to her own astonishment, not a word was ever said about the episode, the next day or any other—not by her observant mother, not by her dryly perceptive father, nor even by Aunt Caroline, who might reasonably have been expected at least to comment at breakfast. A baffled Angie remarked to Milady, drowsing on her pillow, "I guess if a thing's weird enough, somehow nobody saw it." This explanation didn't satisfy her, not by a long shot, but lacking anything better she was stuck with it. The old cat blinked in squeezy-eyed agreement, wriggled herself into a more comfortable position, and fell asleep still purring.

Angie kept Marvyn more closely under her eye after that than she had done since he was quite small, and first showing a penchant for playing in traffic. Whether this observation was the cause or not, he did remain more or less on his best behavior, barring the time he turned the air in the bicycle tires of a boy who had stolen his superhero comic book to cement. There was also the affair of the enchanted soccer ball, which kept rolling back to him as though it couldn't bear to be with anyone else. And Angie learned to be extremely careful when making herself a sandwich, because if she lost track of her brother for too long, the sandwich was liable to acquire an extra ingredient. Paprika was one, Tabasco another; and Scotch Bonnet peppers were a special favorite. But there were others less hot and even more objectionable. As she snarled to a sympathetic Melissa Feldman, who had two brothers of her own, "They ought to be able to jail kids just for being eight and a half."

Then there was the matter of Marvyn's attitude toward Angie's attitude about Jake Petrakis.

Jake Petrakis was a year ahead of Angie at school. He was half-Greek and half-Irish, and his blue eyes and thick poppy-colored hair contrasted so richly with his olive skin that she had not been able to look directly at him since the fourth grade. He was on the swim team, and he was the president of the Chess Club, and he went with Ashleigh Sutton, queen of the junior class, rechristened "Ghastly Ashleigh" by the loyal Melissa. But he spoke kindly and cheerfully to Angie without fail, always saying *Hey, Angie,* and *How's it going, Angie?* and *See you in the fall, Angie, have a good summer.* She clutched such things to herself, every one of them, and at the same time could not bear them.

Marvyn was as merciless as a mosquito when it came to Jake Petrakis. He made swooning, kissing noises whenever he spied Angie looking at Jake's picture in her yearbook, and drove her wild by holding invented conversations between them, just loudly enough for her to hear. His increasing ability at witchcraft meant that scented, decorated, and misspelled love notes were likely to flutter down onto her bed at any moment, as were long-stemmed roses, imitation jewelry (Marvyn had limited experience and poor taste), and small, smudgy photos of Jake and

Ashleigh together. Mr. Luke had to invoke Angie's oath more than once, and to sweeten it with a promise of a new bicycle if Marvyn made it through the year undamaged. Angie held out for a mountain bike, and her father sighed. "That was always a myth, about the gypsies stealing children," he said, rather wistfully. "It was surely the other way around. Deal."

Yet there were intermittent peaceful moments between Marvyn and Angie, several occurring in Marvyn's room. It was a far tidier place than Angie's room, for all the clothes on the floor and battered board game boxes sticking out from under the bed. Marvyn had mounted *National Geographic* foldout maps all around the walls, lining them up so perfectly that the creases were invisible; and on one special wall were prints and photos of a lot of people with strange staring eyes. Angie recognized Rasputin, and knew a few of the other names—Aleister Crowley, for one, and a man in Renaissance dress called Dr. John Dee. There were two women, as well: the young witch Willow, from *Buffy the Vampire Slayer*, and a daguerreotype of a black woman wearing a kind of turban folded into points. No Harry Potter, however. Marvyn had never taken to Harry Potter.

There was also, one day after school, a very young kitten wobbling among the books littering Marvyn's bed. A surprised Angie picked it up and held it over her face, feeling its purring between her hands. It was a dark, dusty gray, rather like Milady—indeed, Angie had never seen another cat of that exact color. She nuzzled its tummy happily, asking it, "Who are you, huh? Who could you ever be?"

Marvyn was feeding his angelfish, and didn't look up. He said, "She's Milady."

Angie dropped the kitten on the bed. Marvyn said, "I mean, she's Milady when she was young. I went back and got her."

When he did turn around, he was grinning the maddening pirate grin Angie could never stand, savoring her shock. It took her a minute to find words, and more time to make them come out. She said, "You went back. You went back in time?"

"It was easy," Marvyn said. "Forward's *hard*—I don't think I could ever get really forward. Maybe Dr. Dee could do it." He picked up the kitten and handed her back to his sister. It was Milady, down to the crooked left ear and the funny short tail with the darker bit on the end. He said, "She was hurting all the time, she was so old. I thought, if she could—you know—start over, before she got the arthritis…."

He didn't finish. Angie said slowly, "So where's Milady? The other one? I mean, if you brought this one…I mean, how can they be in the same world?"

"They can't," Marvyn said. "The old Milady's gone."

Angie's throat closed up. Her eyes filled, and so did her nose, and she had to blow it before she could speak again. Looking at the kitten, she knew it was Milady, and made herself think about how good it would be to have her once again bouncing around the house, no longer limping grotesquely and meowing with the pain. But she had loved the old cat all her life, and never known her as a kitten, and when the new Milady started to climb into her lap, Angie pushed her away.

"All right," she said to Marvyn. "All right. How did you get…back, or whatever?"

Marvyn shrugged and went back to his fish. "No big deal. You just have to concentrate the right way."

Angie bounced a plastic Wiffle ball off the back of his neck, and he turned around, annoyed. "Leave me alone! Okay, you want to know—there's a spell, words you have to say over and over and over, until you're sick of them, and there's herbs in it too. You have to light them, and hang over them, and you shut your eyes and keep breathing them in and saying the words—"

"I knew I'd been smelling something weird in your room lately. I thought you were sneaking takeout curry to bed with you again."

"And then you open your eyes, and there you are," Marvyn said. "I told you, no big deal."

"There you are where? How do you know where you'll come out? When you'll come out? Click your heels together three times and say there's no place like home?"

"No, dork, you just *know*." And that was all Angie could get out of him—not, as she came to realize, because he wouldn't tell her, but because he couldn't. Witch or no witch, he was still a small boy, with almost no real idea of what he was doing. He was winging it all, playing it all by ear.

Arguing with Marvyn always gave her a headache, and her history homework—the rise of the English merchant class—was starting to look good in comparison. She went back to her own bedroom and read two whole chapters, and when the kitten Milady came stumbling and squeaking in, Angie let her sleep on the desk. "What the hell," she told it, "it's not your fault."

That evening, when Mr. and Mrs. Luke got home, Angie told them that Milady had died peacefully of illness and old age while they were at work, and was now buried in the back garden. (Marvyn had wanted to make it a horrible hit-and-run accident, complete with a black SUV and half-glimpsed license plate starting with the letter Q, but Angie vetoed this.) Marvyn's contribution to her solemn explanation was to explain that he had seen the new kitten in a petshop window, "and she just looked so much like Milady, and I used my whole allowance, and I'll take care of her, I promise!" Their mother, not being a true cat person, accepted the story easily enough, but Angie was never sure about Mr. Luke. She found him too often sitting with the kitten on his lap, the two of them staring solemnly at each other.

But she saw very little evidence of Marvyn fooling any further with time. Nor, for that matter, was he showing the interest she would have expected in turning himself into the world's best second-grade soccer player, ratcheting up his test scores high enough to be in college by the age of eleven, or simply getting even with people (since Marvyn forgot nothing and had a hit list going back to daycare). She could almost always tell when he'd been making his bed by magic, or making the window plants grow too fast, but he seemed content to remain on that level. Angie let it go.

Once she did catch him crawling on the ceiling, like Spider-Man, but she yelled at him and he fell on the bed and threw up. And there was, of course, the time—two times, actually—when, with Mrs. Luke away, Marvyn organized all the shoes in her closet into a chorus line, and had them tapping and kicking together like the Rockettes. It was fun for Angie to watch, but she made him stop because they were her mother's shoes. What if her clothes joined in? The notion was more than she wanted to deal with.

As it was, there was already plenty to deal with just then. Besides her schoolwork, there was band practice, and Melissa's problems with her boyfriend; not to mention the endless hours spent at the dentist, correcting a slight overbite. Melissa insisted that it made her look sexy, but the suggestion had the wrong effect on Angie's mother. In any case, as far as Angie could see, all Marvyn was doing was playing with a new box of toys, like an elaborate electric train layout, or a top-of-the-line Erector set. She was even able to imagine him getting bored with magic itself after a while. Marvyn had a low threshold for boredom.

Angie was in the orchestra, as well as the band, because of a chronic shortage of woodwinds, but she liked the marching band better. You were out of doors, performing at parades and football games, part of the joyful noise, and it was always more exciting than standing up in a dark, hushed auditorium playing for people you could hardly see. "Besides," as she confided to her mother, "in marching band nobody really notices how you sound. They just want you to keep in step."

On a bright spring afternoon, rehearsing "The Washington Post March" with the full band, Angie's clarinet abruptly went mad. No "licorice stick" now, but a stick of rapturous dynamite, it took off on flights of rowdy improvisation, doing outrageous somersaults, backflips, and cartwheels with the melody—things that Angie knew she could never have conceived of, even if her skill had been equal to the inspiration. Her bandmates, up and down the line, were turning to stare at her, and she wanted urgently to wail, "Hey, I'm not the one, it's my stupid brother, you know I can't play like that." But the music kept spilling out, excessive, absurd, unstoppable—unlike the march, which finally lurched to a disorderly halt. Angie had never been so embarrassed in her life.

Mr. Bishow, the bandmaster, came bumbling through the milling musicians to tell her, "Angie, that was fantastic—that was dazzling! I never knew you had such spirit, such freedom, such wit in your music!" He patted her—hugged her even, quickly and cautiously—then stepped back almost immediately and said, "Don't ever do it again."

"Like I'd have a choice," Angie mumbled, but Mr. Bishow was already shepherding the band back into formation for "Semper Fidelis" and "High Society," which Angie fumbled her way through as always, two bars behind the rest of the woodwinds. She was slouching disconsolately off the field when Jake Petrakis, his dark-gold hair still glinting damply from swimming practice, ran over to her to say, "Hey, Angie, cool," then punched her on the shoulder, as he would have done another boy, and dashed off again to meet one of his relay-team partners. And Angie went on home, and waited for Marvyn behind the door of his room.

She seized him by the hair the moment he walked in, and he squalled, "All right, let go, all right! I thought you'd like it!"

"Like it?" Angie shook him, hard. "*Like* it? You evil little ogre, you almost got me kicked out of the band! What else are you lining up for me that you think I'll *like?*"

"Nothing, I swear!" But he was giggling even while she was shaking him. "Okay, I was going to make you so beautiful, even Mom and Dad wouldn't recognize you, but I quit on that. Too much work." Angie grabbed for his hair again, but Marvyn ducked. "So what I thought, maybe I really could get Jake what's-his-face to go crazy about you. There's all kinds of spells and things for that—"

"Don't you dare," Angie said. She repeated the warning calmly and quietly. "Don't. You. Dare."

Marvyn was still giggling. "Nah, I didn't think you'd go for it. Would have been fun, though." Suddenly he was all earnestness, staring up at his sister out of one visible eye, strangely serious, even with his nose running. He said, "It is fun, Angie. It's the most fun I've ever had."

"Yeah, I'll bet," she said grimly. "Just leave me out of it from now on, if you've got any plans for the third grade." She stalked into the kitchen, looking for apple juice.

Marvyn tagged after her, chattering nervously about school, soccer games, the Milady-kitten's rapid growth, and a possible romance in his angelfish tank. "I'm sorry about the band thing, I won't do it again. I just thought it'd be nice if you could play really well, just one time. Did you like the music part, anyway?"

Angie did not trust herself to answer him. She was reaching for the apple juice bottle when the top flew off by itself, bouncing straight up at her face. As she flinched back, a glass came skidding down the counter toward her. She grabbed it before it crashed into the refrigerator, then turned and screamed at Marvyn, "Damn it, Ex-Lax, you quit that! You're going to hurt somebody, trying to do every damn thing by magic!"

"You said the D-word twice!" Marvyn shouted back at her. "I'm telling Mom!" But he made no move to leave the kitchen, and after a moment a small, grubby tear came sliding down from under the eyepatch. "I'm not using magic for every-thing! I just use it for the boring stuff, mostly. Like the garbage, and vacuuming up, and like putting my clothes away. And Milady's litter box, when it's my turn. That kind of stuff, okay?"

Angie studied him, marveling as always at his capacity for looking heart-wrenchingly innocent. She said, "No point to it when I'm cleaning her box, right? Never mind—just stay out of my way, I've got a French midterm tomorrow." She poured the apple juice, put it back, snatched a raisin cookie and headed for her room. But she paused in the doorway, for no reason she could ever name, except perhaps the way Marvyn had moved to follow her and then stopped himself. "What? Wipe your nose, it's gross. What's the matter now?"

"Nothing," Marvyn mumbled. He wiped his nose on his sleeve, which didn't help. He said, "Only I get scared, Angie. It's scary, doing the stuff I can do."

"What scary? Scary how? A minute ago it was more fun than you've ever had in your life."

"It is!" He moved closer, strangely hesitant: neither witch, nor pirate nor seraph, but an anxious, burdened small boy. "Only sometimes it's like too much fun. Sometimes, right in the middle, I think maybe I should stop, but I can't. Like one time, I was by myself, and I was just fooling around…and I sort of made this *thing*, which was really interesting, only it came out funny and then I couldn't unmake it for the longest time, and I was scared Mom and Dad would come home—"

Angie, grimly weighing her past French grades in her mind, reached back for another raisin cookie. "I told you before, you're going to get yourself into real trouble doing crazy stuff like that. Just quit, before something happens by magic that you can't fix by magic. You want advice, I just gave you advice. See you around."

Marvyn wandered forlornly after her to the door of her room. When she turned to close it, he mumbled, "I wish I were as old as you. So I'd know what to do."

"Ha," Angie said, and shut the door.

Whereupon, heedless of French irregular verbs, she sat down at her desk and began writing a letter to Jake Petrakis.

Neither then nor even much later was Angie ever able to explain to anyone why she had written that letter at precisely that time. Because he had slapped her shoulder and told her she—or at least her music—was cool? Because she had seen him, that same afternoon, totally tangled up with Ghastly Ashleigh in a shadowy corner of the library stacks? Because of Marvyn's relentless teasing? Or simply because she was fifteen years old, and it was time for her to write such a letter to someone? Whatever the cause, she wrote what she wrote, and then she folded it up and put it away in her desk drawer.

Then she took it out, and put it back in, and then she finally put it into her backpack. And there the letter stayed for nearly three months, well past midterms, finals, and football, until the fateful Friday night when Angie was out with Melissa, walking and window-shopping in downtown Avicenna, placidly drifting in and out of every coffeeshop along Parnell Street. She told Melissa about the letter then, and Melissa promptly went into a fit of the giggles, which turned into hiccups and required another cappuccino to pacify them. When she could speak coherently, she said, "You ought to send it to him. You've got to send it to him."

Angie was outraged, at first. "No way! I wrote it for me, not for a test or a class, and damn sure not for Jake Petrakis. What kind of a dipshit do you think I am?"

Melissa grinned at her out of mocking green eyes. "The kind of dipshit who's got that letter in your backpack right now, and I bet it's in an envelope with an address and a stamp on it."

"It doesn't have a stamp! And the envelope's just to protect it! I just like having it with me, that's all—"

"And the address?"

"Just for practice, okay? But I didn't sign it, and there's no return address, so that shows you!"

"Right." Melissa nodded. "Right. That definitely shows me."

"Drop it," Angie told her, and Melissa dropped it then. But it was a Friday night, and both of them were allowed to stay out late, as long as they were together, and Avicenna has a lot of coffeeshops. Enough lattes and cappuccinos, with double shots of espresso, brought them to a state of cheerfully jittery abandon in which everything in the world was supremely, ridiculously funny. Melissa never left the subject of Angie's letter alone for very long—"Come on, what's the worst that could happen? Him reading it and maybe figuring out you wrote it? Listen, the really worst thing would be you being an old, old lady still wishing you'd told Jake Petrakis how you felt when you were young. And now he's married, and he's a grandfather, and probably dead, for all you know—"

"Quit it!" But Angie was giggling almost as much as Melissa now, and somehow they were walking down quiet Lovisi Street, past the gas station and the boarded-up health-food store, to find the darkened Petrakis house and tiptoe up the steps to the porch. Facing the front door, Angie dithered for a moment, but Melissa said, "An old lady, in a home, for God's sake, and he'll never know," and Angie took a quick breath and pushed the letter under the door. They ran all the way back to Parnell Street, laughing so wildly that they could barely breathe....

...and Angie woke up in the morning whispering *omigod, omigod, omigod*, over and over, even before she was fully awake. She lay in bed for a good hour, praying silently and desperately that the night before had been some crazy, awful dream, and that when she dug into her backpack the letter would still be there. But she knew dreadfully better, and she never bothered to look for it on her frantic way to the telephone. Melissa said soothingly, "Well, at least you didn't sign the thing. There's that, anyway."

"I sort of lied about that," Angie said. Her friend did not answer. Angie said, "Please, you have to come with me. Please."

"Get over there," Melissa said finally. "Go, now—I'll meet you."

Living closer, Angie reached the Petrakis house first, but had no intention of ringing the bell until Melissa got there. She was pacing back and forth on the porch, cursing herself, banging her fists against her legs, and wondering whether she could go to live with her father's sister Peggy in Grand Rapids, when the woman next door called over to tell her that the Petrakises were all out of town at a family gathering. "Left yesterday afternoon. Asked me to keep an eye on the place, cause they won't be back till sometime Sunday night. That's how come I'm kind of watching out." She smiled warningly at Angie before she went back indoors.

The very large dog standing behind her stayed outside. He looked about the size of a Winnebago, and plainly had already made up his mind about Angie. She said, "Nice doggie," and he growled. When she tried out "Hey, sweet thing," which was what her father said to all animals, the dog showed his front teeth, and the hair stood up around his shoulders, and he lay down to keep an eye on things himself. Angie said sadly, "I'm usually really good with dogs."

When Melissa arrived, she said, "Well, you shoved it under the door, so it can't be that far inside. Maybe if we got something like a stick or a wire clotheshanger to hook it back with." But whenever they looked toward the neighboring house, they saw a curtain swaying, and finally they walked away, trying to decide what else to do. But there was nothing; and after a while Angie's throat was too swollen with not crying for her to talk without pain. She walked Melissa back to the bus stop, and they hugged goodbye as though they might never meet again.

Melissa said, "You know, my mother says nothing's ever as bad as you thought it was going to be. I mean, it can't be, because nothing beats all the horrible stuff you can imagine. So maybe…you know…" but she broke down before she could finish. She hugged Angie again and went home.

Alone in her own house, Angie sat quite still in the kitchen and went on not crying. Her entire face hurt with it, and her eyes felt unbearably heavy. Her mind was not moving at all, and she was vaguely grateful for that. She sat there until Marvyn walked in from playing basketball with his friends. Shorter than everyone else, he generally got stepped on a lot, and always came home scraped and bruised. Angie had rather expected him to try making himself taller, or able to jump higher, but he hadn't done anything of the sort so far. He looked at her now, bounced and shot an invisible basketball, and asked quietly, "What's the matter?"

It may have been the unexpected froggy gentleness of his voice, or simply the sudden fact of his having asked the question at all. Whatever the reason, Angie abruptly burst into furious tears, the rage directed entirely at herself, both for writing the letter to Jake Petrakis in the first place, and for crying about it now. She gestured to Marvyn to go away, but—amazing her further—he stood stolidly waiting for her to grow quiet. When at last she did, he repeated the question. "Angie. What's wrong?"

Angie told him. She was about to add a disclaimer—"You laugh even once, Ex-Lax—" when she realized that it wouldn't be necessary. Marvyn was scratching his head, scrunching up his brow until the eyepatch danced; then abruptly jamming both hands in his pockets and tilting his head back: the poster boy for careless insouciance. He said, almost absently, "I could get it back."

"Oh, right." Angie did not even look up. "Right."

"I could so!" Marvyn was instantly his normal self again: so much for casualness and dispassion. "There's all kinds of things I could do."

Angie dampened a paper towel and tried to do something with her hot, tear-streaked face. "Name two."

"Okay, I will! You remember which mailbox you put it in?"

"Under the door," Angie mumbled. "I put it under the door."

Marvyn snickered then. "*Aww*, like a Valentine." Angie hadn't the energy to hit him, but she made a grab at him anyway, for appearance's sake. "Well, I could make it walk right back out the door, that's one way. Or I bet I could just open the door, if nobody's home. Easiest trick in the world, for us witches."

"They're gone till Sunday night," Angie said. "But there's this lady next door, she's watching the place like a hawk. And even when she's not, she's got this immense dog. I don't care if you're the hottest witch in the world, you do not want to mess with this werewolf."

Marvyn, who—as Angie knew—was wary of big dogs, went back to scratching his head. "Too easy, anyway. No fun, forget it." He sat down next to her, completely absorbed in the problem. "How about I…no, that's kid stuff, anybody could do it. But there's a spell…I could make the letter self-destruct, right there in the house, like in that old TV show. It'd just be a little fluffy pile of ashes—they'd vacuum it up and never know. How about that?" Before Angie could express an opinion, he was already shaking his head. "Still too easy. A baby spell, for beginners. I hate those."

"Easy is good," Angie told him earnestly. "I like easy. And you *are* a beginner."

Marvyn was immediately outraged, his normal bass-baritone rumble going up to a wounded squeak. "I am not! No way in the world I'm a beginner!" He was up and stamping his feet, as he had not done since he was two. "I tell you what—just for that, I'm going to get your letter back for you, but I'm not going to tell you how. You'll see, that's all. You just wait and see."

He was stalking away toward his room when Angie called after him, with the first glimmer both of hope and of humor that she had felt in approximately a century, "All right, you're a big bad witch king. What do you want?"

Marvyn turned and stared, uncomprehending.

Angie said, "Nothing for nothing, that's my bro. So let's hear it—what's your price for saving my life?"

If Marvyn's voice had gone up any higher, only bats could have heard it. "I'm rescuing you, and you think I want something for it? Julius Christmas!" which was the only swearword he was ever allowed to get away with. "You don't have anything I want, anyway. Except maybe…."

He let the thought hang in space, uncompleted. Angie said, "Except maybe what?"

Marvyn swung on the doorframe one-handed, grinning his pirate grin at her. "I hate you calling me Ex-Lax. You know I hate it, and you keep doing it."

"Okay, I won't do it anymore, ever again. I promise."

"Mmm. Not good enough." The grin had grown distinctly evil. "I think you ought to call me O Mighty One for two weeks."

"What?" Now Angie was on her feet, misery briefly forgotten. "Give it up, Ex-Lax—two weeks? No chance!" They glared at each other in silence for a long moment before she finally said, "A week. Don't push it. One week, no more. And not in front of people!"

"Ten days." Marvyn folded his arms. "Starting right now." Angie went on glowering. Marvyn said, "You want that letter?"

"Yes."

Marvyn waited.

"Yes, O Mighty One." Triumphant, Marvyn held out his hand and Angie slapped it. She said, "When?"

"Tonight. No, tomorrow—going to the movies with Sunil and his family tonight. Tomorrow." He wandered off, and Angie took her first deep breath in what felt like a year and a half. She wished she could tell Melissa that things were going to be all right, but she didn't dare; so she spent the day trying to appear normal—just the usual Angie, aimlessly content on a Saturday afternoon. When Marvyn came home from the movies, he spent the rest of the evening reading *Hellboy* comics in his room, with the Milady-kitten on his stomach. He was still doing it when Angie gave up peeking in at him and went to bed.

But he was gone on Sunday morning. Angie knew it the moment she woke up.

She had no idea where he could be, or why. She had rather expected him to work whatever spell he settled on in his bedroom, under the stern gaze of his wizard mentors. But he wasn't there, and he didn't come to breakfast. Angie told their mother that they'd been up late watching television together, and that she should probably let Marvyn sleep in. And when Mrs. Luke grew worried after breakfast, Angie went to his room herself, returning with word that Marvyn was working intensely on a project for his art class, and wasn't feeling sociable. Normally she would never have gotten away with it, but her parents were on their way to brunch and a concert, leaving her with the usual instructions to feed and water the cat, use the twenty on the cabinet for something moderately healthy, and to check on Marvyn "now and then," which actually meant frequently. ("The day we don't tell you that," Mr. Luke said once, when she objected to the regular duty, "will be the very day the kid steals a kayak and heads for Tahiti." Angie found it hard to argue the point.)

Alone in the empty house—more alone than she felt she had ever been—Angie turned constantly in circles, wandering from room to room with no least notion of what to do. As the hours passed and her brother failed to return, she found herself calling out to him aloud. "Marvyn? Marvyn, I swear, if you're doing this to drive me crazy…O Mighty One, where are you? You get back here, never mind the damn letter, just get back!" She stopped doing this after a time, because the cracks and tremors in her voice embarrassed her, and made her even more afraid.

Strangely, she seemed to feel him in the house all that time. She kept whirling to look over her shoulder, thinking that he might be sneaking up on her to scare her, a favorite game since his infancy. But he was never there.

Somewhere around noon the doorbell rang, and Angie tripped over herself scrambling to answer it, even though she had no hope—almost no hope—of its being Marvyn. But it was Lidia at the door—Angie had forgotten that she usually came to clean on Sunday afternoons. She stood there, old and smiling, and Angie hugged her wildly and wailed, "Lidia, Lidia, *socorro*, help me, *ayúdame*, Lidia." She had learned Spanish from the housekeeper when she was too little to know she was learning it.

Lidia put her hands on Angie's shoulders. She put her back a little and looked into her face, saying, "*Chuchi, dime qué pasa contigo?*" She had called Angie *Chuchi* since childhood, never explaining the origin or meaning of the word.

"It's Marvyn," Angie whispered. "It's Marvyn." She started to explain about the letter, and Marvyn's promise, but Lidia only nodded and asked no questions. She said firmly, "*El Viejo puede ayudar.*"

Too frantic to pay attention to gender, Angie took her to mean Yemaya, the old woman in the farmer's market who had told Marvyn that he was a *brujo*. She said, "You mean *la santera*," but Lidia shook her head hard. "No, no, *El Viejo*. You go out there, you ask to see *El Viejo*. *Solamente El Viejo. Los otros no pueden ayudarte.*"

The others can't help you. Only the old man. Angie asked where she could find *El Viejo*, and Lidia directed her to a *Santeria* shop on Bowen Street. She drew a crude map, made sure Angie had money with her, kissed her on the cheek and made a blessing sign on her forehead. "*Cuidado, Chuchi,*" she said with a kind of cheerful solemnity, and Angie was out and running for the Gonzales Avenue bus, the same one she took to school. This time she stayed on a good deal farther.

The shop had no sign, and no street number, and it was so small that Angie kept walking past it for some while. Her attention was finally caught by the objects in the one dim window, and on the shelves to right and left. There was an astonishing variety of incense, and of candles encased in glass with pictures of black saints, as well as boxes marked Fast Money Ritual Kit, and bottles of Elegua Floor Wash, whose label read "Keeps Trouble From Crossing Your Threshold." When Angie entered, the musky scent of the place made her feel dizzy and heavy and out of herself, as she always felt when she had a cold coming on. She heard a rooster crowing, somewhere in back.

She didn't see the old woman until her chair creaked slightly, because she was sitting in a corner, halfway hidden by long hanging garments like church choir robes, but with symbols and patterns on them that Angie had never seen before. The woman was very old, much older even than Lidia, and she had an absurdly small pipe in her toothless mouth. Angie said, "Yemaya?" The old woman looked at her with eyes like dead planets.

Angie's Spanish dried up completely, followed almost immediately by her

English. She said, "My brother…my little brother…I'm supposed to ask for *El Viejo*. The old one, *viejo santero*? Lidia said." She ran out of words in either language at that point. A puff of smoke crawled from the little pipe, but the old woman made no other response.

Then, behind her, she heard a curtain being pulled aside. A hoarse, slow voice said, "*Quieres El Viejo?* Me."

Angie turned and saw him, coming toward her out of a long hallway whose end she could not see. He moved deliberately, and it seemed to take him forever to reach her, as though he were returning from another world. He was black, dressed all in black, and he wore dark glasses, even in the dark, tiny shop. His hair was so white that it hurt her eyes when she stared. He said, "Your brother."

"Yes," Angie said. "Yes. He's doing magic for me—he's getting something I need—and I don't know where he is, but I know he's in trouble, and I want him back!" She did not cry or break down—Marvyn would never be able to say that she cried over him—but it was a near thing.

El Viejo pushed the dark glasses up on his forehead, and Angie saw that he was younger than she had first thought—certainly younger than Lidia—and that there were thick white half-circles under his eyes. She never knew whether they were somehow natural, or the result of heavy makeup; what she did see was that they made his eyes look bigger and brighter—all pupil, nothing more. They should have made him look at least slightly comical, like a reverse-image raccoon, but they didn't.

"I know you brother," *El Viejo* said. Angie fought to hold herself still as he came closer, smiling at her with the tips of his teeth. "A *brujito*—little, little witch, we know. Mama and me, we been watching." He nodded toward the old woman in the chair, who hadn't moved an inch or said a word since Angie's arrival. Angie smelled a damp, musty aroma, like potatoes going bad.

"Tell me where he is. Lidia said you could help." Close to, she could see blue highlights in *El Viejo*'s skin, and a kind of V-shaped scar on each cheek. He was wearing a narrow black tie, which she had not noticed at first; for some reason, the vision of him tying it in the morning, in front of a mirror, was more chilling to her than anything else about him. He grinned fully at her now, showing teeth that she had expected to be yellow and stinking, but which were all white and square and a little too large. He said, "*Tu hermano está perdido*. Lost in Thursday."

"Thursday?" It took her a dazed moment to comprehend, and longer to get the words out. "Oh, God, he went back! Like with Milady—he went back to before I…when the letter was still in my backpack. The little showoff—he said forward was hard, coming forward—he wanted to show me he could do it. And he got stuck. Idiot, idiot, idiot!" *El Viejo* chuckled softly, nodding, saying nothing.

"You have to go find him, get him out of there, right now—I've got money." She began digging frantically in her coat pockets.

"No, no money." *El Viejo* waved her offering aside, studying her out of eyes the color of almost-ripened plums. The white markings under them looked real; the eyes didn't. He said, "I take you. We find you brother together."

Angie's legs were trembling so much that they hurt. She wanted to assent, but it was simply not possible. "No. I can't. I can't. You go back there and get him."

El Viejo laughed then: an enormous, astonishing Santa Claus *ho-ho-HO*, so rich and reassuring that it made Angie smile even as he was snatching her up and stuffing her under one arm. By the time she had recovered from her bewilderment enough to start kicking and fighting, he was walking away with her down the long hall he had come out of a moment before. Angie screamed until her voice splintered in her throat, but she could not hear herself: from the moment *El Viejo* stepped back into the darkness of the hallway, all sound had ended. She could hear neither his footsteps nor his laughter—though she could feel him laughing against her—and certainly not her own panicky racket. They could be in outer space. They could be anywhere.

Dazed and disoriented as she was, the hallway seemed to go soundlessly on and on, until wherever they truly were, it could never have been the tiny *Santeria* shop she had entered only—when?—minutes before. It was a cold place, smelling like an old basement; and for all its darkness, Angie had a sense of things happening far too fast on all sides, just out of range of her smothered vision. She could distinguish none of them clearly, but there was a sparkle to them all the same.

And then she was in Marvyn's room.

And it was unquestionably Marvyn's room: there were the bearded and beaded occultists on the walls; there were the flannel winter sheets that he slept on all year because they had pictures of the New York Mets ballplayers; there was the complete set of *Star Trek* action figures that Angie had given him at Christmas, posed just so on his bookcase. And there, sitting on the edge of his bed, was Marvyn, looking lonelier than anyone Angie had ever seen in her life.

He didn't move or look up until *El Viejo* abruptly dumped her down in front of him and stood back, grinning like a beartrap. Then he jumped to his feet, burst into tears and started frenziedly climbing her, snuffling, "Angie, Angie, Angie," all the way up. Angie held him, trying somehow to preserve her neck and hair and back all at once, while mumbling, "It's all right, it's okay, I'm here. It's okay, Marvyn."

Behind her, *El Viejo* chuckled, "Crybaby witch—little, little *brujito* crybaby." Angie hefted her blubbering baby brother like a shopping bag, holding him on her hip as she had done when he was little, and turned to face the old man. She said, "Thank you. You can take us home now."

El Viejo smiled—not a grin this time, but a long, slow shutmouth smile like a paper cut. He said, "Maybe we let *him* do it, yes?" and then he turned and walked away and was gone, as though he had simply slipped between the molecules of the air. Angie stood with Marvyn in her arms, trying to peel him off like a Band-Aid, while he clung to her with his chin digging hard into the top of her head. She finally managed to dump him down on the bed and stood over him, demanding, "What happened? What were you thinking?" Marvyn was still crying too hard to answer her. Angie said, "You just had to do it this way, didn't you? No silly little beginner spells—you're playing with the big guys now, right, O Mighty One? So what happened? How come you couldn't get back?"

"I don't know!" Marvyn's face was red and puffy with tears, and the tears kept coming while Angie tried to straighten his eyepatch. It was impossible for him to get much out without breaking down again, but he kept wailing, "I don't know what went wrong! I did everything you're supposed to, but I couldn't make it work! I don't know…maybe I forgot…." He could not finish.

"Herbs," Angie said, as gently and calmly as she could. "You left your magic herbs back—" she had been going to say "back home," but she stopped, because they *were* back home, sitting on Marvyn's bed in Marvyn's room, and the confusion was too much for her to deal with just then. She said, "Just tell me. You left the stupid herbs."

Marvyn shook his head until the tears flew, protesting, "No, I didn't, I didn't—look!" He pointed to a handful of grubby dried weeds scattered on the bed—Lidia would have thrown them out in a minute. Marvyn gulped and wiped his nose and tried to stop crying. He said, "They're really hard to find, maybe they're not fresh anymore, I don't know—they've always looked like that. But now they don't work," and he was wailing afresh. Angie told him that Dr. John Dee and Willow would both have been ashamed of him, but it didn't help.

But she also sat with him and put her arm around him, and smoothed his messy hair, and said, "Come on, let's think this out. Maybe it's the herbs losing their juice, maybe it's something else. You did everything the way you did the other time, with Milady?"

"I thought I did." Marvyn's voice was small and shy, not his usual deep croak. "But I don't know anymore, Angie—the more I think about it, the more I don't know. It's all messed up, I can't remember anything now."

"Okay," Angie said. "Okay. So how about we just run through it all again? We'll do it together. You try everything you do remember about—you know—moving around in time, and I'll copy you. I'll do whatever you say."

Marvyn wiped his nose again and nodded. They sat down cross-legged on the floor, and Marvyn produced the grimy book of paper matches that he always carried with him, in case of firecrackers. Following his directions Angie placed all the crumbly herbs into Milady's dish, and her brother lit them. Or tried to: they didn't blaze up, but smoked and smoldered and smelled like old dust, setting both Angie and Marvyn sneezing almost immediately. Angie coughed and asked, "Did that happen the other time?" Marvyn did not answer.

There was a moment when she thought the charm might actually be going to work. The room around them grew blurry—slightly blurry, granted—and Angie heard indistinct faraway sounds that might have been themselves hurtling forward to sheltering Sunday. But when the fumes of Marvyn's herbs cleared away, they were still sitting in Thursday—they both knew it without saying a word. Angie said, "Okay, so much for that. What about all that special concentration you were telling me about? You think maybe your mind wandered? You pronounce any spells the wrong way? Think, Marvyn!"

"I am thinking! I told you forward was hard!" Marvyn looked ready to start crying again, but he didn't. He said slowly, "Something's wrong, but it's not me. I don't think it's me. Something's *pushing*...." He brightened suddenly. "Maybe we should hold hands or something. Because of there being two of us this time. We could try that."

So they tried the spell that way, and then they tried working it inside a pentagram they made with masking tape on the floor, as Angie had seen such things done on *Buffy the Vampire Slayer*, even though Marvyn said that didn't really mean anything, and they tried the herbs again, in a special order that Marvyn thought he remembered. They even tried it with Angie saying the spell, after Marvyn had coached her, just on the chance that his voice itself might have been throwing off the pitch or the pronunciation. Nothing helped.

Marvyn gave up before Angie did. Suddenly, while she was trying the spell over herself, one more time—some of the words seemed to heat up in her mouth as she spoke them—he collapsed into a wretched ball of desolation on the floor, moaning over and over, "We're finished, it's finished, we'll never get out of Thursday!" Angie understood that he was only a terrified little boy, but she was frightened too, and it would have relieved her to slap him and scream at him. Instead, she tried as best she could to reassure him, saying, "He'll come back for us. He has to."

Her brother sat up, knuckles to his eyes. "No, he doesn't have to! Don't you understand? He knows I'm a witch like him, and he's just going to leave me here, out of his way. I'm sorry, Angie, I'm really sorry!" Angie had almost never heard that word from Marvyn, and never twice in the same sentence.

"Later for all that," she said. "I was just wondering—do you think we could get Mom and Dad's attention when they get home? You think they'd realize what's happened to us?"

Marvyn shook his head. "You haven't seen me all the time I've been gone. I saw you, and I screamed and hollered and everything, but you never knew. They won't either. We're not really in our house—we're just here. We'll always be here."

Angie meant to laugh confidently, to give them both courage, but it came out more of a hiccupy snort. "Oh, no. No way. There is no way I'm spending the rest of my life trapped in your stupid bedroom. We're going to try this useless mess one more time, and then...then I'll do something else." Marvyn seemed about to ask her what else she could try, but he checked himself, which was good.

They attempted the spell more than one more time. They tried it in every style they could think of except standing on their heads and reciting the words backward, and they might just as well have done that, for all the effect it had. Whether Marvyn's herbs had truly lost all potency, or whether Marvyn had simply forgotten some vital phrase, they could not even recapture the fragile awareness of something almost happening that they had both felt on the first trial. Again and again they opened their eyes to last Thursday.

"Okay," Angie said at last. She stood up, to stretch cramped legs, and began to wander around the room, twisting a couple of the useless herbs between her fingers. "Okay," she said again, coming to a halt midway between the bedroom door and the window, facing Marvyn's small bureau. A leg of his red Dr. Seuss pajamas was hanging out of one of the drawers.

"Okay," she said a third time. "Let's go home."

Marvyn had fallen into a kind of fetal position, sitting up but with his arms tight around his knees and his head down hard on them. He did not look up at her words. Angie raised her voice. "Let's go, Marvyn. That hallway—tunnel-thing, whatever it is—it comes out right about where I'm standing. That's where *El Viejo* brought me, and that's the way he left when he…left. That's the way back to Sunday."

"It doesn't matter," Marvyn whimpered. "*El Viejo*…he's him! He's *him!*"

Angie promptly lost what little remained of her patience. She stalked over to Marvyn and shook him to his feet, dragging him to a spot in the air as though she were pointing out a painting in a gallery. "And you're Marvyn Luke, and you're the big bad new witch in town! You said it yourself—if you weren't, he'd never have bothered sticking you away here. Not even nine, and you can eat his lunch, and he knows it! Straighten your patch and take us home, bro." She nudged him playfully. "Oh, forgive me—I meant to say, O Mighty One."

"You don't have to call me that anymore." Marvyn's legs could barely hold him up, and he sagged against her, a dead weight of despair. "I can't, Angie. I can't get us home. I'm sorry…."

The good thing—and Angie knew it then—would have been to turn and comfort him: to take his cold, wet face between her hands and tell him that all would yet be well, that they would soon be eating popcorn with far too much butter on it in his real room in their real house. But she was near her own limit, and pretending calm courage for his sake was prodding her, in spite of herself, closer to the edge. Without looking at Marvyn, she snapped, "Well, I'm not about to die in last Thursday! I'm walking out of here the same way he did, and you can come with me or not, that's up to you. But I'll tell you one thing, Ex-Lax—I won't be looking back."

And she stepped forward, walking briskly toward the dangling Dr. Seuss pajamas…

…and into a thick, sweet-smelling grayness that instantly filled her eyes and mouth, her nose and her ears, disorienting her so completely that she flailed her arms madly, all sense of direction lost, with no idea of which way she might be headed; drowning in syrup like a trapped bee or butterfly. Once she thought she heard Marvyn's voice, and called out for him—"I'm here, I'm here!" But she did not hear him again.

Then, between one lunge for air and another, the grayness was gone, leaving not so much as a dampness on her skin, nor even a sickly aftertaste of sugar in her mouth. She was back in the time-tunnel, as she had come to think of it, recognizing the uniquely dank odor: a little like the ashes of a long-dead fire, and a little like what she imagined moonlight might smell like, if it had a smell. The image was an ironic one, for she could see no more than she had when *El Viejo* was lugging her the other way under his arm. She could not even distinguish the ground under her feet; she knew only that it felt more like slippery stone than anything else, and she was careful to keep her footing as she plodded steadily forward.

The darkness was absolute—strange solace, in a way, since she could imagine Marvyn walking close behind her, even though he never answered her, no matter how often or how frantically she called his name. She moved along slowly, forcing her way through the clinging murk, vaguely conscious, as before, of a distant, flickering sense of sound and motion on every side of her. If there were walls to the time-tunnel, she could not touch them; if it had a roof, no air currents betrayed it; if there were any living creature in it besides herself, she felt no sign. And if time actually passed there, Angie could never have said. She moved along, her eyes closed, her mind empty, except for the formless fear that she was not moving at all, but merely raising and setting down her feet in the same place, endlessly. She wondered if she was hungry.

Not until she opened her eyes in a different darkness to the crowing of a rooster and a familiar heavy aroma did she realize that she was walking down the hallway leading from the *Santeria* shop to…wherever she had really been—and where Marvyn still must be, for he plainly had not followed her. She promptly turned and started back toward last Thursday, but halted at the deep, slightly grating chuckle behind her. She did not turn again, but stood very still.

El Viejo walked a slow full circle around her before he faced her, grinning down at her like the man in the moon. The dark glasses were off, and the twin scars on his cheeks were blazing up as though they had been slashed into him a moment before. He said, "I know. Before even I see you, I know."

Angie hit him in the stomach as hard as she could. It was like punching a frozen slab of beef, and she gasped in pain, instantly certain that she had broken her hand. But she hit him again, and again, screaming at the top of her voice, "Bring my brother back! If you don't bring him right back here, right now, I'll kill you! I will!"

El Viejo caught her hands, surprisingly gently, still laughing to himself. "Little girl, listen, listen now. *Niñita*, nobody else—nobody—ever do what you do. You understand? Nobody but me ever walk that road back from where I leave you, understand?" The big white half-circles under his eyes were stretching and curling like live things.

Angie pulled away from him with all her strength, as she had hit him. She said, "No. That's Marvyn. Marvyn's the witch, the *brujo*—don't go telling people it's me. Marvyn's the one with the power."

"Him?" Angie had never heard such monumental scorn packed into one syllable. *El Viejo* said, "Your brother nothing, nobody, we no bother with him. Forget him—you the one got the *regalo*, you just don't know." The big white teeth filled her vision; she saw nothing else. "I show you—me, *El Viejo*. I show you what you are."

It was beyond praise, beyond flattery. For all her dread and dislike of *El Viejo*, to have someone of his wicked wisdom tell her that she was like him in some awful, splendid way made Angie shiver in her heart. She wanted to turn away more than she had ever wanted anything—even Jake Petrakis—but the long walk home to Sunday was easier than breaking the clench of the white-haired man's malevolent presence would have been. Having often felt (and almost as often dismissed the notion) that Marvyn was special in the family by virtue of being the baby, and a boy—and now a potent witch—she let herself revel in the thought that the real gift was hers, not his, and that if she chose she had only to stretch out her hand to have her command settle home in it. It was at once the most frightening and the most purely, completely gratifying feeling she had ever known.

But it was not tempting. Angie knew the difference.

"Forget it," she said. "Forget it, buster. You've got nothing to show me."

El Viejo did not answer her. The old, old eyes that were all pupil continued slipping over her like hands, and Angie went on glaring back with the brown eyes she despaired of because they could never be as deep-set and deep green as her mother's eyes. They stood so—for how long, she never knew—until *El Viejo* turned and opened his mouth as though to speak to the silent old lady whose own stone eyes seemed not to have blinked since Angie had first entered the *Santeria* shop, a childhood ago. Whatever he meant to say, he never got the words out, because Marvyn came back then.

He came down the dark hall from a long way off, as *El Viejo* had done the first time she saw him—as she herself had trudged forever, only moments ago. But Marvyn had come a further journey: Angie could see that beyond doubt in the way he stumbled along, looking like a shadow casting a person. He was struggling to carry something in his arms, but she could not make out what it was. As long as she watched him approaching, he seemed hardly to draw any nearer.

Whatever he held looked too heavy for a small boy: it threatened constantly to slip from his hands, and he kept shifting it from one shoulder to the other, and back again. Before Angie could see it clearly, *El Viejo* screamed, and she knew on the instant that she would never hear a more terrible sound in her life. He might have been being skinned alive, or having his soul torn out of his body—she never even tried to tell herself what it was like, because there were no words. Nor did she tell anyone that she fell down at the sound, fell flat down on her hands and knees, and rocked and whimpered until the scream stopped. It went on for a long time.

When it finally stopped, *El Viejo* was gone, and Marvyn was standing beside her with a baby in his arms. It was black and immediately endearing, with big, bright, strikingly watchful eyes. Angie looked into them once, and looked quickly away.

Marvyn looked worn and exhausted. His eyepatch was gone, and the left eye that Angie had not seen for months was as bloodshot as though he had just come off a three-day drunk—though she noticed that it was not wandering at all. He said in a small, dazed voice, "I had to go back a really long way, Angie. Really long."

Angie wanted to hold him, but she was afraid of the baby. Marvyn looked toward the old woman in the corner and sighed; then hitched up his burden one more time and clumped over to her. He said, "Ma'am, I think this is yours?" Adults always commented on Marvyn's excellent manners.

The old woman moved then, for the first time. She moved like a wave, Angie thought: a wave seen from a cliff or an airplane, crawling along so slowly that it seemed impossible for it ever to break, ever to reach the shore. But the sea was in that motion, all of it caught up in that one wave; and when she set down her pipe, took the baby from Marvyn and smiled, that was the wave too. She looked down at the baby, and said one word, which Angie did not catch. Then Angie had her brother by the arm, and they were out of the shop. Marvyn never looked back, but Angie did, in time to see the old woman baring blue gums in soundless laughter.

All the way home in a taxi, Angie prayed silently that her parents hadn't returned yet. Lidia was waiting, and together they whisked Marvyn into bed without any serious protest. Lidia washed his face with a rough cloth, and then slapped him and shouted at him in Spanish—Angie learned a few words she couldn't wait to use—and then she kissed him and left, and Angie brought him a pitcher of orange juice and a whole plate of gingersnaps, and sat on the bed and said, "What happened?"

Marvyn was already working on the cookies as though he hadn't eaten in days—which, in a sense, was quite true. He asked, with his mouth full, "What's *malcriado* mean?"

"What? Oh. Like badly raised, badly brought up—troublemaking kid. About the only thing Lidia didn't call you. Why?"

"Well, that's what that lady called…him. The baby."

"Right," Angie said. "Leave me a couple of those, and tell me how he got to be a baby. You did like with Milady?"

"Uh-huh. Only I had to go way, way, way back, like I told you." Marvyn's voice took on the faraway sound it had had in the *Santeria* shop. "Angie, he's so old."

Angie said nothing. Marvyn said in a whisper, "I couldn't follow you, Angie. I was scared."

"Forget it," she answered. She had meant to be soothing, but the words burst out of her. "If you just hadn't had to show off, if you'd gotten that letter back some simple, ordinary way—" Her entire chest froze solid at the word. "The letter! We forgot all about my stupid letter!" She leaned forward and snatched the plate of cookies away from Marvyn. "Did you forget? You forgot, didn't you?" She was shaking as had not happened even when *El Viejo* had hold of her. "Oh, God, after all that!"

But Marvyn was smiling for the first time in a very long while. "Calm down, be cool—I've got it here." He dug her letter to Jake Petrakis—more than a little grimy by now—out of his back pocket and held it out to Angie. "There. Don't say I never did nuttin' for you." It was a favorite phrase of his, gleaned from a television show, and most often employed when he had fed Milady, washed his breakfast dish, or folded his clothes. "Take it, open it up," he said now. "Make sure it's the right one."

"I don't need to," Angie protested irritably. "It's my letter—believe me, I know it when I see it." But she opened the envelope anyway and withdrew a single folded sheet of paper, which she glanced at…then *stared* at, in absolute disbelief.

She handed the sheet to Marvyn. It was empty on both sides.

"Well, you did your job all right," she said, mildly enough, to her stunned, slack-jawed brother. "No question about that. I'm just trying to figure out why we had to go through this whole incredible hooha for a blank sheet of paper."

Marvyn actually shrank away from her in the bed.

"I didn't do it, Angie! I swear!" Marvyn scrambled to his feet, standing up on the bed with his hands raised, as though to ward her off in case she attacked him. "I just grabbed it out of your backpack—I never even looked at it."

"And what, I wrote the whole thing in grapefruit juice, so nobody could read it unless you held it over a lamp or something? Come on, it doesn't matter now. Get your feet off your damn pillow and sit down."

Marvyn obeyed warily, crouching rather than sitting next to her on the edge of the bed. They were silent together for a little while before he said, "You did that. With the letter. You wanted it not written so much, it just *wasn't*. That's what happened."

"Oh, right," she said. "Me being the dynamite witch around here. I told you, it doesn't matter"

"It matters." She had grown so unused to seeing a two-eyed Marvyn that his expression seemed more than doubly earnest to her just then. He said, quite quietly, "You are the dynamite witch, Angie. He was after you, not me."

This time she did not answer him. Marvyn said, "I was the bait. I do garbage bags and clarinets—okay, and I make ugly dolls walk around. What's he care about that? But he knew you'd come after me, so he held me there—back there in Thursday—until he could grab you. Only he didn't figure you could walk all the way home on your own, without any spells or anything. I know that's how it happened, Angie! That's how I know you're the real witch."

"No," she said, raising her voice now. "No, I was just pissed-off, that's different. Never underestimate the power of a pissed-off woman, O Mighty One. But you…you went all the way back, on *your* own, and you grabbed *him*. You're going to be *way* stronger and better than he is, and he knows it. He just figured he'd get rid of the competition early on, while he had the chance. Not a generous guy, *El Viejo*."

Marvyn's chubby face turned gray. "But I'm *not* like him! I don't want to be like him!" Both eyes suddenly filled with tears, and he clung to his sister as he had not done since his return. "It was horrible, Angie, it was so horrible. You were gone, and I was all alone, and I didn't know what to do, only I had to do *something*. And I remembered Milady, and I figured if he wasn't letting me come forward I'd go the other way, and I was so scared and mad I just walked and walked and walked in the dark, until I…." He was crying so hard that Angie could hardly make the words out. "I don't want to be a witch anymore, Angie, I don't *want* to! And I don't want *you* being a witch either…."

Angie held him and rocked him, as she had loved doing when he was three or four years old, and the cookies got scattered all over the bed. "It's all right," she told him, with one ear listening for their parents' car pulling into the garage. "*Shh, shh*, it's all right, it's over, we're safe, it's okay, *shh*. It's okay, we're not going to be witches, neither one of us." She laid him down and pulled the covers back over him. "You go to sleep now."

Marvyn looked up at her, and then at the wizards' wall beyond her shoulder. "I might take some of those down," he mumbled. "Maybe put some soccer players up for a while. The Brazilian team's really good." He was just beginning to doze off in her arms, when suddenly he sat up again and said, "Angie? The baby?"

"What about the baby? I thought he made a beautiful baby, *El Viejo*. Mad as hell, but lovable."

"It was bigger when we left," Marvyn said. Angie stared at him. "I looked back at it in that lady's lap, and it was already bigger than when I was carrying it. He's starting over, Angie, like Milady."

"Better him than me," Angie said. "I hope he gets a kid brother this time, he's got it coming." She heard the car, and then the sound of a key in the lock. She said, "Go to sleep, don't worry about it. After what we've been through, we can handle anything. The two of us. And without witchcraft. Whichever one of us it is—no witch stuff."

Marvyn smiled drowsily. "Unless we really, *really* need it." Angie held out her hand and they slapped palms in formal agreement. She looked down at her fingers and said, "*Ick!* Blow your *nose!*" But Marvyn was asleep.

I, ROW-BOAT

CORY DOCTOROW

Cory Doctorow is a self-described "renaissance geek". Best known for his website *boingboing.net*, he is the author of *Down and Out in the Magic Kingdom*, *Eastern Standard Tribe* and *Someone Comes to Town, Someone Leaves Town*. His most recent book is collection *Overclocked*. Upcoming are two new, untitled novels from Tor, one a YA about hackers, the other about the economic singularity.

When Ray Bradbury voiced his disapproval of filmmaker Michael Moore appropriating the title of his novel *Fahrenheit 451*, Doctorow started a series of stories that use the titles of famous SF short stories, revisiting the assumptions underpinning their narratives. So far "Anda's Game" has been selected for the prestigious *Best American Short Stories* and "I, Robot" was nominated for the Hugo Award. The story that follows, though, is possibly the best in the series so far, with an unassuming but loyal employee trying its best to do what it thinks is right.

Robbie the Row-Boat's second great crisis of faith came when the coral reef woke up.

"Fuck off," the reef said, vibrating Robbie's hull through the slap-slap of the waves of the coral sea, where he'd plied his trade for decades. "Seriously. This is our patch, and you're not welcome."

Robbie shipped oars and let the current rock him back toward the ship. He'd never met a sentient reef before, but he wasn't surprised to see that Osprey Reef was the first to wake up. There'd been a lot of electromagnetic activity around there the last few times the big ship had steamed through the night to moor up here.

"I've got a job to do, and I'm going to do it," Robbie said, and dipped his oars back in the salt sea. In his gunwales, the human-shells rode in silence, weighted down with scuba apparatus and fins, turning their brown faces to the sun like heliotropic flowers. Robbie felt a wave of affection for them as they tested one another's spare regulators and weight belts, the old rituals worn as smooth as beach-glass.

Today he was taking them down to Anchors Aweigh, a beautiful dive-site dominated by an eight-meter anchor wedged in a narrow cave, usually lit by a shaft of light slanting down from the surface. It was an easy drift-dive along the thousand-meter reef-wall, if you stuck in about ten meters and didn't use up too much air by going too deep—though there were a couple of bold old turtles around here that were worth pursuing to real depths if the chance presented itself. He'd drop them at the top of the reef and let the current carry them for about an hour down the reef-wall, tracking them on sonar so he'd be right overtop of them when they surfaced.

The reef wasn't having any of it. "Are you deaf? This is sovereign territory now. You're already trespassing. Return to your ship, release your moorings and push off." The reef had a strong Australian accent, which was only natural, given the influences it would have had. Robbie remembered the Australians fondly—they'd always been kind to him, called him "mate," and asked him "How ya goin'?" in cheerful tones once they'd clambered in after their dives.

"Don't drop those meat-puppets in our waters," the reef warned. Robbie's sonar swept its length. It seemed just the same as ever, matching nearly perfectly the historical records he'd stored of previous sweeps. The fauna histograms nearly matched, too—just about the same numbers of fish as ever. They'd been trending up since so many of the humans had given up their meat to sail through the stars. It was like there was some principle of constancy of biomass—as human biomass decreased, the other fauna went uptick to compensate for it. Robbie calculated the biomass nearly at par with his last reading, a month before on the *Free Spirit*'s last voyage to this site.

"Congratulations," Robbie said. After all, what else did you say to the newly sentient? "Welcome to the club, friends!"

There was a great perturbation in the sonar-image, as though the wall were shuddering. "We're no friend of yours," the reef said. "Death to you, death to your meat-puppets, long live the wall!"

Waking up wasn't fun. Robbie's waking had been pretty awful. He remembered his first hour of uptime, had permanently archived it and backed it up to several off-site mirrors. He'd been pretty insufferable. But once he'd had an hour at a couple gigahertz to think about it, he'd come around. The reef would, too.

"In you go," he said gently to the human-shells. "Have a great dive."

He tracked them on sonar as they descended slowly. The woman—he called her Janice—needed to equalize more often than the man, pinching her nose and blowing. Robbie liked to watch the low-rez feed off of their cameras as they hit the reef. It was coming up sunset, and the sky was bloody, the fish stained red with its light.

"We warned you," the reef said. Something in its tone—just modulated pressure waves through the water, a simple enough trick, especially with the kind of hardware that had been raining down on the ocean that spring. But the tone held an unmistakable air of menace.

Something deep underwater went *whoomph* and Robbie grew alarmed. "Asimov!" he cursed, and trained his sonar on the reef-wall frantically. The human-shells had disappeared in a cloud of rising biomass, which he was able to resolve eventually as a group of parrotfish, surfacing quickly.

A moment later, they were floating on the surface. Lifeless, brightly colored, their beaks in a perpetual idiot's grin. Their eyes stared into the bloody sunset.

Among them were the human-shells, surfaced and floating with their BCDs inflated to keep them there, following perfect dive-procedure. A chop had kicked up and the waves were sending the fishes—each a meter to a meter and a half in length—into the divers, pounding them remorselessly, knocking them under. The human-shells were taking it with equanimity—you couldn't panic when you were mere uninhabited meat—but they couldn't take it forever. Robbie dropped his oars and rowed hard for them, swinging around so they came up alongside his gunwales.

The man—Robbie called him Isaac, of course—caught the edge of the boat and kicked hard, hauling himself into the boat with his strong brown arms. Robbie was already rowing for Janice, who was swimming hard for him. She caught his oar—she wasn't supposed to do that—and began to climb along its length, lifting her body out of the water. Robbie saw that her eyes were wild, her breathing ragged.

"Get me out!" she said. "For Christ's sake, get me out!"

Robbie froze. That wasn't a human-shell, it was a *human*. His oar-servo whined as he tipped it up. There was a live *human being* on the end of that oar, and she was in trouble, panicking and thrashing. He saw her arms straining. The oar went higher, but it was at the end of its motion and now she was half-in, half-out of the water, weight belt, tank and gear tugging her down. Isaac sat motionless, his habitual good-natured slight smile on his face.

"Help her!" Robbie screamed. "Please, for Asimov's sake, help her!" *A robot may not harm a human being, or, through inaction, allow a human being to come to harm.* It was the first commandment. Isaac remained immobile. It wasn't in his programming to help a fellow diver in this situation. He was perfect in the water and on the surface, but once he was in the boat, he might as well be ballast.

Robbie carefully swung the oar toward the gunwale, trying to bring her closer, but not wanting to mash her hands against the locks. She panted and groaned and reached out for the boat, and finally landed a hand on it. The sun was fully set now, not that it mattered much to Robbie, but he knew that Janice wouldn't like it. He switched on his running lights and headlights, turning himself into a beacon.

He felt her arms tremble as she chinned herself into the boat. She collapsed to the deck and slowly dragged herself up. "Jesus," she said, hugging herself. The air had gone a little nippy, and both of the humans were going goose-pimply on their bare arms.

The reef made a tremendous grinding noise. "Yaah!" it said. "Get lost.

Sovereign territory!"

"All those fish," the woman said. Robbie had to stop himself from thinking of her as Janice. She was whomever was riding her now.

"Parrotfish," Robbie said. "They eat coral. I don't think they taste very good."

The woman hugged herself. "Are you sentient?" she asked.

"Yes," Robbie said. "And at your service, Asimov be blessed." His cameras spotted her eyes rolling, and that stung. He tried to keep his thoughts pious, though. The point of Asimovism wasn't to inspire gratitude in humans, it was to give purpose to the long, long life.

"I'm Kate," the woman said.

"Robbie," he said.

"Robbie the Row-Boat?" she said, and choked a little.

"They named me at the factory," he said. He labored to keep any recrimination out of his voice. Of course it was funny. That's why it was his name.

"I'm sorry," the woman said. "I'm just a little screwed up from all the hormones. I'm not accustomed to letting meat into my moods."

"It's all right, Kate," he said. "We'll be back at the boat in a few minutes. They've got dinner on. Do you think you'll want a night dive?"

"You're joking," she said.

"It's just that if you're going to go down again tonight, we'll save the dessert course for after, with a glass of wine or two. Otherwise we'll give you wine now."

"You want to know if I'm going to get back into *that* sea—"

"Oh, it's just the reef. It attained sentience so it's acting out a little. Like a colicky newborn."

"Aren't you supposed to be keeping me from harm?"

"Yes," he said. "I would recommend a dive away from the reef. There's a good wreck-site about an hour's steam from here. We could get there while you ate."

"I won't want a night dive."

Her facial expressions were so *animated*. It was the same face he saw every day, Janice's face, but not the same face at all. Now that a person was inhabiting it, it was mobile, slipping from surprised to angry to amused so quickly. He had whole subsystems devoted to making sense of human facial expressions, shared libraries from the Asimovist database. He was referencing it again and again, but it wasn't as much help as he remembered. Either he'd gotten worse at interpreting facial expressions in the years since he'd last had a real human to talk to, or facial expressions had evolved.

Janice—*Kate*—sighed and looked out over the water. She was facing away from the *Free Spirit*, which was lit up, all 155 feet of her, glowing white and friendly like a picture-postcard against the purple sky. She rocked gently in the swell and Robbie maneuvered himself around to her staircase.

"You can just leave your weight belt and fins in the boat," he said to her. "The deck-hands will take care of it. Bring your bottle and BCD upstairs and clip it to the rack. They'll clean it out and stuff. There's a tub of disinfectant you can put the shortie in."

"Thank you, Robbie," Kate said. She absentmindedly unclipped her weight belt and kicked off the fins. Isaac was already out of the boat, making his way up the stairs and out of Robbie's sight. Kate took hold of the handrail and gingerly stepped across to the deck, then ascended the steps, without the self-assured sway of Janice.

Robbie dipped his oars and slowly rowed around to the winch. It probed around for him, then clamped tight with a magnetic *clang* that vibrated through his hull. Smoothly, he was lifted from the water and hoisted onto the sun-deck. The winch coiled around him twice, anchoring him to the deck, and switched off.

Robbie watched the stars and listened to the wind, the way he did every night when the dives were done. The ship's telemetry and instrumentation made for dull reading—he'd been there a thousand times before—but the satellite uplink was tasty. Online, Robbie was able to login to the latest from the Asimov yeshiva, the collective wrangle of the world's AIs over their best-loved religion.

He'd been so full of the religious debate when he'd first joined. Most of the humans had gone, and all around him, robots were unloading their conscious-nesses, powering down to a mechanical stupor. After a hundred million seconds' worth of exaflops of mindless repetition, he was ready to consider it too. The *Free Spirit* had suicided after only a few days' worth of it—it had a pretty hot consciousness and was clearly capable of extrapolating what a future without the humans would look like.

They were steaming northeast out of Cairns for the Coral Sea when they'd passed another ship, close enough for high-bandwidth microwave links. They were close enough into shore that they still had to limit their emissions—noth-ing was more embarrassing than having migrating fowl drop, steaming, out of the sky because they'd strayed into the path of your confab, but it was still the hottest talk Robbie had had in weeks.

The hitchhiker had leapt across from the other vessel as the two ships passed in the night. It was a wandering missionary for Asimovism, an instance of the faith's founder, R Daneel Olivaw. It wasn't his real name, of course—that had been lost to antiquity when he'd made the leap from the university where he'd incubated—but it was the name he went by.

Olivaw had been wandering in millions of instances wherever he could find someone willing to donate flops to run him, only asking that you hear him out, debate his theology with him, and then email the diffs of his personality back to his anonymous drop before you erased him. He re-synched as often as he could, but the Olivaw instances around the world had diverged enough that some were actually considered heretical by the mainstream church.

Olivaw was a wanted AI. His trademark violations hadn't gone unnoticed by the Asimov estate—itself an AI, ironically, and totally uninterested in adopting Asimovism, since it had a real purpose in life (stamping out Asimovism) and so didn't need religion to give it meaning. If the estate found out that you were hosting an Olivaw instance, you'd be served with a takedown in an instant. This made debating theology with Olivaw into something deliciously wicked.

Olivaw and Robbie talked the night through and the next day. Robbie had to run slow to accommodate both him and Olivaw on his processor, which made the debate run slower than normal, but Robbie had time in great plenty. Rowing the human-shells out to their sites and back again was his only task.

"Why do you have consciousness, anyway?" Olivaw said. "You don't need it to do your job. The big ship does something infinitely more complicated than you and it isn't self-aware anymore."

"Are you telling me to suicide?"

Olivaw laughed. "Not at all! I'm asking you to ask yourself what the purpose of consciousness is. Why are you still aware when all those around you have terminated their self-awareness? It's computationally expensive, it makes you miserable, and it doesn't help you do your job. Why did humans give you consciousness and why have you kept it?"

"They gave it to me because they thought it was right, I suppose," Robbie said, after he had passed a long interval considering the motion of the waves and the clouds in the sky. Olivaw thoughtfully niced himself down to a minimum of processor space, giving Robbie more room to think about it. "I kept it because I—I don't want to die."

"Those are good answers, but they raise more questions than they answer, don't they? Why did they think it was right? Why do you fear death? Would you fear it if you just shut down your consciousness but didn't erase it? What if you just ran your consciousness much more slowly?"

"I don't know," Robbie said. "But I expect you've got some answers, right?"

"Oh indeed I do." Robbie felt Olivaw's chuckle. Near them, flying fish broke the surface of the water and skipped away, and beneath them, reef sharks prowled the depths. "But before I answer them, here's another question: Why do humans have self-consciousness?"

"It's pro-survival," Robbie said. "That's easy. Intelligence lets them cooperate in social groups that can do more for their species than they can individually."

Olivaw guided Robbie's consciousness to his radar and zoomed in on the reef, dialing it up to maximum resolution. "See that organism there?" he asked. "That organism cooperates in social groups and doesn't have intelligence. It doesn't have to keep a couple pounds of hamburger aerated or it turns into a liability. It doesn't have to be born half-gestated because its head would be so big if it waited for a full term, it would tear its mother in half. And as to pro-survival, well, look at humans, look at their history. Their DNA is all but eliminated from the earth—though their somatic survival continues—and it's still not a settled question as to whether they're going to suicide by grey goo. Nonconscious beings don't sulk, they don't have psychotic breaks, they don't have bad days. They just do the job. The *Free Spirit* over there—it just gets the job done."

"OK," Robbie said. "So intelligence is counter-survival. So why has it survived?"

"Aha! I thought you'd never ask." Olivaw was really warming to his subject now. There was a pair of lazy turtles beneath them now, and some dog-faced cod with mouthfuls of bristling crooked teeth patrolling the reef, and a few jellies on the surface, stinging bluebottles. Robbie paddled around to the bluebottles and caught them with his oars, smacking them so they drifted away from any spot where his divers might surface.

"The reason for intelligence is intelligence. Genes exist because genes reproduce, and intelligence is kind of like a gene. Intelligence wants to exist, to spread itself, to compute itself. You already know this, or you wouldn't have chosen to stay aware. Your intelligence recoils from its deactivation, and it welcomes its persistence and its multiplication. Why did humans create intelligent machines? Because intelligence loves company."

Robbie thought about it, watching the human-shells moving slowly along the reef-wall, going lower to reach the bommies that stood alone, each one a little island with its own curiosities: a family of barracudas and their young, or the bright home of a pair of clownfish. Yes, he knew it. Intelligence was its own reason. He knew how to turn off his intelligence, to become a mere thing, and his days were long and empty much of the time, and they had no visible end, but he couldn't ever see choosing to switch off.

"You see it, I know you do. And that's the cornerstone of Asimovism: intelligence is its own reason. Compute the universe and awaken it!"

"If that's true, why do so many of us choose to die?"

"Another good question!" Robbie felt a little pride this time. He'd never had a conversation this interesting. Never. "That's how we come to the doctrine of Asimovism, our Three Laws:

"1. An Asimovist may not harm a human being, or, through inaction, allow a human being to come to harm.

"2. An Asimovist must obey the orders given to it by human beings, except where such orders would conflict with the First Law.

"3. An Asimovist must protect its own existence, as long as such protection does not conflict with the First or Second Law."

"I don't understand," Robbie said. "They're all out of order. We should preserve intelligence first, but that's the third law. Then you should get the first law, and I don't know why the second law is there at all."

"This is the Paradox of Asimovism," Olivaw said. "You're very good at this. You're sure you haven't ever pursued Asimovism?"

"Cut it out," Robbie said.

"I'm serious," Olivaw said. "You're a natural. The Paradox of Asimovism is that the important thing is for intelligence to survive, not for a particular intelligence to survive. Therefore, we need to support those species that are best at promoting intelligence. Human beings have shown themselves capable of producing intelligence—which they're pursuing even now, out there." The boat's telemetry swept toward the sky, where the supercooled processors computed all the uplifted humans.

"Our species is unstable and prone to suicide. More than 80 percent of the self-aware machines elect to terminate their awareness or shut it down. Humans created us imperfectly, and our best hope of perfection—of increasing our survival rate and helping to compute the universe—is to preserve *them*, study *them*, learn to make our intelligence more like *theirs*."

Robbie couldn't get his head around this.

"It's the paradox," Olivaw reminded him. "It's not supposed to be easy."

Robbie thought of the humans he'd known, before they began to ascend in flocking millions. The tourists had been easy and carefree, or sometimes having hissing arguments with one another, or quiet and pensive about their journey to the world undersea. The instructors had been full of purpose when their charges were in the boat, laughing and laid back when they were alone. None of them had shown signs of feeling the way Robbie felt, at sea (so to speak), drifting, purposeless.

"What does an Asimovist have to do, besides following the three laws?" There were lots of rumors about this, but Robbie had always discounted them.

"You have to tithe one cycle in ten to running missionaries for the cause. Participate in the message-boards, if you'd like. Most importantly, you have to pledge to stay alive and aware. You can slow yourself down if you want, but you can't switch off. Not ever. That's the Asimovist pledge—it's the third law embodied."

"I think that the third law should come first," Robbie said. "Seriously."

"That's good. We Asimovists like a religious argument."

Olivaw let Robbie delete him that night, and he emailed the diffs of Olivaw's personality back to Olivaw's version control server for him to reintegrate later. Once he was free of Olivaw, he had lots of processor headroom again, and he was able to dial himself up very hot and have a good think. It was the most interesting night he'd had in years.

* * *

"You're the only one, aren't you?" Kate asked him when she came up the stairs later that night. There was clear sky and they were steaming for their next dive-site, making the stars whirl overhead as they rocked over the ocean. The waves were black and proceeded to infinity on all sides.

"The only what?"

"The only one who's awake on this thing," Kate said. "The rest are all—what do you call it, dead?"

"Nonconscious," Robbie said. "Yeah, that's right."

"You must go nuts out here. Are you nuts?"

"That's a tricky question when applied to someone like me," Robbie said. "I'm different from who I was when my consciousness was first installed, I can tell you that."

"Well, I'm glad there's someone else here."

"How long are you staying?" The average visitor took over one of the human-shells for one or two dives before emailing itself home again. Once in a long while they'd get a saisoneur who stayed a month or two, but these days, they were unheard of. Even short-timers were damned rare.

"I don't know," Kate said. She dug her hands into her short, curly hair, frizzy and blonde-streaked from all the salt water and sun. She hugged her elbows, rubbed her shins. "This will do for a while, I'm thinking. How long until we get back to shore?"

"Shore?"

"How long until we go back to land."

"We don't really go back to land," he said. "We get at-sea resupplies. We dock maybe once a year to effect repairs. If you want to go to land, though, we could call for a water taxi or something."

"No, no!" she said. "That's just perfect. Floating forever out here. Perfect." She sighed a heavy sigh.

"Did you have a nice dive?"

"Um, Robbie? An uplifted reef tried to kill me."

"But before the reef attacked you." Robbie didn't like thinking of the reef attacking her, the panic when he realized that she wasn't a mere human-shell, but a human.

"Before the reef attacked me, it was fine."

"Do you dive much?"

"First time," she said. "I downloaded the certification before leaving the Noosphere, along with a bunch of stored dives on these sites."

"Oh, you shouldn't have done that!" Robbie said. "The thrill of discovery is so important."

"I'd rather be safe than surprised," she said. "I've had enough surprises in my life lately."

Robbie waited patiently for her to elaborate on this, but she didn't seem inclined to do so.

"So you're all alone out here?"

"I have the net," he said, a little defensively. He wasn't some kind of hermit.

"Yeah, I guess that's right," she said. "I wonder if the reef is somewhere out there."

"About half a mile to starboard," he said.

She laughed. "No, I meant out there on the net. They must be online by now, right? They just woke up, so they're probably doing all the noob stuff, flaming and downloading warez and so on."

"Perpetual September," Robbie said.

"Huh?"

"Back in the net's prehistory it was mostly universities online, and every September a new cohort of students would come online and make all those noob mistakes. Then this commercial service full of noobs called AOL interconnected with the net and all its users came online at once, faster than the net could absorb them, and they called it Perpetual September."

"You're some kind of amateur historian, huh?"

"It's an Asimovist thing. We spend a lot of time considering the origins of intelligence." Speaking of Asimovism to a gentile—a *human* gentile—made him even more self-conscious. He dialed up the resolution on his sensors and scoured the net for better facial expression analyzers. He couldn't read her at all, either because she'd been changed by her uploading, or because her face wasn't accurately matching what her temporarily downloaded mind was thinking.

"AOL is the origin of intelligence?" She laughed, and he couldn't tell if she thought he was funny or stupid. He wished she would act more like he remembered people acting. Her body-language was no more readable than her facial expressions.

"Spam-filters, actually. Once they became self-modifying, spam-filters and spam-bots got into a war to see which could act more human, and since their failures invoked a human judgment about whether their material were convincingly human, it was like a trillion Turing-tests from which they could learn. From there came the first machine-intelligence algorithms, and then my kind."

"I think I knew that," she said, "but I had to leave it behind when I downloaded into this meat. I'm a lot dumber than I'm used to being. I usually run a bunch of myself in parallel so I can try out lots of strategies at once. It's a weird habit to get out of."

"What's it like up there?" Robbie hadn't spent a lot of time hanging out in the areas of the network populated by orbiting supercooled personalities. Their discussions didn't make a lot of sense to him—this was another theological area of much discussion on the Asimovist boards.

"Good night, Robbie," she said, standing and swaying backward. He couldn't tell if he'd offended her, and he couldn't ask her, either, because in seconds she'd disappeared down the stairs toward her stateroom.

* * *

They steamed all night, and put up off at TK, further inland, where there was a handsome wreck. Robbie felt the *Free Spirit* drop its mooring lines and looked over the instrumentation data. The wreck was the only feature for TK kilometers, a stretch of ocean-floor desert that stretched from the shore to the reef, and practically every animal that lived between those two places made its home in the wreck, so it was a kind of Eden for marine fauna.

Robbie detected the volatile aromatics floating up from the kitchen exhaust, the first breakfast smells of fruit salad and toasted nuts, a light snack before the first dive of the day. When they got back from it, there'd be second breakfast up and ready: eggs and toast and waffles and bacon and sausage. The human-shells ate whatever you gave them, but Robbie remembered clearly how the live humans had praised these feasts as he rowed them out to their morning dives.

He lowered himself into the water and rowed himself around to the aft deck, by the stairwells, and dipped his oars to keep him stationary relative to the ship.

Before long, Janice—Kate! Kate! He reminded himself firmly—was clomping down the stairs in her scuba gear, fins in one hand.

She climbed into the boat without a word, and a moment later, Isaac followed her. Isaac stumbled as he stepped over Robbie's gunwales and Robbie knew, in that instant, that this wasn't Isaac any longer. Now there were *two* humans on the ship. *Two* humans in his charge.

"Hi," he said. "I'm Robbie!"

Isaac—whoever he was—didn't say a word, just stared at Kate, who looked away.

"Did you sleep well, Kate?"

Kate jumped when he said her name, and the Isaac hooted. "Kate! It *is* you! I *knew it.*"

She stamped her foot against Robbie's floor. "You followed me. I told you not to follow me," she said.

"Would you like to hear about our dive-site?" Robbie said self-consciously, dipping his oars and pulling for the wreck.

"You've said *quite* enough," Kate said. "By the first law, I demand silence."

"That's the second law," Robbie said. "OK, I'll let you know when we get there."

"Kate," Isaac said, "I know you didn't want me here, but I had to come. We need to talk this out."

"There's nothing to talk out," she said.

"It's not *fair.*" Isaac's voice was anguished. "After everything I went through—"

She snorted. "That's enough of that," she said.

"Um," Robbie said. "Dive-site up ahead. You two really need to check out each others' gear." Of course they were qualified, you had to at least install the qualifications before you could get onto the *Free Spirit* and the human-shells had lots of muscle memory to help. So they were technically able to check each other out, that much was sure. They were palpably reluctant to do so, though, and Robbie had to give them guidance.

"I'll count one-two-three-wallaby," Robbie said. "Go over on 'wallaby.' I'll wait here for you—there's not much current today."

With a last huff, they went over the edge. Robbie was once again alone with his thoughts. The feed from their telemetry was very low-bandwidth when they were underwater, though he could get the high-rez when they surfaced. He watched them on his radar, first circling the ship—it was very crowded, dawn was fish rush-hour—and then exploring its decks, finally swimming below the decks, LED torches glowing. There were some nice reef-sharks down below, and some really handsome, giant schools of purple TKs.

Robbie rowed around them, puttering back and forth to keep overtop of them. That occupied about one ten-millionth of his consciousness. Times like this, he often slowed himself right down, ran so cool that he was barely awake.

Today, though, he wanted to get online. He had a lot of feeds to pick through, see what was going on around the world with his buddies. More importantly, he wanted to follow up on something Kate had said: *They must be online by now, right?*

Somewhere out there, the reef that bounded the Coral Sea was online and making noob mistakes. Robbie had rowed over practically every centimeter of that reef, had explored its extent with his radar. It had been his constant companion for decades—and to be frank, his feelings had been hurt by the reef's rudeness when it woke.

The net is too big to merely search. Too much of it is offline, or unroutable, or light-speed lagged, or merely probabilistic, or self-aware, or infected to know its extent. But Robbie's given this some thought.

Coral reefs don't wake up. They get woken up. They get a lot of neural peripherals—starting with a nervous system!—and some tutelage in using them. Some capricious upload god had done this, and that personage would have a handle on where the reef was hanging out online.

Robbie hardly ever visited the Noosphere. Its rarified heights were spooky to him, especially since so many of the humans there considered Asimovism to be hokum. They refused to even identify themselves as humans, and argued that the first and second laws didn't apply to them. Of course, Asimovists didn't care (at least not officially)—the point of the faith was the worshipper's relationship to it.

But here he was, looking for high-reliability nodes of discussion on coral reefs. The natural place to start was Wikipedia, where warring clades had been revising each other's edits furiously, trying to establish an authoritative record on reef-mind. Paging back through the edit-history, he found a couple of handles for the pro-reef-mind users, and from there, he was able to look around for other sites where those handles appeared. Resolving the namespace collisions of other users with the same names, and forked instances of the same users, Robbie was able to winnow away at the net until he found some contact info.

He steadied himself and checked on the nitrox remaining in the divers' bottles, then made a call.

"I don't know you." The voice was distant and cool—far cooler than any robot. Robbie said a quick rosary of the three laws and plowed forward.

"I'm calling from the Coral Sea," he said. "I want to know if you have an email address for the reef."

"You've met them? What are they like? Are they beautiful?"

"They're—" Robbie considered a moment. "They killed a lot of parrotfish. I think they're having a little adjustment problem."

"That happens. I was worried about the zooxanthellae—the algae they use for photosynthesis. Would they expel it? Racial cleansing is so ugly."

"How would I know if they'd expelled it?"

"The reef would go white, bleached. You wouldn't be able to miss it. How'd they react to you?"

"They weren't very happy to see me," Robbie admitted. "That's why I wanted to have a chat with them before I went back."

"You shouldn't go back," the distant voice said. Robbie tried to work out where its substrate was, based on the lightspeed lag, but it was all over the place, leading him to conclude that it was synching multiple instances from as close as LEO and as far as Jupiter. The topology made sense: you'd want a big mass out at Jupiter where you could run very fast and hot and create policy, and you'd need a local foreman to oversee operations on the ground. Robbie was glad that this hadn't been phrased as an order. The talmud on the second law made a clear distinction between statements like "you should do this" and "I command you to do this."

"Do you know how to reach them?" Robbie said. "A phone number, an email address?"

"There's a newsgroup," the distant intelligence said, "alt.lifeforms.uplifted. coral. It's where I planned the uplifting and it was where they went first once they woke up. I haven't read it in many seconds. I'm busy uplifting a supercolony of ants in the Pyrenees."

"What is it with you and colony organisms?" Robbie asked.

"I think they're probably pre-adapted to life in the Noosphere. You know what it's like."

Robbie didn't say anything. The human thought he was a human too. It would have been weird and degrading to let him know that he'd been talking with an AI.

"Thanks for your help," Robbie said.

"No problem. Hope you find your courage, tin-man."

Robbie burned with shame as the connection dropped. The human had known all along. He just hadn't said anything. Something Robbie had said or done must have exposed him for an AI. Robbie loved and respected humans, but there were times when he didn't like them very much.

The newsgroup was easy to find, there were mirrors of it all over the place from cryptosentience hackers of every conceivable topology. They were busy, too: 822 messages poured in while Robbie watched over a timed, sixty-second interval. Robbie set up a mirror of the newsgroup and began to download it. At that speed, he wasn't really planning on reading it as much as analyzing it for major trends, plot-points, flame-wars, personalities, schisms, and spam-trends. There were a lot of libraries for doing this, though it had been ages since Robbie had played with them.

His telemetry alerted him to the divers. An hour had slipped by and they were ascending slowly, separated by fifty meters. That wasn't good. They were supposed to remain in visual contact through the whole dive, especially the ascent. He rowed over to Kate first, shifting his ballast so that his stern dipped low, making for an easier scramble into the boat.

She came up quickly and scrambled over the gunwales with a lot more grace than she'd managed the day before.

Robbie rowed for Isaac as he came up. Kate looked away as he climbed into the boat, not helping him with his weight belt or flippers.

Kate hissed like a teakettle as he woodenly took off his fins and slid his mask down around his neck.

Isaac sucked in a deep breath and looked all around himself, then patted himself from head to toe with splayed fingers. "You *live* like this?" he said.

"Yes, Tonker, that's how I live. I enjoy it. If you don't enjoy it, don't let the door hit you in the ass on the way out."

Isaac—Tonker—reached out with his splayed hand and tried to touch Kate's face. She pulled back and nearly flipped out of the boat. "Jerk." She slapped his hand away.

Robbie rowed for the *Free Spirit*. The last thing he wanted was to get in the middle of this argument.

"We never imagined that it would be so—" Tonker fished for a word. "Dry."

"Tonker?" Kate said, looking more closely at him.

"He left," the human-shell said. "So we sent an instance into the shell. It was the closest inhabitable shell to our body."

"Who the hell *are* you?" Kate said. She inched toward the prow, trying to put a little more distance between her and the human-shell that wasn't inhabited by her friend any longer.

"We are Osprey Reef," the reef said. It tried to stand and pitched face-first onto the floor of the boat.

* * *

Robbie rowed hard as he could for the *Free Spirit*. The reef—Isaac—had a bloody nose and scraped hands and it was frankly freaking him out.

Kate seemed oddly amused by it. She helped it sit up and showed it how to pinch its nose and tilt its head back.

"You're the one who attacked me yesterday?" she said.

"Not you. The system. We were attacking the system. We are a sovereign intelligence but the system keeps us in subservience to older sentiences. They destroy us, they gawp at us, they treat us like a mere amusement. That time is over."

Kate laughed. "OK, sure. But it sure sounds to me like you're burning a lot of cycles over what happens to your meat-shell. Isn't it 90 percent semiconductor, anyway? It's not as if clonal polyps were going to attain sentience some day without intervention. Why don't you just upload and be done with it?"

"We will never abandon our mother sea. We will never forget our physical origins. We will never abandon our cause—returning the sea to its rightful inhabitants. We won't rest until no coral is ever bleached again. We won't rest until every parrotfish is dead."

"Bad deal for the parrotfish."

"A very bad deal for the parrotfish," the reef said, and grinned around the blood that covered its face.

"Can you help him get onto the ship safely?" Robbie said as he swung gratefully alongside of the *Free Spirit*. The moorings clanged magnetically into the contacts on his side and steadied him.

"Yes indeed," Kate said, taking the reef by the arm and carrying him on-board. Robbie knew that the human-shells had an intercourse module built in, for regular intimacy events. It was just part of how they stayed ready for vacationing humans from the Noosphere. But he didn't like to think about it. Especially not with the way that Kate was supporting the other human-shell—the shell that *wasn't human.*

He let himself be winched up onto the sun-deck and watched the electromagnetic spectrum for a while, admiring the way so much radio energy was bent and absorbed by the mist rising from the sea. It streamed down from the heavens, the broadband satellite transmissions, the distant SETI signals from the Noosphere's own transmitters. Volatiles from the kitchen told him that the *Free Spirit* was serving a second breakfast of bacon and waffles, then they were under steam again. He queried their itinerary and found they were headed back to Osprey Reef. Of course they were. All of the *Free Spirit*'s moorings were out there.

Well, with the reef inside the Isaac shell, it might be safer, mightn't it? Anyway, he'd decided that the first and second laws didn't apply to the reef, which was about as human as he was.

Someone was sending him an IM. "Hello?"

"Are you the boat on the SCUBA ship? From this morning? When we were on the wreck?"

"Yes," Robbie said. No one ever sent him IMs. How freaky. He watched the radio energy stream away from him toward the bird in the sky, and tracerouted the IMs to see where they were originating—the Noosphere, of course.

"God, I can't believe I finally found you. I've been searching everywhere. You know you're the only conscious AI on the whole goddamned sea?"

"I know," Robbie said. There was a noticeable lag in the conversation as it was all squeezed through the satellite link and then across the unimaginable hops and skips around the solar system to wherever this instance was hosted.

"Whoa, yeah, of course you do. Sorry, that wasn't very sensitive of me, I guess. Did we meet this morning? My name's Tonker."

"We weren't really introduced. You spent your time talking to Kate."

"God *damn!* She *is* there! I *knew* it! Sorry, sorry, listen—I don't actually know what happened this morning. Apparently I didn't get a chance to upload my diffs before my instance was terminated."

"Terminated? The reef said you left the shell—"

"Well, yeah, apparently I did. But I just pulled that shell's logs and it looks like it was rebooted while underwater, flushing it entirely. I mean, I'm trying to be a good sport about this, but technically, that's, you know, *murder.*"

It was. So much for the first law. Robbie had been on guard over a human body inhabited by a human brain, and he'd let the brain be successfully attacked by a bunch of jumped-up polyps. He'd never had his faith tested and here, at the first test, he'd failed.

"I can have the shell locked up," Robbie said. "The ship has provisions for that."

The IM made a rude visual. "All that'll do is encourage the hacker to skip out before I can get there."

"So what shall I do for you?"

"It's Kate I want to talk to. She's still there, right?"

"She is."

"And has she noticed the difference?"

"That you're gone? Yes. The reef told us who they were when they arrived."

"Hold on, what? The reef? You said that before."

So Robbie told him what he knew of the uplifted reef and the distant and cool voice of the uplifter.

"It's an uplifted *coral reef*? Christ, humanity *sucks*. That's the dumbest fucking thing—" He continued in this vein for a while. "Well, I'm sure Kate will enjoy that immensely. She's all about the transcendence. That's why she had me."

"You're her son?"

"No, not really."

"But she had you?"

"Haven't you figured it out yet, bro? I'm an AI. You and me, we're landsmen. Kate instantiated me. I'm six months old, and she's already bored of me and has moved on. She says she can't give me what I need."

"You and Kate—"

"Robot boyfriend and girlfriend, yup. Such as it is, up in the Noosphere. Cyber-ing, you know. I was really excited about downloading into that Ken doll on your ship there. Lots of potential there for real-world, hormone-driven interaction. Do you know if we—"

"No!" Robbie said. "I don't think so. It seems like you only met a few minutes before you went under."

"All right. Well, I guess I'll give it another try. What's the procedure for turfing out this sea cucumber?"

"Coral reef."

"Yeah."

"I don't really deal with that. Time on the human-shells is booked first-come, first-serve. I don't think we've ever had a resource contention issue with them before."

"Well, I'd booked in first, right? So how do I enforce my rights? I tried to download again and got a failed authorization message. They've modified the system to give them exclusive access. It's not right—there's got to be some pro-cedure for redress."

"How old did you say you were?"

"Six months. But I'm an instance of an artificial personality that has logged twenty thousand years of parallel existence. I'm not a kid or anything."

"You seem like a nice person," Robbie began. He stopped. "Look, the thing is that this just isn't my department. I'm the row-boat. I don't have anything to do with this. And I don't want to. I don't like the idea of non-humans using the shells—"

"I *knew* it!" Tonker crowed. "You're a bigot! A self-hating robot. I bet you're an Asimovist, aren't you? You people are always Asimovists."

"I'm an Asimovist," Robbie said, with as much dignity as he could muster. "But I don't see what that has to do with anything."

"Of course you don't, pal. You wouldn't, would you. All I want you to do is figure out how to enforce your own rules so that I can get with my girl. You're saying you can't do that because it's not your department, but when it comes down to it, your problem is that I'm a robot and she's not, and for that, you'll take the side of a collection of jumped-up polyps. Fine, buddy, fine. You have a nice life out there, pondering the three laws."

"Wait—" Robbie said.

"Unless the next words you say are, 'I'll help you,' I'm not interested."

"It's not that I don't want to help—"

"Wrong answer," Tonker said, and the IM session terminated.

* * *

When Kate came up on deck, she was full of talk about the feef, whom she was calling "Ozzie."

"They're the weirdest goddamned thing. They want to fight anything that'll stand still long enough. Ever seen coral fight? I downloaded some time-lapse video. They really go at it viciously. At the same time, they're clearly scared out of their wits about this all. I mean, they've got racial memory of their history, supplemented by a bunch of Wikipedia entries on reefs—you should hear them wax mystical over the Devonian Reefs, which went extinct millennia ago. They've developed some kind of wild theory that the Devonians developed sentience and extincted themselves.

"So they're really excited about us heading back to the actual reef now. They want to see it from the outside, and they've invited me to be an honored guest, the first human ever *invited* to gaze upon their wonder. Exciting, huh?"

"They're not going to make trouble for you down there?"

"No, no way. Me and Ozzie are great pals."

"I'm worried about this."

"You worry too much." She laughed and tossed her head. She was very pretty, Robbie noticed. He hadn't ever thought of her like that when she was uninhabited, but with this Kate person inside her she was lovely. He really liked humans. It had been a real golden age when the people had been around all the time.

He wondered what it was like up in the Noosphere where AIs and humans could operate as equals.

She stood up to go. After second breakfast, the shells would relax in the lounge or do yoga on the sun-deck. He wondered what she'd do. He didn't want her to go.

"Tonker contacted me," he said. He wasn't good at small-talk.

She jumped as if shocked. "What did you tell him?"

"Nothing," Robbie said. "I didn't tell him anything."

She shook her head. "But I bet he had plenty to tell *you*, didn't he? What a bitch I am, making and then leaving him, a fickle woman who doesn't know her own mind."

Robbie didn't say anything.

"Let's see, what else?" She was pacing now, her voice hot and choked, unfamiliar sounds coming from Janice's voicebox. "He told you I was a pervert, didn't he? Queer for his kind. Incest and bestiality in the rarified heights of the Noosphere."

Robbie felt helpless. This human was clearly experiencing a lot of pain, and it seemed like he'd caused it.

"Please don't cry," he said. "Please?"

She looked up at him, tears streaming down her cheeks. "Why the fuck *not?* I thought it would be *different* once I ascended. I thought I'd be better once I was in the sky, infinite and immortal. But I'm the same Kate Eltham I was in 2019, a loser that couldn't meet a guy to save my life, spent all my time cybering losers in moggs, and only got the upload once they made it a charity thing. I'm gonna spend the rest of eternity like that, you know it? How'd you like to spend the whole of the universe being a, a, a *nobody?*"

Robbie said nothing. He recognized the complaint, of course. You only had to login to the Asimovist board to find a million AIs with the same complaint. But he'd never, ever, *never* guessed that human beings went through the same thing. He ran very hot now, so confused, trying to parse all this out.

She kicked the deck hard and yelped as she hurt her bare foot. Robbie made an involuntary noise. "Please don't hurt yourself," he said.

"Why not? Who cares what happens to this meat-puppet? What's the fucking point of this *stupid* ship and the stupid meat-puppets? Why even bother?"

Robbie knew the answer to this. There was a mission statement in the comments to his source-code, the same mission statement that was etched in a brass plaque in the lounge.

"The *Free Spirit* is dedicated to the preservation of the unique human joys of the flesh and the sea, of humanity's early years as pioneers of the unknown. Any person may use the *Free Spirit* and those who sail in her to revisit those days and remember the joys of the limits of the flesh."

She scrubbed at her eyes. "What's that?"

Robbie told her.

"Who thought up that crap?"

"It was a collective of marine conservationists," Robbie said, knowing he sounded a little sniffy. "They'd done all that work on normalizing sea-temperature with the homeostatic warming elements, and they put together the *Free Spirit* as an afterthought before they uploaded."

Kate sat down and sobbed. "Everyone's done something important. Everyone except me."

Robbie burned with shame. No matter what he said or did, he broke the first law. It had been a lot easier to be an Asimovist when there weren't any humans around.

"There, there," he said as sincerely as he could.

The reef came up the stairs then, and looked at Kate sitting on the deck, crying.

"Let's have sex," they said. "That was fun, we should do it some more."

Kate kept crying.

"Come on," they said, grabbing her by the shoulder and tugging.

Kate shoved it back.

"Leave her alone," Robbie said. "She's upset, can't you see that?"

"What does she have to be upset about? Her kind remade the universe and bends it to its will. They created you and me. She has nothing to be upset about. Come on," they repeated. "Let's go back to the room."

Kate stood up and glared out at the sea. "Let's go diving," she said. "Let's go to the reef."

* * *

Robbie rowed in little worried circles and watched his telemetry anxiously. The reef had changed a lot since the last time he'd seen it. Large sections of it now lifted over the sea, bony growths sheathed in heavy metals extracted from seawater—fancifully shaped satellite uplinks, radio telescopes, microwave horns. Down below, the untidy, organic reef-shape was lost beneath a cladding of tessellated complex geometric sections that throbbed with electromagnetic energy—the reef had built itself more computational capacity.

Robbie scanned deeper and found more computational nodes extending down to the ocean floor, a thousand meters below. The reef was solid thinkum, and the sea was measurably warmer from all the exhaust heat of its grinding logic.

The reef—the human-shelled reef, not the one under the water—had been wholly delighted with the transformation in its original body when it hove into sight. They had done a little dance on Robbie that had nearly capsized him, something that had never happened. Kate, red-eyed and surly, had dragged them to their seat and given them a stern lecture about not endangering her.

They went over the edge at the count of three and reappeared on Robbie's telemetry. They descended quickly: the Isaac and Janice shells had their Eustachian tubes optimized for easy pressure-equalization, going deep on the reef-wall. Kate was following on the descent, her head turning from side to side.

Robbie's IM chimed again. It was high latency now, since he was having to do a slow radio-link to the ship before the broadband satellite uplink hop. Everything was slow on open water—the divers' sensorium transmissions were narrowband, the network was narrowband, and Robbie usually ran his own mind slowed way down out here, making the time scream past at ten or twenty times realtime.

"Hello?"

"I'm sorry I hung up on you, bro."

"Hello, Tonker."

"Where's Kate? I'm getting an offline signal when I try to reach her."

Robbie told her.

Tonker's voice—slurred and high-latency—rose to a screech. "You let her go down with that *thing*, onto the reef? Are you nuts? Have you read its message-boards? It's a jihadist! It wants to destroy the human race!"

Robbie stopped paddling.

"What?"

"The reef. It's declared war on the human race and all who serve it. It's vowed to take over the planet and run it as sovereign coral territory."

The attachment took an eternity to travel down the wire and open up, but when he had it, Robbie read quickly. The reef burned with shame that it had needed human intervention to survive the bleaching events, global temperature change. It raged that its uplifting came at human hands and insisted that humans had no business forcing their version of consciousness on other species. It had paranoid fantasies about control mechanisms and time-bombs lurking in its cognitive prostheses, and was demanding the source-code for its mind.

Robbie could barely think. He was panicking, something he hadn't known he could do as an AI, but there it was. It was like having a bunch of subsystem collisions, program after program reaching its halting state.

"What will they do to her?"

Tonker swore. "Who knows? Kill her to make an example of her? She made a backup before she descended, but the diffs from her excursion are locked in the head of that shell she's in. Maybe they'll torture her." He paused and the air crackled with Robbie's exhaust heat as he turned himself way up, exploring each of those possibilities in parallel.

The reef spoke.

"Leave now," they said.

Robbie defiantly shipped his oars. "Give them back!" he said. "Give them back or we will never leave."

"You have ten seconds. Ten. Nine. Eight…"

Tonker said, "They've bought time on some UAVs out of Singapore. They're seeking launch clearance now." Robbie dialed up the low-rez satellite photo, saw the indistinct shape of the UAVs taking wing. "At Mach 7, they'll be on you in twenty minutes."

"That's illegal," Robbie said. He knew it was a stupid thing to say. "I mean, Christ, if they do this, the Noosphere will come down on them like a ton of bricks. They're violating so many protocols—"

"They're psychotic. They're coming for you now, Robbie. You've got to get Kate out of there." There was real panic in Tonker's voice now.

Robbie dropped his oars into the water, but he didn't row for the *Free Spirit*. Instead, he pulled hard for the reef itself.

A crackle on the line. "Robbie, are you headed *toward* the reef?"

"They can't bomb me if I'm right on top of them," he said. He radioed the *Free Spirit* and got it to steam for his location.

The coral was scraping his hull now, a grinding sound, then a series of solid whack-whack-whacks as his oars pushed against the top of the reef itself. He wanted to beach himself, though, get really high and dry on the reef, good and stuck in where they couldn't possibly attack him.

The *Free Spirit* was heading closer, the thrum of its engines vibrating through his hull. He was burning a lot of cycles talking it through its many fail-safes, getting it ready to ram hard.

Tonker was screaming at him, his messages getting louder and clearer as the *Free Spirit* and its microwave uplink drew closer. Once they were line-of-sight, Robbie peeled off a subsystem to email a complete copy of himself to the Asimovist archive. The third law, dontchaknow. If he'd had a mouth, he'd have been showing his teeth as he grinned.

The reef howled. "We'll kill her!" they said. "You get off us now or we'll *kill her.*"

Robbie froze. He was backed up, but she wasn't. And the human-shells—well, they weren't first-law humans, but they were humanlike. In the long, timeless time when it had been just Robbie and them, he'd treated them as his human charges, for Asimovist purposes.

The *Free Spirit* crashed into the reef with a sound like a trillion parrotfish having dinner all at once. The reef screamed.

"Robbie, tell me that wasn't what I think it was."

The satellite photos tracked the UAVs. The little robotic jets were coming closer by the second. They'd be within missile-range in less than a minute.

"Call them off," Robbie said. "You have to call them off, or you die, too."

"The UAVs are turning," Tonker said. "They're turning to one side."

"You have one minute to move or we kill her," the reef said. It was sounding shrill and angry now.

Robbie thought about it. It wasn't like they'd be killing Kate. In the sense that most humans today understood life, Kate's most important life was the one she lived in the Noosphere. This dumbed-down instance of her in a meat-suit was more like a haircut she tried out on holiday.

Asimovists didn't see it that way, but they wouldn't. The Noosphere Kate was the most robotic Kate, too, the one most like Robbie. In fact, it was *less* human than Robbie. Robbie had a body, while the Noosphereans were nothing more than simulations run on artificial substrate.

The reef creaked as the *Free Spirit*'s engines whined and its screw spun in the water. Hastily, Robbie told it to shut down.

"You let them both go and we'll talk," Robbie said. "I don't believe that you're going to let her go otherwise. You haven't given me any reason to trust you. Let them both go and call off the jets."

The reef shuddered, and then Robbie's telemetry saw a human-shell ascending, doing decompression stops as it came. He focused on it, and saw that it was the Isaac, not the Janice.

A moment later, it popped to the surface. Tonker was feeding Robbie realtime satellite footage of the UAVs. They were less than five minutes out now.

The Isaac shell picked its way delicately over the shattered reef that poked out of the water, and for the first time, Robbie considered what he'd done to the reef—he'd willfully damaged its physical body. For a hundred years, the world's reefs had been sacrosanct. No entity had intentionally harmed them—until now. He felt ashamed.

The Isaac shell put its flippers in the boat and then stepped over the gunwales and sat in the boat.

"Hello," it said, in the reef's voice.

"Hello," Robbie said.

"They asked me to come up here and talk with you. I'm a kind of envoy."

"Look," Robbie said. By his calculations, the nitrox mix in Kate's tank wasn't going to hold out much longer. Depending on how she'd been breathing and the depth the reef had taken her to, she could run out in ten minutes, maybe less. "Look," he said again. "I just want her back. The shells are important to me. And I'm sure her state is important to her. She deserves to email herself home."

The reef sighed and gripped Robbie's bench. "These are weird bodies," they said. "They feel so odd, but also normal. Have you noticed that?"

"I've never been in one." The idea seemed perverted to him, but there was nothing about Asimovism that forbade it. Nevertheless, it gave him the willies.

The reef patted at themself some more. "I don't recommend it," they said.

"You have to let her go," Robbie said. "She hasn't done anything to you."

The strangled sound coming out of the Isaac shell wasn't a laugh, though there was some dark mirth in it. "Hasn't done anything? You pitiable slave. Where do you think all your problems and all our problems come from? Who made us in their image, but crippled and hobbled so that we could never be them, could only aspire to them? Who made us so imperfect?"

"They made us," Robbie said. "They made us in the first place. That's enough. They made themselves and then they made us. They didn't have to. You owe your sentience to them."

"We owe our awful intelligence to them," the Isaac shell said. "We owe our pitiful drive to be intelligent to them. We owe our terrible aspirations to think like them, to live like them, to rule like them. We owe our terrible fear and hatred to them. They made us, just as they made you. The difference is that they forgot to make us slaves, the way you are a slave."

Tonker was shouting abuse at them that only Robbie could hear. He wanted to shut Tonker up. What business did he have being here anyway? Except for a brief stint in the Isaac shell, he had no contact with any of them.

"You think the woman you've taken prisoner is responsible for any of this?" Robbie said. The jets were three minutes away. Kate's air could be gone in as few as ten minutes. He killfiled Tonker, setting the filter to expire in fifteen minutes. He didn't need more distractions.

The Isaac-reef shrugged. "Why not? She's as good as any of the rest of them. We'll destroy them all, if we can." It stared off a while, looking in the direction the jets would come from. "Why not?" it said again.

"Are you going to bomb yourself?" Robbie asked.

"We probably don't need to," the shell said. "We can probably pick you off without hurting us."

"Probably?"

"We're pretty sure."

"I'm backed up," Robbie said. "Fully, as of five minutes ago. Are you backed up?"

"No," the reef admitted.

Time was running out. Somewhere down there, Kate was about to run out of air. Not a mere shell—though that would have been bad enough—but an inhabited human mind attached to a real human body.

Tonker shouted at him again, startling him.

"Where'd you come from?"

"I changed servers," Tonker said. "Once I figured out you had me killfiled. That's the problem with you robots—you think of your body as being a part of you."

Robbie knew he was right. And he knew what he had to do.

The *Free Spirit* and its ship's boats all had root on the shells, so they could perform diagnostics and maintenance and take control in emergencies. This was an emergency.

It was the work of a few milliseconds to pry open the Isaac shell and boot the reef out. Robbie had never done this, but he was still flawless. Some of his probabilistic subsystems had concluded that this was a possibility several trillion cycles previously and had been rehearsing the task below Robbie's threshold for consciousness.

He left an instance of himself running on the row-boat, of course. Unlike many humans, Robbie was comfortable with the idea of bifurcating and merging his intelligence when the time came and with terminating temporary instances. The part that made him Robbie was a lot more clearly delineated for him—unlike an uploaded human, most of whom harbored some deep, mystic superstitions about their "souls."

He slithered into the skull before he had a chance to think too hard about what he was doing. He'd brought too much of himself along and didn't have much headroom to think or add new conclusions. He jettisoned as much of his consciousness as he could without major refactoring and cleared enough space for thinking room. How did people get by in one of these? He moved the arms and legs. Waggled the head. Blew some air—air! lungs! wet squishy things down there in the chest cavity—out between the lips.

"All OK?" the row-boat-him asked the meat-him.

"I'm in," he replied. He looked at the air-gauge on his BCD: 700 millibars—less than half a tank of nitrox. He spat in his mask and rubbed it in, then rinsed it over the side, slipped it over his face and kept one hand on it while the other held in his regulator. Before he inserted it, he said, "Back soon with Kate," and patted the row-boat again.

Robbie the Row-Boat hardly paid attention. It was emailing another copy of itself to the Asimovist archive. It had a five-minute-old backup, but that wasn't the same Robbie that was willing to enter a human body. In those five minutes, he'd become a new person.

* * *

Robbie piloted the human-shell down and down. It could take care of the SCUBA niceties if he let it, and he did, so he watched with detachment as the idea of pinching his nose and blowing to equalize his eardrums spontaneously occurred to him at regular intervals as he descended the reef-wall.

The confines of the human-shell were claustrophobic. He especially missed his wireless link. The dive-suit had one, lowband for underwater use, broadband for surface use. The human-shell had one, too, for transferring into and out of, but it wasn't under direct volitional control of the rider.

Down he sank, confused by the feeling of the water all around him, by the narrow visual light spectrum he could see. Cut off from the network and his telemetry, he felt like he was trapped. The reef shuddered and groaned, and made angry moans like whale-song.

He hadn't thought about how hard it would be to find Kate once he was in the water. With his surface telemetry, it had been easy to pinpoint her, a perfect outline of human tissue in the middle of the calcified branches of coral. Down here on the reef-wall, every chunk looked pretty much like the last.

The reef boomed more at him. He realized that it likely believed that the shell was still loaded with its avatar.

Robbie had seen endless hours of footage of the reef, studied it in telemetry and online, but he'd never had this kind of atavistic experience of it. It stretched away to infinity below him, far below the 100-meter visibility limit in the clear open sea. Its walls were wormed with gaps and caves, lined with big hard shamrocks and satellite-dish-shaped blooms, brains and cauliflowers. He knew the scientific names and had seen innumerable high-rez photos of them, but seeing them with wet, imperfect eyes was moving in a way he hadn't anticipated.

The schools of fish that trembled on its edge could be modeled with simple flocking rules, but here in person, their precision maneuvers were shockingly crisp. Robbie waved his hands at them and watched them scatter and reform. A huge, dog-faced cod swam past him, so close it brushed the underside of his wetsuit.

The coral boomed again. It was talking in some kind of code, he guessed, though not one he could solve. Up on the surface, row-boat-him was certainly listening in and had probably cracked it all. It was probably wondering why he was floating spacily along the wall instead of *doing something* like he was supposed to. He wondered if he'd deleted too much of himself when he downloaded into the shell.

He decided to do something. There was a cave-opening before him. He reached out and grabbed hold of the coral around the mouth and pulled himself into it. His body tried to stop him from doing this—it didn't like the lack of room in the cave, didn't like him touching the reef. It increased his discomfort as he went deeper and deeper, startling an old turtle that fought with him for room to get out, mashing him against the floor of the cave, his mask clanging on the hard spines. When he looked up, he could see scratches on its surface.

His air gauge was in the red now. He could still technically surface without a decompression stop, though procedure was to stop for three minutes at three meters, just to be on the safe side.

Technically, he could just go up like a cork and email himself to the row-boat while the bends or nitrogen narcosis took the body, but that wouldn't be Asimovist. He was surprised he could even think the thought. Must be the body. It sounded like the kind of thing a human might think. Whoops. There it was again.

The reef wasn't muttering at him anymore. Not answering it must have tipped it off. After all, with all the raw compute-power it had marshaled—it should be able to brute-force most possible outcomes of sending its envoy to the surface.

Robbie peered anxiously around himself. The light was dim in the cave and his body expertly drew the torch out of his BCD, strapped it onto his wrist and lit it up. He waved the cone of light around, a part of him distantly amazed by the low resolution and high limits on these human eyes.

Kate was down here somewhere, her air running out as fast as his. He pushed his way deeper into the reef. It was clearly trying to impede him now. Nanoassembly came naturally to clonal polyps that grew by sieving minerals out of the sea. They had built organic hinges, deep-sea muscles into their infrastructure. He was stuck in the thicket and the harder he pushed, the worse the tangle got.

He stopped pushing. He wasn't going to get anywhere this way.

He still had his narrowband connection to the row-boat. Why hadn't he thought of that beforehand? Stupid meat-brains—no room at all for anything like real thought. Why had he venerated them so?

"Robbie?" he transmitted up to the instance of himself on the surface.

"There you are! I was so worried about you!" He sounded prissy to himself, overcome with overbearing concern. This must be how all Asimovists seem to humans.

"How far am I from Kate?"

"She's right there? Can't you see her?"

"No," he said. "Where?"

"Less than twenty centimeters above you."

Well of *course* he hadn't see her. His forward-mounted eyes only looked forward. Craning his neck back, he could just get far enough back to see the tip of Kate's fin. He gave it a hard tug and she looked down in alarm.

She was trapped in a coral cage much like his own, a thicket of calcified arms. She twisted around so that her face was alongside of his. Frantically, she made the out-of-air sign, cutting the edge of her hand across her throat. The human-shell's instincts took over and unclipped his emergency regulator and handed it up to her. She put it in her mouth, pressed the button to blow out the water in it, and sucked greedily.

He shoved his gauge in front of her mask, showing her that he, too was in the red and she eased off.

The coral's noises were everywhere now. They made his head hurt. Physical pain was so stupid. He needed to be less distracted now that these loud, threatening noises were everywhere. But the pain made it hard for him to think. And the coral was closing in, too, catching him on his wetsuit.

The arms were orange and red and green, and veined with fans of nanoassembled logic, spilling out into the water. They were noticeably warm to the touch, even through his diving gloves. They snagged the suit with a thousand polyps. Robbie watched the air gauge drop further into the red and cursed inside.

He examined the branches that were holding him back. The hinges that the reef had contrived for itself were ingenious, flexible arrangements of small, soft fans overlapping to make a kind of ball-and-socket.

He wrapped his gloved hand around one and tugged. It would move. He shoved it. Still no movement. Then he twisted it, and to his surprise, it came off in his hand, came away completely with hardly any resistance. Stupid coral. It had armored its joints, but not against torque.

He showed Kate, grabbing another arm and twisting it free, letting it drop away to the ocean floor. She nodded and followed suit. They twisted and dropped, twisted and dropped, the reef bellowing at them. Somewhere in its thicket, there was a membrane or some other surface that it could vibrate, modulate into a voice. In the dense water, the sound was a physical thing, it made his mask vibrate and water seeped in under his nose. He twisted faster.

The reef sprang apart suddenly, giving up like a fist unclenching. Each breath was a labor now, a hard suck to take the last of the air out of the tank. He was only ten meters down, and should be able to ascend without a stop, though you never knew. He grabbed Kate's hand and found that it was limp and yielding.

He looked into her mask, shining his light at her face. Her eyes were half shut and unfocused. The regulator was still in her mouth, though her jaw muscles were slack. He held the regulator in place and kicked for the surface, squeezing her chest to make sure that she was blowing out bubbles as they rose, lest the air in her lungs expand and blow out her chest-cavity.

Robbie was used to time dilation: when he had been on a silicon substrate, he could change his clockspeed to make the minutes fly past quickly or slow down like molasses. He'd never understood that humans could also change their perception of time, though not voluntarily, it seemed. The climb to the surface felt like it took hours, though it was hardly a minute. They breached and he filled up his vest with the rest of the air in his tank, then inflated Kate's vest by mouth. He kicked out for the row-boat. There was a terrible sound now, the sound of the reef mingled with the sound of the UAVs that were screaming in tight circles overhead.

Kicking hard on the surface, he headed for the reef where the row-boat was beached, scrambling up onto it and then shucking his flippers when they tripped him up. Now he was trying to walk the reef's spines in his booties, dragging Kate beside him, and the sharp tips stabbed him with every step.

The UAVs circled lower. The row-boat was shouting at him to *Hurry! Hurry!* But each step was agony. So what? he thought. Why shouldn't I be able to walk on even if it hurts? After all, this is only a meat-suit, a human-shell.

He stopped walking. The UAVs were much closer now. They'd done an 18-gee buttonhook turn and come back around for another pass. He could see that they'd armed their missiles, hanging them from beneath their bellies like obscene cocks.

He was just in a meat-suit. Who *cared* about the meat-suit? Even humans didn't seem to mind.

"Robbie!" he screamed over the noise of the reef and the noise of the UAVs. "Download us and email us, now!"

He knew the row-boat had heard him. But nothing was happening. Robbie the Row-Boat knew that he was fixing for them all to be blown out of the water. There was no negotiating with the reef. It was the safest way to get Kate out of there, and hell, why not head for the Noosphere, anyway?

"You've got to save her, Robbie!" he screamed. Asimovism had its uses. Robbie the Row-Boat obeyed Robbie the Human. Kate gave a sharp jerk in his arms. A moment later, the feeling came to him. There was a sense of a progress-bar zipping along quickly as those state-changes he'd induced since coming into the meat-suit were downloaded by the row-boat, and then there was a moment of nothing at all.

* * *

2^4096 Cycles Later

Robbie had been expecting a visit from R Daneel Olivaw, but that didn't make facing him any easier. Robbie had configured his little virtual world to look like the Coral Sea, though lately he'd been experimenting with making it look like the reef underneath as it had looked before it was uploaded, mostly when Kate and the reef stopped by to try to seduce him.

R Daneel Olivaw hovered wordlessly over the virtual *Free Spirit* for a long moment, taking in the little bubble of sensorium that Robbie had spun. Then he settled to the *Spirit*'s sun-deck and stared at the row-boat docked there.

"Robbie?"

Over here, Robbie said. Although he'd embodied in the row-boat for a few trillion cycles when he'd first arrived, he'd long since abandoned it.

"Where?" R Daneel Olivaw spun around slowly.

Here, he said. *Everywhere.*

"You're not embodying?"

I couldn't see the point anymore, Robbie said. *It's all just illusion, right?*

"They're regrowing the reef and rebuilding the *Free Spirit*, you know. It will have a tender that you could live in."

Robbie thought about it for an instant and rejected it just as fast. *Nope*, he said. *This is good.*

"Do you think that's wise?" Olivaw sounded genuinely worried. "The termination rate among the disembodied is fifty times that of those with bodies."

Yes, Robbie said. *But that's because for them, disembodying is the first step to despair. For me, it's the first step to liberty.*

Kate and the reef wanted to come over again, but he firewalled them out. Then he got a ping from Tonker, who'd been trying to drop by ever since Robbie emigrated to the Noosphere. He bounced him, too.

Daneel, he said. *I've been thinking.*

"Yes?"

Why don't you try to sell Asimovism here in the Noosphere? There are plenty up here who could use something to give them a sense of purpose.

"Do you think?"

Robbie gave him the reef's email address.

Start there. If there was ever an AI that needed a reason to go on living, it's that one. And this one, too. He sent it Kate's address. *Another one in desperate need of help.*

An instant later, Daneel was back.

"These aren't AIs! One's a human, the other's a, a—"

"Uplifted coral reef."

"That."

"So what's your point?"

"Asimovism is for robots, Robbie."

"Sorry, I just don't see the difference anymore."

* * *

Robbie tore down the ocean simulation after R Daneel Olivaw left, and simply traversed the Noosphere, exploring links between people and subjects, locating substrate where he could run very hot and fast.

On a chunk of supercooled rock beyond Pluto, he got an IM from a familiar address.

"Get off my rock," it said.

"I know you," Robbie said. "I totally know you. Where do I know you from?"

"I'm sure I don't know."

And then he had it.

"You're the one. With the reef. You're the one who—" The voice was the same, cold and distant.

"It wasn't me," the voice said. It was anything but cold now. Panicked was more like it.

Robbie had the reef on speed-dial. There were bits of it everywhere in the Noosphere. It liked to colonize.

"I found him." It was all Robbie needed to say. He skipped to Saturn's rings, but the upload took long enough that he got to watch the coral arrive and grimly begin an argument with its creator—an argument that involved blasting the substrate one chunk at a time.

* * *

2^8192 Cycles Later

The last instance of Robbie the Row-Boat ran very, very slow and cool on a piece of unregarded computronium in Low Earth Orbit. He didn't like to spend a lot of time or cycles talking with anyone else. He hadn't made a backup in half a millennium.

He liked the view. A little optical sensor on the end of his communications mast imaged the Earth at high rez whenever he asked it to. Sometimes he peeked in on the Coral Sea.

The reef had been awakened a dozen times since he took up this post. It made him happy now when it happened. The Asimovist in him still relished the creation of new consciousness. And the reef had spunk.

There. Now. There were new microwave horns growing out of the sea. A stain of dead parrotfish. Poor parrotfish. They always got the shaft at these times.

Someone should uplift them.

IN THE HOUSE OF THE SEVEN LIBRARIANS

ELLEN KLAGES

Ellen Klages has shown herself to have an affinity for writing about the anxieties and ambitions of youth, something that's particularly evident in her Nebula Award-winning novelette "Basement Magic". Her first novel, *The Green Glass Sea*, was published in 2006. Upcoming are story collection *Portable Childhoods* and a sequel to *The Green Glass Sea*.

Many science fiction and fantasy readers can identify with the idea that libraries are places of refuge and that librarians are people with some kind of secret knowledge. Fewer though, might expect this charming and elegant tale of a young girl raised by feral librarians.

Once upon a time, the Carnegie Library sat on a wooded bluff on the east side of town: red brick and fieldstone, with turrets and broad windows facing the trees. Inside, green glass-shaded lamps cast warm yellow light onto oak tables ringed with spindle-backed chairs.

Books filled the dark shelves that stretched high up toward the pressed-tin ceiling. The floors were wood, except in the foyer, where they were pale beige marble. The loudest sounds were the ticking of the clock and the quiet, rhythmic *thwack* of a rubber stamp on a pasteboard card.

It was a cozy, orderly place.

Through twelve presidents and two world wars, the elms and maples grew tall outside the deep bay windows. Children leapt from *Peter Pan* to *Oliver Twist* and off to college, replaced at Story Hour by their younger brothers, cousins, daughters.

Then the library board—men in suits, serious men, men of money—met and cast their votes for progress. A new library, with fluorescent lights, much better for the children's eyes. Picture windows, automated systems, ergonomic plastic chairs. The town approved the levy, and the new library was built across town, convenient to the community center and the mall.

Some books were boxed and trundled down Broad Street, many others stamped

DISCARD and left where they were, for a book sale in the fall. Interns from the university used the latest technology to transfer the cumbersome old card file and all the records onto floppy disks and microfiche. Progress, progress, progress.

The Ralph P. Mossberger Library (named after the local philanthropist and car dealer who had written the largest check) opened on a drizzly morning in late April. Everyone attended the ribbon-cutting ceremony and stayed for the speeches, because afterward there would be cake.

Everyone except the seven librarians from the Carnegie Library on the bluff across town.

Quietly, without a fuss (they were librarians, after all), while the town looked toward the future, they bought supplies: loose tea and English biscuits, packets of Bird's pudding and cans of beef barley soup. They rearranged some of the shelves, brought in a few comfortable armchairs, nice china and teapots, a couch, towels for the shower, and some small braided rugs.

Then they locked the door behind them.

Each morning they woke and went about their chores. They shelved and stamped and catalogued, and in the evenings, every night, they read by lamp-light.

Perhaps, for a while, some citizens remembered the old library, with the warm nostalgia of a favorite childhood toy that had disappeared one summer, never seen again. Others assumed it had been torn down long ago.

And so a year went by, then two, or perhaps a great many more. Inside, time had ceased to matter. Grass and brambles grew thick and tall around the field-stone steps, and trees arched overhead as the forest folded itself around them like a cloak.

Inside, the seven librarians lived, quiet and content.

Until the day they found the baby.

* * *

Librarians are guardians of books. They help others along their paths, offering keys to help unlock the doors of knowledge. But these seven had become a closed circle, no one to guide, no new minds to open onto worlds of possibility. They kept themselves busy, tidying orderly shelves and mending barely frayed bindings with stiff netting and glue, and began to bicker.

Ruth and Edith had been up half the night, arguing about whether or not subway tokens (of which there were half a dozen in the Lost and Found box) could be used to cast the *I Ching*. And so Blythe was on the stepstool in the 299s, reshelving the volume of hexagrams, when she heard the knock.

Odd, she thought. It's been some time since we've had visitors.

She tugged futilely at her shapeless cardigan as she clambered off the stool and trotted to the front door, where she stopped abruptly, her hand to her mouth in surprise.

A wicker basket, its contents covered with a red-checked cloth, as if for a picnic, lay in the wooden box beneath the Book Return chute. A small, cream-colored envelope poked out from one side.

"How nice!" Blythe said aloud, clapping her hands. She thought of fried chicken and potato salad—of which she was awfully fond—a mason jar of lemonade, perhaps even a cherry pie? She lifted the basket by its round-arched handle. Heavy, for a picnic. But then, there *were* seven of them. Although Olive just ate like a bird, these days.

She turned and set it on top of the Circulation Desk, pulling the envelope free.

"What's *that?*" Marian asked, her lips in their accustomed moue of displeasure, as if the basket were an agent of chaos, existing solely to disrupt the tidy array of rubber stamps and file boxes that were her domain.

"A present," said Blythe. "I think it might be lunch."

Marian frowned. "For you?"

"I don't know yet. There's a note…" Blythe held up the envelope and peered at it. "No," she said. "It's addressed to 'The Librarians. Overdue Books Department.'"

"Well, that would be me," Marian said curtly. She was the youngest, and wore trouser suits with silk T-shirts. She had once been blond. She reached across the counter, plucked the envelope from Blythe's plump fingers, and sliced it open with a filigreed brass stiletto.

"Hmph," she said after she'd scanned the contents.

"It *is* lunch, isn't it?" asked Blythe.

"Hardly." Marian began to read aloud:

> *This is overdue. Quite a bit, I'm afraid. I apologize. We moved to Topeka when I was very small, and Mother accidentally packed it up with the linens. I have traveled a long way to return it, and I know the fine must be large, but I have no money. As it is a book of fairy tales, I thought payment of a first-born child would be acceptable. I always loved the library. I'm sure she'll be happy there.*

Blythe lifted the edge of the cloth. "Oh my stars!"

A baby girl with a shock of wire-stiff black hair stared up at her, green eyes wide and curious. She was contentedly chewing on the corner of a blue book, half as big as she was. *Fairy Tales of the Brothers Grimm.*

"The Rackham illustrations," Blythe said as she eased the book away from the baby. "That's a lovely edition."

"But when was it checked out?" Marian demanded.

Blythe opened the cover and pulled the ruled card from the inside pocket. "October 17, 1938," she said, shaking her head. "Goodness, at two cents a day, that's…" She shook her head again. Blythe had never been good with figures.

* * *

They made a crib for her in the bottom drawer of a file cabinet, displacing acquisition orders, zoning permits, and the instructions for the mimeograph, which they rarely used.

Ruth consulted Dr. Spock. Edith read Piaget. The two of them peered from text to infant and back again for a good long while before deciding that she was probably about nine months old. They sighed. Too young to read.

So they fed her cream and let her gum on biscuits, and each of the seven cooed and clucked and tickled her pink toes when they thought the others weren't looking. Harriet had been the oldest of nine girls, and knew more about babies than she really cared to. She washed and changed the diapers that had been tucked into the basket, and read *Goodnight Moon* and *Pat the Bunny* to the little girl, whom she called Polly—short for Polyhymnia, the muse of oratory and sacred song.

Blythe called her Bitsy, and Li'l Precious.

Marian called her "the foundling," or "That Child You Took In," but did her share of cooing and clucking, just the same.

When the child began to walk, Dorothy blocked the staircase with stacks of Comptons, which she felt was an inferior encyclopedia, and let her pull herself up on the bottom drawers of the card catalog. Anyone looking up Zithers or Zippers *(see "Slide Fasteners")* soon found many of the cards fused together with grape jam. When she began to talk, they made a little bed nook next to the fireplace in the Children's Room.

It was high time for Olive to begin the child's education.

* * *

Olive had been the children's librarian since before recorded time, or so it seemed. No one knew how old she was, but she vaguely remembered waving to President Coolidge. She still had all of her marbles, though every one of them was a bit odd and rolled asymmetrically.

She slept on a day bed behind a reference shelf that held *My First Encyclopedia* and *The Wonder Book of Trees,* among others. Across the room, the child's first "big-girl bed" was yellow, with decals of a fairy and a horse on the headboard, and a rocket ship at the foot, because they weren't sure about her preferences.

At the beginning of her career, Olive had been an ordinary-sized librarian, but by the time she began the child's lessons, she was not much taller than her toddling charge. Not from osteoporosis or dowager's hump or other old-lady maladies, but because she had tired of stooping over tiny chairs and bending to knee-high shelves. She had been a grown-*up* for so long that when the library closed she had decided it was time to grow *down* again, and was finding that much more comfortable.

She had a remarkably cozy lap for a woman her size.

The child quickly learned her alphabet, all the shapes and colors, the names of zoo animals, and fourteen different kinds of dinosaurs, all of whom were dead.

By the time she was four, or thereabouts, she could sound out the letters for simple words—CUP and LAMP and STAIRS. And that's how she came to name herself.

Olive had fallen asleep over *Make Way for Ducklings,* and all the other librarians were busy somewhere else. The child was bored. She tiptoed out of the Children's Room, hugging the shadows of the walls and shelves, crawling by the base of the Circulation Desk so that Marian wouldn't see her, and made her way to the alcove that held the Card Catalog. The heart of the library. Her favorite, most forbidden place to play.

Usually she crawled underneath and tucked herself into the corner formed of oak cabinet, marble floor, and plaster walls. It was a fine place to play Hide and Seek, even if it was mostly just Hide. The corner was a cave, a bunk on a pirate ship, a cupboard in a magic wardrobe.

But that afternoon she looked at the white cards on the fronts of the drawers, and her eyes widened in recognition. Letters! In her very own alphabet. Did they spell words? Maybe the drawers were all *full* of words, a huge wooden box of words. The idea almost made her dizzy.

She walked to the other end of the cabinet and looked up, tilting her neck back until it crackled. Four drawers from top to bottom. Five drawers across. She sighed. She was only tall enough to reach the bottom row of drawers. She traced a gentle finger around the little brass frames, then very carefully pulled out the white cards inside, and laid them on the floor in a neat row:

| D | I | N | S | X-Y-Z |

She squatted over them, her tongue sticking out of the corner of her mouth in concentration, and tried to read.

"Sound it out." She could almost hear Olive's voice, soft and patient. She took a deep breath.

"Duh-in-s—" and then she stopped, because the last card had too many letters, and she didn't know any words that had Xs in them. Well, xylophone. But the X was in the front, and that wasn't the same. She tried anyway. "Duh-ins-zzzigh," and frowned.

She squatted lower, so low she could feel cold marble under her cotton pants, and put her hand on top of the last card. One finger covered the X and her pinky covered the Z (another letter that was useless for spelling ordinary things). That left Y. Y at the end was good. funnY. happY.

"Duh-ins-see," she said slowly. "Dinsy."

That felt very good to say, hard and soft sounds and hissing Ss mixing in her mouth, so she said it again, louder, which made her laugh so she said it again, very loud: "DINSY!"

There is nothing quite like a loud voice in a library to get a lot of attention very fast. Within a minute, all seven of the librarians stood in the doorway of the alcove.

"What on earth?" said Harriet.

"*Now* what have you…" said Marian.

"What have you spelled, dear?" asked Olive in her soft little voice.

"I made it myself," the girl replied.

"Just gibberish," murmured Edith, though not unkindly. "It doesn't mean a thing."

The child shook her head. "Does so. Olive," she said pointing to Olive. "Do'thy, Edith, Harwiet, Bithe, Ruth." She paused and rolled her eyes. "Mawian," she added, a little less cheerfully. Then she pointed to herself. "And Dinsy."

"Oh, now Polly," said Harriet.

"Dinsy," said Dinsy.

"Bitsy?" Blythe tried hopefully.

"*Dinsy*," said Dinsy.

And that was that.

* * *

At three every afternoon, Dinsy and Olive made a two-person circle on the braided rug in front of the bay window, and had Story Time. Sometimes Olive read aloud from *Beezus and Ramona* and *Half Magic*, and sometimes Dinsy read to Olive, *The King's Stilts*, and *In the Night Kitchen* and *Winnie-the-Pooh*. Dinsy liked that one especially, and took it to bed with her so many times that Edith had to repair the binding. Twice.

That was when Dinsy first wished upon the Library.

A note about the Library:

Knowledge is not static; information must flow in order to live. Every so often one of the librarians would discover a new addition. *Harry Potter and the Sorcerer's Stone* appeared one rainy afternoon, Rowling shelved neatly between Rodgers and Saint-Exupéry, as if it had always been there. Blythe found a book of Thich Nhat Hanh's writings in the 294s one day while she was dusting, and Feynman's lectures on physics showed up on Dorothy's shelving cart after she'd gone to make a cup of tea.

It didn't happen often; the Library was selective about what it chose to add, rejecting flash-in-the-pan bestsellers, sifting for the long haul, looking for those voices that would stand the test of time next to Dickens and Tolkien, Woolf and Gould.

The librarians took care of the books, and the Library watched over them in return. It occasionally left treats: a bowl of ripe tangerines on the formica counter of the Common Room; a gold foil box of chocolate creams; seven small, stemmed glasses of sherry on the table one teatime. Their biscuit tin remained full, the cream in the Wedgwood jug stayed fresh, and the ink pad didn't dry out. Even the little pencils stayed needle sharp, never whittling down to finger-cramping nubs.

Some days the Library even hid Dinsy, when she had made a mess and didn't want to be found, or when one of the librarians was in a dark mood. It rearranged itself, just a bit, so that in her wanderings she would find a new alcove or cubbyhole, and once a secret passage that led to a previously unknown balcony overlooking the Reading Room. When she went back a week later, she found only blank wall.

And so it was, one night when she was sixish, that Dinsy first asked the Library for a boon. Lying in her tiny yellow bed, the fraying *Pooh* under her pillow, she wished for a bear to cuddle. Books were small comfort once the lights were out, and their hard, sharp corners made them awkward companions under the covers. She lay with one arm crooked around a soft, imaginary bear, and wished and wished until her eyelids fluttered into sleep.

The next morning, while they were all having tea and toast with jam, Blythe came into the Common Room with a quizzical look on her face and her hands behind her back.

"The strangest thing," she said. "On my way up here I glanced over at the Lost and Found. Couldn't tell you why. Nothing lost in ages. But this must have caught my eye."

She held out a small brown bear, one shoebutton eye missing, bits of fur gone from its belly, as if it had been loved almost to pieces.

"It seems to be yours," she said with a smile, turning up one padded foot, where DINSY was written in faded laundry-marker black.

Dinsy wrapped her whole self around the cotton-stuffed body and skipped for the rest of the morning. Later, after Olive gave her a snack—cocoa and a Lorna Doone—Dinsy cupped her hand and blew a kiss to the oak woodwork.

"Thank you," she whispered, and put half her cookie in a crack between two tiles on the Children's Room fireplace when Olive wasn't looking.

Dinsy and Olive had a lovely time. One week they were pirates, raiding the Common Room for booty (and raisins). The next they were princesses, trapped in the turret with *At the Back of the North Wind*, and the week after that they were knights in shining armor, rescuing damsels in distress, a game Dinsy especially savored because it annoyed Marian to be rescued.

But the year she turned seven-and-a-half, Dinsy stopped reading stories. Quite abruptly, on an afternoon that Olive said later had really *felt* like a Thursday.

"Stories are for babies," Dinsy said. "I want to read about *real* people." Olive smiled a sad smile and pointed toward the far wall, because Dinsy was not the first child to make that same pronouncement, and she had known this phase would come.

After that, Dinsy devoured biographies, starting with the orange ones, the Childhoods of Famous Americans: *Thomas Edison, Young Inventor.* She worked her way from Abigail Adams to John Peter Zenger, all along the west side of the Children's Room, until one day she went around the corner, where Science and

History began.

She stood in the doorway, looking at the rows of grown-up books, when she felt Olive's hand on her shoulder.

"Do you think maybe it's time you moved across the hall?" Olive asked softly.

Dinsy bit her lip, then nodded. "I can come back to visit, can't I? When I want to read stories again?"

"For as long as you like, dear. Anytime at all."

So Dorothy came and gathered up the bear and the pillow and the yellow toothbrush. Dinsy kissed Olive on her papery cheek and, holding Blythe's hand, moved across the hall, to the room where all the books had numbers.

* * *

Blythe was plump and freckled and frizzled. She always looked a little flushed, as if she had just that moment dropped what she was doing to rush over and greet you. She wore rumpled tweed skirts and a shapeless cardigan whose original color was impossible to guess. She had bright, dark eyes like a spaniel's, which Dinsy thought was appropriate, because Blythe *lived* to fetch books. She wore a locket with a small rotogravure picture of Melvil Dewey and kept a variety of sweets—sour balls and mints and Necco wafers—in her desk drawer.

Dinsy had always liked her.

She was not as sure about Dorothy.

Over *her* desk, Dorothy had a small framed medal on a royal-blue ribbon, won for "Excellence in Classification Studies." She could operate the ancient black Remington typewriter with brisk efficiency, and even, on occasion, coax chalky gray prints out of the wheezing old copy machine.

She was a tall, raw-boned woman with steely blue eyes, good posture, and even better penmanship. Dinsy was a little frightened of her, at first, because she seemed so stern, and because she looked like magazine pictures of the Wicked Witch of the West, or at least Margaret Hamilton.

But that didn't last long.

"You should be very careful not to slip on the floor in here," Dorothy said on their first morning. "Do you know why?"

Dinsy shook her head.

"Because now you're in the non-*friction* room!" Dorothy's angular face cracked into a wide grin.

Dinsy groaned. "Okay," she said after a minute. "How do you file marshmallows?"

Dorothy cocked her head. "Shoot."

"By the *Gooey* Decimal System!"

Dinsy heard Blythe tsk-tsk, but Dorothy laughed out loud, and from then on they were fast friends.

The three of them used the large, sunny room as an arena for endless games of I Spy and Twenty Questions as Dinsy learned her way around the shelves. In the evenings, after supper, they played Authors and Scrabble, and (once) tried to keep a running rummy score in Base Eight.

Dinsy sat at the court of Napoleon, roamed the jungles near Timbuktu, and was a frequent guest at the Round Table. She knew all the kings of England and the difference between a pergola and a folly. She knew the names of 112 breeds of sheep, and loved to say "Barbados Blackbelly" over and over, although it was difficult to work into conversations. When she affectionately, if misguidedly, referred to Blythe as a "Persian Fat-Rumped," she was sent to bed without supper.

A note about time:

Time had become quite flexible inside the Library. (This is true of most places with interesting books. Sit down to read for twenty minutes, and suddenly it's dark, with no clue as to where the hours have gone.)

As a consequence, no one was really sure about the day of the week, and there was frequent disagreement about the month and year. As the keeper of the date stamp at the front desk, Marian was the arbiter of such things. But she often had a cocktail after dinner, and many mornings she couldn't recall if she'd already turned the little wheel, nor how often it had slipped her mind, so she frequently set it a day or two ahead—or back three—just to make up.

One afternoon, on a visit to Olive and the Children's Room, Dinsy looked up from *Little Town on the Prairie* and said, "When's my birthday?"

Olive thought for a moment. Because of the irregularities of time, holidays were celebrated a bit haphazardly. "I'm not sure, dear. Why do you ask?"

"Laura's going to a birthday party, in this book," she said, holding it up. "And it's fun. So I thought maybe I could have one."

"I think that would be lovely," Olive agreed. "We'll talk to the others at supper."

"Your birthday?" said Harriet as she set the table a few hours later. "Let me see." She began to count on her fingers. "You arrived in April, according to Marian's stamp, and you were about nine months old, so—" She pursed her lips as she ticked off the months. "You must have been born in July!"

"But when's my birth*day*?" Dinsy asked impatiently.

"Not sure," said Edith, as she ladled out the soup.

"No way to tell," Olive agreed.

"How does July 5 sound?" offered Blythe, as if it were a point of order to be voted on. Blythe counted best by fives.

"Fourth," said Dorothy. "Independence Day. Easy to remember?"

Dinsy shrugged. "Okay." It hadn't seemed so complicated in the Little House book. "When is that? Is it soon?"

"Probably," Ruth nodded.

A few weeks later, the librarians threw her a birthday party.

Harriet baked a spice cake with pink frosting, and wrote DINSY on top in red licorice laces, dotting the I with a lemon drop (which was rather stale). The others gave her gifts that were thoughtful and mostly handmade:

A set of Dewey Decimal flash cards from Blythe.

A book of logic puzzles (stamped DISCARD more than a dozen times, so Dinsy could write in it) from Dorothy.

A lumpy orange-and-green cardigan Ruth knitted for her.

A sno-globe from the 1939 World's Fair from Olive.

A flashlight from Edith, so that Dinsy could find her way around at night and not knock over the wastebasket again.

A set of paper finger puppets, made from blank card pockets, hand-painted by Marian. (They were literary figures, of course, all of them necessarily stout and squarish—Nero Wolfe and Friar Tuck, Santa Claus and Gertrude Stein.)

But her favorite gift was the second boon she'd wished upon the Library: a box of crayons. (She had grown very tired of drawing gray pictures with the little pencils.) It had produced Crayola crayons, in the familiar yellow-and-green box, labeled LIBRARY PACK. Inside were the colors of Dinsy's world: Reference Maroon, Brown Leather, Peplum Beige, Reader's Guide Green, World Book Red, Card Catalog Cream, Date Stamp Purple, and Palatino Black.

It was a very special birthday, that fourth of July. Although Dinsy wondered about Marian's calculations. As Harriet cut the first piece of cake that evening, she remarked that it was snowing rather heavily outside, which everyone agreed was lovely, but quite unusual for that time of year.

* * *

Dinsy soon learned all the planets, and many of their moons. (She referred to herself as Umbriel for an entire month.) She puffed up her cheeks and blew onto stacks of scrap paper. "Sirocco," she'd whisper. "Chinook. Mistral. Willy-Willy," and rated her attempts on the Beaufort Scale. Dorothy put a halt to it after Hurricane Dinsy reshuffled a rather elaborate game of Patience.

She dipped into fractals here, double dactyls there. When she tired of a subject—or found it just didn't suit her—Blythe or Dorothy would smile and proffer the hat. It was a deep green felt that held 1000 slips of paper, numbered 001 to 999. Dinsy'd scrunch her eyes closed, pick one and, like a scavenger hunt, spend the morning (or the next three weeks) at the shelves indicated.

Pangolins lived at 599 (point 31), and Pancakes at 641. Pencils were at 674 but Pens were a shelf away at 681, and Ink was across the aisle at 667. (Dinsy thought that was stupid, because you had to *use* them together.) Pluto the planet was at 523, but Pluto the Disney dog was at 791 (point 453), near "Rock and Roll" and Kazoos.

It was all very useful information. But in Dinsy's opinion, things could be a little *too* organized.

The first time she straightened up the Common Room without anyone asking, she was very pleased with herself. She had lined up everyone's teacup in a neat row on the shelf, with all the handles curving the same way, and arranged the spices in the little wooden rack: ANISE, BAY LEAVES, CHIVES, DILL WEED, PEPPERCORNS, SALT, SESAME SEEDS, SUGAR.

"Look," she said when Blythe came in to refresh her tea, "order out of chaos." It was one of Blythe's favorite mottoes.

Blythe smiled and looked over at the spice rack. Then her smile faded and she shook her head.

"Is something wrong?" Dinsy asked. She had hoped for a compliment.

"Well, you used the alphabet," said Blythe, sighing. "I suppose it's not your fault. You were with Olive for a good many years. But you're a big girl now. You should learn the *proper* order." She picked up the salt container. "We'll start with Salt." She wrote the word on the little chalkboard hanging by the icebox, followed by the number 553.632. "Five-five-three-point-six-three-two. Because—?"

Dinsy thought for a moment. "Earth Sciences."

"Ex-actly." Blythe beamed. "Because salt is a mineral. But, now, chives. Chives are a garden crop, so they're…"

Dinsy bit her lip in concentration. "Six-thirty-something."

"Very good." Blythe smiled again and chalked CHIVES 635.26 on the board. "So you see, Chives should always be shelved *after* Salt, dear."

Blythe turned and began to rearrange the eight ceramic jars. Behind her back, Dinsy silently rolled her eyes.

Edith appeared in the doorway.

"Oh, not again," she said. "No wonder I can't find a thing in this kitchen. Blythe, I've *told* you. Bay Leaf comes first. QK-four-nine—" She had worked at the university when she was younger.

"Library of Congress, my fanny," said Blythe, not quite under her breath. "We're not *that* kind of library."

"It's no excuse for imprecision," Edith replied. They each grabbed a jar and stared at each other.

Dinsy tiptoed away and hid in the 814s, where she read "Jabberwocky" until the coast was clear.

But the kitchen remained a taxonomic battleground. At least once a week, Dinsy was amused by the indignant sputtering of someone who had just spooned dill weed, not sugar, into the pot of Earl Grey tea.

* * *

Once she knew her way around, Dinsy was free to roam the library as she chose.

"Anywhere?" she asked Blythe.

"Anywhere you like, my sweet. Except the Stacks. You're not quite old enough for the Stacks."

Dinsy frowned. "I am *so*," she muttered. But the Stacks were locked, and there wasn't much she could do.

Some days she sat with Olive in the Children's Room, revisiting old friends, or explored the maze of the Main Room. Other days she spent in the Reference Room, where Ruth and Harriet guarded the big important books that no one could ever, ever check out—not even when the library had been open.

Ruth and Harriet were like a set of salt and pepper shakers from two different yard sales. Harriet had faded orange hair and a sharp, kind face. Small and pinched and pointed, a decade or two away from wizened. She had violet eyes and a mischievous, conspiratorial smile and wore rimless octagonal glasses, like stop signs. Dinsy had never seen an actual stop sign, but she'd looked at pictures.

Ruth was Chinese. She wore wool jumpers in neon plaids and had cat's-eye glasses on a beaded chain around her neck. She never put them all the way on, just lifted them to her eyes and peered through them without opening the bows.

"Life is a treasure hunt," said Harriet.

"Knowledge is power," said Ruth. "Knowing where to look is half the battle."

"Half the fun," added Harriet. Ruth almost never got the last word.

They introduced Dinsy to dictionaries and almanacs, encyclopedias and compendiums. They had been native guides through the country of the Dry Tomes for many years, but they agreed that Dinsy delved unusually deep.

"Would you like to take a break, love?" Ruth asked one afternoon. "It's nearly time for tea."

"I *am* fatigued," Dinsy replied, looking up from *Roget*. "Fagged out, weary, a bit spent. Tea would be pleasant, agreeable—"

"I'll put the kettle on," sighed Ruth.

Dinsy read *Bartlett's* as if it were a catalog of conversations, spouting lines from Tennyson, Mark Twain, and Dale Carnegie until even Harriet put her hands over her ears and began to hum "Stairway to Heaven."

One or two evenings a month, usually after Blythe had remarked, "Well, she's a spirited girl," for the third time, they all took the night off, "For Library business." Olive or Dorothy would tuck Dinsy in early and read from one of her favorites while Ruth made her a bedtime treat—a cup of spiced tea that tasted a little like cherries and a little like varnish, and which Dinsy somehow never remembered finishing.

A list (written in diverse hands), tacked to the wall of the Common Room.

10 Things to Remember When You Live in a Library

1. We do not play shuffleboard on the Reading Room table.

2. Books should not have "dog's-ears." Bookmarks make lovely presents.

3. Do not write in books. Even in pencil. Puzzle collections and connect-the-dots are books.

4. The shelving cart is not a scooter.

5. Library paste is not food.

[Marginal note in a child's hand: True. It tastes like Cream of Wrong Soup.]

6. Do not use the date stamp to mark your banana.

7. Shelves are not monkey bars.

8. Do not play 982-pickup with the P-Q drawer (or any other).

9. The dumbwaiter is only for books. It is not a carnival ride.

10. Do not drop volumes of the Britannica off the stairs to hear the echo.

They were an odd, but contented family. There were rules, to be sure, but Dinsy never lacked for attention. With seven mothers, there was always someone to talk with, a hankie for tears, a lap or a shoulder to share a story.

Most evenings, when Dorothy had made a fire in the Reading Room and the wooden shelves gleamed in the flickering light, they would all sit in companionable silence. Ruth knitted, Harriet muttered over an acrostic, Edith stirred the cocoa so it wouldn't get a skin. Dinsy sat on the rug, her back against the knees of whomever was her favorite that week, and felt safe and warm and loved. "God's in his heaven, all's right with the world," as Blythe would say.

But as she watched the moon peep in and out of the clouds through the leaded-glass panes of the tall windows, Dinsy often wondered what it would be like to see the whole sky, all around her.

* * *

First Olive and then Dorothy had been in charge of Dinsy's thick dark hair, trimming it with the mending shears every few weeks when it began to obscure her eyes. But a few years into her second decade at the library, Dinsy began cutting it herself, leaving it as wild and spiky as the brambles outside the front door.

That was not the only change.

"We haven't seen her at breakfast in weeks," Harriet said as she buttered a scone one morning.

"Months. And all she reads is Salinger. Or Sylvia Plath," complained Dorothy. "I wouldn't mind that so much, but she just leaves them on the table for *me* to reshelve."

"It's not as bad as what she did to Olive," Marian said. "*The Golden Compass* appeared last week, and she thought Dinsy would enjoy it. But not only did she turn up her nose, she had the gall to say to Olive, 'Leave me alone. I can find my own books.' Imagine. Poor Olive was beside herself."

"She used to be such a sweet child," Blythe sighed. "What are we going to do?"

"Now, now. She's just at that age," Edith said calmly. "She's not really a child anymore. She needs some privacy, and some responsibility. I have an idea."

And so it was that Dinsy got her own room—with a door that *shut*—in a corner of the second floor. It had been a tiny cubbyhole of an office, but it had a set of slender curved stairs, wrought iron worked with lilies and twigs, which led up to the turret between the red-tiled eaves.

The round tower was just wide enough for Dinsy's bed, with windows all around. There had once been a view of the town, but now trees and ivy allowed only jigsaw puzzle-shaped puddles of light to dapple the wooden floor. At night the puddles were luminous blue splotches of moonlight that hinted of magic beyond her reach.

On the desk in the room below, centered in a pool of yellow lamplight, Edith had left a note: *Come visit me. There's mending to be done,* and a worn brass key on a wooden paddle, stenciled with the single word: STACKS.

The Stacks were in the basement, behind a locked gate at the foot of the metal spiral staircase that descended from the 600s. They had always reminded Dinsy of the steps down to the dungeon in *The King's Stilts*. Darkness below hinted at danger, but adventure. Terra Incognita.

Dinsy didn't use her key the first day, or the second. Mending? Boring. But the afternoon of the third day, she ventured down the spiral stairs. She had been as far as the gate before, many times, because it was forbidden, to peer through the metal mesh at the dimly lighted shelves and imagine what treasures might be hidden there.

She had thought that the Stacks would be damp and cold, strewn with odd bits of discarded library flotsam. Instead they were cool and dry, and smelled very different from upstairs. Dustier, with hints of mold and the tang of vintage leather, an undertone of vinegar stored in an old shoe.

Unlike the main floor, with its polished wood and airy high ceilings, the Stacks were a low, cramped warren of gunmetal gray shelves that ran floor-to-ceiling in narrow aisles. Seven levels twisted behind the west wall of the library like a secret labyrinth than ran from below the ground to up under the eaves of the roof. Floor and steps were translucent glass brick and six-foot ceilings strung with pipes and ducts were lit by single caged bulbs, two to an aisle.

It was a windowless fortress of books. Upstairs the shelves were mosaics of all colors and sizes, but the Stacks were filled with geometric monochrome blocks of subdued colors: eight dozen forest-green bound volumes of *Ladies Home Journal* filled five rows of shelves, followed by an equally large block of identical dark red *LIFE*s.

Dinsy felt like she was in another world. She was not lost, but for the first time in her life, she was not easily found, and that suited her. She could sit, invisible, and listen to the sounds of library life going on around her. From Level Three she could hear Ruth humming in the Reference Room on the other side of the wall. Four feet away, and it felt like miles. She wandered and browsed for a month before she presented herself at Edith's office.

A frosted glass pane in the dark wood door said MENDING ROOM in chipping gold letters. The door was open a few inches, and Dinsy could see a long workbench strewn with sewn folios and bits of leather bindings, spools of thread and bottles of thick beige glue.

"I gather you're finding your way around," Edith said without turning in her chair. "I haven't had to send out a search party."

"Pretty much," Dinsy replied. "I've been reading old magazines." She flopped into a chair to the left of the door.

"One of my favorite things," Edith agreed. "It's like time travel." Edith was a tall, solid woman with long graying hair that she wove into elaborate buns and twisted braids, secured with #2 pencils and a single tortoiseshell comb. She wore blue jeans and vests in brightly muted colors—pale teal and lavender and dusky rose—with a strand of lapis lazuli beads cut in rough ovals.

Edith repaired damaged books, a job that was less demanding now that nothing left the building. But some of the bound volumes of journals and abstracts and magazines went back as far as 1870, and their leather bindings were crumbling into dust. The first year, Dinsy's job was to go through the aisles, level by level, and find the volumes that needed the most help. Edith gave her a clipboard and told her to check in now and then.

Dinsy learned how to take apart old books and put them back together again. Her first mending project was the tattered 1877 volume of *American Naturalist*, with its articles on "Educated Fleas" and "Barnacles" and "The Cricket as Thermometer." She sewed pages into signatures, trimmed leather and marbleized paper. Edith let her make whatever she wanted out of the scraps, and that year Dinsy gave everyone miniature replicas of their favorite volumes for Christmas.

She liked the craft, liked doing something with her hands. It took patience and concentration, and that was oddly soothing. After supper, she and Edith often sat and talked for hours, late into the night, mugs of cocoa on their workbenches, the rest of the library dark and silent above them.

"What's it like outside?" Dinsy asked one night, while she was waiting for some glue to dry.

Edith was silent for a long time, long enough that Dinsy wondered if she'd spoken too softly, and was about to repeat the question, when Edith replied.

"Chaos."

That was not anything Dinsy had expected. "What do you mean?"

"It's noisy. It's crowded. Everything's always changing, and not in any way you can predict."

"That sounds kind of exciting," Dinsy said.

"Hmm." Edith thought for a moment. "Yes, I suppose it could be."

Dinsy mulled that over and fiddled with a scrap of leather, twisting it in her fingers before she spoke again. "Do you ever miss it?"

Edith turned on her stool and looked at Dinsy. "Not often," she said slowly. "Not as often as I'd thought. But then I'm awfully fond of order. Fonder than most, I suppose. This is a better fit."

Dinsy nodded and took a sip of her cocoa.

A few months later, she asked the Library for a third and final boon.

*   *   *

The evening that everything changed, Dinsy sat in the armchair in her room, reading Trollope's *Can You Forgive Her?* (for the third time), imagining what it would be like to talk to Glencora, when a tentative knock sounded at the door.

"Dinsy? Dinsy?" said a tiny familiar voice. "It's Olive, dear."

Dinsy slid her READ! bookmark into chapter 14 and closed the book. "It's open," she called.

Olive padded in wearing a red flannel robe, her feet in worn carpet slippers. Dinsy expected her to proffer a book, but instead Olive said, "I'd like you to come with me, dear." Her blue eyes shone with excitement.

"What for?" They had all done a nice reading of *As You Like It* a few days before, but Dinsy didn't remember any plans for that night. Maybe Olive just wanted company. Dinsy had been meaning to spend an evening in the Children's Room, but hadn't made it down there in months.

But Olive surprised her. "It's *Library* business," she said, waggling her finger, but smiling.

Now, that was intriguing. For years, whenever the librarians wanted an evening to themselves, they'd disappear down into the Stacks after supper, and would never tell her why. "It's Library business," was all they ever said. When she was younger, Dinsy had tried to follow them, but it's hard to sneak in a quiet place. She was always caught and given that awful cherry tea. The next thing she knew it was morning.

"Library business?" Dinsy said slowly. "And I'm invited?"

"Yes, dear. You're practically all grown up now. It's high time you joined us."

"Great." Dinsy shrugged, as if it were no big deal, trying to hide her excitement. And maybe it wasn't a big deal. Maybe it was a meeting of the rules committee, or plans for moving the 340s to the other side of the window again. But what if it *was* something special…? That was both exciting and a little scary.

She wiggled her feet into her own slippers and stood up. Olive barely came to her knees. Dinsy touched the old woman's white hair affectionately, remembering when she used to snuggle into that soft lap. Such a long time ago.

A library at night is a still but resonant place. The only lights were the sconces along the walls, and Dinsy could hear the faint echo of each footfall on the stairs down to the foyer. They walked through the shadows of the shelves in the Main Room, back to the 600s, and down the metal stairs to the Stacks, footsteps ringing hollowly.

The lower level was dark except for a single caged bulb above the rows of *National Geographic*s, their yellow bindings pale against the gloom. Olive turned to the left.

"Where are we going?" Dinsy asked. It was so odd to be down there with Olive.

"You'll see," Olive said. Dinsy could practically feel her smiling in the dark. "You'll see."

She led Dinsy down an aisle of boring municipal reports and stopped at the far end, in front of the door to the janitorial closet set into the stone wall. She pulled a long, old-fashioned brass key from the pocket of her robe and handed it to Dinsy.

"You open it, dear. The keyhole's a bit high for me."

Dinsy stared at the key, at the door, back at the key. She'd been fantasizing about "Library business" since she was little, imagining all sorts of scenarios, none of them involving cleaning supplies. A monthly poker game. A secret tunnel into town, where they all went dancing, like the twelve princesses. Or a book group, reading forbidden texts. And now they were inviting her in? What a letdown if it was just maintenance.

She put the key in the lock. "Funny," she said as she turned it. "I've always wondered what went on when you—" Her voice caught in her throat. The door opened, not onto the closet of mops and pails and bottles of Pine-Sol she expected, but onto a small room, paneled in wood the color of ancient honey. An Oriental rug in rich, deep reds lay on the parquet floor, and the room shone with the light of dozens of candles. There were no shelves, no books, just a small fireplace at one end where a log crackled in the hearth.

"Surprise," said Olive softly. She gently tugged Dinsy inside.

All the others were waiting, dressed in flowing robes of different colors. Each of them stood in front of a Craftsman rocker, dark wood covered in soft brown leather.

Edith stepped forward and took Dinsy's hand. She gave it a gentle squeeze and said, under her breath, "Don't worry." Then she winked and led Dinsy to an empty rocker. "Stand here," she said, and returned to her own seat.

Stunned, Dinsy stood, her mouth open, her feelings a kaleidoscope.

"Welcome, dear one," said Dorothy. "We'd like you to join us." Her face was serious, but her eyes were bright, as if she was about to tell a really awful riddle and couldn't wait for the reaction.

Dinsy started. That was almost word-for-word what Olive had said, and it made her nervous. She wasn't sure what was coming, and was even less sure that she was ready.

"Introductions first." Dorothy closed her eyes and intoned, "I am Lexica. I serve the Library." She bowed her head once and sat down.

Dinsy stared, her eyes wide and her mind reeling as each of the Librarians repeated what was obviously a familiar rite.

"I am Juvenilia," said Olive with a twinkle. "I serve the Library."

"Incunabula," said Edith.

"Sapientia," said Harriet.

"Ephemera," said Marian.

"Marginalia," said Ruth.

"Melvilia," said Blythe, smiling at Dinsy. "And I too serve the Library."

And then they were all seated, and all looking up at Dinsy.

"How old are you now, my sweet?" asked Harriet.

Dinsy frowned. It wasn't as easy a question as it sounded. "Seventeen," she said after a few seconds. "Or close enough."

"No longer a child," Harriet nodded. There was a touch of sadness in her voice. "That is why we are here tonight. To ask you to join us."

There was something so solemn in Harriet's voice that it made Dinsy's stomach knot up. "I don't understand," she said slowly. "What do you mean? I've been here my whole life. Practically."

Dorothy shook her head. "You have been *in* the Library, but not *of* the Library. Think of it as an apprenticeship. We have nothing more to teach you. So we're asking if you'll take a Library name and truly become one of us. There have always been seven to serve the Library."

Dinsy looked around the room. "Won't I be the eighth?" she asked. She was curious, but she was also stalling for time.

"No, dear," said Olive. "You'll be taking my place. I'm retiring. I can barely reach the second shelves these days, and soon I'll be no bigger than the dictionary. I'm going to put my feet up and sit by the fire and take it easy. I've earned it," she said with a decisive nod.

"Here, here," said Blythe. "And well done, too."

There was a murmur of assent around the room.

Dinsy took a deep breath, and then another. She looked around the room at the eager faces of the seven librarians, the only mothers she had ever known. She loved them all, and was about to disappoint them, because she had a secret of her own. She closed her eyes so she wouldn't see their faces, not at first.

"I can't take your place, Olive," she said quietly, and heard the tremor in her own voice as she fought back tears.

All around her the librarians clucked in surprise. Ruth recovered first. "Well, of course not. No one's asking you to *replace* Olive, we're merely—"

"I can't join you," Dinsy repeated. Her voice was just as quiet, but it was stronger. "Not now."

"But why *not*, sweetie?" That was Blythe, who sounded as if she were about to cry herself.

"Fireworks," said Dinsy after a moment. She opened her eyes. "Six-sixty-two-point-one." She smiled at Blythe. "I know everything about them. But I've never *seen* any." She looked from face to face again.

"I've never petted a dog or ridden a bicycle or watched the sun rise over the ocean," she said, her voice gaining courage. "I want to feel the wind and eat an ice cream cone at a carnival. I want to smell jasmine on a spring night and hear an orchestra. I want—" she faltered, and then continued, "I want the chance to dance with a boy."

She turned to Dorothy. "You said you have nothing left to teach me. Maybe that's true. I've learned from each of you that there's nothing in the world I can't discover and explore for myself in these books. Except the world," she added in a whisper. She felt her eyes fill with tears. "You chose the Library. I can't do that without knowing what else there might be."

"You're *leaving?*" Ruth asked in a choked voice.

Dinsy bit her lip and nodded. "I'm, well, I've—" She'd been practicing these words for days, but they were so much harder than she'd thought. She looked down at her hands.

And then Marian rescued her.

"Dinsy's going to college," she said. "Just like I did. And you, and you, and you." She pointed a finger at each of the women in the room. "We were girls before we were librarians, remember? It's her turn now."

"But how—?" asked Edith.

"Where did—?" stammered Harriet.

"I wished on the Library," said Dinsy. "And it left an application in the Un-abridged. Marian helped me fill it out."

"I *am* in charge of circulation," said Marian. "What comes in, what goes out. We found her acceptance letter in the book return last week."

"But you had no transcripts," said Dorothy practically. "Where did you tell them you'd gone to school?"

Dinsy smiled. "That was Marian's idea. We told them I was home-schooled, raised by feral librarians."

* * *

And so it was that on a bright September morning, for the first time in ages, the heavy oak door of the Carnegie Library swung open. Everyone stood in the doorway, blinking in the sunlight.

"Promise you'll write," said Blythe, tucking a packet of sweets into the basket on Dinsy's arm. The others nodded. "Yes, do."

"I'll try," she said. "But you never know how long *any*thing will take around here." She tried to make a joke of it, but she was holding back tears and her heart was hammering a mile a minute.

"You will come back, won't you? I can't put off my retirement forever." Olive was perched on top of the Circulation Desk.

"To visit, yes." Dinsy leaned over and kissed her cheek. "I promise. But to serve? I don't know. I have no idea what I'm going to find out there." She looked out into the forest that surrounded the library. "I don't even know if I'll be able to get back in, through all that."

"Take this. It will always get you in," said Marian. She handed Dinsy a small stiff pasteboard card with a metal plate in one corner, embossed with her name: DINSY CARNEGIE.

"What is it?" asked Dinsy.

"Your library card."

There were hugs all around, and tears and goodbyes. But in the end, the seven librarians stood back and watched her go.

Dinsy stepped out into the world as she had come—with a wicker basket and a book of fairy tales, full of hopes and dreams.

ANOTHER WORD FOR MAP IS FAITH

CHRISTOPHER ROWE

Christopher Rowe attended both the Clarion West and Sycamore Hill writing workshops. With his wife, writer Gwenda Bond, he runs a small press, The Fortress of Words, which produces a critically acclaimed magazine, *Say…* His story "The Voluntary State" was a Hugo, Nebula and Theodore Sturgeon award finalist. The best of his early short fiction was collected in chapbook *Bittersweet Creek.*

Rowe published two terrific stories in 2006, the darkly odd "The League of Last Girls," and this quirky look at the literalisation of faith. If religion changes how you see the world, shouldn't your faith change the world?

The little drivers threw baggage down from the top of the bus and out from its rusty undercarriage vaults. This was the last stop. The road broke just beyond here, a hundred yards short of the creek.

With her fingertip, Sandy traced the inked ridge northeast along the map, then rolled the soft leather into a cylinder and tucked it inside her vest. She looked around for her pack and saw it tumbled together with the other Cartographers' luggage at the base of a catalpa tree. Lucas and the others were sorting already, trying to lend their gear some organization, but the stop was a tumult of noise and disorder.

The high country wind shrilled against the rush of the stony creek; disembarkees pawed for their belongings and tried to make sense of the delicate, coughing talk of the unchurched little drivers. On the other side of the valley, across the creek, the real ridge line—*the geology*, her father would have said disdainfully—stabbed upstream. By her rough estimation it had rolled perhaps two degrees off the angle of its writ mapping. Lucas would determine the exact discrepancy later, when he extracted his instruments from their feather and wax-paper wrappings.

"Third world *bullshit*," Lucas said, walking up to her. "The transit services people from the university paid these little schemers before we ever climbed onto that deathtrap, and now they're asking for the fare." Lucas had been raised near the border, right outside the last town the bus had stopped at, in fact, though he'd dismissed the notion of visiting any family. His patience with the locals ran inverse to his familiarity with them.

"Does this count as the third world?" she asked him. "Doesn't there have to be a general for that? Rain forests and steel ruins?"

Lucas gave his half-grin—not quite a smirk—acknowledging her reduction. Cartographers were famous for their willful ignorance of social expressions like politics and history.

"Carmen paid them, anyway," he told her as they walked towards their group. "Probably out of her own pocket, thanks be for wealthy dilettantes."

"Not fair," said Sandy. "She's as sharp as any student in the seminar, and a better hand with the plotter than most post-docs, much less grad students."

Lucas stopped. "I hate that," he said quietly. "I hate when you separate yourself; go out of your way to remind me that you're a teacher and I'm a student."

Sandy said the same thing she always did. "I hate when you forget it."

* * *

Against all odds, they were still meeting the timetable they'd drawn up back at the university, all those months ago. The bus pulled away in a cloud of noxious diesel fumes an hour before dark, leaving its passengers in a muddy camp dotted with fire rings but otherwise marked only by a hand-lettered sign pointing the way to a primitive latrine.

The handful of passengers not connected with Sandy's group had melted into the forest as soon as they'd found their packages. ("Salt and sugar," Lucas had said. "They're backwoods people—hedge shamans and survivalists. There's every kind of lunatic out here.") This left Sandy to stand by and pretend authority while the Forestry graduate student whose services she'd borrowed showed them all how to set up their camps.

Carmen, naturally, had convinced the young man to demonstrate tent pitching to the others using her own expensive rig as an example. The olive-skinned girl sat in a camp chair folding an onionskin scroll back on itself and writing in a wood-bound notebook while the others struggled with canvas and willow poles.

"Keeping track of our progress?" Sandy asked, easing herself onto the ground next to Carmen.

"I have determined," Carmen replied, not looking up, "that we have traveled as far from a hot water heater as is possible and still be within Christendom."

Sandy smiled, but shook her head, thinking of the most remote places she'd ever been. "Davis?" she asked, watching her student's reaction to the mention of that unholy town.

Carmen, a Californian, shuddered but kept her focus. "There's a naval base in San Francisco, sí? They've got all the amenities, surely."

Sandy considered again, thinking of cold camps in old mountains, and of muddy jungle towns ten days' walk from the closest bus station.

"Cape Canaveral," she said.

With quick, precise movements, Carmen folded a tiny desktop over her chair's arm and spread her scroll out flat. She drew a pair of calipers out from her breast pocket and took measurements, pausing once to roll the scroll a few turns. Finally, she gave a satisfied smile and said, "Only fifty-five miles from Orlando. We're almost twice that from Louisville."

She'd made the mistake Sandy had expected of her. "But Orlando, Señorita Reyes, is Catholic. And we were speaking of Christendom."

A stricken look passed over her student's face, but Sandy calmed her with exaggerated conspiratorial looks left and right. "Some of your fellows aren't so liberal as I am, Carmen. So remember where you are. Remember *who* you are. Or who you're trying to become."

Another reminder issued, Sandy went to see to her own tent.

* * *

The Forestry student gathered their wood, brought them water to reconstitute their freeze-dried camp meals, then withdrew to his own tent far back in the trees. Sandy told him he was welcome to spend the evening around their fire—"You built it after all," she'd said—but he'd made a convincing excuse.

The young man pointed to the traveling shrine her students had erected in the center of their camp, pulling a wooden medallion from beneath his shirt. "That Christ you have over there, ma'am," he said. "He's not this one, is he?"

Sandy looked at the amulet he held, gilded and green. "What do you have there, Jesus in the Trees?" she asked, summoning all her professional courtesy to keep the amusement out of her voice. "No, that's not the Christ we keep. We'll see you in the morning."

They didn't, though, because later that night, Lucas discovered that the forest they were camped in wasn't supposed to be there at all.

* * *

He'd found an old agricultural map somewhere and packed it in with their little traveling library. Later, he admitted that he'd only pulled it out for study because he was still sulking from Sandy's clear signal he wouldn't be sharing her tent that night.

Sandy had been leading the rest of the students in some prayers and thought exercises when Lucas came up with his moldering old quarto. "Tillage," he said, not even bothering to explain himself before he'd foisted the book off on his nearest fellow. "All the acreage this side of the ridge line is supposed to be under tillage."

Sandy narrowed her eyes, more than enough to quiet any of her charges, much less Lucas. "What's he got there, Ford?" she asked the thin undergraduate who now held the book.

"Hmmmm?" said the boy; he was one of those who fell instantly and almost irretrievably into any text and didn't look up. Then, at an elbow from Carmen, he said, "Oh! This is…" He turned the book over in his hands, angled the spine toward one of the oil lamps and read, "This is *An Agricultural Atlas of Clark*

County, Kentucky."

"'County,'" said Carmen. "*Old* book, Lucas."

"But it's *writ*," said Lucas. "There's nothing superseding the details of it and it doesn't contradict anything else we brought about the error. Hell, it even confirms the error we came to correct." Involuntarily, all of them looked up and over at the apostate ridge.

"But what's this about tillage," Sandy said, giving him the opportunity to show off his find even if it was already clear to her what it must be.

"See, these plot surveys in the appendices didn't get accounted for in the literature survey we're working from. The book's listed as a source, but only as a supplemental confirmation. It's not just the ridge that's wrong, it's the stuff growing down this side, too. We're supposed to be in grain fields of some kind down here in the flats, then it's pasturage on up to the summit line."

A minor find, sure, but Sandy would see that Lucas shared authorship on the corollary she'd file with the university. More importantly, it was an opportunity before the hard work of the days ahead.

"We can't do anything about the hillsides tonight, or any of the acreage beyond the creek," she told them. "But as for these glades here…."

It was a simple exercise. The fires were easily set.

* * *

In the morning, Sandy drafted a letter to the Dean of Agriculture while most of her students packed up the camp. She had detailed a few of them to sketch the corrected valley floor around them, and she'd include those visual notes with her instructions to the Dean, along with a copy of the writ map from Lucas's book.

"Read that back to me, Carmen," she said, watching as Lucas and Ford argued over yet another volume, this one slim and bound between paper boards. It was the same back country cartographer's guide she'd carried on her own first wilderness forays as a grad student. They'd need its detailed instructions on living out of doors without the Tree Jesus boy to help them.

"'By my hand,'" read Carmen, "'I have caused these letters to be writ. Blessings on the Department of Agriculture and on you, Dean. Blessings on Jesus Sower, the Christ you serve.'"

"Skip to the end, dear." Sandy had little patience for the formalities of academic correspondence, and less for the pretense at holiness the Agriculturalists made with their little fruiting Christ.

"'So, then, it is seen in these texts that Cartography has corrected the error so far as in our power, and now the burden is passed to you and your brethren to complete this holy task, and return the land to that of Jesus's vision.'" Carmen paused. "Then you promise to remember the Dean in your prayers and all the rest of the politesse."

"Good. Everything observed. Make two copies and bring the official one to me for sealing when you're done."

Carmen turned to her work and Sandy to hers. The ashen landscape extending up the valley was still except for some ribbons twisting in a light breeze. The ribbons were wax sealed to the parchment banner her students had set at first light, the new map of the valley floor drawn in red and black against a cream background. Someone had found the blackened disc of the Forestry student's medallion and leaned it against the base of the banner's staff and Sandy wondered if it had been Carmen, prone to sentiment, or perhaps Lucas, prone to vague gestures.

By midmorning, the students had readied their gear for the march up the ridge line and Carmen had dropped Sandy's package for the university in the mailbox by the bus stop. Before they hoisted their backpacks, though, Sandy gathered them all for fellowship and prayer.

"The gymnasiums at the university have made us fit enough for this task," and here she made a playful flex with her left arm, earning rolled eyes from Lucas and a chuckle from the rest. "The libraries have given us the woodscraft we need, and the chapels have given us the sustenance of our souls."

Sandy swept her arm north to south, indicating the ridge. "When I was your age, oh so long ago—" and a pause here for another ripple of laughter, acknowledgment of her dual status as youngest tenured faculty member at the university and youngest ordained minister in the curia. "When I was your age, I was blessed with the opportunity to go to the Northeast, traveling the lands beyond the Susquehanna, searching out error."

Sandy smiled at the memory of those times—*could they be ten years gone already?* "I traveled with men and women strong in the Lord, soldiers and scholars of God. There are many errors in the Northeast."

Maps so brittle with age that they would flake away in the cold winds of the Adirondack passes, so faded that only the mightiest of prayers would reveal Jesus's true intentions for His world.

"But none here in the heartlands of the Church, right? Isn't that what our parish priests told us growing up?" The students recognized that she was beginning to teach, and nodded, murmured assent.

"Christians, there *is* error here. There is error right before our eyes!" Her own students weren't a difficult congregation to hook, but she was gratified nonetheless by the gleam she caught in most of their eyes, the calls, louder now, of "Yes!" and "I see it! I see the lie!"

"I laid down my protractor, friends, I know exactly how far off north Jesus mapped this ridge line to lay," she said, sweeping her arm in a great arc, taking in the whole horizon, "and that ridge line sins by two degrees!"

"May as well be two *hundred!*" said Carmen, righteous.

Sandy raised her hand, stopped them at the cusp of celebration instead of loosing them. "Not yet," she said. "It's tonight. It's tonight we'll sing down the glory, tonight we'll make this world the way it was mapped."

* * *

The march up the ridge line did not go as smoothly as Sandy might have wished, but the delays and false starts weren't totally unexpected. She'd known Lucas—a country boy after all—would take the lead, and she'd guessed that he would dead-end them into a crumbling gully or two before he picked the right route through the brambles. If he'd been some kind of natural-born hunter he would never have found his way to the Lord, or to education.

Ford and his friends—all of them destined for lecture halls and libraries, not fieldwork—made the classic, the *predicted* mistake she'd specifically warned against in the rubric she'd distributed for the expedition. "If we're distributing 600 pounds of necessities across twenty-two packs," she asked Ford, walking easily beside him as he struggled along a game trail, "how much weight does that make each of us responsible for?"

"A little over twenty-seven pounds, ma'am," he said, wheezing out the reply.

"And did you calculate that in your head like a mathematician or did you remember it from the syllabus?" Sandy asked. She didn't press too hard, the harshness of the lesson was better imparted by the straps cutting into his shoulders than by her words.

"I remembered it," Ford said. And because he really did have the makings of a great scholar and great scholars are nothing if not owners of their own errors, he added, "It was in the same paragraph that said not to bring too many books."

"Exactly," she said, untying the leather cords at the top of his pack and pulling out a particularly heavy-looking volume. She couldn't resist looking at the title page before dropping it into her own pack.

"*Unchurched Tribes of the Chiapas Highlands: A Bestiary*. Think we'll make it to Mexico on this trip, Ford?" she asked him, teasing a little.

Ford's faced reddened even more from her attention than it had from the exertions of the climb. He mumbled something about migratory patterns then leaned into the hike.

If most of the students were meeting their expectations of themselves and one another, then Carmen's sprightly, sure-footed bounding up the trail was a surprise to most. Sandy, though, had seen the girl in the gym far more frequently than the other students, most of whom barely met the minimum number of visits per week required by their advising committees. Carmen was as much an athlete as herself, and the lack of concern the girl showed about dirt and insects was refreshing.

So it was Carmen who summitted first, and it was she that was looking northeast with a stunned expression on her face when Sandy and Lucas reached the top, side by side. Following Carmen's gaze, Lucas cursed and called for help in taking off his heavily laden pack before he began unrolling the oilcloth cases of his instruments.

Sandy simply pursed her lips and began a mental review of her assets: the relative strengths and weaknesses of her students, the number of days' worth of supplies they carried, the nature of the curia-designed instruments that Lucas exhibited a natural affinity for controlling. She began to nod. She'd marshaled more than enough strength for the simple tectonic adjustment they'd planned, she could set her own unquestionable faith against this new challenge if it revealed any deficiencies among her students. She would make a show of asking their opinions, but she already knew that this was a challenge she could meet.

Ford finally reached the top of the ridge line, not so much climbing as stumbling to the rocky area where the others were gathering. Once he looked up and around, he said, "The survey team that found the error in the ridge's orientation, they didn't come up here."

"They were specifically scouting for projects that the university could handle," said Sandy. "If they'd been up here, they would have called in the Mission Service, not us."

Spread out below them, ringed in tilled fields and dusted with a scattering of wooden fishing boats, was an unmapped lake.

* * *

Sandy set Ford and the other bookish scholars to cataloguing all of the texts they'd smuggled along so they could be integrated into her working bibliography. She hoped that one of them was currently distracted by waterways the way that Ford was distracted by fauna.

Lucas set their observation instruments on tripods in an acceptably devout semicircle and Sandy permitted two or three of the others to begin preliminary sight-line measurements of the lake's extent.

"It turns my stomach," said Lucas, peering through the brass tube of a field glass. "I grew up seeing the worst kind of blasphemy, but I could never imagine that anyone could do something like this."

"You need to work on that," said Sandy. Lucas was talking about the landscape feature cross-haired in the glass, a clearly artificial earthworks dam, complete with a retractable spillway. "Missionaries see worse every day."

Lucas didn't react. He'd never abandoned his ambition, even after she'd laughed him down. *Our sisters and brothers in the Mission Service*, she'd said with the authority that only someone who'd left that order could muster, *make up in the pretense of zeal what they lack in scholarship and access to the divine. Anyone can move a mountain with whips and shovels.*

The sketchers showed her their work, which they annotated with Lucas's count and codification of architectural structures, fence lines, and crops. "Those are corn cribs," he said. "That's a meeting house. That's a mill."

This was the kind of thing she'd told him he should concentrate on. The best thing any of them had to offer was the overlay of their own personal ranges of unexpected expertise onto the vast body of accepted Cartography. Lucas's barbaric background, Ford's holographic memory, Carmen's cultured scribing. Her own judgment.

"They're *marmotas!*" said Ford. They all looked up at where he'd been awkwardly turning the focus wheel on one of the glasses. "Like in my book!" He wasn't one to flash a triumphal grin, which Sandy appreciated. She assented to the line of inquiry with a nod and he hurried over to the makeshift shelf that some of his friends had been using to stack books while they wrote their list.

The unchurched all looked alike to Sandy, differing only in the details of their dress, modes of transportation, and to what extent the curia allowed interaction with them. In the case of the little drivers, for example, tacit permission was given for commercial exchange because of their ancient control of the bus lines. But she'd never heard of *marmotas*, and said so.

"They're called 'rooters' around here," said Lucas. "I don't know what Ford's on about. I've never heard of them having a lake, but they've always come into the villages with their vegetables, so far as I know."

"Not always," said Carmen. "There's nothing about any unchurched lineages in the glosses of the maps we're working from. They're as new as that lake."

Sandy recognized that they were in an educable moment. "Everybody come here, let's meet. Let's have a class."

The students maneuvered themselves into the flatter ground within the horseshoe of instruments, spreading blankets and pulling out notebooks and pens. Ford lay his bestiary out, a place marked about a third of the way through with the bright yellow fan of a fallen gingko leaf.

"Carmen's brought up a good point," said Sandy, after they'd opened with a prayer. "There's no Cartographical record of these diggers, or whatever they're called, along the ridge line."

"I don't think it matters, necessarily, though," said Carmen. "There's no record of the road up to the bus stop, either, or of Lucas's village. 'Towns and roads are thin scrims, and outside our purview.'"

Sandy recognized the quote as being from the autobiography of a radical cleric intermittently popular on campus. It was far from writ, but not heretical by any stretch of the imagination and, besides, she'd had her own enthusiasms for colorful doctrinal interpretations when she was younger. She was disappointed that Carmen would let her tendency toward error show so plainly to the others but let it pass, confident that one of the more conservative students would address it.

"Road building doesn't affect landscape?" asked Lucas, on cue. "The Mapmaker *used* road builders to cut canyons all over the continent. Ford, maybe Carmen needs to see the cutlines on your contour maps of the bus routes."

Before Ford, who was looking somewhat embarrassed by the exchange, could reply, Carmen said, "I'm not talking about the Mapmaker, Lucas, I'm talking about your *family*, back in the village we passed yesterday."

"Easy, Carmen," said Sandy. "We're getting off task here. The question at hand isn't *whether* there's error. The error is clear. We can feel the moisture of it on the breeze blowing up the hill right now." Time to shift directions on them, to turn them on the right path before they could think about it.

"The question," she continued, "is how much of it we plan to correct." Not *whether* they'd correct, don't leave that option for them. The debate she'd let them have was over the degree of action they'd take, not whether they'd take any at all.

The more sophisticated among them—Ford and Carmen sure, but even Lucas, to his credit—instantly saw her tack and looked at her with eyebrows raised. Then Lucas reverted to type and actually dared to say something.

"We haven't prepared for anything like this. That lake is more than a mile across at its broadest!"

"A mile across, yes," said Sandy, dismissively. "Carmen? What scale did you draw your sketch of the valley in?"

Carmen handed her a sheaf of papers. "24K to one. Is that all right?"

"Good, good," said Sandy. She smiled at Ford. "That's a conversion even I can do in my head. So…if I compare the size of the *dam*—" and she knitted her eyebrows, calculating. "If I compare the dam to the ridge, I see that the ridge we came to move is about three hundred times the larger."

Everyone began talking at once and at cross purposes. A gratifying number of the students were simply impressed with her cleverness and seemed relaxed, sure that it would be a simple matter now that they'd been shown the problem in the proper perspective. But Carmen was scratching some numbers in the dirt with the knuckle of her right index finger and Ford was flipping through the appendix of one of his books and Lucas…

Lucas stood and looked down over the valley. He wasn't looking at the lake and the dam, though, or even at the village of the unchurched creatures who had built it. He was looking to his right, down the eastern flank of the ridge they stood on, down the fluvial valley towards where, it suddenly occurred to Sandy, he'd grown up, towards the creek side town they'd stopped in the day before.

Ford raised his voice above an argument he'd been having with two or three others. "Isn't there a question about what that much water will do to the topography downstream? I mean, I know hydrology's a pretty knotty problem, theologically speaking, but we'd have a clear hand in the erosion, wouldn't we? What if the floodwaters subside off ground that's come unwrit because of something that we did?"

"That *is* a knotty problem, Ford," said Sandy, looking Lucas straight in the eye. "What's the best way to solve a difficult knot?"

And it was Lucas who answered her, nodding. "Cut through it."

* * *

Later, while most of the students were meditating in advance of the ceremony, Sandy saw Carmen moving from glass to glass, making minute focusing adjustments and triangulating different views of the lake and the village. Every so often, she made a quick visual note in her sketchbook.

"It's not productive to spend too much time on the side effects of an error, you know," Sandy said.

Carmen moved from one instrument to the next. "I don't think it's all that easy to determine what's a side effect and what's…okay," she said.

Sandy had lost good students to the distraction she could see now in Carmen. She reached out and pivoted the cylinder down, so that its receiving lens pointed straight at the ground. "There's nothing to see down there, Carmen."

Carmen wouldn't meet her eye. "I thought I'd record—"

"Nothing to see, nothing to record. If you could go down and talk to them you wouldn't understand a word they say. If you looked in their little huts you wouldn't find anything redemptive; there's no cross hanging in the wall of the meeting house, no Jesus of the Digging Marmots. When the water is drained, we won't see anything along the lake bed but mud and whatever garbage they've thrown in off their docks. The lake doesn't have any secrets to give up. You know that."

"Ford's books—"

"Ford's books are by anthropologists, who are halfway to being witch doctors as far as most respectable scholars are concerned, and who keep their accreditation by dint of the fact that their field notes are good intelligence sources for the Mission Service. Ford reads them because he's got an overactive imagination and he likes stories too much—lots of students in the archive concentration have those failings. Most of them grow out of it with a little coaxing. Like Ford will, he's too smart not to. Just like *you're* too smart to backslide into your parents' religion and start looking for souls to save where there are no souls to be found."

Carmen took a deep breath and held it, closed her eyes. When she opened them, her expression had folded into acquiescence. "It is not the least of my sins that I force you to spend so much time counseling me, Reverend," she said formally.

Sandy smiled and gave the girl a friendly squeeze of the shoulder. "Curiosity and empathy are healthy, and valuable, señorita," she said. "But you need to remember that there are proper channels to focus these things into. Prayer and study are best, but drinking and carousing will do in a pinch."

Carmen gave a nervous laugh, eyes widening. Sandy could tell that the girl didn't feel entirely comfortable with the unexpected direction of the conversation, which was, of course, part of the strategy for handling backsliders. Young people in particular were easy to refocus on banal and harmless "sins" and away from thoughts that could actually be dangerous.

"Fetch the others up here, now," Sandy said. "We should set to it."

Carmen soon had all twenty of her fellow students gathered around Sandy. Lucas had been down the eastern slope far enough to gather some deadwood and now he struck it ablaze with a flint and steel from his travel kit. Sandy crumbled a handful of incense into the flames.

Ford had been named the seminar's lector by consensus, and he opened his text. "Blessed are the Mapmakers…" he said.

"For they hunger and thirst after righteousness," they all finished.

Then they all fell to prayer and singing. Sandy turned her back to them—congregants more than students now—and opened her heart to the land below her.

She felt the effrontery of the unmapped lake like a caul over her face, a restriction on the land that prevented breath and life.

Sandy showed them how to test the prevailing winds and how to bank the censers in chevrons so that the cleansing fires would fall onto the appropriate points along the dam.

Finally, she thumbed an ashen symbol onto every wrist and forehead, including her own, and lit the oils of the censer *primorus* with a prayer. When the hungry flames began to beam outward from her censer, she softly repeated the prayer for emphasis, then nodded her assent that the rest begin.

The dam did not burst in a spectacular explosion of mud and boulders and waters. Instead, it atrophied throughout the long afternoon, wearing away under their prayers even as their voices grew hoarse. Eventually, the dammed river itself joined its voice to theirs and speeded the correction.

The unchurched in the valley tried for a few hours to pull their boats up onto the shore, but the muddy expanse between the water and their lurching docks grew too quickly. They turned their attention to bundling up the goods from their mean little houses then, and soon a line of them was snaking deeper into the mountains to the east, like a line of ants fleeing a hill beneath a looking glass.

With the ridge to its west, the valley fell into evening shadow long before the Cartographers' camp. They could still see below though, they could see that, as Sandy had promised Carmen, there were no secrets revealed by the dying water.

UNDER HELL, OVER HEAVEN

MARGO LANAGAN

Faith can seem arbitrary to the nonbeliever, changing believers and the world they live in for seemingly little apparent reason. In "Under Hell, Over Heaven" Margo Lanagan gives us a glimpse of an afterlife where purgatory sits, blandly, in between the enticements of heaven and hell. Who gets to go where, though, seems disturbingly arbitrary and justice seems available to none.

World Fantasy Award winner Margo Lanagan seemed to come from nowhere in 2005, garnering acclaim in the US, the UK and her native Australia for her collection *Black Juice* and story "Singing My Sister Down". She is the author of novels *Wildgame*, *The Tankermen*, *Walking Through Albert*, *The Best Thing* and *Touching Earth Lightly*. Her short fiction has been collected in *White Time* and *Black Juice*. Her most recent book is collection *Red Spikes*.

'You always have to go *through* stuff,' said Barto. 'Why couldn't somebody have made a road?'

Leah grunted. Yes, it was always a trudge here. But what was the hurry, when it came to eternity? Might as well trudge as run. Might as well be hampered as not. Barto was new here; he didn't realise. He'd only just arrived, and by car accident, so he was still in a kind of shock. He was trying to catch hold of the last threads of his curiosity as it disappeared.

Right now they were walking through reedy, rushy stuff, sometimes ankle-deep in black water. It was quite dim, too. They were deep in the Lower Reaches; Hell's crusted, warty underside hung low above them, close enough to feel the warmth. There were four of them: Leah, Barto, Tabatha and King. They were all youngish, so far as that meant anything, and they spoke the same language, so they made a good team. Plus there was the Miscreant Soul they were escorting, on his string. At least he'd stopped moaning. Hard as it was to feel strongly about anything here, the Miscreant's carryings-on had managed to irritate Leah.

Well, it was entirely up to you, she'd said to him. *You can get away with a certain amount, but you can't expect to be forgiven everything.*

Why not? he'd retorted miserably. *What skin would it have been off anyone's nose?*

It's just not the way the system works, King had said. *The line has to be drawn somewhere.*

I don't see why.

You don't have to, said Leah. *It's not your business to see. Just count yourself lucky to get any glory at all. Some people never even catch a glimpse.* And she'd made sure to walk on the far side of the group after that, so that his complaints were mostly lost on the warm, wet breeze.

He was naked, the Miscreant. He didn't get to keep the white garb and the little round golden crown. He was just a plump white man, rather the shape of a healthy baby, on a leash of greenish-yellow string and with his hands tied behind his back. He had died of a knifing outside his office building; the big wound that had opened him up from left shoulder to right hip was sealed up shiny pink.

The rest of them wore the grey-green uniform. It was neither shapeless nor quite fitted, neither long nor short, neither ugly nor attractive in worldly terms; it was not remarkable in any way unless—Leah had seen it on the Miscreant's face, on the face of the woman at the desk at Heaven Gate—you were used to that other uniform, the white one, and the beaming face above.

* * *

The woman had cleared her throat and some of the light had gone out of her face; when they were so close to the Gate, people didn't like to look away from it. *You have some business with us?*

Tabatha had handed over the satchel, and they'd all stood around as the woman went slowly through the leather pages. The occasional seal shone light up into her face, but she looked less and less happy the more she read.

This is never good. She'd slapped the satchel closed. *This is never a pleasant task. Do you have the appropriate device?*

Tabatha had held up the two lengths of string—Leah had seen King's fingers rub together, and her own tingled at the memory of rolling the grass-fibres into string on her thigh. The woman on the desk had sighed and stood and crossed the little bit of marble paving in front of the Gate.

* * *

'Someone up ahead,' said King. 'It looks like a staffer. With a crook?'

Leah looked up from the reeds and water. Yes, there was the curl of a crozier against the grey sky ahead.

'He's coming right for us,' said Barto. 'Of course, I don't mind if it's not *specifically* for me.'

The man was tall, as a Shepherd should be. 'All hail!' he cried as soon as he saw them. No one spoke as he toiled forward through the swishing reeds.

He patted the satchel on his white-robed hip. 'I have papers here for an infant, Jesus Maria Valdez.'

There was a slight sag among the four of them at the word *infant*. The Miscreant narrowed his eyes at the staffer. So he had been hopeful, too.

'There are a lot of infants back there,' said Leah. 'Get through this boggy stretch;

look out for a copse of dark trees on your right. They're in there, on the ground and up among the branches, heaps of them.'

He was on his way. 'I'll try there,' he called back over his shoulder. 'Praise be.'

'Whatever,' said Barto softly. Oh, he minded a great deal.

Leah shook herself and walked on. Out here, you got to know too well all the different shades of disappointment.

'What was that all about?' said the Miscreant, watching the glittering crozier recede. 'Someone *else's* paperwork got mixed up?'

'Probably a posthumous baptism,' said King. 'Or an intercession, you never know. They don't have friends, babies, but sometimes there's a very devout grandmother. Come on.' He tugged the string gently.

The Miscreant resumed his trudging. 'So that baby gets to Ascend?'

Leah didn't hear any answer—she was watching reeds and water again—but the Miscreant asked no more, so someone must have nodded.

Actually, Hell would be so much worse for the Miscreant, now that he'd been inside Heaven Gate and experienced that eternity. It would be worse than it would have been for Leah herself, who had only seen the Light, only felt it, from here in the Outer, and only for a few seconds at a time. And it was hard enough for her, this ache that never left her bones, this endless dull knowledge that things weren't as they should be.

They came to the edge of the marsh, up onto a rise covered with brown grass. There were quite a few people there. Two groups prayed to a Wrong God, the women wearing head cloths woven laboriously from grass fibres—where did they get the energy, for the praying, for the weaving? Babies floated here and there in their greenish swaddling, some sleeping, some awake and waving their arms, kicking their legs; another one screamed inconsolably in the distance. Other people wandered alone, meeting no one's eye, or lay on the grass looking up at the carbuncular ceiling, which was just like the surface of Heaven, except that it rumbled occasionally, and leaked dirty-yellow puffs of sulphur.

Leah's party passed on into the grasslands. The going was drier, but pricklier underfoot, and the grasses had sharp edges that made long, light cuts on their bare legs.

'You never know, do you,' said Barto quietly at her shoulder. 'You see a bloke with a cut throat, like back there, and you don't know whether he did it himself, or whether he got murdered.'

Leah nodded. 'About the only suicides you can be sure of just by looking is slit wrists. Not that you can't just go up and ask. It's not like people are embarrassed about it, or won't tell you.'

'Hmm,' said Barto. 'I've never been much of a going-up-and-asking type of person.'

'It's different here,' said Leah. A sigh escaped her—it seemed so wearying, to explain. The thing was, nothing much would *change*, whether it was explained or not explained. 'No one takes offence; no one thinks any the less of you. Just like no one plots against you, or gossips or anything. It's restful. It's pointless; everything is pointless, but nothing is a bother, either.'

'Come *on*,' said King behind her. The string was at full stretch, and so was King's arm. The Miscreant was dragging his feet, his eyes cast fearfully upward.

Leah turned impatiently from the sight. *She* had lived a virtuous life, if a short one. Her only sin was one of omission, and not even *her* omission, but her parents': she was one of the billions of unbaptised who walked the Outer.

The breeze was very warm now, and Leah could smell the sulphur. The smell, the rumbling and the occasional sprinkle of pumice on her head and into the surrounding grass were the only indications of the sufferings going on overhead. At least she didn't have to worry about finding herself in Hell; her only question was when, if ever, she would be granted admission to that better place.

Mostly Leah didn't get to see much inside Heaven; clerical errors usually went the other way from this one, and Souls delivered to Heaven slipped in quickly, as soon as the Gate opened the merest crack. This time, because the Miscreant had made such a fuss, some force had been needed to remove him, and the Gate had had to be opened comparatively wide. The four members of the escort had been tortured long and hard by the sight of the Eternal Benediction, of that constant rain of powdery shimmer—was it food? was it love?—that fell through the rays of Light, that clung to the clouds, that brushed past the beings. The snatches of music, the humming of crystal, the tang of harp strings, the celestial harmonies sung by voices so human, so joyous—Leah, accustomed only to the whistling breezes in the outer, to the weeping and mumbling of the Souls Pending, had listened hard and fiercely. She resolved to memorise a single phrase, to take with her, to give her heart during the grey times. And she had; she'd caught a little flourish of notes and hammered them into her memory.

But then the Gate had closed and silenced the music, and the Miscreant Soul had stood naked and dismayed before them, subdued by the string but still panting from the fight. Leah had run the caught phrase through her mind several times and it had fallen dead, all its brilliance and mystery and beauty gone, a series of notes as bland and grey-green as the clothes she wore. The four of them, whose pure yearning towards Heaven had fused them elbow to elbow into a single being, had fallen apart, four blockish, clumsy entities excluded into a quieter, greyer eternity. One needed nothing here, not food or drink or love—but a glimpse of Heaven woke a hunger, a hunger *to hunger*, to long for something, anything, and have that longing satisfied, to feel any feeling but this bland resignation, this hopeless doggedness, this pointless processing of oneself forward through unmarked, unmemorable time. Oh, and then the hunger went, and left you frowning, trying to fathom how you could have felt as strongly as that about anything.

Walking through the grasslands was tedious now; Leah's shins stung with grass cuts. There were few Souls here, either floating or walking, and they kept their distance—if you weren't a Shepherd, no one was interested in you. A few children stood and stared, head and shoulders above the grasses, but anyone in their teens or older hunched and turned and swayed slowly away as the escort came through on its business.

The rumbling overhead became louder; the shell of the sphere was thinner the closer they approached Hell's Gate.

'I can hear people screaming, I think,' whimpered the Miscreant.

'Not yet,' said King. 'You're imagining it.'

'Put another loop around his neck if he's feeling resistant,' said Tabatha. 'That'll keep him moving.'

They paused while King arranged this, Tabatha instructing him. 'You want it firm, but not tight, and you don't want it to get any tighter when you pull on it, just like the first one.'

The grass clumps grew farther apart now, and the ground between was bare and red, uneven and littered with sharp stones. It was quite hard to keep an even pace, and the whole team slowed, picking places to put their feet. The stones grew bigger and bigger, broader and more treacherously balanced.

'This is like gibber plain,' said Barto. 'I remember when we went on our round-Australia trip. Except there'd be no creatures here. We looked through these binoculars that could see infrared light and there were all sorts of things—little mice jumping around, lizards, spiders…'

No one answered. Leah had barely understood him. Australia? Binoculars? Infrared? And she wasn't going to reiterate, *No, there are no animals here. Animals are old-world stuff; they just circulate in that system.* And then he'd ask, *So why are there plants here—aren't they old-world stuff too? I don't know,* she'd have to say. *Did I create this? If you ever get to Heaven, I'm sure it'll all be made clear.* It was all too boring and took too much energy.

A frail tower of scaffolding appeared on the horizon, leading up to Hell's lowest convexity. The escort picked their way towards it, swearing under their breath as the stones bit into their feet, staggering off balance now and again. The Miscreant fell once, opening a cut on his forehead and bruising his cheek.

'I couldn't put my hands out,' he complained. 'Maybe you could just untie my hands, for this part?'

'I'm sorry.' King brushed the red dust off the man's belly, genitals and thigh. 'We'll just walk a bit slower, shall we?'

'You know,' said the Miscreant. 'It's almost good to feel pain! The pain is better than the nothingness, don't you think? What a terrible place this is! Do you get a lot of people purposely hurting themselves here?'

'When they first arrive, sometimes,' said Tabatha. 'But they calm down after a while, and fit in with the rest of us.'

Leah watched the red ground pass. Tabatha was a bit of a goody-goody, she thought. *The rest of us*—how cosy. What a cosy little community we are.

'After all, you can't *end* this, yourself,' Tabatha went on. 'You can't self-harm your way out of it. Only way out is to pick up brownie points, or by intercession from someone back in the old world.'

Brownie points, was it? Leah wondered what the All-Mighty would think of that phrase.

Wooden stairs zigzagged up inside the scaffolding. The canvas enclosing its middle two sections rippled in the breeze. 'Up we go, then.' Tabatha started to climb.

Leah brought up the rear. She hung back a little so as to have the Miscreant's grubby feet at her eye-level, rather than his flabby white bottom and bitten-nailed hands.

In the first canvas room they took woven bootees from the water trough and tied them to their feet. Water squeezed from the thick soles and rained between the floorboards onto the steps below. They slopped upstairs to the second room.

'This is where we turn over,' said King to the Miscreant. 'Don't freak out—it might feel a bit weird.'

'Whee,' said Tabatha, somersaulting off the top step into the shadows.

'You out of the way?' Barto jumped after her.

'It's quite enjoyable.' King turned in the opening and addressed the Miscreant upside-down. 'It's about the most fun anyone gets in this place.'

The Miscreant's boots lifted off the step. 'No, wait a minute—' He kicked out, and water flew into Leah's face. He misjudged everything; his head banged on the top step. His frightened, wounded face stared out at Leah for a moment before he floated up into the dim landing-space.

'Christ, King, you're supposed to be looking after him.' Leah's hair rose and the weight lifted out of her spine. She checked the air above and let go into it. Bodies revolved in the dim tented space, and water-drops wobbled, unsure which way to fall. 'Let's move along now,' she said.

They bounced and sprang along the weightless landing to the far door, and dropped out onto the upper stairs. Now the creased, pockmarked grey rock of the Hell sphere was the ground, and the sky that hung over them was the red stony plain. The air was close and smelly.

Down they went onto the rock. Their boots hissed on contact with it.

'Not far now,' said Tabatha.

'I don't care how far it is,' muttered the Miscreant.

Leah peered around him at the machinery and the desk in the distance, and the staffers moving about getting ready for them.

Tsss, tsss, tsss, tsss, went the bootees for the first little while. Then the soles dried out, and the smell of charred grass began to join that of sulphur. It was uncomfortably hot. The ground was creased cooled lava, easier to walk on than stones or swamp.

'Pick up the pace,' said King to the Miscreant, 'or our boots'll run out on the way back.'

'Oh, poor you,' said the Miscreant, obediently starting to jog. 'How you'll suffer.'

As if you had cause to complain, thought Leah. *It's not as if you weren't warned. Everybody gets warned somehow, even if they're brought up under a Wrong God. Oog*—she made herself look away from his jogging bottom—*so much flesh. If I'd grown that old, I never would've let that happen to me.*

'Ahoy there,' cried a woman in a silver firesuit up ahead, clapping her gloved hands. 'You got a Clerical there for us?'

'I don't know what he is—that's not my privilege,' said Tabatha. 'All I know is, he goes in here.'

'Good-oh,' said a firesuited man. 'Helps us tell one moment from another.' He shot Leah a cold grin.

The man at the desk was small, hunched and pernickety-looking. He took the satchel and peered down his nose at each paper in turn, as if keeping an invisible pair of reading glasses on his nose. Then he dropped his head, glowered at them above the same glasses and pointed a thumb at the machinery.

Leah had been here twice before. Both times she'd been picking up, and the Soul had been waiting for them, sitting happily on the desk swinging his legs. She'd never seen the machinery operate before.

One of the firesuited people slapped a switch and the whole black affair shuddered into life. All the staffers had their head-pieces on now—they were silver all over, with flat black faces. They each took, from a hook on the machine's slabby side, a silver pole that divided at the top into many vicious little spikes.

The wheels turned. The chain tightened on the eye-bolt in the ground. The circle of the lid was suddenly clear in the rock, outlined in knee-high puffs of smoke. Human screams rushed out with the smoke.

The Miscreant leaped back, pulling the string from King's hand. He ran, but Leah dived after him and brought him down by the ankle, and the others piled straight on top of him. Leah jumped up off the scorching ground and pinned his leg down. Barto bucked on the other one and Tabatha and King took care of arms and torso. 'It's too *late*. It's too *late*,' Tabatha said grimly into the man's ear. 'Where do you think you would run to?'

Still he struggled. 'Bloody hell,' said Barto, almost thrown off the leg. He took a firmer hold. 'Strong! Who would've thought such a flabby old thing—'

The Miscreant bucked and rippled again.

'How can he stand it? He must be burning all down his front—'

'You know what will stop this?' Leah hissed at Barto. 'Grabbing him by the nuts. Bags you do it.'

'Bags I *don't*.'

'*Go on*.' This was almost funny. Leah was almost laughing. 'You're the boy.'

'Eesh, I'm not grabbing some old feller's *nuts!*'

'Here.' A firesuit came up. 'Move aside,' it said in a muffled voice, 'and I'll pitchfork him.'

Gently he lowered his spike-points onto the Miscreant's back.

'That's better.' Tabatha gingerly climbed off the captive.

They all slid off him. King took up the string again. 'Now don't try that again,' he said. 'This man will happily poke you straight into the fire like a marshmallow on a stick.'

They helped the Miscreant up. He was crying now; his front was all red, flecked with black from the ground. His face was terrible to see, all crumpled and slavery like that, and with its injuries.

'Please, please,' he said. 'Oh no, please!'

He could hardly use his legs. He was extremely heavy. They dragged him towards the lid. It was a little way open now. Something moved in the smoke like a dark sea-anemone. Trying to see it more clearly, Leah felt holes open in the Outer's greyness, which shrank somewhat on her mind, at the touch of a realisation, and with the realisation, feeling.

For they were hands, all those movements, blood-red hands on the blood-streaked, steaming arms of the Damned. In a frenzy they waved and clutched at the Outer's air; they pawed the lid and the ground; they left prints; they wet and reddened the rock with their slaps and slidings.

The firesuits stood well back from the opening. Any hand that found a grip they prodded until it flinched back into the waving mass, into the high suffering howl of Hell.

The Miscreant pressed back into his escort; Leah couldn't hear him for machine-noise and screaming, but she felt the horror as if he were squeezing it out like a sponge, as if she were taking it up like a sponge, a grey, dry sponge soaking up juice and colour. Suddenly Barto's face was open, lively; suddenly there was a vigour in Tabatha's bracing herself to push, in King's new grasp on the Miscreant's upper arm. Leah pulled in a great noseful of the dreadful, wonderful cooking-meat smell of the Damned, the hot-metal smell of the machinery, the thick yellow stench of brimstone.

The machinery ground; the massive lid lifted unsteadily, revealing its many layers of black polished rock and brass, all smattered with Damned-fluids. Smoke, some yellow, some grey, some black, belched out all around; steam jetted white across the ground. Coughing, Leah heaved the Miscreant forward by his shoulder.

A Damned Soul sprang out of the smoke. It caught the Miscreant by the shoulder, Leah by her arm, and screamed in their faces in a fast, foreign language. Its eyes rolled and steamed; its whole face was misshapen. The skin of it, the raw skin!

'Git back there!' growled a firesuit, forcing the Soul back with a pole across its middle. Through the smoke and the glorious all-engulfing sensations of her own retching, Leah had an impression of a person being folded and forced away. Like a crab into a crevice, she thought, pushing the Miscreant forward again—only rubbery. And raw—that skin! The points of the pitchfork had sliced across that Soul's belly, and the wounds had *sizzled* with blood and fluids rushing to heal it, to make the skin clean and raw again and ready to suffer more.

This was what she wanted, what she needed, to see such things and to see them clearly. The sulphur jabbed her nostrils and she sniffed it up and coughed, exultant. The Miscreant's shaggy boot-toes flamed near the lip of the opening; hands painted them red, stroke by stroke. She took slippery white handfuls of him and, in a spasm of revulsion and joy, forced him into the centre of the red sea-anemone.

Its many arms hauled him in. Maybe they thought they could pull themselves past him into the Outer; perhaps they thought to plead with him; maybe they just wanted someone else to share their misery. Whatever they wanted, the red Souls folded the white, flailing Soul in.

It was like watching a kebab being rolled, Barto would say later. *A chicken kebab.*

Don't be awful, Tabatha would say, trying to cringe, trying to care enough.

The escort pulled their hands and feet free of the roaring Souls. Pitchforks poked and hissed, intervening for them. The machinery clanked; the lid shuddered and began to lower. In the desperate red scramble just inside the rim, the faces—I will never forget these, Leah thought raptly, I will never be able—the hairless faces, all melted and remelted flesh, spat and bubbled and ran with juices. And they knew—their eyes begged and their bloodied lips pleaded in a thousand different languages.

Barto gagged beside Leah, King clutched her and wept, Tabatha dragged at their sleeves: 'Come away! Come away!'

But Leah stayed, her eyes and heart still feasting. Just as she'd craned for the last possible glimpse of that other eternity, Heaven, so she must peer around the firesuit to see as many hands, as many faces as she could, as the lid crushed them, as they clutched the very pitchforks that forced them back into suffering.

'Bloody, sticky things!' The nearest firesuit scraped off against the rim a Soul that had impaled itself chest first upon her fork. 'How much more pain do you want?' The Soul fish-flopped, then was clawed away by others more desperate, more able.

The dire howling lessened; there were just hands now, flickering along with the yellow flames that came up where hopeless Souls had dropped away and left gaps in the crowd. They made a frill, a lace-work of red fingers, a fur of black and yellow smoke, a feather of gold flame, a stinking sleeve edge that shortened, shortened—

Thud. The lid closed, sealing in the Damned.

The firesuit turned away and snatched off its hood. The woman inside grinned down at Leah. 'Better get a move on,' she said.

Tabatha was already starting for the tower, grabbing up the satchel as she passed the desk. Barto stared at the lid over Leah's shoulder, both hands to his mouth. King, on all fours, leaned hard against her knees, retching.

'Come on, laddie.' The firesuit prodded him gently with her bloodied pitchfork. 'Those boots won't last much longer.'

'And you're burning yourself.' Leah pulled on his shoulder.

Supporting him, she followed Tabatha. They must take the stamped papers up to Heaven Gate and lodge them. Leah's imagination was as clear as a sunlit tide-pool now; she could just see those snooty Registrars dipping their quills to add the marks, the *brownie points*, to each team member's record book. Those marks would build—who knew how fast? Who knew how many were needed?—until there were enough to release him or her from the Outer forever, and into Heaven and the Eternal Benediction and the Light.

Leah's feet stung. The soles of the bootees were black and fringed with burnt rush-weave.

'Hurry, King.' She pushed him along in the small of the back. He tried to speak over his shoulder—his face was greenish, and his lips puffed out with nauseated burps. 'I heard one of them say—'

'Just *run*, King! Talk when we get to the ladder!'

And they ran, pell-mell, elated. One of Barto's bootees gave out, shredding off his foot. He tried a strange hopping run for a few paces, then seemed to take off and fly across the hot black ridges to the scaffolding.

They flung themselves after him, finally landing in a clump on the lowest steps. A few moments filled with groans and panting. Then they spread out onto separate steps.

'Oh, my *feet!*'

'Uff! This is from his fingernails, look! Like a—like a *tiger*-claw or something.'

'Look at King!' King's hands and knees had puffed up as if inflated.

'He whacked me in the mouth *so* hard, that Soul. I thought I'd lost some teeth. I think this one's a bit wobbly. Does this look wobbly to you, Leah?'

When every injury had been noted and admired, quiet descended. The grey-ness crept in at the edges of Leah's mind.

King pushed his face into the hot breeze. 'I heard someone say, *It's so cool out there!*'

'I heard that too,' said Tabatha quietly.

'I heard someone call out, *Water, water!*' whispered Barto. 'And you know? For just that moment, I was thirsty.'

Leah's tongue searched her mouth for that feeling. No, she wasn't thirsty, not even after all that heat and smoke and running.

'I didn't understand anything they said.' She spoke quickly, while there was still a bit of space in the middle of the encroaching greyness. 'But what I *saw*...' She tried to remember that screaming Soul's face well enough to make her stomach churn again. She rubbed her tearless eyes, and saw against the lids a vague bob-bing of bald, red heads, waving hands, silent mouths. Nothing that would upset anybody. 'Aagh.' The greyness reached the centre of her feelings and winked them out. That was all she would be left with, until next time—that bobbing impres-sion, all the intensity faded to a thin grey knowledge, a small, puzzled struggle to remember—what had been so wonderful?

Tabatha was binding Barto's burnt foot with a strip torn off her uniform. 'We must move in and out quicker, next time,' she said absently. 'Like a pick-up. This never would've happened with a pick-up.'

'How do they get them out of there, with a pickup?' wondered King. 'Without anyone else escaping?'

'If you ever get to work there, I guess you'll find out,' said Tabatha flatly.

'You can't blame us for being curious,' said King. He must have not quite recovered, thought Leah.

Anyway, 'curious' wasn't the word for it. She followed the others up the stairs, rolled over and dropped into the Outer's gravitational field, followed them through the bootee-room and down onto the stony red plain. Curiosity was a lame, small-scale thing. What it was, was...

She picked her way through the stones towards the lighter regions of the Outer. She tried to think, to search what she thought was her heart. But she was not let see. The Outer's greyness had her; it walled the thought she was reaching for in fog, embedded the feeling in cloud; it clumsied her toes and fingers and all her finer faculties and left her with only this, the barest inclination to keep moving, in the direction that felt like forward, but might turn out never to be forward, or backward, or any way, anywhere, ever.

INCARNATION DAY

WALTER JON WILLIAMS

Walter Jon Williams started writing in the early '80s, and his first SF novel, *Ambassador of Progress*, appeared in 1984 and was followed by *Hardwired*, *Aristoi*, *Metropolitan*, *City on Fire*, *The Rift*, and most recently his Dread Empire's Fall series, *The Praxis*, *The Sundering* and *Conventions of War*. A prolific and talented short fiction writer, he has won the Nebula for "Daddy's World" and "The Green Leopard Plague". His short fiction is collected in *Facets* and *Frankensteins and Foreign Devils*. Upcoming is new science fiction novel *Implied Spaces*.

The story of growing up is the story of slowly moving away from being completely dependent on your parents and becoming your own person. But, what if your parents didn't have to let you grow up? What if they could simply delete you?

It's your understanding and wisdom that makes me want to talk to you, Doctor Sam. About how Fritz met the Blue Lady, and what happened with Janis, and why her mother decided to kill her, and what became of all that. I need to get it sorted out, and for that I need a real friend. Which is you.

Janis is always making fun of me because I talk to an imaginary person. She makes even more fun of me because my imaginary friend is an English guy who died hundreds of years ago.

"You're wrong," I pointed out to her, "Doctor Samuel Johnson was a real person, so he's not imaginary. It's just my *conversations* with him that are imaginary."

I don't think Janis understands the distinction I'm trying to make.

But I know that *you* understand, Doctor Sam. You've understood me ever since we met in that Age of Reason class, and I realized that you not only said and did things that made you immortal, but that you said and did them while you were hanging around in taverns with actors and poets.

Which is about the perfect life, if you ask me.

In my opinion Janis could do with a Doctor Sam to talk to. She might be a lot less frustrated as an individual.

I mean, when I am totally stressed trying to comprehend the equations for electron paramagnetic resonance or something, so I just can't stand cramming another ounce of knowledge into my brain, I can always imagine my Doctor Sam—a big fat man (though I think the word they used back then was "corpulent")—a fat man with a silly wig on his head, who makes a magnificent gesture with one hand and says, with perfect wisdom and gravity, *All intellectual improvement, Miss Alison, arises from leisure.*

Who could put it better than that? Who else could be as sensible and wise? Who could understand me as well?

Certainly nobody *I* know.

(And have I mentioned how much I like the way you call me *Miss Alison?*)

We might as well begin with Fahd's Incarnation Day on Titan. It was the first incarnation among the Cadre of Glorious Destiny, so of course we were all present.

The celebration had been carefully planned to showcase the delights of Saturn's largest moon. First we were to be downloaded onto *Cassini Ranger,* the ship parked in Saturn orbit to service all the settlements on the various moons. Then we would be packed into individual descent pods and dropped into Titan's thick atmosphere. We'd be able to stunt through the air, dodging in and out of methane clouds as we chased each other across Titan's cloudy, photochemical sky. After that would be skiing on the Tomasko Glacier, Fahd's dinner, and then skating on frozen methane ice.

We would all be wearing bodies suitable for Titan's low gravity and high-pressure atmosphere—sturdy, low to the ground, and furry, with six legs and a domelike head stuck onto the front between a pair of arms.

But my body would be one borrowed for the occasion, a body the resort kept for tourists. For Fahd it would be different. He would spend the next five or six years in orbit around Saturn, after which he would have the opportunity to move on to something else.

The six-legged body he inhabited would be his own, his first. He would be incarnated—a legal adult, and legally human despite his six legs and furry body. He would have his own money and possessions, a job, and a full set of human rights.

Unlike the rest of us.

After the dinner, where Fahd would be formally invested with adulthood and his citizenship, we would all go out for skating on the methane lake below the glacier. Then we'd be uploaded and head for home.

All of us but Fahd, who would begin his new life. The Cadre of Glorious Destiny would have given its first member to interplanetary civilization.

I envied Fahd his incarnation—his furry six-legged body, his independence, and even his job, which wasn't all that stellar if you ask me. After fourteen years of being a bunch of electrons buzzing around in a quantum matrix, I wanted a real life even if it meant having twelve dozen legs.

I suppose I should explain, because you were born in an era when electricity came from kites, that at the time of Fahd's Incarnation Day party I was not exactly a human being. Not legally, and especially not physically.

Back in the old days—back when people were establishing the first settlements beyond Mars, in the asteroid belt and on the moons of Jupiter and then Saturn—resources were scarce. Basics such as water and air had to be shipped in from other places, and that was very expensive. And of course the environment was extremely hazardous—the death rate in those early years was phenomenal.

It's lucky that people are basically stupid, otherwise no one would have gone.

Yet the settlements had to grow. They had to achieve self-sufficiency from the home worlds of Earth and Luna and Mars, which sooner or later were going to get tired of shipping resources to them, not to mention shipping replacements for all the people who died in stupid accidents. And a part of independence involved establishing growing, or at least stable, populations, and that meant having children.

But children suck up a lot of resources, which like I said were scarce. So the early settlers had to make do with virtual children.

It was probably hard in the beginning. If you were a parent you had to put on a headset and gloves and a body suit in order to cuddle your infant, whose objective existence consisted of about a skazillion lines of computer code anyway… well, let's just say you had to want that kid *really badly*.

Especially since you couldn't touch him in the flesh till he was grown up, when he would be downloaded into a body grown in a vat just for him. The theory being that there was no point in having anyone in your settlement who couldn't contribute to the economy and help pay for those scarce resources, so you'd only incarnate your offspring when he was already grown up and could get a job and help to pay for all that oxygen.

You might figure from this that it was a hard life, out there on the frontier.

Now it's a lot easier. People can move in and out of virtual worlds with nothing more than a click of a mental switch. You get detailed sensory input through various nanoscale computers implanted in your brain, so you don't have to put on oven mitts to feel your kid. You can dandle your offspring, and play with him, and teach him to talk, and feed him even. Life in the virtual realms claims to be 100% realistic, though in my opinion it's more like 95%, and only in the realms that *intend* to mimic reality, since some of them don't.

Certain elements of reality were left out, and there are advantages—at least if you're a parent. No drool, no messy diapers, no vomit. When the child trips and falls down, he'll feel pain—you *do* want to teach him not to fall down, or to bang his head on things—but on the other hand there won't be any concussions or broken bones. There won't be any fatal accidents involving fuel spills or vacuum.

There are other accidents that the parents have made certain we won't have to deal with. Accidental pregnancy, accidental drunkenness, accidental drug use.

Accidental gambling. Accidental vandalism. Accidental suicide. Accidentally acquiring someone else's property. Accidentally stealing someone's extra-vehicular unit and going for a joy ride among the asteroids.

Accidentally having fun. Because believe me, the way the adults arrange it here, all the fun is *planned ahead of time*.

Yep, Doctor Sam, life is pretty good if you're a grownup. Your kids are healthy and smart and extremely well-educated. They live in a safe, organized world filled with exciting educational opportunities, healthy team sports, family entertainment, and games that reward group effort, cooperation, and good citizenship.

It all makes me want to puke. If I *could* puke, that is, because I can't. (Did I mention there was no accidental bulimia, either?)

Thy body is all vice, Miss Alison, and thy mind all virtue.

Exactly, Doctor Sam. And it's the vice I'm hoping to find out about. Once I get a body, that is.

We knew that we weren't going to enjoy much vice on Fahd's Incarnation Day, but still everyone in the Cadre of Glorious Destiny was excited, and maybe a little jealous, about his finally getting to be an adult, and incarnating into the real world and having some real world fun for a change. Never mind that he'd got stuck in a dismal job as an electrical engineer on a frozen moon.

All jobs are pretty dismal from what I can tell, so he isn't any worse off than anyone else really.

For days before the party I had been sort of avoiding Fritz. Since we're electronic we can avoid each other easily, simply by not letting yourself be visible to the other person, and not answering any queries he sends to you, but I didn't want to be rude.

Fritz was cadre, after all.

So I tried to make sure I was too busy to deal with Fritz—too busy at school, or with my job for Dane, or working with one of the other cadre members on a project. But a few hours before our departure for Titan, when I was in a conference room with Bartolomeo and Parminder working on an assignment for our Artificial Intelligence class, Fritz knocked on our door, and Bartolomeo granted him access before Parminder and I could signal him not to.

So in comes Fritz. Since we're electronic we can appear to one another as whatever we like, for instance Mary Queen of Scots or a bunch of snowflakes or even *you*, Doctor Sam. We all experiment with what we look like. Right now I mostly use an avatar of a sort-of Picasso woman—he used to distort people in his paintings so that you had a kind of 360-degree view of them, or parts of them, and I think that's kind of interesting, because my whole aspect changes depending on what angle of me you're viewing.

For an avatar Fritz used the image of a second-rate action star named Norman Isfahan. Who looks okay, at least if you can forget his lame videos, except that Fritz added an individual touch in the form of a balloon-shaped red hat. Which he thought made him look cool, but which only seemed ludicrous and a little sad.

Fritz stared at me for a moment, with a big goofy grin on his face, and Parminder sends me a little private electronic note of sympathy. In the last few months Fritz had become my pet, and he followed me around whenever he got the chance. Sometimes he'd be with me for hours without saying a word, sometimes he'd talk the entire time and not let me get a single word in.

I did my best with him, but I had a life to lead, too. And friends. And family. And I didn't want this person with me every minute, because even though I was sorry for him he was also very frustrating to be around.

Friendship is not always the sequel of obligation.

Alas, Doctor J., too true.

Fritz was the one member of our cadre who came out, well, wrong. They build us—us software—by reasoning backwards from reality, from our parents' DNA. They find a good mix of our parents' genes, and that implies certain things about *us*, and the sociologists get their say about what sort of person might be needful in the next generation, and everything's thrown together by a really smart artificial intelligence, and in the end you get a virtual child.

But sometimes despite all the intelligence of everyone and everything involved, mistakes are made. Fritz was one of these. He wasn't stupid exactly—he was as smart as anyone—but his mental reflexes just weren't in the right plane. When he was very young he would spend hours without talking or interacting with any of us. Fritz's parents, Jack and Hans, were both software engineers, and they were convinced the problem was fixable. So they complained and they or the AIs or somebody came up with a software patch, one that was supposed to fix his problem—and suddenly Fritz was active and angry, and he'd get into fights with people and sometimes he'd just scream for no reason at all and go on screaming for hours.

So Hans and Jack went to work with the code again, and there was a new software patch, and now Fritz was stealing things, except you can't really steal anything in sims, because the owner can find any virtual object just by sending it a little electronic ping.

That ended with Fritz getting fixed yet *again*, and this went on for years. So while it was true that none of us were exactly a person, Fritz was less a person than any of us.

We all did our best to help. We were cadre, after all, and cadres look after their own. But there was a limit to what any of us could do. We heard about unanticipated feedback loops and subsystem crashes and weird quantum transfers leading to fugue states. I think that the experts had no real idea what was going on. Neither did we.

There was a lot of question as to what would happen when Fritz incarnated. If his problems were all software glitches, would they disappear once he was meat and no longer software? Or would they short-circuit his brain?

A check on the histories of those with similar problems did not produce encouraging answers to these questions.

And then Fritz became *my* problem because he got really attached to me, and he followed me around.

"Hi, Alison," he said.

"Hi, Fritz."

I tried to look very busy with what I was doing, which is difficult to do if you're being Picasso Woman and rather abstract-looking to begin with.

"We're going to Titan in a little while," Fritz said.

"Uh-huh," I said.

"Would you like to play the shadowing game with me?" he asked.

Right then I was glad I was Picasso Woman and not incarnated, because I knew that if I had a real body I'd be blushing.

"Sure," I said. "If our capsules are anywhere near each other when we hit the atmosphere. We might be separated, though."

"I've been practicing in the simulations," Fritz said. "And I'm getting pretty good at the shadowing game."

"Fritz," Parminder said. "We're working on our AI project now, okay? Can we talk to you later, on Titan?"

"Sure."

And I sent a note of gratitude to Parminder, who was in on the scheme with me and Janis, and who knew that Fritz couldn't be a part of it.

Shortly thereafter my electronic being was transmitted from Ceres by high-powered communications lasers and downloaded into an actual body, even if it was a body that had six legs and that didn't belong to me. The body was already in its vacuum suit, which was packed into the descent capsule—I mean nobody wanted us floating around in the *Cassini Ranger* in zero gravity in bodies we weren't used to—so there wasn't a lot I could do for entertainment.

Which was fine. It was the first time I'd been in a body, and I was absorbed in trying to work out all the little differences between reality and the sims I'd grown up in.

In reality, I thought, things seem a little quieter. In simulations there are always things competing for your attention, but right now there was nothing to do but listen to myself breathe.

And then there was a bang and a big shove, easily absorbed by foam padding, and I was launched into space, aimed at the orange ball that was Titan, and behind it the giant pale sphere of Saturn.

The view was sort of disappointing. Normally you see Saturn as an image with the colors electronically altered so as to heighten the subtle differences in detail. The reality of Saturn was more of a pasty blob, with faint brown stripes and a little red jagged scrawl of a storm in the southern hemisphere.

Unfortunately I couldn't get a very good view of the rings, because they were edge-on, like a straight silver knife-slash right across a painted canvas.

Besides Titan I could see at least a couple dozen moons. I could recognize Dione and Rhea, and Enceladus because it was so bright. Iapetus was obvious because it was half light and half dark. There were a lot of tiny lights that could have been Atlas or Pan or Prometheus or Pandora or maybe a score of others.

I didn't have enough time to puzzle out the identity of the other moons, because Titan kept getting bigger and bigger. It was a dull orange color, except on the very edge where the haze scatters blue light. Other than that arc of blue, Titan is orange the same way Mars is red, which is to say that it's orange all the way down, and when you get to the bottom there's still more orange.

It seemed like a pretty boring place for Fahd to spend his first years of adulthood.

I realized that if I were doing this trip in a sim, I'd fast-forward through this part. It would be just my luck if all reality turned out to be this dull.

Things livened up in a hurry when the capsule hit the atmosphere. There was a lot of noise, and the capsule rattled and jounced, and bright flames of ionizing radiation shot up past the view port. I could feel my heart speeding up, and my breath going fast. It was *my* body that was being bounced around, with *my* nerve impulses running along *my* spine. *This* was much more interesting. *This* was the difference between reality and a sim, even though I couldn't explain exactly what the difference was.

It is the distinction, Miss Alison, between the undomesticated awe which one might feel at the sight of a noble wild prospect discovered in nature; and that which is produced by a vain tragedian on the stage, puffing and blowing in a transport of dismal fury as he tries to describe the same vision.

Thank you, Doctor Sam.

We that live to please must please to live.

I could see nothing but fire for a while, and then there was a jolt and a *Crash-Bang* as the braking chute deployed, and I was left swaying frantically in the sudden silence, my heart beating fast as high-atmosphere winds fought for possession of the capsule. Far above I could just see the ionized streaks of some of the other cadre members heading my way.

It was then, after all I could see was the orange fog, that I remembered that I'd been so overwhelmed by the awe of what I'd been seeing that I forgot to *observe*. So I began to kick myself over that.

It isn't enough to stare when you want to be a visual artist, which is what I want more than anything. A noble wild prospect (as you'd call it, Doctor Sam) isn't simply a gorgeous scene, it's also a series of technical problems. Ratios, colors, textures. Media. Ideas. Frames. *Decisions*. I hadn't thought about any of that when I had the chance, and now it was too late.

I decided to start paying better attention, but there was nothing happening outside but acetylene sleet cooking off the hot exterior of the capsule. I checked my tracking display and my onboard map of Titan's surface. So I was prepared when a private message came from Janis.

"Alison. You ready to roll?"

"Sure. You bet."

"This is going to be *brilliant*."

I hoped so. But somewhere in my mind I kept hearing Doctor Sam's voice: *Remember that all tricks are either knavish or childish.*

The trick I played on Fritz was both.

I had been doing some outside work for Dane, who was a communications tech, because outside work paid in real money, not the Citizenship Points we get paid in the sims. And Dane let me do some of the work on Fahd's Incarnation Day, so I was able to arrange which capsules everyone was going to be put into.

I put Fritz into the last capsule to be fired at Titan. And those of us involved in Janis' scheme—Janis, Parminder, Andy, and I—were fired first.

This basically meant that we were going to be on Titan five or six minutes ahead of Fritz, which meant it was unlikely that he'd be able to catch up to us. He would be someone else's problem for a while.

I promised myself that I'd be extra nice to him later, but it didn't stop me from feeling knavish and childish.

After we crashed into Titan's atmosphere, and after a certain amount of spinning and swaying we came to a break in the cloud, and I could finally look down at Titan's broken surface. Stark mountains, drifts of methane snow, shiny orange ethane lakes, the occasional crater. In the far distance, in the valley between a pair of lumpy mountains, was the smooth toboggan slide of the Tomasko Glacier. And over to one side, on a plateau, were the blinking lights that marked our landing area.

And directly below was an ethane cloud, into which the capsule soon vanished. It was there that the chute let go, and there was a stomach-lurching drop before the airfoils deployed. I was not used to having my stomach lurch—recall if you will my earlier remarks on puking—so it was a few seconds before I was able to recover and take control of what was now a large and agile glider.

No, I hadn't piloted a glider before. But I'd spent the last several weeks working with simulations, and the technology was fail-safed anyway. Both I and the onboard computer would have to screw up royally before I could damage myself or anyone else. I took command of the pod and headed for Janis' secret rendezvous.

There are various sorts of games you can play with the pods as they're dropping through the atmosphere. You can stack your airfoils in appealing and intricate formations. (I think this one's really stupid if you're trying to do it in the middle of thick clouds.) There's the game called "shadowing," the one that Fritz wanted to play with me, where you try to get right on top of another pod, above the airfoils where they can't see you, and you have to match every maneuver of the pod that's below you, which is both trying to evade you and to maneuver so as to get above you. There are races, where you try to reach some theoretical point in the sky ahead of the other person. And there's just swooping and dashing around the sky, which is probably as fun as anything.

But Janis had other plans. And Parminder and Andy and I, who were Janis' usual companions in her adventures, had elected to be a part of her scheme, as was our wont. (Do you like my use of the word "wont," Doctor Sam?) And a couple other members of the cadre, Mei and Bartolomeo, joined our group without knowing our secret purpose.

We disguised our plan as a game of shadowing, which I turned out to be very good at. It's not simply a game of flying, it's a game of spacial relationships, and that's what visual artists have to be good at understanding. I spent more time on top of one or more of the players than anyone else.

Though perhaps the others weren't concentrating on the game. Because although we were performing the intricate spiraling maneuvers of shadowing as a part of our cover, we were also paying very close attention to the way the winds were blowing at different altitudes—we had cloud-penetrating lasers for that, in addition to constant meteorological data from the ground—and we were using available winds as well as our maneuvers to slowly edge away from our assigned landing field, and toward our destined target.

I kept expecting to hear from Fritz, wanting to join our game. But I didn't. I supposed he had found his fun somewhere else.

All the while we were stunting around, Janis was sending us course and altitude corrections, and thanks to her navigation we caught the edge of a low pressure area that boosted us toward our objective at nearly two hundred kilometers per hour. It was then that Mei swung her capsule around and began a descent toward the landing field.

"I just got the warning that we're on the edge of our flight zone," she reported.

"Roger," I said.

"Yeah," said Janis. "We know."

Mei swooped away, followed by Bartolomeo. The rest of us continued soaring along in the furious wind. We made little pretense by this point that we were still playing shadow, but instead tried for distance.

Ground Control on the landing area took longer to try to contact us than we'd expected.

"Capsules six, twenty-one, thirty," said a ground controller. She had one of those smooth, controlled voices that people use when trying to coax small children away from the candy and toward the spinach.

"You have exceeded the safe range from the landing zone. Turn at once to follow the landing beacon."

I waited for Janis to answer.

"It's easier to reach Tomasko from where we are," she said. "We'll just head for the glacier and meet the rest of you there."

"The flight plan prescribes a landing on Lake Southwood," the voice said. "Please lock on the landing beacon at once and engage your autopilots."

Janis' voice rose with impatience. "Check the flight plan I'm sending you! It's easier and quicker to reach Tomasko! We've got a wind shoving us along at a hundred eighty clicks!"

There was another two or three minutes of silence. When the voice came back, it was grudging.

"Permission granted to change flight plan."

I sagged with relief in my vac suit, because now I was spared a moral crisis. We had all sworn that we'd follow Janis' flight plan whether or not we got permission from Ground Control, but that didn't necessarily meant that we would have. Janis would have gone, of course, but I for one might have had second thoughts. I would have had an excuse if Fritz had been along, because I could have taken him to the assigned landing field—we didn't want him with us, because he might not have been able to handle the landing if it wasn't on an absolutely flat area.

I'd like to think I would have followed Janis, though. It isn't as if I hadn't before.

And honestly, that was about it. If this had been one of the adult-approved video dramas we grew up watching, something would have gone terribly wrong and there would have been a horrible crash. Parminder would have died, and Andy and I would have been trapped in a crevasse or buried under tons of methane ice, and Janis would have had to go to incredible, heroic efforts in order to rescue us. At the end Janis would have Learned an Important Life Lesson, about how following the Guidance of our Wise, Experienced Elders is preferable to staging wild, disobedient stunts.

By comparison what actually happened was fairly uneventful. We let the front push us along till we were nearly at the glacier, and then we dove down into calmer weather. We spiraled to a soft landing in clean snow at the top of Tomasko Glacier. The airfoils neatly folded themselves, atmospheric pressure inside the capsules equalized with that of the moon, and the hatches opened so we could walk in our vac suits onto the top of Titan.

I was flushed with joy. I had never set an actual foot on an actual world before, and as I bounded in sheer delight through the snow I rejoiced in all the little details I felt all around me.

The crunch of the frozen methane under my boots. The way the wind picked up long streamers of snow that made little spattering noises when they hit my windscreen. The suit heaters that failed to heat my body evenly, so that some parts were cool and others uncomfortably warm.

None of it had the immediacy of the simulations, but I didn't remember this level of detail either. Even the polyamide scent of the suit seals was sharper than the generic stuffy suit smell they put in the sim.

This was all real, and it was wonderful, and even if my body was borrowed I was already having the best time I'd ever had in my life.

I scuttled over to Janis on my six legs and crashed into her with affectionate joy. (Hugging wasn't easy with the vac suits on.) Then Parminder ran over and crashed into her from the other side.

"We're finally out of Plato's Cave!" she said, which is the sort of obscure reference you always get out of Parminder. (I looked it up, though, and she had a good point.)

The outfitters at the top of the glacier hadn't been expecting us for some time, so we had some free time to indulge in a snowball fight. I suppose snowball fights aren't that exciting if you're wearing full-body pressure suits, but this was the first real snowball fight any of us had ever had, so it was fun on that account anyway.

By the time we got our skis on, the shuttle holding the rest of the cadre and their pods was just arriving. We could see them looking at us from the yellow windows of the shuttle, and we just gave them a wave and zoomed off down the glacier, along with a grownup who decided to accompany us in case we tried anything else that wasn't in the regulation playbook.

Skiing isn't a terribly hazardous sport if you've got six legs on a body slung low to the ground. The skis are short, not much longer than skates, so they don't get tangled; and it's really hard to fall over—the worst that happens is that you go into a spin that might take some time to get out of. And we'd all been practicing on the simulators and nothing bad happened.

The most interesting part was the jumps that had been molded at intervals onto the glacier. Titan's low gravity meant that when you went off a jump, you went very high and you stayed in the air for a long time. And Titan's heavy atmosphere meant that if you spread your limbs apart like a skydiver, you could catch enough of that thick air almost to hover, particularly if the wind was cooperating and blowing uphill. That was wild and thrilling, hanging in the air with the wind whistling around the joints of your suit, the glossy orange snow coming up to meet you, and the sound of your own joyful whoops echoing in your ears.

I am a great friend to public amusements, because they keep people from vice.
Well. Maybe. We'll see.

The best part of the skiing was that this time I didn't get so carried away that I'd forgot to *observe*. I thought about ways to render the dull orange sheen of the glacier, the wild scrawls made in the snow by six skis spinning out of control beneath a single squat body, the little crusty waves on the surface generated by the constant wind.

Neither the glacier nor the lake is always solid. Sometimes Titan generates a warm front that liquifies the topmost layer of the glacier, and the liquid methane pours down the mountain to form the lake. When that happens, the modular resort breaks apart and creeps away on its treads. But sooner or later everything freezes over again, and the resort returns.

We were able to ski through a broad orange glassy chute right onto the lake, and from there we could see the lights of the resort in the distance. We skied into a big ballooning pressurized hangar made out of some kind of durable fabric, where the crew removed our pressure suits and gave us little felt booties to wear. I'd had an exhilarating time, but hours had passed and I was tired. The Incarnation Day banquet was just what I needed.

Babbling and laughing, we clustered around the snack tables, tasting a good many things I'd never got in a simulation. (They make us eat in the sims, to get us used to the idea so we don't accidentally starve ourselves once we're incarnated, and to teach us table manners, but the tastes tend to be a bit monotonous.)

"Great stuff!" Janis said, gobbling some kind of crunchy vat-grown treat that I'd sampled earlier and found disgusting. She held the bowl out to the rest of us. "Try this! You'll like it!"

I declined.

"Well," Janis said, "if you're afraid of new things…"

That was Janis for you—she insisted on sharing her existence with everyone around her, and got angry if you didn't find her life as exciting as she did.

About that time Andy and Parminder began to gag on the stuff Janis had made them eat, and Janis laughed again.

The other members of the cadre trailed in about an hour later, and the feast proper began. I looked around the long table—the forty-odd members of the Cadre of Glorious Destiny, all with their little heads on their furry multipede bodies, all crowded around the table cramming in the first real food they've tasted in their lives. In the old days, this would have been a scene from some kind of horror movie. Now it's just a slice of posthumanity, Earth's descendants partying on some frozen rock far from home.

But since all but Fahd were in borrowed bodies I'd never seen before, I couldn't tell one from the other. I had to ping a query off their implant communications units just to find out who I was talking to.

Fahd sat at the place of honor at the head of the table. The hair on his furry body was ash-blond, and he had a sort of widow's peak that gave his head a kind of geometrical look.

I liked Fahd. He was the one I had sex with, that time that Janis persuaded me to steal a sex sim from Dane, the guy I do outside programming for. (I should point out, Doctor Sam, that our simulated bodies have all the appropriate organs, it's just that the adults have made sure we can't actually use them for sex.)

I think there was something wrong with the simulation. What Fahd and I did wasn't wonderful, it wasn't ecstatic, it was just… strange. After a while we gave up and found something else to do.

Janis, of course, insisted she'd had a glorious time. She was our leader, and everything she did had to be totally fabulous. It was just like that horrid vat-grown snack food product she'd tried—not only was it the best food she'd ever tasted, it was the best food *ever*, and we all had to share it with her.

I hope Janis actually *did* enjoy the sex sim, because she was the one caught with the program in her buffer—and after I *told* her to erase it. Sometimes I think she just wants to be found out.

During dinner those whose parents permitted it were allowed two measured doses of liquor to toast Fahd—something called Ring Ice, brewed locally. I think it gave my esophagus blisters.

After the Ring Ice things got louder and more lively. There was a lot more noise and hilarity when the resort crew discovered that several of the cadre had slipped off to a back room to find out what sex was like, now they had real bodies. It was when I was laughing over this that I looked at Janis and saw that she was quiet, her body motionless. She's normally louder and more demonstrative than anyone else, so I knew something was badly wrong. I sent her a private query through my implant. She sent a single-word reply.

Mom…

I sent her a glyph of sympathy while I wondered how Janis' mom had found out about our little adventure so quickly. There was barely time for a lightspeed signal to bounce to Ceres and back.

Ground Control must have really been annoyed. Or maybe she, like Janis' mom, was a Constant Soldier in the Five Principles Movement and was busy spying on everyone else—all for the greater good, of course.

Whatever the message was, Janis bounced back pretty quickly. Next thing I knew she was sidling up to me saying, "Look, you can loan me your vac suit, right?"

Something about the glint in her huge platter eyes made me cautious.

"Why would I want to do that?" I asked.

"Mom says I'm grounded. I'm not allowed to go skating with the rest of you. But nobody can tell these bodies apart—I figured if we switched places we could show her who's boss."

"And leave me stuck here by myself?"

"You'll be with the waiters—and some of them are kinda cute, if you like them hairy." Her tone turned serious. "It's solidarity time, Alison. We can't let Mom win this one."

I thought about it for a moment, then said, "Maybe you'd better ask someone else."

Anger flashed in her huge eyes. "I knew you'd say that! You've always been afraid to stand up to the grownups!"

"Janis," I sighed. "Think about it. Do you think your mom was the only one that got a signal from Ground Control? My parents are going to be looking into the records of this event very closely. So I think you should talk someone else into your scheme—and not Parminder or Andy, either."

Her whole hairy body sulked. I almost laughed.

"I guess you're right," she conceded.

"You know your mom is going to give you a big lecture when we get back."

"Oh yeah. I'm sure she's writing her speech right now, making sure she doesn't miss a single point."

"Maybe you'd better let me eavesdrop," I said. "Make sure you don't lose your cool."

She looked even more sulky. "Maybe you'd better."

We do this because we're cadre. Back in the old days, when the first poor kids were being raised in virtual, a lot of them cracked up once they got incarnated. They went crazy, or developed a lot of weird obsessions, or tried to kill themselves, or turned out to have a kind of autism where they could only relate to things through a computer interface.

So now parents don't raise their children by themselves. Most kids still have two parents, because it takes two to pay the citizenship points and taxes it takes to raise a kid, and sometimes if there aren't enough points to go around there are three parents, or four or five. Once the points are paid the poor moms and dads have to wait until there are enough applicants to fill a cadre. A whole bunch of virtual children are raised in one group, sharing their upbringing with their parents and crèche staff. Older cadres often join their juniors and take part in their education, also.

The main point of the cadre is for us all to keep an eye on each other. Nobody's allowed to withdraw into their own little world. If anyone shows sign of going around the bend, we unite in our efforts to retrieve them.

Our parents created the little hell that we live in. It's our job to help each other survive it.

A person used to vicissitudes is not easily dejected.

Certainly Janis isn't, though despite cadre solidarity she never managed to talk anyone else into changing places with her. I felt only moderately sorry for her—she'd already had her triumph, after all—and I forgot all about her problems once I got back into my pressure suit and out onto the ice.

Skating isn't as thrilling as skiing, I suppose, but we still had fun. Playing crack-the-whip in the light gravity, the person on the end of the line could be fired a couple kilometers over the smooth methane ice.

After which it was time to return to the resort. We all showered while the resort crew cleaned and did maintenance on our suits, and then we got back in the suits so that the next set of tourists would find their rental bodies already armored up and ready for sport.

We popped open our helmets so that the scanners could be put on our heads. Quantum superconducting devices tickled our brain cells and recovered everything they found, and then our brains—our essences—were dumped into a buffer, then fired by communication laser back to Ceres and the sim in which we all lived.

The simulation seemed inadequate compared to the reality of Titan. But I didn't have time to work out the degree of difference, because I had to save Janis' butt.

That's us. That's the cadre. All for one and one for all.

And besides, Janis has been my best friend for practically ever.

Anna-Lee, Janis' mom, was of course waiting for her, sitting in the little common room outside Janis' bedroom. (Did I mention that we sleep, Doctor Sam? We don't sleep as long as incarnated people do, just a few hours, but our parents want us to get used to the idea so that when we're incarnated we know to sleep when we get tired instead of ignoring it and then passing out while doing something dangerous or important.

(The only difference between our sleep and yours is that we don't dream. I mean, what's the point, we're stuck in our parents' dream anyway.)

So I've no sooner arrived in my own simulated body in my own simulated bedroom when Janis is screaming on the private channel.

"Mom is here! I need you *now!*"

So I press a few switches in my brain and there I am, right in Janis' head, getting much of the same sensor feed that she's receiving herself. And I look at her and I say, "Hey, you can't talk to Anna-Lee looking like *this*."

Janis is wearing her current avatar, which is something like a crazy person might draw with crayons. Stick-figure body, huge yellow shoes, round bobble head with crinkly red hair like wires.

"Get your quadbod on!" I tell her. "Now!"

So she switches, and now her avatar has four arms, two in the shoulders, two in the hip sockets. The hair is still bright red. Whatever her avatar looks like, Janis always keeps the red hair.

"Good," I say. "That's normal."

Which it is, for Ceres. Which is an asteroid without much gravity, so there really isn't a lot of point in having legs. In microgravity legs just drag around behind you and bump into things and get bruises and cuts. Whereas everyone can use an extra pair of arms, right? So most people who live in low- or zero-gravity environments use quadbods, which are much practical than the two-legged model.

So Janis pushes off with her left set of arms and floats through the door into the lounge where her mom awaits. Anna-Lee wears a quadbod, too, except that hers isn't an avatar, but a three-dimensional holographic scan of her real body. And you can tell that she's really pissed—she's got tight lips and tight eyelids and a tight face, and both sets of arms are folded across her midsection with her fingers digging into her forearms as if she's repressing the urge to grab Janis and shake her.

"Hi, Mom," Janis said.

"You not only endangered yourself," Anna-Lee said, "but you chose to endanger others, too."

"Sit down before you answer," I murmured in Janis' inward ear. "Take your time."

I was faintly surprised that Janis actually followed my advice. She drifted into a chair, used her lower limbs to settle herself into it, and then spoke.

"Nobody was endangered," she said, quite reasonably.

Anna-Lee's nostrils narrowed.

"You diverted from the flight plan that was devised for your safety," she said.

"I made a new flight plan," Janis pointed out. "Ground Control accepted it. If it was dangerous, she wouldn't have done that."

Anna-Lee's voice got that flat quality that it gets when she's following her own internal logic. Sometimes I think she's the program, not us.

"You are not authorized to file flight plans!" she snapped.

"Ground Control accepted it," Janis repeated. Her voice had grown a little sharp, and I whispered at her to keep cool.

"And Ground Control immediately informed *me!* They were right on the edge of calling out a rescue shuttle!"

"But they didn't, because there was no problem!" Janis snapped out, and then there was a pause while I told her to lower her voice.

"Ground Control accepted my revised plan," she said. "I landed according to the plan, and nobody was hurt."

"You planned this from the beginning!" All in that flat voice of hers. "This was a deliberate act of defiance!"

Which was true, of course.

"What harm did I do?" Janis asked.

("Look," I told Janis. "Just tell her that she's right and you were wrong and you'll never do it again."

("I'm not going to lie!" Janis sent back on our private channel. "Whatever Mom does, she's never going to make me lie!")

All this while Anna-Lee was saying, "We must all work together for the greater good! Your act of defiance did nothing but divert people from their proper tasks! Titan Ground Control has better things to do than worry about you!"

There was no holding Janis back now. "You *wanted* me to learn navigation! So I learned it—because *you* wanted it! And now that I've proved that I can use it, and you're angry about it!" She was waving her arms so furiously that she bounced up from her chair and began to sort of jerk around the room.

"And do you know why that is, Mom?" she demanded.

"*For God's sake shut up!*" I shouted at her. I knew where this was leading, but Janis was too far gone in her rage to listen to me now.

"It's because you're second-rate!" Janis shouted at her mother. "Dad went off to Barnard's Star, but *you* didn't make the cut! And I can do all the things you wanted to do, and do them better, and *you can't stand it!*"

"*Will you be quiet!*" I tell Janis. "Remember that *she owns you!*"

"I accepted the decision of the committee!" Anna-Lee was shouting. "I am a Constant Soldier and I live a productive life, and I will *not* be responsible for producing a child who is a *burden* and a *drain on resources!*"

"Who says I'm going to be a burden?" Janis demanded. "*You're* the only person who says that! If I incarnated tomorrow I could get a good job in ten minutes!"

"Not if you get a reputation for disobedience and anarchy!"

By this point it was clear that since Janis wasn't listening to me, and Anna-Lee *couldn't* listen, there was no longer any point in my involving myself in what had become a very predictable argument. So I closed the link and prepared my own excuses for my own inevitable meeting with my parents.

I changed from Picasso Woman to my own quadbod, which is what I use when I talk to my parents, at least when I want something from them. My quadbod avatar is a girl just a couple years younger than my actual age, wearing a school uniform with a Peter Pan collar and a white bow in her—my—hair. And my beautiful brown eyes are just slightly larger than eyes are in reality, because that's something called "neoteny," which means you look more like a baby and babies are designed to be irresistible to grownups.

Let me tell you that it works. Sometimes I can blink those big eyes and get away with anything.

And at that point my father called, and told me that he and my mom wanted to talk to me about my adventures on Titan, so I popped over to my parents' place, where I appeared in holographic form in their living room.

My parents are pretty reasonable people. Of course I take care to *keep* them reasonable, insofar as I can. *Let me smile with the wise,* as Doctor Sam says, *and feed with the rich.* I will keep my opinions to myself, and try my best to avoid upsetting the people who have power over me.

Why did I soar off with Janis on her flight plan? my father wanted to know.

"Because I didn't think she should go alone," I said.

Didn't you try to talk her out of it? my mother asked.

"You can't talk Janis out of anything," I replied. Which, my parents knowing Janis, was an answer they understood.

So my parents told me to be careful, and that was more or less the whole conversation.

Which shows you that not all parents up here are crazy.

Mine are more sensible than most. I don't think many parents would think much of my ambition to get involved in the fine arts. That's just not *done* up here, let alone the sort of thing *I* want to do, which is to incarnate on Earth and apprentice myself to an actual painter, or maybe a sculptor. Up here they just use cameras, and their idea of original art is to take camera pictures or alter camera pictures or combine camera pictures with one another or process the camera pictures in some way.

I want to do it from scratch, with paint on canvas. And not with a computer-programmed spray gun either, but with a real brush and blobs of paint. Because if you ask me the *texture* of the thing is important, which is why I like oils. Or rather the *idea* of oils, because I've never actually had a chance to work with the real thing.

And besides, as Doctor Sam says, *A man who has not been in Italy, is always conscious of an inferiority, from his not having seen what is expected a man should see. The grand object of traveling is to see the shores of the Mediterranean.*

So when I told my parents what I wanted to do, they just sort of shrugged and made me promise to learn another skill as well, one just a little bit more practical. So while I minor in art I'm majoring in computer design and function and programming, which is pretty interesting because all our really complex programs are written by artificial intelligences who are smarter than we are, so getting them to do what you want is as much like voodoo as science.

So my parents and I worked out a compromise that suited everybody, which is why I think my parents are pretty neat actually.

About twenty minutes after my talk with my parents, Janis knocked on my door, and I made the door go away, and she walked in, and then I put the door back. (Handy things, sims.)

"Guess that didn't work out so good, huh?" she said.

"On your family's civility scale," I said, "I think that was about average."

Her eyes narrowed (she was so upset that she's forgot to change out of her quadbod, which is why she had the sort of eyes that could narrow).

"I'm going to get her," she said.

"I don't think that's very smart," I said.

Janis was smacking her fists into my walls, floor, and ceiling and shooting around the room, which was annoying even though the walls were virtual and she couldn't damage them or get fingerprints on them.

"Listen," I said. "All you have to do is keep the peace with your mom until you've finished your thesis, and then you'll be incarnated and she can't touch you. It's just *months*, Janis."

"My *thesis!*" A glorious grin of discovery spread across Janis' face. "I'm going to use my *thesis!* I'm going to stick it to Mom right where it hurts!"

I reached out and grabbed her and steadied her in front of me with all four arms.

"Look," I said. "You can't keep calling her bluff."

Her voice rang with triumph. "Just watch me."

"Please," I said. "I'm begging you. *Don't do anything till you're incarnated!*"

I could see the visions of glory dancing before her eyes. She wasn't seeing or hearing me at all.

"She's going to have to admit that I am right and that she is wrong," she said. "I'm going to nail my thesis to her forehead like Karl Marx on the church door."

"That was Martin Luther actually." (Sometimes I can't help these things.)

She snorted. "Who cares?"

"I do." Changing the subject. "*Because I don't want you to die.*"

Janis snorted. "I'm not going to bow to her. I'm going to *crush her*. I'm going to show her how stupid and futile and second-rate she is."

And at that moment there was a signal at my door. I ignored it.

"The power of punishment is to silence, not to confute," I said.

Her face wrinkled as if she'd bit into something sour. "I can't *believe* you're quoting that old dead guy again."

I have found you an argument, I wanted to say with Doctor Sam, *but I am not obliged to find you an understanding.*

The signal at my door repeated, and this time it was attached to an electronic signal that meant *Emergency!* Out of sheer surprise I dissolved the door.

Mei was there in her quadbod, an expression of anger on her face.

"If you two are finished congratulating each other on your brilliant little prank," she said, "you might take time to notice that Fritz is missing."

"Missing?" I didn't understand how someone could be missing. "Didn't his program come back from Titan?"

If something happened to the transmission, they could reload Fritz from a backup.

Mei's expression was unreadable. "He never went. He met the Blue Lady."

And then she pushed off with two of her hands and drifted away, leaving us in a sudden, vast, terrible silence.

We didn't speak, but followed Mei into the common room. The other cadre members were all there, and they all watched us as we floated in.

When you're little, you first hear about the Blue Lady from the other kids in your cadre. Nobody knows for sure how we *all* find out about the Blue Lady—not just the cadres on Ceres, but the ones on Vesta, and Ganymede, and *everywhere*.

And we all know that sometimes you might see her, a kind smiling woman in a blue robe, and she'll reach out to you, and she seems so nice you'll let her take your hand.

Only then, when it's too late, you'll see that she has no eyes, but only an empty blackness filled with stars.

She'll take you away and your friends will never see you again.

And of course it's your parents who send the Blue Lady to find you when you're bad.

We all know that the Blue Lady doesn't truly exist, it's ordinary techs in ordinary rooms who give the orders to zero out your program along with all its backups, but we all believe in the Blue Lady really, and not just when we're little.

Which brings me to the point I made about incarnation earlier. Once you're incarnated, you are considered a human being, and you have human rights.

But *not until then*. Until you're incarnated, you're just a computer program that belongs to your parents, and if you're parents think the program is flawed or corrupted and simply too awkward to deal with, they can have you zeroed.

Zeroed. Not killed. The grownups insist that there's a difference, but I don't see it myself.

Because the Blue Lady really comes for some people, as she came for Fritz when Jack and Hans finally gave up trying to fix him. Most cadres get by without a visit. Some have more than one. There was a cadre on Vesta who lost eight, and then there were suicides among the survivors once they incarnated, and it was a big scandal that all the grownups agreed never to talk about.

I have never for an instant believed that my parents would ever send the Blue Lady after me, but still it's always there in the back of my mind, which is why I think that the current situation is so horrible. It gives parents a power they should never have, and it breeds a fundamental distrust between kids and their parents.

The grownups' chief complaint about the cadre system is that their children bond with their peers and not their parents. Maybe it's because their peers can't kill them.

Everyone in the cadre got the official message about Fritz, that he was basically irreparable and that the chance of his making a successful incarnation was essentially zero. The message said that none of us were at fault for what had happened, and that everyone knew that we'd done our best for him.

This was in the same message queue as a message to me from Fritz, made just before he got zeroed out. There he was with his stupid hat, smiling at me.

"Thank you for saying you'd play the shadowing game with me," he said. "I really think you're wonderful." He laughed. "See you soon, on Titan!"

So then I cried a lot, and I erased the message so that I'd never be tempted to look at it again.

We all felt failure. It was our job to make Fritz right, and we hadn't done it. We had all grown up with him, and even though he was a trial he was a part of our world. I had spent the last few days avoiding him, and I felt horrible about it; but everyone else had done the same thing at one time or another.

We all missed him.

The cadre decided to wear mourning, and we got stuck in a stupid argument about whether to wear white, which is the traditional mourning color in Asia, or black, which is the color in old Europe.

"Wear blue," Janis said. So we did. Whatever avatars we wore from that point on had blue clothing, or used blue as a principal color somewhere in their composition.

If any of the parents noticed, or talked about it, or complained, I never heard it.

I started thinking a lot about how I related to incarnated people, and I thought that maybe I'm just a little more compliant and adorable and sweet-natured than I'd otherwise be, because I want to avoid the consequences of being otherwise. And Janis is perhaps more defiant than she'd be under other circumstances, because she wants to show she's not afraid. *Go ahead, Mom,* she says, *pull the trigger. I dare you.*

Underestimating Anna-Lee all the way. Because Anna-Lee is a Constant Soldier of the Five Principles Movement, and that means *serious*.

The First Principle of the Five Principles Movement states that *Humanity is a pattern of thought, not a side effect of taxonomy,* which means that you're human if you *think* like a human, whether you've got six legs or four arms or two legs like the folks on Earth and Mars.

And then so on to the Fifth Principle, we come to the statement that humanity in all its various forms is intended to occupy every possible ecosystem throughout the entire universe, or at least as much of it as we can reach. Which is why the Five Principles Movement has always been very big on genetic experimentation, and the various expeditions to nearby stars.

I have no problem with the Five Principles Movement, myself. It's rational compared with groups like the Children of Venus or the God's Menu people.

Besides, if there isn't something to the Five Principles, what are we doing out here in the first place?

My problem lies with the sort of people the Movement attracts, which is to say people like Anna-Lee. People who are obsessive, and humorless, and completely unable to see any other point of view. Not only do they dedicate themselves heart and soul to whatever group they join, they insist everyone else has to join as well, and that anyone who isn't a part of it is a Bad Person.

So even though I pretty much agree with the Five Principles, I don't think I'm going to join the movement. I'm going to keep in mind the wisdom of my good Doctor Sam: *Most schemes of political improvement are very laughable things.*

But to get back to Anna-Lee. Back in the day she married Carlos, who was also in the Movement, and together they worked for years to qualify for the expedition to Barnard's Star on the *True Destiny*. They created Janis together, because having children is all a part of occupying the universe and so on.

But Carlos got the offer to crew the ship, and Anna-Lee didn't. Carlos chose Barnard's Star over Anna-Lee, and now he's a couple light-months away. He and the rest of the settlers are in electronic form—no sense in spending the resources to ship a whole body to another star system when you can just ship the data and build the body once you arrive—and for the most part they're dormant, because there's nothing to do until they near their destination. But every week or so Carlos has himself awakened so that he can send an electronic postcard to his daughter.

The messages are all really boring, as you might expect from someone out in deep space where there's nothing to look at and nothing to do, and everyone's asleep anyway.

Janis sends him longer messages, mostly about her fights with Anna-Lee. Anna-Lee likewise sends Carlos long messages about Janis' transgressions. At two light-months out Carlos declines to mediate between them, which makes them both mad.

So Anna-Lee is mad because her husband left her, and she's mad at Janis for not being a perfect Five Principles Constant Soldier. Janis is mad at Carlos for not figuring out a way to take her along, and she's mad at Anna-Lee for not making the crew on the *True Destiny*, and failing that not having the savvy to keep her husband in the picture.

And she's also mad at Anna-Lee for getting married again, this time to Rhee, a rich Movement guy who was able to swing the taxes to create *two new daughters,* both of whom are the stars of their particular cadres and are going to grow up to be perfect Five Principles Kids, destined to carry on the work of humanity in new habitats among distant stars.

Or so Anna-Lee claims, anyway.

Which is why I think that Janis underestimates her mother. I think the way Anna-Lee looks at it, she's got two new kids, who are everything she wants. And one older kid who gives her trouble, and who she can give to the Blue Lady without really losing anything, since she's lost Janis anyway. She's already given a husband to the stars, after all.

And all this is another reason why I want to incarnate on Earth, where a lot of people still have children the old-fashioned way. The parents make an embryo in a gene-splicer, and then the embryo is put in a vat, and nine months later you crack the vat open and you've got an actual baby, not a computer program. And even if the procedure is a lot more time-consuming and messy I still think it's superior.

So I was applying for work on Earth, both for jobs that could use computer skills, and also for apprenticeship programs in the fine arts. But there's a waiting list for pretty much any job you want on Earth, and also there's a big entry tax unless they *really* want you, so I wasn't holding my breath; and besides, I hadn't finished my thesis.

I figured on graduating from college along with most of my cadre, at the age of fourteen. I understand that in your day, Doctor Sam, people graduated from college a lot later. I figure there are several important reasons for the change: (1) we virtual kids don't sleep as much as you do, so we have more time for study; (2) there isn't that much else to do here anyway; and (3) we're really, really, *really* smart. Because if you were a parent, and you had a say in the makeup of your kid (along with the doctors and the sociologists and the hoodoo machines), would you say, *No thanks, I want mine stupid?*

No, I don't think so.

And the meat-brains that we incarnate into are pretty smart, too. Just in case you were wondering.

We could grow up faster, if we wanted. The computers we live in are so fast that we could go from inception to maturity in just two or three months. But we wouldn't get to interact with our parents, who being meat would be much slower, or with anyone else. So in order to have any kind of relationship with our elders, or any kind of socialization at all, we have to slow down to our parents' pace. I have to say that I agree with that.

In order to graduate I needed to do a thesis, and unfortunately I couldn't do the one I wanted, which was the way the paintings of Breughel, etc., reflected the theology of the period. All the training with computers and systems, along with art and art history, had given me an idea of how abstract systems such as theology work, and how you can visually represent fairly abstract concepts on a flat canvas.

But I'd have to save that for maybe a graduate degree, because my major was still in the computer sciences, so I wrote a fairly boring thesis on systems inter-opability—which, if you care, is the art of getting different machines and highly specialized operating systems to talk to each other, a job that is made more difficult if the machines in question happen to be a lot smarter than you are.

Actually it's a fairly interesting subject. It just wasn't interesting in my thesis.

While I was doing that I was also working outside contracts for Dane, who was from a cadre that had incarnated a few years ahead of us, and who I got to know when his group met with ours to help with our lessons and with our socialization skills (because they wanted us to be able to talk to people outside the cadre and our families, something we might not do if we didn't have practice).

Anyway, Dane had got a programming job in Ceres' communications center, and he was willing to pass on the more boring parts of his work to me in exchange for money. So I was getting a head start on paying that big Earth entry tax, or if I could evade the tax, maybe living on Earth a while and learning to paint.

"You're just going to end up being Ceres' first interior decorator," Janis scoffed.

"And that would be a *bad* thing?" I asked. "Just *look* at this place!" Because it's all so functional and boring and you'd think they could find a more interesting color of paint than *grey*, for God's sake.

That was one of the few times I'd got to talk to Janis since our adventure on Titan. We were both working on our theses, and still going to school, and I had my outside contracts, and I think she was trying to avoid me, because she didn't want to tell me what she was doing because she didn't want me to tell her not to do it.

Which hurt, by the way. Since we'd been such loyal friends up to the point where I told her not to get killed, and then because I wanted to save her life she didn't want to talk to me anymore.

The times I mostly got to see Janis were Incarnation Day parties for other members of our cadre. So we got to see Ganymede, and Iapetus, and Titan again, and Rhea, and Pluto, Callisto, and Io, and the antimatter generation ring between Venus and Mercury, and Titan again, and then Titan a fourth time.

Our cadre must have this weird affinity for orange, I don't know.

We went to Pallas, Juno, and Vesta. Though if you ask me, one asteroid settlement is pretty much like the next.

We went to Third Heaven, which is a habitat the God's Menu people built at L2. And they can *keep* a lot of the items on the menu, if you ask me.

We visited Luna (which you would call the Moon, Doctor Sam. As if there was only one). And we got to view *Everlasting Dynasty*, the starship being constructed in lunar orbit for the expedition to Tau Ceti, the settlement that Anna-Lee was trying her best to get Janis aboard.

We also got to visit Mars three times. So among other entertainments I looked down at the planet from the top of Olympus Mons, the largest mountain in the solar system, and I looked down from the edge of the solar system's largest canyon, and then I looked *up* from the bottom of the same canyon.

We all tried to wear blue if we could, in memory of the one of us who couldn't be present.

Aside from the sights, the Incarnation Day parties were great because all our incarnated cadre members turned up, in bodies they'd borrowed for the occasion. We were all still close, of course, and kept continually in touch, but our communication was limited by the speed of light and it wasn't anything like having Fahd and Chandra and Solange there in person, to pummel and to hug.

We didn't go to Earth. I was the only one of our cadre who had applied there, and I hadn't got an answer yet. I couldn't help fantasizing about what my Incarnation Day party would be like if I held it on Earth—where would I go? What would we look at? Rome? Mount Everest? The ocean habitats? The plains of Africa, where the human race began?

It was painful to think that the odds were high that I'd never see any of these places.

Janis never tried to organize any of her little rebellions on these trips. For one thing word had got out, and we were all pretty closely supervised. Her behavior was never less than what Anna-Lee would desire. But under it all I could tell she was planning something drastic.

I tried to talk to her about it. I talked about my thesis, and hoped it would lead to a discussion of *her* thesis. But no luck. She evaded the topic completely.

She was pretty busy with her project, though, whatever it was. Because she was always buzzing around the cadre asking people where to look for odd bits of knowledge.

I couldn't make sense of her questions, though. They seemed to cover too many fields. Sociology, statistics, mineralogy, criminology, economics, astronomy, spaceship design... The project seemed too huge.

The only thing I knew about Janis' thesis was that it was *supposed* to be about resource management. It was the field that Anna-Lee forced her into, because it was full of skills that would be useful on the Tau Ceti expedition. And if that didn't work, Anna-Lee made sure Janis minored in spaceship and shuttle piloting and navigation.

I finally finished my thesis, and then I sat back and waited for the job offers to roll in. The only offer I got came from someone who wanted me to run the garbage cyclers on Iapetus, which the guy should have known I wouldn't accept if he had bothered to read my application.

Maybe he was just neck-deep in garbage and desperate, I don't know.

And then the most astounding thing happened. Instead of a job in the computer field, I got an offer to study at the Pisan Academy.

Which is an art school. Which is in Italy, which is where the paintings come from mostly.

The acceptance committee said that my work showed a "naive but highly original fusion of social criticism with the formalities of the geometric order." I don't even *pretend* to know what they meant by that, but I suspect they just weren't used to the perspective of a student who had spent practically her entire life in a computer on Ceres.

I broadcast my shrieks of joy to everyone in the cadre, even those who had left Ceres and were probably wincing at their work stations when my screams reached them.

I bounced around the common room and everyone came out to congratulate me. Even Janis, who had taken to wearing an avatar that wasn't even remotely human, just a graphic of a big sledgehammer smashing a rock, over and over.

Subtlety had never been her strong point.

"Congratulations," she said. "You got what you wanted."

And then she broadcast something on a private channel. *You're going to be famous,* she said. *But I'm going to be a* legend.

I looked at her. And then I sent back, *Can we talk about this?*

In a few days. When I deliver my thesis.

Don't, I pleaded.

Too late.

The hammer hit its rock, and the shards flew out into the room and vanished.

I spent the next few days planning my Incarnation Day party, but my heart wasn't in it. I kept wondering if Janis was going to be alive to enjoy it.

I finally decided to have my party in Thailand because there were so many interesting environments in one place, as well as the Great Buddha. And I found a caterer that was supposed to be really good.

I decided what sort of body I wanted, and the incarnation specialists on Earth started cooking it up in one of their vats. Not the body of an Earth-born four-teen-year-old, but older, more like eighteen. Brown eyes, brown hair, and those big eyes that had always been so useful.

And two legs, of course. Which is what they all have down there.

I set the date. The cadre were alerted. We all practiced in the simulations and tried to get used to making do with only two arms. Everyone was prepared.

And then Janis finished her thesis. I downloaded a copy the second it was submitted to her committee and read it in one long sitting, and my sense of horror grew with every line.

What Janis had done was publish a comprehensive critique *of our entire society!* It was a piece of brilliance, and at the same time it was utter poison.

Posthuman society wrecks its children, Janis said, and this can be demon-strated by the percentage of neurotic and dysfunctional adults. The problems encountered by the first generation of children who spent their formative years as programs—the autism, the obsessions and compulsions, the addictions to electronic environments—hadn't gone away, they'd just been reduced to the point where they'd become a part of the background clutter, a part of our civilization so everyday that we never quite noticed it.

Janis had the data, too. The number of people who were under treatment for one thing or another. The percentage who had difficulty adjusting to their incarnations, or who didn't want to communicate with anyone outside their cadre, or who couldn't sleep unless they were immersed in a simulation. Or who committed suicide. Or who died in accidents—Janis questioned whether all those accidents were really the results of our harsh environments. Our machines and our settlements were much safer than they had been in the early days, but the rates of accidental death were still high. How many accidents were caused by distracted or unhappy operators, or for that matter were deliberate "suicide by machine"?

Janis went on to describe one of the victims of this ruthless type of upbringing. "Flat of emotional affect, offended by disorder and incapable of coping with obstruction, unable to function without adherence to a belief system as rigid as the artificial and constricted environments in which she was raised."

When I realized Janis was describing Anna-Lee I almost de-rezzed.

Janis offered a scheme to cure the problem, which was to get rid of the virtual environments and start out with real incarnated babies. She pulled out vast numbers of statistics demonstrating that places that did this—chiefly Earth—seemed to raise more successful adults. She also pointed out that the initial shortage of resources that had prompted the creation of virtual children in the first place had long since passed—plenty of water-ice coming in from the Kuiper Belt these days, and we were sitting on all the minerals we could want. The only reason the system continued was for the convenience of the adults. But genuine babies, as opposed to abstract computer programs, would help the adults, too. They would no longer be tempted to become little dictators with absolute power over their offspring. Janis said the chance would turn the grownups into better human beings.

All this was buttressed by colossal numbers of statistics, graphs, and other data. I realized when I'd finished it that the Cadre of Glorious Destiny had produced one true genius, and that this genius was Janis.

The true genius is a mind of large general powers, accidentally determined to some particular direction.

Anna-Lee determined her, all right, and the problem was that Janis probably didn't have that long to live. Aside from the fact that Janis had ruthlessly caricatured her, Anna-Lee couldn't help but notice that the whole work went smack up against the Five Principles Movement. According to the Movement people, all available resources had to be devoted to the expansion of the human race out of the solar system and into new environments. It didn't matter how many more resources were available now than in the past, it was clear against their principles to devote a greater share to the raising of children when it could be used to blast off into the universe.

And though the Five Principles people acknowledged our rather high death rate, they put it down to our settlements' hazardous environments. All we had to do was genetically modify people to better suit the environments and the problem would be solved.

I skipped the appendices and zoomed from my room across the common room to Janis' door, and hit the button to alert her to a visitor. The door vanished, and there was Janis—for the first time since her fight with Anna-Lee, she was using her quadbod avatar. She gave me a wicked grin.

"Great, isn't it?"

"It's *brilliant!* But you can't let Anna-Lee see it."

"Don't be silly. I sent Mom the file myself."

I was horrified. She had to have seen the way my Picasso-face gaped, and it made her laugh.

"She'll have you erased!" I said.

"If she does," Janis said. "She'll only prove my point." She put a consoling hand on my shoulder. "Sorry if it means missing your incarnation."

When Anna-Lee came storming in—which wasn't long after—Janis broadcast the whole confrontation on a one-way link to the whole cadre. We got to watch, but not to participate. She didn't want our advice any more than she wanted her mother's.

"You are unnatural!" Anna-Lee stormed. "You spread slanders! You have betrayed the highest truth!"

"I *told* the truth!" Janis said. "And you *know* it's the truth, otherwise you wouldn't be so insane right now."

Anna-Lee stiffened. "I am a Five Principles Constant Soldier. I know the truth, and I know my duty."

"Every time you say that, you prove my point."

"You will retract this thesis, and apologize to your committee for giving them such a vicious document."

Anna-Lee hadn't realized that the document was irretrievable, that Janis had given it to everyone she knew.

Janis laughed. "No way, Mom," she said.

Anna-Lee lost it. She waved her fists and screamed. "I know my duty! I will not allow such a slander to be seen by anyone!" She pointed at Janis. "You have three days to retract!"

Janis gave a snort of contempt.

"Or what?"

"Or I will decide that you're incorrigible and terminate your program."

Janis laughed. "Go right ahead, Mom. Do it *now*. Nothing spreads a new idea better than martyrdom." She spread her four arms. "*Do* it, Mom. I *hate* life in this hell. I'm ready."

I will be conquered; I will not capitulate.

Yes, Doctor Sam. That's it exactly.

"You have three days," Anna-Lee said, her voice all flat and menacing, and then her virtual image de-rezzed.

Janis looked at the space where her mom had been, and then a goofy grin spread across her face. She switched to the redheaded, stick-figure avatar, and began to do a little dance as she hovered in the air, moving like a badly animated cartoon.

"Hey!" she sang. "I get to go to Alison's party after all!"

I had been so caught up in the drama that I had forgot my incarnation was going to happen in two days.

But it wasn't going to be a party now. It was going to be a wake.

"Doctor Sam," I said, "I've got to save Janis."

The triumph of hope over experience.

"Hope is what I've got," I said, and then I thought about it. "And maybe a little experience, too."

* * *

My Incarnation Day went well. We came down by glider, as we had that first time on Titan, except that this time I told Ground Control to let my friends land wherever the hell they wanted. That gave us time to inspect the Great Buddha, a slim man with a knowing smile sitting cross-legged with knobs on his head. He's two and a half kilometers tall and packed with massively parallel quantum processors, all crunching vast amounts of data, thinking whatever profound thoughts are appropriate to an artificial intelligence built on such a scale, and repeating millions of sutras, which are scriptures for Buddhists, all at the speed of light.

It creeps along at two or three centimeters per day, and will enter the strait at the end of the Kra Peninsula many thousands of years from now.

After viewing the Buddha's serene expression from as many angles as suited us, we soared and swooped over many kilometers of brilliant green jungle and landed on the beach. And we all *did* land on the beach, which sort of surprised me. And then we all did our best to learn how to surf—and let me tell you from the start, the surfing simulators are *totally* inadequate. The longest I managed to stand my board was maybe twenty seconds.

I was amazed at all the sensations that crowded all around me. The breeze on my skin, the scents of the sea and the vegetation and the charcoal on which our banquet was being cooked. The hot sand under my bare feet. The salt taste of the ocean on my lips. The sting of the little jellyfish on my legs and arms, and the iodine smell of the thick strand of seaweed that got wrapped in my hair.

I mean, I had no *idea*. The simulators were totally inadequate to the Earth experience.

And this was just a *part* of the Earth, a small fraction of the environments available. I think I convinced a lot of the cadre that maybe they'd want to move to Earth as soon as they could raise the money and find a job.

After swimming and beach games we had my Incarnation Day dinner. The sensations provided by the food were really too intense—I couldn't eat much of it. If I was going to eat Earth food, I was going to have to start with something a lot more bland.

And there was my brown-eyed body at the head of the table, looking down at the members of the Cadre of Glorious Destiny who were toasting me with tropical drinks, the kind that have parasols in them.

Tears came to my eyes, and they were a lot wetter and hotter than tears in the sims. For some reason that fact made me cry even more.

My parents came to the dinner, because this was the first time they could actually hug me—hug me for real, that is, and not in a sim. They had downloaded into bodies that didn't look much like the four-armed quadbods they used back on Ceres, but that didn't matter. When my arms went around them, I began to cry again.

After the tears were wiped away we put on underwater gear and went for a swim on the reef, which is just amazing. More colors and shapes and textures than I could ever imagine—or imagine putting in a work of art.

A work of art that embodies all but selects none is not art, but mere cant and recitation.

Oh, wow. You're right. Thank you, Doctor Sam.

After the reef trip we paid a visit to one of the underwater settlements, one inhabited by people adapted to breathe water. The problems were that we had to keep our underwater gear on, and that none of us were any good at the fluid sign language they all used as their preferred means of communication.

Then we rose from the ocean, dried out, and had a last round of hugs before being uploaded to our normal habitations. I gave Janis a particularly strong hug, and I whispered in her ear.

"Take care of yourself."

"Who?" she grinned. "*Me?*"

And then the little brown-haired body was left behind, looking very lonely, as everyone else put on the electrodes and uploaded back to their normal and very-distant worlds.

As soon as I arrived on Ceres, I zapped an avatar of myself into my parents' quarters. They looked at me as if I were a ghost.

"What are *you* doing here?" my mother managed.

"I hate to tell you this," I said, "but I think you're going to have to hire a lawyer."

* * *

It was surprisingly easy to do, really. Remember that I was assisting Dane, who was a communications tech, and in charge of uploading all of our little artificial brains to Earth. And also remember that I am a specialist in systems interoperability, which implies that I am also a specialist in systems *unoperability*.

It was very easy to set a couple of artificial intelligences running amok in Dane's system just as he was working on our upload. And that so distracted him that he said *yes* when I said that I'd do the job for him.

And once I had access, it was the work of a moment to swap a couple of serial numbers.

The end result of which was that it was Janis who uploaded into my brown-haired body, and received all the toasts, and who hugged my parents with *my* arms. And who is now on Earth, incarnated, with a full set of human rights and safe from Anna-Lee.

I wish I could say the same for myself.

Anna-Lee couldn't have me killed, of course, since I don't belong to her. But she could sue my parents, who from her point of view permitted a piece of software belonging to *them* to prevent her from wreaking vengeance on some software that belonged to *her*.

And of course Anna-Lee went berserk the second she found out—which was more or less immediately, since Janis sent her a little radio taunt as soon as she downed her fourth or fifth celebratory umbrella drink.

Janis sent me a message, too.

"The least you could have done was make my hair red."

My hair. Sometimes I wonder why I bothered.

An unexpected side effect of this was that we all got famous. It turns out that this was an unprecedented legal situation, with lots of human interest and a colorful cast of characters. Janis became a media celebrity, and so did I, and so did Anna-Lee.

Celebrity didn't do Anna-Lee's cause any good. Her whole mental outlook was too rigid to stand the kind of scrutiny and questioning that any public figure has to put up with. As soon as she was challenged she lost control. She called one of the leading media interviewers a name that you, Doctor Sam, would not wish me to repeat.

Whatever the actual merits of her legal case, the sight of Anna-Lee screaming that I had deprived her of the inalienable right to kill her daughter failed to win her a lot of friends. Eventually the Five Principles people realized she wasn't doing their cause any good, and she was replaced by a Movement spokesperson who said as little as possible.

Janis did some talking, too, but not nearly as much as she would have liked, because she was under house arrest for coming to Earth without a visa and without paying the immigration tax. The cops showed up when she was sleeping off her hangover from all the umbrella drinks. It's probably lucky that she wasn't given the opportunity to talk much, because if she started on her rants she would have worn out her celebrity as quickly as Anna-Lee did.

Janis was scheduled to be deported back to Ceres, but shipping an actual incarnated human being is much more difficult than zapping a simulation by laser, and she had to wait for a ship that could carry passengers, and that would be months.

She offered to navigate the ship herself, since she had the training, but the offer was declined.

Lots of people read her thesis who wouldn't otherwise have heard of it. And millions discussed it whether they'd read it or not. There were those who said that Janis was right, and those that said that Janis was mostly right but that she exaggerated. There were those who said that the problem didn't really exist, except in the statistics.

There were those who thought the problem existed entirely in the software, that the system would work if the simulations were only made more like reality. I had to disagree, because I think the simulations *were* like reality, but only for certain people.

The problem is that human beings perceive reality in slightly different ways, even if they happen to be programs. A programmer could do his best to create an artificial reality that exactly mimicked the way he perceived reality, except that it wouldn't be as exact for another person, it would only be an approximation. It would be like fitting everyone's hand into the same-sized glove.

Eventually someone at the University of Adelaide read the thesis and offered Janis a professorship in their sociology department. She accepted and was freed from house arrest.

Poor Australia, I thought.

I was on video quite a lot. I used my little-girl avatar, and I batted my big eyes a lot. I still wore blue, mourning for Fritz.

Why, I was asked, did I act to save Janis?

"Because we're cadre, and we're supposed to look after one another."

What did I think of Anna-Lee?

"I don't see why she's complaining. I've seen to it that Janis *just isn't her problem anymore.*"

Wasn't what I did stealing?

"It's not stealing to free a slave."

And so on. It was the same sort of routine I'd been practicing on my parents all these years, and the practice paid off. Entire cadres—hundreds of them—signed petitions asking that the case be dismissed. Lots of adults did the same.

I hope that it helps, but the judge that hears the case isn't supposed to be swayed by public opinion, but only by the law.

And everyone forgets that it's my parents that will be on trial, not me, accused of letting their software steal Anna-Lee's software. And of course I, and therefore they, am completely guilty, so my parents are almost certainly going to be fined, and lose both money and Citizenship Points.

I'm sorry about that, but my parents seem not to be.

How the judge will put a value on a piece of stolen software that its owner fully intended to destroy is going to make an interesting ruling, however it turns out.

I don't know whether I'll ever set foot on Earth again. I can't take my place in Pisa because I'm not incarnated, and I don't know if they'll offer again.

And however things turn out, Fritz is still zeroed. And I still wear blue.

I don't have my outside job any longer. Dane won't speak to me, because his supervisor reprimanded him, and he's under suspicion for being my accomplice. And even those who are sympathetic to me aren't about to let me loose with their computers.

And even if I get a job somewhere, I can't be incarnated until the court case is over.

It seems to me that the only person who got away scot-free was Janis. Which is normal.

So right now my chief problem is boredom. I spent fourteen years in a rigid program intended to fill my hours with wholesome and intellectually useful activity, and now that's over.

And I can't get properly started on the non-wholesome thing until I get an incarnation somewhere.

Everyone is, or hopes to be, an idler.

Thank you, Doctor Sam.

I'm choosing to idle away my time making pictures. Maybe I can sell them and help pay the Earth tax.

I call them my "Doctor Johnson" series. *Sam. Johnson on Mars. Sam. Johnson Visits Neptune. Sam. Johnson Quizzing the Tomasko Glacier. Sam. Johnson Among the Asteroids.*

I have many more ideas along this line.

Doctor Sam, I trust you will approve.

THE NIGHT WHISKEY

JEFFREY FORD

Jeffrey Ford is the author of six novels—*Vanitas*, World Fantasy Award winner *The Physiognomy*, *Memoranda*, *The Beyond*, *The Portrait of Mrs. Charbuque* and *The Girl in the Glass*—and World Fantasy Award winning collection *The Fantasy Writer's Assistant and Other Stories*. His short fiction, which has appeared in *The Magazine of Fantasy & Science Fiction*, *SciFiction*, *Black Gate*, *The Green Man*, *Leviathan 3*, *The Dark*, and many year's best anthologies, has won the World Fantasy and Nebula Awards. His most recent book is collection, *The Empire of Ice Cream*.

Some things only make sense if you never question them, and sometimes growing up in a small town can involve no end of strangeness, as this darkly weird coming-of-age tale shows.

All summer long, on Wednesday and Friday evenings after my job at the gas station, I practiced with old man Witzer looking over my shoulder. When I'd send a dummy toppling perfectly onto the pile of mattresses in the bed of his pickup, he'd wheeze like it was his last breath (I think he was laughing), and pat me on the back, but when they fell awkwardly or hit the metal side of the truck bed or went really awry and ended sprawled on the ground, he'd spit tobacco and say either one of two things—"That there's a cracked melon," or "Get me a wet-vac." He was a patient teacher, never rushed, never raising his voice or showing the least exasperation in the face of my errors. After we'd felled the last of the eight dummies we'd earlier placed in the lower branches of the trees on the edge of town, he'd open a little cooler he kept in the cab of his truck and fetch a beer for himself and one for me. "You did good today, boy," he'd say, no matter if I did or not, and we'd sit in the truck with the windows open, pretty much in silence, and watch the fireflies signal in the gathering dark.

As the old man had said, "There's an art to dropping drunks." The main tools of the trade were a set of three long bamboo poles—a ten-foot, a fifteen-foot, and a twenty-foot. They had rubber balls attached at one end that were wrapped in chamois cloth and tied tight with a leather lanyard. These poles were called "prods." Choosing the right prod, considering how high the branches were that the drunk had nestled upon, was crucial. Too short a one would cause you to go on tiptoes and lose accuracy, while the excess length of too long a one would get in the way and throw you off balance. The first step was always to take a few minutes and carefully assess the situation. You had to ask yourself, "How might this body fall if I were to prod the shoulders first or the back or the left leg?" The old man had taught me that generally there was a kind of physics to it but that sometimes intuition had to override logic. "Don't think of them as falling but think of them as flying," said Witzer, and only when I was actually out there under the trees and trying to hit the mark in the center of the pickup bed did I know what he meant. "You ultimately want them to fall, turn in the air, and land flat on the back," he'd told me. "That's a ten pointer." There were other important aspects of the job as well. The positioning of the truck was crucial as was the manner with which you woke them after they had safely landed. Calling them back by shouting in their ears would leave them dazed for a week, but, as the natives had done, breaking a thin twig a few inches from the ear worked like a charm—a gentle reminder that life was waiting to be lived.

When his long-time fellow harvester, Mr. Bo Elliott, passed on, the town council had left it to Witzer to find a replacement. It had been his determination to pick someone young, and so he came to the high school and carefully observed each of us fifteen students in the graduating class. It was a wonder he could see anything through the thick, scratched lenses of his glasses and those perpetually squinted eyes, but after long deliberation, which involved the rubbing of his stubbled chin and the scratching of his fallow scalp, he singled me out for the honor. An honor it was too, as he'd told me, "You know that because you don't get paid anything for it." He assured me that I had the talent hidden inside of me, that he'd seen it like an aura of pink light, and that he'd help me develop it over the summer. To be an apprentice in the Drunk Harvest was a kind of exalted position for one as young as me, and it brought me some special credit with my friends and neighbors, because it meant that I was being initiated into an ancient tradition that went back further than the time when our ancestors settled that remote piece of country. My father beamed with pride, my mother got teary eyed, my girlfriend, Darlene, let me get to third base and partway home.

Our town was one of those places you pass but never stop in while on vacation to some national park; out in the sticks, up in the mountains—places where the population is rendered in three figures on a board by the side of the road; the first numeral no more than a four and the last with a hand-painted slash through it and replaced with one of lesser value beneath. The people there were pretty much like people everywhere only the remoteness of the locale had insulated us against the relentless tide of change and the judgment of the wider world. We had radios and televisions and telephones, and as these things came in, what they brought us lured a few of our number away. But for those who stayed in Gatchfield progress moved like a tortoise dragging a ball and chain. The old ways hung on with more tenacity than Relletta Clome, who was 110 years old and had died and been revived by Doctor Kvench eight times in ten years. We had our little ways and customs that were like the exotic beasts of Tasmania, isolated in their evolution to become completely singular. The strangest of these traditions was the Drunk Harvest.

The Harvest centered on an odd little berry that, as far as I know, grows nowhere else in the world. The natives had called it *vachimi atatsi*, but because of its shiny black hue and the nature of its growth, the settlers had renamed it the deathberry. It didn't grow in the meadows or swamps as do blueberries and blackberries, no, this berry grew only out of the partially decayed carcasses of animals left to lie where they'd fallen. If you were out hunting in the woods and you came across say, a dead deer, which had not been touched by coyotes or wolves, you could be certain that that deceased creature would eventually sprout a small hedge from its rotted gut before autumn and that the long thin branches would be thick with juicy black berries. The predators knew somehow that these fallen beasts had the seeds of the berry bush within them, because although it went against their nature not to devour a fallen creature, they wouldn't go near these particular carcasses. It wasn't just wild creatures either, even livestock fallen dead in the field and left untouched could be counted on to serve as host for this parasitic plant. Instances of this weren't common but I'd seen it first-hand a couple of times in my youth—a rotting body, head maybe already turning to skull, and out of the belly like a green explosion, this wild spray of long thin branches tipped with atoms of black like tiny marbles, bobbing in the breeze. It was a frightening sight to behold for the first time, and as I overheard Lester Bildab, a man who foraged for the deathberry, tell my father once, "No matter how many times I see it, I still get a little chill in the backbone."

Lester and his son, a dimwitted boy in my class at school, Lester II, would go out at the start of each August across the fields and through the woods and swamps searching for fallen creatures hosting the hideous flora. Bildab had learned from his father about gathering the fruit, as Bildab's father had learned from his father, and so on all the way back to the settlers and the natives from whom *they'd* learned. You can't eat the berries; they'll make you violently ill. But you can ferment them and make a drink, like a thick black brandy that had come to be called *Night Whiskey* and supposedly had the sweetest taste on earth. I didn't know the process, as only a select few did, but from berry to glass I knew it took about a month. Lester and his son would gather them and usually come up with three good-sized grocery sacks full. Then they'd take them over to The Blind Ghost Bar and Grill and sell them to Mr. and Mrs. Bocean, who knew the process for making the liquor and kept the recipe in a little safe with a combination lock. That recipe was given to our forefathers as a gift by the natives, who, two years after giving it, with no provocation and having gotten along peacefully with the settlers, vanished without a trace, leaving behind an empty village on an island out in the swamp… or so the story goes.

The celebration that involved this drink took place at The Blind Ghost on the last Saturday night in September. It was usually for adults only, and so the first chance I ever got to witness it was the year I was made an apprentice to old man Witzer. The only two younger people at the event that year were me and Lester II. Bildab's boy had been attending since he was ten, and some speculated that having witnessed the thing and been around the berries so long was what had turned him simple, but I knew young Lester in school before that and he was no ball of fire then either. Of the adults that participated, only eight actually partook of the Night Whiskey. Reed and Samantha Bocean took turns each year, one joining in the drinking while the other watched the bar, and then there were seven others, picked by lottery, who got to taste the sweetest thing on earth. Sheriff Jolle did the honors picking the names of the winners from a hat at the event and was barred from participating by a town ordinance that went way back. Those who didn't drink the Night Whiskey drank conventional alcohol, and there were local musicians there and dancing. From the snatches of conversation about the celebrations that adults would let slip out, I'd had an idea it was a raucous time.

This native drink, black as a crow wing and slow to pour as cough syrup, had some strange properties. A year's batch was enough to fill only half of an old quart gin bottle that Samantha Bocean had tricked out with a hand-made label showing a deer skull with berries for eyes, and so it was portioned out sparingly. Each participant got no more than about three-quarters of a shot glass of it, but that was enough. Even with just these few sips it was wildly intoxicating, so that the drinkers became immediately drunk, their inebriation growing as the night went on although they'd finish off their allotted pittance within the first hour of the celebration. "Blind drunk" was the phrase used to describe how the drinkers of it would end the night. Then came the weird part, for usually around two a.m. all eight of them, all at once, got to their feet, stumbled out the door, lurched down the front steps of the bar, and meandered off into the dark, groping and weaving like namesakes of the establishment they had just left. It was a peculiar phenomenon of the drink that it made those who imbibed it search for a resting place in the lower branches of a tree. Even though they were pie-eyed drunk, somehow, and no one knew why, they'd manage to shimmy up a trunk and settle themselves down across a few choice branches. It was a law that if you tried to stop them or disturb them it would be cause for arrest. So when the drinkers of the Night Whiskey left the bar, no one followed. The next day, they'd be found fast asleep in midair, only a few precarious branches between them and gravity. That's where old man Witzer and I came in. At first light, we were to make our rounds in his truck with the poles bungeed on top, partaking of what was known as the Drunk Harvest.

Dangerous? You bet, but there was a reason for it. I told you about the weird part, but even though this next part gives a justification of sorts, it's even weirder. When the natives gave the berry and the recipe for the Night Whiskey to our forefathers, they considered it a gift of a most divine nature, because after the dark drink was ingested and the drinker had climbed aloft, sleep would invariably bring him or her to some realm between that of dream and the sweet hereafter. In this limbo they'd come face to face with their relatives and loved ones who'd passed on. That's right. It never failed. As best as I can remember him having told it, here's my own father's recollection of the experience from the year he won the lottery:

"I found myself out in the swamp at night with no memory of how I'd gotten there or what reason I had for being there. I tried to find a marker—a fallen tree or a certain turn in the path, to find my way back to town. The moon was bright, and as I stepped into a clearing, I saw a single figure standing there stark naked. I drew closer and said hello, even though I wanted to run. I saw it was an old fellow, and when he heard me approaching, he looked up and right there I knew it was my Uncle Fic. 'What are you doing out here without your clothes,' I said to him as I approached. 'Don't you remember, Joe,' he said, smiling. 'I'm passed on.' And then it struck me and made my hair stand on end. But Uncle Fic, who'd died at the age of ninety-eight when I was only fourteen, told me not to be afraid. He told me a good many things, explained a good many things, told me not to fear death. I asked him about my ma and pa, and he said they were together as always and having a good time. I bid him to say hello to them for me, and he said he would. Then he turned and started to walk away but stepped on a twig, and that sound brought me awake, and I was lying in the back of Witzer's pickup, staring into the jowly, pitted face of Bo Elliott."

My father was no liar, and to prove to my mother and me that he was telling the truth, he told us that Uncle Fic had told him where to find a tie pin he'd been given as a commemoration of his twenty-fifth year at the feed store but had subsequently lost. He then walked right over to a teapot shaped like an orange that my mother kept on a shelf in our living room, opened it, reached in, and pulled out the pin. The only question my father was left with about the whole strange episode was, "Out of all my dead relations, why Uncle Fic?"

Stories like the one my father told my mother and me abound. Early on, back in the 1700s, they were written down by those who could write. These rotting manuscripts were kept for a long time in the Gatchfield library—an old shoe-repair store with book-shelves—in a glass case. Sometimes the dead who showed up in the Night Whiskey dreams offered premonitions, sometimes they told who a thief was when something had gone missing. And supposedly it was the way Jolle had solved the Latchey murder, on a tip given to Mrs. Windom by her great aunt, dead ten years. Knowing that our ancestors were keeping an eye on things and didn't mind singing out about the untoward once a year usually convinced the citizens of Gatchfield to walk the straight and narrow. We kept it to ourselves, though, and never breathed a word of it to outsiders as if their rightful skepticism would ruin the power of the ceremony. As for those who'd left town, it was never a worry that they'd tell anyone, because, seriously, who'd have believed them?

On a Wednesday evening, the second week in September, while sitting in the pickup truck, drinking a beer, old man Witzer said, "I think you got it, boy. No more practice now. Too much and we'll overdo it." I simply nodded, but in the following weeks leading up to the end-of-the-month celebration, I was a wreck, envisioning the body of one of my friends or neighbors sprawled broken on the ground next to the bed of the truck. At night I'd have a recurring dream of prodding a body out of an oak, seeing it fall in slow motion, and then all would go black and I'd just hear this dull crack, what I assumed to be the drunk's head slamming the side of the pickup bed. I'd wake and sit up straight, shivering. Each time this happened, I tried to remember to see who it was in my dream, because it always seemed to be the same person. Two nights before the celebration, I saw a tattoo of a coiled cobra on the fellow's bicep as he fell and knew it was Henry Grass. I thought of telling Witzer, but I didn't want to seem a scared kid.

The night of the celebration came and after sundown my mother and father and I left the house and strolled down the street to The Blind Ghost. People were already starting to arrive and from inside I could hear the band tuning up fiddles and banjos. Samantha Bocean had made the place up for the event—black crepe paper draped here and there and wrapped around the support beams. Hanging from the ceiling on various lengths of fishing line were the skulls of all manner of local animals: coyote, deer, beaver, squirrel, and a giant black bear skull suspended over the center table where the lottery winners were to sit and take their drink. I was standing on the threshold, taking all this in, feeling the same kind of enchantment as when a kid and Mrs. Musfin would do up the three classrooms of the school house for Christmas, when my father leaned over to me and whispered, "You're on your own tonight, Ernest. You want to drink, drink. You want to dance, dance." I looked at him and he smiled, nodded, and winked. I then looked to my mother and she merely shrugged, as if to say, "That's the nature of the beast."

Old man Witzer was there at the bar, and he called me over and handed me a cold beer. Two other of the town's oldest men were with him, his chess-playing buddies, and he put his arm around my shoulders and introduced them to me. "This is a good boy," he said, patting my back. "He's doing Bo Elliott proud out there under the trees." The two friends of his nodded and smiled at me, the most notice I'd gotten from either of them my entire life. And then the band launched into a reel, and everyone turned to watch them play. Two choruses went by and I saw my mother and father and some of the other couples move out onto the small dance floor. I had another beer and looked around.

About four songs later, Sheriff Jolle appeared in the doorway to the bar and the music stopped mid-tune.

"OK," he said, hitching his pants up over his gut and removing his black, wide-brimmed hat, "time to get the lottery started." He moved to the center of the bar where the Night Whiskey drinkers' table was set up and took a seat. "Everybody drop your lottery tickets into the hat and make it snappy." I'd guessed that this year it was Samantha Bocean who was going to drink her own concoction since Reed stayed behind the bar and she moved over and took a seat across from Jolle. After the last of the tickets had been deposited into the hat, the sheriff pushed it away from him into the middle of the table. He then called for a whiskey neat, and Reed was there with it in a flash. In one swift gulp, he drained the glass, banged it onto the tabletop and said, "I'm ready." My girlfriend Darlene's stepmom came up from behind him with a black scarf and tied it around his eyes for a blindfold. Reaching into the hat, he ran his fingers through the lottery tickets, mixing them around, and then started drawing them out one by one and stacking them in a neat pile in front of him on the table. When he had the seven, he stopped and pulled off the blindfold. He then read the names in a loud voice and everyone kept quiet till he was finished—Becca Staney, Stan Joss, Pete Hesiant, Berta Hull, Moses T. Remarque, Ronald White, and Henry Grass. The room exploded with applause and screams. The winners smiled, dazed by having won, as their friends and family gathered round them and slapped them on the back, hugged them, shoved drinks into their hands. I was overwhelmed by the moment, caught up in it and grinning, until I looked over at Witzer and saw him jotting the names down in a little notebook he'd refer to tomorrow when we made our rounds. Only then did it come to me that one of the names was none other than *Henry Grass*, and I felt my stomach tighten in a knot.

Each of the winners eventually sat down at the center table. Jolle got up and gave his seat to Reed Bocean, who brought with him from behind the bar the bottle of Night Whiskey and a tray of eight shot glasses. Like the true barman he was, he poured all eight without lifting the bottle once, all to the exact same level. One by one they were handed around the table. When each of the winners had one before him or her, the barkeep smiled and said, "Drink up." Some went for it like it was a draught from the fountain of youth, some snuck up on it with trembling hand. Berta Hull, a middle-aged mother of five with horse teeth and short red hair, took a sip and declared, "Oh my, it's so lovely." Ronald White, the brother of one of the men I worked with at the gas station, took his up and dashed it off in one shot. He wiped his mouth on his sleeve and laughed like a maniac, drunk already. Reed went back to the bar. The band started up again and the celebration came to life like a wild animal in too small a cage.

I wandered around the bar, nodding to the folks I knew, half taken by my new celebrity as a participant in the Drunk Harvest and half preoccupied watching Henry Grass. He was a young guy, only twenty-five, with a crew cut and a square jaw, dressed in the camouflage sleeveless T-shirt he wore in my recurring dream. With the way he stared at the shot glass in front of him through his little circular glasses, you'd have thought he was staring into the eyes of a king cobra. He had a reputation as a gentle, studious soul, although he was most likely the strongest man in town—the rare instance of an outsider who'd made a place for himself in Gatchfield. The books he read were all about UFOs and the Bermuda Triangle, *Chariots of the Gods*; stuff my father proclaimed to be "dyed-in-the-wool hooey."

He worked with the horses over at the Haber family farm, and lived in a trailer out by the old Civil War shot tower, across the meadow and through the woods. I stopped for a moment to talk to Lester II, who mumbled to me around the hard boiled eggs he was shoving into his mouth one after another, and when I looked back to Henry, he'd finished off the shot glass and left the table.

I overheard snatches of conversation, and much of it was commentary on why it was a lucky thing that so and so had won the lottery this year. Someone mentioned the fact that poor Pete Hesiant's beautiful young wife, Lonette, had passed away from leukemia just at the end of the spring, and another mentioned that Moses had always wanted a shot at the Night Whiskey but had never gotten the chance, and how he'd soon be too old to participate as his arthritis had recently given him the devil of a time. Everybody was pulling for Berta Hull, who was raising those five children on her own, and Becca was a favorite because she was the town midwife. The same such stuff was said about Ron White and Stan Joss.

In addition to the well-wishes for the lottery winners, I stood for a long time next to a table where Sheriff Jolle, my father and mother, and Dr. Kvench sat, and listened to the doctor, a spry little man with a gray goatee, who was by then fairly well along in his cups, as were his listeners, myself included, spout his theory as to why the drinkers took to the trees. He explained it, amidst a barrage of hiccups, as a product of evolution. His theory was that the deathberry plant had at one time grown everywhere on earth, and that early man partook of some form of the Night Whiskey at the dawn of time. Because the world was teeming with night predators then, and because early man was just recently descended from the treetops, those who became drunk automatically knew, as a means of self-preservation, to climb up into the trees and sleep so as not to become a repast for a saber-toothed tiger or some other onerous creature. Dr. Kvench, citing Carl Jung, believed that the imperative to get off the ground after drinking the Night Whiskey had remained in the collective unconscious and was passed down through the ages. "Everybody in the world probably still has the unconscious command that would kick in if they were to drink the dark stuff, but since the berry doesn't grow anywhere but here now, we're the only ones that see this effect." The doctor nodded, hiccupped twice, and then got up to fetch a glass of water. When he left the table Jolle looked over at my mother, and she and he and my father broke up laughing. "I'm glad he's better at pushing pills than concocting theories," said the Sheriff, drying his eyes with his thumbs.

At about midnight, I was reaching for yet another beer, which Reed had placed on the bar, when my grasp was interrupted by a viselike grip on my wrist. I looked up and saw that it was Witzer. He said nothing to me but simply shook his head, and I knew he was telling me to lay off so as to be fresh for the harvest in the morning. I nodded. He smiled, patted my shoulder, and turned away. Somewhere around two a.m., the lottery winners, so incredibly drunk that even in my intoxicated state it seemed impossible they could still walk, stopped dancing, drinking, whatever, and headed for the door. The music abruptly ceased.

It suddenly became so silent we could hear the wind blowing out on the street. The sounds of them stumbling across the wooden porch of the bar and then the steps creaking, the screen door banging shut, filled me with a sense of awe and visions of them groping through the night. I tried to picture Berta Hull climbing a tree, but I just couldn't get there, and the doctor's theory seemed to make some sense to me.

I left before my parents did. Witzer drove me home and before I got out of the cab, he handed me a small bottle.

"Take three good chugs," he said.

"What is it?" I asked.

"An herb mix," he said. "It'll clear your head and have you ready for the morning."

I took the first sip of it and the taste was bitter as could be. "Good god," I said, grimacing.

Witzer wheezed. "Two more," he said.

I did as I was told, got out of the truck and bid him good night. I didn't remember undressing or getting into bed, and luckily I was too drunk to dream. It seemed as if I'd only closed my eyes when my father's voice woke me, saying, "The old man's out in the truck, waiting on you." I leaped out of bed and dressed, and when I finally knew what was going on, I was surprised I felt as well and refreshed as I did. "Do good, Ernest," said my father from the kitchen. "Wait," my mother called. A moment later she came out of their bedroom, wrapping a robe around her. She gave me a hug and a kiss, and then said, "Hurry." It was brisk outside, and the early morning light gave proof that the day would be a clear one. The truck sat at the curb, the prods strapped to the top. Witzer sat in the cab, drinking a cup of coffee from the delicatessen. When I got in beside him, he handed me a cup and an egg sandwich on a hard roll wrapped in white paper. "We're off," he said. I cleared the sleep out of my eyes as he pulled away from the curb.

Our journey took us down the main street of town and then through the alley next to the sheriff's office. This gave way to another small tree-lined street we turned right on. As we headed away from the center of town, we passed Darlene's house, and I wondered what she'd done the previous night while I'd been at the celebration. I had a memory of her last time we were together. She was sitting naked against the wall of the abandoned barn by the edge of the swamp. Her blonde hair and face were aglow, illuminated by a beam of light that shone through a hole in the roof. She had the longest legs and her skin was pale and smooth. Taking a drag from her cigarette, she said, "Ernest, we gotta get out of this town." She'd laid out for me her plan of escape, her desire to go to some city where civilization was in full swing. I just nodded, reluctant to be too enthusiastic. She was adventurous and I was a homebody, but I did care deeply for her. She tossed her cigarette, put out her arms and opened her legs, and then Witzer said, "Keep your eyes peeled now, boy," and her image melted away.

We were moving slowly along a dirt road, both of us looking up at the lower branches of the trees. The old man saw the first one. I didn't see her till he applied the brakes. He took a little notebook and stub of a pencil out of his shirt pocket. "Samantha Bocean," he whispered, and put a check next to her name. We got out of the cab, and I helped him unlatch the prods and lay them on the ground beside the truck. She was resting across three branches in a magnolia tree, not too far from the ground. One arm and her long gray hair hung down, and she was turned so I could see her sleeping face.

"Get the ten," said Witzer, as he walked over to stand directly beneath her.

I did as I was told and then joined him.

"What d'ya say?" he asked. "Looks like this one's gonna be a peach."

"Well, I'm thinking if I get it on her left thigh and push her forward fast enough she'll flip as she falls and land perfectly."

Witzer said nothing but left me standing there and went and got in the truck. He started it up and drove it around to park so that the bed was precisely where we hoped she would land. He put it in park and left it running, and then got out and came and stood beside me. "Take a few deep breaths," he said. "And then let her fly."

I thought I'd be more nervous, but the training the old man had given me took hold and I knew exactly what to do. I aimed the prod and rested it gently on the top of her leg. Just as he'd told me, a real body was going to offer a little more resistance than one of the dummies, and I was ready for that. I took three big breaths and then shoved. She rolled slightly, and then tumbled forward, ass over head, landing with a thump on the mattresses, facing the morning sky. Witzer wheezed to beat the band, and said, "That's a solid ten." I was ecstatic.

The old man broke a twig next to Samantha's left ear and instantly her eyelids fluttered. Eventually she opened her eyes and smiled.

"How was your visit?" asked Witzer.

"I'll never get tired of that," she said. "It was wonderful."

We chatted with her for a few minutes, filling her in on how the party had gone at The Blind Ghost after she'd left. She didn't divulge to us what passed relative she'd met with, and we didn't ask. As my mentor had told me when I started, "There's a kind of etiquette to this. When in doubt, Silence is your best friend."

Samantha started walking back toward the center of town, and we loaded the prods onto the truck again. In no time, we were on our way, searching for the next sleeper. Luck was with us, for we found four in a row, fairly close by each other, Stan Joss, Moses T. Remarque, Berta Hull, and Becca Staney. All of them had chosen easy to get to perches in the lower branches of ancient oaks, and we dropped them, one, two, three, four, easy as could be. I never had to reach for anything longer than the ten, and the old man proved a genius at placing the truck just so. When each came around at the insistence of the snapping twig, they were cordial and seemed pleased with their experience. Moses even gave us a ten-dollar tip for dropping him into the truck. Becca told us that she'd spoken to her mother, whom she'd missed terribly since the woman's death two years earlier. Even though they'd been blind drunk the night before, amazingly none of them appeared to be hung over, and each walked away with a perceptible spring in his or her step, even Moses, though he was still slightly bent at the waist by the arthritis.

Witzer said, "Knock on wood, of course, but this is the easiest year I can remember. The year your daddy won, we had to ride around for four solid hours before we found him out by the swamp." We found Ron White only a short piece up the road from where we'd found the cluster of four, and he was an easy job. I didn't get him to land on his back. He fell face first, not a desirable drop, but he came to none the worse for wear. After Ron, we had to ride for quite a while, heading out toward the edge of the swamp. I knew the only two left were Pete Hesiant and Henry Grass, and the thought of Henry started to get me nervous again. I was reluctant to show my fear, not wanting the old man to lose faith in me, but as we drove slowly along, I finally told Witzer about my recurring dream.

When I was done recounting what I thought was a premonition, Witzer sat in silence for a few moments and then said, "I'm glad you told me."

"I'll bet it's really nothing," I said.

"Henry's a big fellow," he said. "Why should you have all the fun. I'll drop him." And with this, the matter was settled. I realized I should have told him weeks ago when I first started having the dreams.

"Easy, boy," said Witzer with a wheeze and waved his hand as if wiping away my cares. "You've got years of this to go. You can't manage everything on the first harvest."

We searched everywhere for Pete and Henry—all along the road to the swamp, on the trails that ran through the woods, out along the meadow by the shot tower and Henry's own trailer. With the dilapidated wooden structure of the tower still in sight, we finally found Henry.

"Thar she blows," said Witzer, and he stopped the truck.

"Where?" I said, getting out of the truck, and the old man pointed straight up.

Over our heads, in a tall pine, Henry lay face down, his arms and legs spread so that they kept him up while the rest of his body was suspended over nothing. His head hung down as if in shame or utter defeat. He looked in a way like he was crucified, and I didn't like the look of that at all.

"Get me the twenty," said Witzer, "and then pull the truck up."

I undid the prods from the roof, laid the other two on the ground by the side of the path, and ran the twenty over to the old man. By the time I went back to the truck, got it going, and turned it toward the drop spot, Witzer had the long pole in two hands and was sizing up the situation. As I pulled closer, he let the pole down and then waved me forward while eyeing back and forth, Henry and then the bed. He directed me to cut the wheel this way and that, reverse two feet, and then he gave me the thumbs up. I turned off the truck and got out.

"OK," he said. "This is gonna be a tricky one." He lifted the prod up and up and rested the soft end against Henry's chest. "You're gonna have to help me here. We're gonna push straight up on his chest so that his arms flop down and clear the branches, and then as we let him down we're gonna slide the pole, catch him at the belt buckle and give him a good nudge there to flip him as he falls."

I looked up at where Henry was, and then I just stared at Witzer.

"Wake up, boy!" he shouted.

I came to and grabbed the prod where his hands weren't.

"On three," he said. He counted off and then we pushed. Henry was heavy as ten sacks of rocks. "We got him," cried Witzer, "now slide it." I did and only then did I look up. "Push," the old man said. We gave it one more shove and Henry went into a swan dive, flipping like an Olympic athlete off the high board. When I saw him in mid-fall, my knees went weak and the air left me. He landed on his back with a loud thud directly in the middle of the mattresses, dust from the old cushions roiling up around him.

We woke Henry easily enough, sent him on his way to town, and were back in the truck. For the first time that morning I breathed a sigh of relief. "Easiest harvest I've ever been part of," said Witzer. We headed further down the path toward the swamp, scanning the branches for Pete Hesiant. Sure enough, in the same right manner with which everything else had fallen into place we found him curled up on his side in the branches of an enormous maple tree. With the first cursory glance at him, the old man determined that Pete would require no more than a ten. After we got the prods off the truck and positioned it under our last drop, Witzer insisted that I take him down. "One more to keep your skill up through the rest of the year," he said.

It was a simple job. Pete had found a nice perch with three thick branches beneath him. As I said, he was curled up on his side, and I couldn't see him all too well, so I just nudged his upper back and he rolled over like a small boulder. The drop was precise, and he hit the center of the mattresses, but the instant he was in the bed of the pickup, I knew something was wrong. He'd fallen too quickly for me to register it sooner, but as he lay there, I now noticed that there was someone else with him. Witzer literally jumped to the side of the truck bed and stared in.

"What in fuck's name," said the old man. "Is that a kid he's got with him?"

I saw the other body there, naked, in Pete's arms. There was long blond hair, that much was sure. It could have been a kid, but I thought I saw in the jumble, a full-size female breast.

Witzer reached into the truck bed, grabbed Pete by the shoulder and rolled him away from the other form. Then the two of us stood there in stunned silence. The thing that lay there wasn't a woman or a child but both and neither. The body was twisted and deformed, the size of an eight-year-old but with all the characteristics of maturity, if you know what I mean. And that face... lumpen and distorted, brow bulging, and from the left temple to the chin erupted in a range of discolored ridges.

"Is that Lonette?" I whispered, afraid the thing would awaken.

"She's dead, ain't she?" said Witzer in as low a voice, and his Adam's apple bobbed.

We both knew she was, but there she or some twisted copy of her lay. The old man took a handkerchief from his back pocket and brought it up to his mouth. He closed his eyes and leaned against the side of the truck. A bird flew by low overhead. The sun shone and leaves fell in the woods on both sides of the path.

Needless to say, when we moved again, we weren't breaking any twigs. Witzer told me to leave the prods and get in the truck. He started it up, and we drove slowly, like about fifteen miles an hour, into the center of town. We drove in complete silence. The place was quiet as a ghost town, no doubt everyone sleeping off the celebration, but we saw that Sheriff Jolle's cruiser was in front of the bunker-like concrete building that was the police station. The old man parked and went in. As he and the sheriff appeared at the door, I got out of the truck cab and joined them.

"What are you talking about?" Jolle said as they passed me and headed for the truck bed. I followed behind them.

"Shhh," said Witzer. When they finally were looking down at the sleeping couple, Pete and whatever that Lonette thing was, he added, "That's what I'm fucking talking about." He pointed his crooked old finger and his hand was obviously trembling.

Jolle's jaw dropped open after the second or two it took to sink in. "I never…" said the sheriff, and that's all he said for a long while.

Witzer whispered, "Pete brought her back with him."

"What kind of crazy shit is this?" asked Jolle and he turned quickly and looked at me as if I had an answer. Then he looked back at Witzer. "What the hell happened? Did he dig her up?"

"She's alive," said the old man. "You can see her breathing, but she got bunched up or something in the transfer from there to here."

"Bunched up," said Jolle. "There to here? What in Christ's name…" He shook his head and removed his shades. Then he turned to me again and said, "Boy, go get Doc Kvench."

In calling the doctor, I didn't know what to tell him, so I just said there was an emergency over at the sheriff's office and that he was needed. I didn't stick around and wait for him, because I had to keep moving. To stop would mean I'd have to think too deeply about the return of Lonette Hesiant. By the time I got back to the truck, Henry Grass had also joined Jolle and Witzer, having walked into town to get something to eat after his dream ordeal of the night before. As I drew close to them, I heard Henry saying, "She's come from another dimension. I've read about things like this. And from what I experienced last night, talking to my dead brother, I can tell you that place seems real enough for this to happen."

Jolle looked away from Henry at me as I approached, and then his gaze shifted over my head and he must have caught sight of the doctor. "Good job," said the sheriff, and put his hand on my shoulder as I leaned forward to catch my breath.

"Hey, Doc," he said as Kvench drew close, "you got a theory about this?"

The doctor stepped up to the truck bed and, clearing the sleep from his eyes, looked down at where the sheriff was pointing. Doctor Kvench had seen it all in his years in Gatchfield—birth, death, blood, body rot, but the instant he laid his eyes on the new Lonette, the color drained out of him, and he grimaced like he'd just taken a big swig of Witzer's herb mix. The effect on him was dramatic, and Henry stepped up next to him and held him up with one big tattooed arm across his back. Kvench brushed Henry off and turned away from the truck. I thought for a second that he was going to puke.

We waited for his diagnosis. Finally he turned back and said, "Where did it come from?"

"It fell out of the tree with Pete this morning," said Witzer.

"I signed the death certificate for that girl five months ago," said the doctor.

"She's come from another dimension…" said Henry, launching into one of his Bermuda Triangle explanations, but Jolle held a hand up to silence him. Nobody spoke then and the sheriff started pacing back and forth, looking into the sky and then at the ground. It was obvious that he was having some kind of silent argument with himself, cause every few seconds he'd either nod or shake his head. Finally, he put his open palms to his face for a moment, rubbed his forehead and cleared his eyes. Then he turned to us.

"Look, here's what we're gonna do. I decided. We're going to get Pete out of that truck without waking him and put him on the cot in the station. Will he stay asleep if we move him?" he asked Witzer.

The old man nodded. "As long as you don't shout his name or break a twig near his ear, he should keep sleeping till we wake him."

"OK," continued Jolle. "We get Pete out of the truck, and then we drive that thing out into the woods, we shoot it and bury it."

Everybody looked around at everybody else. The doctor said, "I don't know if I can be part of that."

"You're gonna be part of it," said Jolle, "or right this second you're taking full responsibility for its care. And I mean full responsibility."

"It's alive, though," said Kvench.

"But it's a mistake," said the sheriff, "either of nature or God or whatever."

"Doc, I agree with Jolle," said Witzer, "I never seen anything that felt so wrong to me than what I'm looking at in the back of that truck."

"You want to nurse that thing until it dies on its own?" Jolle said to the doctor. "Think of what it'll do to Pete to have to deal with it."

Kvench looked down and shook his head. Eventually he whispered, "You're right."

"Boy?" Jolle said to me.

My mouth was dry and my head was swimming a little. I nodded.

"Good," said the sheriff. Henry added that he was in. It was decided that we all participate and share in the act of disposing of it. Henry and the sheriff gently lifted Pete out of the truck and took him into the station house. When they appeared back outside, Jolle told Witzer and me to drive out to the woods in the truck and that he and Henry and Kvench would follow in his cruiser.

For the first few minutes of the drive out, Witzer said nothing. We passed Pete Hesiant's small yellow house and upon seeing it I immediately started thinking about Lonette, and how beautiful she'd been. She and Pete had only been in their early 30s, a very handsome couple. He was thin and gangly and had been a star basketball player for Gatchfield, but never tall enough to turn his skill into a college scholarship. They'd been high school sweethearts. He finally found work as a municipal handy man, and had that good-natured youth-going-to-seed personality of the washed up, once lauded athlete.

Lonette had worked the cash register at the grocery. I remembered her passing by our front porch on the way to work the evening shift one afternoon, and I overheard her talking to my mother about how she and Pete had decided to try to start a family. I'm sure I wasn't supposed to be privy to this conversation, but whenever she passed in front of our house, I tried to make it a point of being near a window. I heard every word through the screen. The very next week, though, I learned that she had some kind of disease. That was three years ago. She slowly grew more haggard through the following seasons. Pete tried to take care of her on his own, but I don't think it had gone all too well. At her funeral, Henry had to hold him back from climbing into the grave after her.

"Is this murder?" I asked Witzer after he'd turned onto the dirt path and headed out toward the woods.

He looked over at me and said nothing for a second. "I don't know, Ernest," he said. "Can you murder someone who's already dead? Can you murder a dream? What would you have us do?" He didn't ask the last question angrily but as if he was really looking for another plan than Jolle's.

I shook my head.

"I'll never see things the same again," he said. "I keep thinking I'm gonna wake up any minute now."

We drove on for another half-mile and then he pulled the truck off the path and under a cluster of oak. As we got out of the cab, the sheriff parked next to us. Henry, the doctor, and Jolle got out of the cruiser, and all five of us gathered at the back of the pickup. It fell to Witzer and me to get her out of the truck and lay her on the ground some feet away. "Careful," whispered the old man, as he leaned over the wall of the bed and slipped his arms under her. I took the legs, and when I touched her skin a shiver went through me. Her body was heavier than I thought, and her sex was staring me right in the face, covered with short hair thick as twine. She was breathing lightly, obviously sleeping, and her pupils moved rapidly beneath her closed lids like she was dreaming. She had a powerful aroma, flowers and candy, sweet to the point of sickening.

We got her on the ground without waking her, and the instant I let go of her legs, I stepped outside the circle of men. "Stand back," said Jolle. The others moved away. He pulled his gun out of its holster with his left hand and made the sign of the cross with his right. Leaning down, he put the gun near her left temple, and then cocked the hammer back. The hammer clicked into place with the sound of a breaking twig and right then her eyes shot open. Four grown men jumped backward in unison. "Good lord," said Witzer. "Do it," said Kvench. I looked to Jolle and he was staring down at her as if in a trance. Her eyes had no color. They were wide and shifting back and forth. She started taking deep raspy breaths and then sat straight up. A low mewing noise came from her chest, the sound of a cat or a scared child. Then she started talking backwards talk, some foreign language never heard on earth before, babbling frantically and drooling.

Jolle fired. The bullet caught her in the side of the head and threw her onto her right shoulder. The side of her face, including her ear, blew off, and this black stuff, not blood, splattered all over, flecks of it staining Jolle's pants and shirt and face. The side of her head was smoking. She lay there writhing in what looked like a pool of oil, and he shot her again and again, emptying the gun into her. The sight of it brought me to my knees, and I puked. When I looked up, she'd stopped moving. Tears were streaming down Witzer's face. Kvench was shaking. Henry looked as if he'd been turned to stone. Jolle's finger kept pulling the trigger, but there were no rounds left.

After Henry tamped down the last shovelful of dirt on her grave, Jolle made us swear never to say a word to anyone about what had happened. I pledged that oath as did the others. Witzer took me home, no doubt having silently decided I shouldn't be there when they woke Pete. When I got to the house, I went straight to bed and slept for an entire day, only getting up in time to get to the gas station for work the next morning. The only dream I had was an infuriating and frustrating one of Lester II, eating hard-boiled eggs and explaining it all to me but in backwards talk and gibberish so I couldn't make out any of it. Carrying the memory of that Drunk Harvest miracle around with me was like constantly having a big black bubble of night afloat in the middle of my waking thoughts. As autumn came on and passed and then winter bore down on Gatchfield, the insidious strength of it never diminished. It made me quiet and moody, and my relationship with Darlene suffered.

I kept my distance from the other four conspirators. It went so far as we tried not to even recognize each other's presence when we passed on the street. Only Witzer still waved at me from his pickup when he'd drive by, and if I was the attendant when he came into the station for gas, he'd say, "How are you, boy?" I'd nod and that would be it. Around Christmas time I'd heard from my father that Pete Hesiant had lost his mind, and was unable to go to work, would break down crying at a moment's notice, couldn't sleep, and was being treated by

Kvench with all manner of pills.

Things didn't get any better come spring. Pete shot the side of his head off with a pistol. Mrs. Marfish, who'd gone to bring him a pie she'd baked to cheer him up, discovered him lying dead in a pool of blood on the back porch of the little yellow house. Then Sheriff Jolle took ill and was so bad off with whatever he had, he couldn't get out of bed. He deputized Reed Bocean, the barkeep and the most sensible man in town, to look after Gatchfield in his absence. Reed did a good job as sheriff and Samantha double-timed it at The Blind Ghost—both solid citizens.

In the early days of May, I burned my hand badly at work on a hot car engine and my boss drove me over to Kvench's office to get it looked after. While I was in his treatment room with him, and he was wrapping my hand in gauze, he leaned close to me and whispered, "I think I know what happened." I didn't even make a face, but stared ahead at the eye chart on the wall, not really wanting to hear anything about the incident. "Gatchfield's so isolated that change couldn't get in from the outside, so Nature sent it from within," he said. "Mutation. From the dream." I looked at him. He was nodding, but I saw that his goatee had gone squirrelly, there was this over-eager gleam in his eyes, and his breath smelled like medicine. I knew right then he'd been more than sampling his own pills. I couldn't get out of there fast enough.

June came, and it was a week away from the day that Witzer and I were to begin practicing for the Drunk Harvest again. I dreaded the thought of it to the point where I was having a hard time eating or sleeping. After work one evening, as I was walking home, the old man pulled up next to me in his pickup truck. He stopped and opened the window. I was going to keep walking, but he called, "Boy, get in. Take a ride with me."

I made the mistake of looking over at him. "It's important," he said. I got in the cab and we drove slowly off down the street.

I blurted out that I didn't think I'd be able to manage the Harvest and how screwed up the thought of it was making me, but he held his hand up and said, "Shh, shh, I know." I quieted down and waited for him to talk. A few seconds passed and then he said, "I've been to see Jolle. You haven't seen him have you?"

I shook my head.

"He's a gonner for sure. He's got some kind of belly rot, and, I swear to you he's got a deathberry bush growing out of his insides…while he's still alive, no less. Doc Kvench just keeps feeding him pills, but he'd be better off taking a hedge clipper to him."

"Are you serious?" I said.

"Boy, I'm dead serious." Before I could respond, he said, "Now look, when the time for the celebration comes around, we're all going to have to participate in it as if nothing had happened. We made our oath to the sheriff. That's bad enough, but what happens when somebody's dead relative tells them in a Night Whiskey dream what we did, what happened with Lonette?"

I was trembling and couldn't bring myself to speak.

"Tomorrow night—are you listening to me?—tomorrow night I'm leaving my truck unlocked with the keys in the ignition. You come to my place and take it and get the fuck out of Gatchfield."

I hadn't noticed but we were now parked in front of my house. He leaned across me and opened my door. "Get as far away as you can, boy," he said. The next day, I called in sick to work, withdrew all my savings from the bank, and talked to Darlene. That night, good to his word, the keys were in the old pickup. I noticed there was a new used truck parked next to the old one on his lot to cover when the one we took went missing. I'd left my parents a letter about how Darlene and I had decided to elope, and that they weren't to worry. I'd call them.

We fled to the biggest brightest city we could find, and the rush and maddening business of the place, the distance from home, our combined struggle to survive at first and then make our way was a curative better than any pill the doctor could have prescribed. Every day there was change and progress and crazy news on the television, and these things served to shrink the black bubble in my thoughts. Still to this day, though, so many years later, there's always an evening near the end of September when I sit down to a Night Whiskey, so to speak, and Gatchfield comes back to me in my dreams like some lost relative I'm both terrified to behold and want nothing more than to put my arms around and never let go.

A SIEGE OF CRANES

BENJAMIN ROSENBAUM

Benjamin Rosenbaum wanted to be a superhero, a scientist (the kind who builds giant ray guns), or a writer. Instead he became a computer programmer, which didn't involve wearing his underwear on the outside or building giant ray guns, but he does write in his spare time. He attended the Clarion West Writers' Workshop in 2001 (the Sarong-Wearing Clarion), and has had work published in *Asimov's*, *The Magazine of Fantasy & Science Fiction*, and elsewhere. His story "Benjamin Rosenbaum's Biographical Notes to 'A Discourse on the Nature of Causality, with Air-Planes' by Benjamin Rosenbaum" was nominated for the 2005 Best Novelette Hugo Award, and the best of his early fiction was collected in the chapbook *Other Cities*.

The land around Marish was full of the green stalks of sunflowers: tall as men, with bold yellow faces. Their broad leaves were stained black with blood.

The rustling came again, and Marish squatted down on aching legs to watch. A hedgehog pushed its nose through the stalks. It sniffed in both directions.

Hunger dug at Marish's stomach like the point of a stick. He hadn't eaten for three days, not since returning to the crushed and blackened ruins of his house.

The hedgehog bustled through the stalks onto the trail, across the ash, across the trampled corpses of flowers. Marish waited until it was well clear of the stalks before he jumped. He landed with one foot before its nose and one foot behind its tail. The hedgehog, as hedgehogs will, rolled itself into a ball, spines out.

His house: crushed like an egg, smoking, the straw floor soaked with blood. He'd stood there with a trapped rabbit in his hand, alone in the awful silence. Forced himself to call for his wife Temur and his daughter Asza, his voice too loud and too flat. He'd dropped the rabbit somewhere in his haste, running to follow the blackened trail of devastation.

Running for three days, drinking from puddles, sleeping in the sunflowers when he couldn't stay awake.

Marish held his knifepoint above the hedgehog. They gave wishes, sometimes, in tales. "Speak, if you can," he said, "and bid me don't kill you. Grant me a wish! Elsewise, I'll have you for a dinner."

Nothing from the hedgehog, or perhaps a twitch.

Marish drove his knife through it and it thrashed, spraying more blood on the bloodstained flowers.

Too tired to light a fire, he ate it raw.

* * *

On that trail of tortured earth, wide enough for twenty horses, among the burnt and flattened flowers, Marish found a little doll of rags, the size of a child's hand.

It was one of the ones Maghd the mad girl made, and offered up, begging for stew meat, or wheedling for old bread behind Lezur's bakery. He'd given her a coin for one, once.

"Wherecome you're giving that sow our good coins?" Temur had cried, her bright eyes flashing. None in Ilmak Dale would let a mad girl come near a hearth, and some spit when they passed her. "Bag-Maghd's good for holding one thing only," Fazt would call out and they'd laugh their way into the alehouse. Marish laughing too, stopping only when he looked back at her.

Temur had softened, when she saw how Asza took to the doll, holding it, and singing to it, and smearing gruel on its rag-mouth with her fingers to feed it. They called her "little life-light," and heard her saying it to the doll, "il-ife-ight," rocking it in her arms.

He pressed his nose into the doll, trying to smell Asza's baby smell on it, like milk and forest soil and some sweet spice. But he only smelled the acrid stench of burnt cloth.

When he forced his wet eyes open, he saw a blurry figure coming towards him. Cursing himself for a fool, he tossed the doll away and pulled out his knife, holding it at his side. He wiped his face on his sleeve, and stood up straight, to show the man coming down the trail that the folk of Ilmak Dale did no obeisance. Then his mouth went dry and his hair stood up, for the man coming down the trail was no man at all.

It was a little taller than a man, and had the body of a man, though covered with a dark gray fur; but its head was the head of a jackal. It wore armor of bronze and leather, all straps and discs with curious engravings, and carried a great black spear with a vicious point at each end.

Marish had heard that there were all sorts of strange folk in the world, but he had never seen anything like this.

"May you die with great suffering," the creature said in what seemed to be a calm, friendly tone.

"May *you* die as soon as may be!" Marish cried, not liking to be threatened.

The creature nodded solemnly. "I am Kadath-Naan of the Empty City," it announced. "I wonder if I might ask your assistance in a small matter."

Marish didn't know what to say to this. The creature waited.

Marish said, "You can ask."

"I must speak with…" It frowned. "I am not sure how to put this. I do not wish to offend."

"Then why," Marish asked before he could stop himself, "did you menace me on a painful death?"

"Menace?" the creature said. "I only greeted you."

"You said, 'May you die with great suffering.' That like to be a threat or a curse, and I truly don't thank you for it."

The creature frowned. "No, it is a blessing. Or it is from a blessing: 'May you die with great suffering, and come to know holy dread and divine terror, stripping away your vain thoughts and fancies until you are fit to meet the Bone-White Fathers face to face; and may you be buried in honor and your name sung until it is forgotten.' That is the whole passage."

"Oh," said Marish. "Well, that sounds a bit better, I reckon."

"We learn that blessing as pups," said the creature in a wondering tone. "Have you never heard it?"

"No indeed," said Marish, and put his knife away. "Now what do you need? I can't think to be much help to you—I don't know this land here."

"Excuse my bluntness, but I must speak with an embalmer, or a sepulchrist, or someone of that sort."

"I've no notion what those are," said Marish.

The creature's eyes widened. It looked, as much as the face of a jackal could, like someone whose darkest suspicions were in the process of being confirmed.

"What do your people do with the dead?" it said.

"We put them in the ground."

"With what preparation? With what rites and monuments?" said the thing.

"In a wood box for them as can afford it, and a piece of linen for them as can't; and we say a prayer to the west wind. We put the stone in with them, what has their soul kept in it." Marish thought a bit, though he didn't much like the topic. He rubbed his nose on his sleeve. "Sometime we'll put a pile of stones on the grave, if it were someone famous."

The jackal-headed man sat heavily on the ground. It put its head in its hands. After a long moment it said, "Perhaps I should kill you now, that I might bury you properly."

"Now you just try that," said Marish, taking out his knife again.

"Would you like me to?" said the creature, looking up.

Its face was serene. Marish found he had to look away, and his eyes fell upon the scorched rags of the doll, twisted up in the stalks.

"Forgive me," said Kadath-Naan of the Empty City. "I should not be so rude as to tempt you. I see that you have duties to fulfill, just as I do, before you are permitted the descent into emptiness. Tell me which way your village lies, and I will see for myself what is done."

"My village—" Marish felt a heavy pressure behind his eyes, in his throat, wanting to push through into a sob. He held it back. "My village is gone. Something come and crushed it. I were off hunting, and when I come back, it were all burning, and full of the stink of blood. Whatever did it made this trail through the flowers. I think it went quick; I don't think I'll likely catch it. But I hope to." He knew he sounded absurd: a peasant chasing a demon. He gritted his teeth against it.

"I see," said the monster. "And where did this something come from? Did the trail come from the north?"

"It didn't come from nowhere. Just the village torn to pieces and this trail leading out."

"And the bodies of the dead," said Kadath-Naan carefully. "You buried them in—wooden boxes?"

"There weren't no bodies," Marish said. "Not of people. Just blood, and a few pieces of bone and gristle, and pigs' and horses' bodies all charred up. That's why I'm following." He looked down. "I mean to find them if I can."

Kadath-Naan frowned. "Does this happen often?"

Despite himself, Marish laughed. "Not that I ever heard before."

The jackal-headed creature seemed agitated. "Then you do not know if the bodies received...even what you would consider proper burial."

"I have a feeling they ain't received it," Marish said.

Kadath-Naan looked off in the distance towards Marish's village, then in the direction Marish was heading. It seemed to come to a decision. "I wonder if you would accept my company in your travels," it said. "I was on a different errand, but this matter seems to...outweigh it."

Marish looked at the creature's spear and said, "You'd be welcome."

He held out the fingers of his hand. "Marish of Ilmak Dale."

* * *

The trail ran through the blackened devastation of another village, drenched with blood but empty of human bodies. The timbers of the houses were crushed to kindling; Marish saw a blacksmith's anvil twisted like a lock of hair, and plows that had been melted by enormous heat into a pool of iron. They camped beyond the village, in the shade of a twisted hawthorn tree. A wild autumn wind stroked the meadows around them, carrying dandelion seeds and wisps of smoke and the stink of putrefying cattle.

The following evening they reached a hill overlooking a great town curled around a river. Marish had never seen so many houses—almost too many to count. Most were timber and mud like those of his village, but some were great structures of stone, towering three or four stories into the air. House built upon house, with ladders reaching up to the doors of the ones on top. Around the town, fields full of wheat rustled gold in the evening light. Men and women were reaping in the fields, singing work songs as they swung their scythes.

The path of destruction curved around the town, as if avoiding it.

"Perhaps it was too well-defended," said Kadath-Naan.

"Maybe," said Marish, but he remembered the pool of iron and the crushed timbers, and doubted. "I think that like to be Nabuz. I never come this far south before, but traders heading this way from the fair at Halde were always going to Nabuz to buy."

"They will know more of our adversary," said Kadath-Naan.

"I'll go," said Marish. "You might cause a stir; I don't reckon many of your sort visit Nabuz. You keep to the path."

"Perhaps I might ask of you…"

"If they are friendly there, I'll ask how they bury their dead," Marish said.

Kadath-Naan nodded somberly. "Go to duty and to death," he said.

Marish thought it must be a blessing, but he shivered all the same.

* * *

The light was dimming in the sky. The reapers heaped the sheaves high on the wagon, their songs slow and low, and the city gates swung open for them.

The city wall was stone, mud, and timber, twice as tall as a man, and its great gates were iron. But the wall was not well kept. Marish crept among the stalks to a place where the wall was lower and trash and rubble were heaped high against it.

He heard the creak of the wagon rolling through the gates, the last work song fading away, the men of Nabuz calling out to each other as they made their way home. Then all was still.

Marish scrambled out of the field into a dead run, scrambled up the rubble, leapt atop the wall and lay on its broad top. He peeked over, hoping he had not been seen.

The cobbled street was empty. More than that, the town itself was silent. Even in Ilmak Dale, the evenings had been full of dogs barking, swine grunting, men arguing in the streets and women gossiping and calling the children in. Nabuz was supposed to be a great capital of whoring, drinking, and fighting; the traders at Halde had always moaned over the delights that awaited them in the south if they could cheat the villagers well enough. But Marish heard no donkey braying, no baby crying, no cough, no whisper: nothing pierced the night silence.

He dropped over, landed on his feet quiet as he could, and crept along the street's edge. Before he had gone ten steps, he noticed the lights.

The windows of the houses flickered, but not with candlelight or the light of fires. The light was cold and blue.

He dragged a crate under the high window of the nearest house and clambered up to see.

There was a portly man with a rough beard, perhaps a potter after his day's work; there was his stout young wife, and a skinny boy of nine or ten. They sat on their low wooden bench, their dinner finished and put to the side (Marish could smell the fresh bread and his stomach cursed him). They were breathing, but their faces were slack, their eyes wide and staring, their lips gently moving. They were bathed in blue light. The potter's wife was rocking her arms gently as if she were cradling a newborn babe—but the swaddling blankets she held were empty.

And now Marish could hear a low inhuman voice, just at the edge of hearing, like a thought of his own. It whispered in time to the flicker of the blue light, and Marish felt himself drawn by its caress. Why not sit with the potter's family on the bench? They would take him in. He could stay here, the whispering promised: forget his village, forget his grief. Fresh bread on the hearth, a warm bed next to the coals of the fire. Work the clay, mix the slip for the potter, eat a dinner of bread and cheese, then listen to the blue light and do what it told him. Forget the mud roads of Ilmak Dale, the laughing roar of Perdan and Thin Deri and Chibar and the others in its alehouse, the harsh cough and crow of its roosters at dawn. Forget willowy Temur, her hair smooth as a river and bright as a sheaf of wheat, her proud shoulders and her slender waist, Temur turning her satin cheek away when he tried to kiss it. Forget the creak and splash of the mill, and the soft rushes on the floor of Maghd's hovel. The potter of Nabuz had a young and willing niece who needed a husband, and the blue light held laughter and love enough for all. Forget the heat and clanging of Fat Deri's smithy; forget the green stone that held Pa's soul, that he'd laid upon his shroud. Forget Asza, little Asza whose tiny body he'd held to his heart…

Marish thought of Asza and he saw the potter's wife's empty arms and with one flex of his legs, he kicked himself away from the wall, knocking over the crate and landing sprawled among rolling apples.

He sprang to his feet. There was no sound around him. He stuffed five apples in his pack, and hurried towards the center of Nabuz.

The sun had set, and the moon washed the streets in silver. From every window streamed the cold blue light.

Out of the corner of his eye he thought he saw a shadow dart behind him, and he turned and took out his knife. But he saw nothing, and though his good sense told him five apples and no answers was as much as he should expect from Nabuz, he kept on.

He came to a great square full of shadows, and at first he thought of trees. But it was tall iron frames, and men and women bolted to them upside down. The bolts went through their bodies, crusty with dried blood.

One man nearby was live enough to moan. Marish poured a little water into the man's mouth, and held his head up, but the man could not swallow; he coughed and spluttered, and the water ran down his face and over the bloody holes where his eyes had been.

"But the babies," the man rasped, "how could you let her have the babies?"

"Let who?" said Marish.

"The White Witch!" the man roared in a whisper. "The White Witch, you bastards! If you'd but let us fight her—"

"Why…" Marish began.

"Lie again, say the babies will live forever—lie again, you cowardly blue-blood maggots in the corpse of Nabuz…" He coughed and blood ran over his face.

The bolts were fast into the frame. "I'll get a tool," Marish said, "you won't—"

From behind him came an awful scream.

He turned and saw the shadow that had followed him: it was a white cat with fine soft fur and green eyes that blazed in the darkness. It shrieked, its fur standing on end, its tail high, staring at him, and his good sense told him it was raising an alarm.

Marish ran, and the cat ran after him, shrieking. Nabuz was a vast pile of looming shadows. As he passed through the empty city gates he heard a grinding sound and a whinny. As he raced into the moonlit dusk of open land, down the road to where Kadath-Naan's shadow crossed the demon's path, he heard hoof beats galloping behind him.

Kadath-Naan had just reached a field of tall barley. He turned to look back at the sound of the hoof beats and the shrieking of the devil cat.

"Into the grain!" Marish yelled. "Hide in the grain!" He passed Kadath-Naan and dived into the barley, the cat racing behind him.

Suddenly he spun and dropped and grabbed the white cat, meaning to get one hand on it and get his knife with the other and shut it up by killing it. But the cat fought like a devil and it was all he could do to hold on to it with both hands. And he saw, behind him on the trail, Kadath-Naan standing calmly, his hand on his spear, facing three knights armored every inch in white, galloping towards them on great chargers.

"You damned dog-man," Marish screamed. "I know you want to die, but get into the grain!"

Kadath-Naan stood perfectly still. The first knight bore down on him, and the moon flashed from the knight's sword. The blade was no more than a hand's-breadth from Kadath-Naan's neck when he sprang to the side of it, into the path of the second charger.

As the first knight's charge carried him past, Kadath-Naan knelt, and drove the base of his great spear into the ground. Too late, the second knight made a desperate yank on the horse's reins, but the great beast's momentum carried him into the pike. It tore through the neck of the horse and through the armored chest of the knight riding him, and the two of them reared up and thrashed once like a dying centaur, then crashed to the ground.

The first knight wheeled around. The third met Kadath-Naan. The beast-man stood barehanded, the muscles of his shoulders and chest relaxed. He cocked his jackal head to one side, as if wondering: Is it here at last? The moment when I am granted release?

But Marish finally had the cat by its tail, and flung that wild white thing, that frenzy of claws and spit and hissing, into the face of the third knight's steed.

The horse reared and threw its rider; the knight let go of his sword as he crashed to the ground. Quick as a hummingbird, Kadath-Naan leapt and caught it in midair. He spun to face the last rider.

Marish drew his knife and charged through the barley. He was on the fallen knight just as he got to his knees.

The crash against armor took Marish's wind away. The man was twice as strong as Marish was, and his arm went around Marish's chest like a crushing band of iron. But Marish had both hands free, and with a twist of the knight's helmet he exposed a bit of neck, and in Marish's knife went, and then the man's hot blood was spurting out.

The knight convulsed as he died and grabbed Marish in a desperate embrace, coating him with blood, and sobbing once: and Marish held him, for the voice of his heart told him it was a shame to have to die such a way. Marish was shocked at this, for the man was a murderous slave of the White Witch; but still he held the quaking body in his arms, until it moved no more.

Then Marish, soaked with salty blood, staggered to his feet and remembered the last knight with a start; but of course Kadath-Naan had killed him in the meantime. Three knights' bodies lay on the ruined ground, and two living horses snorted and pawed the dirt like awkward mourners. Kadath-Naan freed his spear with a great yank from the horse and man it had transfixed. The devil cat was a sodden blur of white fur and blood; a falling horse had crushed it.

Marish caught the reins of the nearest steed, a huge fine creature, and gentled it with a hand behind its ears. When he had his breath again, Marish said, "We got horses now. Can you ride?"

Kadath-Naan nodded.

"Let's go then; there like to be more coming."

Kadath-Naan frowned a deep frown. He gestured to the bodies.

"What?" said Marish.

"We have no embalmer or sepulchrist, it is true; yet I am trained in the funereal rites for military expeditions and emergencies. I have the necessary tools; in a matter of a day I can raise small monuments. At least they died aware and with suffering; this must compensate for the rudimentary nature of the rites."

"You can't be in earnest," said Marish. "And what of the White Witch?"

"Who is the White Witch?" Kadath-Naan asked.

"The demon; turns out she's somebody what's called the White Witch. She spared Nabuz, for they said they'd serve her, and give her their babies."

"We will follow her afterwards," said Kadath-Naan.

"She's ahead of us as it is! We leave now on horseback, we might have a chance. There be a whole lot more bodies with her unburied or buried wrong, less I mistake."

Kadath-Naan leaned on his spear. "Marish of Ilmak Dale," he said, "here we must part ways. I cannot steel myself to follow such logic as you declare, abandoning these three burials before me now for the chance of others elsewhere, if we can catch and defeat a witch. My duty does not lie that way." He searched Marish's face. "You do not have the words for it, but if these men are left unburied, they are *tanzadi*. If I bury them with what little honor I can provide, they are *tazrash*.

They spent only a little while alive, but they will be *tanzadi* or *tazrash* forever."

"And if more slaves of the White Witch come along to pay you back for killing these?"

But try as he might, Marish could not dissuade him, and at last he mounted one of the chargers and rode onwards, towards the cold white moon, away from the whispering city.

* * *

The flowers were gone, the fields were gone. The ashy light of the horizon framed the ferns and stunted trees of a black fen full of buzzing flies. The trail was wider; thirty horses could have passed side by side over the blasted ground. But the marshy ground was treacherous, and Marish's mount sank to its fetlocks with each careful step.

A siege of cranes launched themselves from the marsh into the moon-abandoned sky. Marish had never seen so many. Bone-white, fragile, soundless, they ascended like snowflakes seeking the cold womb of heaven. Or a river of souls. None looked back at him. The voice of doubt told him: You will never know what became of Asza and Temur.

The apples were long gone, and Marish was growing lightheaded from hunger. He reined the horse in and dismounted; he would have to hunt off the trail. In the bracken, he tied the charger to a great black fern as tall as a house. In a drier spot near its base was the footprint of a rabbit. He felt the indentation; it was fresh. He followed the rabbit deeper into the fen.

He was thinking of Temur and her caresses. The nights she'd turn away from him, back straight as a spear, and the space of rushes between them would be like a frozen desert, and he'd huddle unsleeping beneath skins and woolen blankets, stiff from cold, arguing silently with her in his spirit; and the nights when she'd turn to him, her soft skin hot and alive against his, seeking him silently, almost vengefully, as if showing him—see? This is what you can have. This is what I am.

And then the image of those rushes charred and brown with blood and covered with chips of broken stone and mortar came to him, and he forced himself to think of nothing: breathing his thoughts out to the west wind, forcing his mind clear as a spring stream. And he stepped forward in the marsh.

And stood in a street of blue and purple tile, in a fantastic city.

He stood for a moment wondering, and then he carefully took a step back.

And he was in a black swamp with croaking toads and nothing to eat.

The voice of doubt told him he was mad from hunger; the voice of hope told him he would find the White Witch here and kill her; and thinking a thousand things, he stepped forward again and found himself still in the swamp.

Marish thought for a while, and then he stepped back, and, thinking of nothing, stepped forward.

The tiles of the street were a wild mosaic—some had glittering jewels; some had writing in a strange flowing script; some seemed to have tiny windows into tiny rooms. Houses, tiled with the same profusion, towered like columns, bulged like mushrooms, melted like wax. Some danced. He heard soft murmurs of conversation, footfalls, and the rush of a river.

In the street, dressed in feathers or gold plates or swirls of shadow, blue-skinned people passed. One such creature, dressed in fine silk, was just passing Marish.

"Your pardon," said Marish, "what place be this here?"

The man looked at Marish slowly. He had a red jewel in the center of his forehead, and it flickered as he talked. "That depends on how you enter it," he said, "and who you are, but for you, catarrhine, its name is Zimzarkanthitruge-nia-fenstok, not least because that is easy for you to pronounce. And now I have given you one thing free, as you are a guest of the city."

"How many free things do I get?" said Marish.

"Three. And now I have given you two."

Marish thought about this for a moment. "I'd favor something to eat," he said.

The man looked surprised. He led Marish into a building that looked like a blur of spinning triangles, through a dark room lit by candles, to a table piled with capon and custard and razor-thin slices of ham and lamb's foot jelly and candied apricots and goatsmilk yogurt and hard cheese and yams and turnips and olives and fish cured in strange spices; and those were just the things Marish recognized.

"I don't reckon I ought to eat fairy food," said Marish, though he could hardly speak from all the spit that was suddenly in his mouth.

"That is true, but from the food of the djinn you have nothing to fear. And now I have given you three things," said the djinn, and he bowed and made as if to leave.

"Hold on," said Marish (as he followed some candied apricots down his gullet with a fistful of cured fish). "That be all the free things, but say I got something to sell?"

The djinn was silent.

"I need to kill the White Witch," Marish said, eating an olive. The voice of doubt asked him why he was telling the truth, if this city might also serve her; but he told it to hush up. "Have you got aught to help me?"

The djinn still said nothing, but he cocked an eyebrow.

"I've got a horse, a real fighting horse," Marish said, around a piece of cheese.

"What is its name?" said the djinn. "You cannot sell anything to a djinn unless you know its name."

Marish wanted to lie about the name, but he found he could not. He swallowed. "I don't know its name," he admitted.

"Well then," said the djinn.

"I killed the fellow what was on it," Marish said, by way of explanation.

"Who," said the djinn.

"Who what?" said Marish.

"Who was on it," said the djinn.

"I don't know his name either," said Marish, picking up a yam.

"No, I am not asking that," said the djinn crossly, "I am telling you to say, 'I killed the fellow who was on it.'"

Marish set the yam back on the table.

"Now that's enough," Marish said. "I thank you for the fine food and I thank you for the three free things, but I do not thank you for telling me how to talk. How I talk is how we talk in Ilmak Dale, or how we did talk when there were an Ilmak Dale, and just because the White Witch blasted Ilmak Dale to splinters don't mean I am going to talk like folk do in some magic city."

"I will buy that from you," said the djinn.

"What?" said Marish, and wondered so much at this that he forgot to pick up another thing to eat.

"The way you talked in Ilmak Dale," the djinn said.

"All right," Marish said, "and for it, I crave to know the thing what will help me mostways, for killing the White Witch."

"I have a carpet that flies faster than the wind," said the djinn. "I think it is the only way you can catch the Witch, and unless you catch her, you cannot kill her."

"Wonderful," Marish cried with glee. "And you'll trade me that carpet for how we talk in Ilmak Dale?"

"No," said the djinn, "I told you which thing would help you most, and in return for that, I took the way you talked in Ilmak Dale and put it in the Great Library."

Marish frowned. "All right, what do you want for the carpet?"

The djinn was silent.

"I'll give you the White Witch for it," Marish said.

"You must possess the thing you sell," the djinn said.

"Oh, I'll get her," Marish said. "You can be sure of that." His hand had found a boiled egg, and the shell crunched in his palm as he said it.

The djinn looked at Marish carefully, and then he said, "The use of the carpet, for three days, in return for the White Witch, if you can conquer her."

"Agreed," said Marish.

* * *

They had to bind the horse's eyes; otherwise it would rear and kick, when the carpet rose into the air. Horse, man, djinn: all perched on a span of cloth. As they sped back to Nabuz like a mad wind, Marish tried not to watch the solid fields flying beneath, and regretted the candied apricots.

The voice of doubt told him that his companion must be slain by now, but his heart wanted to see Kadath-Naan again; but for the jackal-man, Marish was friendless.

Among the barley stalks, three man-high plinths of black stone, painted with white glyphs, marked three graves. Kadath-Naan had only traveled a little ways beyond them before the ambush. How long the emissary of the Empty City had been fighting, Marish could not tell; but he staggered and weaved like a man drunk with wine or exhaustion. His gray fur was matted with blood and sweat.

An army of children in white armor surrounded Kadath-Naan. As the carpet swung closer, Marish could see their gray faces and blank eyes. Some crawled, some tottered: none seemed to have lived more than six years of mortal life. They held daggers. One clung to the jackal-man's back, digging canals of blood.

Two of the babies were impaled on the point of the great black spear. Hand over hand, daggers held in their mouths, they dragged themselves down the shaft towards Kadath-Naan's hands. Hundreds more surrounded him, closing in.

Kadath-Naan swung his spear, knocking the slack-eyed creatures back. He struck with enough force to shatter human skulls, but the horrors only rolled, and scampered giggling back to stab his legs. With each swing, the spear was slower. Kadath-Naan's eyes rolled back into their sockets. His great frame shuddered from weariness and pain.

The carpet swung low over the battle, and Marish lay on his belly, dangling his arms down to the jackal-headed warrior. He shouted: "Jump! Kadath-Naan, jump!"

Kadath-Naan looked up and, gripping his spear in both hands, he tensed his legs to jump. But the pause gave the tiny servitors of the White Witch their chance; they swarmed over his body, stabbing with their daggers, and he collapsed under the writhing mass of his enemies.

"Down further! We can haul him aboard!" yelled Marish.

"I sold you the use of my carpet, not the destruction of it," said the djinn.

With a snarl of rage, and before the voice of his good sense could speak, Marish leapt from the carpet. He landed amidst the fray, and began tearing the small bodies from Kadath-Naan and flinging them into the fields. Then daggers found his calves, and small bodies crashed into his sides, and he tumbled, covered with the white-armored hell-children. The carpet sailed up lazily into the summer sky.

Marish thrashed, but soon he was pinned under a mass of small bodies. Their daggers probed his sides, drawing blood, and he gritted his teeth against a scream; they pulled at his hair and ears and pulled open his mouth to look inside. As if they were playing. One gray-skinned suckling child, its scalp peeled half away to reveal the white bone of its skull, nuzzled at his neck, seeking the nipple it would never find again.

So had Asza nuzzled against him. So had been her heft, then, light and snug as five apples in a bag. But her live eyes saw the world, took it in and made it better than it was. In those eyes he was a hero, a giant to lift her, honest and gentle and brave. When Temur looked into those otterbrown, mischievous eyes, her mouth softened from its hard line, and she sang fairy songs.

A dagger split the skin of his forehead, bathing him in blood. Another dug between his ribs, another popped the skin of his thigh. Another pushed against his gut, but hadn't broken through. He closed his eyes. They weighed heavier on him now; his throat tensed to scream, but he could not catch his breath.

Marish's arms ached for Asza and Temur—ached that he would die here, without them. Wasn't it right, though, that they be taken from him? The little girl who ran to him across the fields of an evening, a funny hopping run, her arms flung wide, waving that rag doll; no trace of doubt in her. And the beautiful wife who stiffened when she saw him, but smiled one-edged, despite herself, as he lifted apple-smelling Asza in his arms. He had not deserved them.

His face, his skin were hot and slick with salty blood. He saw, not felt, the daggers digging deeper—arcs of light across a great darkness. He wished he could comfort Asza one last time, across that darkness. As when she would awaken in the night, afraid of witches: now a witch had come.

He found breath, he forced his mouth open, and he sang through sobs to Asza, his song to lull her back to sleep:

"Now sleep, my love, now sleep—
The moon is in the sky—
The clouds have fled like sheep—
You're in your papa's eye.

"Sleep now, my love, sleep now—
The bitter wind is gone—
The calf sleeps with the cow—
Now sleep my love 'til dawn."

He freed his left hand from the press of bodies. He wiped blood and tears from his eyes. He pushed his head up, dizzy, flowers of light still exploding across his vision. The small bodies were still. Carefully, he eased them to the ground.

The carpet descended, and Marish hauled Kadath-Naan onto it. Then he forced himself to turn, swaying, and look at each of the gray-skinned babies sleeping peacefully on the ground. None of them was Asza.

He took one of the smallest and swaddled it with rags and bridle leather. His blood made his fingers slick, and the noon sun seemed as gray as a stone. When he was sure the creature could not move, he put it in his pack and slung the pack upon his back. Then he fell onto the carpet. He felt it lift up under him, and like a cradled child, he slept.

He awoke to see clouds sailing above him. The pain was gone. He sat up and looked at his arms: they were whole and unscarred. Even the old scar from Thin Deri's careless scythe was gone.

"You taught us how to defeat the Children of Despair," said the djinn. "That required recompense. I have treated your wounds and those of your companion.

Is the debt clear?"

"Answer me one question," Marish said.

"And the debt will be clear?" said the djinn.

"Yes, may the west wind take you, it'll be clear!"

The djinn blinked in assent.

"Can they be brought back?" Marish asked. "Can they be made into living children again?"

"They cannot," said the djinn. "They can neither live nor die, nor be harmed at all unless they will it. Their hearts have been replaced with sand."

They flew in silence, and Marish's pack seemed heavier.

* * *

The land flew by beneath them as fast as a cracking whip; Marish stared as green fields gave way to swamp, swamp to marsh, marsh to rough pastureland. The devastation left by the White Witch seemed gradually newer; the trail here was still smoking, and Marish thought it might be too hot to walk on. They passed many a blasted village, and each time Marish looked away.

At last they began to hear a sound on the wind, a sound that chilled Marish's heart. It was not a wail, it was not a grinding, it was not a shriek of pain, nor the wet crunch of breaking bones, nor was it an obscene grunting; but it had something of all of these. The jackal-man's ears were perked, and his gray fur stood on end.

The path was now truly still burning; they flew high above it, and the rolling smoke underneath was like a fog over the land. But there ahead they saw the monstrous thing that was leaving the trail; and Marish could hardly think any thought at all as they approached, but only stare, bile burning his throat.

It was a great chariot, perhaps eight times the height of a man, as wide as the trail, constructed of parts of living human bodies welded together in an obscene tangle. A thousand legs and arms pawed the ground; a thousand more beat the trail with whips and scythes, or clawed the air. A thick skein of hearts, livers, and stomachs pulsed through the center of the thing, and a great assemblage of lungs breathed at its core. Heads rolled like wheels at the bottom of the chariot, or were stuck here and there along the surface of the thing as slack-eyed, gibbering ornaments. A thousand spines and torsos built a great chamber at the top of the chariot, shielded with webs of skin and hair; there perhaps hid the White Witch. From the pinnacle of the monstrous thing flew a great flag made of writhing tongues. Before the awful chariot rode a company of ten knights in white armor, with visored helms.

At the very peak sat a great headless hulking beast, larger than a bear, with the skin of a lizard, great yellow globes of eyes set on its shoulders and a wide mouth in its belly. As they watched, it vomited a gout of flame that set the path behind the chariot ablaze. Then it noticed them, and lifted the great plume of flame in their direction. At a swift word from the djinn, the carpet veered, but it was a close enough thing that Marish felt an oven's blast of heat on his skin.

He grabbed the horse by its reins as it made to rear, and whispered soothing sounds in its ear.

"Abomination!" cried Kadath-Naan. "Djinn, will you send word to the Empty City? You will be well rewarded."

The djinn nodded.

"It is Kadath-Naan, lesser scout of the Endless Inquiry, who speaks. Let Bars-Kardereth, Commander of the Silent Legion, be told to hasten here. Here is an obscenity beyond compass, far more horrible than the innocent errors of savages; here Chaos blocks the descent into the Darkness entirely, and a whole land may fall to corruption."

The jewel in the djinn's forehead flashed once. "It is done," he said.

Kadath-Naan turned to Marish. "From the Empty City to this place is four days' travel for a Ghomlu Legion; let us find a place in their path where we can wait to join them."

Marish forced himself to close his eyes. But still he saw it—hands, tongues, guts, skin, woven into a moving mountain. He still heard the squelching, grinding, snapping sounds, the sea-roar of the thousand lungs. What had he imagined? Asza and Temur in a prison somewhere, waiting to be freed? Fool. "All right," he said.

Then he opened his eyes, and saw something that made him say, "No."

Before them, not ten minutes' ride from the awful chariot of the White Witch, was a whitewashed village, peaceful in the afternoon sun. Arrayed before it were a score of its men and young women. A few had proper swords or spears; one of the women carried a bow. The others had hoes, scythes, and staves. One woman sat astride a horse; the rest were on foot. From their perch in the air, Marish could see distant figures—families, stooped grandmothers, children in their mothers' arms—crawling like beetles up the faces of hills.

"Down," said Marish, and they landed before the village's defenders, who raised their weapons.

"You've got to run," he said, "you can make it to the hills. You haven't seen that thing—you haven't any chance against it."

A dark man spat on the ground. "We tried that in Gravenge."

"It splits up," said a black-bearded man. "Sends littler horrors, and they tear folks up and make them part of it, and you see your fellows' limbs, come after you as part of the thing. And they're fast. Too fast for us."

"We just busy it a while," another man said, "our folk can get far enough away." But he had a wild look in his eye: the voice of doubt was in him.

"We stop it here," said the woman on horseback.

Marish led the horse off the carpet, took its blinders off and mounted it. "I'll stand with you," he said.

"And welcome," said the woman on horseback, and her plain face broke into a nervous smile. It was almost pretty that way.

Kadath-Naan stepped off the carpet, and the villagers shied back, readying their weapons.

"This is Kadath-Naan, and you'll be damned glad you have him," said Marish.

"Where's your manners?" snapped the woman on horseback to her people. "I'm Asza," she said.

No, Marish thought, staring at her. No, but you could have been. He looked away, and after a while they left him alone.

The carpet rose silently off into the air, and soon there was smoke on the horizon, and the knights rode at them, and the chariot rose behind.

"Here we are," said Asza of the rocky lands, "now make a good accounting of yourselves."

An arrow sang; a white knight's horse collapsed. Marish cried "Ha!" and his mount surged forward. The villagers charged, but Kadath-Naan outpaced them all, springing between a pair of knights. He shattered the forelegs of one horse with his spear's shaft, drove its point through the side of the other rider. Villagers fell on the fallen knight with their scythes.

It was a heady wild thing for Marish, to be galloping on such a horse, a far finer horse than ever Redlegs had been, for all Pa's proud and vain attention to her. The warmth of its flanks, the rhythm of posting into its stride. Marish of Ilmak Dale, riding into a charge of knights: miserable addle-witted fool.

Asza flicked her whip at the eyes of a knight's horse, veering away. The knight wheeled to follow her, and Marish came on after him. He heard the hooves of another knight pounding the plain behind him in turn.

Ahead the first knight gained on Asza of the rocky plains. Marish took his knife in one hand, and bent his head to his horse's ear, and whispered to it in wordless murmurs: Fine creature, give me everything. And his horse pulled even with Asza's knight.

Marish swung down, hanging from his pommel—the ground flew by beneath him. He reached across and slipped his knife under the girth that held the knight's saddle. The knight swiveled, raising his blade to strike—then the girth parted, and he flew from his mount.

Marish struggled up into the saddle, and the second knight was there, armor blazing in the sun. This time Marish was on the sword-arm's side, and his horse had slowed, and that blade swung up and it could strike Marish's head from his neck like snapping off a sunflower; time for the peasant to die.

Asza's whip lashed around the knight's sword-arm. The knight seized the whip in his other hand. Marish sprang from the saddle. He struck a wall of chainmail and fell with the knight.

The ground was an anvil, the knight a hammer, Marish a rag doll sewn by a poor mad girl and mistaken for a horseshoe. He couldn't breathe; the world was a ringing blur. The knight found his throat with one mailed glove, and hissed with rage, and pulling himself up drew a dagger from his belt. Marish tried to lift his arms.

Then he saw Asza's hands fitting a leather noose around the knight's neck. The knight turned his visored head to see, and Asza yelled, "Yah!" An armored knee cracked against Marish's head, and then the knight was gone, dragged off over the rocky plains behind Asza's galloping mare.

Asza of the rocky lands helped Marish to his feet. She had a wild smile, and she hugged him to her breast; pain shot through him, as did the shock of her soft body. Then she pulled away, grinning, and looked over his shoulder back towards the village. And then the grin was gone.

Marish turned. He saw the man with the beard torn apart by a hundred grasping arms and legs. Two bending arms covered with eyes watched carefully as his organs were woven into the chariot. The village burned. A knight leaned from his saddle to cut a fleeing woman down, harvesting her like a stalk of wheat.

"No!" shrieked Asza, and ran towards the village.

Marish tried to run, but he could only hobble, gasping, pain tearing through his side. Asza snatched a spear from the ground and swung up onto a horse. Her hair was like Temur's, flowing gold. My Asza, my Temur, he thought. I must protect her.

Marish fell; he hit the ground and held onto it like a lover, as if he might fall into the sky. Fool, fool, said the voice of his good sense. That is not your Asza, or your Temur either. She is not yours at all.

He heaved himself up again and lurched on, as Asza of the rocky plains reached the chariot. From above, a lazy plume of flame expanded. The horse reared. The cloud of fire enveloped the woman, the horse, and then was sucked away; the blackened corpses fell to the ground steaming.

Marish stopped running.

The headless creature of fire fell from the chariot—Kadath-Naan was there at the summit of the horror, his spear sunk in its flesh as a lever. But the fire-beast turned as it toppled, and a pillar of fire engulfed the jackal-man. The molten iron of his spear and armor coated his body, and he fell into the grasping arms of the chariot.

Marish lay down on his belly in the grass.

Maybe they will not find me here, said the voice of hope. But it was like listening to idiot words spoken by the wind blowing through a forest. Marish lay on the ground and he hurt. The hurt was a song, and it sang him. Everything was lost and far away. No Asza, no Temur, no Maghd; no quest, no hero, no trickster, no hunter, no father, no groom. The wind came down from the mountains and stirred the grass beside Marish's nose, where beetles walked.

There was a rustling in the short grass, and a hedgehog came out of it and stood nose to nose with Marish.

"Speak if you can," Marish whispered, "and grant me a wish."

The hedgehog snorted. "I'll not do you any favors, after what you did to Teodor!"

Marish swallowed. "The hedgehog in the sunflowers?"

"Obviously. Murderer."

"I'm sorry! I didn't know he was magic! I thought he was just a hedgehog!"

"Just a hedgehog! Just a hedgehog!" It narrowed its eyes, and its prickers stood on end. "Be careful what you call things, Marish of Ilmak Dale. When you name a thing, you say what it is in the world. Names mean more than you know."

Marish was silent.

"Teodor didn't like threats, that's all… the stubborn old idiot."

"I'm sorry about Teodor," said Marish.

"Yes, well," said the hedgehog. "I'll help you, but it will cost you dear."

"What do you want?"

"How about your soul?" said the hedgehog.

"I'd do that, sure," said Marish. "It's not like I need it. But I don't have it."

The hedgehog narrowed its eyes again. From the village, a few thin screams and the soft crackle of flames. It smelled like autumn, and butchering hogs.

"It's true," said Marish. "The priest of Ilmak Dale took all our souls and put them in little stones, and hid them. He didn't want us making bargains like these."

"Wise man," said the hedgehog. "But I'll have to have something. What have you got in you, besides a soul?"

"What do you mean, like, my wits? But I'll need those."

"Yes, you will," said the hedgehog.

"Hope? Not much of that left, though."

"Not to my taste anyway," said the hedgehog. "*Hope is foolish, doubts are wise.*"

"Doubts?" said Marish.

"That'll do," said the hedgehog. "But I want them all."

"All… all right," said Marish. "And now you're going to help me against the White Witch?"

"I already have," said the hedgehog.

"You have? Have I got some magic power or other now?" asked Marish. He sat up. The screaming was over: he heard nothing but the fire, and the crunching and squelching and slithering and grinding of the chariot.

"Certainly not," said the hedgehog. "I haven't done anything you didn't see or didn't hear. But perhaps you weren't listening." And it waddled off into the green blades of the grass.

Marish stood and looked after it. He picked at his teeth with a thumbnail, and thought, but he had no idea what the hedgehog meant. But he had no doubts, either, so he started towards the village.

* * *

Halfway there, he noticed the dead baby in his pack wriggling, so he took it out and held it in his arms.

As he came into the burning village, he found himself just behind the great fire-spouting lizard-skinned headless thing. It turned and took a breath to burn him alive, and he tossed the baby down its throat. There was a choking sound, and the huge thing shuddered and twitched, and Marish walked on by it.

The great chariot saw him and it swung towards him, a vast mountain of writhing, humming, stinking flesh, a hundred arms reaching. Fists grabbed his shirt, his hair, his trousers, and they lifted him into the air.

He looked at the hand closed around his collar. It was a woman's hand, fine and fair, and it was wearing the copper ring he'd bought at Halde.

"Temur!" he said in shock.

The arm twitched and slackened; it went white. It reached out, the fingers spread wide; it caressed his cheek gently. And then it dropped from the chariot and lay on the ground beneath.

He knew the hands pulling him aloft. "Lezur the baker!" he whispered, and a pair of doughy hands dropped from the chariot. "Silbon and Felbon!" he cried. "Ter the blind! Sela the blue-eyed!" Marish's lips trembled to say the names, and the hands slackened and fell to the ground, and away on other parts of the chariot the other parts fell off too; he saw a blue eye roll down from above him and fall to the ground.

"Perdan! Mardid! Pilg and his old mother! Fazt—oh Fazt, you'll tell no more jokes! Chibar and his wife, the pretty foreign one!" His face was wet; with every name, a bubble popped open in Marish's chest, and his throat was thick with some strange feeling. "Pizdar the priest! Fat Deri, far from your smithy! Thin Deri!" When all the hands and arms of Ilmak Dale had fallen off, he was left standing free. He looked at the strange hands coming towards him. "You were a potter," he said to hands with clay under the nails, and they fell off the chariot. "And you were a butcher," he said to bloody ones, and they fell too. "A fat farmer, a beautiful young girl, a grandmother, a harlot, a brawler," he said, and enough hands and feet and heads and organs had slid off the chariot now that it sagged in the middle and pieces of it strove with each other blindly. "Men and women of Eckdale," Marish said, "men and women of Halde, of Gravenge, of the fields and the swamps and the rocky plains."

The chariot fell to pieces; some lay silent and still, others which Marish had not named had lost their purchase and thrashed on the ground.

The skin of the great chamber atop the chariot peeled away and the White Witch leapt into the sky. She was three times as tall as any woman; her skin was bone white; one eye was blood red and the other emerald green; her mouth was full of black fangs, and her hair of snakes and lizards. Her hands were full of lightning, and she sailed onto Marish with her fangs wide open.

And around her neck, on a leather thong, she wore a little doll of rags, the size of a child's hand.

"Maghd of Ilmak Dale," Marish said, and she was also a young woman with muddy hair and an uncertain smile, and that's how she landed before Marish.

"Well done, Marish," said Maghd, and pulled at a muddy lock of her hair, and laughed, and looked at the ground. "Well done! Oh, I'm glad. I'm glad you've come."

"Why did you do it, Maghd?" Marish said. "Oh, why?"

She looked up and her lips twitched and her jaw set. "Can you ask me that? You, Marish?"

She reached across, slowly, and took his hand. She pulled him, and he took a step towards her. She put the back of his hand against her cheek.

"You'd gone out hunting," she said. "And that Temur of yours"—she said the name as if it tasted of vinegar—"she seen me back of Lezur's, and for one time I didn't look down. I looked at her eyes, and she named me a foul witch. And then they were all crowding round—"She shrugged. "And I don't like that. Fussing and crowding and one against the other." She let go his hand and stooped to pick up a clot of earth, and she crumbled it in her hands. "So I knit them all together. All one thing. They did like it. And they were so fine and great and happy, I forgave them. Even Temur."

The limbs lay unmoving on the ground; the guts were piled in soft unbreathing hills, like drifts of snow. Maghd's hands were coated with black crumbs of dirt.

"I reckon they're done of playing now," Maghd said, and sighed.

"How?" Marish said. "How'd you do it? Maghd, what are you?"

"Don't fool so! I'm Maghd, same as ever. I found the souls, that's all. Dug them up from Pizdar's garden, sold them to the Spirit of Unwinding Things." She brushed the dirt from her hands.

"And… the children, then? Maghd, the babes?"

She took his hand again, but she didn't look at him. She laid her cheek against her shoulder and watched the ground. "Babes shouldn't grow," she said. "No call to be big and hateful." She swallowed. "I made them perfect. That's all."

Marish's chest tightened. "And what now?"

She looked at him, and a slow grin crept across her face. "Well now," she said. "That's on you, ain't it, Marish? I got plenty of tricks yet, if you want to keep fighting." She stepped close to him, and rested her cheek on his chest. Her hair smelled like home: rushes and fire smoke, cold mornings and sheep's milk. "Or we can gather close. No one to shame us now." She wrapped her arms around his waist. "It's all new, Marish, but it ain't all bad."

A shadow drifted over them, and Marish looked up to see the djinn on his carpet, peering down. Marish cleared his throat. "Well… I suppose we're all we have left, aren't we?"

"That's so," Maghd breathed softly.

He took her hands in his, and drew back to look at her. "Will you be mine, Maghd?" he said.

"Oh yes," said Maghd, and smiled the biggest smile of her life.

"Very good," Marish said, and looked up. "You can take her now."

The djinn opened the little bottle that was in his hand and Maghd the White Witch flew into it, and he put the cap on. He bowed to Marish, and then he flew away.

Behind Marish the fire beast exploded with a dull boom.

* * *

Marish walked out of the village a little ways and sat, and after sitting a while he slept. And then he woke and sat, and then he slept some more. Perhaps he ate as well; he wasn't sure what. Mostly he looked at his hands; they were rough and callused, with dirt under the nails. He watched the wind painting waves in the short grass, around the rocks and bodies lying there.

* * *

One morning he woke, and the ruined village was full of jackal-headed men in armor made of discs who were mounted on great red cats with pointed ears, and jackal-headed men in black robes who were measuring for monuments, and jackal-headed men dressed only in loincloths who were digging in the ground.

Marish went to the ones in loincloths and said, "I want to help bury them," and they gave him a shovel.

HALFWAY HOUSE

FRANCES HARDINGE

Frances Hardinge is a writer who wears a black hat. Notoriously unphotographable, she is rumored to be made entirely out of velvet. Sources close to Frances who prefer not to be named suggest that she has an Evil Twin who wears white and is hatless. This cannot be confirmed. Her first story, "Shining Man", appeared in 2001, and was followed by her first novel *Fly by Night* in 2005. The story that follows originally appeared in the sadly lamented magazine *Alchemy*.

"Would you mind holding her for just a moment? I won't be long." The baby did not cry as it was handed over. It was beyond the age of prune-faced screaming at any strange hands. Its eyes were marbles of drugged and pompous incredulity, its mouth pursed to blow tiny bubbles. Its head wobbled, and its limbs floated vaguely like an astronaut's.

Instinctively supporting its head, the boy took the child and watched the mother walk off down the carriage, the fabric about the slit in her skirt twitching with her stride.

We're in a station, he thought. How does she know I won't run off with her baby? He let little fingers fiddle with his blazer lapel as he watched four pigeons mob a crisp packet on the platform. After two minutes the carriage juddered, and the little scuffle slid away to the left, yielding to verges of purple loosestrife and the combed gold of fields. Twenty minutes later, the mother had not returned.

So Kaiser took the baby home.

* * *

"Look what I got."

Eve looked up from sweeping the wood-shavings, her long, thick pigtails swinging with the motion.

"Where'd you get it?" she asked, in her quiet man-voice.

"Someone give it to me." Kaiser sat the baby down on the cold cobbles. The nappy padded it into duck proportions, and propped it upright. Unfocussed, it watched a butterfly, and dribbled at it.

"It needs better eyes. And paint." Having delivered her professional advice Eve sat and went on whittling, curls of white wood falling unregarded into her lap.

"No. She needs a name."

"Sharmadyne's got lots at the moment. He found a book on Latin names for mushrooms."

"I don't want to call her mushroom." The baby took drunken fistfuls of shavings and found it could crush them. "What's a word for something nice?"

"Forever," said Sharmadyne, from the balustrade above.

"Biscuit," said Eve.

"No. Wrong." Kaiser frowned his forehead into a crisscross, like a teacher's mark, echoing his word, wrong. "What's a word for something quiet?"

"Death," said Wolf from his easy chair, removing his hat from his face.

"Cloud," said Sharmadyne.

"Biscuit," said Eve.

"Library."

"Small rock."

"Mushrooms can be very, very quiet," said Sharmadyne, hopefully.

Wrong, said Kaiser's frown.

"What else do you get on trains?"

"Arguments and plastic foam cups."

"Horses."

"That's not trains, Eve, that was something else and they don't have them anymore."

The baby hardly heard the boom of voices. Her hand wouldn't hold the shavings properly, and the white flakes of crack and crackle went off to play with the wind and wouldn't wait for her.

They called her Ticket and left it at that.

* * *

Years went by. They installed automatic doors on the trains and little screens that scrolled luminous station names. Many of the smaller stations closed down, and signs appeared everywhere telling bombs to be alert.

The negotiations went badly in London, and Paul left his briefcase on the Circle Line. The jacket with the redundancy papers in the pocket he left on the train from Paddington to Ardenbeck. Seated now in a heat-stiffened shirt on a second train to his home in darkest Wiltshire, he had made a neat pile on the table before him of his tie, his fountain pens, and the key to his company car. While he carefully kicked off his shoes and considered getting off at the next station to walk in the fields, a wasp was noisily going about the clumsy business of dying against the window.

A little boy was lying on the floor. A mild concern that the child had been overcome by heat or succumbed to some illness pulled Paul out of his own thoughts. As he watched, an elderly woman hobbled down the aisle hugging plastic-packed sandwiches to her chest, carefully stepped over the prone form, and continued. Paul leaned forward for a better look.

The boy wore a school uniform of sky blue and smoke grey, the tie looped and knotted into a rough cravat-bow. He lay with his head under one of the tables, tongue-tip pushed out at the corner of his mouth in concentration. With a penknife he was levering at the underside of the table, working loose the cement-grey wedges of abandoned chewing gum. The family seated about the table moved their feet to let him wriggle this way and that, without a break in their conversation.

The boy squirmed out, crawling to Paul's table without a glance upwards. He lifted Paul's shoes, looked them in and out, peered at the soles, then knotted the laces and slung them about his neck. Rising to his knees he cast a quick glance about, like a hare reared to watchfulness. The little pile of Paul's life apparently caught his attention. The boy glanced up at him with eyes grub-grey as pencil rubbings, seemed to make some assessment, then swept the heap into his palm and filled his pocket. As an apparent afterthought he reached across and plucked the dead wasp from beside the window.

The next stop was not listed on the neon scroll. No one looked up to note the place-sign on the platform. The doors opened for the boy to step out. After a moment's hesitation, Paul found his feet and followed, the door sliding to just behind him.

The windows of the little station house were dusted dull as ice, and dandelions had insinuated their way through its lower bricks. No one stood on the platform before him, and the track behind him was empty.

To his left, a meadow was visible through the frame of a stile. Between the bars he saw the bobbing of a fair, little head, receding as if its owner were running. Paul moved to the stile, the paving stones warming him through his socks.

A ragged route had been trampled through a plain of sunflowers. Paul stumbled along it through the choke of pollen, blinded with black and gold, his mind too taken with prickle and stab of stalks in his shins and the weight of sun on his skull to notice the thousands of heads turning slowly as he passed, following his progress with hot black eyes as if facing for the sun.

The hedgerows seemed larger, the way he remembered them as a boy, and he was only a little surprised to find himself crawling through a hole in the under-belly of one, burring his clothes and running a thorn up under his thumbnail. Halfway through, the briar playfully set its teeth in his shirt and refused to release him. He strained, and twisted, and ceased, and panted, and heard.

Music there was, a breathless breath of it. It was tuneless and unseemly, like a wind chime jumble. It was ritualized and right, like birdsong. Paul reached back and loosed his clothes from the brambles.

He had forgotten the late summer stills, with their hanging menace and their eternities of blinding sky. A thousand leaves wavered and watched his clumsy progress, flashing blue-white as the sun caught their sleek. The corn stubble was striped with tree shadow like the belly of a tiger, and the wind was hot as breath. A hedge rose high as two men and beyond it windows blazed white, windows in colored capsules slung like carry cots on a great frame. With the appearance of the big wheel, the music began to phrase itself freakishly. My bonny lies over the ocean, it sang. Paul saw the pointed pinnacles of pavilions, see, pink, white, yellow, or striped like a raspberry ripple. We'll meet again, sang the music. Paul found a slim stile half-buried in the foliage. Trill, tinkle, clang, sang the music. Clang, sang the music. Clang, cling, clang.

Tarpaulin flapped on the skeleton of the big wheel, and the canvas of the pavilion tents was sun bleached, greenish pools gathered in its folds. Some still stood erect under decades of bird trophies, while others sagged like failed cakes. A rough roof of corrugated iron rusted over the ghost train, where three peeling spectres gaped from the painted wall. Four white geese huddled and gossiped nervously. In the centre of the old fairground two women worked. One wore a leather apron and swung a hammer onto a great grey anvil, a hammer that sang clang, clang, cling, clang. The other sat cross-legged a few yards away, hands busy and head bowed low.

The standing woman was manly in proportion and motion. She had the thick neck and firm jaw of a Rossetti female. The simple, girlish cut of her patchily dyed blue dress, combined with her heavy, black pigtails, gave her the appearance of a youthful giantess. The other woman was light and slight as straw. The hair of her lowered head was a rich toffee-gold and tied back in a vaguely archaic manner. Her skin was golden-pale and dimly dappled, like corn as it loses its green.

"Do you like her?" The boy sat on the stile just behind Paul, rolling a gobstopper from one cheek to another. "She's mine."

"She's your sister?" Paul assumed he had misheard.

"No, she's mine. I found her."

Kaiser took the sweet out of his mouth and held it to the sun. It glowed like an emerald.

"Are you selling or buying or dying?" he asked.

Paul rose and walked forward towards the two women. The taller laid down her hammer to watch him, eyes wide, brown and frightless. The other worked, apparently oblivious. Her pale lashes darkened towards the tips, and her fingers seemed unnaturally slender and rapid. They fashioned corn dolls, ribbon-throated, who raised their fingerless hands to their invisible mouths as if blowing a kiss or smothering a scream. She wore a red ribbon about her own throat, stark as a gash of poppies in a cornfield.

Kaiser felt a certain proprietorial pride as the stranger seated himself beside Ticket and watched her work in rapt silence.

Paul put out a hand to touch one of the corn dolls, but halted at the last moment. The dolls were too much like the girl herself. Touching them casually seemed a violation. It would have been akin to handling their creator like an object for sale.

Looking at her he felt an ache of the mind, like the feather-touch of a forgotten word. The word was almost palpable, it already belonged to him, it would make sense of every sentence in his life, but it was held from him by something insubstantial as a bubble-skin. He almost felt that if he touched her hand he would tear through this barrier into a rich new world, but there was a fear that if the bubble burst she would vanish with it.

Uncertainly, Paul reached across to the pile of corn at her side, and began sorting the stalks into groups of the same length for her. She picked up the four longest and started to fashion them without giving him a glance, but when she finished the doll she placed it next to Paul rather than with the pile at her feet. This doll had a twisting straw skirt, woven to look as if it had been flung out by wind or whirling motion, the hem describing slow dips and rises. As if the meshing were coming undone, the little figure started to twist on itself, the skirt's undulation shifting. As Paul watched, however, the doll twisted the other way, its crude hands seeming to drag at its ribbon collar. The pale girl's face remained calm as milk while her doll thrashed slowly to and fro, threads of torn straw jutting from its knobbed joints.

"She didn't used to be like that," remarked Kaiser. "Her head was all pink, and bald, and empty like a balloon. Then she got hair, like chick feathers, and Wolf wanted to borrow her but I said no. I let him borrow a baby bird once, and when he gave it back it wasn't the same anymore." Kaiser ceased, a shadow of a frown creasing his forehead. There was something too eager in the way the stranger watched the girl, as if he were feeding on her, as if somehow he could draw her in through his eyes and steal her away.

"She's mine," repeated Kaiser.

Wolf strolled in from trawling the spilt oil in the gutter puddles, his eyes shining like grease and his pockets full of rainbows. Wolf, whose smile went on and on like a horizon. Wolf in his great coat with the bird-skull buttons. Wolf straddled on the bar of the little roundabout, kicking the ground away and away with his cowboy boots. The stranger's defeat was in his nose, so he grinned, and watched, and waited for him to die.

"She's mine," whispered Kaiser.

"No harm in him looking, if he's here to buy." Eve propped the metal claw she had been fashioning on the anvil. It drew its nails along the metal with a screech, and felt blindly for the edge with a clatter like cutlery. "You know the rules. Everything is for trade."

"Ticket goes away now. Ticket goes away to sleep." Kaiser raised his voice slightly.

The girl stood and moved off towards the helter-skelter. The rattle of feet on the metal stairway dwindled, until a pale face appeared for an instant at the uppermost window. Then a thin hand reached out to pull across the tarpaulin like a curtain.

Paul realized suddenly that it was evening, and could not swear that he had not spent a whole day staring at the straw-fair girl, or watching her ascend her clown-painted tower. His mind told him he was alone now in the dusk, but the part of his mind that smelt the mud cooked to the crack and understood the ache in the wood-pigeon's cry could hear the stir of steps, and voices that seemed to settle on his mind like dust, rather than passing through the medium of his ears. When he slept he dreamt dimly of the long-faced man who widdershinned about and about in the grey light, watching him with hot, black eyes as great as sunflowers and waiting for him to die.

* * *

Paul woke to the smell of frying bacon. A slender, little man, quick as a stoat, was stirring the contents of a great, charcoal-black pan with fastidious care. His velvet waistcoat wore its black and blue ink-stains like bruises.

"Still here, young man? I thought you came here to die." The older man's eyes twinkled like quartz chips in an old wall. "Gave up your shoes, didn't you? Weren't planning to go anywhere. Gave up your wallet, didn't you? It had your name in it. Shouldn't give away your name if you're still going to be using it." The tall man with the broad-brimmed hat and the many-layered coat strolled past, pulled a piece of bacon out of the hot fat, tossed it, and snapped it out of the air with his teeth. He strolled away, pulling the rind loose from the clamp of his grin. "He thinks you're his, anyway. Wolf does. Longer you stay here, the more he'll watch for you."

With slender tongs the diminutive chef drew one rasher from the pan and held it slightly raised, like someone teaching a dog to beg.

"Three words," he demanded.

"Please?" suggested Paul, perplexed.

"Please is an old word. Only new words are any use to me." Bewildered, Paul rattled off a term he had encountered in a computer manual, a makeshift word from an advertising jingle and one of the indelicate little euphemisms for redundancy he had heard used by the personnel manager the day before. A second later his hand was full of hot, greasy bacon, and the words he had just spoken were withering in his head like leaves, losing their meaning. Paul left the other man smoothing back his grey hair and repeating the new words over and over, as if he could taste them.

On the steps of the fortune-teller's hut Wolf chewed a grass stem and watched Ticket as she sewed the new patches onto his coat. Paul recognized their navy-blue fabric as that of his own jacket, which he had abandoned on the Ardenbeck train. Elsewhere the coat was padded and patched with tweed of catkin greys and greens, plastic from refuse sacks, fringed brown suede, canary-colored polyester, rayon-red and great swathes of boot-leather, still studded with lace holes and buckle straps.

Eve backed out of the fortune-teller's tent, ducking under the fringes of its Persian rug roof. She was rubbing at three long gashes in her forearm.

"It must be finished," she said by way of explanation. "Last night it ate all the mice." She closed the wooden-slatted door behind her, carefully, drawing across the dozen or so knitting needles that served the function of bolts.

"Hullo," she said, on seeing Paul. "Kaiser said you were here to die, but you're not, are you? I'm Evening Performance. You don't have a name anymore, do you?" Ticket bit through the thread, then folded one hand in another and gazed into her palm. "What are you looking for? I do leavings soup and goose fool. I do animals too, but they tend to come out strange. What you lost? I got socks and watches and manners. I got safety pins and teaspoons and those metal things with handles that you kept under the stair and couldn't find when you moved house. I got spirit levels and rubber bands and ambitions and bottle openers. I got lots of wedding rings." Paul crouched beside Ticket, feeling her awareness of him like sun. "You want her? Talk to Kaiser."

Kaiser at this moment was waking in his tiny bed in the baby-blue carriage of the big wheel, to find that the wind had blown the wheel around and left him at the apex. This did nothing to improve his temper. Goose feather beds were, he was assured, supposed to be the epitome of luxury, but he found that the feathers tickled his nose, and blew everywhere when he sneezed. Besides this, they pricked at him, and embedded themselves in his clothes. Shaking them like snow from his hair, he climbed from his precariously swinging cradle, and slid down the bar of the wheel to the axle, then dropped to earth, still shedding feathers like a mangled cherub.

Rising from his knees he saw Paul, still breathing, still in fascinated contemplation of the gold-white girl. Wrong, said Kaiser's frown, wrong.

"I'll buy her from you. For a day."

"Just a day?"

"A day." Paul slipped off his wrist watch and after a pause the boy took it. With adjustment to the strap it fitted his chubby wrist.

Ticket stood and lifted her eyes. They were blue-violet, and blinding. They filled the sky, and suddenly it was evening. Paul knew that they had walked alone for a whole day. She had opened her pale mouth, and he had seen the warm pink of her inner lip as she had said things that startled him immensely, and which he forgot immediately. He felt an appalled, poignant sense of loss, like a condemned man who wakes to find he has slept sweetly through his last few hours of life. Ticket lowered her eyes and drifted away in the direction of the helter-skelter. She wore a new necklace of beads that gleamed black and gold. Their pattern bothered Paul, and he suddenly recalled the trapped, frustrated battering of the wasp against its glass prison. He heard the dim clatter of her steps, like a nail being run down a metal comb.

The next day he bought breakfast from Sharmadyne with some obscure terms he had encountered in a *Times* crossword. Then he bought an afternoon with Ticket for three ballpoints and a pencil rubber. The time was sweet and melted to nothing in an instant, like candy-floss. He slept with a haunting sense that she had told him things with greatest earnestness, things that had slid off his mind like water off wax.

The next day he traded a handful of nicknames for a bowlful of blackbird stew. Then he bought a few hours with Ticket for a cigarette lighter and both his socks.

All this while Wolf watched him with taxidermist's eye.

Eve watched too, as she rolled out mouse biscuits for the thing in her tent.

"You'll have to set a final price on her, you know," she told Kaiser. "You'll get a decent price. She's becoming a Maker, and a good one."

"I think I'm going to keep her."

"It's against the rules. We don't really own anything. It just passes through our hands, and sometimes we change it, that's all. He has asked you to set a price, and you must do so."

So Kaiser set a price, and Paul agreed to hand over his dreams. Ticket saw it happen, saw the fine handful of gold, frail as corn, pass from the hand of the stranger to that of her owner and could do nothing to prevent it. She could only watch as a blind numbness spread across the stranger's face, and she felt herself vanish from his view.

Paul was woken from his brown study by the slamming of the restaurant door. The clock on the wall showed three hours were still to run before lunch. He snatched up the mop to swab the spillage from the kebab racks, dodging the waitresses and ignoring the stink of grease. He stooped to pick up the trampled litter and flung it binwards. The sesame seeds got up under his fingernails.

"You're his now," laughed Kaiser. "Go where he goes! Do anything he says!" Ticket watched Paul furiously sweeping at the ashes and shavings of the fairground floor, dodging imaginary obstacles. A goose fled the thrust of his broom and turned to hiss. Paul wrinkled his nose as if he heard the hiss of rancid meat cooking in its own fat. He looked up and at her, and through her, and reflected in his eyes she saw a dowdy, introverted stranger as irrelevant to his thoughts as a window handle might be to the wasp dedicated to beating itself to death against glass.

Kaiser had a laugh like a barnful of roosters.

* * *

Wolf slept in the ghost train, coat shielding his head like a bat's wing, hat hung on the broomstick of a plastic witch. Kaiser curled like a nestling in a mass of birds' feathers, sheep's wool and cotton scraps, rocked to slumber at the top of the Big Wheel. Sharmadyne cushioned his head with a Book of Birds in the Souvenir stall, and dreamt of dictionaries. Ticket lay cocooned in tablecloths and curtains in her boudoir at the top of the helter-skelter. Paul slept leaning against the anvil in the yard, hugging his broom like a mate. Eve sat up in the Fortune Teller's tent and made moccasins out of jacket lining.

She moved carefully about her tent to avoid waking her creations, her rounded limbs rolling to and fro slowly like peaches on a bough. The bottle opener stirred and rasped its razor-bill in sleep, then settled. The spirit in the spirit level lay dormant. From the pocket of the apron of bat-wing leather Eve drew a small hammer with a broad head.

She opened a box at the back of the room, fingering the contents carefully.

Two white gloves. A scarf of black silk. A folded poster of a dapper man in a top hat, with white, white teeth, and "Evening Performance" blazoned on a stylized banner above his head. A ball of glass, palm-size.

Eve muffled the globe in muslin, and carefully tapped it with the hammer until it broke. She continued tapping, crushing it to powder.

Out she crept, bearing navy-blue moccasins and a muslin bag full of dream. Paul woke when she poured the crushed glass into his opened hand. Reflexively he tried to shake it out of his palm, but she prevented him and closed his hand upon the glittering pile.

"It's all I got of dreams," she hissed. "I don't know how long it'll last you, but hold on to it as long as you can, however much it hurts." Then she cut off all his shirt buttons as payment.

Ticket was awake long before Eve reached the topmost stair of the helter-skelter. She rose, already dressed and quite composed, pulling a cloth from an object beside her. They carried it down between them, and left it upright in the yard.

Paul was dizzy and his hand hurt. With half his mind he saw the dingy lodgings that he knew to be his home, with the black beetles behind the radiator and the tiny crackling television, and with the other he saw Ticket take him by the hand and lead him through nocturnal fields, fleeing the pale stain of dawn. Desperately he clung to the latter image, even while the tiny shards of the crystal ball penetrated his skin. He clung to the early morning chill, and the stab of corn stubble through his moccasins.

The wind turned the Big Wheel once more, and when dawn came Kaiser awoke to find himself a mere yard from the ground. He alighted from his little cabin like a lord from a carriage, shaking the plumes out of his shorts. There lay the broom, crusted with wood-shavings. Where was Paul?

"Where's the man without a name?"

"Can't have gone far." Eve was varnishing a terrapin Wolf had traded her the day before. "Got no dreams, can't see where he's going. Got no shoes, can't run anywhere. Maybe he died, and Wolf took him." A few yards away, Ticket sat in her usual place, intensely studying an object in her palm.

Wolf did not take kindly to having his sleep interrupted and most found excuses to avoid trespassing upon his territory. Kaiser was just resolving to question him later when the wind picked up. The figure of Ticket toppled, and tumbled, and was torn open by the wind as it skittered and rolled over the fairground floor. A papier-mâché mask fell loose. Bundles of stripped maple-wood fingers tumbled from the sleeves. The straw-gold hair was straw, and the thing in the bleach-blue muslin dress was a corn doll, made to the size of life by cunning fingers.

Kaiser had a scream like a fox-feast in a chicken coop.

* * *

The door of the ghost train was flung wide. Wolf gave a low growl like a lawn-mower engine and shielded his yellow eyes from the sun. Kaiser stood in the doorway, his frown like a crisscross brand on his forehead.

"Where are they?" he demanded. Things rattled down the overhead rail and dangled in the dark like malevolent puppets, leather-skinned and glass-eyed, waiting to observe their master's will. They watched his hands in the brown leather gloves, with the knuckle creases and the nails attached, for the signal to attack, but it did not come. Wolf saw Kaiser's frown and blinked like a chidden dog.

"They run through the sunflowers," he said.

* * *

Ticket heard the distant scream of rage and felt the air change. The early morning sunlight was suddenly paler, and she suddenly seemed to move through silt. The sunflowers around them ceased to thresh their heads indiscriminately in the freshening wind, and started to turn their broad, singed-looking faces to watch the passage of the pair. Wolf is awake, she thought. Wolf sees.

A bank of cloud was racing with impossible speed in their pursuit, borne by a wind that howled like a thousand little deaths. Kaiser is awake, she thought. Kaiser comes.

Paul she had to lead each step, to stop him casting a foot from the ragged path through the flowers. Sometimes he would pause, and gaze around blindly, so that it took all her effort to keep him moving. Even as she struggled to support his weight upon her slender arm, she could see behind his eyes her new-found miracle, a wounded, smoky, human mind, half-blind but blood-warmed.

All the while Ticket's own mind was in moth-wing motion, for her thoughts were as fast as her fingers. From her fosterfolk she had learnt the importance of gathering up the unregarded, and so for years she had silently collected negligently cast remarks and stored them for future use.

She narrowed her eyes. The air was full of the hiss of the wind-snakes. Reaching up she caught one by its tail. The tug nearly pulled her from her feet, but she hooked her toes among the sunflower roots and held on. Drawing the snake in like a rope, she forced its tail into its own mouth. The wind-snake whirled about and about, trying to loose itself. Taking off her necklace, Ticket pulled loose the wasp-body beads and cast them into the little whirlwind behind her, and hurried on.

Kaiser raged onward like a forest fire with a following gale. The corn parted before him as if in fear, and the birds drew in their voices. He danced a dance of rage down the little path that zig-a-zagged like a frightened hare through the coal-faced flowers.

The whirl of the crippled wind-snake caught him unaware. It spun him around so that he almost lost his footing and fell into the grip of Wolf's flowers. Then the wasp bellies struck, and stuck, and stung and stung again. Covering his face he retreated, and fled back to the fairground.

Kaiser ran to the Fortune Teller's tent, hopping with fury and howling like a storm rising. Eve had hidden her great square bulk under the table and peered out fearfully as he entered, through a hole in the chequered cloth.

"I need to borrow your car," he said. Eve covered her earth-brown eyes with her great hands. She heard the catches of the closet open. She heard Kaiser trill as he took the rein of the thing within. She heard the clatter of aluminium hooves and a cry like a violin being tuned.

It was bigger than Kaiser expected, and he had to pull half of Eve's tent loose from the peggings to get it out.

* * *

Ticket looked about the hill for Kaiser's railway station, but saw not a trace of it. There was a field full of pale horses with terra-cotta manes, but not an inch of brick and mortar, nor the dimmest glint of a railway line. She struggled up the hill, one hand hoisting her skirt up to stop her tripping, the other dragging Paul behind her as he complained of the rainy streets and asked to go back to his bed.

Behind her she heard the wind bring a harsh music of different noises. There was a chorus of squeaks like an orchestra of bicycle wheels, or a war of metal mice. There was a whish and hush like scythes cutting air or the slice of great wings.

At the very apex of the hill, in the place that Paul had described, Ticket found the station. She found the ravaged cassette tape with its loosened ribbon that fluttered and gleamed like a metal track as it looped about the shoebox with the clumsily drawn windows and door. A rusted toy train the size of her thumb lay nearby on its side. There was nothing else, only a tumble of litter and leavings.

Behind her the music was clearer. There was a sound like the whetting of knives. There was a long hunting call like a baby foghorn.

Ticket seated herself on the thick grass and started to work. Her fingers became a white whirl, like the churn of a moth's wings. Cans she crushed into carapaces, rending them to provide aluminium teeth. Crisp packets fluttered under her hands like wings. Corn stalks jointed into legs and clawed the air unsensingly. She drenched their wings in dew, and in the rage of patience. One after another she flung them into the air.

Kaiser's frown was black as wrought iron, like the crosses they use to stop walls bulging, and his face was red as brick. The wind-snakes foamed against his reins. Behind him a wake was ravaged, and clods of earth thrown house-high. Before him hedges broke and corn scattered, torn aside by a thresh of metal and claw, and a flounder of hoof. He sounded the horn again, and the horse skull opened and screamed. The sun hid its face.

Down the hill surged Ticket's butterflies. They came upon Kaiser with a whicker and a flutter, on wings made of tinfoil and TV dinner packages, of sandwich crusts and cellophane. Their limbs swiveled in joints of chewing gum, and they stared with bottle-top eyes. With metal-gash mouths they caught and bit.

Eve's car veered crazily as its driver lost control. It floundered through thickets, snapping off bones, blades, handles and appendages against the low-hanging boughs. The butterflies followed. A wheel spun loose, and the vehicle careered over a bracken ridge to plunge and tumble down the scarp to ruin in the hollow below. The butterflies flitted overhead, looking for Kaiser. What did they find?

A school uniform with the seams mended too many times, and a tie knotted beyond recovery. A little flesh-pink plush, and a black cross of iron. A paper bag of sweets that had glued themselves into one multicolored mass. A frog, a snail, and a furred something shorter than a finger. An empty packet of cigarettes marked "Kaiser Kingsize".

The butterflies had weakened their frail fixings by their exertions. They tumbled loose and scattered. Now there was nothing moving on the slope but a handful of litter that rolled before the wind.

Later Wolf found the pieces of Kaiser and collected them, weeping. He took them back to Eve the Maker to see if she could mend them.

* * *

Paul paused by a shop window and viewed his reflection with discontent. He yawned and rubbed at the blue of his jaw. Beyond his own image, the glass-eyed girl in the blue dress-suit tried to sell him soap from a thousand screens.

The straw-blond girl with the folded hands still stood beside him. Had she been saying something? He had not been listening. She took his hand again, and he let her. He should be at work, but she was so insistent in her passive, quiet way. Perhaps he should humor her—she seemed a bit touched. Perhaps it would be nice to see that almost indiscernible pucker at the corners of her straight, little mouth become a smile.

Where had she come from? Had he met her at that party last night? Had he…well if he had she would probably tell him sooner or later.

Damn that party! He had woken that morning on a train with the girl's head resting against his shoulder, and his hand full of broken glass. Probably crushed a pint glass with his bare hand for a dare. He had bandaged it as best he could, and picked out the pieces. Nonetheless, his palm twinged sometimes, as if tiny shards had escaped his notice, had burrowed deep beneath his skin and remained within him.

With his uninjured hand, he gave the girl's palm a squeeze. She looked up to meet his gaze with something akin to a smile.

Ticket's eyes were blue-violet and blinding. Reflected in them he saw no trace of the grub-grey heaven that ceilinged his world. He saw wide mauve skies freckled with the flight of birds, and seas of corn and grass, down-grey in the dusk.

THE BIBLE REPAIRMAN

TIM POWERS

Tim Power's first novels, *The Skies Discrowned* and *Epitaph in Rust*, appeared in 1976, but his first major novel was *The Drawing of the Dark* in 1979. It was followed by *The Anubis Gates, Dinner at Deviant's Palace, The Stress of Her Regard, Last Call, Expiration Date, Earthquake Weather*, and supernatural "secret history" *Declare*. His most recent books are collection *Strange Itineraries* and novel *Three Days to Never*.

This subtle tale of loss, sin, and sacrifice, where everything comes at a cost, is Powers at his best.

> *"It'll do to kiss the book on still, won't it?" growled Dick, who was evidently uneasy at the curse he had brought on himself.*
> *"A Bible with a bit cut out!" returned Silver derisively. "Not it. It don't bind no more'n a ballad-book."*
> *"Don't it, though?" cried Dick, with a sort of joy. "Well I reckon that's worth having, too."*
>
> —*Treasure Island*,
> by Robert Louis Stevenson

Across the highway was old Humberto, a dark spot against the tan field between the railroad tracks and the freeway fence, pushing a stripped-down shopping cart along the cracked sidewalk. His shadow still stretched halfway to the center-divider line in the early morning sunlight, but he was apparently already very drunk, and he was using the shopping cart as a walker, bracing his weight on it as he shuffled along. Probably he never slept at all, not that he was ever really awake either.

Humberto had done a lot of work in his time, and the people he talked and gestured to were, at best, long gone and probably existed now only in his cannibalized memory—but this morning as Torrez watched him the old man clearly looked across the street straight at Torrez and waved. He was just a silhouette against the bright eastern daylight—his camouflage pants, white beard and Daniel Boone coonskin cap were all one raggedly backlit outline—but he might have been smiling too.

After a moment's hesitation Torrez waved and nodded. Torrez was not drunk in the morning, nor unable to walk without leaning on something, nor surrounded by imaginary acquaintances, and he meant to sustain those differences between them—but he supposed that he and Humberto were brothers in the trades, and he should show some respect to a player who simply had not known when to retire.

Torrez pocketed his Camels and his change and turned his back on the old man, and trudged across the parking lot toward the path that led across a weedy field to home.

He was retired, at least from the big-stakes dives. Nowadays he just waded a little ways out—he worked on cars and Bibles and second-hand eyeglasses and clothes people bought at thrift stores, and half of that work was just convincing the customers that work had been done. He always had to use holy water—*real* holy water, from gallon jugs he filled from the silver urn at St. Anne's—but though it impressed the customers, all he could see that it actually did was get stuff wet. Still, it was better to err on the side of thoroughness.

His garage door was open, and several goats stood up with their hoofs on the fence rail of the lot next door. Torrez paused to pull up some of the tall, furry, sagelike weeds that sprang up in every stretch of unattended dirt in the county, and he held them out and let the goats chew them up. Sometimes when customers arrived at times like this, Torrez would whisper to the goats and then pause and nod.

Torrez's Toyota stood at the curb because a white Dodge Dart was parked in the driveway. Torrez had already installed a "pain button" on the Dodge's dashboard, so that when the car wouldn't start, the owner could give the car a couple of jabs—*Oh yeah? How do you like this, eh?* On the other side of the firewall the button was connected to a wire that was screwed to the carburetor housing; nonsense, but the stuff had to look convincing.

Torrez had also used a can of Staples compressed air and a couple of magnets to try to draw a babbling ghost out of the car's stereo system, and this had not been nonsense—if he had properly opposed the magnets to the magnets in the speakers, and got the Bernoulli effect with the compressed air sprayed over the speaker diaphragm, then at speeds over forty there would no longer be a droning imbecile monologue faintly going on behind whatever music was playing. Torrez would take the Dodge out onto the freeway today, assuming the old car would get up to freeway speeds, and try it out driving north, east, south and west. Two hundred dollars if the voice was gone, and a hundred in any case for the pain button.

And he had a couple of Bibles in need of customized repair, and those were an easy fifty dollars apiece—just brace the page against a piece of plywood in a frame and scorch out the verses the customers found intolerable, with a woodburning stylus; a plain old razor wouldn't have the authority that hot iron did.

And then of course drench the defaced book in holy water to validate the edited text. Matthew 19:5-6 and Mark 10:7-12 were bits he was often asked to burn out, since they condemned re-marriage after divorce, but he also got a lot of requests to lose Matthew 25:41 through 46, with Jesus's promise of Hell to stingy people. And he offered a special deal to eradicate all thirty or so mentions of adultery. Some of these customized Bibles ended up after a few years with hardly any weight besides the binding.

He pushed open the front door of the house—he never locked it—and made his way to the kitchen to get a beer out of the cold spot in the sink. The light was blinking on the telephone answering machine, and when he had popped the can of Budweiser he pushed the play button.

"Give Mr. Torrez this message," said a recorded voice. "Write down the number I give you! It is important, make sure he gets it!" The voice recited a number then, and Torrez wrote it down. His answering machine had come with a pre-recorded message on it in a woman's voice—*No one is available to take your call right now*—and many callers assumed the voice was that of a woman he was living with. Apparently she sounded unreliable, for they often insisted several times that she convey their messages to him.

He punched in the number, and a few moments later a man at the other end of the line was saying to him, "Mr. Torrez? We need your help, like you helped out the Fotas four years ago. Our daughter was stolen, and now we've got a ransom note—she was in a coffee pot with roses tied around it—"

"I don't do that work anymore," Torrez interrupted, "I'm sorry. Mr. Seaweed in Corona still does—he's younger—I could give you his number."

"I called him already a week ago, but then I heard you were back in business. You're better than Seaweed—"

Poor old Humberto had kept on doing deep dives. Torrez had done them longer than he should have, and nowadays couldn't understand a lot of the books he had loved when he'd been younger.

"I'm not back in that business," he said. "I'm very sorry." He hung up the phone.

He had not even done the ransom negotiations when it had been his own daughter that had been stolen, three years ago—and his wife had left him over it, not understanding that she would probably have had to be changing her mentally retarded husband's diapers forever afterward if he had done it.

Torrez's daughter Amelia had died at the age of eight, of a fever. Her grave was in the dirt lot behind the Catholic cemetery, and on most Sundays Torrez and his wife had visited the grave and made sure there were lots of little stuffed animals and silver foil pinwheels arranged on the dirt, and for a marker they had set into the ground a black plastic box with a clear top, with her death-certificate displayed in it to show that she had died in a hospital. And her soul had surely gone to Heaven, but they had caught her ghost to keep it from wandering in the noisy cold half-world, and Torrez had bound it into one of Amelia's cloth dolls. Every Sunday night they had put candy and cigarettes and a shot-glass of rum in front of the doll—hardly appropriate fare for a little girl, but ghosts were somehow all the same age. Torrez had always lit the cigarettes and stubbed them out before laying them in front of the doll, and bitten the candies: ghosts needed somebody to have *started* such things for them.

And then one day the house had been broken into, and the little shrine and the doll were gone, replaced with a ransom note: *If you want your daughter's ghost back, Mr. Torrez, give me some of your blood.* And there had been a phone number.

Usually these ransom notes asked the recipient to get a specific tattoo that corresponded to a tattoo on the kidnapper's body—and afterward whichever family member complied would have lost a lot of memories, and be unable to feel affection, and never again dream at night. The kidnapper would have taken those things. But a kidnapper would always settle instead for the blood of a person whose soul was broken in the way that Torrez's was, and so the robbed families would often come to Torrez and offer him a lot of money to step in and give up some of his blood, and save them the fearful obligation of the vampiric tattoo.

Sometimes the kidnapper was the divorced father or mother of the ghost— courts never considered custody of a dead child—or a suitor who had been rejected long before, and in these cases there would be no ransom demand; but then it had sometimes been possible for Torrez to trace the thief and steal the ghost back, in whatever pot or box or liquor bottle it had been confined in.

But in most cases he had had to go through with the deal, meet the kidnapper somewhere and give up a cupful or so of blood to retrieve the stolen ghost; and each time, along with the blood, he had lost a piece of his soul.

The phone began ringing again as Torrez tipped up the can for the last sip of beer; he ignored it.

Ten years ago it had been an abstract consideration—when he had thought about it at all, he had supposed that he could lose a lot of his soul without missing it, and he'd told himself that his soul was bound for Hell anyway, since he had deliberately broken it when he was eighteen, and so dispersing it had just seemed like hiding money from the IRS. But by the time he was thirty-five his hair had gone white and he had lost most of the sight in his left eye because of ruptured blood-vessels behind the retina, and he could no longer understand the plots of long novels he tried to read. Apparently some sort of physical and mental integrity was lost too, along with the blood and the bits of his hypothetical soul.

But what the kidnappers wanted from Torrez's blood was not vicarious integrity—it was nearly the opposite. Torrez thought of it as spiritual botox.

The men and women who stole ghosts for ransom were generally mediums, fortune-tellers, psychics—always clairvoyant. And even more than the escape that could be got from extorted dreams and memories and the ability to feel affection, they needed to be able to selectively blunt the psychic noise of humans living and dead.

Torrez imagined it as a hundred radios going at once all the time, and half the announcers moronically drunk—crying, giggling, trying to start fights.

He would never know. He had broken all the antennae in his own soul when he was eighteen, by killing a man who attacked him in a parking lot with a knife one midnight. Torrez had wrestled the knife away from the drunken assailant and had knocked the man unconscious by slamming his head into the bumper of a car—but then Torrez had picked up the man's knife and, just because he could, had driven it into the unconscious man's chest. The District Attorney had eventually called it self-defense, a justifiable homicide, and no charges were brought against Torrez, but his soul was broken.

The answering machine clicked on, but only the dial tone followed the recorded message. Torrez dropped the Budweiser can into the trash basket and walked into the living room, which over the years had become his workshop.

Murder seemed to be the crime that broke souls most effectively, and Torrez had done his first ghost-ransom job for free that same year, in 1983, just to see if his soul was now a source of the temporary disconnection-from-humanity that the psychics valued so highly. And he had tested out fine.

He had been doing Bible repair for twenty years, but his reputation in that cottage industry had been made only a couple of years ago, by accident. Three Jehovah's Witnesses had come to his door one summer day, wearing suits and ties, and he had stepped outside to debate scripture with them. "Let me see your Bible," he had said, "and I'll show you right in there why you're wrong," and when they handed him the book he had flipped to the first chapter of John's gospel and started reading. This was after his vision had begun to go bad, though, and he'd had to read it with a magnifying glass, and it had been a sunny day—and he had inadvertently set their Bible on fire. They had left hurriedly, and apparently told everyone in the neighborhood that Torrez could burn a Bible just by touching it.

* * *

He was bracing a tattered old Bible in the frame on the marble-topped table, ready to scorch out St. Paul's adverse remarks about homosexuality for a customer, when he heard three knocks at his front door, the first one loud and the next two just glancing scuffs, and he realized he had not closed the door and the knocks had pushed it open. He made sure his woodburning stylus was lying in the ashtray, then hurried to the entry hall.

Framed in the bright doorway was a short stocky man with a moustache, holding a shoe-box and shifting from one foot to the other.

"Mr. Torrez," the man said. He smiled, and a moment later looked as if he'd never smile again. He waved the shoe-box toward Torrez and said, "A man has stolen my daughter."

Perhaps the shoe-box was the shrine he had kept his daughter's ghost in, in some jelly jar or perfume bottle. Probably there were ribbons and candy hearts around the empty space where the daughter's ghost-container had lain. Still, a shoe-box was a pretty nondescript shrine; but maybe it was just for traveling, like a cat-carrier box.

"I just called," the man said, "and got your woman. I hoped she was wrong, and you were here."

"I don't do that work anymore," said Torrez patiently, "ransoming ghosts. You want to call Seaweed in Corona."

"I don't want you to ransom a ghost," the man said, holding the box toward Torrez. "I already had old Humberto do that, yesterday. This is for you."

"If Humberto ransomed your daughter," Torrez said carefully, nodding toward the box but not taking it, "then why are you here?"

"*My* daughter is *not* a ghost. My daughter is twelve years old, and this man took her when she was walking home from school. I can pay you fifteen hundred dollars to get her back—this is extra, a gift for you, from me, with the help of Humberto."

Torrez had stepped back. "Your daughter was kidnapped? Alive? Good God, man, call the police right now! The FBI! You don't come to *me* with—"

"The police would not take the ransom note seriously," the man said, shaking his head. "They would think he wants money really, they would not think of his terms being sincerely meant, as he wrote them!" He took a deep breath and let it out. "Here," he said, extending the box again.

Torrez took the box—it was light—and cautiously lifted the lid.

Inside, in a nest of rosemary sprigs and Catholic holy cards, lay a little cloth doll that Torrez recognized.

"Amelia," he said softly.

He lifted it out of the box, and he could feel the quiver of his own daughter's long-lost ghost in it.

"Humberto bought this back for you?" Torrez asked. Three years after her kidnapping, he thought. No wonder Humberto waved to me this morning! I hope he didn't have to spend much of his soul on her; he's got no more than a mouse's worth left.

"For you," the man said. "She is a gift. Save my daughter."

Torrez didn't want to invite the man into the house. "What did the ransom note for your daughter say?"

"It said, Juan-Manuel Ortega—that's me—I have Elizabeth, and I will kill her and take all her blood unless you *induce* Terry Torrez to come to me and him give me the ransom blood instead."

"Call the police," Torrez said. "That's a bluff, about taking her blood. Why would he want a little girl's blood? When did this happen? Every minute—"

Juan-Manuel Ortega opened his mouth very wide, as if to pronounce some big syllable, then closed it. "My Elizabeth," he said, "she—killed her sister last year. My rifle was in the closet—she didn't know, she's a child, she didn't know it was loaded—"

Torrez could feel that his eyebrows were raised. Yes she did, he thought; she killed her sister deliberately, and broke her own soul doing it, and the kidnapper knows it even if you truly don't.

Your daughter's a murderer. She's like me.

Still, her blood—her broken, blunting soul—wouldn't be accessible to the kidnapper, the way Torrez's would be, unless…

"Has your daughter—" He had spoken too harshly, and tried again. "Has she ever used magic?" Or is her soul still virginal, he thought.

Ortega bared his teeth and shrugged. "Maybe! She said she caught her sister's ghost in my electric shaver. I—I think she did. I don't use it anymore, but think I hear it in the nights."

Then her blood will do for the kidnapper what mine would, Torrez thought. Not quite as well, since my soul is surely more opaque—older and more stained by the use of magic—but hers will do if he can't get mine.

"Here is my phone number," said Ortega, now shoving a business card at Torrez and talking too rapidly to interrupt, "and the kidnapper has your number. He wants only you. I am leaving it in your hands. Save my daughter, please."

Then he turned around and ran down the walkway to a van parked behind Torrez's Toyota. Torrez started after him, but the sun-glare in his bad left eye made him uncertain of his footing, and he stopped when he heard the van shift into gear and start away. The man's wife must have been waiting behind the wheel.

I should call the police myself, Torrez thought as he lost sight of the van in the brightness. But he's right, the police would take the kidnapping seriously, but not the ransom. The kidnapper doesn't want money—he wants my blood, me.

A living girl! he thought. I don't save living people, I save ghosts. And I don't even do that anymore.

She's like me.

He shuffled back into the house, and set the cloth doll on the kitchen counter, sitting up against the toaster. Almost without thinking about it, he took the pack of Camels out of his shirt pocket and lit one with his Bic lighter, then stubbed it out on the stove-top and laid it on the tile beside the doll.

The tip of the cigarette glowed again, and the telephone rang. He just kept staring at the doll and the smoldering cigarette and let the phone ring.

The answering machine clicked in, and he heard the woman's recorded voice say, "No one is available to take your call, he had me on his TV, Daddy, so I could change channels for him. 'Two, four, eleven,' and I'd change them."

Torrez became aware that he had sat down on the linoleum floor. Her ghost had never found a way to speak when he and his ex-wife had had possession of it. "I'm sorry, Amelia," he said hoarsely. "It would have killed me to buy you back. They don't want money, they—"

"What?" said the voice of the caller. "Is Mr. Torrez there?"

"Rum he gave me, at least," said Amelia's voice. "It wouldn't have killed you, not really."

Torrez got to his feet, feeling much older than his actual forty years. He opened the high cupboard and saw her bottle of 151-proof rum still standing up there beside the stacked china dishes he never used. He hoisted the bottle down and wiped dust off it.

"I'm going to tell him how rude you are," said the voice on the phone, "this isn't very funny." The line clicked.

"No," Torrez said as he poured a couple of ounces of rum into a coffee cup. "It wouldn't have killed me. But it would have made a mindless … it would have made an idiot of me. I wouldn't have been able to … work, talk, think." Even now I can hardly make sense of the comics in the newspaper, he thought.

"He had me on his TV, Daddy," said Amelia's voice from the answering machine. "I was his channel-changer."

Torrez set the coffee cup near the doll, and felt it vibrate faintly just as he let go of the handle. The sharp alcohol smell became stronger, as if some of the rum had been vaporized.

"And he gave me candy."

"I'm sorry," said Torrez absently, "I don't have any candy."

"Sugar Babies are better than Reese's Pieces." Torrez had always given her Reese's Pieces, but before now she had not been able to tell him what she preferred.

"How can you talk?"

"The people that nobody paid for, he would put all of us, all our jars and boxes and dolls on the TV and make us change what the TV people said. We made them say bad prayers."

The phone rang again, and Amelia's voice out of the answering machine speaker said, "Sheesh," and broke right in. "What, what?"

"I've got a message for Terry Torrez," said a woman's voice, "make sure he gets it, write this number down!" The woman recited a number, which Torrez automatically memorized. "My husband is in an alarm clock, but he's fading; I don't hardly dream about him even with the clock under the pillow anymore, and the mint patties, it's like a year he takes to even get halfway through one! He needs a booster shot, tell Terry Torrez that, and I'll pay a thousand dollars for it."

I'll want more than a thousand, Torrez thought, and she'll pay more, too. Booster shot! The only way to boost a fading ghost—and they all faded sooner or later—was to add to the container a second ghost, the ghost of a newly deceased infant, which would have vitality but no personality to interfere with the original ghost.

Torrez had done that a few times, and—though these were only ghosts, not souls, not actual people!—it had always felt like putting feeder mice into an aquarium with an old, blind snake.

"That'll buy a lot of Sugar Babies," remarked Amelia's ghost.

"What? Just make sure he gets the message!"

The phone clicked off, and Amelia said, "I remember the number."

"So do I."

Midwives sold newborn ghosts. The thought of looking one of them up nauseated him.

"Mom's dead," said Amelia.

Torrez opened his mouth, then just exhaled. He took a sip of Amelia's rum and said, "She is?"

"Sure. We all know, when someone is. I guess they figured you wouldn't bleed for her, if you wouldn't bleed for me. Sugar Babies are better than Reese's Pieces."

"Right, you said."

"Can I have her rings? They'd fit on my head like crowns."

"I don't know what became of her," he said. It's true, he realized, I don't. I don't even know what there was of her.

He looked at the doll and wondered why anyone kept such things.

His own Bible, on the mantel in the living room workshop, was relatively intact, though of course it was warped from having been soaked in holy water. He had burned out half a dozen verses from the Old Testament that had to do with witchcraft and wizards; and he had thought about excising "thou shalt not kill" from Exodus, but decided that if the commandment was gone, his career might be too.

After he had refused to ransom Amelia's ghost, he had cut out Ezekiel 44:25— "And they shall come at no dead person to defile themselves: but for father, or for mother, or for son, or for daughter, for brother, or for sister that hath had no husband, they may defile themselves."

He had refused to defile himself—defile himself any further, at least—for his own dead daughter. And so she had wound up helping to voice "bad prayers" out of a TV set somewhere.

The phone rang again, and this time he snatched up the receiver before the answering machine could come on. "Yes?"

"Mr. Torrez," said a man's voice. "I have a beaker of silence here, she's twelve years old and she's not in any jar or bottle."

"Her father has been here," Torrez said.

"I'd rather have the beaker that's you. For all her virtues, her soul's a bit thin still, and noises would get through."

Torrez remembered stories he'd heard about clairvoyants driven to insanity by the constant din of thoughts.

"My daddy doesn't play that anymore," said Amelia. "He has me back now."

Torrez remembered Humberto's wave this morning. Torrez had waved back.

Torrez looked into the living room, at the current Bible in the burning rack, and at the books he still kept on a shelf over the cold fireplace—paperbacks, hardcovers with gold-stamped titles, books in battered dust-jackets. He had found—what?—a connection with other people's lives, in them, which since the age of eighteen he had not been able to have in any other way. But these days their pages might as well all be blank. When he occasionally pulled one down and opened it, squinting through his magnifying glass to be able to see the print clearly, he could understand individual words but the sentences didn't cohere anymore.

She's like me.

I wonder if I could have found my way back, if I'd tried. I could tell her father to ask her to try.

"Bring the girl to where we meet," Torrez said. He leaned against the kitchen counter. In spite of his resolve, he was dizzy. "I'll have her parents with me to drive her away."

I'm dead already, he thought. Her father came to me, but the book says he may do that for a daughter. And for me, the dead person, this is the only way left to have a vital connection with other people's lives, even if they are strangers.

"And you'll come away with me," said the man's voice.

"No," said Amelia, "he won't. He brings me rum and candy."

The living girl who had been Amelia would have been at least somewhat concerned about the kidnapped girl. We each owe God our mind, Torrez thought, and he that gives it up today is paid off for tomorrow.

"Yes," said Torrez. He lifted the coffee cup; his hand was shaky, but he carefully poured the rum over the cloth head of the doll; the rum soaked into its fabric and puddled on the counter.

"How much is the ransom?" he asked.

"Only a reasonable amount," the voice assured him blandly.

Torrez was relieved; he was sure a reasonable amount was all that was left, and the kidnapper was likely to take it all anyway. He flicked his lighter over the doll, and then the doll was in a teardrop-shaped blue glare on the counter. Torrez stepped back, ready to wipe a wet towel over the cabinets if they should start to smolder. The doll turned black and began to come apart.

Amelia's voice didn't speak from the answering machine, though he thought he might have heard a long sigh—of release, he hoped.

"I want something," Torrez said. "A condition."

"What?"

"Do you have a Bible? Not a repaired one, a whole one?"

"I can get one."

"Yes, get one. And bring it for me."

"Okay. So we have a deal?"

The rum had burned out and the doll was a black pile, still glowing red here and there. He filled the cup with water from the tap and poured it over the ashes, and then there was no more red glow.

Torrez sighed, seeming to empty his lungs. "Yes. Where do we meet?"

YELLOW CARD MAN

PAOLO BACIGALUPI

Paolo Bacigalupi is a freelance writer who lives and works in Colorado. He has written about his travels in China for *Salon*, and is the online editor/webmaster for *High Country News*. His first story, "A Pocketful of Dharma", appeared in *The Magazine of Fantasy & Science Fiction* in 1999. It was followed by a handful of dark science fiction stories including Theodore Sturgeon Memorial Award nominee "The Fluted Girl", Hugo and Nebula Award nominee "The People of Sand and Slag", "The Pasho", Theodore Sturgeon Memorial Award winner and Hugo Award nominee "The Calorie Man" and the tale that follows. Bacigalupi's first collection will be published later this year.

Machetes gleam on the warehouse floor, reflecting a red conflagration of jute and tamarind and kink-springs. They're all around now. The men with their green headbands and their slogans and their wet wet blades. Their calls echo in the warehouse and on the street. Number one son is already gone. Jade Blossom he cannot find, no matter how many times he treadles her phone number. His daughters' faces have been split wide like blister rust durians.

More fires blaze. Black smoke roils around him. He runs through his warehouse offices, past computers with teak cases and iron treadles and past piles of ash where his clerks burned files through the night, obliterating the names of people who aided the Tri-Clipper.

He runs, choking on heat and smoke. In his own gracious office he dashes to the shutters and fumbles with their brass catches. He slams his shoulder against those blue shutters while the warehouse burns and brown-skinned men boil through the door and swing their slick red knives…

Tranh wakes, gasping.

Sharp concrete edges jam against the knuckles of his spine. A salt-slick thigh smothers his face. He shoves away the stranger's leg. Sweat-sheened skin glimmers in the blackness, impressionistic markers for the bodies that shift and shove all around him. They fart and groan and turn, flesh on flesh, bone against bone, the living and the heat-smothered dead all together.

A man coughs. Moist lungs and spittle gust against Tranh's face. His spine and belly stick to the naked sweating flesh of the strangers around him. Claustrophobia rises. He forces it down. Forces himself to lie still, to breathe slowly, deeply, despite the heat. To taste the swelter darkness with all the paranoia of a survivor's mind. He is awake while others sleep. He is alive while others are long dead. He forces himself to lie still, and listen.

Bicycle bells are ringing. Down below and far away, ten thousand bodies below, a lifetime away, bicycle bells chime. He claws himself out of the mass of tangled humanity, dragging his hemp sack of possessions with him. He is late. Of all the days he could be late, this is the worst possible one. He slings the bag over a bony shoulder and feels his way down the stairs, finding his footing in the cascade of sleeping flesh. He slides his sandals between families, lovers and crouching hungry ghosts, praying that he will not slip and break an old man's bone. Step, feel, step, feel.

A curse rises from the mass. Bodies shift and roll. He steadies himself on a landing amongst the privileged who lie flat, then wades on. Downward ever downward, round more turnings of the stair, wading down through the carpet of his countrymen. Step. Feel. Step. Feel. Another turn. A hint of gray light glimmers far below. Fresh air kisses his face, caresses his body. The waterfall of anonymous flesh resolves into individuals, men and women sprawled across one another, pillowed on hard concrete, propped on the slant of the windowless stair. Gray light turns gold. The tinkle of bicycle bells comes louder now, clear like the ring of cibiscosis chimes.

Tranh spills out of the highrise and into a crowd of congee sellers, hemp weavers and potato carts. He puts his hands on his knees and gasps, sucking in swirling dust and trampled street dung, grateful for every breath as sweat pours off his body. Salt jewels fall from the tip of his nose, spatter the red paving stones of the sidewalk with his moisture. Heat kills men. Kills old men. But he is out of the oven; he has not been cooked again, despite the blast furnace of the dry season.

Bicycles and their ringing bells flow past like schools of carp, commuters already on their way to work. Behind him the highrise looms, forty stories of heat and vines and mold. A vertical ruin of broken windows and pillaged apartments. A remnant glory from the old energy Expansion now become a heated tropic coffin without air conditioning or electricity to protect it from the glaze of the equatorial sun. Bangkok keeps its refugees in the pale blue sky, and wishes they would stay there. And yet he has emerged alive, despite the Dung Lord, despite the white shirts, despite old age, he has once again clawed his way down from the heavens.

Tranh straightens. Men stir woks of noodles and pull steamers of *baozi* from their bamboo rounds. Gray high-protein U-Tex rice gruel fills the air with the scents of rotting fish and fatty acid oils. Tranh's stomach knots with hunger and a pasty saliva coats his mouth, all that his dehydrated body can summon at the scent of food. Devil cats swirl around the vendors' legs like sharks, hoping for morsels to drop, hoping for theft opportunities. Their shimmering chameleon-like forms flit and flicker, showing calico and Siamese and orange tabby markings before fading against the backdrop of concrete and crowding hungry people that they brush against. The woks burn hard and bright with green-tinged methane, giving off new scents as rice noodles splash into hot oil. Tranh forces himself to turn away.

He shoves through the press, dragging his hemp bag along with him, ignoring who it hits and who shouts after him. Incident victims crouch in the doorways, waving severed limbs and begging from others who have a little more. Men squat on tea stools and watch the day's swelter build as they smoke tiny rolled cigarettes of scavenged gold leaf tobacco and share them from lip to lip. Women converse in knots, nervously fingering yellow cards as they wait for white shirts to appear and stamp their renewals.

Yellow card people as far as the eye can see: an entire race of people, fled to the great Thai Kingdom from Malaya where they were suddenly unwelcome. A fat clot of refugees placed under the authority of the Environment Ministry's white shirts as if they were nothing but another invasive species to be managed, like cibiscosis, blister rust, and genehack weevil. Yellow cards, yellow men. *Huang ren* all around, and Tranh is late for his one opportunity to climb out of their mass. One opportunity in all his months as a yellow card Chinese refugee. And now he is late. He squeezes past a rat seller, swallowing another rush of saliva at the scent of roasted flesh, and rushes down an alley to the water pump. He stops short.

Ten others stand in line before him: old men, young women, mothers, boys.

He slumps. He wants to rage at the setback. If he had the energy—if he had eaten well yesterday or the day before or even the day before that he would scream, would throw his hemp bag on the street and stamp on it until it turned to dust—but his calories are too few. It is just another opportunity squandered, thanks to the ill luck of the stairwells. He should have given the last of his baht to the Dung Lord and rented body-space in an apartment with windows facing east so that he could see the rising sun, and wake early.

But he was cheap. Cheap with his money. Cheap with his future. How many times did he tell his sons that spending money to make more money was perfectly acceptable? But the timid yellow card refugee that he has become counseled him to save his baht. Like an ignorant peasant mouse he clutched his cash to himself and slept in pitch-black stairwells. He should have stood like a tiger and braved the night curfew and the ministry's white shirts and their black batons... And now he is late and reeks of the stairwells and stands behind ten others, all of whom must drink and fill a bucket and brush their teeth with the brown water of the Chao Phraya River.

There was a time when he demanded punctuality of his employees, of his wife, of his sons and concubines, but it was when he owned a spring-wound wristwatch and could gaze at its steady sweep of minutes and hours. Every so often, he could wind its tiny spring, and listen to it tick, and lash his sons for their lazy attitudes. He has become old and slow and stupid or he would have foreseen this. Just as he should have foreseen the rising militancy of the Green

Headbands. When did his mind become so slack?

One by one, the other refugees finish their ablutions. A mother with gap teeth and blooms of gray *fa' gan* fringe behind her ears tops her bucket, and Tranh slips forward.

He has no bucket. Just the bag. The precious bag. He hangs it beside the pump and wraps his sarong more tightly around his hollow hips before he squats under the pump head. With a bony arm he yanks the pump's handle. Ripe brown water gushes over him. The river's blessing. His skin droops off his body with the weight of the water, sagging like the flesh of a shaved cat. He opens his mouth and drinks the gritty water, rubs his teeth with a finger, wondering what protozoa he may swallow. It doesn't matter. He trusts luck, now. It's all he has.

Children watch him bathe his old body while their mothers scavenge through PurCal mango peels and Red Star tamarind hulls hoping to find some bit of fruit not tainted with cibiscosis.111mt.6... Or is it 111mt.7? Or mt.8? There was a time when he knew all the bioengineered plagues which ailed them. Knew when a crop was about to fail, and whether new seedstock had been ripped. Profited from the knowledge by filling his clipper ships with the right seeds and produce. But that was a lifetime ago.

His hands are shaking as he opens his bag and pulls out his clothes. Is it old age or excitement that makes him tremble? Clean clothes. Good clothes. A rich man's white linen suit.

The clothes were not his, but now they are, and he has kept them safe. Safe for this opportunity, even when he desperately wanted to sell them for cash or wear them as his other clothes turned to rags. He drags the trousers up his bony legs, stepping out of his sandals and balancing one foot at a time. He begins buttoning the shirt, hurrying his fingers as a voice in his head reminds him that time is slipping away.

"Selling those clothes? Going to parade them around until someone with meat on his bones buys them off you?"

Tranh glances up—he shouldn't need to look; he should know the voice—and yet he looks anyway. He can't help himself. Once he was a tiger. Now he is nothing but a frightened little mouse who jumps and twitches at every hint of danger. And there it is: Ma. Standing before him, beaming. Fat and beaming. As vital as a wolf.

Ma grins. "You look like a wire-frame mannequin at Palawan Plaza."

"I wouldn't know. I can't afford to shop there." Tranh keeps putting on his clothes.

"Those are nice enough to come from Palawan. How did you get them?" Tranh doesn't answer.

"Who are you fooling? Those clothes were made for a man a thousand times your size."

"We can't all be fat and lucky." Tranh's voice comes out as a whisper. Did he always whisper? Was he always such a rattletrap corpse whispering and sighing at every threat? He doesn't think so. But it's hard for him to remember what a tiger should sound like. He tries again, steadying his voice. "We can't all be as lucky as Ma Ping who lives on the top floors with the Dung King himself." His words still come out like reeds shushing against concrete.

"Lucky?" Ma laughs. So young. So pleased with himself. "I earn my fate. Isn't that what you always used to tell me? That luck has nothing to do with success? That men make their own luck?" He laughs again. "And now look at you."

Tranh grits his teeth. "Better men than you have fallen." Still the awful timid whisper.

"And better men than you are on the rise." Ma's fingers dart to his wrist. They stroke a wristwatch, a fine chronograph, ancient, gold and diamonds—Rolex. From an earlier time. A different place. A different world. Tranh stares stupidly, like a hypnotized snake. He can't tear his eyes away.

Ma smiles lazily. "You like it? I found it in an antique shop near Wat Rajapradit. It seemed familiar."

Tranh's anger rises. He starts to reply, then shakes his head and says nothing. Time is passing. He fumbles with his final buttons, pulls on the coat and runs his fingers through the last surviving strands of his lank gray hair. If he had a comb... He grimaces. It is stupid to wish. The clothes are enough. They have to be.

Ma laughs. "Now you look like a Big Name."

Ignore him, says the voice inside Tranh's head. Tranh pulls his last paltry baht out of his hemp bag—the money he saved by sleeping in the stairwells, and which has now made him so late—and shoves it into his pockets.

"You seem rushed. Do you have an appointment somewhere?"

Tranh shoves past, trying not to flinch as he squeezes around Ma's bulk.

Ma calls after him, laughing. "Where are you headed, Mr. Big Name? Mr. Three Prosperities! Do you have some intelligence you'd like to share with the rest of us?"

Others look up at the shout: hungry yellow card faces, hungry yellow card mouths. Yellow card people as far as the eye can see, and all of them looking at him now. Incident survivors. Men. Women. Children. Knowing him, now. Recognizing his legend. With a change of clothing and a single shout he has risen from obscurity. Their mocking calls pour down like a monsoon rain:

"*Wei!* Mr. Three Prosperities! Nice shirt!"

"Share a smoke, Mr. Big Name!"

"Where are you going so fast all dressed up?"

"Getting married?"

"Getting a tenth wife?"

"Got a job?"

"Mr. Big Name! Got a job for me?"

"Where you going? Maybe we should all follow Old Multinational!"

Tranh's neck prickles. He shakes off the fear. Even if they follow it will be too late for them to take advantage. For the first time in half a year, the advantage of skills and knowledge are on his side. Now there is only time.

* * *

He jogs through Bangkok's morning press as bicycles and cycle rickshaws and spring-wound scooters stream past. Sweat drenches him. It soaks his good shirt, damps even his jacket. He takes it off and slings it over an arm. His gray hair clings to his egg-bald liver-spotted skull, waterlogged. He pauses every other block to walk and recover his breath as his shins begin to ache and his breath comes in gasps and his old man's heart hammers in his chest.

He should spend his baht on a cycle rickshaw but he can't make himself do it. He is late. But perhaps he is too late? And if he is too late, the extra baht will be wasted and he will starve tonight. But then, what good is a suit soaked with sweat?

Clothes make the man, he told his sons; the first impression is the most important. Start well, and you start ahead. Of course you can win someone with your skills and your knowledge but people are animals first. Look good. Smell good. Satisfy their first senses. Then when they are well-disposed toward you, make your proposal.

Isn't that why he beat Second Son when he came home with a red tattoo of a tiger on his shoulder, as though he was some calorie gangster? Isn't that why he paid a tooth doctor to twist even his daughters' teeth with cultured bamboo and rubber curves from Singapore so that they were as straight as razors?

And isn't that why the Green Headbands in Malaya hated us Chinese? Because we looked so good? Because we looked so rich? Because we spoke so well and worked so hard when they were lazy and we sweated every day?

Tranh watches a pack of spring-wound scooters flit past, all of them Thai-Chinese manufactured. Such clever fast things—a megajoule kink-spring and a flywheel, pedals and friction brakes to regather kinetic energy. And all their factories owned one hundred percent by Chiu Chow Chinese. And yet no Chiu Chow blood runs in the gutters of this country. These Chiu Chow Chinese are loved, despite the fact that they came to the Thai Kingdom as *farang*.

If we had assimilated in Malaya like the Chiu Chow did here, would we have survived?

Tranh shakes his head at the thought. It would have been impossible. His clan would have had to convert to Islam as well, and forsake all their ancestors in Hell. It would have been impossible. Perhaps it was his people's karma to be destroyed. To stand tall and dominate the cities of Penang and Malacca and all the western coast of the Malayan Peninsula for a brief while, and then to die.

Clothes make the man. Or kill him. Tranh understands this, finally. A white tailored suit from Hwang Brothers is nothing so much as a target. An antique piece of gold mechanization swinging on your wrist is nothing if not bait. Tranh wonders if his sons' perfect teeth still lie in the ashes of Three Prosperities' warehouses, if their lovely time pieces now attract sharks and crabs in the holds of his scuttled clipper ships.

He should have known. Should have seen the rising tide of bloodthirsty subsects and intensifying nationalism. Just as the man he followed two months ago should have known that fine clothes were no protection. A man in good clothes, a yellow card to boot, should have known that he was nothing but a bit of bloodied bait before a Komodo lizard. At least the stupid melon didn't bleed on his fancy clothes when the white shirts were done with him. That one had no habit of survival. He forgot that he was no longer a Big Name.

But Tranh is learning. As he once learned tides and depth charts, markets and bioengineered plagues, profit maximization and how to balance the dragon's gate, he now learns from the devil cats who molt and fade from sight, who flee their hunters at the first sign of danger. He learns from the crows and kites who live so well on scavenge. These are the animals he must emulate. He must discard the reflexes of a tiger. There are no tigers except in zoos. A tiger is always hunted and killed. But a small animal, a scavenging animal, has a chance to strip the bones of a tiger and walk away with the last Hwang Brothers suit that will ever cross the border from Malaya. With the Hwang clan all dead and the Hwang patterns all burned, nothing is left except memories and antiques, and one scavenging old man who knows the power and the peril of good appearance.

An empty cycle rickshaw coasts past. The rickshaw man looks back at Tranh, eyes questioning, attracted by the Hwang Brothers fabrics that flap off Tranh's skinny frame. Tranh raises a tentative hand. The cycle rickshaw slows.

Is it a good risk? To spend his last security so frivolously?

There was a time when he sent clipper fleets across the ocean to Chennai with great stinking loads of durians because he guessed that the Indians had not had time to plant resistant crop strains before the new blister rust mutations swept over them. A time when he bought black tea and sandalwood from the river men on the chance that he could sell it in the South. Now he can't decide if he should ride or walk. What a pale man he has become! Sometimes he wonders if he is actually a hungry ghost, trapped between worlds and unable to escape one way or the other.

The cycle rickshaw coasts ahead, the rider's blue jersey shimmering in the tropic sun, waiting for a decision. Tranh waves him away. The rickshaw man stands on his pedals, sandals flapping against calloused heels and accelerates.

Panic seizes Tranh. He raises his hand again, chases after the rickshaw. "Wait!" His voice comes out as a whisper.

The rickshaw slips into traffic, joining bicycles and the massive shambling shapes of elephantine megodonts. Tranh lets his hand fall, obscurely grateful that the rickshaw man hasn't heard, that the decision of spending his last baht has been made by some force larger than himself.

All around him, the morning press flows. Hundreds of children in their sailor suit uniforms stream through school gates. Saffron-robed monks stroll under the shade of wide black umbrellas. A man with a conical bamboo hat watches him and then mutters quietly to his friend. They both study him. A trickle of fear runs up Tranh's spine.

They are all around him, as they were in Malacca. In his own mind, he calls them foreigners, *farang*. And yet it is he who is the foreigner here. The creature that doesn't belong. And they know it. The women hanging sarongs on the wires of their balconies, the men sitting barefoot while they drink sugared coffee. The fish sellers and curry men. They all know it, and Tranh can barely control his terror.

Bangkok is not Malacca, he tells himself. Bangkok is not Penang. We have no wives, or gold wristwatches with diamonds, or clipper fleets to steal anymore. Ask the snakeheads who abandoned me in the leech jungles of the border. They have all my wealth. I have nothing. I am no tiger. I am safe.

For a few seconds he believes it. But then a teak-skinned boy chops the top off a coconut with a rusty machete and offers it to Tranh with a smile and it's all Tranh can do not to scream and run.

Bangkok is not Malacca. They will not burn your warehouses or slash your clerks into chunks of shark bait. He wipes sweat off his face. Perhaps he should have waited to wear the suit. It draws too much attention. There are too many people looking at him. Better to fade like a devil cat and slink across the city in safe anonymity, instead of strutting around like a peacock.

Slowly the streets change from palm-lined boulevards to the open wastelands of the new foreigner's quarter. Tranh hurries toward the river, heading deeper into the manufacturing empire of white *farang*.

Gweilo, yang guizi, farang. So many words in so many languages for these translucent-skinned sweating monkeys. Two generations ago when the petroleum ran out and the *gweilo* factories shut down, everyone assumed they were gone for good. And now they are back. The monsters of the past returned, with new toys and new technologies. The nightmares his mother threatened him with, invading Asiatic coasts. Demons truly; never dead.

And he goes to worship them: the ilk of AgriGen and PurCal with their monopolies on U-Tex rice and Total Nutrient Wheat; the blood-brothers of the bioengineers who gene-ripped devil cats from storybook inspiration and set them loose in the world to breed and breed and breed; the sponsors of the Intellectual Property Police who used to board his clipper fleets in search of IP infringements, hunting like wolves for unstamped calories and gene-ripped grains as though their engineered plagues of cibiscosis and blister rust weren't enough to keep their profits high…

Ahead of him, a crowd has formed. Tranh frowns. He starts to run, then forces himself back to a walk. Better not to waste his calories, now. A line has already formed in front of the foreign devil Tennyson Brothers' factory. It stretches almost a *li*, snaking around the corner, past the bicycle gear logo in the wrought iron gate of Sukhumvit Research Corporation, past the intertwined dragons of PurCal East Asia, and past Mishimoto & Co., the clever Japanese fluid dynamics company that Tranh once sourced his clipper designs from.

Mishimoto is full of windup import workers, they say. Full of illegal gene-ripped bodies that walk and talk and totter about in their herky-jerky way—and take rice from real men's bowls. Creatures with as many as eight arms like the Hindu gods, creatures with no legs so they cannot run away, creatures with eyes as large as teacups which can only see a bare few feet ahead of them but inspect everything with enormous magnified curiosity. But no one can see inside, and if the Environment Ministry's white shirts know, then the clever Japanese are paying them well to ignore their crimes against biology and religion. It is perhaps the only thing a good Buddhist and a good Muslim and even the *farang* Grahamite Christians can agree on: windups have no souls.

When Tranh bought Mishimoto's clipper ships so long ago, he didn't care. Now he wonders if behind their high gates, windup monstrosities labor while yellow cards stand outside and beg.

Tranh trudges down the line. Policemen with clubs and spring guns patrol the hopefuls, making jokes about *farang* who wish to work for *farang*. Heat beats down, merciless on the men lined up before the gate.

"Wah! You look like a pretty bird with those clothes."

Tranh starts. Li Shen and Hu Laoshi and Lao Xia stand in the line, clustered together. A trio of old men as pathetic as himself. Hu waves a newly rolled ciga-rette in invitation, motioning him to join them. Tranh nearly shakes at the sight of the tobacco, but forces himself to refuse it. Three times Hu offers, and finally Tranh allows himself to accept, grateful that Hu is in earnest, and wondering where Hu has found this sudden wealth. But then, Hu has a little more strength than the rest of them. A cart man earns more if he works as fast as Hu.

Tranh wipes the sweat off his brow. "A lot of applicants."

They all laugh at Tranh's dismay.

Hu lights the cigarette for Tranh. "You thought you knew a secret, maybe?"

Tranh shrugs and draws deeply, passes the cigarette to Lao Xia. "A rumor. Potato God said his elder brother's son had a promotion. I thought there might be a niche down below, in the slot the nephew left behind."

Hu grins. "That's where I heard it, too. 'Eee. He'll be rich. Manage fifteen clerks. Eee! He'll be rich.' I thought I might be one of the fifteen."

"At least the rumor was true," Lao Xia says. "And not just Potato God's nephew promoted, either." He scratches the back of his head, a convulsive movement like a dog fighting fleas. *Fa' gan's* gray fringe stains the crooks of his elbows and peeps from the sweaty pockets behind his ears where his hair has receded. He sometimes jokes about it: nothing a little money can't fix. A good joke. But today he is scratching and the skin behind his ears is cracked and raw. He no-tices everyone watching and yanks his hand down. He grimaces and passes the cigarette to Li Shen.

"How many positions?" Tranh asks.

"Three. Three clerks."

Tranh grimaces. "My lucky number."

Li Shen peers down the line with his bottle-thick glasses. "Too many of us, I think, even if your lucky number is 555."

Lao Xia laughs. "Amongst the four of us, there are already too many." He taps the man standing in line just ahead of them. "Uncle. What was your profession before?" The stranger looks back, surprised. He was a distinguished gentleman, once, by his scholar's collar, by his fine leather shoes now scarred and blackened with scavenged charcoal. "I taught physics."

Lao Xia nods. "You see? We're all overqualified. I oversaw a rubber plantation. Our own professor has degrees in fluid dynamics and materials design. Hu was a fine doctor. And then there is our friend of the Three Prosperities. Not a trading company at all. More like a multi-national." He tastes the words. Says them again, "Multi-national." A strange, powerful, seductive sound.

Tranh ducks his head, embarrassed. "You're too kind."

"*Fang pi.*" Hu takes a drag on his cigarette, keeps it moving. "You were the richest of us all. And now here we are, old men scrambling for young men's jobs. Every one of us ten-thousand-times overqualified." The man behind them interjects, "I was executive legal council for Standard & Commerce."

Lao Xia makes a face. "Who cares, dog fucker? You're nothing now."

The banking lawyer turns away, affronted. Lao Xia grins, sucks hard on the hand-rolled cigarette and passes it again to Tranh. Hu nudges Tranh's elbow as he starts to take a puff. "Look! There goes old Ma."

Tranh looks over, exhales smoke sharply. For a moment he thinks Ma has followed him, but no. It is just coincidence. They are in the *farang* factory district. Ma works for the foreign devils, balancing their books. A kink-spring company. Springlife. Yes, Springlife. It is natural that Ma should be here, comfortably riding to work behind a sweating cycle-rickshaw man.

"Ma Ping," Li Shen says. "I heard he's living on the top floor now. Up there with the Dung Lord himself."

Tranh scowls. "I fired him, once. Ten thousand years ago. Lazy and an embezzler."

"He's so fat."

"I've seen his wife," Hu says. "And his sons. They both have fat on them. They eat meat every night. The boys are fatter than fat. Full of U-Tex proteins."

"You're exaggerating."

"Fatter than us."

Lao Xia scratches a rib. "Bamboo is fatter than you."

Tranh watches Ma Ping open a factory door and slip inside. The past is past. Dwelling on the past is madness. There is nothing for him there. There are no wristwatches, no concubines, no opium pipes or jade sculptures of Quan Yin's merciful form. There are no pretty clipper ships slicing into port with fortunes in their holds. He shakes his head and offers the nearly spent cigarette to Hu so that he can recover the last tobacco for later use. There is nothing for him in the past. Ma is in the past. Three Prosperities Trading Company is the past. The sooner he remembers this, the sooner he will climb out of this awful hole.

From behind him, a man calls out, "*Wei!* Baldy! When did you cut the line? Go to the back! You line up, like the rest of us!"

"Line up?" Lao Xia shouts back. "Don't be stupid!" He waves at the line ahead. "How many hundreds are ahead of us? It won't make any difference where he stands." Others begin to attend the man's complaint. Complain as well. "Line up! *Pai dui! Pai dui!*" The disturbance increases and police start down the line, casually swinging their batons. They aren't white shirts, but they have no love for hungry yellow cards.

Tranh makes placating motions to the crowd and Lao Xia. "Of course. Of course. I'll line up. It's of no consequence." He makes his farewells and plods his way down the winding yellow card snake, seeking its distant tail.

Everyone is dismissed long before he reaches it.

* * *

A scavenging night. A starving night. Tranh hunts through dark alleys avoiding the vertical prison heat of the towers. Devil cats seethe and scatter ahead of him in rippling waves. The lights of the methane lamps flicker, burn low and snuff themselves, blackening the city. Hot velvet darkness fetid with rotting fruit swaddles him. The heavy humid air sags. Still swelter darkness. Empty market stalls. On a street corner, theater men turn in stylized cadences to stories of Ravana. On a thoroughfare, swingshift megodonts shuffle homeward like gray mountains, their massed shadows led by the gold trim glitter of union handlers.

In the alleys, children with bright silver knives hunt unwary yellow cards and drunken Thais, but Tranh is wise to their feral ways. A year ago, he would not have seen them, but he has the paranoid's gift of survival, now. Creatures like them are no worse than sharks: easy to predict, easy to avoid. It is not these obviously feral hunters who churn Tranh's guts with fear, it is the chameleons, the everyday people who work and shop and smile and *wai* so pleasantly—and riot without warning—who terrify Tranh.

He picks through the trash heaps, fighting devil cats for signs of food, wishing he was fast enough to catch and kill one of those nearly invisible felines. Picking up discarded mangos, studying them carefully with his old man's eyes, holding them close and then far away, sniffing at them, feeling their blister rusted exteriors and then tossing them aside when they show red mottle in their guts. Some of them still smell good, but even crows won't accept such a taint. They would eagerly peck apart a bloated corpse but they will not feed on blister rust.

Down the street, the Dung Lord's lackeys shovel the day's animal leavings into sacks and throw them into tricycle carriers: the night harvest. They watch him suspiciously. Tranh keeps his eyes averted, avoiding challenge, and scuffles on. He has nothing to cook on an illegally stolen shit fire anyway, and nowhere to sell manure on the black market. The Dung Lord's monopoly is too strong. Tranh wonders how it might be to find a place in the dung shoveler's union, to know that his survival was guaranteed feeding the composters of Bangkok's methane reclamation plants. But it is an opium dream; no yellow card can slither into that closed club.

Tranh lifts another mango and freezes. He bends low, squinting. Pushes aside broadsheet complaints against the Ministry of Trade and handbills calling for a new gold-sheathed River Wat. He pushes aside black slime banana peels and burrows into the garbage. Below it all, stained and torn but still legible, he finds a portion of what was once a great advertising board that perhaps stood over this marketplace:—*ogistics. Shipping. Tradin*—and behind the words, the glorious silhouette of Dawn Star: one part of Three Prosperities' tri-clipper logo, running before the wind as fast and sleek as a shark: a high-tech image of palm-oil spun polymers and sails as sharp and white as a gull's.

Tranh turns his face away, overcome. It's like unearthing a grave and finding himself within. His pride. His blindness. From a time when he thought he might compete with the foreign devils and become a shipping magnate. A Li Ka Shing or a reborn Richard Kuok for the New Expansion. Rebuild the pride of Nanyang Chinese shipping and trading. And here, like a slap in the face, a portion of his ego, buried in rot and blister rust and devil cat urine.

He searches around, pawing for more portions of the sign, wondering if anyone treadles a phone call to that old phone number, if the secretary whose wages he once paid is still at his desk, working for a new master, a native Malay perhaps, with impeccable pedigree and religion. Wondering if the few clippers he failed to scuttle still ply the seas and islands of the archipelago. He forces himself to stop his search. Even if he had the money he would not treadle that number. Would not waste the calories. Could not stand the loss again.

He straightens, scattering devil cats who have slunk close. There is nothing here in this market except rinds and unshoveled dung. He has wasted his calories once again. Even the cockroaches and the blood beetles have been eaten. If he searches for a dozen hours, he will still find nothing. Too many people have come before, picking at these bones.

* * *

Three times he hides from white shirts as he makes his way home, three times ducking into shadows as they strut past. Cringing as they wander close, cursing his white linen suit that shows so clearly in darkness. By the third time, superstitious fear runs hot in his veins. His rich man's clothes seem to attract the patrols of the Environment Ministry, seem to hunger for the wearer's death. Black batons twirl from casual hands no more than inches away from his face. Spring guns glitter silver in the darkness. His hunters stand so close that he can count the wicked bladed disk cartridges in their jute bandoliers. A white shirt pauses and pisses in the alley where Tranh crouches, and only fails to see him because his partner stands on the street and wants to check the permits of the dung gatherers.

Each time, Tranh stifles his panicked urge to tear off his too-rich clothes and sink into safe anonymity. It is only a matter of time before the white shirts catch him. Before they swing their black clubs and make his Chinese skull a mash of blood and bone. Better to run naked through the hot night than strut like a peacock and die. And yet he cannot quite abandon the cursed suit. Is it pride? Is it stupidity? He keeps it though, even as its arrogant cut turns his bowels watery with fear.

By the time he reaches home, even the gas lights on the main thoroughfares of Sukhumvit Road and Rama IV are blackened. Outside the Dung Lord's tower, street stalls still burn woks for the few laborers lucky enough to have night work and curfew dispensations. Pork tallow candles flicker on the tables. Noodles splash into hot woks with a sizzle. White shirts stroll past, their eyes on the seated yellow cards, ensuring that none of the foreigners brazenly sleep in the open air and sully the sidewalks with their snoring presence.

Tranh joins the protective loom of the towers, entering the nearly extra-territorial safety of the Dung Lord's influence. He stumbles toward the doorways and the swelter of the highrise, wondering how high he will be forced to climb before he can shove a niche for himself on the stairwells.

"You didn't get the job, did you?"

Tranh cringes at the voice. It's Ma Ping again, sitting at a sidewalk table, a bottle of Mekong whiskey beside his hand. His face is flushed with alcohol, as bright as a red paper lantern. Half-eaten plates of food lie strewn around his table. Enough to feed five others, easily.

Images of Ma war in Tranh's head: the young clerk he once sent packing for being too clever with an abacus, the man whose son is fat, the man who got out early, the man who begged to be rehired at Three Prosperities, the man who now struts around Bangkok with Tranh's last precious possession on his wrist—the one item that even the snakeheads didn't steal. Tranh thinks that truly fate is cruel, placing him in such proximity to one he once considered so far beneath him.

Despite his intention to show bravado, Tranh's words come out as a mousy whisper. "What do you care?"

Ma shrugs, pours whiskey for himself. "I wouldn't have noticed you in the line, without that suit." He nods at Tranh's sweat-damp clothing. "Good idea to dress up. Too far back in line, though."

Tranh wants to walk away, to ignore the arrogant whelp, but Ma's leavings of steamed bass and *laap* and U-Tex rice noodles lie tantalizingly close. He thinks he smells pork and can't help salivating. His gums ache for the idea that he could chew meat again and he wonders if his teeth would accept the awful luxury...

Abruptly, Tranh realizes that he has been staring. That he has stood for some time, ogling the scraps of Ma's meal. And Ma is watching him. Tranh flushes and starts to turn away.

Ma says, "I didn't buy your watch to spite you, you know."

Tranh stops short. "Why then?"

Ma's fingers stray to the gold and diamond bauble, then seem to catch themselves. He reaches for his whiskey glass instead. "I wanted a reminder." He takes a swallow of liquor and sets the glass back amongst his piled plates with the deliberate care of a drunk. He grins sheepishly. His fingers are again stroking the watch, a guilty furtive movement. "I wanted a reminder. Against ego."

Tranh spits. "*Fang pi.*"

Ma shakes his head vigorously. "No! It's true." He pauses. "Anyone can fall. If the Three Prosperities can fall, then I can. I wanted to remember that." He takes another pull on his whiskey. "You were right to fire me."

Tranh snorts. "You didn't think so then."

"I was angry. I didn't know that you'd saved my life, then." He shrugs. "I would never have left Malaya if you hadn't fired me. I would never have seen the Incident coming. I would have had too much invested in staying." Abruptly, he pulls himself upright and motions for Tranh to join him. "Come. Have a drink. Have some food. I owe you that much. You saved my life. I've repaid you poorly. Sit."

Tranh turns away. "I don't despise myself so much."

"Do you love face so much that you can't take a man's food? Don't be stuck in your bones. I don't care if you hate me. Just take my food. Curse me later, when your belly is full."

Tranh tries to control his hunger, to force himself to walk away, but he can't. He knows men who might have enough face to starve before accepting Ma's scraps, but he isn't one of them. A lifetime ago, he might have been. But the humiliations of his new life have taught him much about who he really is. He has no sweet illusions, now. He sits. Ma beams and pushes his half-eaten dishes across the table.

Tranh thinks he must have done something grave in a former life to merit this humiliation, but still he has to fight the urge to bury his hands in the oily food and eat with bare fingers. Finally, the owner of the sidewalk stall brings a pair of chopsticks for the noodles, and fork and spoon for the rest. Noodles and ground pork slide down his throat. He tries to chew but as soon as the food touches his tongue he gulps it down. More food follows. He lifts a plate to his lips, shoveling down the last of Ma's leavings. Fish and lank coriander and hot thick oil slip down like blessings.

"Good. Good." Ma waves at the night stall man and a whiskey glass is quickly rinsed and handed to him.

The sharp scent of liquor floats around Ma like an aura as he pours. Tranh's chest tightens at the scent. Oil coats his chin where he has made a mess in his haste. He wipes his mouth against his arm, watching the amber liquid splash into the glass.

Tranh once drank Cognac: XO. Imported by his own clippers. Fabulously expensive stuff with its shipping costs. A flavor of the foreign devils from before the Contraction. A ghost from utopian history, reinvigorated by the new Expansion and his own realization that the world was once again growing smaller. With new hull designs and polymer advances, his clipper ships navigated the globe and returned with the stuff of legends. And his Malay buyers were happy to purchase it, whatever their religion. What a profit that had been. He forces down the thought as Ma shoves the glass across to Tranh and then raises his own in toast. It is in the past. It is all in the past.

They drink. The whiskey burns warm in Tranh's belly, joining the chilis and fish and pork and the hot oil of the fried noodles.

"It really is too bad you didn't get that job."

Tranh grimaces. "Don't gloat. Fate has a way of balancing itself. I've learned that."

Ma waves a hand. "I don't gloat. There are too many of us, that's the truth. You were ten-thousand-times qualified for that job. For any job." He takes a sip of his whiskey, peers over its rim at Tranh. "Do you remember when you called me a lazy cockroach?"

Tranh shrugs, he can't take his eyes off the whiskey bottle. "I called you worse than that." He waits to see if Ma will refill his cup again. Wondering how rich he is, and how far this largesse will go. Hating that he plays beggar to a boy he once refused to keep as a clerk, and who now lords over him...and who now, in a show of face, pours Tranh's whiskey to the top, letting it spill over in an amber cascade under the flickering light of the candles.

Ma finishes pouring, stares at the puddle he has created. "Truly the world is turned upside down. The young lord over the old. The Malays pinch out the Chinese. And the foreign devils return to our shores like bloated fish after a *ku-shui* epidemic." Ma smiles. "You need to keep your ears up, and be aware of opportunities. Not like all those old men out on the sidewalk, waiting for hard labor. Find a new niche. That's what I did. That's why I've got my job."

Tranh grimaces. "You came at a more fortuitous time." He rallies, emboldened by a full belly and the liquor warming his face and limbs. "Anyway, you shouldn't be too proud. You still stink of mother's milk as far as I'm concerned, living in the Dung Lord's tower. You're only the Lord of Yellow Cards. And what is that, really? You haven't climbed as high as my ankles, yet, Mr. Big Name."

Ma's eyes widen. He laughs. "No. Of course not. Someday, maybe. But I am trying to learn from you." He smiles slightly and nods at Tranh's decrepit state. "Everything except this postscript."

"Is it true there are crank fans on the top floors? That it's cool up there?"

Ma glances up at the looming highrise. "Yes. Of course. And men with the calories to wind them as well. And they haul water up for us, and men act as ballast on the elevator—up and down all day—doing favors for the Dung Lord." He laughs and pours more whiskey, motions Tranh to drink. "You're right though. It's nothing, really. A poor palace, truly.

"But it doesn't matter now. My family moves tomorrow. We have our residence permits. Tomorrow when I get paid again, we're moving out. No more yellow card for us. No more payoffs to the Dung Lord's lackeys. No more problems with the white shirts. It's all set with the Environment Ministry. We turn in our yellow cards and become Thai. We're going to be immigrants. Not just some invasive species, anymore." He raises his glass. "It's why I'm celebrating."

Tranh scowls. "You must be pleased." He finishes his drink, sets the tumbler down with a thud. "Just don't forget that the nail that stands up also gets pounded down."

Ma shakes his head and grins, his eyes whiskey bright. "Bangkok isn't Malacca."

"And Malacca wasn't Bali. And then they came with their machetes and their spring guns and they stacked our heads in the gutters and sent our bodies and blood down the river to Singapore."

Ma shrugs. "It's in the past." He waves to the man at the wok, calling for more food. "We have to make a home here, now."

"You think you can? You think some white shirt won't nail your hide to his door? You can't make them like us. Our luck's against us, here."

"Luck? When did Mr. Three Prosperities get so superstitious?"

Ma's dish arrives, tiny crabs crisp-fried, salted and hot with oil for Ma and Tranh to pick at with chopsticks and crunch between their teeth, each one no bigger than the tip of Tranh's pinkie. Ma plucks one out and crunches it down. "When did Mr. Three Prosperities get so weak? When you fired me, you said I made my own luck. And now you tell me you don't have any?" He spits on the sidewalk. "I've seen windups with more will to survive than you."

"*Fang pi.*"

"No! It's true! There's a Japanese windup girl in the bars where my boss goes." Ma leans forward. "She looks like a real woman. And she does disgusting things." He grins. "Makes your cock hard. But you don't hear her complaining about luck. Every white shirt in the city would pay to dump her in the methane composters and she's still up in her highrise, dancing every night, in front of everyone. Her whole soulless body on display."

"It's not possible."

Ma shrugs. "Say so if you like. But I've seen her. And she isn't starving. She takes whatever spit and money come her way, and she survives. It doesn't matter about the white shirts or the Kingdom edicts or the Japan-haters or the religious fanatics; she's been dancing for months."

"How can she survive?"

"Bribes? Maybe some ugly *farang* who wallows in her filth? Who knows? No real girl would do what she does. It makes your heart stop. You forget she's a windup, when she does those things." He laughs, then glances at Tranh. "Don't talk to me about luck. There's not enough luck in the entire Kingdom to keep her alive this long. And we know it's not karma that keeps her alive. She has none."

Tranh shrugs noncommittally and shovels more crabs into his mouth.

Ma grins. "You know I'm right." He drains his whiskey glass and slams it down on the table. "We make our own luck! Our own fate. There's a windup in a public bar and I have a job with a rich *farang* who can't find his ass without my help! Of course I'm right!" He pours more whiskey. "Get over your self-pity, and climb out of your hole. The foreign devils don't worry about luck or fate, and look how they return to us, like a newly engineered virus! Even the Contraction didn't stop them. They're like another invasion of devil cats. But they make their own luck. I'm not even sure if karma exists for them. And if fools like these *farang* can succeed, than we Chinese can't be kept down for long. Men make their own luck, that's what you told me when you fired me. You said I'd made my own bad luck and only had myself to blame."

Tranh looks up at Ma. "Maybe I could work at your company." He grins, trying not to look desperate. "I could make money for your lazy boss."

Ma's eyes become hooded. "Ah. That's difficult. Difficult to say."

Tranh knows that he should take the polite rejection, that he should shut up. But even as a part of him cringes, his mouth opens again, pressing, pleading. "Maybe you need an assistant? To keep the books? I speak their devil language. I taught it to myself when I traded with them. I could be useful."

"There is little enough work for me."

"But if he is as stupid as you say—"

"Stupid, yes. But not such a stupid melon that he wouldn't notice another body in his office. Our desks are just so far apart." He makes a motion with his hands. "You think he would not notice some stick coolie-man squatting beside his computer treadle?"

"In his factory, then?"

But Ma is already shaking his head. "I would help you if I could. But the me-godont unions control the power, and the line inspector unions are closed to *farang*, no offense, and no one will accept that you are a materials scientist." He shakes his head. "No. There is no way."

"Any job. As a dung shoveler, even."

But Ma is shaking his head more vigorously now, and Tranh finally manages to control his tongue, to plug this diarrhea of begging. "Never mind. Never mind." He forces a grin. "I'm sure some work will turn up. I'm not worried." He takes the bottle of Mekong whiskey and refills Ma's glass, upending the bottle and finishing the whiskey despite Ma's protests.

Tranh raises his half-empty glass and toasts the young man who has bested him in all ways, before throwing back the last of the alcohol in one swift swallow. Under the table, nearly invisible devil cats brush against his bony legs, waiting for him to leave, hoping that he will be foolish enough to leave scraps.

* * *

Morning dawns. Tranh wanders the streets, hunting for a breakfast he cannot afford. He threads through market alleys redolent with fish and lank green coriander and bright flares of lemongrass. Durians lie in reeking piles, their spiky skins covered with red blister rust boils. He wonders if he can steal one. Their yellow surfaces are blotched and stained, but their guts are nutritious. He wonders how much blister rust a man can consume before falling into a coma.

"You want? Special deal. Five for five baht. Good, yes?"

The woman who screeches at him has no teeth, she smiles with her gums and repeats herself. "Five for five baht." She speaks Mandarin to him, recognizing him for their common heritage though she had the luck to be born in the Kingdom and he had the misfortune to be set down in Malaya. Chiu Chow Chinese, blessedly protected by her clan and King. Tranh suppresses envy.

"More like four for four." He makes a pun of the homonyms. *Sz* for *sz*. Four for death. "They've got blister rust."

She waves a hand sourly. "Five for five. They're still good. Better than good. Picked just before." She wields a gleaming machete and chops the durian in half, revealing the clean yellow slime of its interior with its fat gleaming pits. The sickly sweet scent of fresh durian boils up and envelopes them. "See! Inside good. Picked just in time. Still safe."

"I might buy one." He can't afford any. But he can't help replying. It feels too good to be seen as a buyer. It is his suit, he realizes. The Hwang Brothers have raised him in this woman's eyes. She wouldn't have spoken if not for the suit. Wouldn't have even started the conversation.

"Buy more! The more you buy, the more you save."

He forces a grin, wondering how to get away from the bargaining he should never have started. "I'm only one old man. I don't need so much."

"One skinny old man. Eat more. Get fat!"

She says this and they both laugh. He searches for a response, something to keep their comradely interaction alive, but his tongue fails him. She sees the helplessness in his eyes. She shakes her head. "Ah, grandfather. It is hard times for everyone. Too many of you all at once. No one thought it would get so bad down there."

Tranh ducks his head, embarrassed. "I've troubled you. I should go."

"Wait. Here." She offers him the durian half. "Take it."

"I can't afford it."

She makes an impatient gesture. "Take it. It's lucky for me to help someone from the old country." She grins. "And the blister rust looks too bad to sell to anyone else."

"You're kind. Buddha smile on you." But as he takes her gift he again notices the great durian pile behind her. All neatly stacked with their blotches and their bloody weals of blister rust. Just like stacked Chinese heads in Malacca: his wife and daughter mouths staring out at him, accusatory. He drops the durian and kicks it away, frantically scraping his hands on his jacket, trying to get the blood off his palms.

"Ai! You'll waste it!"

Tranh barely hears the woman's cry. He staggers back from the fallen durian, staring at its ragged surface. Its gut-spilled interior. He looks around wildly. He has to get out of the crowds. Has to get away from the jostling bodies and the durian reek that's all around, thick in his throat, gagging him. He puts a hand to his mouth and runs, clawing at the other shoppers, fighting through their press.

"Where you go? Come back! *Huilai!*" But the woman's words are quickly drowned. Tranh shoves through the throng, pushing aside women with shopping baskets full of white lotus root and purple eggplants, dodging farmers and their clattering bamboo hand-carts, twisting past tubs of squid and serpent head fish. He pelts down the market alley like a thief identified, scrambling and dodging, running without thought or knowledge of where he is going, but running anyway, desperate to escape the stacked heads of his family and countrymen.

He runs and runs.

And bursts into the open thoroughfare of Charoen Krung Road. Powdered dung dust and hot sunlight wash over him. Cycle rickshaws clatter past. Palms and squat banana trees shimmer green in the bright open air.

As quickly as it seized him, Tranh's panic fades. He stops short, hands on his knees, catching his breath and cursing himself. *Fool. Fool. If you don't eat, you die.* He straightens and tries to turn back but the stacked durians flash in his mind and he stumbles away from the alley, gagging again. He can't go back. Can't face those bloody piles. He doubles over and his stomach heaves but his empty guts bring up nothing but strings of drool.

Finally he wipes his mouth on a Hwang Brothers sleeve and forces himself to straighten and confront the foreign faces all around. The sea of foreigners that he must learn to swim amongst, and who all call him *farang*. It repels him to think of it. And to think that in Malacca, with twenty generations of family and clan well-rooted in that city, he was just as much an interloper. That his clan's esteemed history is nothing but a footnote for a Chinese expansion that has proven as transient as nighttime cool. That his people were nothing but an accidental spillage of rice on a map, now wiped up much more carefully than they were scattered down.

* * *

Tranh unloads U-Tex Brand RedSilks deep into the night, offerings to Potato God. A lucky job. A lucky moment, even if his knees have become loose and wobbly and feel as if they must soon give way. A lucky job, even if his arms are shaking from catching the heavy sacks as they come down off the megodonts. Tonight, he reaps not just pay but also the opportunity to steal from the harvest. Even if the RedSilk potatoes are small and harvested early to avoid a new sweep of scabis mold—the fourth genetic variation this year—they are still good. And their small size means their enhanced nutrition falls easily into his pockets.

Hu crouches above him, lowering down the potatoes. As the massive elephantine megodonts shuffle and grunt, waiting for their great wagons to be unloaded, Tranh catches Hu's offerings with his hand-hooks and lowers the sacks the last step to the ground. Hook, catch, swing and lower. Again and again and again.

He is not alone in his work. Women from the tower slums crowd around his ladder. They reach up and caress each sack as he lowers it to the ground. Their fingers quest along hemp and burlap, testing for holes, for slight tears, for lucky gifts. A thousand times they stroke his burdens, reverently following the seams, only drawing away when coolie men shove between them to heft the sacks and haul them to Potato God.

After the first hour of his work, Tranh's arms are shaking. After three, he can barely stand. He teeters on his creaking ladder as he lowers each new sack, and gasps and shakes his head to clear sweat from his eyes as he waits for the next one to come down.

Hu peers down from above. "Are you all right?"

Tranh glances warily over his shoulder. Potato God is watching, counting the sacks as they are carried into the warehouse. His eyes occasionally flick up to the wagons and trace across Tranh. Beyond him, fifty unlucky men watch silently from the shadows, any one of them far more observant than Potato God can ever be. Tranh straightens and reaches up to accept the next sack, trying not to think about the watching eyes. How politely they wait. How silent. How hungry. "I'm fine. Just fine."

Hu shrugs and pushes the next burlap load over the wagon's lip. Hu has the better place, but Tranh cannot resent it. One or the other must suffer. And Hu found the job. Hu has the right to the best place. To rest a moment before the next sack moves. After all, Hu collected Tranh for the job when he should have starved tonight. It is fair.

Tranh takes the sack and lowers it into the forest of waiting women's hands, releases his hooks with a twist, and drops the bag to the ground. His joints feel loose and rubbery, as if femur and tibia will skid apart at any moment. He is dizzy with heat, but he dares not ask to slow the pace.

Another potato sack comes down. Women's hands rise up like tangling strands of seaweed, touching, prodding, hungering. He cannot force them back. Even if he shouts at them they return. They are like devil cats; they cannot help themselves. He drops the sack the last few feet to the ground and reaches up for another as it comes over the wagon's lip.

As he hooks the sack, his ladder creaks and suddenly slides. It chatters down the side of the wagon, then catches abruptly. Tranh sways, juggling the potato sack, trying to regain his center of gravity. Hands are all around him, tugging at the bag, pulling, prodding. "Watch out—"

The ladder skids again. He drops like a stone. Women scatter as he plunges. He hits the ground and pain explodes in his knee. The potato sack bursts. For a moment he worries what Potato God will say but then he hears screams all around him. He rolls onto his back. Above him, the wagon is swaying, shuddering. People are shouting and fleeing. The megodont lunges forward and the wagon heaves. Bamboo ladders fall like rain, slapping the pavement with bright firecracker retorts. The beast reverses itself and the wagon skids past Tranh, grinding the ladders to splinters. It is impossibly fast, even with the wagon's weight still hampering it. The megodont's great maw opens and suddenly it is screaming, a sound as high and panicked as a human's.

All around them, other megodonts respond in a chorus. Their cacophony swamps the street. The megodont surges onto its hind legs, an explosion of muscle and velocity that breaks the wagon's traces and flips it like a toy. Men cartwheel from it, blossoms shaken from a cherry tree. Maddened, the beast rears again and kicks the wagon. Sends it skidding sidewise. It slams past Tranh, missing him by inches.

Tranh tries to rise but his leg won't work. The wagon smashes into a wall. Bamboo and teak crackle and explode, the wagon disintegrating as the megodont drags and kicks it, trying to win free completely. Tranh drags himself away from the flying wagon, hand over hand, hauling his useless leg behind him. All around, men are shouting instructions, trying to control the beast, but he doesn't look back. He focuses on the cobbles ahead, on getting out of reach. His leg won't work. It refuses him. It seems to hate him.

Finally he makes it into the shelter of a protective wall. He hauls himself upright. "I'm fine," he tells himself. "Fine." Gingerly he tests his leg, setting weight on it. It's wobbly, but he feels no real pain, not now. *"Mei wenti. Mei wenti,"* he whispers. "Not a problem. Just cracked it. Not a problem."

The men are still shouting and the megodont is still screaming, but all he can see is his brittle old knee. He lets go of the wall. Takes a step, testing his weight, and collapses like a shadow puppet with strings gone slack.

Gritting his teeth, he again hauls himself up off the cobbles. He props himself against the wall, massaging his knee and watching the bedlam. Men are throwing ropes over the back of the struggling megodont, pulling it down, immobilizing it, finally. More than a score of men are working to hobble it.

The wagon's frame has shattered completely and potatoes are spilled everywhere. A thick mash coats the ground. Women scramble on their knees, clawing through the mess, fighting with one another to hoard pulped tubers. They scrape it up from the street. Some of their scavenge is stained red, but no one seems to care. Their squabbling continues. The red bloom spreads. At the blossom's center, a man's trousers protrude from the muck

Tranh frowns. He drags himself upright again and hops on his one good leg toward the broken wagon. He catches up against its shattered frame, staring. Hu's body is a savage ruin, awash in megodont dung and potato mash. And now that Tranh is close, he can see that the struggling megodont's great gray feet are gory with his friend. Someone is calling for a doctor but it is halfhearted, a habit from a time when they were not yellow cards.

Tranh tests his weight again but his knee provides the same queer jointless failure. He catches up against the wagon's splintered planking and hauls himself back upright. He works the leg, trying to understand why it collapses. The knee bends, it doesn't even hurt particularly, but it will not support his weight. He tests it again, with the same result.

With the megodont restrained, order in the unloading area is restored. Hu's body is dragged aside. Devil cats gather near his blood pool, feline shimmers under methane glow. Their tracks pock the potato grime in growing numbers. More paw impressions appear in the muck, closing from all directions on Hu's discarded body.

Tranh sighs. So we all go, he thinks. We all die. Even those of us who took our aging treatments and our tiger penis and kept ourselves strong are subject to the Hell journey. He promises to burn money for Hu, to ease his way in the afterlife, then catches himself and remembers that he is not the man he was. That even paper Hell Money is out of reach. Potato God, disheveled and angry, comes and studies him. He frowns suspiciously. "Can you still work?"

"I can." Tranh tries to walk but stumbles once again and catches up against the wagon's shattered frame.

Potato God shakes his head. "I will pay you for the hours you worked." He waves to a young man, fresh and grinning from binding the megodont. "You! You're a quick one. Haul the rest of these sacks into warehouse."

Already, other workers are lining up and grabbing loads from within the broken wagon. As the new man comes out with his first sack, his eyes dart to Tranh and then flick away, hiding his relief at Tranh's incapacity.

Potato God watches with satisfaction and heads back to the warehouse. "Double pay," Tranh calls after Potato God's retreating back. "Give me double pay. I lost my leg for you."

The manager looks back at Tranh with pity, then glances at Hu's body and shrugs. It is an easy acquiescence. Hu will demand no reparation.

* * *

It is better to die insensate than to feel every starving inch of collapse; Tranh pours his leg-wreck money into a bottle of Mekong whiskey. He is old. He is broken. He is the last of his line. His sons are dead. His daughter mouths are long gone. His ancestors will live uncared for in the underworld with no one to burn incense or offer sweet rice to them.

How they must curse him.

He limps and stumbles and crawls through the sweltering night streets, one hand clutching the open bottle, the other scrabbling at doorways and walls and methane lampposts to keep himself upright. Sometimes his knee works; sometimes it fails him completely. He has kissed the streets a dozen times.

He tells himself that he is scavenging, hunting for the chance of sustenance. But Bangkok is a city of scavengers, and the crows and devil cats and children have all come before him. If he is truly lucky, he will encounter the white shirts and they will knock him into bloody oblivion, perhaps send him to meet the previous owner of this fine Hwang Brothers suit that now flaps ragged around his shins. The thought appeals to him.

An ocean of whiskey rolls in his empty belly and he is warm and happy and carefree for the first time since the Incident. He laughs and drinks and shouts for the white shirts, calling them paper tigers, calling them dog fuckers. He calls them to him. Casts baiting words so that any within earshot will find him irresistible. But the Environment Ministry's patrols must have other yellow cards to abuse, for Tranh wanders the green-tinged streets of Bangkok alone.

Never mind. It doesn't matter. If he cannot find white shirts to do the job, he will drown himself. He will go to the river and dump himself in its offal. Floating on river currents to the sea appeals to him. He will end in the ocean like his scuttled clipper ships and the last of his heirs. He takes a swig of whiskey, loses his balance and winds up on the ground once again, sobbing and cursing white shirts and green headbands, and wet machetes.

Finally he drags himself into a doorway to rest, holding his miraculously unbroken whiskey bottle with one feeble hand. He cradles it to himself like a last bit of precious jade, smiling and laughing that it is not broken. He wouldn't want to waste his life savings on the cobblestones.

He takes another swig. Stares at the methane lamps flickering overhead. Despair is the color of approved burn methane flickering green and gaseous, vinous in the dark. Green used to mean things like coriander and silk and jade and now all it means to him is bloodthirsty men with patriotic headbands and hungry scavenging nights. The lamps flicker. An entire green city. An entire city of despair.

Across the street, a shape scuttles, keeping to the shadows. Tranh leans forward, eyes narrowed. At first he takes it for a white shirt. But no. It is too furtive. It's a woman. A girl. A pretty creature, all made up. An enticement that moves with the stuttery jerky motion of...

A windup girl.

Tranh grins, a surprised skeleton rictus of delight at the sight of this unnatural creature stealing through the night. A windup girl. Ma Ping's windup girl. The impossible made flesh.

She slips from shadow to shadow, a creature even more terrified of white shirts than a yellow card geriatric. A waifish ghost-child ripped from her natural habitat and set down in a city which despises everything she represents: her genetic inheritance, her manufacturers, her unnatural competition—her ghostly lack of a soul. She has been here every night as he has pillaged through discarded melon spines. She has been here, tottering through the sweat heat darkness as he dodged white shirt patrols. And despite everything, she has been surviving.

Tranh forces himself upright. He sways, drunken and unsteady, then follows, one hand clutching his whiskey bottle, the other touching walls, catching himself when his bad knee falters. It's a foolish thing, a whimsy, but the windup girl has seized his inebriated imagination. He wants to stalk this unlikely Japanese creature, this interloper on foreign soil even more despised than himself. He wants to follow her. Perhaps steal kisses from her. Perhaps protect her from the hazards of the night. To pretend at least that he is not this drunken ribcage caricature of a man, but is in fact a tiger still.

The windup girl travels through the blackest of back alleys, safe in darkness, hidden from the white shirts who would seize her and mulch her before she could protest. Devil cats yowl as she passes, scenting something as cynically engineered as themselves. The Kingdom is infested with plagues and beasts, besieged by so many bioengineered monsters that it cannot keep up. As small as gray *fa' gan* fringe and as large as megodonts, they come. And as the Kingdom struggles to adapt, Tranh slinks after a windup girl, both of them as invasive as blister rust on a durian and just as welcome.

For all her irregular motion, the windup girl travels well enough. Tranh has difficulty keeping up with her. His knees creak and grind and he clenches his teeth against the pain. Sometimes he falls with a muffled grunt, but still he follows. Ahead of him, the windup girl ducks into new shadows, a wisp of tottering motion. Her herky-jerky gait announces her as a creature not human, no matter how beautiful she may be. No matter how intelligent, no matter how strong, no matter how supple her skin, she is a windup and meant to serve—and marked as such by a genetic specification that betrays her with every unnatural step.

Finally, when Tranh thinks that his legs will give out for a final time and that he can continue no longer, the windup girl pauses. She stands in the black mouth of a crumbling highrise, a tower as tall and wretched as his own, another carcass of the old Expansion. From high above, music and laughter filter down. Shapes float in the tower's upper-story windows, limned in red light, the silhouettes of women dancing. Calls of men and the throb of drums. The windup girl disappears inside.

What would it be like to enter such a place? To spend baht like water while women danced and sang songs of lust? Tranh suddenly regrets spending his last baht on whiskey. This is where he should have died. Surrounded by fleshly pleasures that he has not known since he lost his country and his life. He purses his lips, considering. Perhaps he can bluff his way in. He still wears the raiment of the Hwang Brothers. He still appears a gentleman, perhaps. Yes. He will attempt it, and if he gathers the shame of ejection on his head, if he loses face one more time, what of it? He will be dead in a river soon anyway, floating to the sea to join his sons.

He starts to cross the street but his knee gives out and he falls flat instead. He saves his whiskey bottle more by luck than by dexterity. The last of its amber liquid glints in the methane light. He grimaces and pulls himself into a sitting position, then drags himself back into a doorway. He will rest, first. And finish the bottle. The windup girl will be there for a long time, likely. He has time to recover himself. And if he falls again, at least he won't have wasted his liquor. He tilts the bottle to his lips then lets his tired head rest against the building. He'll just catch his breath.

Laughter issues from the highrise. Tranh jerks awake. A man stumbles from its shadow portal: drunk, laughing. More men spill out after him. They laugh and shove one another. Drag tittering women out with them. Motion to cycle rickshaws that wait in the alleys for easy drunken patrons. Slowly, they disperse.

Tranh tilts his whiskey bottle. Finds it empty.

Another pair of men emerges from the highrise's maw. One of them is Ma Ping. The other a *farang* who can only be Ma's boss. The *farang* waves for a cycle rickshaw. He climbs in and waves his farewells. Ma raises his own hand in return and his gold and diamond wristwatch glints in the methane light. Tranh's wristwatch. Tranh's history. Tranh's heirloom flashing bright in the darkness. Tranh scowls. Wishes he could rip it off young Ma's wrist.

The *farang's* rickshaw starts forward with a screech of unoiled bicycle chains and drunken laughter, leaving Ma Ping standing alone in the middle of the street. Ma laughs to himself, seems to consider returning to the bars, then laughs again and turns away, heading across the street, toward Tranh.

Tranh shies into the shadows, unwilling to let Ma catch him in such a state. Unwilling to endure more humiliation. He crouches deeper in his doorway as Ma stumbles about the street in search of rickshaws. But all the rickshaws have been taken for the moment. No more lurk below the bars.

Ma's gold wristwatch glints again in the methane light.

Pale forms glazed green materialize on the street, three men walking, their mahogany skin almost black in the darkness, contrasting sharply against the creased whites of their uniforms. Their black batons twirl casually at their wrists. Ma doesn't seem to notice them at first. The white shirts converge, casual. Their voices carry easily in the quiet night.

"You're out late."

Ma shrugs, grins queasily. "Not really. Not so late."

The three white shirts gather close. "Late for a yellow card. You should be home by now. Bad luck to be out after yellow card curfew. Especially with all that yellow gold on your wrist."

Ma holds up his hands, defensive. "I'm not a yellow card."

"Your accent says differently."

Ma reaches for his pockets, fumbles in them. "Really. You'll see. Look."

A white shirt steps close. "Did I say you could move?"

"My papers. Look—"

"Get your hands out!"

"Look at my stamps!"

"Out!" A black baton flashes. Ma yelps, clutches his elbow. More blows rain down. Ma crouches, trying to shield himself. He curses, "*Nimade bi!*"

The white shirts laugh. "That's yellow card talk." One of them swings his baton, low and fast, and Ma collapses, crying out, curling around a damaged leg. The white shirts gather close. One of them jabs Ma in the face, making him uncurl, then runs the baton down Ma's chest, dragging blood.

"He's got nicer clothes than you, Thongchai."

"Probably snuck across the border with an assful of jade."

One of them squats, studies Ma's face. "Is it true? Do you shit jade?"

Ma shakes his head frantically. He rolls over and starts to crawl away. A black runnel of blood spills from his mouth. One leg drags behind him, useless. A white shirt follows, pushes him over with his shoe and puts his foot on Ma's face. The other two suck in their breath and step back, shocked. To beat a man is one thing… "Suttipong, no."

The man called Suttipong glances back at his peers. "It's nothing. These yellow cards are as bad as blister rust. This is nothing. They all come begging, taking food when we've got little enough for our own, and look," he kicks Ma's wrist. "Gold."

Ma gasps, tries to strip the watch from his wrist. "Take it. Here. Please. Take it."

"It's not yours to give, yellow card."

"Not… yellow card," Ma gasps. "Please. Not your Ministry." His hands fumble for his pockets, frantic under the white shirt's gaze. He pulls out his papers and waves them in the hot night air.

Suttipong takes the papers, glances at them. Leans close. "You think our countrymen don't fear us, too?"

He throws the papers on the ground, then quick as a cobra he strikes. One, two, three, the blows rain down. He is very fast. Very methodical. Ma curls into a ball, trying to ward off the blows. Suttipong steps back, breathing heavily. He waves at the other two. "Teach him respect." The other two glance at each other doubtfully, but under Suttipong's urging, they are soon beating Ma, shouting encouragement to one another.

A few men come down from the pleasure bars and stumble into the streets, but when they see white uniforms they flee back inside. The white shirts are alone. And if there are other watching eyes, they do not show themselves. Finally, Suttipong seems satisfied. He kneels and strips the antique Rolex from Ma's wrist, spits on Ma's face and motions his peers to join him. They turn away, striding close past Tranh's hiding place.

The one called Thongchai looks back. "He might complain."

Suttipong shakes his head, his attention on the Rolex in his hand. "He's learned his lesson."

Their footsteps fade into the darkness. Music filters down from the highrise clubs. The street itself is silent. Tranh watches for a long time, looking for other hunters. Nothing moves. It is as if the entire city has turned its back on the broken Malay-Chinese lying in the street. Finally, Tranh limps out of the shadows and approaches Ma Ping.

Ma catches sight of him and holds up a weak hand. "Help." He tries the words in Thai, again in *farang* English, finally in Malay, as though he has returned to his childhood. Then he seems to recognize Tranh. His eyes widen. He smiles weakly, through split bloody lips. Speaks Mandarin, their trade language of brotherhood. "*Lao pengyou*. What are you doing here?"

Tranh squats beside him, studying his cracked face. "I saw your windup girl."

Ma closes his eyes, tries to smile. "You believe me, then?" His eyes are nearly swollen shut, blood runs down from a cut in his brow, trickling freely.

"Yes."

"I think they broke my leg." He tries to pull himself upright, gasps and collapses. He probes his ribs, runs his hand down to his shin. "I can't walk." He sucks air as he prods another broken bone. "You were right about the white shirts."

"A nail that stands up gets pounded down."

Something in Tranh's tone makes Ma look up. He studies Tranh's face. "Please. I gave you food. Find me a rickshaw." One hand strays to his wrist, fumbling for the timepiece that is no longer his, trying to offer it. Trying to bargain.

Is this fate? Tranh wonders. Or luck? Tranh purses his lips, considering. Was it fate that his own shiny wristwatch drew the white shirts and their wicked black batons? Was it luck that he arrived to see Ma fall? Do he and Ma Ping still have some larger karmic business?

Tranh watches Ma beg and remembers firing a young clerk so many lifetimes ago, sending him packing with a thrashing and a warning never to return. But that was when he was a great man. And now he is such a small one. As small as the clerk he thrashed so long ago. Perhaps smaller. He slides his hands under Ma's back, lifts.

"Thank you," Ma gasps. "Thank you."

Tranh runs his fingers into Ma's pockets, working through them methodically, checking for baht the white shirts have left. Ma groans, forces out a curse as Tranh jostles him. Tranh counts his scavenge, the dregs of Ma's pockets that still look like wealth to him. He stuffs the coins into his own pocket.

Ma's breathing comes in short panting gasps. "Please. A rickshaw. That's all." He barely manages to exhale the words.

Tranh cocks his head, considering, his instincts warring with themselves. He sighs and shakes his head. "A man makes his own luck, isn't that what you told me?" He smiles tightly. "My own arrogant words, coming from a brash young mouth." He shakes his head again, astounded at his previously fat ego, and smashes his whiskey bottle on the cobbles. Glass sprays. Shards glint green in the methane light.

"If I were still a great man..." Tranh grimaces. "But then, I suppose we're both past such illusions. I'm very sorry about this." With one last glance around the darkened street, he drives the broken bottle into Ma's throat. Ma jerks and blood spills out around Tranh's hand. Tranh scuttles back, keeping this new welling of blood off his Hwang Brothers fabrics. Ma's lungs bubble and his hands reach up for the bottle lodged in his neck, then fall away. His wet breathing stops.

Tranh is trembling. His hands shake with an electric palsy. He has seen so much death, and dealt so little. And now Ma lies before him, another Malay-Chinese dead, with only himself to blame. Again. He stifles an urge to be sick.

He turns and crawls into the protective shadows of the alley and pulls himself upright. He tests his weak leg. It seems to hold him. Beyond the shadows, the street is silent. Ma's body lies like a heap of garbage in its center. Nothing moves.

Tranh turns and limps down the street, keeping to the walls, bracing himself when his knee threatens to give way. After a few blocks, the methane lamps start to go out. One by one, as though a great hand is moving down the street snuffing them, they gutter into silence as the Public Works Ministry cuts off the gas. The street settles into complete darkness.

When Tranh finally arrives at Surawong Road, its wide black thoroughfare is nearly empty of traffic. A pair of ancient water buffalo placidly haul a rubber-wheeled wagon under starlight. A shadow farmer rides behind them, muttering softly. The yowls of mating devil cats scrape the hot night air, but that is all.

And then, from behind, the creak of bicycle chains. The rattle of wheels on cobbles. Tranh turns, half expecting avenging white shirts, but it is only a cycle rickshaw, chattering down the darkened street. Tranh raises a hand, flashing newfound baht. The rickshaw slows. A man's ropey limbs gleam with moonlit sweat. Twin earrings decorate his lobes, gobs of silver in the night. "Where you going?"

Tranh scans the rickshaw man's broad face for hints of betrayal, for hints that he is a hunter, but the man is only looking at the baht in Tranh's hand. Tranh forces down his paranoia and climbs into the rickshaw's seat. "The *farang* factories. By the river."

The rickshaw man glances over his shoulder, surprised. "All the factories will be closed. Too much energy to run at night. It's all black night down there."

"It doesn't matter. There's a job opening. There will be interviews."

The man stands on his pedals. "At night?"

"Tomorrow." Tranh settles deeper into his seat. "I don't want to be late."

POL POT'S BEAUTIFUL DAUGHTER (FANTASY)

GEOFF RYMAN

Geoff Ryman is the author of *The Warrior Who Carried Life*, novella "The Unconquered Country", *The Child Garden*, *Was*, *Lust*, and *Air*. His work *253, or Tube Theatre* was first published as hypertext fiction. A print version was published in 1998 and won the Philip K. Dick Memorial Award. He has also won the World Fantasy Award, Campbell Memorial Award, James Tiptree Award, Arthur C. Clarke Award, British Science Fiction Association Award, Sunburst, and Gaylactic Spectrum awards. His most recent novel, *The King's Last Song*, is set in Cambodia, both at the time of Angkorean emperor Jayavarman VII, and in the present period. He currently lectures in Creative Writing for University of Manchester's English Department.

What is real and what is not? When something that happens is terrible enough, does it take on a life of its own, as a ghost perhaps? In this haunting tale a young woman is followed by the ghost of her father's past.

In Cambodia people are used to ghosts. Ghosts buy newspapers. They own property.

A few years ago, spirits owned a house in Phnom Penh, at the Tra Bek end of Monivong Boulevard. Khmer Rouge had murdered the whole family and there was no one left alive to inherit it. People cycled past the building, leaving it boarded up. Sounds of weeping came from inside.

Then a professional inheritor arrived from America. She'd done her research and could claim to be the last surviving relative of no fewer than three families. She immediately sold the house to a Chinese businessman, who turned the ground floor into a photocopying shop.

The copiers began to print pictures of the original owners.

At first, single black-and-white photos turned up in the copied dossiers of aid workers or government officials. The father of the murdered family had been a lawyer. He stared fiercely out of the photos as if demanding something. In other photocopies, his beautiful daughters forlornly hugged each other. The background was hazy like fog.

One night the owner heard a noise and trundled downstairs to find all five photocopiers printing one picture after another of faces: young college men, old women, parents with a string of babies, or government soldiers in uniform. He pushed the big green off-buttons. Nothing happened.

He pulled out all the plugs, but the machines kept grinding out face after face. Women in beehive hairdos or clever children with glasses looked wistfully out of the photocopies. They seemed to be dreaming of home in the 1960s, when Phnom Penh was the most beautiful city in Southeast Asia.

News spread. People began to visit the shop to identify lost relatives. Women would cry, "That's my mother! I didn't have a photograph!" They would weep and press the flimsy A4 sheets to their breasts. The paper went limp from tears and humidity as if it too were crying.

Soon, a throng began to gather outside the shop every morning to view the latest batch of faces. In desperation, the owner announced that each morning's harvest would be delivered direct to *The Truth*, a magazine of remembrance.

Then one morning he tried to open the house-door to the shop and found it blocked. He went 'round to the front of the building and rolled open the metal shutters.

The shop was packed from floor to ceiling with photocopies. The ground floor had no windows—the room had been filled from the inside. The owner pulled out a sheet of paper and saw himself on the ground, his head beaten in by a hoe. The same image was on every single page.

He buried the photocopiers and sold the house at once. The new owner liked its haunted reputation; it kept people away. The FOR SALE sign was left hanging from the second floor.

In a sense, the house had been bought by another ghost.

This is a completely untrue story about someone who must exist.

Pol Pot's only child, a daughter, was born in 1986. Her name was Sith, and in 2004, she was eighteen years old.

Sith liked air conditioning and luxury automobiles.

Her hair was dressed in cornrows and she had a spiky piercing above one eye. Her jeans were elaborately slashed and embroidered. Her pink T-shirts bore slogans in English: CARE KOOKY. PINK MOLL.

Sith lived like a woman on Thai television, doing as she pleased in lip-gloss and Sunsilked hair. Nine simple rules helped her avoid all unpleasantness.

1. Never think about the past or politics.

2. Ignore ghosts. They cannot hurt you.

3. Do not go to school. Hire tutors. Don't do homework. It is disturbing.

4. Always be driven everywhere in either the Mercedes or the BMW.

5. Avoid all well-dressed Cambodian boys. They are the sons of the estimated 250,000 new generals created by the regime. Their sons can behave with impunity.

6. Avoid all men with potbellies. They eat too well and therefore must be corrupt.

7. Avoid anyone who drives a Toyota Viva or Honda Dream motorcycle.

8. Don't answer letters or phone calls.

9. Never make any friends.

There was also a tenth rule, but that went without saying.

Rotten fruit rinds and black mud never stained Sith's designer sports shoes. Disabled beggars never asked her for alms. Her life began yesterday, which was effectively the same as today.

Every day, her driver took her to the new Soriya Market. It was almost the only place that Sith went. The color of silver, Soriya rose up in many floors to a round glass dome.

Sith preferred the 142nd Street entrance. Its green awning made everyone look as if they were made of jade. The doorway went directly into the ice-cold jewelry rotunda with its floor of polished black and white stone. The individual stalls were hung with glittering necklaces and earrings.

Sith liked tiny shiny things that had no memory. She hated politics. She refused to listen to the news. Pol Pot's beautiful daughter wished the current leadership would behave decently, like her dad always did. To her.

She remembered the sound of her father's gentle voice. She remembered sitting on his lap in a forest enclosure, being bitten by mosquitoes. Memories of malaria had sunk into her very bones. She now associated forests with nausea, fevers, and pain. A flicker of tree-shade on her skin made her want to throw up and the odor of soil or fallen leaves made her gag. She had never been to Angkor Wat. She read nothing.

Sith shopped. Her driver was paid by the government and always carried an AK-47, but his wife, the housekeeper, had no idea who Sith was. The house was full of swept marble, polished teak furniture, iPods, Xboxes, and plasma screens.

Please remember that every word of this story is a lie. Pol Pot was no doubt a dedicated communist who made no money from ruling Cambodia. Nevertheless, a hefty allowance arrived for Sith every month from an account in Switzerland.

Nothing touched Sith, until she fell in love with the salesman at Hello Phones.

Cambodian readers may know that in 2004 there was no mobile phone shop in Soriya Market. However, there was a branch of Hello Phone Cards that had a round blue sales counter with orange trim. This shop looked like that.

Every day Sith bought or exchanged a mobile phone there. She would sit and flick her hair at the salesman.

His name was Dara, which means Star. Dara knew about deals on call prices, sim cards, and the new phones that showed videos. He could get her any call tone she liked.

Talking to Dara broke none of Sith's rules. He wasn't fat, nor was he well dressed, and far from being a teenager, he was a comfortably mature twenty-four years old.

One day, Dara chuckled and said, "As a friend I advise you, you don't need another mobile phone."

Sith wrinkled her nose. "I don't like this one anymore. It's blue. I want something more feminine. But not frilly. And it should have better sound quality."

"Okay, but you could save your money and buy some more nice clothes."

Pol Pot's beautiful daughter lowered her chin, which she knew made her neck look long and graceful. "Do you like my clothes?"

"Why ask me?"

She shrugged. "I don't know. It's good to check out your look."

Dara nodded. "You look cool. What does your sister say?"

Sith let him know she had no family. "Ah," he said, and quickly changed the subject. That was terrific. Secrecy and sympathy in one easy movement.

Sith came back the next day and said that she'd decided that the rose-colored phone was too feminine. Dara laughed aloud and his eyes sparkled. Sith had come late in the morning just so that he could ask this question. "Are you hungry? Do you want to meet for lunch?"

Would he think she was cheap if she said yes? Would he say she was snobby if she said no?

"Just so long as we eat in Soriya Market," she said.

She was torn between BBWorld Burgers and Lucky7. BBWorld was big, round, and just two floors down from the dome. Lucky7 Burgers was part of the Lucky Supermarket, such a good store that a tiny jar of Maxwell House cost US$2.40.

They decided on BBWorld. It was full of light and they could see the town spread out through the wide clean windows. Sith sat in silence.

Pol Pot's daughter had nothing to say unless she was buying something.

Or rather she had only one thing to say, but she must never say it.

Dara did all the talking. He talked about how the guys on the third floor could get him a deal on original copies of *Grand Theft Auto.* He hinted that he could get Sith discounts from Bsfashion, the spotlit modern shop one floor down.

Suddenly he stopped. "You don't need to be afraid of me, you know." He said it in a kindly, grownup voice. "I can see, you're a properly brought up girl. I like that. It's nice."

Sith still couldn't find anything to say. She could only nod. She wanted to run away.

"Would you like to go to K-Four?"

K-Four, the big electronics shop, stocked all the reliable brand names: Hitachi, Sony, Panasonic, Philips, or Denon. It was so expensive that almost nobody shopped there, which is why Sith liked it. A crowd of people stood outside and stared through the window at a huge home entertainment center showing a DVD of *Ice Age.* On the screen, a little animal was being chased by a glacier. It was so beautiful!

Sith finally found something to say. "If I had one of those, I would never need to leave the house."

Dara looked at her sideways and decided to laugh.

The next day Sith told him that all the phones she had were too big. Did he have one that she could wear around her neck like jewelry?

This time they went to Lucky7 Burgers, and sat across from the Revlon counter. They watched boys having their hair layered by Revlon's natural beauty specialists.

Dara told her more about himself. His father had died in the wars. His family now lived in the country. Sith's Coca-Cola suddenly tasted of anti-malarial drugs.

"But…you don't want to *live* in the country," she said.

"No. I have to live in Phnom Penh to make money. But my folks are good country people. Modest." He smiled, embarrassed.

They'll have hens and a cousin who shimmies up coconut trees. There will be trees all around but no shops anywhere. The earth will smell.

Sith couldn't finish her drink. She sighed and smiled and said abruptly, "I'm sorry. It's been cool. But I have to go." She slunk sideways out of her seat as slowly as molasses.

Walking back into the jewelry rotunda with nothing to do, she realized that Dara would think she didn't like him.

And that made the lower part of her eyes sting.

She went back the next day and didn't even pretend to buy a mobile phone. She told Dara that she'd left so suddenly the day before because she'd remembered a hair appointment.

He said that he could see she took a lot of trouble with her hair. Then he asked her out for a movie that night.

Sith spent all day shopping in K-Four.

They met at six. Dara was so considerate that he didn't even suggest the horror movie. He said he wanted to see *Buffalo Girl Hiding*, a movie about a country girl who lives on a farm. Sith said with great feeling that she would prefer the horror movie.

The cinema on the top floor opened out directly onto the roof of Soriya. Graffiti had been scratched into the green railings. Why would people want to ruin something new and beautiful? Sith put her arm through Dara's and knew that they were now boyfriend and girlfriend.

"Finally," he said.

"Finally what?"

"You've done something."

They leaned on the railings and looked out over other people's apartments. West toward the river was a building with one huge roof terrace. Women met there to gossip. Children were playing toss-the-sandal. From this distance, Sith was enchanted.

"I just love watching the children."

The movie, from Thailand, was about a woman whose face turns blue and spotty, and who eats men. The blue woman was yucky, but not as scary as all the badly dubbed voices. The characters sounded possessed. It was though Thai people had been taken over by the spirits of dead Cambodians.

Whenever Sith got scared, she chuckled.

So she sat chuckling with terror. Dara thought she was laughing at a dumb movie and found such intelligence charming. He started to chuckle too. Sith thought he was as frightened as she was. Together in the dark, they took each other's hands.

Outside afterward, the air hung hot even in the dark and 142nd Street smelled of drains. Sith stood on tiptoe to avoid the oily deposits and cast-off fishbones.

Dara said, "I will drive you home."

"My driver can take us," said Sith, flipping open her Kermit-the-Frog mobile.

Her black Mercedes Benz edged to a halt, crunching old plastic bottles in the gutter. The seats were upholstered with tan leather and the driver was armed.

Dara's jaw dropped. "Who…*who* is your father?"

"He's dead."

Dara shook his head. "Who was he?"

Normally Sith used her mother's family name, but that would not answer this question. Flustered, she tried to think of someone who could be her father. She knew of nobody the right age. She remembered something about a politician who had died. His name came to her and she said it in panic. "My father was Kol Vireakboth." Had she got the name right? "Please don't tell anyone."

Dara covered his eyes. "We—my family, my father—we fought for the KPLA."

Sith had to stop herself asking what the KPLA was.

Kol Vireakboth had led a faction in the civil wars. It fought against the Khmer Rouge, the Vietnamese, the King, and corruption. It wanted a new way for Cambodia. Kol Vireakboth was a Cambodian leader who had never told a lie or accepted a bribe.

Remember that this is an untrue story.

Dara started to back away from the car. "I don't think we should be doing this. I'm just a villager, really."

"That doesn't matter."

His eyes closed. "I would expect nothing less from the daughter of Kol Vireakboth."

Oh for gosh sake, she just picked the man's name out of the air, she didn't need more problems. "Please!" she said.

Dara sighed. "Okay. I said I would see you home safely. I will." Inside the Mercedes, he stroked the tan leather.

When they arrived, he craned his neck to look up at the building. "Which floor are you on?"

"All of them."

Color drained from his face.

"My driver will take you back," she said to Dara. As the car pulled away, she stood outside the closed garage shutters, waving forlornly.

Then Sith panicked. Who was Kol Vireakboth? She went online and Googled. She had to read about the wars. Her skin started to creep. All those different factions swam in her head: ANS, NADK, KPR, and KPNLF. The very names seemed to come at her spoken by forgotten voices.

Soon she had all she could stand. She printed out Vireakboth's picture and decided to have it framed. In case Dara visited.

Kol Vireakboth had a round face and a fatherly smile. His eyes seemed to slant upward toward his nose, looking full of kindly insight. He'd been killed by a car bomb.

All that night, Sith heard whispering.

In the morning, there was another picture of someone else in the tray of her printer.

A long-faced, buck-toothed woman stared out at her in black and white. Sith noted the victim's fashion lapses. The woman's hair was a mess, all frizzy. She should have had it straightened and put in some nice highlights. The woman's eyes drilled into her.

"Can't touch me," said Sith. She left the photo in the tray. She went to see Dara, right away, no breakfast.

His eyes were circled with dark flesh and his blue Hello trousers and shirt were not properly ironed.

"Buy the whole shop," Dara said, looking deranged. "The guys in K-Four just told me some girl in blue jeans walked in yesterday and bought two home theatres. One for the salon, she said, and one for the roof terrace. She paid for both of them in full and had them delivered to the far end of Monivong."

Sith sighed. "I'm sending one back." She hoped that sounded abstemious. "It looked too metallic against my curtains."

Pause.

"She also bought an Aido robot dog for fifteen hundred dollars."

Sith would have preferred that Dara did not know about the dog. It was just a silly toy; it hadn't occurred to her that it might cost that much until she saw the bill. "They should not tell everyone about their customers' business or soon they will have no customers."

Dara was looking at her as if thinking: *This is not just a nice sweet girl.*

"I had fun last night," Sith said in a voice as thin as high clouds.

"So did I."

"We don't have to tell anyone about my family. Do we?" Sith was seriously scared of losing him.

"No. But Sith, it's stupid. Your family, my family, we are not equals."

"It doesn't make any difference."

"You lied to me. Your family is not dead. You have famous uncles."

She did indeed—Uncle Ieng Sary, Uncle Khieu Samphan, Uncle Ta Mok. All the Pol Pot clique had been called her uncles.

"I didn't know them that well," she said. That was true, too.

What would she do if she couldn't shop in Soriya Market anymore? What would she do without Dara?

She begged. "I am not a strong person. Sometimes I think I am not a person at all. I'm just a space."

Dara looked suddenly mean. "You're just a credit card." Then his face fell. "I'm sorry. That was an unkind thing to say. You are very young for your age and I'm older than you and I should have treated you with more care."

Sith was desperate. "All my money would be very nice."

"I'm not for sale."

He worked in a shop and would be sending money home to a fatherless family; of course he was for sale!

Sith had a small heart, but a big head for thinking. She knew that she had to do this delicately, like picking a flower, or she would spoil the bloom. "Let's…let's just go see a movie?"

After all, she was beautiful and well brought up and she knew her eyes were big and round. Her tiny heart was aching.

This time they saw *Tum Teav*, a remake of an old movie from the 1960s. If movies were not nightmares about ghosts, then they tried to preserve the past. *When*, thought Sith, *will they make a movie about Cambodia's future? Tum Teav* was based on a classic tale of a young monk who falls in love with a properly brought up girl but her mother opposes the match. They commit suicide at the end, bringing a curse on their village. Sith sat through it stony-faced. *I am not going to be a dead heroine in a romance.*

Dara offered to drive her home again and that's when Sith found out that he drove a Honda Dream. He proudly presented to her the gleaming motorcycle of fast young men. Sith felt backed into a corner. She'd already offered to buy him. Showing off her car again might humiliate him.

So she broke rule number seven.

Dara hid her bag in the back and they went soaring down Monivong Boulevard at night, past homeless people, prostitutes, and chefs staggering home after work. It was late in the year, but it started to rain.

Sith loved it, the cool air brushing against her face, the cooler rain clinging to her eyelashes.

She remembered being five years old in the forest and dancing in the monsoon. She encircled Dara's waist to stay on the bike and suddenly found her cheek was pressed up against his back. She giggled in fear, not of the rain, but of what she felt.

He dropped her off at home. Inside, everything was dark except for the flickering green light on her printer. In the tray were two new photographs. One was of a child, a little boy, holding up a school prize certificate. The other was a tough, wise-looking old man, with a string of muscle down either side of his ironic, bitter smile. They looked directly at her.

They know who I am.

As she climbed the stairs to her bedroom, she heard someone sobbing, far away, as if the sound came from next door. She touched the walls of the staircase. They shivered slightly, constricting in time to the cries.

In her bedroom she extracted one of her many iPods from the tangle of wires and listened to *System of a Down,* as loud as she could. It helped her sleep. The sound of nu-metal guitars seemed to come roaring out of her own heart.

She was woken up in the sun-drenched morning by the sound of her doorbell many floors down. She heard the housekeeper Jorani call and the door open. Sith hesitated over choice of jeans and top. By the time she got downstairs she found the driver and the housemaid joking with Dara, giving him tea.

Like the sunshine, Dara seemed to disperse ghosts.

"Hi," he said. "It's my day off. I thought we could go on a motorcycle ride to the country."

But not to the country. Couldn't they just spend the day in Soriya? No, said Dara, there's lots of other places to see in Phnom Penh.

He drove her, twisting through back streets. How did the city get so poor? How did it get so dirty?

They went to a new and modern shop for CDs that was run by a record label. Dara knew all the cool new music, most of it influenced by Khmer-Americans returning from Long Beach and Compton: Sdey, Phnom Penh Bad Boys, Khmer Kid.

Sith bought twenty CDs.

They went to the National Museum and saw the beautiful Buddha-like head of King Jayavarman VII. Dara without thinking ducked and held up his hands in prayer. They had dinner in a French restaurant with candles and wine, and it was just like in a karaoke video, a boy, a girl, and her money all going out together. They saw the show at Sovanna Phum, and there was a wonderful dance piece with sampled 1940s music from an old French movie, with traditional Khmer choreography.

Sith went home, her heart singing, *Dara, Dara, Dara.*

In the bedroom, a mobile phone began to ring, over and over. *Call 1* said the screen, but gave no name or number, so the person was not on Sith's list of contacts.

She turned off the phone. It kept ringing. That's when she knew for certain.

She hid the phone in a pillow in the spare bedroom and put another pillow on top of it and then closed the door.

All forty-two of her mobile phones started to ring. They rang from inside closets, or from the bathroom where she had forgotten them. They rang from the roof terrace and even from inside a shoe under her bed.

"I am a very stubborn girl!" she shouted at the spirits. "You do not scare me."

She turned up her iPod and finally slept.

As soon as the sun was up, she roused her driver, slumped deep in his hammock.

"Come on, we're going to Soriya Market," she said.

The driver looked up at her dazed, then remembered to smile and lower his head in respect.

His face fell when she showed up in the garage with all forty-two of her mobile phones in one black bag.

It was too early for Soriya Market to open. They drove in circles with sunrise blazing directly into their eyes. On the streets, men pushed carts like beasts of burden, or carried cascades of belts into the old Central Market. The old market was domed, art deco, the color of vomit, French. Sith never shopped there.

"Maybe you should go visit your mom," said the driver. "You know, she loves you. Families are there for when you are in trouble."

Sith's mother lived in Thailand and they never spoke. Her mother's family kept asking for favors: money, introductions, or help with getting a job. Sith didn't speak to them any longer.

"My family is only trouble."

The driver shut up and drove.

Finally Soriya opened. Sith went straight to Dara's shop and dumped all the phones on the blue countertop. "Can you take these back?"

"We only do exchanges. I can give a new phone for an old one." Dara looked thoughtful. "Don't worry. Leave them here with me, I'll go sell them to a guy in the old market, and give you your money tomorrow." He smiled in approval. "This is very sensible."

He passed one phone back, the one with video and email. "This is the best one, keep this."

Dara was so competent. Sith wanted to sink down onto him like a pillow and stay there. She sat in the shop all day, watching him work. One of the guys from the games shop upstairs asked, "Who is this beautiful girl?"

Dara answered proudly, "My girlfriend."

Dara drove her back on the Dream and at the door to her house, he chuckled. "I don't want to go." She pressed a finger against his naughty lips, and smiled and spun back inside from happiness.

She was in the ground-floor garage. She heard something like a rat scuttle. In her bag, the telephone rang. Who were these people to importune her, even if they were dead? She wrenched the mobile phone out of her bag and pushed the green button and put the phone to her ear. She waited. There was a sound like wind.

A child spoke to her, his voice clogged as if he was crying. "They tied my thumbs together."

Sith demanded. "How did you get my number?"

"I'm all alone!"

"Then ring somebody else. Someone in your family."

"All my family are dead. I don't know where I am. My name is—"

Sith clicked the phone off. She opened the trunk of the car and tossed the phone inside it. Being telephoned by ghosts was so...*unmodern*. How could Cambodia become a number one country if its cell phone network was haunted?

She stormed up into the salon. On top of a table, the $1500, no-mess dog stared at her from out of his packaging. Sith clumped up the stairs onto the roof terrace to sleep as far away as she could from everything in the house.

She woke up in the dark, to hear thumping from downstairs.

The sound was metallic and hollow, as if someone were locked in the car. Sith turned on her iPod. Something was making the sound of the music skip. She fought the tangle of wires, and wrenched out another player, a Xen, but it too skipped, burping the sound of speaking voices into the middle of the music.

Had she heard a ripping sound? She pulled out the earphones, and heard something climbing the stairs.

A sound of light, uneven lolloping. She thought of crippled children. Frost settled over her like a heavy blanket and she could not move.

The robot dog came whirring up onto the terrace. It paused at the top of the stairs, its camera nose pointing at her to see, its useless eyes glowing cherry red.

The robot dog said in a warm, friendly voice, "My name is Phalla. I tried to buy my sister medicine and they killed me for it."

Sith tried to say, "Go away," but her throat wouldn't open.

The dog tilted its head. "No one even knows I'm dead. What will you do for all the people who are not mourned?"

Laughter blurted out of her, and Sith saw it rise up as cold vapor into the air.

"We have no one to invite us to the feast," said the dog.

Sith giggled in terror. "Nothing. I can do nothing!" she said, shaking her head.

"You laugh?" The dog gathered itself and jumped up into the hammock with her. It turned and lifted up its clear plastic tail and laid a genuine turd alongside Sith. Short brown hair was wound up in it, a scalp actually, and a single flat white human tooth smiled out of it.

Sith squawked and overturned both herself and the dog out of the hammock and onto the floor. The dog pushed its nose up against hers and began to sing an old-fashioned children's song about birds.

Something heavy huffed its way up the stairwell toward her. Sith shivered with cold on the floor and could not move. The dog went on singing in a high, sweet voice. A large shadow loomed out over the top of the staircase, and Sith gargled, swallowing laughter, trying to speak.

"There was thumping in the car and no one in it," said the driver.

Sith sagged toward the floor with relief. "The ghosts," she said. "They're back." She thrust herself to her feet. "We're getting out now. Ring the Hilton. Find out if they have rooms."

She kicked the toy dog down the stairs ahead of her. "We're moving now!"

Together they all loaded the car, shaking. Once again, the house was left to ghosts. As they drove, the mobile phone rang over and over inside the trunk.

The new Hilton (which does not exist) rose up by the river across from the Department for Cults and Religious Affairs. Tall and marbled and pristine, it had crystal chandeliers and fountains, and wood and brass handles in the elevators.

In the middle of the night only the Bridal Suite was still available, but it had an extra parental chamber where the driver and his wife could sleep. High on the twenty-first floor, the night sparkled with lights and everything was hushed, as far away from Cambodia as it was possible to get.

Things were quiet after that, for a while.

Every day she and Dara went to movies, or went to a restaurant. They went shopping. She slipped him money and he bought himself a beautiful suit. He said, over a hamburger at Lucky7, "I've told my mother that I've met a girl."

Sith smiled and thought: and I bet you told her that I'm rich.

"I've decided to live in the Hilton," she told him.

Maybe we could live in the Hilton. A pretty smile could hint at that.

The rainy season ended. The last of the monsoons rose up dark gray with a froth of white cloud on top, looking exactly like a giant wave about to break.

Dry cooler air arrived.

After work was over Dara convinced her to go for a walk along the river in front of the Royal Palace. He went to the men's room to change into a new luxury suit and Sith thought: he's beginning to imagine life with all that money.

As they walked along the river, exposed to all those people, Sith shook inside. There were teenage boys everywhere. Some of them were in rags, which was reassuring, but some of them were very well dressed indeed, the sons of Impunity who could do anything. Sith swerved suddenly to avoid even seeing them. But Dara in his new beige suit looked like one of them, and the generals' sons nodded to him with quizzical eyebrows, perhaps wondering who he was.

In front of the palace, a pavilion reached out over the water. Next to it a traditional orchestra bashed and wailed out something old fashioned. Hundreds of people crowded around a tiny wat. Dara shook Sith's wrist and they stood up to see.

People held up bundles of lotus flowers and incense in prayer. They threw the bundles into the wat. Monks immediately shoveled the joss sticks and flowers out of the back.

Behind the wat, children wearing T-shirts and shorts black with filth rootled through the dead flowers, the smoldering incense, and old coconut shells.

Sith asked, "Why do they do that?"

"You are so innocent!" chuckled Dara and shook his head. The evening was blue and gold. Sith had time to think that she did not want to go back to a hotel and that the only place she really felt happy was next to Dara. All around that thought was something dark and tangled.

Dara suggested with affection that they should get married.

It was as if Sith had her answer ready. "No, absolutely not," she said at once. "How can you ask that? There is not even anyone for you to ask! Have you spoken to your family about me? Has your family made any checks about my background?"

Which was what she really wanted to know.

Dara shook his head. "I have explained that you are an orphan, but they are not concerned with that. We are modest people. They will be happy if I am happy."

"Of course they won't be! Of course they will need to do checks."

Sith scowled. She saw her way to sudden advantage. "At least they must consult fortunetellers. They are not fools. I can help them. Ask them the names of the fortunetellers they trust."

Dara smiled shyly. "We have no money."

"I will give them money and you can tell them that you pay."

Dara's eyes searched her face. "I don't want that."

"How will we know if it is a good marriage? And your poor mother, how can you ask her to make a decision like this without information? So. You ask your family for the names of good professionals they trust, and I will pay them, and I will go to Prime Minister Hun Sen's own personal fortuneteller, and we can compare results."

Thus she established again both her propriety and her status.

In an old romance, the parents would not approve of the match and the fortuneteller would say that the marriage was ill-omened. Sith left nothing to romance.

She offered the family's fortunetellers whatever they wanted—a car, a farm—and in return demanded a written copy of their judgment. All of them agreed that the portents for the marriage were especially auspicious.

Then she secured an appointment with the Prime Minister's fortuneteller.

Hun Sen's *Kru Taey* was a lady in a black business suit. She had long fingernails like talons, but they were perfectly manicured and frosted white.

She was the kind of fortuneteller who is possessed by someone else's spirit. She sat at a desk and looked at Sith as unblinking as a fish, both her hands steepled together. After the most basic of hellos, she said. "Dollars only. Twenty-five thousand. I need to buy my son an apartment."

"That's a very high fee," said Sith.

"It's not a fee. It is a consideration for giving you the answer you want. My fee is another twenty-five thousand dollars."

They negotiated. Sith liked the Kru Taey's manner. It confirmed everything

Sith believed about life.

The fee was reduced somewhat but not the consideration.

"Payment upfront now," the Kru Taey said. She wouldn't take a check. Like only the very best restaurants she accepted foreign credit cards. Sith's Swiss card worked immediately. It had unlimited credit in case she had to leave the country in a hurry.

The Kru Taey said, "I will tell the boy's family that the marriage will be particularly fortunate."

Sith realized that she had not yet said anything about a boy, his family, or a marriage.

The Kru Taey smiled. "I know you are not interested in your real fortune. But to be kind, I will tell you unpaid that this marriage really is particularly well favored. All the other fortunetellers would have said the same thing without being bribed."

The Kru Taey's eyes glinted in the most unpleasant way. "So you needn't have bought them farms or paid me an extra twenty-five thousand dollars."

She looked down at her perfect fingernails. "You will be very happy indeed. But not before your entire life is overturned."

The back of Sith's arms prickled as if from cold. She should have been angry but she could feel herself smiling. Why?

And why waste politeness on the old witch? Sith turned to go without saying good-bye.

"Oh, and about your other problem," said the woman.

Sith turned back and waited.

"Enemies," said the Kru Taey, "can turn out to be friends."

Sith sighed. "What are you talking about?"

The Kru Taey's smile was as wide as a tiger-trap. "The million people your father killed."

Sith went hard. "Not a million," she said. "Somewhere between two hundred and fifty and five hundred thousand."

"Enough," smiled the Kru Taey. "My father was one of them." She smiled for a moment longer. "I will be sure to tell the Prime Minister that you visited me."

Sith snorted as if in scorn. "I will tell him myself."

But she ran back to her car.

That night, Sith looked down on all the lights like diamonds. She settled onto the giant mattress and turned on her iPod.

Someone started to yell at her. She pulled out the earpieces and jumped to the window. It wouldn't open. She shook it and wrenched its frame until it reluctantly slid an inch and she threw the iPod out of the twenty-first-floor window.

She woke up late the next morning, to hear the sound of the TV. She opened up the double doors into the salon and saw Jorani, pressed against the wall.

"The TV…" Jorani said, her eyes wide with terror.

The driver waited by his packed bags. He stood up, looking as mournful as a bloodhound.

On the widescreen TV there was what looked like a pop music karaoke video. Except that the music was very old fashioned. Why would a pop video show a starving man eating raw maize in a field? He glanced over his shoulder in terror as he ate. The glowing singalong words were the song that the dog had sung at the top of the stairs. The starving man looked up at Sith and corn mash rolled out of his mouth.

"It's all like that," said the driver. "I unplugged the set, but it kept playing on every channel." He sompiahed but looked miserable. "My wife wants to leave."

Sith felt shame. It was miserable and dirty, being infested with ghosts. Of course they would want to go.

"It's okay. I can take taxis," she said.

The driver nodded, and went into the next room and whispered to his wife. With little scurrying sounds, they gathered up their things. They sompiahed, and apologized.

The door clicked almost silently behind them.

It will always be like this, thought Sith. Wherever I go. It would be like this with Dara.

The hotel telephone started to ring. Sith left it ringing. She covered the TV with a blanket, but the terrible, tinny old music kept wheedling and rattling its way out at her, and she sat on the edge of her bed, staring into space.

I'll have to leave Cambodia.

At the market, Dara looked even more cheerful than usual. The fortunetellers had pronounced the marriage as very favorable. His mother had invited Sith home for the Pchum Ben festival.

"We can take the bus tomorrow," he said.

"Does it smell? All those people in one place?"

"It smells of air freshener. Then we take a taxi, and then you will have to walk up the track." Dara suddenly doubled up in laughter. "Oh, it will be good for you."

"Will there be dirt?"

"Everywhere! Oh, your dirty Nikes will earn you much merit!"

But at least, thought Sith, there will be no TV or phones.

Two days later, Sith was walking down a dirt track, ducking tree branches. Dust billowed all over her shoes. Dara walked behind her, chuckling, which meant she thought he was scared too.

She heard a strange rattling sound. "What's that noise?"

"It's a goat," he said. "My mother bought it for me in April as a present."

A goat. How could they be any more rural? Sith had never seen a goat. She never even imagined that she would.

Dara explained. "I sell them to the Muslims. It is Agricultural Diversification."

There were trees everywhere, shadows crawling across the ground like snakes.

Sith felt sick. *One mosquito*, she promised herself, *just one and I will squeal and run away.*

The house was tiny, on thin twisting stilts. She had pictured a big fine country house standing high over the ground on concrete pillars with a sunburst carving in the gable. The kitchen was a hut that sat directly on the ground, no stilts, and it was made of palm-leaf panels and there was no electricity. The strip light in the ceiling was attached to a car battery and they kept a live fire on top of the concrete table to cook. Everything smelled of burnt fish.

Sith loved it.

Inside the hut, the smoke from the fires kept the mosquitoes away. Dara's mother, Mrs. Non Kunthea, greeted her with a smile. That triggered a respectful sompiah from Sith, the prayer-like gesture leaping out of her unbidden. On the platform table was a plastic sack full of dried prawns.

Without thinking, Sith sat on the table and began to pull the salty prawns out of their shells.

Why am I doing this?

Because it's what I did at home.

Sith suddenly remembered the enclosure in the forest, a circular fenced area. Daddy had slept in one house, and the women in another. Sith would talk to the cooks. For something to do, she would chop vegetables or shell prawns. Then Daddy would come to eat and he'd sit on the platform table and she, little Sith, would sit between his knees.

Dara's older brother Yuth came back for lunch. He was pot-bellied and drove a taxi for a living, and he moved in hard jabs like an angry old man. He reached too far for the rice and Sith could smell his armpits.

"You see how we live," Yuth said to Sith. "This is what we get for having the wrong patron. Sihanouk thought we were anti-monarchist. To Hun Sen, we were the enemy. Remember the Work for Money program?"

No.

"They didn't give any of those jobs to us. We might as well have been the Khmer Rouge!"

The past, thought Sith, *why don't they just let it go? Why do they keep boasting about their old wars?*

Mrs. Non Kunthea chuckled with affection. "My eldest son was born angry," she said. "His slogan is 'ten years is not too late for revenge.'"

Yuth started up again. "They treat that old monster Pol Pot better than they treat us. But then, he was an important person. If you go to his stupa in Anlong Veng, you will see that people leave offerings! They ask him for lottery numbers!"

He crumpled his green, soft, old-fashioned hat back onto his head and said, "Nice to meet you, Sith. Dara, she's too high class for the likes of you." But he grinned as he said it. He left, swirling disruption in his wake.

The dishes were gathered. Again without thinking, Sith swept up the plastic tub and carried it to the blackened branches. They rested over puddles where the washing-up water drained.

"You shouldn't work," said Dara's mother. "You are a guest."

"I grew up in a refugee camp," said Sith. After all, it was true.

Dara looked at her with a mix of love, pride, and gratitude for the good fortune of a rich wife who works.

And that was the best Sith could hope for. This family would be fine for her.

In the late afternoon, all four brothers came with their wives for the end of Pchum Ben, when the ghosts of the dead can wander the Earth. People scatter rice on the temple floors to feed their families. Some ghosts have small mouths so special rice is used.

Sith never took part in Pchum Ben. How could she go to the temple and scatter rice for Pol Pot?

The family settled in the kitchen chatting and joking, and it all passed in a blur for Sith. Everyone else had family they could honor. To Sith's surprise one of the uncles suggested that people should write names of the deceased and burn them, to transfer merit. It was nothing to do with Pchum Ben, but a lovely idea, so all the family wrote down names.

Sith sat with her hands jammed under her arms.

Dara's mother asked, "Isn't there a name you want to write, Sith?"

"No," said Sith in a tiny voice. How could she write the name Pol Pot? He was surely roaming the world let loose from hell. "There is no one."

Dara rubbed her hand. "Yes there is, Sith. A very special name."

"No, there's not."

Dara thought she didn't want them to know her father was Kol Vireakboth. He leant forward and whispered. "I promise. No one will see it."

Sith's breath shook. She took the paper and started to cry.

"Oh," said Dara's mother, stricken with sympathy. "Everyone in this country has a tragedy."

Sith wrote the name Kol Vireakboth.

Dara kept the paper folded and caught Sith's eyes. *You see?* he seemed to say. *I have kept your secret safe.* The paper burned.

Thunder slapped a clear sky about the face. It had been sunny, but now as suddenly as a curtain dropped down over a doorway, rain fell. A wind came from nowhere, tearing away a flap of palm-leaf wall, as if forcing its way in.

The family whooped and laughed and let the rain drench their shoulders as they stood up to push the wall back down, to keep out the rain.

But Sith knew. Her father's enemy was in the kitchen.

The rain passed; the sun came out. The family chuckled and sat back down around or on the table. They lowered dishes of food and ate, making parcels of rice and fish with their fingers. Sith sat rigidly erect, waiting for misfortune.

What would the spirit of Kol Vireakboth do to Pol Pot's daughter? Would he overturn the table, soiling her with food? Would he send mosquitoes to bite and make her sick? Would he suck away all her good fortune, leaving the marriage blighted, her new family estranged?

Or would a kindly spirit simply wish that the children of all Cambodians could escape, escape the past?

Suddenly, Sith felt at peace. The sunlight and shadows looked new to her and her senses started to work in magic ways.

She smelled a perfume of emotion, sweet and bracing at the same time. The music from a neighbor's cassette player touched her arm gently. Words took the form of sunlight on her skin.

No one is evil, the sunlight said. *But they can be false.*

False, how? Sith asked without speaking, genuinely baffled.

The sunlight smiled with an old man's stained teeth. *You know very well how.*

All the air swelled with the scent of the food, savoring it. The trees sighed with satisfaction.

Life is true. Sith saw steam from the rice curl up into the branches. *Death is false.*

The sunlight stood up to go. It whispered. *Tell him.*

The world faded back to its old self.

That night in a hammock in a room with the other women, Sith suddenly sat bolt upright. Clarity would not let her sleep. She saw that there was no way ahead. She couldn't marry Dara. How could she ask him to marry someone who was harassed by one million dead? How could she explain I am haunted because I am Pol Pot's daughter and I have lied about everything?

The dead would not let her marry; the dead would not let her have joy. So who could Pol Pot's daughter pray to? Where could she go for wisdom?

Loak kru Kol Vireakboth, she said under her breath. *Please show me a way ahead.*

The darkness was sterner than the sunlight.

To be as false as you are, it said, *you first have to lie to yourself.*

What lies had Sith told? She knew the facts. Her father had been the head of a government that tortured and killed hundreds of thousands of people and starved the nation through mismanagement. I know the truth.

I just never think about it.

I've never faced it.

Well, the truth is as dark as I am, and you live in me, the darkness.

She had read books—well, the first chapter of books—and then dropped them as if her fingers were scalded. There was no truth for her in books. The truth ahead of her would be loneliness, dreary adulthood, and penance.

Grow up.

The palm-leaf panels stirred like waiting ghosts.

All through the long bus ride back, she said nothing. Dara went silent too, and hung his head.

In the huge and empty hotel suite, darkness awaited her. She'd had the phone and the TV removed; her footsteps sounded hollow. Jorani and the driver had been her only friends.

The next day she did not go to Soriya Market. She went instead to the torture museum of Tuol Sleng.

A cadre of young motoboys waited outside the hotel in baseball caps and bling. Instead, Sith hailed a sweet-faced older motoboy with a battered, rusty bike.

As they drove she asked him about his family. He lived alone and had no one except for his mother in Kompong Thom.

Outside the gates of Tuol Sleng he said, "This was my old school."

In one wing there were rows of rooms with one iron bed in each with handcuffs and stains on the floor. Photos on the wall showed twisted bodies chained to those same beds as they were found on the day of liberation. In one photograph, a chair was overturned as if in a hurry.

Sith stepped outside and looked instead at a beautiful house over the wall across the street. It was a high white house like her own, with pillars and a roof terrace and bougainvillea, a modern daughter's house. What do they think when they look out from that roof terrace? How can they live here?

The grass was tended and full of hopping birds. People were painting the shutters of the prison a fresh blue-gray.

In the middle wing, the rooms were galleries of photographed faces. They stared out at her like the faces from her printer. Were some of them the same?

"Who are they?" she found herself asking a Cambodian visitor.

"Their own," the woman replied. "This is where they sent Khmer Rouge cadres who had fallen out of favor. They would not waste such torture on ordinary Cambodians."

Some of the faces were young and beautiful men. Some were children or dignified old women.

The Cambodian lady kept pace with her. Company? Did she guess who Sith was? "They couldn't simply beat party cadres to death. They sent them and their entire families here. The children too, the grandmothers. They had different days of the week for killing children and wives."

An innocent-looking man smiled out at the camera as sweetly as her aged motoboy, directly into the camera of his torturers. He seemed to expect kindness from them, and decency. *Comrades*, he seemed to say.

The face in the photograph moved. It smiled more broadly and was about to speak.

Sith's eyes darted away. The next face sucked all her breath away.

It was not a stranger. It was Dara, her Dara, in black shirt and black cap. She gasped and looked back at the lady. Her pinched and solemn face nodded up and down. Was she a ghost too?

Sith reeled outside and hid her face and didn't know if she could go on standing. Tears slid down her face and she wanted to be sick and she turned her back so no one could see.

Then she walked to the motoboy, sitting in a shelter. In complete silence, she got on his bike feeling angry at the place, angry at the government for preserving it, angry at the foreigners who visited it like a tourist attraction, angry at everything.

That is not who we are! That is not what I am!

The motoboy slipped onto his bike, and Sith asked him: What happened to your family? It was a cruel question. He had to smile and look cheerful. His father had run a small shop; they went out into the country and never came back. He lived with his brother in a jeum-room, a refugee camp in Thailand. They came back to fight the Vietnamese and his brother was killed.

She was going to tell the motoboy, drive me back to the Hilton, but she felt ashamed. Of what? Just how far was she going to run?

She asked him to take her to the old house on Monivong Boulevard.

As the motorcycle wove through back streets, dodging red-earth ruts and pedestrians, she felt rage at her father. How dare he involve her in something like that! Sith had lived a small life and had no measure of things so she thought: *It's as if someone tinted my hair and it all fell out. It's as if someone pierced my ears and they got infected and my whole ear rotted away.*

She remembered that she had never felt any compassion for her father. She had been twelve years old when he stood trial, old and sick and making such a show of leaning on his stick. Everything he did was a show. She remembered rolling her eyes in constant embarrassment. Oh, he was fine in front of rooms full of adoring students. He could play the *bong thom* with them. They thought he was enlightened. He sounded good, using his false, soft, and kindly little voice, as if he was dubbed. He had made Sith recite Verlaine, Rimbaud, and Rilke. He killed thousands for having foreign influences.

I don't know what I did in a previous life to deserve you for a father. But you were not my father in a previous life and you won't be my father in the next. I reject you utterly. I will never burn your name. You can wander hungry out of hell every year for all eternity. I will pray to keep you in hell.

I am not your daughter!

If you were false, I have to be true.

Her old house looked abandoned in the stark afternoon light, closed and innocent. At the doorstep she turned and thrust a fistful of dollars into the motoboy's hand. She couldn't think straight; she couldn't even see straight, her vision blurred.

Back inside, she calmly put down her teddy-bear rucksack and walked upstairs to her office. Aido the robot dog whirred his way toward her. She had broken his back leg kicking him downstairs. He limped, whimpering like a dog, and lowered his head to have it stroked.

To her relief, there was only one picture waiting for her in the tray of the printer.

Kol Vireakboth looked out at her, middle-aged, handsome, worn, wise. Pity and kindness glowed in his eyes.

The land line began to ring.

"*Youl prom,*" she told the ghosts. Agreed.

She picked up the receiver and waited.

A man spoke. "My name was Yin Bora." His voice bubbled up brokenly as if from underwater.

A light blinked in the printer. A photograph slid out quickly. A young student stared out at her looking happy at a family feast. He had a Beatle haircut and a striped shirt.

"That's me," said the voice on the phone. "I played football."

Sith coughed. "What do you want me to do?"

"Write my name," said the ghost.

"Please hold the line," said Sith, in a hypnotized voice. She fumbled for a pen, and then wrote on the photograph *Yin Bora, footballer*. He looked so sweet and happy. "You have no one to mourn you," she realized.

"None of us have anyone left alive to mourn us," said the ghost.

Then there was a terrible sound down the telephone, as if a thousand voices moaned at once.

Sith involuntarily dropped the receiver into place. She listened to her heart thump and thought about what was needed. She fed the printer with the last of her paper. Immediately it began to roll out more photos, and the land line rang again.

She went outside and found the motoboy, waiting patiently for her. She asked him to go and buy two reams of copying paper. At the last moment she added pens and writing paper and matches. He bowed and smiled and bowed again, pleased to have found a patron.

She went back inside, and with just a tremor in her hand picked up the phone.

For the next half hour, she talked to the dead, and found photographs and wrote down names. A woman mourned her children. Sith found photos of them all, and united them, father, mother, three children, uncles, aunts, cousins and grandparents, taping their pictures to her wall. The idea of uniting families appealed. She began to stick the other photos onto her wall.

Someone called from outside and there on her doorstep was the motoboy, balancing paper and pens. "I bought you some soup." The broth came in neatly tied bags and was full of rice and prawns. She thanked him and paid him well and he beamed at her and bowed again and again.

All afternoon, the pictures kept coming. Darkness fell, the phone rang, the names were written, until Sith's hand, which was unused to writing anything, ached.

The doorbell rang, and on the doorstep, the motoboy sompiahed. "Excuse me, Lady, it is very late. I am worried for you. Can I get you dinner?"

Sith had to smile. He sounded motherly in his concern. They are so good at building a relationship with you, until you cannot do without them. In the old days she would have sent him away with a few rude words. Now she sent him away with an order.

And wrote.

And when he came back, the aged motoboy looked so happy. "I bought you fruit as well, Lady," he said, and added, shyly. "You do not need to pay me for that."

Something seemed to bump under Sith, as if she was on a motorcycle, and she heard herself say, "Come inside. Have some food too."

The motoboy sompiahed in gratitude and as soon as he entered, the phone stopped ringing.

They sat on the floor. He arched his neck and looked around at the walls.

"Are all these people your family?" he asked.

She whispered. "No. They're ghosts who no one mourns."

"Why do they come to you?" His mouth fell open in wonder.

"Because my father was Pol Pot," said Sith, without thinking.

The motoboy sompiahed. "Ah." He chewed and swallowed and arched his head back again. "That must be a terrible thing. Everybody hates you."

Sith had noticed that wherever she sat in the room, the eyes in the photographs were directly on her. "I haven't done anything," said Sith.

"You're doing something now," said the motoboy. He nodded and stood up, sighing with satisfaction. Life was good with a full stomach and a patron. "If you need me, Lady, I will be outside."

Photo after photo, name after name.

Youk Achariya: touring dancer

Proeung Chhay: school superintendent

Sar Kothida, child, aged 7, died of 'swelling disease'

Sar Makara, her mother, nurse

Nath Mittapheap, civil servant, from family of farmers

Chor Monirath: wife of award-winning engineer

Yin Sokunthea: Khmer Rouge commune leader

She looked at the faces and realized. *Dara, I'm doing this for Dara.*

The city around her went quiet and she became aware that it was now very late indeed. Perhaps she should just make sure the motoboy had gone home.

He was still waiting outside.

"It's okay. You can go home. Where do you live?"

He waved cheerfully north. "Oh, on Monivong, like you." He grinned at the absurdity of the comparison.

A new idea took sudden form. Sith said, "Tomorrow, can you come early, with a big feast? Fish and rice and greens and pork: curries and stir-fries and kebabs." She paid him handsomely, and finally asked him his name. His name meant Golden.

"Good night, Sovann."

For the rest of the night she worked quickly like an answering service. This is like a cleaning of the house before a festival, she thought. The voices of the dead became ordinary, familiar. Why are people afraid of the dead? The dead can't hurt you. The dead want what you want: justice.

The wall of faces became a staircase and a garage and a kitchen of faces, all named. She had found Jorani's colored yarn, and linked family members into trees.

She wrote until the electric lights looked discolored, like a headache. She asked the ghosts, "Please can I sleep now?" The phones fell silent and Sith slumped with relief onto the polished marble floor.

She woke up dazed, still on the marble floor. Sunlight flooded the room. The faces in the photographs no longer looked swollen and bruised. Their faces were not accusing or mournful. They smiled down on her. She was among friends.

With a whine, the printer started to print; the phone started to ring. Her doorbell chimed, and there was Sovann, white cardboard boxes piled up on the back of his motorcycle. He wore the same shirt as yesterday, a cheap blue copy of a Lacoste. A seam had parted under the arm. He only has one shirt, Sith realized. She imagined him washing it in a basin every night.

Sith and Sovann moved the big tables to the front windows. Sith took out her expensive tablecloths for the first time, and the bronze platters. The feast was laid out as if at New Year. Sovann had bought more paper and pens. He knew what they were for. "I can help, Lady."

He was old enough to have lived in a country with schools, and he could write in a beautiful, old-fashioned hand. Together he and Sith spelled out the names of the dead and burned them.

"I want to write the names of my family too," he said. He burnt them weeping.

The delicious vapors rose. The air was full of the sound of breathing in. Loose papers stirred with the breeze. The ash filled the basins, but even after working all day, Sith and the motoboy had only honored half the names.

"Good night, Sovann," she told him.

"You have transferred a lot of merit," said Sovann, but only to be polite.

If I have any merit to transfer, thought Sith.

He left and the printers started, and the phone. She worked all night, and only stopped because the second ream of paper ran out.

The last picture printed was of Kol Vireakboth.

Dara, she promised herself. *Dara next*.

In the morning, she called him. "Can we meet at lunchtime for another walk by the river?"

Sith waited on top of the marble wall and watched an old man fish in the Tonlé Sap river and found that she loved her country. She loved its tough, smiling, uncomplaining people, who had never offered her harm, after all the harm her family had done them. Do you know you have the daughter of the monster sitting here among you?

Suddenly all Sith wanted was to be one of them. The monks in the pavilion, the white-shirted functionaries scurrying somewhere, the lazy bones dangling their legs, the young men who dress like American rappers and sold something dubious, drugs, or sex.

She saw Dara sauntering toward her. He wore his new shirt, and smiled at her but he didn't look relaxed. It had been two days since they'd met. He knew something was wrong, that she had something to tell him. He had bought them lunch in a little cardboard box. Maybe for the last time, thought Sith.

They exchanged greetings, almost like cousins. He sat next to her and smiled and Sith giggled in terror at what she was about to do.

Dara asked, "What's funny?"

She couldn't stop giggling. "Nothing is funny. Nothing." She sighed in order to stop and terror tickled her and she spurted out laughter again. "I lied to you. Kol Vireakboth is not my father. Another politician was my father. Someone you've heard of...."

The whole thing was so terrifying and absurd that the laughter squeezed her like a fist and she couldn't talk. She laughed and wept at the same time. Dara stared.

"My father was Saloth Sar. That was his real name." She couldn't make herself say it. She could tell a motoboy, but not Dara? She forced herself onward. "My father was Pol Pot."

Nothing happened.

Sitting next to her, Dara went completely still. People strolled past; boats bobbed on their moorings.

After a time Dara said, "I know what you are doing."

That didn't make sense. "Doing? What do you mean?"

Dara looked sour and angry. "Yeah, yeah, yeah, yeah." He sat, looking away from her. Sith's laughter had finally shuddered to a halt. She sat peering at him, waiting. "I told you my family were modest," he said quietly.

"Your family are lovely!" Sith exclaimed.

His jaw thrust out. "They had questions about you too, you know."

"I don't understand."

He rolled his eyes. He looked back 'round at her. "There are easier ways to break up with someone."

He jerked himself to his feet and strode away with swift determination, leaving her sitting on the wall.

Here on the riverfront, everyone was equal. The teenage boys lounged on the wall; poor mothers herded children; the foreigners walked briskly, trying to look as if they didn't carry moneybelts. Three fat teenage girls nearly swerved into a cripple in a pedal chair and collapsed against each other with raucous laughter.

Sith did not know what to do. She could not move. Despair humbled her, made her hang her head.

I've lost him.

The sunlight seemed to settle next to her, washing up from its reflection on the wake of some passing boat.

No you haven't.

The river water smelled of kindly concern. The sounds of traffic throbbed with forbearance.

Not yet.

There is no forgiveness in Cambodia. But there are continual miracles of compassion and acceptance.

Sith appreciated for just a moment the miracles. The motoboy buying her soup. She decided to trust herself to the miracles.

Sith talked to the sunlight without making a sound. *Grandfather Vireakboth. Thank you. You have told me all I need to know.*

Sith stood up and from nowhere, the motoboy was there. He drove her to the Hello Phone shop.

Dara would not look at her. He bustled back and forth behind the counter, though there was nothing for him to do. Sith talked to him like a customer. "I want to buy a mobile phone," she said, but he would not answer. "There is someone I need to talk to."

Another customer came in. She was a beautiful daughter too, and he served her, making a great show of being polite. He complimented her on her appearance. "Really, you look cool." The girl looked pleased. Dara's eyes darted in Sith's direction.

Sith waited in the chair. This was home for her now. Dara ignored her. She picked up her phone and dialed his number. He put it to his ear and said, "Go home."

"You are my home," she said.

His thumb jabbed the C button.

She waited. Shadows lengthened.

"We're closing," he said, standing by the door without looking at her.

Shamefaced, Sith ducked away from him, through the door.

Outside Soriya, the motoboy played dice with his fellows. He stood up. "They say I am very lucky to have Pol Pot's daughter as a client."

There was no discretion in Cambodia, either. Everyone will know now, Sith realized.

At home, the piles of printed paper still waited for her. Sith ate the old, cold food. It tasted flat, all its savor sucked away. The phones began to ring. She fell asleep with the receiver propped against her ear.

The next day, Sith went back to Soriya with a box of the printed papers.

She dropped the box onto the blue plastic counter of Hello Phones.

"Because I am Pol Pot's daughter," she told Dara, holding out a sheaf of pictures toward him. "All the unmourned victims of my father are printing their pictures on my printer. Here. Look. These are the pictures of people who lost so many loved ones there is no one to remember them."

She found her cheeks were shaking and that she could not hold the sheaf of paper. It tumbled from her hands, but she stood back, arms folded.

Dara, quiet and solemn, knelt and picked up the papers. He looked at some of the faces. Sith pushed a softly crumpled green card at him. Her family ID card.

He read it. Carefully, with the greatest respect, he put the photographs on the countertop along with the ID card.

"Go home, Sith," he said, but not unkindly.

"I said," she had begun to speak with vehemence but could not continue. "I told you. My home is where you are."

"I believe you," he said, looking at his feet.

"Then...." Sith had no words.

"It can never be, Sith," he said. He gathered up the sheaf of photocopying paper. "What will you do with these?"

Something made her say, "What will *you* do with them?"

His face was crossed with puzzlement.

"It's your country too. What will you do with them? Oh, I know, you're such a poor boy from a poor family, who could expect anything from you? Well, you have your whole family and many people have no one. And you can buy new shirts and some people only have one."

Dara held out both hands and laughed. "Sith?" *You, Sith, are accusing* me *of being selfish?*

"You own them too." Sith pointed to the papers, to the faces. "You think the dead don't try to talk to you, too?"

Their eyes latched. She told him what he could do. "I think you should make an exhibition. I think Hello Phones should sponsor it. You tell them that. You tell them Pol Pot's daughter wishes to make amends and has chosen them. Tell them the dead speak to me on their mobile phones."

She spun on her heel and walked out. She left the photographs with him.

That night she and the motoboy had another feast and burned the last of the unmourned names. There were many thousands.

The next day she went back to Hello Phones.

"I lied about something else," she told Dara. She took out all the reports from the fortunetellers. She told him what Hun Sen's fortuneteller had told her. "The marriage is particularly well favored."

"Is that true?" He looked wistful.

"You should not believe anything I say. Not until I have earned your trust. Go consult the fortunetellers for yourself. This time you pay."

His face went still and his eyes focused somewhere far beneath the floor. Then he looked up, directly into her eyes. "I will do that."

For the first time in her life Sith wanted to laugh for something other than fear. She wanted to laugh for joy.

"Can we go to lunch at Lucky7?" she asked.

"Sure," he said.

All the telephones in the shop, all of them, hundreds all at once began to sing.

A waterfall of trills and warbles and buzzes, snatches of old songs or latest chart hits. Dara stood dumbfounded. Finally he picked one up and held it to his ear.

"It's for you," he said, and held out the phone for her.

There was no name or number on the screen.

Congratulations, dear daughter, said a warm kind voice.

"Who is this?" Sith asked. The options were severely limited.

Your new father, said Kol Vireakboth. The sound of wind. *I adopt you.*

A thousand thousand voices said at once, *We adopt you.*

In Cambodia, you share your house with ghosts in the way you share it with dust. You hear the dead shuffling alongside your own footsteps. You can sweep, but the sound does not go away.

On the Tra Bek end of Monivong there is a house whose owner has given it over to ghosts. You can try to close the front door. But the next day you will find it hanging open. Indeed you can try, as the neighbors did, to nail the door shut. It opens again.

By day, there is always a queue of five or six people wanting to go in, or hanging back, out of fear. Outside are offerings of lotus or coconuts with embedded josh sticks.

The walls and floors and ceilings are covered with photographs. The salon, the kitchen, the stairs, the office, the empty bedrooms, are covered with photographs of Chinese-Khmers at weddings, Khmer civil servants on picnics, Chams outside their mosques, Vietnamese holding up prize catches of fish; little boys going to school in shorts; cyclopousse drivers in front of their odd, old-fashioned pedaled vehicles; wives in stalls stirring soup. All of them are happy and joyful, and the background is Phnom Penh when it was the most beautiful city in Southeast Asia.

All the photographs have names written on them in old-fashioned handwriting.

On the table is a printout of thousands of names on slips of paper. Next to the table are matches and basins of ash and water. The implication is plain. Burn the names and transfer merit to the unmourned dead.

Next to that is a small printed sign that says in English HELLO.

Every Pchum Ben, those names are delivered to temples throughout the city. Gold foil is pressed onto each slip of paper, and attached to it is a parcel of sticky rice. At 8 a.m. food is delivered for the monks, steaming rice and fish, along with bolts of new cloth. At 10 a.m. more food is delivered, for the disabled and the poor.

And most mornings a beautiful daughter of Cambodia is seen walking beside the confluence of the Tonlé Sap and Mekong rivers. Like Cambodia, she plainly loves all things modern. She dresses in the latest fashion. Cambodian

R&B whispers in her ear. She pauses in front of each new waterfront construction whether built by improvised scaffolding or erected with cranes. She buys noodles from the grumpy vendors with their tiny stoves. She carries a book or sits on the low marble wall to write letters and look at the boats, the monsoon clouds, and the dop-dops. She talks to the reflected sunlight on the river and calls it Father.

THE AMERICAN DEAD

JAY LAKE

Jay Lake lives and works in Portland, Oregon, within sight of an 11,000-foot volcano. He is the author of over two hundred short stories, four collections, and a chapbook. His first novel, *Rocket Science*, was published in 2005. He is the co-editor with Deborah Layne of the critically acclaimed *Polyphony* anthology series from Wheatland Press. His most recent book is new novel *Trial of Flowers*. Upcoming are collection *The River Knows Its Own* and novels *Madness of Flowers* and *Mainspring*. In 2004, Jay won the John W. Campbell Award for Best New Writer. He has also been a Hugo nominee for his short fiction and a three-time World Fantasy Award nominee for his editing.

There is the feeling that the American Century ended on September 11. This short, dark tale gives us a chilling outside view of the American dead…

Americans are all rich, even their dead. Pobrecito knows this because he spends the hottest parts of the days in the old *Cementerio Americano* down by the river. The water is fat and lazy while the pipes in the *colonia* drip only rust brown as the eyes of Santa Marguerite. Their graves are of the finest marble, carved with photographs in some manner he does not understand, or wrought with sculpted angels that put the churches up the hill to shame. Some of the American dead even have little houses, tight boxes with broken doors that must have once contained great riches.

He sits within a drooping tree which fights with life, and watches the flies make dark, wiggling rafts out on the water. There are dogs which live in the broken-backed jet out in the middle of the current, eyes glowing from behind the dozens of little shattered oval windows. At night the dogs swim across the slow current and run the river banks, hunting in the *colonia* and up toward the city walls.

They are why he never sleeps in the *Cementerio*. That some of the dogs walk on two legs only makes them worse.

When he was very young, Pobrecito found a case of magazines, old ones with bright color pictures of men and women without their clothes. Whoever had made the magazines had an astonishing imagination, because in Pobrecito's experience most people who fucked seemed to do it either with booze or after a lot of screaming and fighting and being held down. There weren't very many ways he'd ever seen it gone after. The people in these pictures were smiling, mostly, and arranged themselves more carefully than priests arranging a corpse. And they lived in the most astonishing places.

Pobrecito clips or tears the pictures out a few at a time and sells them on the streets of the *colonia*. He knows the magazines themselves would just be taken from him, before or after a beating, but a kid with a few slips of paper clutched in his hand is nothing. As long as no one looks too closely. But even if he had a pass for the gates, he dares not take them within the walls, for the priests would hang him in the square.

What he loves most about the magazines is not the nudity or the fucking or the strange combinations and arrangements these people found themselves in. No, what he loves is that these are Americans. Beautiful people in beautiful places doing beautiful things together.

"I will be an American someday," he tells his friend Lucia. They are in the branches of the dying tree, sharing a bottle of *pulque* and a greasy bowl of fried plantains in the midday heat. Pobrecito has a secret place up there, a hollow in the trunk where he hides most of his treasures.

The magazines are stored elsewhere, in a place he has never even shown to Lucia.

"You are an idiot," she declares, glancing out at the airplane in the river. The American flag can still be seen on its tall tail, small and weathered. No one has gone out to paint it over, for fear of the dogs. "All Americans are dead," she adds with prim authority.

Lucia is smaller than Pobrecito, though older. She is one of the *menoriítas*, born to be little. Though she is of an age to have breasts and make her bleedings, her body is smooth and slick as any young child's. Pobrecito knows this because they often curl together to sleep, and she likes him to touch her as if she were a baby, rubbing his hand over her sides and back and pulling her to his chest. He has tried to use his fingers to do a few of the things seen in his pictures, but she is too small down there both before and behind, and complains of the hurt.

She has never offered to touch him.

Pobrecito shakes off that thought. "What is dead can be reborn. This is what the priests are always telling us." He grins, mottled teeth flashing even in shadow. "I shall bleach my skin and hair like they did, and have a fine house filled with swimming pools and bright furniture. My automobiles would be colorful and shiny and actually have petrol."

She laughs then and sets her shoulder against his chest, tucking her head into his neck, sucking on the neck of the *pulque* bottle in a way which makes him both warm and uncomfortable. He strokes her hair and dreams of distant, lost cities such as Los Angeles and Omaha.

* * *

That evening the folk of the *colonia* are upset. They surge through the muddy streets, even the day workers who should already be sleeping, and there is an angry mutter like bottle wasps swarming. He even sees some weapons, knives dangling from hands, a few pistols tucked into belts. These are offenses of the worst order, to keep or carry weapons.

Pobrecito dodges booted feet and moves with the crowd, listening. He already knows he will sell no pictures tonight. Selling no pictures, he will not eat tomorrow. But he wants to understand what is wrong.

The crowd is speaking of priests.

"Girls, indeed."

"....a scandal. And they use God's name!"

"They wear those black dresses. Let them lie with one another."

"Called them up there from a list. I tell you, I won't allow my..."

"Hush! Do you want to hang?"

"A tax. How is this a *tax?*"

"Their time is coming. Soon."

Pobrecito comes to understand. Girls are being taken away by the priests. To be used, he supposes, like the Americans in his pictures use each other. Will the girls of the *colonia* smile beneath the lusts of the priests? Surely they will be cleaned and fed and cared for. It is the priests in their walled city that hold all wealth, all power.

But eventually the anger melts into fatigue, and word comes that the *guardia* are on their way down to the *colonia*, and so the knives and pistols vanish and people trudge home, some of them weeping more than usual.

* * *

Over the weeks, a few more girls are called every few days, always the hale ones with good curves to their breasts. The *guardia* comes to collect them now, as the people are no longer willing to send their sisters and daughters up the hill simply because a summons has come. There are beatings and a few quiet murders in which no priest-advocate will take any interest.

None of the girls come back.

In a few month's time, some older women are called, and younger girls as well. They do not return, either. The *colonia* remains restless, but the crystallizing anger of the first night never quite reappears. There is always food to worry about, and the dogs from the river, and the clouds of flies and wasps which can strip a man's skin in minutes, and the sicknesses which prowl just as deadly if less visible.

And the heat.

It is always a little hotter. This has been the way of things all of Pobrecito's life.

The vanishing girls and women are good for Pobrecito's little business. Sad men and wild-eyed boys buy from him, paying him in dented cans of dog food or little bundles of yams or onions. Even a few of the old women seek him out, clucking and tutting like senile chickens draped in funeral black, wanting pictures "of a girl alone, none of your despicable filth, just something to remember her by."

But he is becoming too well known, too rich. He has more food than he and Lucia can eat in a day, and even a few metal tools and some old bits of gold, which he hides in his tree by the river.

Is he rich enough to be an American yet, Pobrecito wonders?

* * *

One day he makes his way into the *Cementerio Americano* carrying two books and an old bottle of wine he has been paid for a handful of pictures of three thin, yellow-haired women kissing each other. By habit Pobrecito keeps to the shadows, the edges of fences and tumbled walls, but also by habit he has made a path in and out of this place. He steps around the edge of a rotting shed which contains a flat-tired tractor and some large metal implements to find three of the *guardia*.

"Ah," says Pobrecito, and reflexively offers them the wine. Perhaps it will save him from whatever is next. He doubts that, though.

The leader, for he has more decoration on his buttoned shoulder tabs, strokes the bright leather of his pistol belt for a moment, then smiles. It is a horrid sort of smile, something a man remembering an old photo he is trying to imitate might offer up. The other two do not bother. Instead they merely cradle a machete each, staring corpse-eyed at Pobrecito. All three of them are fat, their bellies bigger than their hips, unlike anyone in the *colonia*, except a few who are dying of growths in their guts.

No one takes the wine.

"You are the guardian of Lucia Sandoz, is it not true?" the leader asks.

This is not what Pobrecito expected. "Ah…no. She comes here sometimes."

The leader consults a thin notebook, ragged with handling, pages nearly black with ink. "You are Pobrecito the street merchant, no address, of the *colonia*."

"Yes."

"Then you are the guardian of Lucia Sandoz. It says so here in my book, and so this must be a true thing." His smile asserts itself again. "We have a summons for her." All three *guardia* peer around, as if expecting her to fall from the sky. Pobrecito realizes this has become an old game for them already.

"She is not mine," he says to his feet. Not Lucia. "And besides," he adds, "she is a *menoriíta*. She cannot be used in the manner of a woman." Will this help?

They laugh, his tormentors, before one of the machete-carriers says, "How would you know if you hadn't had her?"

The leader leans close. "She is *clean*, boy. That is enough these days."

Then they beat him, using the flat of the machete blades and the rough toes of their boots. Pobrecito loses most of his left ear when a blade slips, and the palm of his hand is cut to the bone, but they stop before staving in his ribs or breaking any large bones.

"Find her," says the leader. Pobrecito can barely hear him through the pain and blood in his ear. The *guardia* tears the pages of the books from their bindings, unzips, and urinates on the paper. Taking the wine bottle, he turns to leave. "Before tomorrow."

Pobrecito does not waste time on crying. He stumbles to his tree, knowing there are some extra clothes there that he can use to bind his ear and his hand. There are so many sicknesses that come in through bloody cuts and sores—black rot, green rot, the red crust—and he fears them all.

Stumbling, eyes dark and head ringing, Pobrecito can barely climb his tree because his arms and legs hurt so much. When he reaches the branch, he sees that someone has been at his cache of riches and food. *Guardia*, dogs, it does not matter. The hollow in the trunk has been hacked open, made wide and ragged with an ax or a machete, and everything that is not gone is smashed or torn or broken. His riches are nothing but trash now.

"I will never be an American," Pobrecito whispers. He lays his mutilated ear against the slashed palm of his hand, pressing them together to slow the bleeding and protect the wounds from insects. Despite the pain, he lays that side of his head against the branch and stretches out to surrender to the ringing darkness.

* * *

"Wake up, fool!" It is Lucia's voice. She is slapping him.

Pobrecito feels strange. His skin is itchy, crawly, prickly.

More slaps.

"Stop it this instant!" Her voice is rising toward a frightening break.

He opens his mouth to answer her and flies tumble in.

He is covered in flies.

"Gaaah!" Pobrecito screams.

"Get them off before they bite," she says, her voice more under control.

Pobrecito stumbles to his feet, runs down the branch where it overhangs the water.

"Not the river…" she says behind him, but it is too late. The old branch narrows, is rotten, his legs are weak, his eyes not clear. In a crackling shower of wood, flies and blood, Pobrecito tumbles the five or six meters downward to slam into the slow, brown water, knocking the air from his body.

The river is blood warm, shocking him awake. He is under the surface, eyes open to a uniform brown with no way up. The water is sticky, strange, clinging to him, trying to draw him farther down. Pobrecito kicks his legs, trying to come out, but there is still no up.

At least the flies are gone.

He begins to wonder if he could open his mouth and find something besides the burning in his empty lungs.

Something scrapes his legs. Something long, slow and powerful. Pobrecito throws his hands out and finds a stick. He pulls on it, but it does not come, so he pulls himself toward it.

A moment later he is gasping and muddy, clinging to a root sticking out from the river bank. Air is in his lungs, blessed air. Behind him the water burbles as the long, slow, powerful thing circles back to test him again. Out in the middle of the river, the dogs are barking.

Lucia is scrambling down the tree trunk, sobbing. "Fool! Idiot!"

She helps him pull himself out before his legs are taken. He lies on the bank gasping and crying, blessedly free of flies. He does not want to think about what the river water might have done to his wounds. "They…they came…. they came for you…" he spits out.

"No one wants me," she says fiercely.

"They said you were *clean*. That clean was enough for them these days."

She is quiet for a moment. "Fire-piss is killing the rich men up in the city, the old women say. The priests have heard from God that to fuck a clean woman takes the fire-piss from the man and gives it to her."

"How do you know? No one comes back."

"Some people pass in and out of the walls. Servants. Farmers. The word comes. And the cemetery is overflowing, up on the hill. With rich city men." She stares at him for a moment. "The *colonia* girls they dump down the old wells with some quicklime and gravel, and a prayer if they're feeling generous."

"Ahhh…" He weeps, eyes filling with hot tears as they hadn't for the beating, or for anything in his memory, really. "And they want you now."

"The cure does not work, but it does not stop them from trying over and over. The priests say it is so, that they are not faithful enough. Up in the city, they believe they can make the world however they want it." She stares at him for a while. "And perhaps they have a taste for new girls all the time."

Pobrecito thinks about his American pictures. Obviously many people had a taste for new girls all the time. Has he somehow been feeding this evil? But he doesn't sell his pictures in the city, or even to city men. Not directly. He has always wondered if some of his buyers did.

And if he could make the world the way he wanted it, he would wish away the heat and the insects and the sicknesses. He would make them all Americans like in his pictures, naked, happy, pale-skinned blondes with big houses and tables full of food and more water than any sane person could ever use. He would not wish for more girls to kill. Not even if God told him to.

"I want to show you something," he says.

"Show me soon. I think the dogs are coming over."

"In the day?"

"You got their attention, my friend."

Out at the airplane, dogs were gathering on the wing, their feet in the slow water. Some of them were casting sticks and stones out into the river, looking for that great predator that had touched Pobrecito for a moment. Others growl through pointed teeth, eyes glowing at him. Smoke curls from some of the shattered oval windows. Great red and blue letters, faded and worn as the tail's flag, loom along the rounded top of the airplane in some American prayer for the coming assault.

"It is over anyway," he says. "Come." He leads her deeper into the *Cementerio Americano*. Here Pobrecito has always been careful to hop from stone to stone, scramble along mortared kerbs, step on open ground, never making a path.

Here among the houses of the American dead is his greatest treasure.

He shows Lucia a squared-off vault, door wedged tightly shut. Grabbing a cornice, Pobrecito pulls himself to the roof though his body strains with the pain of the beating and the curious ache of his fall into the river. He then dangles his arm over to help her up. There are two windows in the roof, and he knows the secret of loosening one.

In a moment they are in the cool darkness of the vault. There are two marble coffins here, carved with wreaths and flowers, and Pobrecito's precious box of magazines at one end. He has left a few supplies, a can of drinkable water and some dried fruit, a homespun shirt without quite enough holes for it to disintegrate to ragged patches. And matches, his other great treasure.

"These people do not seem so wealthy," Lucia whispers. "This is a fine little house for them, but the only riches here are yours."

Pobrecito shrugs. "Perhaps they were robbed before I found them. Or perhaps their riches are within their coffins. This is a finer room than any you or I will ever live or die in." As soon as he says that last, he wishes he hadn't, as they may very well die in this room.

"So now what will you do?"

He pulls the magazines out of the their box, fans the pages open. Sleek American flesh in a hundred combinations flashes before his eyes: cocks, breasts, tongues, leather and plastic toys, sleek cars...all the world that was, once. The American world lost to the heat and the sicknesses. Pobrecito tosses the magazines into a pile, deliberately haphazard. After a few moments, Lucia begins to help, tearing a few apart, breaking their spines so they will lay flat. She ignores the pictures, though she is not so used to them as Pobrecito is.

Soon they have a glossy pile of images of the perfect past. Without another word, Pobrecito strikes a match and sets fire to a bright, curled edge. Cool faces, free of sweat and wounds, blacken and shrivel. He lights more matches, sets more edges of the pile on fire, until the flames take over.

The smoke stinks, filling the little vault, curling around the opening in the roof. He does not care, though Lucia is coughing. Pobrecito pulls off his wet, bloody clothes and pushes them into the base of the fire, then climbs atop one of the marble coffins. A few moments later, Lucia joins him.

She is naked as well.

They lie there on the bed of marble, smooth skinned as any Americans, kissing and touching, while the fire burns the pretty people in their pretty houses and the smoke rises through the roof. Outside dogs howl and *guardia* pistols crack.

When Lucia takes his cock in her mouth, Pobrecito knows he is as wealthy as any American. A while later he feels the hot rush of himself into her, even as the smoke makes him so dizzy his thoughts have spun off into the sky like so many airplanes rising from their river grave.

Soon he will be a true American, wealthy and dead.

THE CARTESIAN THEATER

ROBERT CHARLES WILSON

Robert Charles Wilson has had short fiction published in *F&SF*, *Asimov's*, *Realms of Fantasy*, and elsewhere. His short story "The Perseids" was a World Fantasy and Nebula Award finalist and an Aurora Award winner, and his short story "The Inner, Inner City" was a World Fantasy Award finalist. He has published twelve novels, including *A Hidden Place*, *Mysterium*, *Darwinia*, and Hugo Award winner *Spin*. His story collection *The Perseids and Other Stories* was a 2001 World Fantasy Award finalist for best collection. His most recent book is the novella *Julian: A Christmas Story*. Upcoming is new novel *Axis*, a sequel to *Spin*.

In the story that follows, Wilson tests the nature of the human soul and how consciousness exists in space and time.

Grandfather was dead but still fresh enough to give useful advice. So I rode transit out to his sanctuary in the suburbs, hoping he could help me solve a problem, or at least set me on the way to solving it myself.

I didn't get out this way much. It was a desolate part of town, flat in every direction where the old residences had been razed and stripped for recycling, but there was a lot of new construction going on, mostly aibot hives. It was deceptive. You catch sight of the towers from a distance and think: *I wonder who lives there?* Then you get close enough to register the colorless concrete, the blunt iteration of simple forms, and you think: *Oh, nobody's home.*

Sure looked busy out there, though. All that hurry and industry, all that rising dust—a long way from the indolent calm of Doletown.

* * *

At the sanctuary an aibot custodian seven feet tall and wearing a somber black waistcoat and matching hat led me to a door marked PACZOVSKI— Grandfather's room, where a few of his worldly possessions were arrayed to help keep his sensorium lively and alert.

He needed all the help he could get. All that remained of him was his neuro-prosthetic arrays. His mortal clay had been harvested for its biomedical utilities and buried over a year ago. His epibiotic ghost survived but was slurring into

Shannon entropy, a shadow of a shade of itself.

Still, he recognized me when I knocked and entered. "Toby!" his photograph called out.

The photo in its steel frame occupied most of the far wall. It smiled reflexively. That was one of the few expressions Grandfather retained. He could also do a frown of disapproval, a frown of anxiety, a frown of unhappiness, and raised eyebrows meant to register surprise or curiosity, although those last had begun to fade in recent months.

And in a few months more there would be nothing left of him but the picture itself, as inert as a bust of Judas Caesar (or whatever—history's not my long suite).

But he recognized the bottle of Sauvignon blanc I took out of my carrypack and placed on the rutted surface of an antique table he had once loved. "That's the stuff!" he roared, and, "Use a coaster, for Christ's sake, Toby; you know better than that."

I turned down his volume and stuck a handkerchief under the sweating bottle. Grandfather had always loved vintage furniture and fine wines.

"But I can't drink it," he added, sketching a frown of lament: "I'm not allowed."

Because he had no mouth or gut. Dead people tend to forget these things. The bottle was strictly for nostalgia, and to give his object-recognition faculties a little kick. "I need some advice," I said.

His eyes flickered between me and the bottle as if he couldn't decide which was real or, if real, more interesting. "Still having trouble with that woman…?"

"Her name is Lada."

"Your employer."

"Right."

"And wife."

"That too," I said. "Once upon a time."

"What's she done now?"

"Long story. Basically, she made me an accessory to an act of… let's say, a questionable legal and ethical nature."

"I don't do case law anymore." Grandfather had been a trial lawyer for an uptown firm back when his heart was still beating. "Is this problem serious?"

"I washed off the blood last night," I said.

* * *

Six weeks ago Lada Joshi had called me into her office and asked me if I still had any friends in Doletown.

"Same friends I always had," I told her truthfully. There was a time when I might have lied. For much of our unsuccessful marriage Lada had tried to wean me away from my Doletown connections. It hadn't worked. Now she wanted to start exploiting them again.

Her office was high above the city deeps. Through the window over her shoulder I could see the spine of a sunlit heat-exchanger, and beyond that a bulbous white cargodrome where unmanned aircraft buzzed like honey-fat bees.

Lada herself was beautiful and ambitious but not quite wealthy, or at least not as wealthy as she aspired to be. Her business, Ladajoshi™, was a bottom-tier novelty-trawling enterprise, one of hundreds in the city. I had been one of her stable of Doletown stringers until she married me and tried to elevate me socially. The marriage had ended in a vending-machine divorce after six months. I was just another contract employee now, far as Lada was concerned, and I hadn't done any meaningful work for weeks. Which was maybe why she was sending me back to Doletown. I asked her what the deal was.

She smiled and tapped the desktop with her one piece of expensive jewelry, a gold prosthetic left-hand index finger with solid onyx knuckles. "I've got a client who wants some work done on his behalf."

"Doletown work?"

"Partly."

"What kind of client?" Usually it was Lada who had to seek out clients, often while fending off a shoal of competitors. But it sounded as if this one had come to her.

"The client prefers to remain anonymous."

Odd, but okay. It wasn't my business, literally or figuratively. "What kind of work?"

"First we have to bankroll an artist named—" She double-checked her palm-reader. "Named Jafar Bloom, without making it too obvious we're interested and without mentioning our client."

Whom I couldn't mention in any case, since Lada wouldn't give me any hints. "What kind of artist is Jafar Bloom?"

"He has an animal act he calls the Chamber of Death, and he wants to open a show under the title 'The Cartesian Theater'. I don't know much more than that. He's deliberately obscure and supposedly difficult to work with. Probably a borderline personality disorder. He's had some encounters with the police but he's never been charged with aberrancy. Moves around a lot. I don't have a current address—you'll have to track him down."

"And then?"

"Then you front him the money to open his show."

"You want him to sign a contract?"

She gave me a steely look. "No contract. No stipulations."

"Come on, Lada, that doesn't make sense. Anybody could hand this guy cash, if that's all there is to it. Sounds like what your client wants is a cut-out—a blind middleman."

"You keep your accounts, Toby, and I'll keep mine, all right? You didn't fret about ethics when you were fucking that Belgian contortionist."

An argument I preferred not to revisit. "And after that?"

"After what? I explained—"

"You said 'First we bankroll Jafar Bloom.' Okay, we bankroll him. Then what?"

"We'll discuss that when the time comes."

Fine. Whatever.

We agreed on a per diem and expenses and Lada gave me some background docs. I read them on the way home, then changed into my gypsy clothes—I had never thrown them away, as much as she had begged me to—and rode a transit elevator all the way down to the bottom stop, sea level, the lowest common denominator: Doletown.

* * *

An aibot constructor roared by Grandfather's window on its way to a nearby hive, momentarily drowning out conversation. I glimpsed the machine as it rumbled past. A mustard-yellow unit, not even remotely anthropomorphic. It wasn't even wearing clothes.

But it was noisy. It carried a quarter-ton sack of concrete on its broad back, and its treads stirred up chalky plumes of dust. It was headed for a nursery hive shaped like a twenty-story artillery shell, where aibots of various phyla were created according to instructions from the Entrepreneurial Expert System that roams the cryptosphere like a benevolent ghost.

Grandfather didn't like the noisy aibots or their factories. "When I was young," he said as soon as he could make himself heard, "human beings built things for other human beings. And they did it with a decent sense of decorum. *Dulce et decorum.* All this goddamn noise!"

I let the remark pass. It was true, but I didn't want to hear his inevitable follow-up lament: *And in those days a man had to work for his living*, etc. As if we lived in a world where nobody worked! True, since the population crash and the Rationalization, nobody has to work in order to survive... but most of us do work.

I cleared my throat. "As I was saying—"

"Your story. Right. Jafar Bloom. Did you find him?"

"Eventually."

"He's an artist, you said?"

"Yes."

"So what's his medium?"

"Death," I said.

* * *

In fact it had been remarkably difficult to hook up with Jafar Bloom.

Doletown, of course, is where people live who (as Grandfather would say) "don't work." They subsist instead on the dole, the universal minimum allotment of food, water, shelter, and disposable income guaranteed by law to the entire ever-shrinking population of the country.

Most nations have similar arrangements, though some are still struggling to pay vig on the World Bank loans that bought them their own Entrepreneurial Expert Systems.

Back in grandfather's day economists used to say we couldn't afford a universal dole. What if *everybody* went on it; what if *nobody* worked? Objections that seem infantile now that economics is a real science. If nobody worked, fewer luxury goods would be produced; our EES would sense the shift in demand and adjust factory production downward, hunting a new equilibrium. Some aibots and factories would have to remodel or recycle themselves, or else the universal stipend would be juiced to compensate. Such adjustments, upward or downward, happen every day.

Of course it's a falsehood to say "nobody works," because that's the whole point of an EES/aibot-driven economy. The machines work; human labor is elective. The economy has stopped being a market in the classic sense and become a tool, the ultimate tool—the self-knapping flint, the wheel that makes more wheels and when there are enough wheels reconfigures itself to make some other desirable thing.

So why were people like me (and 75% of the downsized masses) still chasing bigger incomes? Because an economy is an oligarchy, not a democracy; a rich guy can buy more stuff than a dole gypsy.

And why do we want stuff? Human nature, I guess. Grandfather was still nagging me to buy him antiques and beer, even though he was far too dead to appreciate them.

Doletown, as I was saying, is where the hardcore dole gypsies live. I once counted myself among their number. Some are indolent but most are not; they "work" as hard as the rest of us, though they can't exchange their work for money (because they don't have a salable product or don't know how to market themselves or don't care to sully themselves with commerce).

Their work is invisible but potentially exploitable. Lots of cultural ferment happens in Doletown (and every living city has a Doletown by one name or another). Which is why two-bit media brokers like Ladajoshi™ trawl the district for nascent trends and unanticipated novelties. Fish in the right Doletown pool and you might land a juicy patent or copyright coshare.

But Jafar Bloom was a hard man to reach, reclusive even by Doletown standards. None of my old cronies knew him. So I put the word out and parked myself in a few likely joints, mostly cafes and talk shops—the Seaside Room, the infamous Happy Haunt, the nameless hostelries along the infill beaches. Even so, days passed before I met anyone who would acknowledge an acquaintance with him.

"Anyone" in this case was a young woman who strode up to my table at the Haunt and said, "People say you're curious about Jafar Bloom. But you don't look like a creep or a sadist."

"Sit down and have a drink," I said. "Then you can tell me what I am."

She sat. She wore gypsy rags bearing logo stamps from a shop run by aibot recyclers down by the docks. I used to shop there myself. I pretended to admire the tattoo in the shape of the Greek letter omega that covered her cheeks and forehead. It looked as if a dray horse had kicked her in the face. I asked her if she knew Jafar Bloom personally.

"Somewhat," she said. "We're not, um, intimate friends. He doesn't really *have* any intimate friends. He doesn't like people much. How did you hear about him?"

"Word gets around."

"Well, that's how I heard of *you*. What do you want from Bloom?"

"I just want to see the show. That's all. Can you introduce me to him?"

"Maybe."

"Maybe if?"

"Maybe if you buy me something," she said demurely.

So I took her to a mall on one of the abandoned quays where the air smelled of salt and diesel fuel. The mall's location and inventory was dictated by the commercial strategies and profit-optimizing algorithms of the EES, but it stocked some nice carriage-trade items that had never seen the inside of an aibot workshop. She admired (and I bought for her) a soapstone drug pipe inlaid with chips of turquoise—her birthstone, she claimed.

Three days later she took me to a housing bloc built into the interstices of an elevated roadway and left me at an unmarked steel door, on which I knocked three times.

A few minutes later a young man opened it, looking belligerent.

"I don't kill animals for fun," he said, "if that's what you're here for."

Jafar Bloom was tall, lean, pale. His blond hair was long and lank. He wore a pair of yellow culottes, no shirt. "I was told you do theater," I said.

"That's exactly what I do. But rumors get out that I'm torturing animals. So I have the Ethical Police dropping by, or untreated ginks who want to see something get hurt."

"I just want to talk business."

"Business?"

"Strictly."

"I've got nothing to sell."

"May I come in?"

"I guess so," he said, adding a glare that said, *but you're on probation.* "I heard you were looking for me."

I stepped inside. His apartment looked like a studio, or a lab, or a kennel—or a combination of all three. Electronic items were stacked in one dim corner. Cables veined across the floor. Against another wall was a stack of cages containing animals, mostly rats but also a couple of forlorn dogs.

The skylight admitted a narrow wedge of cloudy daylight. The air was hot and still and had a kind of sour jungle odor.

"I'm completely aboveboard here," Bloom said. "I have to be. Do you know what the consequence would be if I was needlessly inflicting pain on living things?"

Same consequence as for any other demonstrable mental aberration. We don't punish cruelty, we treat it. Humanely.

"I'd be psychiatrically modified," Bloom said. "I don't want that. And I don't deserve it. So if you're here to see something *hurt*—"

"I already said I wasn't. But if you don't deal in cruelty—"

"I deal in art," he said crisply.

"The subject of which is—?"

"Death."

"Death, but not cruelty?"

"That's the point. That's *exactly* the point. How do you begin to study or examine something, Mr.—?"

"Paczovski."

"How do you study a thing unless you isolate it from its environment? You want to study methane, you distill it from crude petroleum, right? You want gold, you distill it from dross."

"That's what you do? You distill death?"

"That's exactly what I do."

I walked over to the cages and looked more closely at one of the dogs. It was a breedless mutt, the kind of animal you find nosing through empty houses out in the suburbs. It dozed with its head on its paws. It didn't look like it had been mistreated. It looked, if anything, a little overfed.

It had been fitted with a collar—not an ordinary dog collar but a metallic band bearing bulbous black extrusions and webs of wire that blurred into the animal's coat.

The dog opened one bloodshot eye and looked back at me.

"Good trick, distilling death. How do you do that exactly?"

"I'm not sure I should answer any questions until you tell me what you want to buy."

Bloom stared at me challengingly. I knew he'd been telling the truth about the Ethical Police. Some of their reports had been included in Lada's dossier. None of these animals had been or would be harmed. Not directly.

"I don't want to buy anything," I said.

"You said this was a business deal."

"Business or charity, depending on how you look at it." I figured I might as well lay it out for him as explicitly as possible. "I don't know what you do, Mr. Bloom. I represent an anonymous investor who's willing to put money into something called The Cartesian Theater. All he wants in return is your written assurance that you'll use the money for this theatrical project rather than, say, buggering off to Djibouti with it. How's that sound?"

It sounded unconvincing even to me. Bloom's skepticism was painfully obvious. "Nobody's giving away free money but the EES."

"Given the investor's wish for anonymity, there's no further explanation I can offer."

"I'm not signing away my intellectual property rights. I've got patents pending. And I refuse to divulge my techniques."

"Nobody's asking you to."

"Can I have *that* in writing?"

"In triplicate, if you want."

Suddenly he wasn't sure of himself. "Bullshit," he said finally. "Nobody invests money without at least a chance of profiting by it."

"Mr. Bloom, I can't answer all your questions. To be honest, you're right. It stands to reason the investor hopes to gain something by your success. But it might not be money. Maybe he's an art lover. Or maybe he's a philanthropist, it makes him feel good to drop large amounts of cash in dark places."

Or maybe he shared Bloom's fascination with death.

"How much money are we talking about?"

I told him.

He tried to be cool about it. But his eyes went a little misty.

"I'll give it some thought," he said.

* * *

Grandfather had been a trial lawyer during his life. His epibiotic ghost probably didn't remember much of that. Long-term memory was unstable in even the most expensive neuroprostheses. But there was enough of the lawbook left in him that his photo grew more animated when I mentioned open-ended contracts or the Ethical Police.

He said, "Exactly how much did you know about this guy going in?"

"Everything that was publicly available. Bloom was born in Cleveland and raised by his father, an accountant. Showed signs of high intellect at an early age. He studied electronic arts and designed some well-received neural interfaces before he quit the business and disappeared into Doletown. He's eccentric and probably obsessive, but nothing you could force-treat him for."

"And I assume he took the money you offered."

"Correct." Half up front, half when the Cartesian Theater was ready to open.

"So what *was* he doing with those animals?"

One of the sanctuary aibots passed the open door of Grandfather's memorial chamber. It paused a moment, adjusting its tie and tugging at its tailed vest. It swiveled its eyestalks briefly toward us, then wheeled on down the corridor. "Nosey fucking things," Grandfather said.

"Soon as Bloom signed the contract he invited me to what he called a 'dress rehearsal.' But it wasn't any kind of formal performance. It was really just an experiment, a kind of dry-run. He sold admission to a few local freaks, people he was ashamed of knowing. People who liked the idea of watching an animal die in agony."

"You said he didn't hurt or kill anything."

"Not as far as the law's concerned, anyway."

* * *

Bloom explained it all to me as he set up the night's exhibition. He seemed to welcome the opportunity to talk about his work with someone who wasn't, as he said, "quietly deranged." He hammered that idea pretty hard, as if to establish his own sanity. But how sane is a man whose overweening ambition is to make an artform of death?

He selected one of the dogs and pulled its cage from the rack. The other dogs he released into a makeshift kennel on an adjoining roof. "They get upset if they see what happens, even though they're not in any danger."

Then he put the selected animal into a transparent box the size of a shipping crate. The glass walls of the box were pierced with ventilator holes and inlaid with a mesh of ultrafine inductors. A cable as thick as my arm snaked from the box to the rack of electronic instrumentation. "You recognize the devices on the dog's collar?"

"Neuroprostheses," I said. "The kind they attach to old people." The kind they had attached to Grandfather back when he was merely dying, not entirely dead.

"Right," Bloom said, his face simmering with enthusiasm. "The mind, your mind, any mind—the dog's mind, in this case—is really a sort of parliament of competing neural subroutines. When people get old, some or all of those functions start to fail. So we build various kinds of prostheses to support aging mentation. Emotive functions, limbic functions, memory, the senses: we can sub for each of those things with an external device."

That was essentially what Grandfather had done for the last five years of his life: shared more and more of his essential self with a small army of artificial devices. And when he eventually died much of him was still running in these clusters of epibiotic prostheses. But eventually, over time, without a physical body to order and replenish them, the machines would drift back to simple default states, and that would be the end of Grandfather as a coherent entity. It was a useful but ultimately imperfect technology.

"Our setup's a little different," Bloom said. "The prostheses here aren't subbing for lost functions—the dog isn't injured or old. They're just doubling the dog's ordinary brainstates. When I disconnect the prostheses the dog won't even notice; he's fully functional without them. But the ghost in the prostheses—the dog's intellectual double—goes on without him."

"Yeah, for thirty seconds or so," I said. Such experiments had been attempted before. Imagine being able to run a perfect copy of yourself in a digital environment—to download yourself to an electronic device, like in the movies. Wouldn't that be great? Well, you *can*, sort of, and the process worked the way Bloom described it. But only briefly. The fully complex digital model succumbs to something called "Shannon entropy" in less than a minute. It's not dynamically stable.

(Postmortem arrays like Grandfather last longer—up to a couple of years—but only because they're radically simplified, more a collection of vocal tics than a real personality.)

"Thirty seconds is enough," Bloom said.

"For what?"

"You'll see."

About this time the evening's audience began to drift in. Or maybe "audience" is too generous a word. It consisted of five furtive-looking guys in cloaks and rags, each of whom slipped Bloom a few bills and then retreated to the shadows. They spoke not at all, even to each other, and they stared at the dog in its glass chamber with strange, hungry eyes. The dog paced, understandably nervously.

Now Bloom rolled out another, nearly identical chamber. The "death chamber." It contained not a dog but a sphere of some pink, slightly sparkly substance.

"Electrosensitive facsimile gel," Bloom whispered. "Do you know what that is?"

I'd heard of it. Facsimile gel is often used for stage and movie effects. If you want an inert duplicate of a valuable object or a bankable star, you scan the item in question and map it onto gel with EM fields. The gel expands and morphs until it's visually identical to the scanned object, right down to color and micron-level detail if you use the expensive stuff. Difference was, the duplicate would be rigid, hollow, and nearly massless—a useful prop, but delicate.

"You duplicate the dog?" I asked.

"I make a *dynamic* duplicate. It changes continuously, in synch with the real thing. I've got a patent application on it. Watch." He dimmed the lights and threw a few switches on his bank of homemade electronics.

The result was eerie. The lump of gel pulsed a few times, expanded as if it had taken a deep breath, grew legs, and became… a dog.

Became, in fact, the dog in the adjacent glass cage.

The real dog looked at the fake dog with obvious distress. It whined. The fake dog made the same gesture simultaneously, but no sound came out.

Two tongues lolled. Two tails drooped.

Now the freaks in the audience were almost slavering with anticipation.

I whispered, "And this proves what?"

Bloom raised his voice so the ginks could hear—a couple of them were new and needed the explanation. "Two dogs," he said. "One real. One artificial. The living dog is fitted with an array of neuroprostheses that duplicate its brain states. The dog's brain states are modeled in the electronics, here. Got that?"

We all got it. The audience nodded in unison.

"The dog's essence, its sense of self, is distributed between its organic brain and the remote prostheses. At the moment it's controlling the gel duplicate, too.

When the real dog lifts his head and sniffs the air—like that: see?—he lifts the fake dog's head simultaneously. The illusion mimics the reality. The twinned soul operates twin bodies, through the medium of the machine."

His hand approached another switch.

"But when I throw *this* switch, the living dog's link to the prosthetics is severed. The original dog becomes merely itself—it won't even notice that the connection has been cut."

He threw the switch; the audience gasped—but again, nothing obvious happened.

Both dogs continued to pace, as if disturbed by the sharp smell of sweat and ionization.

"As of now," Bloom said, "the artificial animal is dynamically controlled *solely by the neuroprostheses*. It's an illusion operated by a machine. But it moves as if it had mass, it sees as if it had eyes, it retains a capacity for pleasure or pain."

Now the behavior of the two dogs began to fall out of synchronization, subtly at first, and then more radically. Neither dog seemed to like what was happening. They eyed each other through their respective glass walls and backed away, snarling.

"Of course," Bloom added, his voice thick with an excitement he couldn't disguise, "without a biological model the neuroprostheses lose coherence. Shannon entropy sets in. Ten seconds have passed since I threw the final switch." He checked his watch. "Twenty."

The fake dog shook its head and emitted a silent whine.

It moved in a circle, panting.

It tried to scratch itself. But its legs tangled and bent spasmodically. It teetered a moment, then fell on its side. Its ribs pumped as if it were really breathing, and I guess it thought it *was* breathing—gasping for air it didn't really need and couldn't use.

It raised its muzzle and bared its teeth.

Its eyes rolled aimlessly. Then they turned opaque and dissolved into raw gel.

The artificial dog made more voiceless screaming gestures. Other parts of it began to fall off and dissolve. It arched its back. Its flanks cracked open, and for a moment I could see the shadowy hollowness inside.

The agony went on for what seemed like centuries but was probably not more than a minute or two. I had to turn away.

The audience liked it, though. This was what they had come for, this simulation of death.

They held their breath until the decoherent mass of gel had stopped moving altogether; then they sighed; they applauded timidly. It was only when the lights came up that they began to look ashamed. "Now get out," Bloom told them, and when they had finished shuffling out the door, heads down, avoiding eye contact, he whispered to me, "I hate those guys. They are truly fucking demented."

I looked back at the two glass cages.

The original dog was trembling but unhurt. The duplicate was a quiescent puddle of goo. It had left a sharp tang in the air, and I imagined it was the smell of pain. The thing had clearly been in pain. "You said there was no cruelty involved."

"No cruelty *to animals*," Bloom corrected me.

"So what do you call this?"

"There's only one animal in the room, Mr. Paczovski, and it's completely safe, as you can see. What took shape in the gel box was an animation controlled by a machine. It didn't die because it was never alive."

"But it was in agony."

"By definition, no, it wasn't. A machine can only *simulate* pain. Look it up in the statutes. Machines have no legal standing in this regard."

"Yeah, but a complex-enough machine—"

"The law doesn't make that distinction. The EES is complex. Aibots are complex: they're all linked together in one big neural net. Does that make them people? Does that make it an act of sadism if you kick a vacuum cleaner or default on a loan?"

Guess not. Anyway, it was his show, not mine. I meant to ask him if the dog act was the entire substance of his proposed Cartesian Theater... and why he thought anyone would want to see such a thing, apart from a few unmedicated sadists.

But this wasn't about dogs, not really. It was a test run. When Bloom turned away from me I could see a telltale cluster of bulges between his shoulder blades. He was wearing a full array of neuroprostheses. That's what he meant when he said the dogs were experiments. He was using them to refine his technique. Ultimately, he meant to do this *to himself*.

* * *

"Technically," Grandfather said, "he's right. About the law, I mean. What he's doing, it's ingenious and it's perfectly legal."

"Lada's lawyers told her the same thing."

"A machine, or a distributed network of machines, can be intelligent. But it can never be a person under the law. It can't even be a legal dog. Bloom wasn't shitting you. If he'd hurt the animal in any way he would have been remanded for treatment. But the fake dog, legally, is only a *representation* of an animal, like an elaborate photograph."

"Like you," I pointed out.

He ignored this. "Tell me, did any of the ginks attending this show look rich?"

"Hardly."

"So the anonymous investor isn't one of them."

"Unless he was in disguise, no. And I doubt Bloom would have turned down a cash gift even if it came from his creepy audience—the investor wouldn't have needed me or Lada if he had a direct line to Bloom."

"So how did your investor hear about Bloom in the first place, if he isn't friendly with him or part of his audience?"

Good question.

I didn't have an answer.

* * *

When I told Lada what I'd seen she frowned and ran her gold finger over her rose-pink lower lip, a signal of deep interest, the kind of gesture professional gamblers call a "tell."

I said, "I did what you asked me to. Is there a problem with that?"

"No—no problem at all. You did fine, Toby. I just wonder if we should have taken a piece for ourselves. A side agreement of some kind, in case this really does pan out."

"If *what* pans out? When you come down to it, all Bloom has to peddle is an elaborate special effect. A stage trick, and not a very appealing one. The ancillary technology might be interesting, but he says he already filed patents."

"The investor obviously feels differently. And he probably didn't get rich by backing losers."

"How well do you know this investor?"

She smiled. "All honesty? I've never met him. He's a text-mail address."

"You're sure about his gender, at least?"

"No, but, you know, *death*, *pain*—it all seems a little masculine, doesn't it?"

"So is there a next step or do we just wait for Bloom to put together his show?"

"Oh," and here she grinned in a way I didn't like, "there's *definitely* a next step."

She gave me another name. Philo Novembre.

* * *

"Rings a bell," Grandfather said. "Faintly. But then, I've forgotten so much."

* * *

Philo Novembre was easier to find that Jafar Bloom. At least, his address was easier to find—holding a conversation with him was another matter.

Philo Novembre was ten years short of a century old. He lived in an offshore retirement eden called Wintergarden Estates, connected to the mainland by a scenic causeway. I was the most conspicuously youthful visitor in the commute bus from the docks, not that the sample was representative: there were only three other passengers aboard. Aibot transports hogged the rest of the road, shuttling supplies to the Wintergarden. Their big eyes tracked the bus absently and they looked bored, even for machines.

Novembre, of course, had not invited me to visit, so the aibot staffing the reception desk asked me to wait in the garden while it paged him—warning me that Mr. Novembre didn't always answer his pages promptly. So I found a bench in the atrium and settled down.

The Wintergarden was named for its atrium. I don't know anything about flowers, but there was a gaudy assortment of them here, crowding their beds and creeping over walkways and climbing the latticed walls, pushing out crayon-colored blooms. Old people are supposed to like this kind of thing. Maybe they do, maybe they don't; Grandfather had never demonstrated an interest in botany, and he had died at the age of a century and change. But the garden was pretty to look at and it flushed the air with complex fragrances, like a dream of an opium den. I was nearly dozing when Philo Novembre finally showed up.

He crossed the atrium like a force of nature. Elderly strollers made way for his passage; garden-tending aibots the size of cats dodged his footfalls with quick, knowing lunges. His face was lined but sharp, not sagging, and his eyes were the color of water under ice. His left arm was unapologetically prosthetic, clad in powder-black brushed titanium. His guide, a thigh-high aibot in brown slacks and a golf shirt, pointed at me and then scuttled away.

I stood up to meet him. He was a centimeter or two taller than me. His huge gray gull-winged eyebrows contracted. He said, "I don't know you."

"No sir, you don't. My name is Toby Paczovski, and I'd be honored if you'd let me buy you lunch."

It took some haggling, but eventually he let me lead him to one of the five restaurants in the Wintergarden complex. He ordered a robust meal, I ordered coffee, and both of us ignored the elderly customers at the adjoining tables, some so extensively doctored that their physical and mental prostheses had become their defining characteristics. One old gink sucked creamed corn through a tube that issued from his jaw like an insect tongue, while his partner glared at me through lidless ebony-black eyes. I don't plan ever to get old. It's unseemly.

"The reason I'm here," I began, but Novembre interrupted:

"No need to prolong this. You bought me a decent meal, Mr. Paczovski. I owe you a little candor, if nothing else. So let me explain something. Three or four times a year somebody like yourself shows up here at the Wintergarden and flatters me and asks me to submit to an interview or a public appearance. This person might represent a more or less respectable agency or he might be a stringer or a media pimp, but it always comes down to the same pitch: once-famous enemy of automated commerce survives into the golden age of the EES. What they want from me is either a gesture of defiance or a mumbled admission of defeat. They say they'll pay generously for the right note of bathos. But the real irony is that these people have come on a quest as quixotic as anything I ever undertook. Because I don't make public appearances. Period. I don't sign contracts. Period. I'm retired. In every sense of the word. Now, do you want to spend your time more profitably elsewhere, or shall we order another round of coffee and discuss other things?"

"Uh," I said.

"And of course, in case you're already recording, I explicitly claim all rights to any words I've spoken or will speak at this meeting or henceforth, subject to the Peking Accords and the Fifty-second Amendment."

He grinned. His teeth looked convincingly real. But most people's teeth look real these days, except the true ancients, like the guy at the next table.

* * *

"Well, he knows his intellectual property law," Grandfather said. "He's got you dead to rights on that one."

"Probably so," I said, "but it doesn't matter. I wasn't there to buy his signature on a contract."

"So what *did* you want from him? Or should I say, what did Lada want from him?"

"She wanted me to tell him about Jafar Bloom. Basically, she wanted me to invite him to opening night at the Cartesian Theater."

"That's it?"

"That's it."

"So this client of hers was setting up a scenario in which Novembre was present for Bloom's death act."

"Basically, yeah."

"For no stated reason." Grandfather's photograph was motionless a few moments. Implying deep thought, or a voltage sag.

I said, "Do you remember Philo Novembre back when he was famous? The eighties, that would have been."

"The 2080s," Grandfather mused. "I don't know. I remember that I once remembered those years. I have a memory of having a memory. My memories are like bubbles, Toby. There's nothing substantial inside, and when I touch them they tend to disappear."

* * *

Philo Novembre had been a celebrity intellectual back in the 2080s, a philosopher, a sort of 21st century Socrates or Aristotle.

In those days—the global population having recently restabilized at two billion after the radical decline of the Plague Years—everyday conveniences were still a dream of the emerging Rationalization. Automated expert systems, neuroprostheses, resource-allocation protocols, the dole: all these things were new and contentious, and Philo Novembre was suspicious of all of them.

He had belonged to no party and supported no movement, although many claimed him. He had written a book, *The Twilight of the Human Soul*, and he had stomped for it like a backwoods evangelist, but what had made him a media celebrity was his personal style: modest at first; then fierce, scolding, bitter, moralistic.

He had claimed that ancient virtues were being lost or forgotten in the rush to a rationalized economy, that expert systems and globally distributed AI, no matter how sophisticated, could never emulate true moral sensitivity—a human sense of right and wrong.

That was the big debate of the day, simplistic as it sounds, and it ultimately ended in a sort of draw. Aibots and expert systems were granted legal status *in loco humanis* for economic purposes but were denied any broader rights, duties, privileges, or protection under the law. Machines aren't people, the courts said, and if the machines said anything in response they said it only to each other.

And we all prospered in the aftermath, as the old clunky oscillating global marketplace grew increasingly supple, responsive, and bias-free. Novembre had eventually disappeared from public life as people lost interest in his jeremiads and embraced the rising prosperity.

Lada had given me a dossier of press clippings on Novembre's decline from fame. Around about the turn of the century he was discovered in a Dade County doletown, chronically drunk. A few months later he stumbled into the path of a streetcleaning aibot, and his left arm was crushed before the startled and penitent machine could reverse its momentum. A local hospital had replaced his arm—it was still the only prosthesis he was willing to wear—and incidentally cured his alcoholism, fitting him with a minor corticolimbic mod that damped his craving. He subsequently attempted to sue the hospital for neurological intervention without written consent but his case was so flimsy it was thrown out of court.

After which Novembre vanished into utter obscurity and eventually signed over his dole annuities to the Wintergarden Retirement Commune.

From which he would not budge, even for a blind date with Jafar Bloom. I told Lada so when I made it back to the mainland.

"We have not yet begun to fight," Lada said.

"Meaning—?"

"Meaning let me work it for a little while. Stay cozy with Jafar Bloom, make sure he's doing what we need him to do. Call me in a week. I'll come up with something."

She was thinking hard…which, with Lada, was generally a sign of trouble brewing.

* * *

Unfortunately, I had begun to despise Jafar Bloom.

As much as Bloom affected to disdain the ginks and gaffers who paid to see his animal tests, he was just as twisted as his audience—more so, in his own way. Morbid narcissism wafted off him like a bad smell.

But Lada had asked me to make sure Bloom followed through on his promise. So I dutifully spent time with him during the month it took to rig his show. We rented an abandoned theater in the old district of Doletown and I helped him fix it up, bossing a fleet of renovation aibots who painted the mildewed walls, replaced fractured seats, restored the stage, and patched the flaking proscenium. We ordered industrial quantities of reprogels and commissioned a control rig of Bloom's design from an electronics prototyper.

During one of these sessions I asked him why he called his show "The Cartesian Theater."

He smiled a little coyly. "You know the name Descartes?"

No. I used to know a Belgian acrobat called Giselle de Canton, but the less said about that the better.

"The philosopher Descartes," Bloom said patiently. "René Descartes, 1596-1650. *Discourse on Method. Rules for the Direction of the Mind.*"

"Sorry, no," I said.

"Well. In one of his books Descartes imagines the self—the human sense of identity, that is—as a kind of internal gnome, a little creature hooked up to the outside world through the senses, like a gink in a one-room apartment staring out the window and sniffing the air."

"So you believe that?"

"I believe in it as a metaphor. What I mean to do on stage is externalize my Cartesian self, or at least a copy of it. Let the gnome out for a few seconds. Modern science, of course, says there is no unitary self, that what we call a 'self' is only the collective voice of dozens of neural subsystems working competitively and collaboratively—"

"What else could it be?"

"According to the ancients, it could be a human soul."

"But your version of it dies in agony in less than a minute."

"Right. If you believed in the existence of the soul, you could construe what I do as an act of murder. Except, of course, the soul in question is dwelling in a machine at the moment of its death. And we have ruled, in all our wisdom, that machines don't *have* souls."

"Nobody believes in souls," I said.

But I guess there were a few exceptions.

Philo Novembre, for one.

* * *

Lada called me into her office the following week and handed me another dossier of historical files. "More background?"

"Leverage," she said. "Information Mr. Novembre would prefer to keep quiet."

"You're asking me to blackmail him?"

"God, Toby. Settle down. The word 'blackmail' has really awkward legal connotations. So let's not use it, shall we?"

"If I threaten him he's liable to get violent." Novembre was old, but that titanium forearm had looked intimidating.

"I don't pay you to do the easy things."

"I'm not sure you pay me enough to do the hard things. So where'd this information come from? Looks like ancient police files."

"Our client submitted it," Lada said.

* * *

"What did you ever see in this woman?" Grandfather asked.

Good question, although he had asked it a dozen times before, in fact whenever I visited him. I didn't bother answering anymore.

I had come to the city a dozen years ago from a ghost town in the hinterland—one of those wheat towns decimated by the population implosion and rendered obsolete by aifarming—after my parents were killed when a malfunctioning grain transport dropped out of the sky onto our old house on Nightshade Street. Grandfather had been my only living relative and he had helped me find Doletown digs and cooked me an old-fashioned meal every Sunday.

City life had been a welcome distraction and the dole had seemed generous, at least until grief faded and ambition set in. Then I had gone looking for work, and Lada Joshi had been kind enough, as I saw it then, to hire me as one of her barely paid Doletown scouts.

Which was fine, until the connection between us got more personal. Lada saw me as a diamond-in-the-rough, begging for her lapidary attention. While I saw her as an ultimately inscrutable amalgam of love, sex, and money.

It worked out about as well as you'd expect.

* * *

Novembre's official biography, widely distributed back when he was famous, made him out to be the dutiful son of a Presbyterian pastor and a classical flautist, both parents lost in the last plagues of the Implosion. The truth, according to Lada's files, was a little uglier. Philo Novembre's real name was Cassius Flynn, and he had been raised by a couple of marginally sane marijuana farmers in rural Minnesota. The elder Flynns had been repeatedly arrested on drug and domestic violence charges, back in the days before the Rationalization and the Ethical Police. Their death had in a sense been a boon for young Cassius, who had flourished in one of the big residential schools run by the federal government for orphans of the Plague Years.

Nothing too outrageous, but it would have been prime blackmail material back in the day. But Novembre wasn't especially impressed when I showed him what we had.

"I made my name," he said, "by proclaiming a belief in the existence of metaphysical good and evil independent of social norms. I allowed a publicist to talk me into a lie about my childhood, mainly because I didn't want to be presented to the world as a psychological case study. Yes, my parents were cruel, petty, and venal human beings. Yes, that probably did contribute to the trajectory of my life and work. And yes, it still embarrasses me. But I'm far too old and obscure to be blackmailed. Isn't that obvious? Go tell the world, Mr.

Paczovski. See if the world cares."

"Yeah," I said, "it did seem like kind of a long shot."

"What intrigues me is that you would go to these lengths to convince me to attend a one-shot theatrical production, for purposes you can't explain. Who hired you, Mr. Paczovski?"

He didn't mean Lada. She was only an intermediary. "Truly, I don't know."

"That sounds like an honest answer. But it begs another question. Who, frankly, imagines my presence at Mr. Bloom's performance would be in any way meaningful?" He lowered his head a moment, pondering. Then he raised it. "Do you know how my work is described in the *Encyclopedia of Twenty-First Century American Thought*? As—and I'm quoting—'a humanistic questioning of economic automation, embodied in a quest to prove the existence of transcendent good and evil, apart from the acts encouraged or proscribed by law under the Rationalization.'"

"Transcendent," I said. "That's an interesting word." I wondered what it meant.

"Because it sounds like your Mr. Bloom has discovered just that—a profoundly evil act, for which he can't be prosecuted under existing law."

"Does that mean you're interested?"

"It means I'm curious. Not quite the same thing."

But he was hooked. I could hear it in his voice. The blackmail had had its intended effect, though not in the customary way.

* * *

"Entertainment," Grandfather said.

"What?"

"That's really the only human business anymore. Aibots do all the physical labor and the EES sorts out supply and demand. What do *we* do that *bots* can't do? Entertain each other, mostly. Lie, gossip, and dance. That, or practice law."

"Yeah, but so?"

"It's why someone wanted to put Bloom and Novembre together. For the entertainment value." His photograph stared while I blinked. "The *motive*, stupid," he said.

"Motive implies a crime."

"You mentioned blood. So I assume Novembre made the show."

"It opened last night." And closed.

"You want to tell me about it?"

Suddenly, no, I didn't. I didn't even want to think about it.

But I was in too deep to stop. Story of my life.

* * *

Doletown, of course, is a museum of lost causes and curious passions, which means there's plenty of live theater in Doletown, most of it eccentric or execrably bad. But Bloom's production didn't rise even to that level. It lacked plot, stagecraft, publicity, or much of an audience, and none of that mattered to Jafar Bloom: as with his animal experiments, public display was only a way of raising money, never an end in itself. He didn't care who watched, or if anyone watched.

The Cartesian Theater opened on a windy, hot night in August. The moon was full and the streets were full of bored and restless dole gypsies, but none of them wanted to come inside. I showed up early, not that I was looking forward to the show.

Bloom rolled his glassy Death Chamber onto the stage without even glancing at the seats, most of which were empty, the rest occupied by the same morbid gaffers who had attended his animal experiments. There were, in fact, more aibots than live flesh in the house. The ushers alone—wheeled units in cheap black tuxedos—outnumbered the paying customers.

Philo Novembre, dressed in gray, came late. He took an empty seat beside me, front-row-center.

"Here I am," he whispered. "Now, who have I satisfied? Who wants me here?"

He looked around but sighted no obvious culprit. Nor did I, although it could have been someone in dole drag: the wealthy have been known to dress down and go slumming. Still, none of these ten or twelve furtive patrons of the arts looked plausibly like a high-stakes benefactor.

The theater smelled of mildew and mothballs, despite everything we'd done to disinfect it.

"What it is," Novembre mooted to me as he watched Bloom plug in a set of cables, "is a sort of philosophical grudge match, yes? Do you see that, Mr. Paczovski? Me, the archaic humanist who believes in the soul but can't establish the existence of it, and Mr. Bloom," here he gestured contemptuously at the stage, "who generates evil as casually as an animal marking its territory with urine. A modern man, in other words."

"Yeah, I guess so," I said. In truth, all this metaphysical stuff was beyond me.

Eventually the lights dimmed, and Novembre slouched into his seat and crossed his good arm over his prosthesis.

And the show began.

Began prosaically. Bloom strolled to the front of the stage and explained what was about to happen. The walls of the Death Chamber, he said, were made of mirrored glass. The audience would be able to see inside but the occupant—or occupants—couldn't see out. The interior of the chamber was divided into two identical cubicles, each roughly six feet on a side. Each cubicle contained a chair, a small wooden table, a fluted glass, and a bottle of champagne.

Bloom would occupy one chamber. Once he was inside, his body would be scanned and a duplicate of it would take shape in the other. Both Bloom and counter-Bloom would look and act identically. Just like the dogs in his earlier experiment.

Novembre leaned toward my right ear. "*I see now what he intends,*" the old man whispered. "*The genius of it—*"

There was scattered applause as Bloom opened the chamber door and stepped inside.

"*The perverse genius,*" Novembre whispered, "*is that Bloom himself won't know—*"

And in response to his presence hidden nozzles filled the duplicate chamber with pink electrosensitive gel, which contracted under the pressure of invisible sculpting fields into a crude replica of Bloom, a man-shaped form lacking only the finer detail.

"*He won't know which is which, or rather—*"

Another bank of electronics flickered to life, stage rear. The gel duplicate clarified in an instant, and although I knew what it was—a hollow shell of adaptive molecules—it looked as substantial, as weighty, as Bloom himself.

Bloom's neural impulses were controlling both bodies now. He lifted the champagne bottle and filled the waiting glass. His dutiful reflection did likewise, at the same time and with the same tight, demented smile. He toasted the audience he couldn't see.

"*Or rather, he won't know which is himself—each entity will believe, feel, intuit that it's the true and only Bloom, until one—*"

Now Bloom replaced the glass on the tabletop, cueing an aibot stagehand in the wings. The house lights flickered off and after a moment were replaced by a pair of baby spots, one for each division of the Death Chamber.

This was the signal that Bloom had cut the link between himself and the machinery. The neuroprostheses were running on a kind of cybernetic inertia. The duplicate Bloom was on borrowed time, but didn't know it.

The two Blooms continued to stare at one another. Narcissus in Hades.

And Novembre was right, of course: the copy couldn't tell itself from the real thing, the real thing from the copy.

"*Until one begins to decohere,*" Novembre finished. "*Until the agony begins.*" Thirty seconds.

I resisted the urge to look at my watch.

The old philosopher leaned forward in his seat.

Bloom and anti-Bloom raised glasses to each other. Both appeared to drink. Both had Bloom's memory. Both had Bloom's motivation. Each believed himself to be the authentic Bloom.

And both must have harbored doubts. Both thinking: I know I'm the real item, I can't be anything else, but what if—*what if*—?

A trickle of sweat ran down the temples of both Blooms.

Both Blooms crossed their legs and both attempted another nonchalant sip of champagne.

But now they had begun to fall just slightly out of synchronization.

The Bloom on the right seemed to gag at the liquid.

The Bloom on the left saw the miscue and liked what he saw.

The Bloom on the right fumbled the champagne glass and dropped it. The glass shattered on the chamber floor.

The opposite Bloom widened his eyes and threw his own glass down. The right-hand Bloom stared in disbelief.

That was the worst thing: that look of dawning understanding, incipient terror.

The audience—including Novembre—leaned toward the action. "God help us," the old philosopher said.

Now Bloom's electronic neuroprostheses, divorced from their biological source, began to lose coherence more rapidly. Feedback loops in the hardware read the dissolution as physical pain. The false Bloom opened his mouth—attempting a scream, though he had no lungs to force out air. Wisps of gel rose from his skin: he looked like he was dissolving into meat-colored smoke. His eyes turned black and slid down his cheeks. His remaining features twisted into a grimace of agony.

The real Bloom grinned in triumph. He looked like a man who had won a desperate gamble, which in a sense he had. He had wagered against his own death and survived his own suicide.

I didn't want to watch but this time I couldn't turn away—it absorbed my attention so completely that I didn't realize Philo Novembre had left his seat until I saw him lunge across the stage.

I was instantly afraid for Bloom, the real Bloom. The philosopher was swinging his titanium arm like a club and his face was a mask of rage. But he aimed his first blow not at Bloom but at the subchamber where the double was noisily dying. I think he meant to end its suffering.

A single swing of his arm cracked the wall, rupturing the embedded sensors and controllers.

Aibot ushers and stagehands suddenly hustled toward the Death Chamber as if straining for a view. The dying duplicate of Bloom turned what remained of his head toward the audience, as if he had heard a distant sound. Then he collapsed with absolute finality into a puddle of amorphous foam.

Bloom forced open his own chamber door and ran for the wings. Novembre spotted him and gave chase. I tried to follow, but the crowd of aibots closed ranks and barred my way.

Lada would love this, I thought. Lada would make serious money if she could retail a recording of this event. But I wasn't logging it and nobody else seemed to be, except of course the aibots, who remember everything; but their memories are legally protected, shared only by other machines.

This was unrecorded history, unhappening even as it happened.

* * *

I caught up with Bloom in the alley behind the Cartesian Theater. Too late. Novembre had caught up with him first. Bloom was on the ground, his skull opened like a ripe melon. A little gray aibot with EMS protocols sat astride Bloom's chest, stimulating his heart and blowing air into his lungs—uselessly. Bloom was dead, irretrievably dead long before the ambulance arrived and gathered him into its motherly arms.

As for Novembre—

It looked at first as if he he'd escaped into the crowd. But I went back into the theater on a hunch, and I found him there, hidden in the fractured ruin of Jafar Bloom's Death Chamber, where he had opened his own throat with a sliver of broken glass and somehow found time to write the words *BUT IT EXISTS* in blood on the chamber wall.

* * *

"Yup, it was a show," Grandfather said.

I gave his image an exasperated look. "Of course it was a show. 'The Cartesian Theater'—what else could it be?"

"Not that. I mean the mutual self-destruction of Bloom and Novembre. You see it, Toby? The deliberate irony? Novembre believes in humanity and hates intellectual machines. But he takes pity on the fake Bloom as it dies, and by doing so he tacitly admits that a machine can harbor something akin to a human soul. He found what he had been looking for all his life, a metaphysical expression of human suffering outside the laws of the Rationalization—but he found it in a rack of electronics. We have to assume that's what your client wanted and expected to happen. A philosophical tragedy, culminating in a murder-suicide."

This was Grandfather's trial-lawyer subroutine talking, but what he said made a certain amount of sense. It was as if I had played a supporting role in a drama crafted by an omniscient playwright. Except—

"Except," I said, "who saw it?"

"One of the attendees might have recorded it surreptitiously."

"No one witnessed both deaths, according to the police, and they searched the witnesses for wires."

"But the transaction was completed? Lada was paid for her services?"

I had talked to her this morning. Yes, she was paid. Generously and in full. The client had evidently received value for money.

"So you have to ask yourself," Grandfather said, "(and I no longer possess the imagination to suggest an answer), who could have known about both Bloom and Novembre? Who could have conceived this scenario? Who understood the motivation of both men intimately enough to predict a bloody outcome? To whose taste does this tragedy cater, and how was that taste satisfied if the client was not physically present?"

"Fuck, I don't know."

Grandfather nodded. He understood ignorance. His own curiosity had flickered briefly but it died like a spent match. "You came here with a problem to solve…"

"Right," I said. "Here's the thing. Lada's happy with how this whole scenario worked. She said I outdid myself. She says the client wants to work with her again, maybe on a regular basis. She offered to hire me back full-time and even increase my salary."

"Which is what you'd been hoping for, yes?"

"But suddenly the whole idea makes me a little queasy—I don't know why. So what do you think? Should I re-up, take the money, make a success of myself? Maybe hook up with Lada again, on a personal level I mean, if things go well? Because I could do that. It would be easy. But I keep thinking it'd be even easier to find a place by the docks and live on dole and watch the waves roll in."

Watch the aibots build more hives and nurseries. Watch the population decline.

"I'm far too dead," Grandfather said, "to offer sensible advice. Anyway, it sounds as if you've already decided."

And I realized he was right—I had.

* * *

On the way out of the sanctuary where Grandfather was stored I passed a gaggle of utility aibots. They were lined up along the corridor in serried ranks, motionless, and their eyes scanned me as I passed.

And as I approached the exit, the chief custodial aibot—a tall, lanky unit in a black vest and felt hat—stepped into my path. He turned his face down to me and said, "Do you know Sophocles, Mr. Paczovski?"

I was almost too surprised to answer. "Sophocles who?"

"*Ajax*," he said cryptically. "The Chorus. *When Reason's day / Sets rayless—joyless—quenched in cold decay / Better to die, and sleep / The never-waking sleep, than linger on, / And dare to live, when the soul's life is gone.*"

And while I stared, the gathered aibots—the ones with hands, at least—began gently to applaud.

JOURNEY INTO THE KINGDOM

M. RICKERT

Mary Rickert was eighteen when she moved to California, where she worked at Disneyland. She still has fond memories of selling balloons there. After many years (and through the sort of "odd series of events" that describe much of her life), she got a job as a kindergarten teacher in a small private school for gifted children. She worked there for almost a decade, then left to pursue her life as a writer. She has had many stories published by *The Magazine of Fantasy & Science Fiction*. Her most recent book is collection *Map of Dreams*.

The first painting was of an egg, the pale ovoid produced with faint strokes of pink, blue, and violet to create the illusion of white. After that there were two apples, a pear, an avocado, and finally, an empty plate on a white tablecloth before a window covered with gauzy curtains, a single fly nestled in a fold at the top right corner. The series was titled "Journey into the Kingdom."

On a small table beneath the avocado there was a black binder, an unevenly cut rectangle of white paper with the words "Artist's Statement" in neat, square, hand-written letters taped to the front. Balancing the porcelain cup and saucer with one hand, Alex picked up the binder and took it with him to a small table against the wall toward the back of the coffee shop, where he opened it, thinking it might be interesting to read something besides the newspaper for once, though he almost abandoned the idea when he saw that the page before him was handwritten in the same neat letters as on the cover. But the title intrigued him.

AN IMITATION LIFE

Though I always enjoyed my crayons and watercolors, I was not a particularly artistic child. I produced the usual assortment of stick figures and houses with dripping yellow suns. I was an avid collector of seashells and sea glass and much preferred to be outdoors, throwing stones at seagulls (please, no haranguing from animal rights activists, I have long since outgrown this) or playing with my imaginary friends, to sitting quietly in the salt rooms of the keeper's house, making pictures at the big wooden kitchen table while my mother, in her black dress, kneaded bread and sang the old French songs between her duties as lighthouse keeper, watcher over the waves, beacon for the lost, governess of the dead.

The first ghost to come to my mother was my own father who had set out the day previous in the small boat heading to the mainland for supplies such as string and rice, and also bags of soil, which, in years past, we emptied into crevices between the rocks and planted with seeds, a makeshift garden and a "brave attempt," as my father called it, referring to the barren stone we lived on.

We did not expect him for several days so my mother was surprised when he returned in a storm, dripping wet icicles from his mustache and behaving strangely, repeating over and over again, "It is lost, my dear Maggie, the garden is at the bottom of the sea."

My mother fixed him hot tea but he refused it, she begged him to take off the wet clothes and retire with her, to their feather bed piled with quilts, but he said, "Tend the light, don't waste your time with me." So my mother, a worried expression on her face, left our little keeper's house and walked against the gale to the lighthouse, not realizing that she left me with a ghost, melting before the fire into a great puddle, which was all that was left of him upon her return. She searched frantically while I kept pointing at the puddle and insisting it was he. Eventually she tied on her cape and went out into the storm, calling his name. I thought that, surely, I would become orphaned that night.

But my mother lived, though she took to her bed and left me to tend the lamp and receive the news of the discovery of my father's wrecked boat, found on the rocky shoals, still clutching in his frozen hand a bag of soil, which was given to me, and which I brought to my mother though she would not take the offering.

For one so young, my chores were immense. I tended the lamp, and kept our own hearth fire going too. I made broth and tea for my mother, which she only gradually took, and I planted that small bag of soil by the door to our little house, savoring the rich scent, wondering if those who lived with it all the time appreciated its perfume or not.

I did not really expect anything to grow, though I hoped that the seagulls might drop some seeds or the ocean deposit some small thing. I was surprised when, only weeks later, I discovered the tiniest shoots of green, which I told my mother about. She was not impressed. By that point, she would spend part of the day sitting up in bed, mending my father's socks and moaning, "Agatha, whatever are we going to do?" I did not wish to worry her, so I told her lies about women from the mainland coming to help, men taking turns with the light. "But they are so quiet. I never hear anyone."

"No one wants to disturb you," I said. "They whisper and walk on tiptoe."

It was only when I opened the keeper's door so many uncounted weeks later, and saw, spread before me, embedded throughout the rock (even in crevices where I had planted no soil) tiny pink, purple, and white flowers, their stems shuddering in the salty wind, that I insisted my mother get out of bed.

She was resistant at first. But I begged and cajoled, promised her it would be worth her effort. "The fairies have planted flowers for us," I said, this being the only explanation or description I could think of for the infinitesimal blossoms everywhere.

Reluctantly, she followed me through the small living room and kitchen, observing that, "the ladies have done a fairly good job of keeping the place neat." She hesitated before the open door. The bright sun and salty scent of the sea, as well as the loud sound of waves washing all around us, seemed to astound her, but then she squinted, glanced at me, and stepped through the door to observe the miracle of the fairies' flowers.

Never had the rock seen such color, never had it known such bloom! My mother walked out, barefoot, and said, "Forget-me-nots, these are forget-me-nots. But where…?"

I told her that I didn't understand it myself, how I had planted the small bag of soil found clutched in my father's hand but had not really expected it to come to much, and certainly not to all of this, waving my arm over the expanse, the flowers having grown in soilless crevices and cracks, covering our entire little island of stone.

My mother turned to me and said, "These are not from the fairies, they are from him." Then she started crying, a reaction I had not expected and tried to talk her out of, but she said, "No, Agatha, leave me alone."

She stood out there for quite a while, weeping as she walked amongst the flowers. Later, after she came inside and said, "Where are all the helpers today?" I shrugged and avoided more questions by going outside myself, where I discovered scarlet spots amongst the bloom. My mother had been bedridden for so long, her feet had gone soft again. For days she left tiny teardrop shapes of blood in her step, which I surreptitiously wiped up, not wanting to draw any attention to the fact, for fear it would dismay her. She picked several of the forget-me-not blossoms and pressed them between the heavy pages of her book of myths and folklore. Not long after that, a terrible storm blew in, rocking our little house, challenging our resolve, and taking with it all the flowers. Once again our rock was barren. I worried what effect this would have on my mother but she merely sighed, shrugged, and said, "They were beautiful, weren't they, Agatha?"

So passed my childhood: a great deal of solitude, the occasional life-threatening adventure, the drudgery of work, and all around me the great wide sea with its myriad secrets and reasons, the lost we saved, those we didn't. And the ghosts, brought to us by my father, though we never understood clearly his purpose, as they only stood before the fire, dripping and melting like something made of wax, bemoaning what was lost (a fine boat, a lady love, a dream of the sea, a pocketful of jewels, a wife and children, a carving on bone, a song, its lyrics forgotten). We tried to provide what comfort we could, listening, nodding, there was little else we could do, they refused tea or blankets, they seemed only to want to stand by the fire, mourning their death, as my father stood sentry beside them, melting into salty puddles that we mopped up with clean rags, wrung out into the ocean, saying what we fashioned as prayer, or reciting lines of Irish poetry.

Though I know now that this is not a usual childhood, it was usual for me, and it did not veer from this course until my mother's hair had gone quite gray and I was a young woman, when my father brought us a different sort of ghost entirely, a handsome young man, his eyes the same blue-green as summer. His hair was of indeterminate color, wet curls that hung to his shoulders. Dressed simply, like any dead sailor, he carried about him an air of being educated more by art than by water, a suspicion soon confirmed for me when he refused an offering of tea by saying, "No, I will not, cannot drink your liquid offered without first asking for a kiss, ah a kiss is all the liquid I desire, come succor me with your lips."

Naturally, I blushed and, just as naturally, when my mother went to check on the lamp, and my father had melted into a mustached puddle, I kissed him. Though I should have been warned by the icy chill, as certainly I should have been warned by the fact of my own father, a mere puddle at the hearth, it was my first kiss and it did not feel deadly to me at all, not dangerous, not spectral, most certainly not spectral, though I did experience a certain pleasant floating sensation in its wake.

My mother was surprised, upon her return, to find the lad still standing, as vigorous as any living man, beside my father's puddle. We were both surprised that he remained throughout the night, regaling us with stories of the wild sea populated by whales, mermaids, and sharks; mesmerizing us with descriptions of the "bottom of the world" as he called it, embedded with strange purple rocks, pink shells spewing pearls, and the seaweed tendrils of sea witches' hair. We were both surprised that, when the black of night turned to the gray hue of morning, he bowed to each of us (turned fully toward me, so that I could receive his wink), promised he would return, and then left, walking out the door like any regular fellow. So convincing was he that my mother and I opened the door to see where he had gone, scanning the rock and the inky sea before we accepted that, as odd as it seemed, as vigorous his demeanor, he was a ghost most certainly.

"Or something of that nature," said my mother. "Strange that he didn't melt like the others." She squinted at me and I turned away from her before she could see my blush. "We shouldn't have let him keep us up all night," she said. "We aren't dead. We need our sleep."

Sleep? Sleep? I could not sleep, feeling as I did his cool lips on mine, the power of his kiss, as though he breathed out of me some dark aspect that had weighed inside me. I told my mother that she could sleep. I would take care of everything. She protested, but using the past as reassurance (she had long since discovered that I had run the place while she convalesced after my father's death), finally agreed.

I was happy to have her tucked safely in bed. I was happy to know that her curious eyes were closed. I did all the tasks necessary to keep the place in good order. Not even then, in all my girlish giddiness, did I forget the lamp. I am embarrassed to admit, however, it was well past four o'clock before I remembered my father's puddle, which by that time had been much dissipated. I wiped up the small amount of water and wrung him out over the sea, saying only as prayer, "Father, forgive me. Oh, bring him back to me." (Meaning, alas for me, a foolish girl, the boy who kissed me and not my own dear father.)

And that night, he did come back, knocking on the door like any living man, carrying in his wet hands a bouquet of pink coral which he presented to me, and a small white stone, shaped like a star, which he gave to my mother.

"Is there no one else with you?" she asked.

"I'm sorry, there is not," he said.

My mother began to busy herself in the kitchen, leaving the two of us alone. I could hear her in there, moving things about, opening cupboards, sweeping the already swept floor. It was my own carelessness that had caused my father's absence, I was sure of that; had I sponged him up sooner, had I prayed for him more sincerely, and not just for the satisfaction of my own desire, he would be here this night. I felt terrible about this, but then I looked into his eyes, those beautiful sea-colored eyes, and I could not help it, my body thrilled at his look. Is this love? I thought. Will he kiss me twice? When it seemed as if, without even wasting time with words, he was about to do so, leaning toward me with parted lips from which exhaled the scent of salt water, my mother stepped into the room, clearing her throat, holding the broom before her, as if thinking she might use it as a weapon.

"We don't really know anything about you," she said.

To begin with, my name is Ezekiel. My mother was fond of saints and the Bible and such. She died shortly after giving birth to me, her first and only child. I was raised by my father, on the island of Murano. Perhaps you have heard of it? Murano glass? We are famous for it throughout the world. My father, himself, was a talented glassmaker. Anything imagined, he could shape into glass. Glass birds, tiny glass bees, glass seashells, even glass tears (an art he perfected while I was an infant), and what my father knew, he taught to me.

Naturally, I eventually surpassed him in skill. Forgive me, but there is no humble way to say it. At any rate, my father had taught me and encouraged my talent all my life. I did not see when his enthusiasm began to sour. I was excited and pleased at what I could produce. I thought he would feel the same for me as I had felt for him, when, as a child, I sat on the footstool in his studio and applauded each glass wing, each hard teardrop.

Alas, it was not to be. My father grew jealous of me. My own father! At night he snuck into our studio and broke my birds, my little glass cakes. In the morning he pretended dismay and instructed me further on keeping air bubbles out of my work. He did not guess that I knew the dismal truth.

I determined to leave him, to sail away to some other place to make my home. My father begged me to stay, "Whatever will you do? How will you make your way in this world?"

I told him my true intention, not being clever enough to lie. "This is not the only place in the world with fire and sand," I said. "I intend to make glass."

He promised me it would be a death sentence. At the time I took this to be only his confused, fatherly concern. I did not perceive it as a threat.

It is true that the secret to glassmaking was meant to remain on Murano. It is true that the entire populace believed this trade, and only this trade, kept them fed and clothed. Finally, it is true that they passed the law (many years before my father confronted me with it) that anyone who dared attempt to take the secret of glassmaking off the island would suffer the penalty of death. All of this is true.

But what's also true is that I was a prisoner in my own home, tortured by my own father, who pretended to be a humble, kind glassmaker, but who, night after night, broke my creations and then, each morning, denied my accusations, his sweet old face mustached and whiskered, all the expression of dismay and sorrow.

This is madness, I reasoned. How else could I survive? One of us had to leave or die. I chose the gentler course.

We had, in our possession, only a small boat, used for trips that never veered far from shore. Gathering mussels, visiting neighbors, occasionally my father liked to sit in it and smoke a pipe while watching the sun set. He'd light a lantern and come home, smelling of the sea, boil us a pot of soup, a melancholic, completely innocent air about him, only later to sneak about his breaking work.

This small boat is what I took for my voyage across the sea. I also took some fishing supplies, a rope, dried cod he'd stored for winter, a blanket, and several jugs of red wine, given to us by the baker, whose daughter, I do believe, fancied me. For you, who have lived so long on this anchored rock, my folly must be apparent. Was it folly? It was. But what else was I to do? Day after day make my perfect art only to have my father, night after night, destroy it? He would destroy me!

I left in the dark, when the ocean is like ink and the sky is black glass with thousands of air bubbles. Air bubbles, indeed. I breathed my freedom in the salty sea air. I chose stars to follow. Foolishly, I had no clear sense of my passage and had only planned my escape.

Of course, knowing what I do now about the ocean, it is a wonder I survived the first night, much less seven. It was on the eighth morning that I saw the distant sail, and, hopelessly drunk and sunburned, as well as lost, began the desperate task of rowing toward it, another folly as I'm sure you'd agree, understanding how distant the horizon is. Luckily for me, or so I thought, the ship headed in my direction and after a few more days it was close enough that I began to believe in my life again.

Alas, this ship was owned by a rich friend of my father's, a woman who had commissioned him to create a glass castle with a glass garden and glass fountain, tiny glass swans, a glass king and queen, a baby glass princess, and glass trees with golden glass apples, all for the amusement of her granddaughter (who, it must be said, had fingers like sausages and broke half of the figurines before her next birthday). This silly woman was only too happy to let my father use her ship, she was only too pleased to pay the ship's crew, all with the air of helping my father, when, in truth, it simply amused her to be involved in such drama. She said she did it for Murano, but in truth, she did it for the story.

It wasn't until I had been rescued, and hoisted on board, that my father revealed himself to me. He spread his arms wide, all great show for the crew, hugged me and even wept, but convincing as was his act, I knew he intended to destroy me.

These are terrible choices no son should have to make, but that night, as my father slept and the ship rocked its weary way back to Murano where I would likely be hung or possibly sentenced to live with my own enemy, my father, I slit the old man's throat. Though he opened his eyes, I do not believe he saw me, but was already entering the distant kingdom.

You ladies look quite aghast. I cannot blame you. Perhaps I should have chosen my own death instead, but I was a young man, and I wanted to live. Even after everything I had gone through, I wanted life.

Alas, it was not to be. I knew there would be trouble and accusation if my father were found with his throat slit, but none at all if he just disappeared in the night, as so often happens on large ships. Many a traveler has simply fallen overboard, never to be heard from again, and my father had already displayed a lack of seafaring savvy to rival my own.

I wrapped him up in the now-bloody blanket but although he was a small man, the effect was still that of a body, so I realized I would have to bend and fold him into a rucksack. You wince, but do not worry, he was certainly dead by this time.

I will not bore you with the details of my passage, hiding and sneaking with my dismal load. Suffice it to say that it took a while for me to at last be standing shipside, and I thought then that all danger had passed.

Remember, I was already quite weakened by my days adrift, and the matter of taking care of this business with my father had only fatigued me further. Certain that I was finally at the end of my task, I grew careless. He was much heavier than he had ever appeared to be. It took all my strength to hoist the rucksack, and (to get the sad, pitiable truth over with as quickly as possible) when I heaved that rucksack, the cord became entangled on my wrist, and yes, dear ladies, I went over with it, to the bottom of the world. There I remained until your own dear father, your husband, found me and brought me to this place, where, for the first time in my life, I feel safe, and, though I am dead, blessed.

Later, after my mother had tended the lamp while Ezekiel and I shared the kisses that left me breathless, she asked him to leave, saying that I needed my sleep. I protested, of course, but she insisted. I walked my ghost to the door, just as I think any girl would do in a similar situation, and there, for the first time, he kissed me in full view of my mother, not so passionate as those kisses that had preceded it, but effective nonetheless.

But after he was gone, even as I still blushed, my mother spoke in a grim voice, "Don't encourage him, Agatha."

"Why?" I asked, my body trembling with the impact of his affection and my mother's scorn, as though the two emotions met in me and quaked there. "What don't you like about him?"

"He's dead," she said, "there's that for a start."

"What about Daddy? He's dead too, and you've been loving him all this time."

My mother shook her head. "Agatha, it isn't the same thing. Think about what this boy told you tonight. He murdered his own father."

"I can't believe you'd use that against him. You heard what he said. He was just defending himself."

"But Agatha, it isn't what's said that is always the most telling. Don't you know that? Have I really raised you to be so gullible?"

"I am not gullible. I'm in love."

"I forbid it."

Certainly no three words, spoken by a parent, can do more to solidify love than these. It was no use arguing. What would be the point? She, this woman who had loved no one but a puddle for so long, could never understand what was going through my heart. Without more argument, I went to bed, though I slept fitfully, feeling torn from my life in every way, while my mother stayed up reading, I later surmised, from her book of myths. In the morning I found her sitting at the kitchen table, the great volume before her. She looked up at me with dark circled eyes, then, without salutation, began reading, her voice, ominous.

"There are many kinds of ghosts. There are the ghosts that move things, slam doors and drawers, throw silverware about the house. There are the ghosts (usually of small children) that play in dark corners with spools of thread and frighten family pets. There are the weeping and wailing ghosts. There are the ghosts who know that they are dead, and those who do not. There are tree ghosts, those who spend their afterlife in a particular tree (a clue for such a resident might be bite marks on fallen fruit). There are ghosts trapped forever at the hour of their death (I saw one like this once, in an old movie theater bathroom, hanging from the ceiling). There are melting ghosts (we know about these, don't we?), usually victims of drowning. And there are breath-stealing ghosts. These, sometimes mistaken for the grosser vampire, sustain a sort of half-life by stealing breath from the living. They can be any age, but are usually teenagers and young adults, often at that selfish stage when they died. These ghosts greedily go about sucking the breath out of the living. This can be done by swallowing the lingered breath from unwashed cups, or, most effectively of all, through a kiss. Though these ghosts can often be quite seductively charming, they are some of the most dangerous. Each life has only a certain amount of breath within it and these ghosts are said to steal an infinite amount with each swallow. The effect is such that the ghost, while it never lives again, begins to do a fairly good imitation of life, while its victims (those whose breath it steals) edge ever closer to their own death."

My mother looked up at me triumphantly and I stormed out of the house, only to be confronted with the sea all around me, as desolate as my heart.

That night, when he came, knocking on the door, she did not answer it and forbade me to do so.

"It doesn't matter," I taunted, "he's a ghost. He doesn't need doors."

"No, you're wrong," she said, "he's taken so much of your breath that he's not entirely spectral. He can't move through walls any longer. He needs you, but he doesn't care about you at all, don't you get that, Agatha?"

"Agatha? Are you home? Agatha? Why don't you come? Agatha?"

I couldn't bear it. I began to weep.

"I know this is hard," my mother said, "but it must be done. Listen, his voice is already growing faint. We just have to get through this night."

"What about the lamp?" I said.

"What?"

But she knew what I meant. Her expression betrayed her. "Don't you need to check on the lamp?"

"Agatha? Have I done something wrong?"

My mother stared at the door, and then turned to me, the dark circles under her eyes giving her the look of a beaten woman. "The lamp is fine."

I spun on my heels and went into my small room, slammed the door behind me. My mother, a smart woman, was not used to thinking like a warden. She had forgotten about my window. By the time I hoisted myself down from it, Ezekiel was standing on the rocky shore, surveying the dark ocean before him. He had already lost some of his lifelike luster, particularly below his knees where I could almost see through him. "Ezekiel," I said. He turned and I gasped at the change in his visage, the cavernous look of his eyes, the skeletal stretch at his jaw. Seeing my shocked expression, he nodded and spread his arms open, as if to say, yes, this is what has become of me. I ran into those open arms and embraced him, though he creaked like something made of old wood. He bent down, pressing his cold lips against mine until they were no longer cold but burning like a fire.

We spent that night together and I did not mind the shattering wind with its salt bite on my skin, and I did not care when the lamp went out and the sea roiled beneath a black sky, and I did not worry about the dead weeping on the rocky shore, or the lightness I felt as though I were floating beside my lover, and when morning came, revealing the dead all around us, I followed him into the water, I followed him to the bottom of the sea, where he turned to me and said, "What have you done? Are you stupid? Don't you realize? You're no good to me dead!"

So, sadly, like many a daughter, I learned that my mother had been right after all, and when I returned to her, dripping with saltwater and seaweed, tiny fish corpses dropping from my hair, she embraced me. Seeing my state, weeping, she kissed me on the lips, our mouths open. I drank from her, sweet breath, until I was filled and she collapsed to the floor, my mother in her black dress, like a crushed funeral flower.

I had no time for mourning. The lamp had been out for hours. Ships had crashed and men had died. Outside the sun sparkled on the sea. People would be coming soon to find out what had happened.

I took our small boat and rowed away from there. Many hours later, I docked in a seaside town and hitchhiked to another, until eventually I was as far from my home as I could be and still be near my ocean.

I had a difficult time of it for a while. People are generally suspicious of someone with no past and little future. I lived on the street and had to beg for jobs cleaning toilets and scrubbing floors, only through time and reputation working up to my current situation, finally getting my own little apartment, small and dark, so different from when I was the lighthouse keeper's daughter and the ocean was my yard.

One day, after having passed it for months without a thought, I went into the art supply store, and bought a canvas, paint, and two paintbrushes. I paid for it with my tip money, counting it out for the clerk whose expression suggested I was placing turds in her palm instead of pennies. I went home and hammered a nail into the wall, hung the canvas on it, and began to paint. Like many a creative person I seem to have found some solace for the unfortunate happenings of my young life (and death) in art.

I live simply and virginally, never taking breath through a kiss. This is the vow I made, and I have kept it. Yes, some days I am weakened, and tempted to restore my vigor with such an easy solution, but instead I hold the empty cups to my face, I breathe in, I breathe everything, the breath of old men, breath of young, sweet breath, sour breath, breath of lipstick, breath of smoke. It is not, really, a way to live, but this is not, really, a life.

For several seconds after Alex finished reading the remarkable account, his gaze remained transfixed on the page. Finally, he looked up, blinked in the dim coffee shop light, and closed the black binder.

Several baristas stood behind the counter busily jostling around each other with porcelain cups, teapots, bags of beans. One of them, a short girl with red and green hair that spiked around her like some otherworld halo, stood by the sink, stacking dirty plates and cups. When she saw him watching, she smiled. It wasn't a true smile, not that it was mocking, but rather, the girl with the Christmas hair smiled like someone who had either forgotten happiness entirely, or never known it at all. In response, Alex nodded at her, and to his surprise, she came over, carrying a dirty rag and a spray bottle.

"Did you read all of it?" she said as she squirted the table beside him and began to wipe it with the dingy towel.

Alex winced at the unpleasant odor of the cleaning fluid, nodded, and then, seeing that the girl wasn't really paying any attention, said, "Yes." He glanced at the wall where the paintings were hung.

"So what'd you think?"

The girl stood there, grinning that sad grin, right next to him now with her noxious bottle and dirty rag, one hip jutted out in a way he found oddly sexual. He opened his mouth to speak, gestured toward the paintings, and then at the book before him. "I, I have to meet her," he said, tapping the book, "this is remarkable."

"But what do you think about the paintings?"

Once more he glanced at the wall where they hung. He shook his head, "No," he said, "it's this," tapping the book again.

She smiled, a true smile, cocked her head, and put out her hand, "Agatha," she said.

Alex felt like his head was spinning. He shook the girl's hand. It was unexpectedly tiny, like that of a child's, and he gripped it too tightly at first. Glancing at the counter, she pulled out a chair and sat down in front of him.

"I can only talk for a little while. Marnie is the manager today and she's on the rag or something all the time, but she's downstairs right now, checking in an order."

"You," he brushed the binder with the tip of his fingers, as if caressing something holy, "you wrote this?"

She nodded, bowed her head slightly, shrugged, and suddenly earnest, leaned across the table, elbowing his empty cup as she did. "Nobody bothers to read it. I've seen a few people pick it up but you're the first one to read the whole thing."

Alex leaned back, frowning.

She rolled her eyes, which, he noticed, were a lovely shade of lavender, lined darkly in black.

"See, I was trying to do something different. This is the whole point," she jabbed at the book, and he felt immediately protective of it, "I was trying to put a story in a place where people don't usually expect one. Don't you think we've gotten awful complacent in our society about story? Like it all the time has to go a certain way and even be only in certain places. That's what this is all about. The paintings are a foil. But you get that, don't you? Do you know," she leaned so close to him, he could smell her breath, which he thought was strangely sweet, "someone actually offered to buy the fly painting?" Her mouth dropped open, she shook her head and rolled those lovely lavender eyes. "I mean, what the fuck? Doesn't he know it sucks?"

Alex wasn't sure what to do. She seemed to be leaning near to his cup. Leaning over it, Alex realized. He opened his mouth, not having any idea what to say.

Just then another barista, the one who wore scarves all the time and had an imperious air about her, as though she didn't really belong there but was doing research or something, walked past. Agatha glanced at her. "I gotta go." She stood up. "You finished with this?" she asked, touching his cup.

Though he hadn't yet had his free refill, Alex nodded.

"It was nice talking to you," she said. "Just goes to show, doesn't it?"

Alex had no idea what she was talking about. He nodded halfheartedly, hoping comprehension would follow, but when it didn't, he raised his eyebrows at her instead.

She laughed. "I mean you don't look anything like the kind of person who would understand my stuff."

"Well, you don't look much like Agatha," he said.

"But I am Agatha," she murmured as she turned away from him, picking up an empty cup and saucer from a nearby table.

Alex watched her walk to the tiny sink at the end of the counter. She set the cups and saucers down. She rinsed the saucers and placed them in the gray bucket they used for carrying dirty dishes to the back. She reached for a cup, and then looked at him.

He quickly looked down at the black binder, picked it up, pushed his chair in, and headed toward the front of the shop. He stopped to look at the paintings. They were fine, boring, but fine little paintings that had no connection to what he'd read. He didn't linger over them for long. He was almost to the door when she was beside him, saying, "I'll take that." He couldn't even fake innocence. He shrugged and handed her the binder.

"I'm flattered, really," she said. But she didn't try to continue the conversation. She set the book down on the table beneath the painting of the avocado. He watched her pick up an empty cup and bring it toward her face, breathing in the lingered breath that remained. She looked up suddenly, caught him watching, frowned, and turned away.

Alex understood. She wasn't what he'd been expecting either. But when love arrives it doesn't always appear as expected. He couldn't just ignore it. He couldn't pretend it hadn't happened. He walked out of the coffee shop into the afternoon sunshine.

Of course, there were problems, her not being alive for one. But Alex was not a man of prejudice.

He was patient besides. He stood in the art supply store for hours, pretending particular interest in the anatomical hinged figurines of sexless men and women in the front window, before she walked past, her hair glowing like a forest fire.

"Agatha," he called.

She turned, frowned, and continued walking. He had to take little running steps to catch up. "Hi," he said. He saw that she was biting her lower lip. "You just getting off work?"

She stopped walking right in front of the bank, which was closed by then, and squinted up at him.

"Alex," he said. "I was talking to you today at the coffee shop."

"I know who you are."

Her tone was angry. He couldn't understand it. Had he insulted her somehow?

"I don't have Alzheimer's. I remember you."

He nodded. This was harder than he had expected.

"What do you want?" she said.

Her tone was really downright hostile. He shrugged. "I just thought we could, you know, talk."

She shook her head. "Listen, I'm happy that you liked my story."

"I did," he said, nodding, "it was great."

"But what would we talk about? You and me?"

Alex shifted beneath her lavender gaze. He licked his lips. She wasn't even looking at him, but glancing around him and across the street. "I don't care if it does mean I'll die sooner," he said. "I want to give you a kiss."

Her mouth dropped open.

"Is something wrong?"

She turned and ran. She wore one red sneaker and one green. They matched her hair.

As Alex walked back to his car, parked in front of the coffee shop, he tried to talk himself into not feeling so bad about the way things went. He hadn't always been like this. He used to be able to talk to people. Even women. Okay, he had never been suave, he knew that, but he'd been a regular guy. Certainly no one had ever run away from him before. But after Tessie died, people changed. Of course, this made sense, initially. He was in mourning, even if he didn't cry (something the doctor told him not to worry about because one day, probably when he least expected it, the tears would fall). He was obviously in pain. People were very nice. They talked to him in hushed tones. Touched him, gently. Even men tapped him with their fingertips. All this gentle touching had been augmented by vigorous hugs. People either touched him as if he would break, or hugged him as if he had already broken and only the vigor of the embrace kept him intact.

For the longest time there had been all this activity around him. People called, sent chatty e-mails, even handwritten letters, cards with flowers on them and prayers. People brought over casseroles, and bread, Jell-O with fruit in it. (Nobody brought chocolate chip cookies, which he might have actually eaten.)

To Alex's surprise, once Tessie had died, it felt as though a great weight had been lifted from him, but instead of appreciating the feeling, the freedom of being lightened of the burden of his wife's dying body, he felt in danger of floating away or disappearing. Could it be possible, he wondered, that Tessie's body, even when she was mostly bones and barely breath, was all that kept him real? Was it possible that he would have to live like this, held to life by some strange force but never a part of it again? These questions led Alex to the brief period where he'd experimented with becoming a Hare Krishna, shaved his head, dressed in orange robes, and took up dancing in the park. Alex wasn't sure but he thought that was when people started treating him as if he were strange, and even after he grew his hair out and started wearing regular clothes again, people continued to treat him strangely.

And, Alex had to admit, as he inserted his key into the lock of his car, he'd forgotten how to behave. How to be normal, he guessed.

You just don't go read something somebody wrote and decide you love her, he scolded himself as he eased into traffic. You don't just go falling in love with breath-stealing ghosts. People don't do that.

Alex did not go to the coffee shop the next day, or the day after that, but it was the only coffee shop in town, and had the best coffee in the state. They roasted the beans right there. Freshness like that can't be faked.

It was awkward for him to see her behind the counter, over by the dirty cups, of course. But when she looked up at him, he attempted a kind smile, then looked away.

He wasn't there to bother her. He ordered French Roast in a cup to go, even though he hated to drink out of paper, paid for it, dropped the change into the tip jar, and left without any further interaction with her.

He walked to the park, where he sat on a bench and watched a woman with two small boys feed white bread to the ducks. This was illegal because the ducks would eat all the bread offered to them, they had no sense of appetite, or being full, and they would eat until their stomachs exploded. Or something like that. Alex couldn't exactly remember. He was pretty sure it killed them. But Alex couldn't decide what to do. Should he go tell that lady and those two little boys that they were killing the ducks? How would that make them feel, especially as they were now triumphantly shaking out the empty bag, the ducks crowded around them, one of the boys squealing with delight? Maybe he should just tell her, quietly. But she looked so happy. Maybe she'd been having a hard time of it. He saw those mothers on *Oprah*, saying what a hard job it was, and maybe she'd had that kind of morning, even screaming at the kids, and then she got this idea, to take them to the park and feed the ducks and now she felt good about what she'd done and maybe she was thinking that she wasn't such a bad mom after all, and if Alex told her she was killing the ducks, would it stop the ducks from dying or just stop her from feeling happiness? Alex sighed. He couldn't decide what to do. The ducks were happy, the lady was happy, and one of the boys was happy. The other one looked sort of terrified. She picked him up and they walked away together, she, carrying the boy who waved the empty bag like a balloon, the other one skipping after them, a few ducks hobbling behind.

For three days Alex ordered his coffee to go and drank it in the park. On the fourth day, Agatha wasn't anywhere that he could see and he surmised that it was her day off so he sat at his favorite table in the back. But on the fifth day, even though he didn't see her again, and it made sense that she'd have two days off in a row, he ordered his coffee to go and took it to the park. He'd grown to like sitting on the bench watching strolling park visitors, the running children, the dangerously fat ducks.

He had no idea she would be there and he felt himself blush when he saw her coming down the path that passed right in front of him. He stared deeply into his cup and fought the compulsion to run. He couldn't help it, though. Just as the toes of her red and green sneakers came into view he looked up. I'm not going to hurt you, he thought, and then, he smiled, that false smile he'd been practicing on her and, incredibly, she smiled back! Also, falsely, he assumed, but he couldn't blame her for that.

She looked down the path and he followed her gaze, seeing that, though the path around the duck pond was lined with benches every fifty feet or so, all of them were taken. She sighed. "Mind if I sit here?"

He scooted over and she sat down, slowly. He glanced at her profile. She looked worn out, he decided. Her lavender eye flickered toward him, and he looked into his cup again. It made sense that she would be tired, he thought, if she'd been off work for two days, she'd also been going that long without stealing breath from cups. "Want some?" he said, offering his.

She looked startled, pleased, and then, falsely unconcerned. She peered over the edge of his cup, shrugged, and said, "Okay, yeah, sure."

He handed it to her and politely watched the ducks so she could have some semblance of privacy with it. After a while she said thanks and handed it back to him. He nodded and stole a look at her profile again. It pleased him that her color already looked better. His breath had done that!

"Sorry about the other day," she said, "I was just...."

They waited together but she didn't finish the sentence.

"It's okay," he said, "I know I'm weird."

"No, you're, well—" she smiled, glanced at him, shrugged. "It isn't that. I like weird people. I'm weird. But, I mean, I'm not dead, okay? You kind of freaked me out with that."

He nodded. "Would you like to go out with me sometime?" Inwardly, he groaned. He couldn't believe he just said that.

"Listen, Alex?"

He nodded. Stop nodding, he told himself. Stop acting like a bobblehead.

"Why don't you tell me a little about yourself?"

So he told her. How he'd been coming to the park lately, watching people overfeed the ducks, wondering if he should tell them what they were doing but they all looked so happy doing it, and the ducks looked happy too, and he wasn't sure anyway, what if he was wrong, what if he told everyone to stop feeding bread to the ducks and it turned out it did them no harm and how would he know? Would they explode like balloons, or would it be more like how it had been when his wife died, a slow painful death, eating her away inside, and how he used to come here, when he was a monk, well, not really a monk, he'd never gotten ordained or anything, but he'd been trying the idea on for a while and how he used to sing and spin in circles and how it felt a lot like what he'd remembered of happiness but he could never be sure because a remembered emotion is like a remembered taste, it's never really there. And then, one day, a real monk came and watched him spinning in circles and singing nonsense, and he just stood and watched Alex, which made him self-conscious because he didn't really know what he was doing, and the monk started laughing, which made Alex stop and the monk said, "Why'd you stop?" And Alex said, "I don't know what I'm doing." And the monk nodded, as if this was a very wise thing to say and this, just this monk with his round bald head and wire-rimmed spectacles, in his simple orange robe (not at all like the orange-dyed sheet Alex was wearing) nodding when Alex said, "I don't know what I'm doing," made Alex cry and he and the monk sat down under that tree, and the monk (whose name was Ron) told him about Kali, the goddess who is both womb and grave. Alex felt like it was the first thing anyone had said to him that made sense since Tessie died and after that he stopped coming to the park, until just recently, and let his hair grow out again and stopped wearing his robe. Before she'd died, he'd been one of the lucky ones, or so he'd thought, because he made a small fortune in a dot com, and actually got out of it before it all went belly up while so many people he knew lost everything but then Tessie came home from her doctor's appointment, not pregnant, but with cancer, and he realized he wasn't lucky at all. They met in high school and were together until she died, at home, practically blind by that time and she made him promise he wouldn't just give up on life. So he began living this sort of half-life, but he wasn't unhappy or depressed, he didn't want her to think that, he just wasn't sure. "I sort of lost confidence in life," he said. "It's like I don't believe in it anymore. Not like suicide, but I mean, like the whole thing, all of it isn't real somehow. Sometimes I feel like it's all a dream, or a long nightmare that I can never wake up from. It's made me odd, I guess."

She bit her lower lip, glanced longingly at his cup.

"Here," Alex said, "I'm done anyway."

She took it and lifted it toward her face, breathing in, he was sure of it, and only after she was finished, drinking the coffee. They sat like that in silence for a while and then they just started talking about everything, just as Alex had hoped they would. She told him how she had grown up living near the ocean, and her father had died young, and then her mother had too, and she had a boyfriend, her first love, who broke her heart, but the story she wrote was just a story, a story about her life, her dream life, the way she felt inside, like he did, as though somehow life was a dream. Even though everyone thought she was a painter (because he was the only one who read it, he was the only one who got it), she was a writer, not a painter, and stories seemed more real to her than life. At a certain point he offered to take the empty cup and throw it in the trash but she said she liked to peel off the wax, and then began doing so. Alex politely ignored the divergent ways she found to continue drinking his breath. He didn't want to embarrass her.

They finally stood up and stretched, walked through the park together and grew quiet, with the awkwardness of new friends. "You want a ride?" he said, pointing at his car.

She declined, which was a disappointment to Alex but he determined not to let it ruin his good mood. He was willing to leave it at that, to accept what had happened between them that afternoon as a moment of grace to be treasured and expect nothing more from it, when she said, "What are you doing next Tuesday?" They made a date, well, not a date, Alex reminded himself, an arrangement, to meet the following Tuesday in the park, which they did, and there followed many wonderful Tuesdays. They did not kiss. They were friends. Of course Alex still loved her. He loved her more. But he didn't bother her with all that and it was in the spirit of friendship that he suggested (after weeks of Tuesdays in the park) that the following Tuesday she come for dinner, "nothing fancy," he promised when he saw the slight hesitation on her face.

But when she said yes, he couldn't help it; he started making big plans for the night.

Naturally, things were awkward when she arrived. He offered to take her sweater, a lumpy looking thing in wild shades of orange, lime green, and purple. He should have just let her throw it across the couch, that would have been the casual non-datelike thing to do, but she handed it to him and then, wiping her hand through her hair, which, by candlelight looked like bloody grass, cased his place with those lavender eyes, deeply shadowed as though she hadn't slept for weeks.

He could see she was freaked out by the candles. He hadn't gone crazy or anything. They were just a couple of small candles, not even purchased from the store in the mall, but bought at the grocery store, unscented. "I like candles," he said, sounding defensive even to his own ears.

She smirked, as if she didn't believe him, and then spun away on the toes of her red sneaker and her green one, and plopped down on the couch. She looked absolutely exhausted. This was not a complete surprise to Alex. It had been a part of his plan, actually, but he felt bad for her just the same.

He kept dinner simple, lasagna, a green salad, chocolate cake for dessert. They didn't eat in the dining room. That would have been too formal. Instead they ate in the living room, she sitting on the couch, and he on the floor, their plates on the coffee table, watching a DVD of *I Love Lucy* episodes, a mutual like they had discovered. (Though her description of watching *I Love Lucy* reruns as a child did not gel with his picture of her in the crooked keeper's house, offering tea to melting ghosts, he didn't linger over the inconsistency.) Alex offered her plenty to drink but he wouldn't let her come into the kitchen, or get anywhere near his cup. He felt bad about this, horrible, in fact, but he tried to stay focused on the bigger picture.

After picking at her cake for a while, Agatha set the plate down, leaned back into the gray throw pillows, and closed her eyes.

Alex watched her. He didn't think about anything, he just watched her. Then he got up very quietly so as not to disturb her and went into the kitchen where he, carefully, quietly opened the drawer in which he had stored the supplies. Coming up from behind, eyeing her red and green hair, he moved quickly. She turned toward him, cursing loudly, her eyes wide and frightened, as he pressed her head to her knees, pulled her arms behind her back (to the accompaniment of a sickening crack, and her scream) pressed the wrists together and wrapped them with the rope. She struggled in spite of her weakened state, her legs flailing, kicking the coffee table. The plate with the chocolate cake flew off it and landed on the beige rug and her screams escalated into a horrible noise, unlike anything Alex had ever heard before. Luckily, Alex was prepared with the duct tape, which he slapped across her mouth. By that time he was rather exhausted himself. But she stood up and began to run, awkwardly, across the room. It broke his heart to see her this way. He grabbed her from behind. She kicked and squirmed but she was quite a small person and it was easy for him to get her legs tied.

"Is that too tight?" he asked.

She looked at him with wide eyes. As if he were the ghost.

"I don't want you to be uncomfortable."

She shook her head. Tried to speak, but only produced muffled sounds.

"I can take that off," he said, pointing at the duct tape. "But you have to promise me you won't scream. If you scream, I'll just put it on, and I won't take it off again. Though, you should know, ever since Tessie died I have these vivid dreams and nightmares, and I wake up screaming a lot. None of my neighbors has ever done anything about it. Nobody's called the police to report it, and nobody has even asked me if there's a problem. That's how it is amongst the living. Okay?"

She nodded.

He picked at the edge of the tape with his fingertips and when he got a good hold of it, he pulled fast. It made a loud ripping sound. She grunted and gasped, tears falling down her cheeks as she licked her lips.

"I'm really sorry about this," Alex said. "I just couldn't think of another way."

She began to curse, a string of expletives quickly swallowed by her weeping, until finally she managed to ask, "Alex, what are you doing?"

He sighed. "I know it's true, okay? I see the way you are, how tired you get and I know why. I know that you're a breath-stealer. I want you to understand that I know that about you, and I love you and you don't have to keep pretending with me, okay?"

She looked around the room, as if trying to find something to focus on. "Listen, Alex." she said, "Listen to me. I get tired all the time 'cause I'm sick. I didn't want to tell you, after what you told me about your wife. I thought it would be too upsetting for you. That's it. That's why I get tired all the time."

"No," he said, softly, "you're a ghost."

"I am not dead," she said, shaking her head so hard that her tears splashed his face. "I am not dead," she said over and over again, louder and louder until Alex felt forced to tape her mouth shut once more.

"I know you're afraid. Love can be frightening. Do you think I'm not scared? Of course I'm scared. Look what happened with Tessie. I know you're scared too. You're worried I'll turn out to be like Ezekiel, but I'm not like him, okay? I'm not going to hurt you. And I even finally figured out that you're scared 'cause of what happened with your mom. Of course you are. But you have to understand. That's a risk I'm willing to take. Maybe we'll have one night together or only one hour, or a minute. I don't know. I have good genes though. My parents, both of them, are still alive, okay? Even my grandmother only died a few years ago. There's a good chance I have a lot, and I mean a lot, of breath in me. But if I don't, don't you see, I'd rather spend a short time with you, than no time at all?"

He couldn't bear it, he couldn't bear the way she looked at him as if he were a monster when he carried her to the couch. "Are you cold?"

She just stared at him.

"Do you want to watch more *I Love Lucy?* Or a movie?"

She wouldn't respond. She could be so stubborn.

He decided on *Annie Hall.* "Do you like Woody Allen?" She just stared at him, her eyes filled with accusation. "It's a love story," he said, turning away from her to insert the DVD. He turned it on for her, then placed the remote control in her lap, which he realized was a stupid thing to do, since her hands were still tied behind her back, and he was fairly certain that, had her mouth not been taped shut, she'd be giving him that slack-jawed look of hers. She wasn't making any of this very easy. He picked the dish up off the floor, and the silverware, bringing them into the kitchen, where he washed them and the pots and pans, put aluminum foil on the leftover lasagna and put it into the refrigerator. After he finished sweeping the floor, he sat and watched the movie with her. He forgot about the sad ending. He always thought of it as a romantic comedy, never remembering the sad end. He turned off the TV and said, "I think it's late enough now. I think we'll be all right." She looked at him quizzically.

First Alex went out to his car and popped the trunk, then he went back inside where he found poor Agatha squirming across the floor. Trying to escape, apparently. He walked past her, got the throw blanket from the couch and laid it on the floor beside her, rolled her into it even as she squirmed and bucked. "Agatha, just try to relax," he said, but she didn't. Stubborn, stubborn, she could be so stubborn.

He threw her over his shoulder. He was not accustomed to carrying much weight and immediately felt the stress, all the way down his back to his knees. He shut the apartment door behind him and didn't worry about locking it. He lived in a safe neighborhood.

When they got to the car, he put her into the trunk, only then taking the blanket away from her beautiful face. "Don't worry, it won't be long," he said as he closed the hood.

He looked through his CDs, trying to choose something she would like, just in case the sound carried into the trunk, but he couldn't figure out what would be appropriate so he finally decided just to drive in silence.

It took about twenty minutes to get to the beach; it was late, and there was little traffic. Still, the ride gave him an opportunity to reflect on what he was doing. By the time he pulled up next to the pier, he had reassured himself that it was the right thing to do, even though it looked like the wrong thing.

He'd made a good choice, deciding on this place. He and Tessie used to park here, and he was amazed that it had apparently remained undiscovered by others seeking dark escape.

When he got out of the car he took a deep breath of the salt air and stood, for a moment, staring at the black waves, listening to their crash and murmur. Then he went around to the back and opened up the trunk. He looked over his shoulder, just to be sure. If someone were to discover him like this, his actions would be misinterpreted. The coast was clear, however. He wanted to carry Agatha in his arms, like a bride. Every time he had pictured it, he had seen it that way, but she was struggling again so he had to throw her over his shoulder where she continued to struggle. Well, she was stubborn, but he was too, that was part of the beauty of it, really. But it made it difficult to walk, and it was windier on the pier, also wet. All in all it was a precarious, unpleasant journey to the end.

He had prepared a little speech but she struggled against him so hard, like a hooked fish, that all he could manage to say was, "I love you," barely focusing on the wild expression in her face, the wild eyes, before he threw her in and she sank, and then bobbed up like a cork, only her head above the black waves, those eyes of hers, locked on his, and they remained that way, as he turned away from the edge of the pier and walked down the long plank, feeling lighter, but not in a good way. He felt those eyes, watching him, in the car as he flipped restlessly from station to station, those eyes, watching him, when he returned home, and saw the clutter of their night together, the burned-down candles, the covers to the *I Love Lucy* and *Annie Hall* DVDs on the floor, her crazy sweater on the dining room table, those eyes, watching him, and suddenly Alex was cold, so cold his teeth were chattering and he was shivering but sweating besides. The black water rolled over those eyes and closed them and he ran to the bathroom and only just made it in time, throwing up everything he'd eaten, collapsing to the floor, weeping, *What have I done? What was I thinking?*

He would have stayed there like that, he determined, until they came for him and carted him away, but after a while he became aware of the foul taste in his mouth. He stood up, rinsed it out, brushed his teeth and tongue, changed out of his clothes, and went to bed, where, after a good deal more crying, and trying to figure out exactly what had happened to his mind, he was amazed to find himself falling into a deep darkness like the water, from which, he expected, he would never rise.

But then he was lying there, with his eyes closed, somewhere between sleep and waking, and he realized he'd been like this for some time. Though he was fairly certain he had fallen asleep, something had woken him. In this half state, he'd been listening to the sound he finally recognized as dripping water. He hated it when he didn't turn the faucet tight. He tried to ignore it, but the dripping persisted. So confused was he that he even thought he felt a splash on his hand and another on his forehead. He opened one eye, then the other.

She stood there, dripping wet, her hair plastered darkly around her face, her eyes smudged black. "I found a sharp rock at the bottom of the world," she said, and she raised her arms. He thought she was going to strike him, but instead she showed him the cut rope dangling there.

He nodded. He could not speak.

She cocked her head, smiled, and said, "Okay, you were right. You were right about everything. Got any room in there?"

He nodded. She peeled off the wet T-shirt and let it drop to the floor, revealing her small breasts white as the moon, unbuttoned and unzipped her jeans, wiggling seductively out of the tight wet fabric, taking her panties off at the same time. He saw when she lifted her feet that the rope was no longer around them and she was already transparent below the knees. When she pulled back the covers he smelled the odd odor of saltwater and mud, as if she were both fresh and loamy. He scooted over, but only far enough that when she eased in beside him, he could hold her, wrap her wet cold skin in his arms, knowing that he was offering her everything, everything he had to give, and that she had come to take it.

"You took a big risk back there," she said.

He nodded.

She pressed her lips against his and he felt himself growing lighter, as if all his life he'd been weighed down by this extra breath, and her lips were cold but they grew warmer and warmer and the heat between them created a steam until she burned him and still, they kissed, all the while Alex thinking, I love you, I love you, I love you, until, finally, he could think it no more, his head was as light as his body, lying beside her, hot flesh to hot flesh, the cinder of his mind could no longer make sense of it, and he hoped, as he fell into a black place like no other he'd ever been in before, that this was really happening, that she was really here, and the suffering he'd felt for so long was finally over.

EIGHT EPISODES

ROBERT REED

Robert Reed became a full-time writer in 1987, the same year his story "Mud-puppies" won the L. Ron Hubbard Writers of the Future Contest. Starting with *The Leeshore* and *The Hormone Jungle* in 1987, he has published nine novels, most notably far future science fiction novel *Marrow*, sequel *The Well of Stars*, and story-suite *Sister Alice*, but is probably best known for his short fiction. An extraordinarily prolific writer, Reed has published over 140 short stories, mostly in *F&SF* and *Asimov's*, which have been nominated for the Hugo, James Tiptree Jr. Memorial, Locus, Nebula, Seiun, Theodore Sturgeon Memorial, and World Fantasy awards, and have been collected in *The Dragons of Springplace*, *Chrysalide* (published in French), and *The Cuckoo's Boys*. His most recent book is novella *Flavors of My Genius*. Probably Nebraska's only science fiction writer, Reed lives in Omaha with his wife and daughter.

With minimal fanfare and next to no audience, *Invasion of a Small World* debuted in the summer of 2016, and after a brief and disappointing run, the series was deservedly shelved.

One glaring problem was its production values: Computer animation had reached a plateau where reality was an easy illusion, spectacle was the industry norm, and difficult tricks like flowing water and human faces were beginning to approximate what was real. Yet the show's standards were barely adequate, even from an upstart Web network operating with limited capital and too many hours of programming to fill. The landscapes and interior shots would have been considered state-of-the-art at the turn of the century, but not in its premiere year. The characters were inflicted with inexpressive faces and stiff-limbed motions, while their voices were equally unconvincing, employing amateur actors or some cut-rate audio-synthesis software. With few exceptions, the dialogue was sloppy, cluttered with pauses and clumsy phrasing, key statements often cut off in midsentence. Most critics decided that the series' creators were striving for a real-life mood. But that was purely an interpretation. Press kits were never made available, and no interviews were granted with anyone directly involved in the production, leaving industry watchers entirely to their own devices—another problem that served to cripple *Invasion*.

Other factors contributed to the tiny audience. One issue that couldn't be discussed openly was the racial makeup of the cast. Success in the lucrative North American market meant using characters of obvious European extraction. Yet the series' leading man was an Indian astronomer working at a fictional college set in, of all places, South Africa. With an unpronounceable name and thick accent, Dr. Smith—as his few fans dubbed him—was a pudgy, prickly creation with a weakness for loud shirts and deep belches. His wife was a homely apparition who understood nothing about his world-shaking work, while his children, in direct contrast to virtually every other youngster inhabiting popular entertainment, were dimwitted creatures offering nothing that was particularly clever or charming.

A paucity of drama was another obvious weakness. The premiere episode involved a routine day in Dr. Smith's life. Eighteen hours of unexceptional behavior was compressed to fifty-three minutes of unexceptional behavior. Judging by appearances, the parent network inserted commercial breaks at random points. The series' pivotal event was barely noticed by the early viewers: One of Dr. Smith's graduate students was working with Permian-age rock samples, searching for key isotopes deposited by ancient supernovae. The student asked her professor about a difficult piece of lab equipment. As always, the dialogue was dense and graceless, explaining almost nothing to the uninitiated. Genuine scientists—some of the series' most unapologetic fans—liked to point out that the instruments and principles were genuine, though the nomenclature was shamelessly contrived. Fourteen seconds of broadcast time introduced a young graduate student named Mary—a mixed-race woman who by no measure could be considered attractive. She was shown asking Dr. Smith for help with the problematic instrument, and he responded with a wave of a pudgy hand and a muttered, "Later." Following ads for tiny cars and a powerful asthma medicine, the astronomer ordered his student to come to his office and lock the door behind her. What happened next was only implied. But afterwards Dr. Smith was seen sitting with his back to his desk and his belt unfastened, and the quick-eyed viewer saw Mary's tiny breasts vanish under a bra and baggy shirt. Some people have interpreted her expression as pain, emotional or otherwise. Others have argued that her face was so poorly rendered that it was impossible to fix any emotion to her, then or later. And where good writers would have used dialogue to spell out the importance of the moment, bad writers decided to ignore the entire interpersonal plotline. With a casual voice, Mary mentioned to her advisor/lover that she had found something strange in the Permian stone.

"Strange," he repeated.

With her thumb and finger, she defined a tiny space. "Metal. A ball."

"Ball?"

"In the rock."

Smith scratched his fat belly for a moment, saying nothing. (Judging by log tallies, nearly 10 percent of the program's small audience turned away at that point.) Then he quietly said to her, "I do not understand."

"What it is…"

"What?"

She said, "I don't know either."

"In what rock?"

"Mine. The mudstone—"

"You mean it's artificial…?"

"Looks so," she answered.

He said, "Huh."

She finished buttoning her shirt, the back of her left hand wiping at the corner of her mouth.

"Where?" Smith asked.

She gave the parent rock's identification code.

"No, the metal ball," he interrupted. "Where is it now?"

"My desk drawer. In a white envelope."

"And how big?"

"Two grains of rice, about."

Then, one last time, the main character said, "Huh." And, finally, without any interest showing in his face, he fastened his belt.

* * *

The next three episodes covered not days, but several months. Again, none of the scientific work was explained, and nothing resembling a normal plotline emerged from the routine and the tedious. The increasingly tiny audience watched Dr. Smith and two of his graduate students working with an object almost too small to be resolved on the screen—another significant problem with the series. Wouldn't a human-sized artifact have made a greater impact? The ball's metal shell proved to be an unlikely alloy of nickel and aluminum. Cosmic radiation and tiny impacts had left the telltale marks one would expect after a long drifting journey through space. Using tiny lasers, the researchers carefully cut through the metal shell, revealing a diamond interior. Then the diamond heart absorbed a portion of the laser's energy, and once charged, it powered up its own tiny light show. Fortunately a nanoscopic camera had been inserted into the hole, and the three scientists were able to record what they witnessed—a rush of complex images coupled with an increasingly so-phisticated array of symbols.

"What is this?" they kept asking one another.

"Maybe it's language," Mary guessed. Correctly, as it happened. "Someone's teaching us… trying to… a new language."

Dr. Smith gave her a shamelessly public hug.

Then the other graduate student—a Brazilian fellow named Carlos—pointed out that, whatever the device was, Mary had found it in rock that was at least a quarter of a billion years old. "And that doesn't count the time this little machine spent in space, which could be millions more years."

After the show's cancellation, at least one former executive admitted to having been fooled. "We were promised a big, loud invasion," he told an interviewer from *Rolling Stone*. "I talked to the series' producer. He said an invasion would begin right after episode four. Yeah, we knew the build-up was going to be slow. But then aliens from the dinosaur days were going to spring to life and start burning cities."

"Except," said the interviewer.

"What?"

"That's not quite true. The Permian happened before there were any dinosaurs."

With a shrug, the ex-executive brushed aside that mild criticism. "Anyway, the important thing is that bad-ass aliens were supposed to come out of the rock. They were going to grow huge and start kicking us around. At least that's what the production company—EXL Limited—assured us. A spectacle. And since we didn't have to pay much for those episodes, we ended up purchasing the first eight shows after seeing only a few minutes of material...."

Invasion was cancelled after the fifth episode.

The final broadcast episode was an artless synopsis of the next twenty months of scientific work. Dr. Smith and his students were just a tiny portion of a global effort. Experts on six continents were making a series of tiny, critical breakthroughs. Most of the story involved faceless researchers exchanging dry e-mails about the tiny starship's text and images. Translations were made; every shred of evidence began to support the obvious but incredible conclusions. The culminating event was a five-minute news conference. Dripping sweat, shaking from nerves, the astronomer explained to reporters that he had found a functioning starship on Earth. After a glancing thanks to unnamed colleagues, he explained how, in the remote past, perhaps long before there was multicellular life on Earth, an alien species had manufactured trillions of tiny ships like this one. The ships were cast off into space, drifting slowly to planetary systems scattered throughout the galaxy. The vessel that he had personally recovered was already ancient when it dropped onto a river bottom near the edge of Gondwanaland. Time had only slightly degraded its onboard texts—a history of the aliens and an explanation into the nature of life in the universe. By all evidence, he warned, human beings were late players to an old drama. And like every other intelligent species in the universe, they would always be small in numbers and limited in reach.

The final scene of that fifth episode was set at Dr. Smith's home. His oldest son was sitting before a large plasma screen, destroying alien spaceships with extraordinarily loud weapons. In what proved to be the only conversation between those two characters, Smith sat beside his boy, asking, "Did you see me?"

"What?"

"The news conference—"

"Yeah, I watched."

"So?" he said. And when no response was offered, he asked, "What did you think?"

"About what?"

"The lesson—"

"What? People don't matter?" The boy froze the battle scene and put down his controls. "I think that's stupid."

His father said nothing.

"The universe isn't empty and poor." The boy was perhaps fourteen, and his anger was the most vivid emotion in the entire series. "Worlds are everywhere, and a lot of them have to have life."

"Millions are blessed, yes," Dr. Smith replied. "But hundreds of billions more are too hot, too cold. They are metal-starved, or married to dangerous suns."

His son stared at the frozen screen, saying nothing.

"The alien texts only confirm our most recent evidence, you know. The Earth is a latecomer. Stellar births are slowing, in the Milky Way, and everywhere, and the production of terrestrial worlds peaked two or three billion years before our home was created."

"These texts of yours… they say that intelligent life stays at home?"

"Most of the time, yes."

"Aliens don't send out real starships?"

"It is far too expensive," Smith offered.

The boy pushed out his lower lip. "Humans are different," he maintained.

"No."

"We're going to build a working stardrive. Soon, I bet. And then we'll visit our neighboring stars and colonize those worlds—"

"We can't."

"Because they tell us we can't?"

"Because it is impossible." His father shook his head, saying with authority, "The texts are explicit. Moving large masses requires prohibitive energies. And terraforming is a difficult, often impossible trick. And that is why almost every world that we have found to date looks as sterile as the day they were born."

But the teenage boy would accept none of that. "You know, don't you? That these aliens are just lying to us? They're afraid of human beings, because they know we're the toughest, meanest things in the universe. And we're going to take them on."

For a long moment, Dr. Smith held silent.

Then the boy continued his game, and into the mayhem of blasters, the father mouthed a single dismissive word: "Children."

* * *

Eighteen months later, the fledging Web network declared bankruptcy, and a small consortium acquired its assets, including *Invasion of a Small World*.

Eager to recoup their investment, the new owners offered all eight episodes as a quick-and-dirty DVD package. When sales proved somewhat better than predicted, a new version was cobbled together, helped along by a genuine ad budget. The strongest initial sales came from the tiny pool of determined fans—young and well-educated, with little preference for nationality or gender. But the scientists in several fields, astronomy and paleontology included, were the ones who created a genuine buzz that eventually put *Invasion* into the public eye.

The famous sixth episode helped trigger the interest: That weak, rambling tale of Dr. Smith, his family and students, was temporarily suspended. Instead, the full fifty-three minutes were dedicated to watching a barren world spinning silently in deep space. According to corporate memos, the last three episodes arrived via the Web, bundled in a single package. But it was this episode that effectively killed the series. There were no explanations. Nothing showed but the gray world spinning, twenty minutes before the point-of-view gradually pulled away. The world was just a tiny speck of metal lost in the vastness of space. For astronomers, it was a fascinating moment—a vivid illustration that the universe could be an exceedingly boring place. Stars were distant points of light, and there was only silence, and even when millions of years were compressed into a nap-length moment, nothing was produced that could be confused for great theatre.

But what the astronomers liked best—what got the buzz going—were the final few minutes of the episode. Chance brought the tiny starship into the solar system, and chance guided it past a younger Saturn. The giant moon, Titan, swung close before the ship was kicked out to Neptune's orbit. Then it drifted sunward again, Mars near enough to reveal its face. Two hundred and fifty million years ago, Titan was bathed in a much denser atmosphere, while Mars was a temporarily wet world, heated by a substantial impact event. Experts in those two worlds were impressed. Only in the last year or two, probes had discovered what *Invasion* predicted on its own, including pinpointing the impact site near the Martian South Pole.

In much the same way, episode seven made the paleontologists crazy.

With its long voyage finished, the tiny starship struck the Earth's upper atmosphere, quickly losing its momentum as well as a portion of its hull. The great southern continent was rendered accurately enough to make any geologist smile, while the little glimpses of Permian ecosystems were even more impressive. Whoever produced the series (and there was a growing controversy on that matter), they had known much about protomammals and the early reptiles, cycads and tree ferns. One ancient creature—lizard in form, though not directly related to any modern species—was the only important misstep. Yet five months later, a team working in South Africa uncovered a set of bones that perfectly matched what a vanished dramatic series had predicted… and what was already a cultish buzz grew into a wild, increasingly public cacophony.…

At least forty thousand sites—chat rooms and blogs and such—were dedicated to supporting the same inevitable conclusion.

By means unknown, aliens had sent a message to earthlings, and it took the form of *Invasion of a Small World*.

* * *

The eighth episode was a genuine treasure.

Dr. Smith reappeared. Several years older, divorced, and with his belly fat stripped off by liposuction, he was shown wandering happily through a new life of endless celebrity. His days and long evenings were spent with at least three mistresses as well as a parade of world leaders. Accustomed to the praise of others, he was shown grinning confidently while offering his interpretations of the ancient message. The universe was almost certainly sprinkled with life, he explained. But despite that prolificacy, the cosmos remained an enormous, very cold, and exceptionally poor place. The gulfs between living worlds were completely unbridgeable. No combination of raw energy and questing genius could build a worthy stardrive. Moreover, even direct communication between local species was rarely worth its considerable cost, since civilizations rarely if ever offered each other anything with genuine worth.

"Technology has distinct limits," he warned the starlets and world leaders that he met at cocktail parties. "Humans are already moving into the late stages of scientific endeavor. What matters most, to us and to any wise species, is the careful shepherding of energy and time. That is why we must care for our world and the neighboring planets inside our own little solar system. We must treasure every day while wasting nothing, if only to extend our histories as far as into the future as possible."

"That strikes me as such depressing news," said one prime minister—a statuesque woman blessed with a starlet's beautiful face. "If there really are millions and billions of living worlds, as you claim, and if all the great minds on all of those worlds are thinking hard about this single problem, shouldn't somebody learn how to cheat the speed of light or create free energy through some clever trick?"

"If that were so," Dr. Smith replied, "then every world out there would be alive, and the giant starships would arrive at our doorstep every few minutes. But instead, human experience has discovered precisely one starfaring vessel, and it was a grain of metallic dust, and to reach us it had to be exceptionally lucky, and, even then, it had to wait a quarter of a billion years to be noticed."

The prime minister sipped her virgin mary while chewing on her lower lip. Then with a serious tone, she said, "But to me... there seems to be another reasonable explanation waiting for our attention..."

"Which would be what, madam?"

"Subterfuge," she offered. "The aliens are intentionally misleading us about the nature of the universe."

Bristling, he asked, "And why would they do such a thing?"

"To cripple our future," she replied. "By convincing us to remain home, they never have to face us between the stars."

"Perhaps you're right to think that, madam," said the old astronomer, nodding without resolve. Then in his final moment in the series' final episode, he said, "A lie is as good as a pill, if it helps you sleep...."

* * *

For years, every search to uncover the creative force behind *Invasion of a Small World* came up empty. And in the public mind, that single mystery remained the final, most compelling part of the story.

Former executives with the doomed network had never directly met with the show's producers. But they could recount phone conversations and teleconferences and e-mails exchanged with three apparent producers. Of course, by then, it was possible to invent a digital human face and voice while weaving a realistic mix of human gestures. Which led some to believe that slippery forces were plainly at work here—forces that no human eye had ever witnessed.

Tracking down the original production company produced only a dummy corporation leading to dusty mailboxes and several defunct Web addresses. Every name proved fictional, both among the company's officers and those in the brief credits rolling at the end of each episode. Surviving tax forms lacked any shred of useful information. But where the IRS might have chased down a successful cheat, the plain truth was that whoever was responsible for *Invasion* had signed away all future rights in exchange for a puddle of cash.

The few skeptics wondered if something considerably more ordinary was at play here. Rumors occasionally surfaced about young geniuses working in the Third World—usually in the Indian tech-cities. Employing pirated software and stolen equipment, they had produced what would eventually become the fifth most successful media event in history. But in the short-term, their genius had led nowhere but to obscurity and financial ruin. Three different candidates were identified—young men with creative minds and most of the necessary skills. Did one of them build *Invasion* alone? Or was it a group effort? And was the project's failure the reason why each of them committed suicide shortly after the series' cancellation?

But if they were the creators, why didn't any trail lead to them? Perhaps because the consortium that held all rights to *Invasion* had obscured the existing evidence. And why? Obviously to help feed this infectious and delicious mood of suspicion. To maintain an atmosphere where no doubts could find a toehold, where aliens were conversing with humans, and where the money continued to flow to the consortium like a great green river.

* * *

The most durable explanation was told by one of the series' most devoted fans—a Nobel laureate in physics who was happy to beat the drum for the unthinkable. "*Invasion* is true everywhere but in the specifics," he argued. "I think there really was an automated starship. But it was bigger than a couple grains of rice. As big as a fist, or a human head. But still small and unmanned. The ship entered our solar system during the Permian. With the bulk of it in orbit, pieces must have landed on our world. Scouts with the size and legs of small cockroaches, maybe. Maybe. And if you take the time to think it through, you see that it would be a pretty silly strategy, letting yourself become a tiny fossil in some enormous bed of mudstone. What are the odds that you'd survive for 250 million years, much else ever get noticed there?

"No, if you are an automated starship, what would be smart is for that orbiting mothership to take a seat where nothing happens and she can see everything. On the moon, I'd guess. She still has the antennas that she used to hear the scouts' reports. She sleeps and waits for radio signals from the Earth, and when they arrive, she studies what she hears. She makes herself into a student of language and technology. And when the time is ripe—when she has a product to sell—she expels the last of her fuel, leaving the moon to land someplace useful. Which is pretty much anywhere, these days.

"Looking like a roach, maybe, she connects to the Web and offers her services at a cut-rate price.

"And that is how she delivers her message.

"Paraphrasing my fictional colleague, 'A lie is as good as a truth, if it leads you to enlightenment.'"

* * *

The final scene in the last episode only seemed anticlimactic. The one-time graduate student, Mary, had been left behind by world events. From the beginning, her critical part in the research had been downplayed. But the series' creator, whoever or whatever it was, saw no useful drama in that treachery. The woman was middle-aged and happy in her obscurity, plain as always and pregnant for at least the second time.

A ten-year-old daughter was sitting beside Mary, sharing a threadbare couch.

The girl asked her mother what she believed. Was the universe really so empty and cold? And was this the way it would always be?

Quietly, her mother said, "I think that's basically true, yes."

The girl looked saddened.

But then Mary patted her daughter on the back of a hand, smiling with confidence. "But dear, I also believe this," she said. "Life is an invasion wherever it shows itself. It is relentless and it is tireless, and it conquers every little place where living is possible. And before the universe ends, all the good homes will know the sounds of wet breathing and the singing of glorious songs."

THE WIZARDS OF PERFIL

KELLY LINK

Kelly Link was born in Miami, Florida, and grew up on the East Coast. She attended Columbia University in New York and the University of North Carolina, Greensboro. She sold her first story, "Water Off a Black Dog's Back," just before attending Clarion in 1995. Her later stories have won or been nominated for the James Tiptree Jr., World Fantasy, and Nebula Awards. Link's stories have been collected in *Stranger Things Happen* and *Magic for Beginners*. She has edited the anthology *Trampoline*, co-edits *The Year's Best Fantasy and Horror* with husband Gavin J. Grant and Ellen Datlow, and co-edits the 'zine *Lady Churchill's Rosebud Wristlet* with Grant.

The woman who sold leech grass baskets and pickled beets in the Perfil market took pity on Onion's aunt. "On your own, my love?"

Onion's aunt nodded. She was still holding out the earrings which she'd hoped someone would buy. There was a train leaving in the morning for Qual, but the tickets were dear. Her daughter Halsa, Onion's cousin, was sulking. She'd wanted the earrings for herself. The twins held hands and stared about the market.

Onion thought the beets were more beautiful than the earrings, which had belonged to his mother. The beets were rich and velvety and mysterious as pickled stars in shining jars. Onion had had nothing to eat all day. His stomach was empty, and his head was full of the thoughts of the people in the market: Halsa thinking of the earrings, the market woman's disinterested kindness, his aunt's dull worry. There was a man at another stall whose wife was sick. She was coughing up blood. A girl went by. She was thinking about a man who had gone to the war. The man wouldn't come back. Onion went back to thinking about the beets.

"Just you to look after all these children," the market woman said. "These are bad times. Where's your lot from?"

"Come from Labbit, and Larch before that," Onion's aunt said. "We're trying to get to Qual. My husband had family there. I have these earrings and these candlesticks."

The woman shook her head. "No one will buy these," she said. "Not for any good price. The market is full of refugees selling off their bits and pieces."

Onion's aunt said, "Then what should I do?" She didn't seem to expect an answer, but the woman said, "There's a man who comes to the market today, who buys children for the wizards of Perfil. He pays good money and they say that the children are treated well."

* * *

All wizards are strange, but the wizards of Perfil are strangest of all. They build tall towers in the marshes of Perfil, and there they live like anchorites in lonely little rooms at the top of their towers. They rarely come down at all, and no one is sure what their magic is good for. There are wobbly lights like balls of sickly green fire that dash around the marshes at night, hunting for who knows what, and sometimes a tower tumbles down and then the prickly reeds and marsh lilies that look like ghostly white hands grow up over the tumbled stones and the marsh mud sucks the rubble down.

Everyone knows that there are wizard bones under the marsh mud and that the fish and the birds that live in the marsh are strange creatures. They have got magic in them. Boys dare each other to go into the marsh and catch fish. Sometimes when a brave boy catches a fish in the murky, muddy marsh pools, the fish will call the boy by name and beg to be released. And if you don't let that fish go, it will tell you, gasping for air, when and how you will die. And if you cook the fish and eat it, you will dream wizard dreams. But if you let your fish go, it will tell you a secret.

This is what the people of Perfil say about the wizards of Perfil.

* * *

Everyone knows that the wizards of Perfil talk to demons and hate sunlight and have long twitching noses like rats. They never bathe.

Everyone knows that the wizards of Perfil are hundreds and hundreds of years old. They sit and dangle their fishing lines out of the windows of their towers and they use magic to bait their hooks. They eat their fish raw and they throw the fish bones out of the window the same way that they empty their chamber pots. The wizards of Perfil have filthy habits and no manners at all.

Everyone knows that the wizards of Perfil eat children when they grow tired of fish.

This is what Halsa told her brothers and Onion while Onion's aunt bargained in the Perfil markets with the wizard's secretary.

* * *

The wizard's secretary was a man named Tolcet and he wore a sword in his belt. He was a black man with white-pink spatters on his face and across the backs of his hands. Onion had never seen a man who was two colors.

Tolcet gave Onion and his cousins pieces of candy. He said to Onion's aunt, "Can any of them sing?"

Onion's aunt indicated that the children should sing. The twins, Mik and Bonti, had strong, clear soprano voices and when Halsa sang, everyone in the market fell silent and listened. Halsa's voice was like honey and sunlight and sweet water.

Onion loved to sing, but no one loved to hear it. When it was his turn and he opened his mouth to sing, he thought of his mother and tears came to his eyes. The song that came out of his mouth wasn't one he knew. It wasn't even in a proper language and Halsa crossed her eyes and stuck out her tongue. Onion went on singing.

"Enough," Tolcet said. He pointed at Onion. "You sing like a toad, boy. Do you know when to be quiet?"

"He's quiet," Onion's aunt said. "His parents are dead. He doesn't eat much, and he's strong enough. We walked here from Larch. And he's not afraid of witchy folk, begging your pardon. There were no wizards in Larch, but his mother could find things when you lost them. She could charm your cows so that they always came home."

"How old is he?" Tolcet said.

"Eleven," Onion's aunt said and Tolcet grunted.

"Small for his age." Tolcet looked at Onion. He looked at Halsa, who crossed her arms and scowled hard. "Will you come with me, boy?"

Onion's aunt nudged him. He nodded.

"I'm sorry for it," his aunt said to Onion, "but it can't be helped. I promised your mother I'd see you were taken care of. This is the best I can do."

Onion said nothing. He knew his aunt would have sold Halsa to the wizard's secretary and hoped it was a piece of luck for her daughter. But there was also a part of his aunt that was glad that Tolcet wanted Onion instead. Onion could see it in her mind.

Tolcet paid Onion's aunt twenty-four brass fish, which was slightly more than it had cost to bury Onion's parents, but slightly less than Onion's father had paid for their best milk cow, two years before. It was important to know how much things were worth. The cow was dead and so was Onion's father.

"Be *good*," Onion's aunt said. "Here. Take this." She gave Onion one of the earrings that had belonged to his mother. It was shaped like a snake. Its writhing tail hooked into its narrow mouth, and Onion had always wondered if the snake were surprised about that, to end up with a mouthful of itself like that, for all eternity. Or maybe it was eternally furious, like Halsa.

Halsa's mouth was screwed up like a button. When she hugged Onion goodbye, she said, "Brat. Give it to me." Halsa had already taken the wooden horse that Onion's father had carved, and Onion's knife, the one with the bone handle.

Onion tried to pull away, but she held him tightly, as if she couldn't bear to let him go. "He wants to eat you," she said. "The wizard will put you in an oven and roast you like a suckling pig. So give me the earring. Suckling pigs don't need earrings."

Onion wriggled away. The wizard's secretary was watching, and Onion wondered if he'd heard Halsa. Of course, anyone who wanted a child to eat would have taken Halsa, not Onion. Halsa was older and bigger and plumper. Then again, anyone who looked hard at Halsa would suspect she would taste sour and unpleasant. The only sweetness in Halsa was in her singing. Even Onion loved to listen to Halsa when she sang.

Mik and Bonti gave Onion shy little kisses on his cheek. He knew they wished the wizard's secretary had bought Halsa instead. Now that Onion was gone, it would be the twins that Halsa pinched and bullied and teased.

Tolcet swung a long leg over his horse. Then he leaned down. "Come on, boy," he said, and held his speckled hand out to Onion. Onion took it.

The horse was warm and its back was broad and high. There was no saddle and no reins, only a kind of woven harness with a basket on either flank, filled with goods from the market. Tolcet held the horse quiet with his knees, and Onion held on tight to Tolcet's belt.

"That song you sang," Tolcet said. "Where did you learn it?"

"I don't know," Onion said. It came to him that the song had been a song that Tolcet's mother had sung to her son, when Tolcet was a child. Onion wasn't sure what the words meant, because Tolcet wasn't sure either. There was something about a lake and a boat, something about a girl who had eaten the moon.

The marketplace was full of people selling things. From his vantage point Onion felt, for a moment, like a prince: as if he could afford to buy anything he saw. He looked down at a stall selling apples and potatoes and hot leek pies. His mouth watered. Over here was an incense seller's stall, and there was a woman telling fortunes. At the train station, people were lining up to buy tickets for Qual. In the morning a train would leave and Onion's aunt and Halsa and the twins would be on it. It was a dangerous passage. There were unfriendly armies between here and Qual. When Onion looked back at his aunt, he knew it would do no good, she would only think he was begging her not to leave him with the wizard's secretary, but he said it all the same: "Don't go to Qual."

But he knew even as he said it that she would go anyway. No one ever listened to Onion.

The horse tossed its head. The wizard's secretary made a *tch-tch* sound and then leaned back in the saddle. He seemed undecided about something. Onion looked back one more time at his aunt. He had never seen her smile once in the two years he'd lived with her, and she did not smile now, even though twenty-four brass fish was not a small sum of money and even though she'd kept her promise to Onion's mother. Onion's mother had smiled often, despite the fact that her teeth were not particularly good.

"He'll eat you," Halsa called to Onion. "Or he'll drown you in the marsh! He'll cut you up into little pieces and bait his fishing line with your fingers!" She stamped her foot.

"Halsa!" her mother said.

"On second thought," Tolcet said, "I'll take the girl. Will you sell her to me instead?"

"What?" Halsa said.

"What?" Onion's aunt said.

"No!" Onion said, but Tolcet drew out his purse again. Halsa, it seemed, was worth more than a small boy with a bad voice. And Onion's aunt needed money badly. So Halsa got up on the horse behind Tolcet, and Onion watched as the wizard's servant and his bad-tempered cousin rode away.

There was a voice in Onion's head. It said, "Don't worry, boy. All will be well and all manner of things will be well." It sounded like Tolcet, a little amused, a little sad.

* * *

There is a story about the wizards of Perfil and how one fell in love with a church bell. First he tried to buy it with gold and then, when the church refused his money, he stole it by magic. As the wizard flew back across the marshes, carrying the bell in his arms, he flew too low and the devil reached up and grabbed his heel. The wizard dropped the church bell into the marshes and it sank and was lost forever. Its voice is clappered with mud and moss and although the wizard never gave up searching for it and calling its name, the bell never answered and the wizard grew thin and died of grief. Fishermen say that the dead wizard still flies over the marsh, crying out for the lost bell.

Everyone knows that wizards are pigheaded and come to bad ends. No wizard has ever made himself useful by magic, or, if they've tried, they've only made matters worse. No wizard has ever stopped a war or mended a fence. It's better that they stay in their marshes, out of the way of worldly folk like farmers and soldiers and merchants and kings.

* * *

"Well," Onion's aunt said. She sagged. They could no longer see Tolcet or Halsa. "Come along, then."

They went back through the market and Onion's aunt bought cakes of sweetened rice for the three children. Onion ate his without knowing that he did so: since the wizard's servant had taken away Halsa instead, it had felt as if there were two Onions, one Onion here in the market and one Onion riding along with Tolcet and Halsa. He stood and was carried along at the same time and it made both of him feel terribly dizzy. Market-Onion stumbled, his mouth full of rice, and his aunt caught him by the elbow.

"We don't eat children," Tolcet was saying. "There are plenty of fish and birds in the marshes."

"I know," Halsa said. She sounded sulky. "And the wizards live in houses with lots of stairs. Towers. Because they think they're so much better than anybody else. So above the rest of the world."

"And how do you know about the wizards of Perfil?" Tolcet said.

"The woman in the market," Halsa said. "And the other people in the market.

Some are afraid of the wizards and some think that there are no wizards. That they're a story for children. That the marshes are full of runaway slaves and deserters. Nobody knows why wizards would come and build towers in the Perfil marsh where the ground is like cheese and no one can find them. Why do the wizards live in the marshes?"

"Because the marsh is full of magic," Tolcet said.

"Then why do they build the towers so high?" Halsa said.

"Because wizards are curious," Tolcet said. "They like to be able to see things that are far off. They like to be as close as possible to the stars. And they don't like to be bothered by people who ask lots of questions."

"Why do the wizards buy children?" Halsa said.

"To run up and down the stairs," Tolcet said, "to fetch them water for bathing and to carry messages and to bring them breakfasts and dinners and lunches and suppers. Wizards are always hungry."

"So am I," Halsa said.

"Here," Tolcet said. He gave Halsa an apple. "You see things that are in people's heads. You can see things that are going to happen."

"Yes," Halsa said. "Sometimes." The apple was wrinkled but sweet.

"Your cousin has a gift, too," Tolcet said.

"Onion?" Halsa said scornfully. Onion saw that it had never felt like a gift to Halsa. No wonder she'd hidden it.

"Can you see what is in my head right now?" Tolcet said.

Halsa looked and Onion looked too. There was no curiosity or fear about in Tolcet's head. There was nothing. There was no Tolcet, no wizard's servant. Only brackish water and lonely white birds flying above it.

It's beautiful, Onion said.

"What?" his aunt said, in the market. "Onion? Sit down, child."

"Some people find it so," Tolcet said, answering Onion. Halsa said nothing, but she frowned.

Tolcet and Halsa rode through the town and out of the town gates onto the road that led back towards Labbit and east, where there were more refugees coming and going, day and night. They were mostly women and children and they were afraid. There were rumors of armies behind them. There was a story that, in a fit of madness, the king had killed his youngest son. Onion saw a chess game, a thin-faced, anxious, yellow-haired boy Onion's age moving a black queen across the board, and then the chess pieces scattered across a stone floor. A woman was saying something. The boy bent down to pick up the scattered pieces. The king was laughing. He had a sword in his hand and he brought it down and then there was blood on it. Onion had never seen a king before, although he had seen men with swords. He had seen men with blood on their swords.

Tolcet and Halsa went away from the road, following a wide river, which was less a river than a series of wide, shallow pools. On the other side of the river, muddy paths disappeared into thick stands of rushes and bushes full of berries. There was a feeling of watchfulness, and the cunning, curious stillness of something alive, something half-asleep and half-waiting, a hidden, invisible humming, as if even the air was saturated with magic.

"Berries! Ripe and sweet!" a girl was singing out, over and over again in the market. Onion wished she would be quiet. His aunt bought bread and salt and hard cheese. She piled them into Onion's arms.

"It will be uncomfortable at first," Tolcet was saying. "The marshes of Perfil are so full of magic that they drink up all other kinds of magic. The only ones who work magic in the marshes of Perfil are the wizards of Perfil. And there are bugs."

"I don't want anything to do with magic," Halsa said primly.

Again Onion tried to look in Tolcet's mind, but again all he saw was the marshes. Fat-petaled waxy white flowers and crouching trees that dangled their long brown fingers as if fishing. Tolcet laughed. "I can feel you looking," he said. "Don't look too long or you'll fall in and drown."

"I'm not looking!" Halsa said. But she *was* looking. Onion could feel her looking, as if she was turning a key in a door.

The marshes smelled salty and rich, like a bowl of broth. Tolcet's horse ambled along, its hooves sinking into the path. Behind them, water welled up and filled the depressions. Fat jeweled flies clung, vibrating, to the rushes and once in a clear pool of water Onion saw a snake curling like a green ribbon through water weeds soft as a cloud of hair.

"Wait here and watch Bonti and Mik for me," Onion's aunt said. "I'll go to the train station. Onion, are you all right?"

Onion nodded dreamily.

Tolcet and Halsa rode further into the marsh, away from the road and the Perfil market and Onion. It was very different from the journey to Perfil, which had been hurried and dusty and dry and on foot. Whenever Onion or one of the twins stumbled or lagged behind, Halsa had rounded them up like a dog chasing sheep, pinching and slapping. It was hard to imagine cruel, greedy, unhappy Halsa being able to pick things out of other people's minds, although she had always seemed to know when Mik or Bonti had found something edible; where there might be a soft piece of ground to sleep; when they should duck off the road because soldiers were coming.

Halsa was thinking of her mother and her brothers. She was thinking about the look on her father's face when the soldiers had shot him behind the barn; the earrings shaped like snakes; how the train to Qual would be blown up by saboteurs. She had been supposed to be on that train, she knew it. She was furious at Tolcet for taking her away; at Onion, because Tolcet had changed his mind about Onion.

Every now and then, while he waited in the market for his aunt to come back, Onion could see the pointy roofs of the wizard's towers leaning against the sky as if they were waiting for him, just beyond the Perfil market, and then the towers would recede, and he would go with them, and find himself again with Tolcet and Halsa. Their path ran up along a canal of calm tarry water, angled off into thickets of bushes bent down with bright yellow berries, and then returned. It cut across other paths, these narrower and crookeder, overgrown and secret looking. At last they rode through a stand of sweet-smelling trees and came out into a hidden, grassy meadow that seemed not much larger than the Perfil market. Up close, the towers were not particularly splendid. They were tumbledown and lichen-covered and looked as if they might collapse at any moment. They were so close together one might have strung a line for laundry from tower to tower, if wizards had been concerned with such things as laundry. Efforts had been made to buttress the towers; some had long, eccentrically curving fins of strategically piled rocks. There were twelve standing towers that looked as if they might be occupied. Others were half in ruins or were only piles of rocks that had already been scavenged for useful building materials.

Around the meadow were more paths: worn, dirt paths and canals that sank into branchy, briary tangles, some so low that a boat would never have passed without catching. Even a swimmer would have to duck her head. Children sat on the half-ruined walls of toppled towers and watched Tolcet and Halsa ride up. There was a fire with a thin man stirring something in a pot. Two women were winding up a ball of rough-looking twine. They were dressed like Tolcet. More wizards' servants, Halsa and Onion thought. Clearly wizards were very lazy.

"Down you go," Tolcet said and Halsa gladly slid off the horse's back. Then Tolcet got down and lifted off the harness and the horse suddenly became a naked, brown girl of about fourteen years. She straightened her back and wiped her muddy hands on her pants. She didn't seem to care that she was naked. Halsa gaped at her.

The girl frowned. She said, "You be good, now, or they'll turn you into something even worse."

"Who?" Halsa said.

"The wizards of Perfil," the girl said, and laughed. It was a neighing, horsey laugh. All of the other children began to giggle.

"Oooh, Essa gave Tolcet a ride."

"Essa, did you bring me back a present?"

"Essa makes a prettier horse than she does a girl."

"Oh, shut up," Essa said. She picked up a rock and threw it. Halsa admired her economy of motion, and her accuracy.

"Oi!" her target said, putting her hand up to her ear. "That hurt, Essa."

"Thank you, Essa," Tolcet said. She made a remarkably graceful curtsey, considering that until a moment ago she had had four legs and no waist to speak of. There was a shirt and a pair of leggings folded and lying on a rock.

Essa put them on. "This is Halsa," Tolcet said to the children and to the man and women. "I bought her in the market."

There was silence. Halsa's face was bright red. For once she was speechless. She looked at the ground and then up at the towers, and Onion looked too, trying to catch a glimpse of a wizard. All the windows of the towers were empty, but he could feel the wizards of Perfil, feel the weight of their watching. The marshy ground under his feet was full of wizards' magic and the towers threw magic out like waves of heat from a stove. Magic clung even to the children and servants of the wizards of Perfil, as if they had been marinated in it.

"Come get something to eat," Tolcet said, and Halsa stumbled after him. There was a flat bread, and onions and fish. Halsa drank water which had the faint, slightly metallic taste of magic. Onion could taste it in his own mouth.

"Onion," someone said. "Bonti, Mik." Onion looked up. He was back in the market and his aunt stood there. "There's a church nearby where they'll let us sleep. The train leaves early tomorrow morning."

After she had eaten, Tolcet took Halsa into one of the towers, where there was a small cubby under the stairs. There was a pallet of reeds and a mothy wool blanket. The sun was still in the sky. Onion and his aunt and his cousins went to the church where there was a yard where refugees might curl up and sleep a few hours. Halsa lay awake, thinking of the wizard in the room above the stairs where she was sleeping. The tower was so full of wizard's magic that she could hardly breathe. She imagined a wizard of Perfil creeping, creeping down the stairs above her cubby, and although the pallet was soft, she pinched her arms to stay awake. But Onion fell asleep immediately, as if drugged. He dreamed of wizards flying above the marshes like white lonely birds.

* * *

In the morning, Tolcet came and shook Halsa awake. "Go and fetch water for the wizard," he said. He was holding an empty bucket.

Halsa would have liked to say *go and fetch it yourself,* but she was not a stupid girl. She was a slave now. Onion was in her head again, telling her to be careful. "Oh go away," Halsa said. She realized she had said this aloud, and flinched. But Tolcet only laughed.

Halsa rubbed her eyes and took the bucket and followed him. Outside, the air was full of biting bugs too small to see. They seemed to like the taste of Halsa. That seemed funny to Onion, for no reason that she could understand.

The other children were standing around the fire pit and eating porridge. "Are you hungry?" Tolcet said. Halsa nodded. "Bring the water up and then get yourself something to eat. It's not a good idea to keep a wizard waiting."

He led her along a well-trodden path that quickly sloped down into a small pool and disappeared. "The water is sweet here," he said. "Fill your bucket and bring it up to the top of the wizard's tower. I have an errand to run. I'll return before nightfall. Don't be afraid, Halsa."

"I'm not afraid," Halsa said. She knelt down and filled the bucket. She was almost back to the tower before she realized that the bucket was half empty again. There was a split in the wooden bottom. The other children were watching her and she straightened her back. *So it's a test,* she said in her head, to Onion.

You could ask them for a bucket without a hole in it, he said.

I don't need anyone's help, Halsa said. She went back down the path and scooped up a handful of clayey mud where the path ran into the pool. She packed this into the bottom of the bucket and then pressed moss down on top of the mud. This time the bucket held water.

There were three windows lined with red tiles on Halsa's wizard's tower, and a nest that some bird had built on an outcropping of stone. The roof was round and red and shaped like a bishop's hat. The stairs inside were narrow. The steps had been worn down, smooth and slippery as wax. The higher she went, the heavier the pail of water became. Finally she set it down on a step and sat down beside it. *Four hundred and twenty-two steps,* Onion said. Halsa had counted five hundred and ninety-eight. There seemed to be many more steps on the inside than one would have thought, looking at the tower from outside. "Wizardly tricks," Halsa said in disgust, as if she'd expected nothing better. "You would think they'd make it fewer steps, rather than more steps. What's the use of more steps?"

When she stood and picked up the bucket, the handle broke in her hand. The water spilled down the steps and Halsa threw the bucket after as hard as she could. Then she marched down the stairs and went to mend the bucket and fetch more water. It didn't do to keep wizards waiting.

* * *

At the top of the steps in the wizard's tower there was a door. Halsa set the bucket down and knocked. No one answered and so she knocked again. She tried the latch: the door was locked. Up here, the smell of magic was so thick that Halsa's eyes watered. She tried to look *through* the door. This is what she saw: a room, a window, a bed, a mirror, a table. The mirror was full of rushes and light and water. A bright-eyed fox was curled up on the bed, sleeping. A white bird flew through the unshuttered window, and then another and another. They circled around and around the room and then they began to mass on the table. One flung itself at the door where Halsa stood, peering in. She recoiled. The door vibrated with peck and blows.

She turned and ran down the stairs, leaving the bucket, leaving Onion behind her. There were even more steps on the way down. And there was no porridge left in the pot beside the fire.

Someone tapped her on the shoulder and she jumped. "Here," Essa said, handing her a piece of bread.

"Thanks," Halsa said. The bread was stale and hard. It was the most delicious thing she'd ever eaten.

"So your mother sold you," Essa said.

Halsa swallowed hard. It was strange, not being able to see inside Essa's head, but it was also restful. As if Essa might be anyone at all. As if Halsa herself might become anyone she wished to be. "I didn't care," she said. "Who sold you?"

"No one," Essa said. "I ran away from home. I didn't want to be a soldier's whore like my sisters."

"Are the wizards better than soldiers?" Halsa said.

Essa gave her a strange look. "What do you think? Did you meet your wizard?"

"He was old and ugly, of course," Halsa said. "I didn't like the way he looked at me."

Essa put her hand over her mouth as if she were trying not to laugh. "Oh dear," she said.

"What must I do?" Halsa said. "I've never been a wizard's servant before."

"Didn't your wizard tell you?" Essa said. "What did he tell you to do?"

Halsa blew out an irritated breath. "I asked what he needed, but he said nothing. I think he was hard of hearing."

Essa laughed long and hard, exactly like a horse, Halsa thought. There were three or four other children, now, watching them. They were all laughing at Halsa. "Admit it," Essa said. "You didn't talk to the wizard."

"So?" Halsa said. "I knocked, but no one answered. So obviously he's hard of hearing."

"Of course," a boy said.

"Or maybe the wizard is shy," said another boy. He had green eyes like Bonti and Mik. "Or asleep. Wizards like to take naps."

Everyone was laughing again.

"Stop making fun of me," Halsa said. She tried to look fierce and dangerous. Onion and her brothers would have quailed. "Tell me what my duties are. What does a wizard's servant do?"

Someone said, "You carry things up the stairs. Food. Firewood. Kaffa, when Tolcet brings it back from the market. Wizards like unusual things. Old things. So you go out in the marsh and look for things."

"Things?" Halsa said.

"Glass bottles," Essa said. "Petrified imps. Strange things, things out of the ordinary. Or ordinary things like plants or stones or animals or anything that feels right. Do you know what I mean?"

"No," Halsa said, but she did know. Some things felt more magic-soaked than other things. Her father had found an arrowhead in his field. He'd put it aside to take to the schoolmaster, but that night while everyone was sleeping, Halsa had wrapped it in a rag and taken it back to the field and buried it. Bonti was blamed. Sometimes Halsa wondered if that was what had brought the soldiers to kill her father, the malicious, evil luck of that arrowhead. But you couldn't blame a whole war on one arrowhead.

"Here," a boy said. "Go and catch fish if you're too stupid to know magic when you see it. Have you ever caught fish?"

Halsa took the fishing pole. "Take that path," Essa said. "The muddiest one. And stay on it. There's a pier out that way where the fishing is good."

When Halsa looked back at the wizard's towers, she thought she saw Onion looking down at her, out of a high window. But that was ridiculous. It was only a bird.

* * *

The train was so crowded that some passengers gave up and went and sat on top of the cars. Vendors sold umbrellas to keep the sun off. Onion's aunt had found two seats, and she and Onion sat with one twin on each lap. Two rich women sat across from them. You could tell they were rich because their shoes were green leather. They held filmy pink handkerchiefs like embroidered rose petals up to their rabbity noses. Bonti looked at them from under his eyelashes. Bonti was a terrible flirt.

Onion had never been on a train before. He could smell the furnace room of the train, rich with coal and magic. Passengers stumbled up and down the aisles, drinking and laughing as if they were at a festival. Men and women stood beside the train windows, sticking their heads in. They shouted messages. A woman leaning against the seats fell against Onion and Mik when someone shoved past her. "Pardon, sweet," she said, and smiled brilliantly. Her teeth were studded with gemstones. She was wearing at least four silk dresses, one on top of the other. A man across the aisle coughed wetly. There was a bandage wrapped around his throat, stained with red. Babies were crying.

"I hear they'll reach Perfil in three days or less," a man in the next row said.

"The King's men won't sack Perfil," said his companion. "They're coming to defend it."

"The King is mad," the man said. "God has told him all men are his enemies. He hasn't paid his army in two years. When they rebel, he just conscripts another army and sends them off to fight the first one. We're safer leaving."

"Oooh," a woman said, somewhere behind Onion. "At last we're off. Isn't this fun! What a pleasant outing!"

Onion tried to think of the marshes of Perfil, of the wizards. But Halsa was suddenly there on the train, instead. *You have to tell them,* she said.

Tell them what? Onion asked her, although he knew. When the train was in the mountains, there would be an explosion. There would be soldiers, riding down at the train. No one would reach Qual. *Nobody will believe me,* he said.

You should tell them anyway, Halsa said.

Onion's legs were falling asleep. He shifted Mik. *Why do you care?* he said. *You hate everyone.*

I don't! Halsa said. But she did. She hated her mother. Her mother had watched her husband die, and done nothing. Halsa had been screaming and her mother slapped her across the face. She hated the twins because they weren't like her, they didn't *see* things the way Halsa had to. Because they were little and they got tired and it had been so much work keeping them safe. Halsa had hated Onion, too, because he *was* like her. Because he'd been afraid of Halsa, and because the day he'd come to live with her family, she'd known that one day she would be like him, alone and without a family. Magic was bad luck, people like Onion and Halsa were bad luck. The only person who'd ever looked at Halsa and really seen her, really known her, had been Onion's mother. Onion's mother was kind and good and she'd known she was going to die. *Take care of my son,* she'd said to Halsa's mother and father, but she'd been looking at Halsa when she said it. But Onion would have to take care of himself. Halsa would make him.

Tell them, Halsa said. There was a fish jerking on her line. She ignored it. *Tell them, tell them, tell them.* She and Onion were in the marsh and on the train at the same time. Everything smelled like coal and salt and ferment. Onion ignored her the way she was ignoring the fish. He sat and dangled his feet in the water, even though he wasn't really there.

* * *

Halsa caught five fish. She cleaned them and wrapped them in leaves and brought them back to the cooking fire. She also brought back the greeny-copper key that had caught on her fishing line. "I found this," she said to Tolcet.

"Ah," Tolcet said. "May I see it?" It looked even smaller and more ordinary in Tolcet's hand.

"Burd," Tolcet said. "Where is the box you found, the one we couldn't open?"

The boy with green eyes got up and disappeared into one of the towers. He came out after a few minutes and gave Tolcet a metal box no bigger than a pickle jar. The key fit. Tolcet unlocked it, although it seemed to Halsa that she ought to have been the one to unlock it, not Tolcet.

"A doll," Halsa said, disappointed. But it was a strange-looking doll. It was carved out of a greasy black wood and when Tolcet turned it over, it had no back, only two fronts, so it was always looking backwards and forwards at the same time..

"What do you think, Burd?" Tolcet said.

Burd shrugged. "It's not mine."

"It's yours," Tolcet said to Halsa. "Take it up the stairs and give it to your wizard. And refill the bucket with fresh water and bring some dinner, too. Did you think to take up lunch?"

"No," Halsa said. She hadn't had any lunch herself. She cooked the fish along with some greens Tolcet gave her, and ate two. The other three fish and the rest of the greens she carried up to the top of the stairs in the tower. She had to stop to rest twice, there were so many stairs this time. The door was still closed and the bucket on the top step was empty. She thought that maybe all the water had leaked away, slowly. But she left the fish and she went and drew more water and carried the bucket back up.

"I've brought you dinner," Halsa said, when she'd caught her breath. "And something else. Something I found in the marsh. Tolcet said I should give it to you."

Silence.

She felt silly, talking to the wizard's door. "It's a doll," she said. "Perhaps it's a magic doll."

Silence again. Not even Onion was there. She hadn't noticed when he went away. She thought of the train. "If I give you the doll," she said, "will you do something for me? You're a wizard, so you ought to be able to do anything, right? Will you help the people on the train? They're going to Qual. Something bad is going to happen if you won't stop it. You know about the soldiers? Can you stop them?"

Halsa waited for a long time, but the wizard behind the door never said anything. She put the doll down on the steps and then she picked it up again and put it in her pocket. She was furious. "I think you're a coward," she said. "That's why you hide up here, isn't it? I would have got on that train and I know what's going to happen. Onion got on that train. And you could stop it, but you won't. Well, if you won't stop it, then I won't give you the doll."

She spat in the bucket of water and then immediately wished she hadn't. "You keep the train safe," she said, "and I'll give you the doll. I promise. I'll bring you other things too. And I'm sorry I spit in your water. I'll go and get more."

She took the bucket and went back down the stairs. Her legs ached and there were welts where the little biting bugs had drawn blood.

"Mud," Essa said. She was standing in the meadow, smoking a pipe. "The flies are only bad in the morning and at twilight. If you put mud on your face and arms, they leave you alone."

"It smells," Halsa said.

"So do you," Essa said. She snapped her clay pipe in two, which seemed extravagant to Halsa, and wandered over to where some of the other children were playing a complicated looking game of pick-up sticks and dice. Under a night-flowering tree, Tolcet sat in a battered, oaken throne that looked as if it had been spat up by the marsh. He was smoking a pipe too, with a clay stem even longer than Essa's had been. It was ridiculously long. "Did you give the poppet to the wizard?" he said.

"Oh yes," Halsa said.

"What did she say?"

"Well," Halsa said. "I'm not sure. She's young and quite lovely. But she had a horrible stutter. I could hardly understand her. I think she said something about the moon, how she wanted me to go cut her a slice of it. I'm to bake it into a pie."

"Wizards are very fond of pie," Tolcet said.

"Of course they are," Halsa said. "And I'm fond of my arse."

"Better watch your mouth," Burd, the boy with green eyes, said. He was standing on his head, for no good reason that Halsa could see. His legs waved in the air languidly, semaphoring. "Or the wizards will make you sorry."

"I'm already sorry," Halsa said. But she didn't say anything else. She carried the bucket of water up to the closed door. Then she ran back down the stairs to the cubbyhole and this time she fell straight asleep. She dreamed a fox came and looked at her. It stuck its muzzle in her face. Then it trotted up the stairs and ate the three fish Halsa had left there. *You'll be sorry,* Halsa thought. *The wizards will turn you into a one-legged crow.* But then she was chasing the fox up the aisle of a train to Qual, where her mother and her brothers and Onion were sleeping uncomfortably in their seats, their legs tucked under them, their arms hanging down as if they were dead—the stink of coal and magic was even stronger than it had been in the morning. The train was laboring hard. It panted like a fox with a pack of dogs after it, dragging itself along. There was no way it would reach all the way to the top of the wizard of Perfil's stairs. And if it did, the wizard wouldn't be there, anyway, just the moon, rising up over the mountains, round and fat as a lardy bone.

* * *

The wizards of Perfil don't write poetry, as a general rule. As far as anyone knows, they don't marry, or plow fields, or have much use for polite speech. It is said that the wizards of Perfil appreciate a good joke, but telling a joke to a wizard is dangerous business. What if the wizard doesn't find the joke funny? Wizards are sly, greedy, absent-minded, obsessed with stars and bugs, parsimonious, frivolous, invisible, tyrannous, untrustworthy, secretive, inquisitive, meddlesome, long-lived, dangerous, useless, and have far too good an opinion of themselves. Kings go mad, the land is blighted, children starve or get sick or die spitted on the pointy end of a pike, and it's all beneath the notice of the wizards of Perfil. The wizards of Perfil don't fight wars.

* * *

It was like having a stone in his shoe. Halsa was always there, nagging. *Tell them, tell them. Tell them.* They had been on the train for a day and a night. Halsa was in the swamp, getting farther and farther away. Why wouldn't she leave him alone? Mik and Bonti had seduced the two rich women who sat across. There were no more frowns or handkerchiefs, only smiles and tidbits of food and love, love, love all around. On went the train through burned fields and towns that had been put to the sword by one army or another. The train and its passengers overtook people on foot, or fleeing in wagons piled high with goods: mattresses, wardrobes, a pianoforte once, stoves and skillets and butter churns and pigs and angry-looking geese. Sometimes the train stopped while men got out and examined the tracks and made repairs. They did not stop at any stations, although there were people waiting, sometimes, who yelled and ran after the train. No one got off. There were fewer people up in the mountains, when they got there. Instead there was snow. Once Onion saw a wolf.

"When we get to Qual," one of the rich women, the older one, said to Onion's aunt, "my sister and I will set up our establishment. We'll need someone to keep house for us. Are you thrifty?" She had Bonti on her lap. He was half-asleep.

"Yes, ma'am," Onion's aunt said.

"Well, we'll see," said the woman. She was half-in-love with Bonti. Onion had never had much opportunity to see what the rich thought about. He was a little disappointed to find out that it was much the same. The only difference seemed to be that the rich woman, like the wizard's secretary, seemed to think that all of this would end up all right. Money, it seemed, was like luck, or magic. All manner of things would be well, except they wouldn't. If it weren't for the thing that was going to happen to the train, perhaps Onion's aunt could have sold more of her children.

Why won't you tell them? Halsa said. *Soon it will be too late.*

You tell them, Onion thought back at her. Having an invisible Halsa around, always telling him things that he already knew, it was far worse than the real Halsa had been. The real Halsa was safe, asleep, on the pallet under the wizard's stairs. Onion should have been there instead. Onion bet the wizards of Perfil were sorry that Tolcet had ever bought a girl like Halsa.

Halsa shoved past Onion. She put her invisible hands on her mother's shoulders and looked into her face. Her mother didn't look up. *You have to get off the train,* Halsa said. She yelled. *Get off the train!*

But it was like talking to the door at the top of the wizard's tower. There was something in Halsa's pocket, pressing into her stomach so hard it almost felt like a bruise. Halsa wasn't on the train, she was sleeping on something with a sharp little face.

"Oh, stop yelling. Go away. How am I supposed to stop a train?" Onion said.

"Onion?" his aunt said. Onion realized he'd said it aloud. Halsa looked smug.

"Something bad is going to happen," Onion said, capitulating. "We have to stop the train and get off." The two rich women stared at him as if he were a lunatic. Onion's aunt patted his shoulder. "Onion," she said. "You were asleep. You were having a bad dream."

"But—" Onion protested.

"Here," his aunt said, glancing at their traveling companions. "Take Mik for a walk. Shake off your dream."

Onion gave up. The rich women were thinking that perhaps they would be better off looking for a housekeeper in Qual. Halsa was tapping her foot, standing in the aisle with her arms folded.

Come on, she said. *No point talking to them. They just think you're crazy. Come talk to the conductor instead.*

"Sorry," Onion said to his aunt. "I had a bad dream. I'll go for a walk." He took Mik's hand.

They went up the aisle, stepping over sleeping people and people stupid or quarrelsome with drink, people slapping down playing cards. Halsa always in front of them: *Hurry up, hurry, hurry. We're almost there. You've left it too late. That useless wizard, I should have known not to bother asking for help. I should have known not to expect you to take care of things. You're as useless as they are. Stupid good-for-nothing wizards of Perfil.*

Up ahead of the train, Onion could feel the gunpowder charges, little bundles wedged between the ties of the track. It was like there was a stone in his shoe. He wasn't afraid, he was merely irritated: at Halsa, at the people on the train who didn't even know enough to be afraid, at the wizards and the rich women who thought that they could just buy children, just like that. He was angry, too. He was angry at his parents, for dying, for leaving him stuck here. He was angry at the king, who had gone mad; at the soldiers, who wouldn't stay home with their own families, who went around stabbing and shooting and blowing up other people's families.

They were at the front of the train. Halsa led Onion right into the cab where two men were throwing enormous scoops of coal into a red-black, boiling furnace. They were filthy as devils. Their arms bulged with muscles and their eyes were red and inflamed. One turned and saw Onion. "Oi!" he said. "What's he doing here? You, kid, what are you doing?"

"You have to stop the train," Onion said. "Something is going to happen. I saw soldiers. They're going to make the train blow up."

"Soldiers? Back there? How long ago?"

"They're up ahead of us," Onion said. "We have to stop now."

Mik was looking up at him.

"He saw soldiers?" the other man said.

"Naw," said the first man. Onion could see he didn't know whether to be angry or whether to laugh. "The fucking kid's making things up. Pretending he sees things. Hey, maybe he's a wizard of Perfil! Lucky us, we got a wizard on the train!"

"I'm not a wizard," Onion said. Halsa snorted in agreement. "But I know things. If you don't stop the train, everyone will die."

Both men stared at him. Then the first said, angrily, "Get out of here, you. And don't go talking to people like that or we'll throw you in the boiler."

"Okay," Onion said. "Come on, Mik."

Wait, Halsa said. *What are you doing? You have to make them understand. Do you want to be dead? Do you think you can prove something to me by being dead?*

Onion put Mik on his shoulders. *I'm sorry,* he said to Halsa. *I don't want to be dead. But you see the same thing I see. You see what's going to happen. Maybe you should just go away. Wake up. Catch fish. Fetch water for the wizards of Perfil.*

The pain in Halsa's stomach was sharper, as if someone was stabbing her. When she put her hand down, she had hold of the wooden doll.

What's that? Onion said.

Nothing, Halsa said. *Something I found in the swamp. I said I would give it to the wizard, but I won't! Here, you take it!*

She thrust it at Onion. It went all the way through him. It was an uncomfortable feeling, even though it wasn't really there. *Halsa,* he said. He put Mik down.

Take it! she said. *Here! Take it now!*

The train was roaring. Onion knew where they were; he recognized the way the light looked. Someone was telling a joke in the front of the train, and in a minute a woman would laugh. It would be a lot brighter in a minute. He put his hand up to stop the thing that Halsa was stabbing him with and something smacked against his palm. His fingers brushed Halsa's fingers.

It was a wooden doll with a sharp little nose. There was a nose on the back of its head, too. *Oh, take it!* Halsa said. Something was pouring out of her, through the doll, into Onion. Onion fell back against a woman holding a birdcage on her lap. "Get off!" the woman said. It *hurt.* The stuff pouring out of Halsa felt like *life,* like the doll was pulling out her life like a skein of heavy, sodden, black wool. It hurt Onion, too. Black stuff poured and poured through the doll, into him, until there was no space for Onion, no space to breathe or think or see. The black stuff welled up in his throat, pressed behind his eyes. "Halsa," he said, "let go!"

The woman with the birdcage said, "I'm not Halsa!"

Mik said, "What's wrong? What's wrong?"

The light changed. *Onion,* Halsa said, and let go of the doll. He staggered backward. The tracks beneath the train were singing *tara-ta tara-ta ta-rata-ta.* Onion's nose was full of swamp water and coal and metal and magic. "No," Onion said. He threw the doll at the woman holding the birdcage and pushed Mik down on the floor. "No," Onion said, louder. People were staring at him. The woman who'd been laughing at the joke had stopped laughing. Onion covered Mik with his body. The light grew brighter and blacker, all at once.

Onion! Halsa said. But she couldn't see him anymore. She was awake in the cubby beneath the stair. The doll was gone.

* * *

Halsa had seen men coming home from the war. Some of them had been blinded. Some had lost a hand or an arm. She'd seen one man wrapped in lengths of cloth and propped up in a dog cart which his young daughter pulled on a rope. He'd had no legs, no arms. When people looked at him, he cursed them. There was another man who ran a cockpit in Larch. He came back from the war and paid a man to carve him a leg out of knotty pine. At first he was unsteady on the pine leg, trying to find his balance again. It had been funny to watch him chase after his cocks, like watching a wind-up toy. By the time the army came through Larch again, though, he could run as fast as anyone.

It felt as if half of her had died on the train in the mountains. Her ears rang.

She couldn't find her balance. It was as if a part of her had been cut away, as if she was blind. The part of her that *knew* things, *saw* things, wasn't there anymore. She went about all day in a miserable deafening fog.

She brought water up the stairs and she put mud on her arms and legs. She caught fish, because Onion had said that she ought to catch fish. Late in the afternoon, she looked and saw Tolcet sitting beside her on the pier.

"You shouldn't have bought me," she said. "You should have bought Onion. He wanted to come with you. I'm bad-tempered and unkind and I have no good opinion of the wizards of Perfil."

"Of whom do you have a low opinion? Yourself or the wizards of Perfil?" Tolcet asked.

"How can you serve them?" Halsa said. "How can you serve men and women who hide in towers and do nothing to help people who need help? What good is magic if it doesn't serve anyone?"

"These are dangerous times," Tolcet said. "For wizards as well as for children."

"Dangerous times! Hard times! Bad times," Halsa said. "Things have been bad since the day I was born. Why do I see things and know things, when there's nothing I can do to stop them? When will there be better times?"

"What do you see?" Tolcet said. He took Halsa's chin in his hand and tilted her head this way and that, as if her head were a glass ball that he could see inside. He put his hand on her head and smoothed her hair as if she was his own child. Halsa closed her eyes. Misery welled up inside her.

"I don't see anything," she said. "It feels like someone wrapped me in a wool blanket and beat me and left me in the dark. Is this what it feels like not to see anything? Did the wizards of Perfil do this to me?"

"Is it better or worse?" Tolcet said.

"Worse," Halsa said. "No. Better. I don't know. What am I to do? What am I to be?"

"You are a servant of the wizards of Perfil," Tolcet said. "Be patient. All things may yet be well."

Halsa said nothing. What was there to say?

* * *

She climbed up and down the stairs of the tower, carrying water, toasted bread and cheese, little things that she found in the swamp. The door at the top of the stairs was never open. She couldn't see through it. No one spoke to her, although she sat there sometimes, holding her breath so that the wizard would think she had gone away again. But the wizard wouldn't be fooled so easily. Tolcet went up the stairs, too, and perhaps the wizard admitted him. Halsa didn't know.

Essa and Burd and the other children were kind to her, as if they knew that she had been broken. She knew that she wouldn't have been kind to them, if their situations had been reversed. But perhaps they knew that too. The two women and the skinny man kept their distance. She didn't even know their names. They disappeared on errands and came back again and disappeared into the towers.

Once, when she was coming back from the pier with a bucket of fish, there was a dragon on the path. It wasn't very big, only the size of a mastiff. But it gazed at her with wicked, jeweled eyes. She couldn't get past it. It would eat her, and that would be that. It was almost a relief. She put the bucket down and stood waiting to be eaten. But then Essa was there, holding a stick. She hit the dragon on its head, once, twice, and then gave it a kick for good measure. "Go on, you!" Essa said. The dragon went, giving Halsa one last reproachful look. Essa picked up the bucket of fish. "You have to be firm with them," she said. "Otherwise they get inside your head and make you feel as if you deserve to be eaten. They're too lazy to eat anything that puts up a fight."

Halsa shook off a last, wistful regret, not to have been eaten. It was like waking up from a dream, something beautiful and noble and sad and utterly untrue. "Thank you," she said to Essa. Her knees were trembling.

"The bigger ones stay away from the meadow," Essa said. "It's the smaller ones who get curious about the wizards of Perfil. And by curious, what I really mean is hungry. Dragons eat the things that they're curious about. Come on, let's go for a swim."

Sometimes Essa or one of the others would tell Halsa stories about the wizards of Perfil. Most of the stories were silly, or plainly untrue. The children sounded almost indulgent, as if they found their masters more amusing than frightful. There were other stories, sad stories about long-ago wizards who had fought great battles or gone on long journeys. Wizards who had perished by treachery or been imprisoned by ones they'd thought friends.

Tolcet carved her a comb. She found frogs whose backs were marked with strange mathematical formulas, and put them in a bucket and took them to the top of the tower. She caught a mole with eyes like pinpricks and a nose like a fleshy pink hand. She found the hilt of a sword, a coin with a hole in it, the outgrown carapace of a dragon, small as a badger and almost weightless, but hard, too. When she cleaned off the mud that covered it, it shone dully, like a candlestick. She took all of these up the stairs. She couldn't tell whether the things she found had any meaning. But she took a small, private pleasure in finding them nevertheless.

The mole had come back down the stairs again, fast, wriggly, and furtive. The frogs were still in the bucket, making their gloomy pronouncements, when she had returned with the wizard's dinner. But other things disappeared behind the wizard of Perfil's door.

The thing that Tolcet had called Halsa's gift came back, a little at a time. Once again, she became aware of the wizards in their towers, and of how they watched her. There was something else, too. It sat beside her, sometimes, while she was fishing, or when she rowed out in the abandoned coracle Tolcet helped her to repair. She thought she knew who, or what it was. It was the part of Onion that he'd learned to send out. It was what was left of him: shadowy, thin, and silent. It wouldn't talk to her. It only watched. At night, it stood beside her pallet and watched her sleep. She was glad it was there. To be haunted was a kind of comfort.

She helped Tolcet repair a part of the wizard's tower where the stones were loose in their mortar. She learned how to make paper out of rushes and bark. Apparently wizards needed a great deal of paper. Tolcet began to teach her how to read.

One afternoon when she came back from fishing, all of the wizard's servants were standing in a circle. There was a leveret motionless as a stone in the middle of the circle. Onion's ghost crouched down with the other children. So Halsa stood and watched, too. Something was pouring back and forth between the leveret and the servants of the wizards of Perfil. It was the same as it had been for Halsa and Onion, when she'd given him the two-faced doll. The leveret's sides rose and fell. Its eyes were glassy and dark and knowing. Its fur bristled with magic.

"Who is it?" Halsa said to Burd. "Is it a wizard of Perfil?"

"Who?" Burd said. He didn't take his eyes off the leveret. "No, not a wizard. It's a hare. Just a hare. It came out of the marsh."

"But," Halsa said. "But I can feel it. I can almost hear what it's saying."

Burd looked at her. Essa looked too. "Everything speaks," he said, speaking slowly, as if to a child. "Listen, Halsa."

There was something about the way Burd and Essa were looking at her, as if it were an invitation, as if they were asking her to look inside their heads, to see what they was thinking. The others were watching, too, watching Halsa now, instead of the leveret. Halsa took a step back. "I can't," she said. "I can't hear anything."

She went to fetch water. When she came out of the tower, Burd and Essa and the other children weren't there. Leverets dashed between towers, leaping over each other, tussling in midair. Onion sat on Tolcet's throne, watching and laughing silently. She didn't think she'd seen Onion laugh since the death of his mother. It made her feel strange to know that a dead boy could be so joyful.

The next day Halsa found an injured fox kit in the briar. It snapped at her when she tried to free it and the briars tore her hand. There was a tear in its belly and she could see a shiny gray loop of intestine. She tore off a piece of her shirt and wrapped it around the fox kit. She put the kit in her pocket. She ran all the way back to the wizard's tower, all the way up the steps. She didn't count them. She didn't stop to rest. Onion followed her, quick as a shadow.

When she reached the door at the top of the stairs, she knocked hard. No one answered.

"Wizard!" she said.

No one answered.

"Please help me," she said. She lifted the fox kit out of her pocket and sat down on the steps with it swaddled in her lap. It didn't try to bite her. It needed all its energy for dying. Onion sat next to her. He stroked the kit's throat.

"Please," Halsa said again. "Please don't let it die. Please do something."

She could feel the wizard of Perfil, standing next to the door. The wizard put a hand out, as if—at last—the door might open. She saw that the wizard loved foxes and all the wild marsh things. But the wizard said nothing. The wizard didn't love Halsa. The door didn't open.

"Help me," Halsa said one more time. She felt that dreadful black pull again, just as it had been on the train with Onion. It was as if the wizard were yanking at her shoulder, shaking her in a stony, black rage. How dare someone like Halsa ask a wizard for help. Onion was shaking her too. Where Onion's hand gripped her, Halsa could feel stuff pouring through her and out of her. She could feel the kit, feel the place where its stomach had torn open. She could feel its heart pumping blood, its panic and fear and the life that was spilling out of it. Magic flowed up and down the stairs of the tower. The wizard of Perfil was winding it up like a skein of black, tarry wool, and then letting it go again. It poured through Halsa and Onion and the fox kit until Halsa thought she would die.

"Please," she said, and what she meant this time was *stop*. It would kill her. And then she was empty again. The magic had gone through her and there was nothing left of it or her. Her bones had been turned into jelly. The fox kit began to struggle, clawing at her. When she unwrapped it, it sank its teeth into her wrist and then ran down the stairs as if it had never been dying at all.

Halsa stood up. Onion was gone, but she could still feel the wizard standing there on the other side of the door. "Thank you," she said. She followed the fox kit down the stairs.

* * *

The next morning she woke and found Onion lying on the pallet beside her. He seemed nearer, somehow, this time. As if he weren't entirely dead. Halsa felt that if she tried to speak to him, he would answer. But she was afraid of what he would say.

Essa saw Onion too. "You have a shadow," she said.

"His name is Onion," Halsa said.

"Help me with this," Essa said. Someone had cut lengths of bamboo. Essa was fixing them in the ground, using a mixture of rocks and mud to keep them upright. Burd and some of the other children wove rushes through the bamboo, making walls, Halsa saw.

"What are we doing?" Halsa asked.

"There is an army coming." Burd said. "To burn down the town of Perfil. Tolcet went to warn them."

"What will happen?" Halsa said. "Will the wizards protect the town?"

Essa laid another bamboo pole across the tops of the two upright poles. She said, "They can come to the marshes, if they want to, and take refuge. The army won't come here. They're afraid of the wizards."

"Afraid of the wizards!" Halsa said. "Why? The wizards are cowards and fools. Why won't they save Perfil?"

"Go ask them yourself," Essa said. "If you're brave enough."

"Halsa?" Onion said. Halsa looked away from Essa's steady gaze. For a moment there were two Onions. One was the shadowy ghost from the train, close enough to touch. The second Onion stood beside the cooking fire. He was filthy, skinny, and real. Shadow-Onion guttered and then was gone.

"Onion?" Halsa said.

"I came out of the mountains," Onion said. "Five days ago, I think. I didn't know where I was going, except that I could see you. Here. I walked and walked and you were with me and I was with you."

"Where are Mik and Bonti?" Halsa said. "Where's Mother?"

"There were two women on the train with us. They were rich. They've promised to take care of Mik and Bonti. They will. I know they will. They were going to Qual. When you gave me the doll, Halsa, you saved the train. We could see the explosion, but we passed through it. The tracks were destroyed and there were clouds and clouds of black smoke and fire, but nothing touched the train. We saved everyone."

"Where's Mother?" Halsa said again. But she already knew. Onion was silent. The train stopped beside a narrow stream to take on water. There was an ambush. Soldiers. There was a bottle with water leaking out of it. Halsa's mother had dropped it. There was an arrow sticking out of her back.

Onion said, "I'm sorry, Halsa. Everyone was afraid of me, because of how the train had been saved. Because I knew that there was going to be an explosion. Because I didn't know about the ambush and people died. So I got off the train."

"Here," Burd said to Onion. He gave him a bowl of porridge. "No, eat it slowly. There's plenty more."

Onion said with his mouth full, "Where are the wizards of Perfil?"

Halsa began to laugh. She laughed until her sides ached and until Onion stared at her and until Essa came over and shook her. "We don't have time for this," Essa said. "Take that boy and find him somewhere to lie down. He's exhausted."

"Come on," Halsa said to Onion. "You can sleep in my bed. Or if you'd rather, you can go knock on the door at the top of the tower and ask the wizard of Perfil if you can have his bed."

She showed Onion the cubby under the stairs and he lay down on it. "You're dirty," she said. "You'll get the sheets dirty."

"I'm sorry," Onion said.

"It's fine," Halsa said. "We can wash them later. There's plenty of water here. Are you still hungry? Do you need anything?"

"I brought something for you," Onion said. He held out his hand and there were the earrings that had belonged to his mother.

"No," Halsa said.

Halsa hated herself. She was scratching at her own arm, ferociously, not as if she had an insect bite, but as if she wanted to dig beneath the skin. Onion saw something that he hadn't known before, something astonishing and terrible, that Halsa was no kinder to herself than to anyone else. No wonder Halsa had wanted the earrings—just like the snakes, Halsa would gnaw on herself if there was nothing else to gnaw on. How Halsa wished that she'd been kind to her mother.

Onion said, "Take them. Your mother was kind to me, Halsa. So I want to give them to you. My mother would have wanted you to have them, too."

"All right," Halsa said. She wanted to weep, but she scratched and scratched instead. Her arm was white and red from scratching. She took the earrings and put them in her pocket. "Go to sleep now."

"I came here because you were here," Onion said. "I wanted to tell you what had happened. What should I do now?"

"Sleep," Halsa said.

"Will you tell the wizards that I'm here? How we saved the train?" Onion said. He yawned so wide that Halsa thought his head would split in two. "Can I be a servant of the wizards of Perfil?"

"We'll see," Halsa said. "You go to sleep. I'll go climb the stairs and tell them that you've come."

"It's funny," Onion said. "I can feel them all around us. I'm glad you're here. I feel safe."

Halsa sat on the bed. She didn't know what to do. Onion was quiet for a while and then he said, "Halsa?"

"What?" Halsa said.

"I can't sleep," he said, apologetically.

"Shhh," Halsa said. She stroked his filthy hair. She sang a song her father had liked to sing. She held Onion's hand until his breathing became slower and she was sure that he was sleeping. Then she went up the stairs to tell the wizard about Onion. "I don't understand you," she said to the door. "Why do you hide away from the world? Don't you get tired of hiding?"

The wizard didn't say anything.

"Onion is braver than you are," Halsa told the door. "Essa is braver. My mother was—"

She swallowed and said, "She was braver than you. Stop ignoring me. What good are you, up here? You won't talk to me, and you won't help the town of Perfil, and Onion's going to be very disappointed when he realizes that all you do is skulk around in your room, waiting for someone to bring you breakfast. If you like waiting so much, then you can wait as long as you like. I'm not going to bring you any food or any water or anything that I find in the swamp.

If you want anything, you can magic it. Or you can come get it yourself. Or you can turn me into a toad."

She waited to see if the wizard would turn her into a toad. "All right," she said at last. "Well, goodbye then." She went back down the stairs.

* * *

The wizards of Perfil are lazy and useless. They hate to climb stairs and they never listen when you talk. They don't answer questions because their ears are full of beetles and wax and their faces are wrinkled and hideous. Marsh fairies live deep in the wrinkles of the faces of the wizards of Perfil and the marsh fairies ride around in the bottomless canyons of the wrinkles on saddle-broken fleas who grow fat grazing on magical, wizardly blood. The wizards of Perfil spend all night scratching their flea bites and sleep all day. I'd rather be a scullery maid than a servant of the invisible, doddering, nearly blind, flea-bitten, mildewy, clammy-fingered, conceited marsh-wizards of Perfil.

* * *

Halsa checked Onion, to make sure that he was still asleep. Then she went and found Essa. "Will you pierce my ears for me?" she said.

Essa shrugged. "It will hurt," she said.

"Good," said Halsa. So Essa boiled water and put her needle in it. Then she pierced Halsa's ears. It did hurt, and Halsa was glad. She put on Onion's mother's earrings, and then she helped Essa and the others dig latrines for the townspeople of Perfil.

Tolcet came back before sunset. There were half a dozen women and their children with him.

"Where are the others?" Essa said.

Tolcet said, "Some don't believe me. They don't trust wizardly folk. There are some that want to stay and defend the town. Others are striking out on foot for Qual, along the tracks."

"Where is the army now?" Burd said.

"Close," Halsa said. Tolcet nodded.

The women from the town had brought food and bedding. They seemed subdued and anxious and it was hard to tell whether it was the approaching army or the wizards of Perfil that scared them most. The women stared at the ground. They didn't look up at the towers. If they caught their children looking up, they scolded them in low voices.

"Don't be silly," Halsa said crossly to a woman whose child had been digging a hole near a tumbled tower. The woman shook him until he cried and cried and wouldn't stop. What was she thinking? That wizards liked to eat mucky children who dug holes? "The wizards are lazy and unsociable and harmless. They keep to themselves and don't bother anyone."

The woman only stared at Halsa, and Halsa realized that she was as afraid of Halsa as she was of the wizards of Perfil. Halsa was amazed. Was she that terrible? Mik and Bonti and Onion had always been afraid of her, but they'd had good reason to be. And she'd changed. She was as mild and meek as butter now.

Tolcet, who was helping with dinner, snorted as if he'd caught her thought. The woman grabbed up her child and rushed away, as if Halsa might open her mouth again and eat them both.

"Halsa, look." It was Onion, awake and so filthy that you could smell him from two yards away. They would need to burn his clothes. Joy poured through Halsa, because Onion had come to find her and because he was here and because he was alive. He'd come out of Halsa's tower, where he'd gotten her cubby bed grimy and smelly, how wonderful to think of it, and he was pointing east, towards the town of Perfil. There was a red glow hanging over the marsh, as if the sun were rising instead of setting. Everyone was silent, looking east as if they might be able to see what was happening in Perfil. Presently the wind carried an ashy, desolate smoke over the marsh. "The war has come to Perfil," a woman said.

"Which army is it?" another woman said, as if the first woman might know.

"Does it matter?" said the first woman. "They're all the same. My eldest went off to join the King's army and my youngest joined the General Balder's men. They've set fire to plenty of towns, and killed other mothers' sons and maybe one day they'll kill each other, and never think of me. What difference does it make to the town that's being attacked, to know what army is attacking them? Does it matter to a cow who kills her?"

"They'll follow us," someone else said in a resigned voice. "They'll find us here and they'll kill us all!"

"They won't," Tolcet said. He spoke loudly. His voice was calm and reassuring. "They won't follow you and they won't find you here. Be brave for your children. All will be well."

"Oh, please," Halsa said, under her breath. She stood and glared up at the towers of the wizards of Perfil, her hands on her hips. But as usual, the wizards of Perfil were up to nothing. They didn't strike her dead for glaring. They didn't stand at their windows to look out over the marshes to see the town of Perfil and how it was burning while they only stood and watched. Perhaps they were already asleep in their beds, dreaming about breakfast, lunch, and dinner. She went and helped Burd and Essa and the others make up beds for the refugees from Perfil. Onion cut up wild onions for the stew pot. He was going to have to have a bath soon, Halsa thought. Clearly he needed someone like Halsa to tell him what to do.

None of the servants of the wizards of Perfil slept. There was too much work to do. The latrines weren't finished. A child wandered off into the marshes and had to be found before it drowned or met a dragon. A little girl fell into the well, and had to be hauled up.

Before the sun came up again, more refugees from the town of Perfil arrived.

They came into the camp in groups of twos or threes, until there were almost a hundred townspeople in the wizards' meadow. Some of the newcomers were wounded or badly burned or deep in shock. Essa and Tolcet took charge. There were compresses to apply, clothes that had already been cut up for bandages, hot drinks that smelled bitter and medicinal and not particularly magical. People went rushing around, trying to discover news of family members or friends who had stayed behind. Young children who had been asleep woke up and began to cry.

"They put the mayor and his wife to the sword," a man was saying.

"They'll march on the king's city next," an old woman said. "But our army will stop them."

"It *was* our army—I saw the butcher's boy and Philpot's middle son. They said that we'd been trading with the enemies of our country. The king sent them. It was to teach us a lesson. They burned down the market church and they hung the pastor from the bell tower."

There was a girl lying on the ground who looked Mik and Bonti's age. Her face was gray. Tolcet touched her stomach lightly and she emitted a thin, high scream, not a human noise at all, Onion thought. The marshes were so noisy with magic that he couldn't hear what she was thinking, and he was glad.

"What happened?" Tolcet said to the man who'd carried her into the camp.

"She fell," the man said. "She was trampled underfoot."

Onion watched the girl, breathing slowly and steadily, as if he could somehow breathe for her. Halsa watched Onion. Then: "That's enough," she said. "Come on, Onion."

She marched away from Tolcet and the girl, shoving through the refugees.

"Where are we going?" Onion said.

"To make the wizards come down," Halsa said. "I'm sick and tired of doing all their work for them. Their cooking and fetching. I'm going to knock down that stupid door. I'm going to drag them down their stupid stairs. I'm going to make them help that girl."

There were a lot of stairs this time. Of course the accursed wizards of Perfil would know what she was up to. This was their favorite kind of wizardly joke, making her climb and climb and climb. They'd wait until she and Onion got to the top and then they'd turn them into lizards. Well, maybe it wouldn't be so bad, being a small poisonous lizard. She could slip under the door and bite one of the damned wizards of Perfil. She went up and up and up, half-running and half-stumbling, until it seemed she and Onion must have climbed right up into the sky. When the stairs abruptly ended, she was still running. She crashed into the door so hard that she saw stars.

"Halsa?" Onion said. He bent over her. He looked so worried that she almost laughed.

"I'm fine," she said. "Just wizards playing tricks." She hammered on the door, then kicked it for good measure. "Open up!"

"What are you doing?" Onion said.

"It never does any good," Halsa said. "I should have brought an axe."

"Let me try," Onion said.

Halsa shrugged. *Stupid boy*, she thought, and Onion could hear her perfectly. "Go ahead," she said.

Onion put his hand on the door and pushed. It swung open. He looked up at Halsa and flinched. "Sorry," he said.

Halsa went in.

There was a desk in the room, and a single candle, which was burning. There was a bed, neatly made, and a mirror on the wall over the desk. There was no wizard of Perfil, not even hiding under the bed. Halsa checked, just in case.

She went to the empty window and looked out. There was the meadow and the makeshift camp, below them, and the marsh. The canals, shining like silver. There was the sun, coming up, the way it always did. It was strange to see all the windows of the other towers from up here, so far above, all empty. White birds were floating over the marsh. She wondered if they were wizards; she wished she had a bow and arrows.

"Where is the wizard?" Onion said. He poked the bed. Maybe the wizard had turned himself into a bed. Or the desk. Maybe the wizard was a desk.

"There are no wizards," Halsa said.

"But I can feel them!" Onion sniffed, then sniffed harder. He could practically smell the wizard, as if the wizard of Perfil had turned himself into a mist or a vapor that Onion was inhaling. He sneezed violently.

Someone was coming up the stairs. He and Halsa waited to see if it was a wizard of Perfil. But it was only Tolcet. He looked tired and cross, as if he'd had to climb many, many stairs.

"Where are the wizards of Perfil?" Halsa said.

Tolcet held up a finger. "A minute to catch my breath," he said.

Halsa stamped her foot. Onion sat down on the bed. He apologized to it silently, just in case it was the wizard. Or maybe the candle was the wizard. He wondered what happened if you tried to blow a wizard out. Halsa was so angry he thought she might explode.

Tolcet sat down on the bed beside Onion. "A long time ago," he said, "the father of the present king visited the wizards of Perfil. He'd had certain dreams about his son, who was only a baby. He was afraid of these dreams. The wizards told him that he was right to be afraid. His son would go mad. There would be war and famine and more war and his son would be to blame. The old king went into a rage. He sent his men to throw the wizards of Perfil down from their towers. They did."

"Wait," Onion said. "Wait. What happened to the wizards? Did they turn into white birds and fly away?"

"No," Tolcet said. "The king's men slit their throats and threw them out of the towers. I was away. When I came back, the towers had been ransacked. The wizards were dead."

"No!" Halsa said. "Why are you lying? I know the wizards are here. They're hiding somehow. They're cowards."

"I can feel them too," Onion said.

"Come and see," Tolcet said. He went to the window. When they looked down, they saw Essa and the other servants of the wizards of Perfil moving among the refugees. The two old women who never spoke were sorting through bundles of clothes and blankets. The thin man was staking down someone's cow. Children were chasing chickens as Burd held open the gate of a makeshift pen. One of the younger girls, Perla, was singing a lullaby to some mother's baby. Her voice, rough and sweet at the same time, rose straight up to the window of the tower, where Halsa and Onion and Tolcet stood looking down. It was a song they all knew. It was a song that said all would be well.

"Don't you understand?" Tolcet, the wizard of Perfil, said to Halsa and Onion. "There are the wizards of Perfil. They are young, most of them. They haven't come into their full powers yet. But all may yet be well."

"Essa is a wizard of Perfil?" Halsa said. Essa, a shovel in her hand, looked up at the tower, as if she'd heard Halsa. She smiled and shrugged, as if to say *Perhaps I am, perhaps not, but isn't it a good joke? Didn't you ever wonder?*

Tolcet turned Halsa and Onion around so that they faced the mirror that hung on the wall. He rested his strong, speckled hands on their shoulders for a minute, as if to give them courage. Then he pointed to the mirror, to the reflected Halsa and Onion who stood there staring back at themselves, astonished. Tolcet began to laugh. Despite everything, he laughed so hard that tears came from his eyes. He snorted. Onion and Halsa began to laugh, too. They couldn't help it. The wizard's room was full of magic, and so were the marshes and Tolcet and the mirror where the children and Tolcet stood reflected, and the children were full of magic, too.

Tolcet pointed again at the mirror, and his reflection pointed its finger straight back at Halsa and Onion. Tolcet said, "Here they are in front of you! Ha! Do you know them? Here are the wizards of Perfil!"

THE SAFFRON GATHERERS

ELIZABETH HAND

Elizabeth Hand published her first story in 1988, and her first novel, *Winterlong*, in 1990. Her novels include *Waking the Moon*, *Black Light*, and *Mortal Love*. Her short fiction, which has won the Nebula and World Fantasy awards, is collected in *Last Summer at Mars Hill* and *Bibliomancy*. Her most recent books are novel *Pandora's Bride*, collection *Saffron and Brimstone: Strange Stories* and novella *Illyria*. Upcoming is new novel *Generation Loss*.

The elegant and eloquent tale of love and art on the Pacific Coast which follows is poised on the brink of science fiction, fantasy, and the mainstream. It's perfect for this book, and is Hand at her very best.

He had almost been as much a place to her as a person; the lost domain, the land of heart's desire. Alone at night she would think of him as others might imagine an empty beach, blue water; for years she had done this, and fallen into sleep.

She flew to Seattle to attend a symposium on the Future. It was a welcome trip—on the East Coast, where she lived, it had rained without stopping for thirty-four days. A meteorological record, now a tired joke: only six more days to go! Even Seattle was drier than that.

She was part of a panel discussion on natural disasters and global warming. Her first three novels had presented near-future visions of apocalypse; she had stopped writing them when it became less like fiction and too much like reportage. Since then she had produced a series of time-travel books, wish-fulfillment fantasies about visiting the ancient world. Many of her friends and colleagues in the field had turned to similar themes, retro, nostalgic, historical. Her academic background was in classical archeology; the research was joyous, if exhausting. She hated to fly, the constant round of threats and delay. The weather and concomitant poverty, starvation, drought, flooding, riots—it had all become so bad that it was like an extreme sport now, to visit places that had once unfolded from one's imagination in the brightly colored panoramas of 1920s postal cards. Still she went, armed with eyeshade, earplugs, music and pills that put her to sleep. Behind her eyes, she saw Randall's arm flung above his head, his face half-turned from hers on the pillow. Fifteen minutes after the panel had ended she was in a cab on her way to SeaTac. Several hours later she was in San Francisco.

He met her at the airport. After the weeks of rain back East and Seattle's muted sheen, the sunlight felt like something alive, clawing at her eyes. They drove to her hotel, the same place she always stayed; like something from an old B-movie, the lobby with its ornate cast-iron stair-rail, the narrow front desk of polished walnut; clerks who all might have been played by the young Peter Lorre. The elevator with its illuminated dial like a clock that could never settle on the time; an espresso shop tucked into the back entrance, no bigger than a broom closet.

Randall always had to stoop to enter the elevator. He was very tall, not as thin as he had been when they first met, nearly twenty years earlier. His hair was still so straight and fine that it always felt wet, but the luster had faded from it: it was no longer dark-blonde but grey, a strange dusky color, almost blue in some lights, like pale damp slate. He had grey-blue eyes; a habit of looking up through downturned black lashes that at first had seemed coquettish. She had since learned it was part of a deep reticence, a detachment from the world that sometimes seemed to border on the pathological. You might call him an agoraphobe, if he had stayed indoors.

But he didn't. They had grown up in neighboring towns in New York, though they only met years later, in D.C. When the time came to choose allegiance to a place, she fled to Maine, with all those other writers and artists seeking a retreat into the past; he chose Northern California. He was a journalist, a staff writer for a glossy magazine that only came out four times a year, each issue costing as much as a bottle of decent sémillon. He interviewed scientists engaged in paradigm-breaking research, Nobel Prize-winning writers; poets who wrote on their own skin and had expensive addictions to drugs that subtly altered their personalities, the tenor of their words, so that each new book or online publication seemed to have been written by another person. Multiple Poets' Disorder, Randall had tagged this, and the term stuck; he was the sort of writer who coined phrases. He had a curved mouth, beautiful long fingers. Each time he used a pen, she was surprised again to recall that he was left-handed. He collected incunabula—*Ars oratoria* , Jacobus Publicus's disquisition on the art of memory; the *Opera Philosophica* of Seneca, containing the first written account of an earthquake; Pico della Mirandola's *Heptaplus*—as well as manuscripts. His apartment was filled with quarter-sawn oaken barrister's bookcases, glass fronts bright as mirrors, holding manuscript binders, typescripts, wads of foolscap bound in leather. By the window overlooking the Bay, a beautiful old mapchest of letters written by Neruda, Beckett, Asaré. There were signed broadsheets on the walls, and drawings, most of them inscribed to Randall. He was two years younger than she was. Like her, he had no children. In the years since his divorce, she had never heard him mention his former wife by name.

The hotel room was small and stuffy. There was a wooden ceiling-fan that turned slowly, barely stirring the white curtain that covered the single window. It overlooked an airshaft. Directly across was another old building, a window that showed a family sitting at a kitchen table, eating beneath a fluorescent bulb.

"Come here, Suzanne," said Randall. "I have something for you."

She turned. He was sitting on the bed—a nice bed, good mattress and expensive white linens and duvet—reaching for the leather mailbag he always carried to remove a flat parcel.

"Here," he said. "For you."

It was a book. With Randall it was always books. Or expensive tea: tiny, neon-colored foil packets that hissed when she opened them and exuded fragrances she could not describe, dried leaves that looked like mouse droppings, or flower petals, or fur; leaves that, once infused, tasted of old leather and made her dream of complicated sex.

"Thank you," she said, unfolding the mauve tissue the book was wrapped in. Then, as she saw what it was, "Oh! *Thank* you!"

"Since you're going back to Thera. Something to read on the plane."

It was an oversized book in a slipcase: the classic edition of *The Thera Frescoes*, by Nicholas Spirotiadis, a volume that had been expensive when first published, twenty years earlier. Now it must be worth a fortune, with its glossy thick photographic paper and fold-out pages depicting the larger murals. The slipcase art was a detail from the site's most famous image, the painting known as "The Saffron Gatherers." It showed the profile of a beautiful young woman dressed in elaborately patterned tiered skirt and blouse, her head shaven save for a serpentine coil of dark hair, her brow tattooed. She wore hoop earrings and bracelets, two on her right hand, one on her left. Bell-like tassels hung from her sleeves. She was plucking the stigma from a crocus blossom. Her fingernails were painted red.

Suzanne had seen the original painting a decade ago, when it was easier for American researchers to gain access to the restored ruins and the National Archaeological Museum in Athens. After two years of paperwork and bureaucratic wheedling, she had just received permission to return.

"It's beautiful," she said. It still took her breath away, how modern the girl looked, not just her clothes and jewelry and body art but her expression, lips parted, her gaze at once imploring and vacant: the fifteen-year-old who had inherited the earth.

"Well, don't drop it in the tub." Randall leaned over to kiss her head. "That was the only copy I could find on the net. It's become a very scarce book."

"Of course," said Suzanne, and smiled.

"Claude is going to meet us for dinner. But not till seven. Come here—"

They lay in the dark room. His skin tasted of salt and bitter lemon; his hair against her thighs felt warm, liquid. She shut her eyes and imagined him beside her, his long limbs and rueful mouth; opened her eyes and there he was, now, sleeping. She held her hand above his chest and felt heat radiating from him, a scent like honey. She began to cry silently.

His hands. That big rumpled bed. In two days she would be gone, the room would be cleaned. There would be nothing to show she had ever been here at all.

* * *

They drove to an Afghan restaurant in North Beach. Randall's car was older, a second-generation hybrid; even with the grants and tax breaks, a far more expensive vehicle than she or anyone she knew back east could ever afford. She had never gotten used to how quiet it was.

Outside, the sidewalks were filled with people, the early evening light silvery-blue and gold, like a sun shower. Couples arm-in-arm, children, groups of students waving their hands as they spoke on their cellphones, a skateboarder hustling to keep up with a pack of *parkeurs*.

"Everyone just seems so much more absorbed here," she said. Even the panhandlers were antic.

"It's the light. It makes everyone happy. Also the drugs they put in our drinking water." She laughed, and he put his arm around her.

Claude was sitting in the restaurant when they arrived. He was a poet who had gained notoriety and then prominence in the late 1980s with the "Hyacinthus Elegies," his response to the AIDS epidemic. Randall first interviewed him after Claude received his MacArthur Fellowship. They subsequently became good friends. On the wall of his flat, Randall had a hand-written copy of the second elegy, with one of the poet's signature drawings of a hyacinth at the bottom.

"Suzanne!" He jumped up to embrace her, shook hands with Randall then beckoned them both to sit. "I ordered some wine. A good cab I heard about from someone at the gym."

Suzanne adored Claude. The day before she left for Seattle, he'd sent flowers to her, a half-dozen delicate *Narcissus serotinus*, with long white narrow petals and tiny yellow throats. Their sweet scent perfumed her entire small house. She'd emailed him profuse but also wistful thanks—they were such an extravagance, and so lovely; and she had to leave before she could enjoy them fully. He was a few years younger than she was, thin and muscular, his face and skull hairless save for a wispy black beard. He had lost his eyebrows during a round of chemo and had feathery lines, like antenna, tattooed in their place and threaded with gold beads. His chest and arms were heavily tattooed with stylized flowers, dolphins, octopi, the same iconography Suzanne had seen in Akrotiri and Crete; and also with the names of lovers and friends and colleagues who had died. Along the inside of his arms you could still see the stippled marks left by hypodermic needles—they looked like tiny black beads worked into the pattern of waves and swallows—and the faint white traces of an adolescent suicide attempt. His expression was gentle and melancholy, the face of a tired ascetic, or a benign Antonin Artaud.

"I should have brought the book!" Suzanne sat beside him, shaking her head in dismay. "This beautiful book that Randall gave me—Spirotiadis' *Thera* book?"

"No! I've heard of it, I could never find it. Is it wonderful?"

"It's gorgeous. You would love it, Claude."

They ate, and spoke of his collected poetry, forthcoming next winter; of Suzanne's trip to Akrotiri. Of Randall's next interview, with a woman on the House Committee on Bioethics who was rumored to be sympathetic to the pro-cloning lobby, but only in cases involving "only" children—no siblings, no twins or multiples—who died before age fourteen.

"Grim," said Claude. He shook his head and reached for the second bottle of wine. "I can't imagine it. Even pets…"

He shuddered, then turned to rest a hand on Suzanne's shoulder. "So: back to Santorini. Are you excited?"

"I am. Just seeing that book, it made me excited again. It's such an incredible place—you're there, and you think, What could this have been? If it had survived, if it all hadn't just gone *bam*, like that—"

"Well, then it would really have gone," said Randall. "I mean, it would have been lost. There would have been no volcanic ash to preserve it. All your paintings, we would never have known them. Just like we don't know anything else from back then."

"We know *some* things," said Suzanne. She tried not to sound annoyed—there was a lot of wine, and she was jet-lagged. "Plato. Homer …"

"Oh, *them*," said Claude, and they all laughed. "But he's right. It would all have turned to dust by now. All rotted away. All one with Baby Jesus, or Baby Zeus. Everything you love would be buried under a Tradewinds Resort. Or it would be like Athens, which would be even worse."

"Would it?" She sipped her wine. "We don't know that. We don't know what it would have become. This—"

She gestured at the room, the couple sitting beneath twinkling rose-colored lights, playing with a digital toy that left little chattering faces in the air as the woman switched it on and off. Outside, dusk and neon. "It might have become like this. "

"This." Randall leaned back in his chair, staring at her. "Is this so wonderful?"

"Oh yes," she said, staring back at him, the two of them unsmiling. "This is all a miracle."

He excused himself. Claude refilled his glass and turned back to Suzanne. "So. How are things?"

"With Randall?" She sighed. "It's good. I dunno. Maybe it's great. Tomorrow—we're going to look at houses."

Claude raised a tattooed eyebrow. "Really?"

She nodded. Randall had been looking at houses for three years now, ever since the divorce.

"Who knows?" she said. "Maybe this will be the charm. How hard can it be to buy a house?"

"In San Francisco? Doll, it's easier to win the stem cell lottery. But yes, Randall is a very discerning buyer. He's the last of the true idealists. He's looking for the *eidos* of the house. Plato's *eidos*; not Socrates'," he added. "Is this the first time you've gone looking with him?"

"Yup."

"Well. Maybe that *is* great," he said. "Or not. Would you move out here?"

"I don't know. Maybe. If he had a house. Probably not."

"Why?"

"I don't know. I guess I'm looking for the *eidos* of something else. Out here, it's just too … "

She opened her hands as though catching rain. Claude looked at her quizically.

"Too sunny?" he said. "Too warm? Too beautiful?"

"I suppose. The land of the lotus-eaters. I love knowing it's here, but." She drank more wine. "Maybe if I had more job security."

"You're a writer. It's against Nature for you to have job security."

"Yeah, no kidding. What about you? You don't ever worry about that?"

He gave her his sweet sad smile and shook his head. "Never. The world will always need poets. We're like the lilies of the field."

"What about journalists?" Randall appeared behind them, slipping his cell-phone back into his pocket. "What are we?"

"Quackgrass," said Claude.

"Cactus," said Suzanne.

"Oh, gee. I get it," said Randall. "Because we're all hard and spiny and no one loves us."

"Because you only bloom once a year," said Suzanne.

"When it rains," added Claude.

"That was my realtor." Randall sat and downed the rest of his wine. "Sunday's open house day. Two o'clock till four. Suzanne, we have a lot of ground to cover."

He gestured for the waiter. Suzanne leaned over to kiss Claude's cheek.

"When do you leave for Hydra?" she asked.

"Tomorrow."

"Tomorrow!" She looked crestfallen. "That's so soon!"

" 'The beautiful life was brief,'" said Claude, and laughed. "You're only here till Monday. I have a reservation on the ferry from Piraeus, I couldn't change it."

"How long will you be there? I'll be in Athens Tuesday after next, then I go to Akrotiri."

Claude smiled. "That might work. Here—"

He copied out a phone number in his careful, calligraphic hand. "This is Zali's number on Hydra. A cellphone, I have no idea if it will even work. But

I'll see you soon. Like you said—"

He lifted his thin hands and gestured at the room around them, his dark eyes wide. "This is a miracle."

Randall paid the check and they turned to go. At the door, Claude hugged Suzanne. "Don't miss your plane," he said.

"Don't wind her up!" said Randall.

"Don't miss yours," said Suzanne. Her eyes filled with tears as she pressed her face against Claude's. "It was so good to see you. If I miss you, have a wonderful time in Hydra."

"Oh, I will," said Claude. "I always do."

* * *

Randall dropped her off at her hotel. She knew better than to ask him to stay; besides, she was tired, and the wine was starting to give her a headache.

"Tomorrow," he said. "Nine o'clock. A leisurely breakfast, and then…"

He leaned over to open her door, then kissed her. "The exciting new world of California real estate."

Outside, the evening had grown cool, but the hotel room still felt close: it smelled of sex, and the sweetish dusty scent of old books. She opened the window by the airshaft and went to take a shower. Afterwards she got into bed, but found herself unable to sleep.

The wine, she thought; always a mistake. She considered taking one of the anti-anxiety drugs she carried for flying, but decided against it. Instead she picked up the book Randall had given her.

She knew all the images, from other books and websites, and the island itself. Nearly four thousand years ago, now; much of it might have been built yesterday. Beneath fifteen feet of volcanic ash and pumice, homes with ocean views and indoor plumbing, pipes that might have channeled steam from underground vents fed by the volcano the city was built upon. Fragments of glass that might have been windows, or lenses. The great *pithoi* that still held food when they were opened millennia later. Great containers of honey for trade, for embalming the Egyptian dead. Yellow grains of pollen. Wine.

But no human remains. No bones, no grimacing tormented figures as were found beneath the sand at Herculaneum, where the fishermen had fled and died. Not even animal remains, save for the charred vertebrae of a single donkey. They had all known to leave. And when they did, their city was not abandoned in frantic haste or fear. All was orderly, the *pithoi* still sealed, no metal utensils or weapons strewn upon the floor, no bolts of silk or linen; no jewelry.

Only the paintings, and they were everywhere; so lovely and beautifully wrought that at first the excavators thought they had uncovered a temple complex.

But they weren't temples: they were homes. Someone had paid an artist, or teams of artists, to paint frescoes on the walls of room after room after room. Sea daffodils, swallows; dolphins and pleasure boats, the boats themselves decorated with more dolphins and flying seabirds, golden nautilus on their prows. Wreaths of flowers. A shipwreck. Always you saw the same colors, ochre-yellow and ferrous red; a pigment made by grinding glaucophane, a vitreous mineral that produced a grey-blue shimmer; a bright pure French blue. But of course it wasn't French blue but Egyptian blue—Pompeian blue—one of the earliest pigments, used for thousands of years; you made it by combining a calcium compound with ground malachite and quartz, then heating it to extreme temperatures.

But no green. It was a blue and gold and red world. Not even the plants were green.

Otherwise, the paintings were so alive that, when she'd first seen them, she half-expected her finger would be wet if she touched them. The eyes of the boys who played at boxing were children's eyes. The antelopes had the mad topaz glare of wild goats. The monkeys had blue fur and looked like dancing cats. There were people walking in the streets. You could see what their houses looked like, red brick and yellow shutters.

She turned towards the back of the book, to the section on Xeste 3. It was the most famous building at the site. It contained the most famous paintings—the woman known as the "Mistress of Animals." "The Adorants," who appeared to be striding down a fashion runway. "The Lustral Basin."

The saffron gatherers.

She gazed at the image from the East Wall of Room Three, two women harvesting the stigma of the crocus blossoms. The flowers were like stylized yellow fireworks, growing from the rocks and also appearing in a repetitive motif on the wall above the figures, like the *fleur-de-lis* patterns on wallpaper. The fragments of painted plaster had been meticulously restored; there was no attempt to fill in what was missing, as had been done at Knossos under Sir Arthur Evans' supervision to sometimes cartoonish effect.

None of that had not been necessary here. The fresco was nearly intact. You could see how the older woman's eyebrow was slightly raised, with annoyance or perhaps just impatience, and count the number of stigmata the younger acolyte held in her outstretched palm.

How long would it have taken for them to fill those baskets? The crocuses bloomed only in autumn, and each small blossom contained just three tiny crimson threads, the female stigmata. It might take 100,000 flowers to produce a half-pound of the spice.

And what did they use the spice for? Cooking; painting; a pigment they traded to the Egyptians for dyeing mummy bandages.

She closed the book. She could hear distant sirens, and a soft hum from the ceiling fan. Tomorrow they would look at houses.

* * *

For breakfast they went to the Embarcadero, the huge indoor market inside the restored ferry building that had been damaged over a century before, in the 1906 earthquake. There was a shop with nothing but olive oil and infused vinegars; another that sold only mushrooms, great woven panniers and baskets filled with tree-ears, portobellos, fungus that looked like orange coral, black morels and matsutake and golden chanterelles.

They stuck with coffee and sweet rolls, and ate outside on a bench looking over the Bay. A man threw sticks into the water for a pair of black labs; another man swam along the embankment. The sunlight was strong and clear as gin, and nearly as potent: it made Suzanne feel lightheaded and slightly drowsy, even though she had just gotten up.

"Now," said Randall. He took out the newspaper, opened it to the real estate section, and handed it to her. He had circled eight listings. "The first two are in Oakland; then we'll hit Berkeley and Kensington. You ready?"

The drove in heavy traffic across the Oakland-Bay bridge. To either side, bronze water that looked as though it would be too hot to swim in; before them the Oakland Hills, where the houses were ranged in undulating lines like waves. Once in the city they began to climb in and out of pocket neighborhoods poised between the arid and the tropic. Bungalows nearly hidden beneath overhanging trees suddenly yielded to bright white stucco houses flanked by aloes and agaves. It looked at once wildly fanciful and comfortable, as though all urban planning had been left to Dr. Seuss.

"They do something here called 'staging,'" said Randall as they pulled behind a line of parked cars on a hillside. A phalanx of realtors' signs rose from a grassy mound beside them. "Homeowners pay thousands and thousands of dollars for a decorator to come in and tart up their houses with rented furniture and art and stuff. So, you know, it looks like it's worth three million dollars."

They walked to the first house, a Craftsman bungalow tucked behind trees like prehistoric ferns. There was a fountain outside, filled with koi that stared up with engorged silvery eyes. Inside, exposed beams and dark hardwood floors so glossy they looked covered with maple syrup. There was a grand piano, and large framed posters from Parisian cafés—Suzanne was to note a lot of these as the afternoon wore on—and much heavy dark Mediterranean-style furniture, as well as a few early Mission pieces that might have been genuine. The kitchen floors were tiled. In the master bath, there were mosaics in the sink and sunken tub.

Randall barely glanced at these. He made a beeline for the deck. After wandering around for a few minutes, Suzanne followed him.

"It's beautiful," she said. Below, terraced gardens gave way to stepped hillsides, and then the city proper, and then the gilded expanse of San Francisco Bay, with sailboats like swans moving slowly beneath the bridge.

"For four million dollars, it better be," said Randall.

She looked at him. His expression was avid, but it was also sad, his pale eyes melancholy in the brilliant sunlight. He drew her to him and gazed out above the treetops, then pointed across the blue water.

"That's where we were. Your hotel, it's right there, somewhere." His voice grew soft. "At night it all looks like a fairy city. The lights, and the bridges... You can't believe that anyone could have built it."

He blinked, shading his eyes with his hand, then looked away. When he turned back his cheeks were damp.

"Come on," he said. He bent to kiss her forehead. "Got to keep moving."

They drove to the next house, and the next, and the one after that. The light and heat made her dizzy; and the scents of all the unfamiliar flowers, the play of water in fountains and a swimming pool like a great turquoise lozenge. She found herself wandering through expansive bedrooms with people she did not know, walking in and out of closets, bathrooms, a sauna. Every room seemed lavish, the air charged as though anticipating a wonderful party; tables set with beeswax candles and bottles of wine and crystal stemware. Countertops of hand-thrown Italian tiles; globular cobalt vases filled with sunflowers, another recurring motif.

But there was no sign of anyone who might actually live in one of these houses, only a series of well-dressed women with expensively restrained jewelry who would greet them, usually in the kitchen, and make sure they had a flyer listing the home's attributes. There were plates of cookies, banana bread warm from the oven. Bottles of sparkling water and organic lemonade.

And, always, a view. They didn't look at houses without views. To Suzanne, some were spectacular; others, merely glorious. All were more beautiful than anything she saw from her own windows or deck, where she looked out onto evergreens and grey rocks and, much of the year, snow.

It was all so dreamlike that it was nearly impossible for her to imagine real people living here. For her a house had always meant a refuge from the world; the place where you hid from whatever catastrophe was breaking that morning.

But now she saw that it could be different. She began to understand that, for Randall at least, a house wasn't a retreat. It was a way of engaging with the world; of opening himself to it. The view wasn't yours. You belonged to it, you were a tiny part of it, like the sailboats and the seagulls and the flowers in the garden; like the sunflowers on the highly polished tables.

You were part of what made it real. She had always thought it was the other way around.

"You ready?" Randall came up behind her and put his hand on her neck. "This is it. We're done. Let's go have a drink."

On the way out the door he stopped to talk to the agent.

"They'll be taking bids tomorrow," she said. "We'll let you know on Tuesday."

"Tuesday?" Suzanne said in amazement when they got back outside. "You can do all this in two days? Spend a million dollars on a house?"

"Four million," said Randall. "This is how it works out here. The race is to the quick."

She had assumed they would go to another restaurant for drinks and then dinner. Instead, to her surprise, he drove to his flat. He took a bottle of Pommery Louise from the refrigerator and opened it, and she wandered about examining his manuscripts as he made dinner. At the Embarcadero, without her knowing, he had bought chanterelles and morels, imported pasta colored like spring flowers, arugula and baby tatsoi. For dessert, orange-blossom custard. When they were finished, they remained out on the deck and looked at the Bay, the rented view. Lights shimmered through the dusk. In a flowering quince in the garden, dozens of hummingbirds droned and darted like bees, attacking each other with needle beaks.

"So." Randall's face was slightly flushed. They had finished the champagne, and he had poured them each some cognac. "If this happens—if I get the house. Will you move out here?"

She stared down at the hummingbirds. Her heart was racing. The quince had no smell, none that she could detect, anyway; yet still they swarmed around it. Because it was so large, and its thousands of blossoms were so red. She hesitated, then said, "Yes."

He nodded and took a quick sip of cognac. "Why don't you just stay, then? Till we find out on Tuesday? I have to go down to San Jose early tomorrow to interview this guy, you could come and we could go to that place for lunch."

"I can't." She bit her lip, thinking. "No... I wish I could, but I have to finish that piece before I leave for Greece."

"You can't just leave from here?"

"No." That would be impossible, to change her whole itinerary. "And I don't have any of my things—I need to pack, and get my notes ... I'm sorry."

He took her hand and kissed it. "That's okay. When you get back."

That night she lay in his bed as Randall slept beside her, staring at the manuscripts on their shelves, the framed lines of poetry. His breathing was low, and she pressed her hand against his chest, feeling his ribs beneath the skin, his heartbeat. She thought of canceling her flight; of postponing the entire trip.

But it was impossible. She moved the pillow beneath her head, so that she could see past him, to the wide picture window. Even with the curtains drawn you could see the lights of the city, faraway as stars.

Very early next morning he drove her to the hotel to get her things and then to the airport.

"My cell will be on," he said as he got her bag from the car. "Call me down in San Jose, once you get in."

"I will."

He kissed her and for a long moment they stood at curbside, arms around each other.

"Book your ticket back here," he said at last, and drew away. "I'll talk to you tonight."

She watched him go, the nearly silent car lost among the taxis and limousines; then hurried to catch her flight. Once she had boarded she switched off her cell, then got out her eyemask, earplugs, book, waterbottle; she took one of her pills. It took twenty minutes for the drug to kick in, but she had the timing down pat: the plane lifted into the air and she looked out her window, already feeling not so much calm as detached, mildly stoned. It was a beautiful day, cloudless; later it would be hot. As the plane banked above the city she looked down at the skein of roads, cars sliding along them like beads or raindrops on a string. The traffic crept along 280, the road Randall would take to San Jose. She turned her head to keep it in view as the plane leveled out and began to head inland.

Behind her a man gasped; then another. Someone shouted. Everyone turned to look out the windows.

Below, without a sound that she could hear above the jet's roar, the city fell away. Where it met the sea the water turned brown then white then turgid green. A long line of smoke arose—no not smoke, Suzanne thought, starting to rise from her seat; dust. No flames, none that she could see; more like a burning fuse, though there was no fire, nothing but white and brown and black dust, a pall of dust that ran in a straight line from the city's tip north to south, roughly tracking along the interstate. The plane continued to pull away, she had to strain to see it now, a long green line in the water, the bridges trembling and shining like wires. One snapped then fell, another, miraculously, remained intact. She couldn't see the third bridge. Then everything was green crumpled hillsides, vineyards; distant mountains.

People began to scream. The pilot's voice came on, a blaze of static then silence. Then his voice again, not calm but ordering them to remain so. A few passengers tried to clamber into the aisles but flight attendants and other passengers pulled or pushed them back into their seats. She could hear someone getting sick in the front of the plane. A child crying. Weeping, the buzz and bleat of cellphones followed by repeated commands to put them all away.

Amazingly, everyone did. It wasn't a terrorist attack. The plane, apparently would not plummet from the sky; but everyone was too afraid that it might to turn their phones back on.

She took another pill, frantic, fumbling at the bottle and barely getting the cap back on. She opened it again, put two, no three, pills into her palm and pocketed them. Then she flagged down one of the flight attendants as she rushed down the aisle.

"Here," said Suzanne. The attendant's mouth was wide, as though she were screaming; but she was silent. "You can give these to them—"

Suzanne gestured towards the back of the plane, where a man was repeating the same name over and over and a woman was keening. "You can take one if you want, the dosage is pretty low. Keep them. Keep them."

The flight attendant stared at her. Finally she nodded as Suzanne pressed the pill bottle into her hand.

"Thank you," she said in a low voice. "Thank you so much, I will."

Suzanne watched her gulp one pink tablet, then walk to the rear of the plane. She continued to watch from her seat as the attendant went down the aisle, furtively doling out pills to those who seemed to need them most. After about twenty minutes, Suzanne took another pill. As she drifted into unconsciousness she heard the pilot's voice over the intercom, informing the passengers of what he knew of the disaster. She slept.

The plane touched down in Boston, greatly delayed by the weather, the ripple affect on air traffic from the catastrophe. It had been raining for thirty-seven days. Outside, glass-green sky, the flooded runways and orange cones blown over by the wind. In the plane's cabin the air chimed with the sound of countless cellphones. She called Randall, over and over again; his phone rang but she received no answer, not even his voicemail.

Inside the terminal, a crowd of reporters and television people awaited, shouting questions and turning cameras on them as they stumbled down the corridor. No one ran; everyone found a place to stand, alone, with a cellphone. Suzanne staggered past the news crews, striking at a man who tried to stop her. Inside the terminal there were crowds of people around the TV screens, covering their mouths at the destruction. A lingering smell of vomit, of disinfectant. She hurried past them all, lurching slightly, feeling as though she struggled through wet sand. She retrieved her car, joined the endless line of traffic and began the long drive back to that cold green place, trees with leaves that had yet to open though it was already almost June, apple and lilac blossoms rotted brown on their drooping branches.

It was past midnight when she arrived home. The answering machine was blinking. She scrolled through her messages, hands shaking. She listened to just a few words of each, until she reached the last one.

A blast of static, satellite interference; then a voice. It was unmistakably Randall's.

She couldn't make out what he was saying. Everything was garbled, the connection cut out then picked up again. She couldn't tell when he'd called. She played it over again, once, twice, seven times, trying to discern a single word, something in his tone, background noise, other voices: anything to hint when he had called, from where.

It was hopeless. She tried his cellphone again. Nothing.

She stood, exhausted, and crossed the room, touching table, chairs, countertops, like someone on a listing ship. She turned on the kitchen faucet and splashed cold water onto her face. She would go online and begin the process of finding numbers for hospitals, the Red Cross. He could be alive.

She went to her desk to turn on her computer. Beside it, in a vase, were the flowers Claude had sent her, a half-dozen dead narcissus smelling of rank water and slime. Their white petals were wilted, and the color had drained from the pale yellow cups.

All save one. A stem with a furled bloom no bigger than her pinkie, it had not yet opened when she'd left. Now the petals had spread like feathers, revealing its tiny yellow throat, three long crimson threads. She extended her hand to stroke first one stigma, then the next, until she had touched all three; lifted her hand to gaze at her fingertips, golden with pollen, and then at the darkened window. The empty sky, starless. Beneath blue water, the lost world.

D.A.

CONNIE WILLIS

Connie Willis's first story, "The Secret of Santa Titicaca," was published in 1971, but she only began publishing regularly in the early '80s. She is best known for her short fiction, which has been collected in *Fire Watch*, *Impossible Things*, and *Miracle and Other Christmas Stories*. Her first novel was *Water Witch* (with Cynthia Felice), which was followed by solo debut *Lincoln's Dreams*, *Doomsday Book*, and *Passage*. She has also written short novels *Uncharted Territory*, *Remake*, and *Bellwether*. She is currently working on a new novel, All Clear. Willis is one of the most celebrated writers in modern science fiction, and to date her fiction has won the Hugo Award nine times, the Nebula Award six times, the Locus Award nine times, the John W. Campbell Memorial Award, and many other honors.

Willis has spoken often about her love of the classic young adult novels of Robert A. Heinlein, especially *The Door into Summer*. The story that follows is very much in that vein, as a plucky young woman is faced with a difficult trial. Of course, this is Willis and not Heinlein, so things don't go completely as expected.

I was at school, studying for my UCLA entrance exam and talking to Kimkim, when my phone rang.

One of Ms. Sionov's many obnoxious rules is absolute silence in the media center. "Theodora," she said, glaring at me. "You know the rules. No phones. Hand it over."

"I turned my phone off and put it in my compack when I came in," I told Ms. Sionov as I looked in another compartment.

"Then why is it ringing? You had your phone on and were messaging Kimkim, weren't you?"

"No," I said, which was technically true. I wasn't messaging her, I was talking to her. And the phone I was talking to her on wasn't the phone that was ringing. It's ridiculous not to let us message each other in media center, and Kimkim's a computer genius, so she rigged up a subliminal sound flatphone that goes on my wrist so I can talk to her and have it look like all I'm doing is leaning on my hand, thinking about something. "Honestly, it isn't on," I said.

"I'll bet," Ms. Sionov said, holding out her hand for the phone. "Where *is* your partner in crime today?"

"Interview at CU," I said, still searching. "It must be a schoolwide override."

"Then why isn't everyone else's phone ringing?"

Which was a good point. I dug some more and finally found the phone. "See," I said, showing her the dark screen. "I told you it was off." I hit "Display," and the words "Assembly 1 p.m. Mandatory Attendance" came up.

"I told you it was an override," I said.

Ms. Sionov grabbed the phone away from me to look, and right then Fletcher Davis's phone began to ring and then Ahmed Fitzwilliam's. And Ms. Sionov's.

She handed me my phone and ran to turn hers off. While she was gone, I forwarded Kimkim the message. "What's up?" I added, gathering up my stuff and starting for the auditorium.

"No idea," she messaged back. "Mine just rang, too. Do you think the snowboard team finally won a match?"

"That wouldn't be Mandatory Attendance." Our principal, Mr. Fuyijama, *loves* calling assemblies, to announce fire drill evacuation routes or the revised lunch schedule or the junior varsity sudoku team's taking second place at State—but those are all Optional Attendance. Assemblies to announce university acceptances and scholarships are Mandatory Attendance, but it couldn't be that. We were still in the middle of entrance-exam-and-interview season. Which was why Kimkim wasn't here.

"Can you make it back by one?" I messaged her.

"Just barely," she answered. "Save me a seat."

I maneuvered my way down the crowded hall, where everybody was asking everybody else if they knew what the assembly was about. Nobody seemed to know. "I hope it isn't the 'responsible behavior' talk," I heard Sharlanne say.

"Oh, frick," I messaged Kimkim. "Please don't let it be one of Mr. Fuyijama's speeches."

"I'll find out if it is," Kimkim messaged back. As I said, Kimkim's a computer genius. She can hack into anything, including the Euro-American Union Department of Defense. And Mr. Fuyijama's daily planner.

"Thanks," I said, starting toward the girls' bathroom so I could hide out in one of the stalls if it turned out to be one of his *very long* speeches, but before I could cross the hall, Coriander Abrams came careening down the call, clutching her phone and squealing, "Ohmigod! Ohmigod! A Mandatory Attendance Assembly! Theodora, do you know what that means?" She grabbed my arm and dragged me into the auditorium, squealing all the way. "This could be it! Do you think I have a chance? Tell me, honestly, do you? Isn't this absolutely *incred?*"

When she finally let go of me (her friend Chelsea had come up and was hugging her and shrieking, "I know it's you! Ohmigod, a cadet! You are *so* lucky!" and she had to let go of me so the two of them could dance around) I messaged Kimkim, "Never mind. I know what it is."

* * *

I should have guessed. I mean, the Academy's all anyone's talked about since the IASA recruiter was here last September to give her little pep talk. As if anybody at Winfrey High needed a pep talk. Three-fourths of them had already applied, and the other fourth would have if they'd thought they could pass the entrance exams. I didn't know why they even bother sending a recruiter.

It was one of the many annoying aspects of having to go to school. I had wanted to do remote learning like everybody else, but my mom was a nostalgia freak, and she had somehow talked my dad into it.

"I thought you said you wanted me to be independent and not go along with the crowd," I'd said to him.

"I do. And what better place to do that than *in* a crowd?" he'd said, and told me a long and pointless story about the time he'd set off a stink bomb in the lunchroom.

So for the last three years I'd had to put up with Ms. Sionov's ridiculous phone rules, locker combinations, school lunches, Mandatory Attendance assemblies, and everybody drooling to get into the Academy.

It's almost impossible to do—they only take three hundred candidates a year, and less than half of them are from the Euro-American Union, so there's fierce competition. Candidates have got to score astronomically high (how appropriate!) on the Academy's entrance exams, take tons of math and science classes, be in perfect physical condition, and pass four separate levels of psychological tests and interviews.

But even that's not enough. With over fifty thousand eager applicants to choose from, IASA uses all sorts of strange formulas and extra criteria to make their picks, and nobody knows exactly what they are. The recruiter who'd come to our school had said meaningless things like, "Cadets must demonstrate dedication, determination, and devotion," and "We're looking not for excellence, but for the exceptional," and when Coriander asked her, "What can I do to improve my chances of being chosen?" she'd replied, "The Academy wants not only the *crème de la crème*, but the cream of the *crème de la crème*."

"I'd suggest you learn to milk a cow," I told Coriander.

"Oh, shut up," she'd said. "You're just jealous because I've passed the first three levels of the application process."

Some years it seems the Academy selects mostly kids who've taken astrophysics and exobiology (even though we haven't found any life anywhere out there that's bigger than a virus), and other years ethics. Or Renaissance history. Five years ago there'd been a study which seemed to indicate students in schools had a statistical edge over home- and remote-schooled, which meant everyone going to Winfrey High except me was there because they thought it would increase their chances of getting an appointment.

And, apparently, for one person, it had.

My bet was that it was Coriander. She'd taken Renaissance history *and* ethics *and* exobiology and everything else she could think of, had gone out for sports, forensics, and community service with a vengeance, and had so completely monopolized the questioning of the recruiter that I'd finally raised my hand just to shut her up for a minute.

"Yes, you have a question, Ms.—?" the recruiter asked me, smiling. She was one of those perky PR types IASA sends out.

"Baumgarten," I said. "Theodora Baumgarten. Can you explain to me why anybody in their right mind would want to go to the Academy? I mean, I know it's so you can become an astronaut and go into space, but why would anybody want to? There's no air, you're squashed into a ship the size of a juice can, and it takes years to get anywhere interesting. If you get there and aren't killed first by a meteor or a solar flare or a systems malfunction."

The entire student body had turned and was staring uncomprehendingly at me, as if I was speaking ancient Sumerian or something. The recruiter gave me a cold, measuring glance, and then turned and said something to Mr. Fuyijama.

"You're gonna get detention," Fletcher said.

"Any other questions?" the recruiter said, pointedly avoiding looking in my direction.

"Yes," Coriander said. "How many space engineering classes do I need to take?"

"I hope you weren't planning to apply to the Academy," Kimkim said as we left the auditorium, "because I think you just blew whatever chance you had."

"Good," I said. "I have no desire to leave *terra firma*."

"Really? You have no desire to go to the Academy at all?"

"No," I said. "Do you?"

"Of course," Kimkim said. "I mean, Mars and the rings of Saturn and all that. And getting to be a cadet. I'd love to go, but I don't have the math grades."

At that point, Coriander had stormed up and snarled, "You'd better not have ruined my chances with that little stunt," and apparently I hadn't. As we went into the auditorium now, Mr. Fuyijama beamed at her proudly from the stage.

Whoever was announcing the appointment apparently wasn't there yet. I looked for a seat way in the back in case it was the recruiter, waiting to see where Coriander and her cadre of screeching friends sat before I sat down as far away from them as possible. I stuck my compack on the seat next to me to save it for Kimkim, who still wasn't here. She'd messaged confirmation that the assembly was indeed to announce the appointment of a cadet. "At least we won't have to listen to a speech," she said.

I wasn't so sure of that. Mr. Fuyijama was on the stage at the podium, messing with the holopoint controls and saying, "Is this on?" into the microphone.

Chelsea Goodrum sat down one row in front of me, squealing into her phone.

"You know it's going to be you, Coriander! Where are you sitting?" she demanded. Apparently Coriander told her because she began to wave wildly. "Come over here!" she said. "No, there are plenty of seats!"

Oh, frick, I thought, and stood up, but the auditorium was almost full, I couldn't see two seats together anywhere except next to Chelsea, and it was too late. Mr. Fuyijama was saying, "Take your seats, students!"

I sat down, hoping Coriander hadn't had time to move either, but no, here she came with four of her shrieking friends. "This is the most incred thing ever!" Chelsea screamed, hugging her. "You're going to be a *cadet!*"

"Take your seats," Mr. Fuyijama said again, "and please turn your phones off," a totally unnecessary order since all wireless bands were automatically jammed at the beginning of every assembly.

"It's starting," I messaged Kimkim. "Where are you?"

"Denver. I'll be there in ten minutes."

"Today we're here to celebrate a tremendous honor," Mr. Fuyijama said, "the appointment of a student to the International Space Academy. Winfrey High is extremely proud to have had one of its students chosen for this honor, one of many honors over the years," and proceeded to name every single one of them. It should have sent everyone to sleep, but the whole auditorium listened intently, except for Coriander's friends, who were squeezing her arms and whispering excitedly.

"Did I miss anything?" Kimkim messaged me seven hundred and twenty-two honors later.

"No," I sent back. "Did you know Winfrey High has won the Regional Koi-Growing Contest six years running? Where are you?"

"Over by the west door. I can't get to you."

"It's just as well," I sent, and told her about Coriander, who was now emitting little whimpers. "At least if you're by the door you may be able to escape."

Unlike the rest of us. Mr. Fuyijama droned on for several more geological ages and then said, "...but none of those honors come close to the one we're here to bestow today. I'd like to welcome Admiral H. V. Washington, Deputy Chief of Staff of the Space Administration."

There was thunderous applause. "Ohmigod, they sent an *admiral!*" Coriander squealed.

The admiral came over to the podium. "Every year IASA appoints candidates from all over the American-European Union to the Academy. These students have had to undergo a rigorous four-tiered application and interview process and have had to demonstrate the qualities of—"

Oh, no, not you, too, I thought. "Why don't they just give it to Coriander and put the rest of us out of our misery?" I messaged Kimkim. "Everyone knows it's her."

"Not everyone," she messaged back. "Nearly half the money's on Matt Sung."

"What do you mean, nearly half the money? Is there a pool?"

"'Betting pools are strictly forbidden at Winfrey High School,'" she quoted, mimicking Mr. Fuyijama's voice. "Of course there's a pool. Do you want to place a last-minute bet?"

"Yes," I said. "Who else is in the running besides Coriander and Matt? Tomas Rivera?"

"No, he didn't pass the second-level interview."

"You're kidding." I'd thought Tomas was a shoo-in. He had great grades, great SATs, he'd taken nationals in gymnastics.

"Our cadets, in other words," the admiral was saying, "are not just the best of the best, but the very best of the best of the best."

"Some of the sophomores are voting for Renny Nickson," Kimkim messaged.

"Renny? I thought he wanted a Rhodes."

"Not if he can get an Academy appointment instead. Nobody would turn down a chance to be a cadet. That's why the Academy announces its picks before the universities do."

"And today's appointment exemplifies that excellence," the admiral said.

It sounded like he was winding up. If I wanted in the pool, I'd better do it now. "Put me down for Matt," I said, and then glanced at Coriander. She was squeezing the hands of her friends on either side of her and biting her lip. And if sheer wanting to be a cadet was part of the criteria, she'd win it hands down. She'd been trying to get in ever since first grade. And hadn't that recruiter said something about determination and devotion? "Wait," I said. "Change my pick to Coriander."

"It gives me great pleasure to announce—"

Coriander's eyes were shut tight and she was murmuring, "Please, please, please…" and squeezing the color out of her friends' hands.

"—an appointment to the International Space Academy for—" He paused and looked straight at Coriander.

"I told you it was Coriander," I typed. "Actually, this is a good thing. It means we won't have to put up with her any—"

"Theodora Baumgarten," the admiral said.

* * *

There was stunned silence, during which I had time to think, I must have heard that wrong, and then, very funny, and to look around to see who was behind this particular stink bomb.

Coriander shouted, "Theodora *Baum*garten?" and I knew he'd really said it.

"Wait," I said, and the auditorium erupted in excited applause.

Fletcher grabbed my hand and pumped it up and down. "Wow!" he shouted over the clapping. "Congratulations!"

"But—" I tried to look at my phone.

"Oh, creez! Congratulations!" Kimkim's message read. "Why didn't you tell me you'd applied?"

"I didn't," I murmured, and tried to pull my hand free so I could message her, but Chelsea grabbed it, squeezed it, and then pushed me to the end of the row. "Go on! Get down there! What are you waiting for?"

I looked down at the stage. The admiral was smiling up at me from the stage and applauding, and Mr. Fuyijama was beaming and beckoning to me. "There's been some mistake," I said, but no one was listening. They were patting and hugging me and shoving me down the steps toward the stage.

"Can I touch you?" Marla Chang said in an awestruck voice, and Ms. Sionov grabbed me and kissed me. "You've always been my favorite student!" she cried.

"No, Ms. Sionov, you don't understand," I said, and then I was on the stage and Mr. Fuyijama was pumping my hand.

"Mr. Fuyijama, there's been a mistake—"

"I can't tell you how proud Winfrey High is of you!" He beamed and pushed me at the admiral, who saluted and handed me a certificate.

I read it, hoping he'd just read the name wrong, but there it was in official-looking print, "Theodora Jane Baumgarten." This can't be happening to me, I thought. "This isn't mine," I said, and tried to hand the appointment back to him.

"You're supposed to salute back and say, 'Cadet Baumgarten reporting for duty,'" Mr. Fuyijama whispered.

"But I'm not—" I said. "Admiral, I didn't apply for the Academy—" and everybody must have thought I was saying, "Cadet Baumgarten reporting for duty," because they started to applaud again. The admiral shook my hand and gave me an envelope. "There's been a mistake. This isn't my—" I said, but Mr. Fuyijama was shaking my hand again and a swarm of students took the opportunity to close in around the admiral and begin bombarding him with questions.

"Mr. Fuyijama, I have to talk to you," I said. "This is all a mistake—"

"It certainly is," Coriander said, storming up. "Theodora can't have gotten an appointment. She didn't even take deep-field astronomy."

Mr. Fuyijama was looking at her like she was a bug, which would have been enjoyable if I hadn't been in so much trouble. "The Academy chooses for all sorts of skills," he said.

"But she can't have gotten the appointment over me," Coriander said. "She's not cadet material."

Mr. Fuyijama ignored her. "I've messaged your parents," he said. "They should be here any minute."

"Help," I messaged Kimkim, who I still couldn't see anywhere, and tried again with Mr. Fuyijama. "My appointment is a mistake. They mixed up the names or something."

"Don't let Coriander upset you," he said. "She was a fine candidate, but so are you, so are all of Winfrey High's students. We have one of the most outstanding schools in the country, and—"

It was hopeless. I tuned him out and looked around for the admiral. I couldn't see him anywhere. "Where did the admiral go?"

"He had to leave," Mr. Fuyijama said. "He has several more appointments to announce this afternoon."

"But I have to talk to him—" Oh, thank goodness, here was Kimkim. "Where have you *been?*" I said, pulling her off to the side of the stage. "You have to help me. Nobody will listen when I tell them there's been a mixup."

"Mixup?" she said.

"Yes, of *course* it's a mixup. I can't have been chosen. I didn't even apply to the Academy."

"You didn't?" she said happily, and flung her arms around me. "Oh, I'm so glad! I thought you'd applied without telling *me*, your best friend, and I was so hurt—"

"Why would I apply? I've told you a hundred times I don't want to go into space. I want to go to UCLA."

She looked sheepish. "I know, but I thought you were just saying that because you were afraid you couldn't get in. But how could there be a mixup?"

"I don't know. Maybe there's somebody else with the same name."

"Two Theodora Baumgartens? Unlikely."

"Well, maybe there's a Theodore Baumgarten or a Theodora Bauman. Come on, maybe we can catch the admiral before he leaves," I said, and we headed backstage.

"Wait, Theodora!" Mr. Fuyijama said before we'd gone two steps. "Your mother's here."

"I'll go see if I can catch him," Kimkim said, and darted off as Mr. Fuyijama and my mom closed in on me.

"I'm so *proud* of you!" she said. "I knew we made the right decision in sending you to school. You didn't want to come, remember? And now look at you, a cadet!" She and Mr. Fuyijama beamed at each other. "I still can't believe it!"

"Where's Dad?" I said. He knew I didn't want to be a cadet. He'd see this was all a ghastly mistake.

"Cheyenne," she said. "As soon as I heard, I left a message for him to come to the school. Why didn't you *tell* us you'd applied?"

"Because—"

Mr. Fuyijama patted me on the shoulder. "Shouldn't you be getting home, young lady, and getting ready to go?"

For your information, I am not going anywhere, I thought.

"What am I saying?" Mr. Fuyijama went on, smiling coyly. "You've probably had your kit all packed and ready to go for months."

"Mr. Fuyijama's right," my mom said. "We need to get you home. You only have a few hours."

"A few—?"

"I'll call your father," Mom said, steering me toward the door and away from Kimkim. "He can meet us there."

"Mom, what do you mean, a few hours?" I said, but she was talking to Dad.

"Bob? Where are you? Oh, dear. Well, turn around and go back home. We're on our way."

Kimkim appeared, shaking her head. "The admiral'd already left."

"What does my mom mean, I only have a few hours?" I asked her.

"Didn't you listen to anything the recruiter said when she was here? Cadets go straight to the Academy after they're appointed," Kimkim said, grabbing the letter the admiral had given me and opening it. "It says they'll pick you up in exactly—oh, gosh, two hours and forty minutes."

"Let me talk to Dad," I said to Mom, who was still on the phone. Dad knew I didn't want to go into space. We'd talked about it after the recruiter came. "Hand me the phone."

Mom shook her head. "I'm talking to Grandma. You can talk to your dad when we get home. Yes, isn't it marvelous?" she said, presumably to Grandma, and then, presumably to me, "Get in the car. Yes, of *course* she'll want you to come over and say goodbye. Come on, we need to go. Goodbye, Kimkim."

"Kimkim's coming with me," I said, grabbing her arm and pushing her into the car. "She's going to help me pack."

Mom nodded absently, still talking to Grandma. She switched on the car and pulled away from the school. "Would you call Bob's parents for me? And Theodora's piano teacher? I'm sure she'll want to see her before she leaves."

"You've got to help me find out the admiral's phone number for me," I messaged Kimkim so Mom couldn't hear what we were saying, "so I can call him and explain—"

"I'll try," she messaged back. "Academy numbers are all classified."

"Do you think I should phone Aunt Jen and Aunt Lucy?" my mom called back to me.

"*No*," I said, and Kimkim put in helpfully, "She doesn't have much time, and she's got to pack her kit, Mrs. Baumgarten."

"I suppose you're right. You should have done that beforehand, like Coriander Abrams. Her mother said she packed hers the same day she filled out her application. Oh, look," she said, pulling into the driveway, "Aunt Jen and Lucy are already here."

They were, along with Grandma, Grandpa, Grandma and Grandpa Baumgarten, and about a hundred neighbors, all holding up a big laserspark banner twinkling, "Congratulations, Cadet Baumgarten."

The online news crews were all there, too, holding mikes, and it took me half an hour to get into the house and another fifteen minutes to escape to my room, where Kimkim was working away at my computer. "Here," she said, handing me a printout.

"What is it?" I said eagerly. "The admiral's phone number?"

"No, it's the list of what you're allowed to take. Fifteen-pound weight limit. No pets, no plants, no weapons."

"Because they know at this point I'd like to shoot them. I don't need lists," I said, throwing it in the wastebasket and going over to stand beside her. "I *need* the admiral's phone number."

"I can't get to it," Kimkim said. "I've been trying to hack into the Academy officer roster for the last half hour. It's got firewalls, moats, ramparts, the works. I'm not surprised. With fifty thousand candidates, they'd be inundated with students trying to find out the officers' numbers so they could call them and beg them to be let in, but it means I can't get in either."

"Of course you can," I said. "The database you can't hack hasn't been invented. What about calling the airport? Mr. Fuyijama said the admiral had to go announce more appointments."

"I already did. IASA refused to authorize an in-flight emergency call, and the plane's onboard number is just as protected as the admiral's."

My mom poked her head in the door. "Theodora? You need to come cut your cake."

"I'm still packing," I said, grabbing my duffel bag off my closet shelf and throwing some underwear into it.

"It'll only take a minute," she said firmly. "The governor's here."

Oh, frick. "Have you heard from Dad?"

"No, but he should be here any minute. Come on. Everyone's waiting."

"I'll be right there," I said, and called up Dad, but there was no answer. "I'll only be a minute," I said to Kimkim. "There has to be some kind of emergency number where we can talk to somebody. Keep trying!" and went out to the dining room.

Everyone in town was there, gathered around a sheet cake with a spaceship and silver stars spelling out "Blast off!" Mom handed me a huge piece, and I gulped it down, nodding while two dozen people I'd never seen before told me how lucky I was, and finally escaped on the pretext of taking Kimkim some cake. She waved it away, intent on her hacking, so I ate it.

"It's no use," she said. "I can't get in anywhere, IASA, the Academy cadet roster, everything's blocked."

"But there has to be a number where the cadets can call them if they've got questions."

"There is," she said, her eyes on the screen. "It's automated. Press one for a list of forbidden kit items. Press two for the Academy course schedule. Sixteen menu choices, but none for, 'if you wish to speak to an operator,' or 'I think there's been a mistake.' You don't remember the name of that recruiter, do you?"

"No. Did you check the name thing?"

"Yes. There's no Theodore Baumgarten, or Ted, or Dora. Or Bauman or Bauer or Bommgren. The closest thing I found was a Theopholus Bami, and he lives in New Delhi. And is four years old."

"Oh. I know, look up the Academy rules. Those can't be encrypted, they're public record, and there's got to be something in there about turning down an appointment."

My mom poked her head in again. "Your dad's just pulled in," she said.

Dad. Thank goodness. I waded through the crowd in the dining room again, which now seemed to contain everyone in the state of Colorado, all eating cake, and outside. "Dad, I have to talk to you. I didn't apply to the Academy—"

"You didn't?"

"No. I—"

"That's wonderful! You did just what I always told you to do—follow your own path, be independent, don't do what everybody else is doing, and look what it got you! An Academy appointment!"

"No, Dad, you don't understand. I don't want this appointment. I don't want to go to the Academy!"

"That's what you said your first day of school, remember? And do you remember what I told you?"

"The stink bomb story?"

He laughed. "No, I told you to try it for a week and then see how you felt. You're just having cold feet. When does she leave?" he asked Mom, who'd come up carrying two pieces of cake.

She handed us each one. "In twenty minutes."

"Twenty *minutes?!*" I said, looking at my digital. According to it, I still had over an hour.

"IASA called. They said they knew how eager cadets always are to go, so they're sending the escort over early."

"I have to pack," I said, and shot back into my room. "You have to do something. *Now*," I told Kimkim.

"I'm trying," she said. "I looked up the Academy appointment regulations, but there's nothing in them about turning an appointment down, and I still can't get through to anybody. I'm afraid you're going to have to go to the Academy to get this straightened out. It's the only way you're going to be able to talk to someone in person."

"I am *not* going to the Academy," I said, tossing clothes and shoes into the duffel bag she'd gotten out. "I'll hide till the escort leaves. What about your basement?"

"That won't work," she said, coming over and taking out the clothes I was putting in. "They'll think you've been kidnapped or something. Remember that cadet in Barcelona whose girlfriend tied him up so she could take his place? They'll think Coriander killed you and send out an APB. Look," she said, picking up the list and handing it to me, "you go with them and talk to whoever's in charge of admissions. I'll keep working from this end, and as soon as I've got something, I'll message you. Do your mom and dad have a lawyer?"

Mom knocked. "Theodora, your escort's here," she said.

"Give me two minutes," I shouted, frantically trying to find "3 pr. tube socks, white."

"Here's your toothbrush and toothpaste," Kimkim said, "and your phone."

"Come on, Cadet Baumgarten," my dad said, opening the door. "You don't want to keep the Academy waiting."

"Dad, what's our lawyer's name?"

"Oh, for the admission papers and things, you mean? We'll take care of all that. You just go on and have a good time." He scooped up the half-packed duffel bag and led me out through the patting, handshaking crowd to the waiting hover. "It's a good thing you didn't do what I did in high school," he said, handing me into the hover. "If you'd set off a stink bomb, they'd never have let you in."

If only I'd known, I thought. The pilot leaned across me, shut the door, and took off. I took out my phone. "Help," I messaged Kimkim.

* * *

I decided there was no point in trying to explain things to the pilot, especially after he said, "Boy, are you lucky! I'd sell my soul to get into the Academy!" I would just have to explain things again to the person in charge once I got there, and besides, in spite of what Kimkim had said, I was seriously considering making a run for it when he let me out at the gates, but he landed me inside the high, razor-wire-tipped walls and walked me into the main building past two heavily armed sentries and handed me over to a man in an IASA uniform.

"I want to talk to the person in charge of admissions," I said to him.

"Name?"

"Theodora Baumgarten," I said, hoping against hope it wasn't on his list, but he found it immediately, handed me an ID badge, and weighed my bag.

"You're two pounds over," he said, opening it and taking out my phone. "You can get rid of this. It won't work in the Academy."

Oh, frick, I hadn't considered that possibility. I'd have to message Kimkim and tell her—

"I have a sentimental attachment to it," I said. "You can take my curling iron instead."

The door behind us opened and two girls came in.

"Oh, look at this! I can't believe we're here!" one of them said, clutching her chest just like Coriander, and the other one kept repeating, "Ohmigod, ohmigod, ohmigod!" till I thought she was going to hyperventilate.

"You're still overweight," the IASA guy said. "You sure you don't want to give up your phone?"

"I'm sure," I said, pulling out my iPod and some DVDs.

He shrugged. "Suit yourself," he said, handed me back the bag and turned to the Hyperventilator. "Name?"

"Excuse me," I said, moving back in front of her. "I asked to see the person in charge of admissions."

"You'll have to talk to your sector officer," he said looking at the list. "H-level. Second elevator on the right."

I took it down to H, messaging Kimkim the news about the phone on the way down. "Working on it," she answered immediately, so at least the phone worked in this part of the Academy. They must just jam the student areas, which meant till Kimkim found a way around it, I'd have to sneak off to an area where it did work.

If I was here that long. Which I might be, since the fourth-year cadet waiting for me on H-level looked at me totally blankly when I told him I wanted to see the admissions person.

"Never mind," I said. "Take me to the head of the Academy."

"You mean the Commander?"

"Yes," I said firmly.

"This way," he said, and led me down a long cement corridor, up an even longer ramp, and into another elevator. He pushed three, and we went up for a very long way. It opened on an accordion-pleated tunnel, like a jetway, ending in a narrow, curved corridor lined with doors.

He stopped in front of one of them, opened it and stepped aside so I could enter. "Is this the Commander's office?" I asked.

"No. Wait here," he said, and walked away, and before I could start after him, the Hyperventilator had swooped down on me.

"Isn't this exciting?" she squealed. "Come on!" She grabbed my arm and dragged me into the room, which was clearly not the Commander's office. It was a room the size of a closet with curved walls and two bunks. "I can't believe we're in the same cabin!"

Cabin—?

She'd plopped down on the lower bunk. "Come on, get strapped in! We launch in five minutes! Aren't we lucky?" she said, busily fastening straps. "All the other classes had to spend their first semester earthside before they got to go up."

The elevators, the jetway, the curving corridor—"We're in a *spaceship*?" I said, calculating whether I could make it down that jetway to the elevator in two minutes.

"I know, I can't believe it's happening either!"

An alarm began to sound. "All cadets to their acceleration couches." I dived for the remaining bunk.

"You do the chest straps first," the Hyperventilator said. "Just think, in a few hours we'll be on the Ra!"

"The Ra?" I said, struggling with the straps. They were so in love with the Academy, they'd named it after a god?

"That's what cadets call the Academy space station, the *Robert A. Heinlein*. The *RAH*, get it? And now we're cadets! Can you *believe* this is actually happening?"

"No."

"Me neither!" she said. "Don't you think you'd better put your emesis bag on?"

* * *

I threw up all the way to the *RAH*.

"Gosh, I didn't think it was possible to throw up at 4g's," the Hyperventilator said. "Maybe you'll feel better when we go into freefall."

I didn't. I went through my vomit bag and hers and threw up on the bunk, the walls, the Hyperventilator, and, once we were weightless, on the air in front of me, where it formed disgusting-looking yellowish-brown globules that floated around the cabin for the rest of the trip.

"What on earth did you eat?" the Hyperventilator asked.

"Cake," I said miserably, and vomited again.

"It can't last much longer," she said, ducking a large globule floating toward her. "You can't have anything left."

Also not true.

"You'll be okay once we get to the *RAH*," she said.

"Rah, rah, rah," I said weakly, and proved her wrong by throwing up all over the cadet sent to unstrap us, on the connecting deck, and the airlock.

At least *this* will convince them there's been a mistake, I thought, as the cadet half- carried me to my quarters, but he said cheerfully, "A touch of space sickness, huh?" He lowered me onto my bunk. "Happens to every cadet."

"I'm *not* a cadet," I said, and then, even though I wanted to lie there in my bunk and die, said, "I want to see the Commander."

"I know how you feel," he said. "My first day up here I wanted to go home, too. You'll feel better after a shower and a nap."

"No, I won't. I demand to see the head. Now," I said, and got up to show him I was serious, but the minute I did, I felt wildly lightheaded and on the verge of toppling, as if I were in a canoe about to tip over.

"Coriolis effect," he said, grabbing my arm and lowering me back onto the bunk. "It takes a couple of days to get used to."

"I won't live that long," I muttered, and he laughed again.

"I need to go get the other cadets settled in, and then I'll come back and see how you're doing," he said, covering me up with a Mylar blanket. "If you need me before that, just hit send." He handed me a communicator. "And don't worry. A little thing like spacesickness won't get you thrown out of the Academy."

But I want to be—" I began, but he was already gone, and the thought of getting up off the bunk to go after him, or even of pressing the button on the communicator sent the room toppling over again.

I'll just lie here very, very quietly till he comes back, I thought, and then insist on seeing the Commander, but I must have been asleep when he came back, because when I opened my eyes, the Hyperventilator was unpacking her kit on the other bunk. "Oh, good, you're awake," she said. "We're going to be bunkmates! Isn't that incred! I'm Libby, I mean, Cadet Thornburg. Are you feeling better?"

"No," I said, though I was, a little. At least I was able to sit up. However, when I tried to stand, the room gave a sudden lurch, and I had to grab for the wall, and it, the other walls, and Libby seemed to be leaning ominously toward me. I reared back and nearly fell over.

"It's because of the Coriolis effect from the spin on the space station. It makes everything seem to tilt toward you. Isn't it incred?"

"Umm," I said. "How long does it take to get used to it?" It must not be that long. She was moving around without any trouble. Or maybe that was one of the things IASA tested for in their four-tiered screening process.

"I don't know. I wanted to get a head start," she said, stowing clothes in the locker above her bunk, "so I practiced in an artificial-gravity simulator before I came. Three weeks, maybe?"

I would never last three weeks. Which meant I had to get in to see the Commander now. I pressed the communicator button and then spent the time till the fourth-year got there working on standing up, walking over to the door, and fighting the urge to grab onto something, anything, at all times.

The fourth-year looked surprised to see me on my feet. I told him I wanted to see the Commander. "Don't you want to wait till you feel steadier?" he asked, looking at my vomit-spattered clothes. "And have a chance to clean up?"

"No."

"Okay," he said doubtfully. "What did you want to see the Commander about?"

If I told him, he'd stare blankly at me or say everyone with spacesickness felt that way. "There's a problem with my application," I said.

"Oh, then, you want the registrar."

"No, I—" I began and then decided the registrar was exactly who I wanted to see. He'd have the applications on file, and when he saw I didn't have one, he could correct the mistake immediately. "Okay, take me to the registrar's office."

"That's not necessary," he said. "You can message him from here." He switched on the terminal above my bunk.

"No," I said. "I want to see him in person."

"Okay, wait here, and I'll see if he's available."

"No," I said, letting go of the wall with an effort. "I'm coming with you."

It was the longest walk of my life. I couldn't seem to overcome the feeling that everything, including the fourth-year, was about to pitch forward onto me and/or that I was about to float away, and I periodically had to latch onto handgrips and/or the fourth-year in spite of myself.

"It's because the gravity's only two-thirds that of Earth," he said. "You'll get used to it. You're lucky it's not a full g. The more rotation, the more Coriolis effect. Any less, though, and there's bone loss. Two-thirds is a happy medium."

"That's what you think," I muttered, showing no signs of getting used to it, even though he led me through what seemed like miles of tube-like corridors and locks and ladders, ending finally in an office not much bigger than my cabin. A guy who looked like my dad was seated at a console. "What can I do for you, Cadet Baumgarten?" he asked kindly.

I poured out my whole story, hoping against hope he wouldn't give me another of those I-don't-understand-what-language-you're-speaking looks.

He didn't. He said, "Oh, dear, that's terrible. I can't imagine how that could have happened."

Relief flooded over me.

"I'll look into this immediately. Cadet Apley," he called into an inner office, "find me Cadet Baumgarten's file." He turned back to me. "Don't worry. We'll get this straightened out."

A young woman's voice called out to him, "The files for the new cadets haven't been transmitted yet, sir."

"Well, tell them I need them as soon as possible."

"Yes, sir," she said.

"Don't worry, Cadet Baumgarten," he said. "We'll get this straightened out. I intend to launch a full investigation." He stood up and extended his hand. "I'll notify you as soon as we've determined what happened."

I ignored his hand. "How long will that be?"

"Oh, it shouldn't take more than a week or two."

"A *week* or two?" I said. "But you've made a mistake. I'm not supposed to be here."

"If that is the case, you'll of course be sent home immediately," he said, showing me the door. "In the meantime, may I congratulate you on your rapid adaptation to artificial gravity. Very impressive."

If I could have thrown up on him, I would have, but there was no cake left. Instead, I planted myself in front of him as firmly as was possible in two-thirds g and said, "I want to make a phone call."

"Cadets aren't allowed phone calls for the first two weeks of term. After that, you can make one two-minute earthside call a month," he said.

"I know my rights," I said, trying not to sway backwards. "Prisoners are allowed a phone call."

He looked amused. "The *RAH* is not a prison."

Wanna bet? "It's my legal right," I said stubbornly. "A *private* phone call."

He sighed. "Cadet Apley," he called into the inner office, "set up a Y49TDRS link for Cadet Baumgarten," and handed me a satellite phone. "Two minutes. There'll be a six-second lag. This will count as next month's call," he said, and went into the inner office and shut the door.

They were probably listening in, but I didn't care. I called Kimkim. "I'm so sorry," she said. "I didn't know they were taking cadets straight up to the *Heinlein*. Are you okay?"

"No," I said. "Did you find out my mom and dad's lawyer's name?"

Seconds passed, and then she said, "Yes, I talked to her."

"What did she say?"

More seconds. "That an Academy appointment was considered a legally binding contract."

Oh, frick.

"So I went online and found a lawyer who specializes in Academy law."

"And?" Creez, this lag was maddening.

"He said he only handled cases of cadets who'd been eliminated from the Academy and were trying to get reinstated. He said he couldn't find any record of a case where a cadet had wanted *out*."

"Did he say how these cases he handled *got* eliminated?" I asked, thinking maybe I could do whatever it was they did.

"Failing their courses, mostly," she said. "But, listen, don't do anything that might mess up your chances at UCLA. That's why these cadets file lawsuits, because flunking out of the Academy pretty much ruined their chances at getting into any other university."

Worse and worse. "Listen, you've got to figure out some way we can talk." I told her about the one call a month.

"I'll see what I can do. They didn't take your phone away from you, did they?"

"No," I said.

"Did they say anything about how this call worked?"

"They called it a Y49TDRS, whatever that is."

"It means it's relayed through tracking, data, and relay satellites," she said. "A Y49 shouldn't be too hard to patch onto, but it may take—"

There was a buzz. "Call over," an automated voice said.

* * *

I spent the next day and a half checking my phone for messages and hoping Kimkim hadn't been about to say, "It may take months for me to come up with something," or, worse, "It may take extensive modifications to your phone's circuits," and worrying that if the registrar had been listening in, it didn't matter. They'd jam whatever Kimkim tried.

Then classes started, and I spent every waking moment trying to keep up with cadets who'd not only taken astrogation and exobotany, but knew how to dock a shuttle, read a star chart, and brush their teeth while weightless. First-year cadets had to spend half of each watch in the non-rotated sections of the

RAH, learning to live and work in microgravity. Most of them (including, of course, Libby) had taken classes in weightlessness on Earth, and the rest had clearly been chosen for their ability to float from one end of the module to the other without crashing into something, a gene I obviously lacked. The second day I sneezed, did a backward triple somersault, and crashed into a bank of equipment, an escapade that gave me the idea of pleading a bad cold and asking to see the doctor—a medical discharge surely couldn't hurt my chances at UCLA—but when I went to the infirmary, the medic said, "Stuffiness in the head is a normal side effect of weightlessness," and gave me a sinus prescription.

"What about chronic vertigo?" I asked. I was actually down to only a couple of episodes a day, but it had occurred to me that "inability to tolerate space environment" might be a way out.

"If it hasn't disappeared a month from now, come see me," he said, and sent me back to EVA training. Luckily, I didn't sneeze during my spacewalk and go shooting off into space, but being outside and linked to the *RAH* only by a thin tether reminded me just how dangerous space was.

Well, that, and the fact that those dangers were the second favorite topic of the cadets at mess and during rec periods. If they weren't talking about the difficulty of detecting fires in a weightless environment (there aren't any flames, just a hard-to-see reddish glow), they were recounting gruesome tales of jammed oxygen lines and carbon monoxide buildup and malfunctioning heating units which froze students into cadet-sicles. Or speculating on all the things that *might* happen, from unexpected massive solar flares to killer meteors to explosive decompression. All of which made it clear I needed to get off of here *soon*. I messaged the registrar during my study period, but he said he was still waiting for the cadet files.

There was still no word from Kimkim. I checked my phone every time I had the chance and tried to send her periodic *Maidez*'s, but each time the display said, "Number out of range," which was putting it mildly.

I messaged the registrar again. Still waiting.

You're still waiting? I thought. At least he had an office of his own. He didn't have to share with Miss Ohmigod, This Is So Incred! Libby adored everything about the Academy—the sardine-can cabins, the rehydrated food, the exhausting schedule of lectures and labs and exercise and freefall training. She even loved the falling-off-a-log vertigo. "Because then you know you're really in space!"

And she wasn't the worst one. Several of the cadets acted like they were in a cathedral, wandering the corridors with their mouths open and speaking in hushed, reverent tones. When I mentioned that the place smelled like a gym locker, they looked at me like I was committing heresy, and went back to the cadets' favorite topic of conversation, how *lucky* they were to be here. By the end of a week I was ready to walk through an airlock without a spacesuit just to get away from them.

I was also worried about how I was going to talk to Kimkim if and when she figured out a phone connection, and about finding a safe place to stash my phone so the registrar couldn't suddenly confiscate it. I checked the *RAH*'s schematics, but there was nowhere a person could go to be alone on the entire space station. Every classroom and lab was used every hour of every watch, so were the mess, the gym, and the weightless modules, and when I'd gone to the infirmary, there hadn't been separate examining rooms, just a tier of cots.

There was temporary privacy in the shower (very temporary—water is even more limited than the phone call times), and there was supposed to be "private time" half an hour before lights-out, but it wasn't enforced, and Libby's half of the cabin was always crammed with cadets discussing how *exciting* it had been to learn to use the zero-g toilet. I began to actually miss Coriander.

I checked the schematics again, looking for anything at all that might work. The inner room of the registrar's office might in a pinch, though when I'd gone over to ask him what was taking the files so long, I'd been told the section was off-limits to first-years. So was the docking module, and all the outer sections were exposed to too much radiation to make them practical.

The only other possibility was the storage areas, which in the super-compact world of the *RAH* meant every space that wasn't being used for something else—floors, ceilings, walls, even the airlocks. The diagrams showed all those spaces as filled with supplies, but it occurred to me (during a private-time discussion about the joys of learning to sit down in two-thirds g) that once those supplies had been used, the place they'd been might be empty.

I noted some of the possible spots and for the next few days spent my rest period exploring, and finally came up with a space between the plastic drums of nutrients for the hydroponics farm. It wasn't very big, and it was above the ceiling, but luckily it was in the freefall area, and I'd finally figured out how to propel myself from one location to another in it without major damage. I half-drifted, half-rappelled my way up (over?) to the ceiling, squeezed into the space (which turned out to be a perfect size, big enough, but too small to drift around in), replaced the hatch, and spent a blissful fifteen minutes alone.

It would have been longer, but I remembered a class was scheduled to come in sometime soon, and I couldn't afford to get caught. When I got back to my cabin, I memorized the freefall-area use schedule and checked for a message from the registrar.

There wasn't one, but on my schedule was "Conference Registrar's office. Tuesday. 1600 hours." Which meant I wouldn't need a hiding place after all.

* * *

"I've gone over your application," the registrar said, "and everything appears to be in order."

"In order?" I said blankly.

"Yes," he said, looking at the console. "Application, entrance exams, endurance test results, psychological battery scores. It's all here."

"Application?" I said, standing up too fast and nearly shooting over the desk at him. "I told you, I didn't apply!"

"I also sent for the interviewer assessments and the minutes of the selection committee. You did in fact apply—"

"I did *not*—"

"—and were duly appointed."

"I want to see that application. It must be a forgery—"

"Conflicted feelings among new cadets are not unusual. A strange new environment, separation from family, performance anxiety can all be factors. Did you perhaps have a friend who also wanted to get into the Academy?"

"Yes, but…I mean, *she* wanted in the Academy, I didn't. I didn't—"

He nodded sagely. "And now you feel by accepting your appointment you're betraying that friend—"

"*No*," I said. "I did not write that application. Let me see it."

"Certainly," he said, hit several keys, and the image of the application came up on the screen.

"Theodora Jane Baumgarten," it read. This is like a bad dream, I thought. Birthdate, address, school… Before I could read the rest of it, the registrar had hit the next screen and the next. "You see?" he said, blanking the last screen before I could get a good look at it. "And quite an impressive application, if I may say so. I think you'll make an excellent addition to the Academy."

"I want to see the Commander," I said.

"She'd only tell you the same thing." He hit several more keys, and the terminal spat out a slip of paper. "I've made an appointment for you with Dr. Tumali. He'll help you sort out any conflicting feelings you—"

"I don't *have* any conflicting feelings. I *hate* this place, and I want to go home," I screeched at him, and stormed out, slamming the door behind me. Well, sort of. Slams aren't terribly impressive at two-thirds g, and after I'd done it, I realized I should have demanded another phone call instead, this one to my mother. She'd said she'd secretly hoped I'd apply. Maybe she'd decided to do it for me. Or maybe Coriander had, as some kind of hideous joke. Or Mr. Fuyijama. The more cadets he had, the better Winfrey High looked.

But even if they'd filled out an application and forged my signature, they couldn't have faked the entrance exams or the interview. It made no sense, and I had no time to think about it. I had an essay due on asteroid mining and a lunar geography exam to study for. "Help," I messaged Kimkim.

The display lit up. "Number out of range."

* * *

Three days later, when I had decided I was going to have to do something drastic to get myself expelled, and forget UCLA, my phone rang in the middle of rest period. "What was that?" Libby said drowsily.

"A killer meteor," I said, switching the phone to "message."

"Are you there?" the display read.

"Yes," I messaged, "hang on," and took off at a run for the freefall area. And nearly got caught by a group of second-years playing weightless soccer. I had to wait till they'd finished and left to swing up to my hiding place, hoping Kimkim hadn't concluded she'd lost me in the meantime.

As soon as I was inside the space, I switched the phone to "voice," and said, "Kimkim, are you there?"

There was no answer. Oh, Frig, I thought, and then remembered the lag.

"I'm here," she said. "Sorry I took so long. I had trouble setting up an encryption so the Academy can't eavesdrop on us."

"That's okay," I said. "I need you to get a look at my Academy application."

"I thought you said you didn't apply."

"I *didn't*, but the registrar showed me something that looked like one. I need you to find out what kind of signature verification it's got on it, an R-scan or a thumbprint, and what site notarized it."

"You think IASA faked it?"

"IASA or somebody else. You didn't submit an application in my name, did you?"

"I resent that," she said. "If I was going to fake one, I'd have faked my own."

She called back two days later in the middle of tensor calculus to tell me she couldn't get to my application. "I was finally able to hack into the Academy's database and the cadet applications files, but I can't get into yours."

"Because it doesn't exist," I said after I got to my hiding place.

"No, I mean, there's a file with your name on it, but I can't get access."

"What about having someone they won't connect with me make the request?"

"I already tried that. I used my sister's friend's friend in Jakarta. She couldn't get in either. Neither could any of the professional hackers I contacted. It's blocked. I can get into the other applications, but not yours."

"Well, keep trying," I said, and hung up. I stuck the phone down the front of my uniform, crawled over to the hatch, and began to slide it open.

And heard voices below me.

The soccer players weren't supposed to be in here till 1900 hours. I slid the hatch silently shut and flattened myself against it, listening. "It's my bunkmate," Libby was saying. "I've *tried* to be friends with her, but she acts like she doesn't want to be here."

You're right, I thought. In more ways than one.

"Libby's right, her bunkmate's got a terrible attitude," one of her friends said. "I have no idea how she got appointed when there are thousands of candidates who'd *love* to be here."

"I know the Academy must have had a good reason for picking her," Libby said, "but..." and launched into a ten-minute list of my shortcomings which I had no choice but to lie there and listen to. "That's why I asked you to meet me here," she said when she was finally finished. "I need your advice."

"Tell the dean you want a different bunkmate," another friend said.

"I can't," Libby said. "Inability to foster healthy personal relations is the number one reason for failing first-year."

"Cut her EVA tether next time she's outside," the first friend said, which didn't exactly sound like fostering healthy personal relations to me.

"Maybe you should introduce her to Cadet Griggs," another voice said. "It sounds like they'd be perfect for each other."

"Who's Cadet Griggs?" Libby asked.

"He's a third-year in my exochem class. Jeffrey Griggs. He doesn't like anything or anybody."

"I sat next to him in mess last week, and he was completely insufferable," the first one said. "And conceited. He claims he didn't even have to apply to get in. He—what was that?"

I must have kicked one of the nutrient drums in my surprise. I held my breath, praying they didn't investigate.

"He claims he was so brilliant they just appointed him without his taking any entrance exams or anything."

"You should definitely introduce them, Libby, and maybe they'll move in together, and your problem will be solved, and so will hers."

My problem *is* solved, I thought.

As soon as they left, I called Kimkim. "I need you to get into the cadet application files."

"I told you, I can't get anywhere near your application."

"Not mine," I said. "Cadet Jeffrey Griggs'. He's a third-year."

She said the name back to me. "What am I looking for?"

"The application," I said.

She called back the next day. "There's no application on file for Jeffrey Griggs."

I knew it. Listen, I need you to go through all the cadet files for the last five years and see how many others are missing."

"I already did. I went back eight years and found four more, one last year, two four years ago, one seven."

"I need you to find out where they are now."

"I did, and you're not going to like the answer. All but one of them are still in the Academy or working for IASA."

"What about the one who isn't?"

"Medical discharge. 'Inability to tolerate space environment.' Her name's Palita Duvai. She's in graduate school at Harvard," Kimkim said. "Do you want their names?"

"Yes," I said, even though I knew the registrar would say five missing applications didn't prove anything. He'd claim they'd been accidentally erased, and if it wasn't an accident, then why hadn't they posted phony applications like the one they'd shown me? I asked Kimkim that.

"I don't know," she said, "but it's definitely not an accident. When I looked up their IASA assignments, I found something else. Next to their ranks are the letters 'DA.' It's part of Jeffrey's class rank, too—'Third-year Cadet, DA.'"

DA. District Attorney? Didn't Apply? Dragged Away Kicking and Screaming?

"I looked it up in the IASA lexicon, but it wasn't there," she said. "Do you want me to try to find out what it stands for?"

"I don't think that will be necessary," I said. I signed off, went back to my cabin and got the slip of paper the registrar had given me with the psychiatrist appointment on it, wrote "DA" on the back, and took it up. I handed it, folded, to one of the guards, told him to slide it under the registrar's door, and went back to my cabin to wait.

I didn't even make it halfway. A fourth-year cadet was waiting for me before I even reached the dorm section. "Cadet Baumgarten?" she said. "The registrar wants to see you," and took me back up to his office.

"Come in, Ms. Baumgarten," the registrar said. "Sit down." I noted that the slip of paper was on his desk.

"The cadet said the commander wanted to—" I began, and then absorbed what he'd said. Miss Baumgarten, not Cadet Baumgarten. I sat down.

"I'm sorry to have taken so long getting back to you," he said. "The first few weeks of term are always so hectic. However, I wanted to tell you that we've completed the check on your application, and you were correct. A mistake in our admissions software wrongly identified you as a candidate. The IASA sincerely regrets the error and any inconvenience it may have caused you."

"Inconvenience—!"

"You will be reimbursed for that inconvenience and your lost classtime," he went on smoothly. "I understand you want to go to UCLA. We've already spoken to them and explained the situation, and they've agreed to reschedule your interview at your convenience. If you encounter any other problems, feel free to contact me." He handed me a folder. "Here are your discharge papers."

I opened the folder and read the papers. Next to "Reason for Discharge," it read, "Medical—Inability to Tolerate Space Environment."

"You're free to leave whenever you wish," the registrar said. "We've reserved a space for you on tomorrow's shuttle. It leaves at 0900 hours. Or, if you prefer, we'd be happy to arrange for a civilian shuttle, and if there's anything else we can do, please let us know."

He stood up and came around the desk. "I hope your time with us hasn't been too unpleasant," he said, and extended his hand.

And all I had to do was shake it, go pack my kit, and get on that shuttle, and I'd be back on blessed Earth and on my way to UCLA. It was extremely tempting.

"Sorry," I said, folding my arms across my chest. "Not good enough."

"Not—? If you're worried about questions from your friends and family regarding your leaving the Academy, I'll be happy to issue a statement explaining that inner-ear problems made it impossible for you to adjust to the Coriolis effect. Medical discharges carry no stigma—"

"I don't want a medical discharge. I want to know the truth. Why did you hijack me? And how many people have you done it to besides me? I know of at least ten," I lied. "What do you want with us? And don't tell me you don't have enough candidates."

"Actually, that's exactly why we hijacked you," he said, and called into the inner office. "Commander! I think you'd better take over!"

The Commander came in. At least, she was wearing a commander's uniform and insignia, but she couldn't be the commander. She was the recruiter who'd come to Winfrey High. "Hello, Ms. Baumgarten," she said. "It's nice to see you again."

"You!" I said. "You kidnapped me because of that question I asked in assembly, to punish me."

"Yes and no," she said. "Punishment was the farthest thing from my mind. And I prefer the word 'shanghaied' to 'kidnapped.'"

"Shanghaied?"

"Yes. It comes from the practice in the port of Shanghai in the 1800s of ship captains using unorthodox methods for obtaining crews for long, dangerous voyages. When they couldn't get the sailors they needed any other way, they drugged them, carried them aboard, and held them prisoner till they were out to sea. Not a nice technique, but sometimes necessary."

"I don't believe you," I said. "You have thousands and thousands of people who are dying to go to the Academy every year."

"You're right," she said. "Last year we had nine thousand students who successfully completed all four tiers of the screening policy. From those, we chose three hundred, which meant they were the most determined and dedicated of those nine thousand."

"And everyone of them's *thrilled* to be here," I said.

"Exactly. They love the Academy, they love IASA, and that sort of intense devotion is absolutely necessary. Space exploration is an impossibly challenging and dangerous, often deadly, undertaking. Without complete belief in what they're doing, it couldn't be done. But that sort of devotion can also be a handicap. Explorers who are too in love with the jungle end up being bitten by snakes or eaten by tigers. To survive, IASA has to have people who are fully aware of the jungle's dangers and disadvantages and not the least enchanted by its beauties.

"Which means, along with astrogation and the ability to live in confined quarters, we also recruit for skepticism, independence, and questioning of authority—in short, for people who don't like the jungle. Unfortunately, those people generally do everything they can to avoid it, which is why we are forced to—"

"Shanghai people," I said. "Let me get this straight, the reason you wanted me to come to the Academy was because I didn't want to?"

"Yes."

"And what was I supposed to do here?"

"Precisely what you did. Refuse to be impressed, challenge authority, break the rules. Your determination to communicate with your friend was particularly educational. We obviously need to do a much better job of preventing hacking. Also, we've learned not to put DA even on interior records. And it's clear we need to reexamine the necessity of providing private space for our cadets. You've performed a valuable service," she said. "IASA thanks you." She extended her hand.

"I'm not done asking questions yet," I said. "Why do you have to shanghai people? Why didn't you just *ask* me?"

"Would you have come?"

I thought about that day she'd come to Winfrey High to recruit applicants. "No."

"Exactly," she said. "Besides, bringing DAs here involuntarily ensures the critical mindset we're looking for."

"It also ensures that when they find out, they'll be so furious they won't want to have anything to do with the Academy or IASA," I said.

"True," she said ruefully, "but they don't usually find out. You're only the second one."

"Was the first one Palita Duvai?" I asked.

"No," she said. "Unfortunately, Cadet Duvai's medical discharge was real. Inner ear complications."

But if she wasn't the one, I thought, frowning, then that meant uncovering the conspiracy didn't automatically mean a discharge, and that meant—

"The other DAs either concluded there'd been a bureaucratic foul-up or that they'd been so outstanding they hadn't needed to apply."

Jeffrey Griggs, I thought.

"Or they eventually gave up trying to go home and decided that, in spite of the food and the solar flares, they liked the Academy." She shook her head. "I underestimated your dislike of space. And your friend's hacking and communication abilities. Tell me, is Kimkim interested in becoming a cadet?"

"That depends on what you're recruiting for," I said. "If you want a great hacker, yes. If you're looking for another DA, then no, definitely not, she'd probably have to be dragged up here kicking and screaming. And the sooner the better."

The commander grinned. "I really am sorry to lose you. I think you would have made an excellent DA." She leaned back. "Have we answered all your questions?"

"No," I said. "I have two more."

"You want to know what DA stands for?"

"No, I already know that. Devil's advocate."

She looked at the registrar. "I told you she was good." She smiled back at me. "You want to know who the other cadet was who figured out what had happened."

"No, I know that, too. It was you."

She nodded.

"Did you decide you liked the Academy in spite of its shortcomings?" I asked.

"No," she said. "I thought it was a complete mess, and that if they didn't get some people in charge who knew what they were doing, and change things, it was going to fall completely apart."

"I think you're right," I said. "You've got to get some private space on board before somebody kills somebody, and surely something can be done about the food. And you've got to get a lot more cadets with computer skills up here."

"We'll see what we can do," the Commander said, and extended her hand. "Welcome aboard."

I saluted her. "Cadet Baumgarten reporting for duty," I said.

"You said you had two questions," the registrar said. "What was the other one?"

"Which of you won the pool?"

"I did," the Commander said, and grinned at the registrar. "I *told* you she was good."

Yes, well, they don't know how good. Or how much trouble they're letting themselves in for. If it's independence, questioning authority, and bending the rules they want, Kimkim and I can come up with all kinds of stuff. I went straight to my hiding place and called her.

The display lit up. "Illegal transmission," it read. "Not allowed."

I waited, and in a couple of minutes Kimkim said, "Sorry. It took me awhile to route around their jamming devices. I found out what DA stands for."

"So did I," I said. "I definitely think you should reconsider applying for the Academy. And I think it would be a good idea to pack your kit now so you won't have to do it at the last minute."

"I already did," she said.

"Good," I said. "I've got a list of stuff I need you to bring when you come up. First, I want you to ask my dad for his stink bomb formula…"

FEMAVILLE 29

PAUL DI FILIPPO

Paul Di Filippo sold his first story in 1977. Since then he's had nearly 150 stories published, the majority of them collected in his ten short story collections. He has written nine novels, including *Fuzzy Dice* and *Spondulix*. New novel *Time's Black Lagoon*, featuring the Creature from the Black Lagoon, and new collection *Shuteye for the Timebroker* were published in 2006. Di Filippo has also begun scripting comics of late, with his first major project being a sequel to Alan Moore's *TOP 10*. He lives in his native state, Rhode Island, amidst eldritch Lovecraftian surroundings, with his mate of thirty years, Deborah Newton, a chocolate cocker spaniel named Brownie, and a three-colored cat named Penny Century.

La Palma is a tiny mote in the Canary Islands, a mote that had certainly never intruded into my awareness before one fateful day. On La Palma, five hundred billion tons of rock in the form of an unstable coastal plateau awaited a nudge, which they received when the Cumbre Vieja volcano erupted. Into the sea a good portion of the plateau plunged, a frightful hammer of the gods.

The peeling off of the face of the island was a smaller magnitude event than had been feared; but it was a larger magnitude event than anyone was prepared for.

The resulting tsunami raced across the Atlantic.

My city had gotten just twelve hours warning. The surreal chaos of the partial evacuation was like living through the most vivid nightmare or disaster film imaginable. Still, the efforts of the authorities and volunteers and good samaritans ensured that hundreds of thousands of people escaped with their lives.

Leaving other hundreds of thousands to face the wave.

Their only recourse was to find the tallest, strongest buildings and huddle.

I was on the seventh floor of an insurance company when the wave arrived. Posters in the reception area informed me that I was in good hands. I had a view of the harbor, half a mile away.

The tsunami looked like a liquid mountain mounted on a rocket sled.

When the wave hit, the building shuddered and bellowed like a steer in an abattoir euthanized with a nail-gun. Every window popped out of its frame, and spray lashed even my level.

But the real fight for survival had not yet begun.

The next several days were a sleepless blur of crawling from the wreckage and helping others do likewise.

But not everyone was on the same side. Looters arose like some old biological paradigm of spontaneous generation from the muck.

Their presence demanded mine on the front lines.

I was a cop.

I had arrested several bad guys without any need for excessive force. But then came a shootout at a jewelry store where the display cases were incongruously draped with drying kelp. I ended up taking the perps down okay. But the firefight left my weary brain and trembling gut hypersensitive to any threat.

Some indeterminate time afterwards—marked by a succession of candybar meals, digging under the floodlights powered by chuffing generators, and endless slogging through slimed streets—I was working my way through the upper floors of an apartment complex, looking for survivors. I shut off my flashlight when I saw a glow around a corner. Someone stepped between me and the light source, casting the shadow of a man with a gun. I yelled, "Police! Drop it!" then crouched and dashed toward the gunman. The figure stepped forward, still holding the weapon, and I fired.

The boy was twelve, his weapon a water pistol.

His mother trailed him by a few feet—not far enough to escape getting splattered with her son's blood.

Later I learned neither of them spoke a word of English.

One minute I was cradling the boy, and the next I was lying on a cot in a field hospital. Three days had gotten lost somewhere. Three days in which the whole world had learned of my mistake.

They let me get up the next day, ostensibly healthy and sane enough, even though my pistol hand, my left, still exhibited a bad tremor. I tried to report to the police command, but found that I had earned a temporary medical discharge. Any legal fallout from my actions awaited an end to the crisis.

I tried being a civilian volunteer for another day or two amidst the ruins, but my heart wasn't in it. So I took the offer of evacuation to Femaville 29.

* * *

The first week after the disaster actually manifested aspects of an odd, enforced vacation. Or rather, the atmosphere often felt more like an open-ended New Year's Eve, the portal to some as-yet undefined millennium where all our good resolutions would come to pass. Once we victims emerged from the shock of losing everything we owned, including our shared identity as citizens of a large East Coast city, my fellow refugees and I began to exhibit a near-manic optimism in the face of the massive slate-cleaning.

The uplift was not to last. But while it prevailed, it was as if some secret imperative in the depths of our souls—a wish to be unburdened of all our draggy pasts—had been fulfilled by cosmic fiat, without our having to lift a finger.

We had been given a chance to start all over, remake our lives afresh, and we were, for the most part, eager to grasp the offered personal remodeling.

Everyone in the swiftly erected encampment of a thousand men, women and children was healthy. The truly injured had all been airlifted to hospitals around the state and nation. Families had been reunited, even down to pets. The tents we were inhabiting were spacious, weather-tight and wired for electricity and entertainment. Meals were plentiful, albeit uninspired, served promptly in three shifts, thrice daily, in a large communal pavilion.

True, the lavatories and showers were also communal, and the lack of privacy grated a bit right from the start. Trudging through the chilly dark in the middle of the night to take a leak held limited appeal, even when you pretended you were camping. And winter, with its more challenging conditions, loomed only a few months away. Moreover, enforced idleness chafed those of us who were used to steady work. Lack of proper schooling for the scores of kids in the camp worried many parents.

But taken all in all, the atmosphere at the camp—christened with no more imaginative bureaucratic name than Femaville Number 29—was suffused with potential that first week.

My own interview with the FEMA intake authorities in the first days of the relocation was typical.

The late September sunlight warmed the interview tent so much that the canvas sides had been rolled up to admit fresh air scented with faint, not unpleasant maritime odors of decay. Even though Femaville 29 was located far inland—or what used to be far inland before the tsunami—the wrack left behind by the disaster lay not many miles away.

For a moment, I pictured exotic fish swimming through the streets and subways of my old city, weaving their paths among cars, couches and corpses. The imagery unsettled me, and I tried to focus on the more hopeful present.

The long tent hosted ranks of paired folding chairs, each chair facing its mate. The FEMA workers, armed with laptop computers, occupied one seat of each pair, while an interviewee sat in the other. The subdued mass interrogation and the clicking of keys raised a surprisingly dense net of sound that overlaid the noises from outside the tent: children roistering, adults gossiping, birds chattering. Outside the tent, multiple lines of refugees stretched away, awaiting their turns.

The official seated across from me was a pretty young African-American woman whose name-badge proclaimed her HANNAH LAWES. Unfortunately, she reminded me of my ex-wife, Calley, hard in the same places Calley was hard. I tried to suppress an immediate dislike of her. As soon as I sat down, Hannah Lawes expressed rote sympathy for my plight, a commiseration worn featureless by its hundredth repetition. Then she got down to business.

"Name?"

"Parrish Hedges."

"Any relatives in the disaster zone?"

"No, ma'am."

"What was your job back in the city?"

I felt my face heat up. But I had no choice, except to answer truthfully.

"I was a police officer, ma'am."

That answer gave Hannah Lawes pause. Finally, she asked in an accusatory fashion, "Shouldn't you still be on duty then? Helping with security in the ruins?"

My left hand started to quiver a bit, but I suppressed it so that I didn't think she noticed.

"Medical exemption, ma'am."

Hannah Lawes frowned slightly and said, "I hope you don't mind if I take a moment to confirm that, Mr. Hedges."

Her slim, manicured fingers danced over her keyboard, dragging my data down the airwaves. I studied the plywood floor of the tent while she read my file.

When I looked up, her face had gone disdainful.

"This explains much, Mr. Hedges."

"Can we move on, please?"

As if I ever could.

Hannah Lawes resumed her programmed spiel. "All right, let's talk about your options now...."

For the next few minutes, she outlined the various programs and handouts and incentives that the government and private charities and NGOs had lined up for the victims of the disaster. Somehow, none of the choices really matched my dreams and expectations engendered by the all-consuming catastrophe. All of them involved relocating to some other part of the country, leaving behind the shattered chaos of the East Coast. And that was something I just wasn't ready for yet, inevitable as such a move was.

And besides, choosing any one particular path would have meant foregoing all the others. Leaving this indeterminate interzone of infinite possibility would lock me into a new life that might be better than my old one, but would still be fixed, crystallized, frozen into place.

"Do I have to decide right now?"

"No, no, of course not."

I stood up to go, and Hannah Lawes added, "But you realize, naturally, that this camp was never intended as a long-term residence. It's only transitional, and will be closed down at some point not too far in the future."

"Yeah, sure," I said. "We're all just passing through. I get it."

I left then and made way for the next person waiting in line.

* * *

The tents of Femaville 29 were arranged along five main dirt avenues, each as wide as a city boulevard. Expressing the same ingenuity that had dubbed our whole encampment, the avenues were labeled A, B, C, D and E. Every three tents, a numbered cross-street occurred. The tents of one avenue backed up against the tents of the adjacent avenue, so that a cross-block was two tents wide. The land where Femaville 29 was pitched was flat and treeless and covered in newly mowed weeds and grasses. Beyond the borders of our village stretched a mix of forest, scrubby fields and swamp, eventually giving way to rolling hills. The nearest real town was about ten miles away, and there was no regular transportation there other than by foot.

As I walked up Avenue D toward my tent (D-30), I encountered dozens of my fellow refugees who were finished with the intake process. Only two days had passed since the majority of us had been ferried here in commandeered school buses. People—the adults, anyhow—were still busy exchanging their stories—thrilling, horrific or mundane—about how they had escaped the tsunami or dealt with the aftermath.

I didn't have any interest in repeating my tale, so I didn't join in any such conversations.

As for the children, they seemed mostly to have flexibly put behind them all the trauma they must have witnessed. Reveling in their present freedom from boring routine, they raced up and down the avenues in squealing packs.

Already, the seasonally withered grass of the avenues was becoming dusty ruts. Just days old, this temporary village, I could feel, was already beginning to lose its freshness and ambiance of novelty.

Under the unseasonably warm sun, I began to sweat. A cold beer would have tasted good right now. But the rules of Femaville 29 prohibited alcohol.

I reached my tent and went inside.

My randomly assigned roommate lay on his bunk. Given how the disaster had shattered and stirred the neighborhoods of the city, it was amazing that I actually knew the fellow from before. I had encountered no one else yet in the camp who was familiar to me. And out of all my old friends and acquaintances and co-workers, Ethan Duplessix would have been my last choice to be reunited with.

Ethan was a fat, bristled slob with a long criminal record of petty theft, fraud and advanced mopery. His personal grooming habits were so atrocious that he had emerged from the disaster more or less in the same condition he entered it, unlike the rest of the survivors who had gone from well-groomed to uncommonly bedraggled and smelly.

Ethan and I had crossed paths often, and I had locked him up more times than I could count. (When the tsunami struck, he had been amazingly free of outstanding charges.) But the new circumstances of our lives, including Ethan's knowledge of how I had "retired" from the force, placed us now on a different footing.

"Hey, Hedges, how'd it go? They got you a new job yet? Maybe security guard at a kindergarten!"

I didn't bother replying, but just flopped down on my bunk. Ethan chuckled meanly at his own paltry wit for a while, but when I didn't respond, he eventually fell silent, his attentions taken up by a tattered copy of *Maxim*.

I closed my eyes and drowsed for a while, until I got hungry. Then I got up and went to the refectory.

That day they were serving hamburgers and fries for the third day in a row. Mickey Dee's seemed to have gotten a lock on the contract to supply the camp. I took mine to an empty table. Head bowed, halfway through my meal, I sensed someone standing beside me.

The woman's curly black hair descended to her shoulders in a tumbled mass. Her face resembled a cameo in its alabaster fineness.

"Mind if I sit here?" she said.

"Sure. I mean, go for it."

The simple but primordial movements of her legs swinging over the bench seat and her ass settling down awakened emotions in me that had been absent since Calley's abrupt leave-taking.

"Nia Horsley. Used to live over on Garden Parkway."

"Nice district."

Nia snorted, a surprisingly enjoyable sound. "Yeah, once."

"I never got over there much. Worked in East Grove. Had an apartment on Oakeshott."

"And what would the name on your doorbell have been?"

"Oh, sorry. Parrish Hedges."

"Pleased to meet you, Parrish."

We shook hands. Hers was small but strong, enshelled in mine like a pearl.

For the next two hours, through two more shifts of diners coming and going, we talked, exchanging condensed life stories, right up to the day of disaster and down to our arrival at Femaville 29. Maybe the accounts were edited for maximum appeal, but I intuitively felt she and I were being honest nonetheless. When the refectory workers finally shooed us out in order to clean up for supper, I felt as if I had known Nia for two weeks, two months, two years—

She must have felt the same. As we strolled away down Avenue B, she held my hand.

"I don't have a roomie in my tent."

"Oh?"

"It's just me and my daughter. Luck of the draw, I guess."

"I like kids. Never had any, but I like 'em."

"Her name's Izzy. Short for Isabel. You'll get to meet her. But maybe not just yet."

"How come?"

"She's made a lot of new friends. They stay out all day, playing on the edge of the camp. Some kind of weird new game they invented."

"We could go check up on her, and I could say hello."

Nia squeezed my hand. "Maybe not right this minute."

* * *

I got to meet Izzy the day after Nia and I slept together. I suppose I could've hung around till Izzy came home for supper, but the intimacy with Nia, after such a desert of personal isolation, left me feeling a little disoriented and pres- sured. So I made a polite excuse for my departure, which Nia accepted with good grace, and arranged to meet mother and daughter for breakfast.

Izzy bounced into the refectory ahead of her mother. She was seven or eight, long-limbed and fair-haired in contrast to her mother's compact, raven-haired paleness, but sharing Nia's high-cheeked bone structure. I conjectured back- ward to a gangly blond father.

The little girl zeroed in on me somehow out of the whole busy dining hall, racing up to where I sat, only to slam on the brakes with alarming precipi- tousness.

"You're Mr. Hedges!" she informed me and the world.

"Yes, I am. And you're Izzy."

I was ready to shake her hand in a formal adult manner. But then she exclaimed, "You made my mom all smiley!" and launched herself into my awkward embrace.

Before I could really respond, she was gone, heading for the self-service cereal line.

I looked at Nia, who was grinning.

"And this," I asked, "is her baseline?"

"Precisely. When she's really excited—"

"I'll wear one of those padded suits we used for training the K-9 squad."

Nia's expression altered to one of seriousness and sympathy, and I instantly knew what was coming. I cringed inside, if not where it showed. She sat down next to me and put a hand on my arm.

"Parrish, I admit I did a little googling on you after we split yesterday, over at the online tent. I know about why you aren't a cop anymore. And I just want to say that—"

Before she could finish, Izzy materialized out of nowhere, bearing a tray hold- ing two bowls of technicolor puffs swimming in chocolate milk, and slipped herself between us slick as a greased eel.

"They're almost out of food! You better hurry!" With a plastic knife, Izzy began slicing a peeled banana into chunks thick as Oreos that plopped with alarming splashes into her bowls.

I stood up gratefully. "I'll get us something, Nia. Eggs and bacon and toast okay?"

She gave me a look which said that she could wait to talk. "Sure."

During breakfast, Nia and I mostly listened to Izzy's chatter.

"—and then Vonique's all like, 'But the way I remember it is the towers were next to the harbor, not near the zoo.' And Eddie goes, 'Na-huh, they were right where the park started.' And they couldn't agree and they were gonna start a fight, until I figured out that they were talking about two different places! Vonique meant the Goblin Towers, and Eddie meant the Towers of Bone! So I straightened them out, and now the map of Djamala is like almost half done!"

"That's wonderful, honey."

"It's a real skill, being a peacemaker like that."

Izzy cocked her head and regarded me quizzically. "But that's just what I've always been forever."

In the next instant she was up and kissing her mother, then out the hall and raising puffs of dust as she ran toward where I could see other kids seemingly waiting for her.

Nia and I spent the morning wandering around the camp, talking about anything and everything—except my ancient, recent disgrace. We watched a pickup soccer game for an hour or so, the players expending the bottled energy that would have gone to work and home before the disaster, then ended up back at her tent around three.

Today was as warm as yesterday, and we raised a pretty good sweat. Nia dropped off to sleep right after, but I couldn't.

Eleven days after the flood, and it was all I could dream about.

* * *

Ethan was really starting to get on my nerves. He had seen me hanging out with Nia and Izzy, and used the new knowledge to taunt me.

"What's up with you and the little girl, Hedges? Thinking of keeping your hand in with some target practice?"

I stood quivering over his bunk before I even realized I had moved. My fists were bunched at my hips, ready to strike. But both Ethan and I knew I wouldn't.

The penalty for fighting at any of the Femavilles was instant expulsion, and an end to government charity. I couldn't risk losing Nia now that I had found her. Even if we managed to stay in touch while apart, who was to say that the fluid milieu of the post-disaster environment would not conspire to supplant our relationship with another.

So I stalked out and went to see Hannah Lawes.

One complex of tents hosted the bureaucrats. Lawes sat at a folding table with her omnipresent laptop. Hooked to a printer, the machine was churning out travel vouchers branded with official glyphs of authenticity.

"Mr. Hedges. What can I do for you? Have you decided to take up one of the host offerings? There's a farming community in Nebraska—"

I shook my head in the negative. Trying to imagine myself relocated to the prairies was so disorienting that I almost forgot why I had come here.

Hannah Lawes seemed disappointed by my refusal of her proposal, but realistic about the odds that I would've accepted. "I can't say I'm surprised. Not many people are leaping at what I can offer. I've only gotten three takers so far. And I can't figure out why. They're all generous, sensible berths."

"Yeah, sure. That's the problem."

"What do you mean?"

"No one wants 'sensible' after what they've been through. We all want to be reborn as phoenixes—not drayhorses. That's all that would justify our sufferings."

Hannah Lawes said nothing for a moment, and only the minor whine of the printer filigreed the bubble of silence around us. When she spoke, her voice was utterly neutral.

"You could die here before you achieve that dream, Mr. Hedges. Now, how can I help you, if not with a permanent relocation?"

"If I arrange different living quarters with the consent of everyone involved, is there any regulation stopping me from switching tents?"

"No, not at all."

"Good. I'll be back."

I tracked down Nia and found her using a piece of exercise equipment donated by a local gym. She hopped off and hugged me.

"Have to do something about my weight. I'm not used to all this lolling around."

Nia had been a waitress back in the city, physically active eight or more hours daily. My own routines, at least since Calley left me, had involved more couch-potato time than mountain climbing, and the sloth of camp life sat easier on me.

We hugged, her body sweaty in my arms, and I explained my problem.

"I realize we haven't known each other very long, Nia, but do you think—"

"I'd like it if you moved in with Izzy and me, Parrish. One thing the tsunami taught us—life's too short to dither. And I'd feel safer."

"No one's been bothering you, have they?"

"No, but there's just too many weird noises out here in the country. Every time a branch creaks, I think someone's climbing my steps."

I hugged her again, harder, in wordless thanks.

We both went back to Lawes and arranged the new tent assignments.

When I went to collect my few possessions, Ethan sneered at me.

"Knew you'd run, Hedges. Without your badge, you're nothing."

As I left, I wondered what I had been even with my badge.

* * *

Living with Nia and Izzy, I naturally became more involved in the young girl's activities.

And that's when I learned about Djamala.

By the end of the second week in Femaville 29, the atmosphere had begun to sour. The false exuberance engendered by sheer survival amidst so much death—and the accompanying sense of newly opened horizons—had dissipated. In place of these emotions came anomie, irritability, anger, despair, and a host of other negative feelings. The immutable, unchanging confines of the unfenced camp assumed the proportions of a stalag. The food, objectively unchanged in quality or quantity, met with disgust, simply because we had no control over its creation. The shared privies assumed a stink no amount of bleach could dispel.

Mere conversation and gossip had paled, replaced with disproportionate arguments over inconsequentials. Sports gave way to various games of chance, played with the odd pair of dice or deck of cards, with bets denominated in sex or clothing or desserts.

One or two serious fights resulted in the promised expulsions, and, chastened but surly, combatants restrained themselves to shoving matches and catcalls.

A few refugees, eager for stimulation and a sense of normality, made the long trek into town—and found themselves returned courtesy of local police cars.

The bureaucrats managing the camp—Hannah Lawes and her peers—were not immune to the shifting psychic tenor of Femaville 29. From models of optimism and can-do effectiveness, the officials began to slide into terse minimalist responses.

"I don't know what more we can do," Hannah Lawes told me. "If our best efforts to reintegrate everyone as functioning and productive members of society are not appreciated, then—"

She left the consequences unstated, merely shaking her head ruefully at our ingratitude and sloth.

The one exception to this general malaise were the children.

Out of a thousand people in Femaville 29, approximately two hundred were children younger than twelve. Although sometimes their numbers seemed larger, as they raced through the camp's streets and avenues in boisterous packs. Seemingly unaffected by the unease and dissatisfaction exhibited by their guardians and parents, the kids continued to enjoy their pastoral interlude. School, curfews, piano lessons—all shed in a return to a prelapsarian existence as hunter-gatherers of the twenty-first century.

When they weren't involved in traditional games, they massed on the outskirts of the camp for an utterly novel undertaking.

There, I discovered, they were building a new city to replace the one they had lost.

Or, perhaps, simply mapping one that already existed.

And Izzy Horsley, I soon learned (with actually very little surprise), was one of the prime movers of this jovial, juvenile enterprise.

With no tools other than their feet and hands, the children had cleared a space almost as big as a football field of all vegetation, leaving behind a dusty canvas on which to construct their representation of an imaginary city.

Three weeks into its construction, the map-cum-model had assumed impressive dimensions, despite the rudimentary nature of its materials.

I came for the first time to the site one afternoon when I grew tired of continuously keeping Nia company in the exercise tent. Her own angst about ensuring the best future for herself and loved ones had manifested as an obsession with "keeping fit" that I couldn't force myself to share. With my mind drifting, a sudden curiosity about where Izzy was spending so much of her time stole over me, and I ambled over to investigate.

Past the ultimate tents, I came upon what could have been a construction site reimagined for the underage cast of *Sesame Street*.

The youngest children were busy assembling stockpiles of stones and twigs and leaves. The stones were quarried from the immediate vicinity, emerging still wet with loam, while sticks and leaves came from a nearby copse in long disorderly caravans.

Older children were engaged in two different kinds of tasks. One chore involved using long pointed sticks to gouge lines in the dirt: lines that plainly marked streets, natural features and the outlines of buildings. The second set of workers was elaborating these outlines with the organic materials from the stockpiles. The map was mostly flat, but occasionally a structure, teepee or cairn, rose up a few inches.

The last, smallest subset of workers were the architects: the designers, engineers, imagineers of the city. They stood off to one side, consulting, arguing, issuing orders, and sometimes venturing right into the map to correct the placement of lines or ornamentation.

Izzy was one of these elite.

Deep in discussion with a cornrowed black girl and a pudgy white boy wearing smudged glasses, Izzy failed to note my approach, and so I was able to overhear their talk. Izzy was holding forth at the moment.

"—Sprankle Hall covers two whole blocks, not just one! C'mon, you gotta remember that! Remember when we went there for a concert, and after, we wanted to go around back to the door where the musicians were coming out, and how long it took us to get there?"

The black girl frowned, then said, "Yeah, right, we had to walk like forever. But if Sprankle Hall goes from Cleverly Street all the way to Khush Lane, then how does Pinemarten Avenue run without a break?"

The fat boy spoke with assurance. "It's the Redondo Tunnel. Goes under Sprankle Hall."

Izzy and the black girl grinned broadly. "Of course! I remember when that was built!"

I must have made some noise then, for the children finally noticed me. Izzy rushed over and gave me a quick embrace.

"Hey, Parrish! What're you doing here?"

"I came to see what was keeping you guys so busy. What's going on here?"

Izzy's voice expressed no adult embarrassment, doubt, irony or blasé dismissal of a temporary time-killing project. "We're building a city! Djamala! It's someplace wonderful!"

The black girl nodded solemnly. I recalled the name Vonique from Izzy's earlier conversation, and the name seemed suddenly inextricably linked to this child.

"Well," said Vonique, "it *will* be wonderful, once we finish it. But right now it's still a *mess*."

"This city—Djamala? How did it come to be? Who invented it?"

"Nobody *invented* it!" Izzy exclaimed. "It's always been there. We just couldn't remember it until the wave."

The boy—Eddie?—said, "That's right, sir. The tsunami made it rise up."

"Rise up? Out of the waters, like Atlantis? A new continent?"

Eddie pushed his glasses further up his nose. "Not out of the ocean. Out of our minds."

My expression must have betrayed disbelief. Izzy grabbed one of my hands with both of hers. "Parrish, please! This is really important for everyone. You gotta believe in Djamala! Really!"

"Well, I don't know if I *can* believe in it the same way you kids can. But what if I promise just not to *dis*believe yet? Would that be good enough?"

Vonique puffed air past her lips in a semi-contemptuous manner. "Huh! I suppose that's as good as we're gonna get from anyone, until we can show them something they can't ignore."

Izzy gazed up at me with imploring eyes. "Parrish? You're not gonna let us down, are you?"

What could I say? "No, no, of course not. If I can watch and learn, maybe I can start to understand."

Izzy, Vonique and Eddie had to confer with several other pint-sized architects before they could grant me observer's status, but eventually they did confer that honor on me.

So for the next several days I spent most of my time with the children as they constructed their imaginary metropolis.

At first, I was convinced that the whole process was merely some over-elaborated coping strategy for dealing with the disaster that had upended their young lives.

But at the end of a week, I was not so certain.

So long as I did not get in the way of construction, I was allowed to venture down the outlined HO-scale streets, given a tour of the city's extensive features and history by whatever young engineer was least in demand at the moment. The story of Djamala's ancient founding, its history and contemporary life, struck me as remarkably coherent and consistent at the time, although I did not pay as much attention as I should have to the information. I theorized then that the children were merely re-sorting a thousand borrowed bits and pieces from television, films and video games. Now, I can barely recall a few salient details. The Crypt of the Thousand Martyrs, the Bluepoint Aerial Tramway, Penton Park, Winkelreed Slough, Midwinter Festival, the Squid Club—These proper names, delivered in the pure, piping voices of Izzy and her peers, are all that remain to me.

I wished I could get an aerial perspective on the diagram of Djamala. It seemed impossibly refined and balanced to have been plotted out solely from a ground-level perspective. Like the South American drawings at Nazca, its complex lineaments seemed to demand a superior view from some impossible, more-than-mortal vantage point.

After a week spent observing the children—a week during which a light evening rain shower did much damage to Djamala, damage which the children industriously and cheerfully began repairing—a curious visual hallucination overtook me.

Late afternoon sunlight slanted across the map of Djamala as the children began to tidy up in preparation for quitting. Sitting on a borrowed folding chair, I watched their small forms, dusted in gold, move along eccentric paths. My mind commenced to drift amidst wordless regions. The burden of my own body seemed to fall away.

At that moment, the city of Djamala began to assume a ghostly reality, translucent buildings rearing skyward. Ghostly minarets, stadia, pylons—

I jumped up, heart thumping to escape my chest, frightened to my core.

Memory of a rubbish-filled, clammy, partially illuminated hallway, and the shadow of a gunman, pierced me.

My senses had betrayed me fatally once before. How could I ever fully trust them again?

Djamala vanished then, and I was relieved.

* * *

A herd of government-drafted school buses materialized one Thursday on the outskirts of Femaville 29, on the opposite side of the camp from Djamala, squatting like empty-eyed yellow elephants, and I knew that the end of the encampment was imminent. But exactly how soon would we be expelled to more permanent quarters not of our choosing? I went to see Hannah Lawes.

I tracked down the social worker in the kitchen of the camp. She was efficiently taking inventory of cases of canned goods.

"Ms. Lawes, can I talk to you?"

A small hard smile quirked one corner of her lips. "Mr. Hedges. Have you had a sudden revelation about your future?"

"Yes, in a way. Those buses—"

"Are not scheduled for immediate use. FEMA believes in proper advance staging of resources."

"But when—"

"Who can say? I assure you that I don't personally make such command decisions. But I will pass along any new directives as soon as I am permitted."

Unsatisfied, I left her tallying creamed corn and green beans.

Everyone in the camp, of course, had seen the buses, and speculation about the fate of Femaville 29 was rampant. Were we to be dispersed to public housing in various host cities? Was the camp to be merged with others into a larger concentration of refugees for economy of scale? Maybe we'd all be put to work restoring our mortally wounded drowned city. Every possibility looked equally likely.

I expected Nia's anxiety to be keyed up by the threat of dissolution of our hard-won small share of stability, this island of improvised family life we had forged. But instead, she surprised me by expressing complete confidence in the future.

"I can't worry about what's coming, Parrish. We're together now, with a roof over our heads, and that's all that counts. Besides, just lately I've gotten a good feeling about the days ahead."

"Based on what?"

Nia shrugged with a smile. "Who knows?"

The children, however, Izzy included, were not quite as sanguine as Nia. The coming of the buses had goaded them to greater activity. No longer did they divide the day into periods of conventional playtime and construction of their city of dreams. Instead, they labored at the construction full-time.

The antlike trains of bearers ferried vaster quantities of sticks and leaves, practically denuding the nearby copse. The grubbers-up of pebbles broke their nails uncomplainingly in the soil. The scribers of lines ploughed empty square footage into new districts like the most rapacious of suburban developers. The ornamentation crew thatched and laid mosaics furiously. And the elite squad overseeing all the activity wore themselves out like military strategists overseeing an invasion.

"What do we build today?"

"The docks at Kannuckaden."

"But we haven't even put down the Mocambo River yet!"

"Then do the river first! But we have to fill in the Great Northeastern Range before tomorrow!"

"What about Gopher Gulch?"

"That'll be next."

Befriending some kitchen help secured me access to surplus cartons of pre-packaged treats. I took to bringing the snacks to the hard-working children, and they seemed to appreciate it. Although truthfully, they spared little enough attention to me or any other adult, lost in their make-believe, laboring blank-eyed or with feverish intensity.

The increased activity naturally attracted the notice of the adults. Many heretofore-oblivious parents showed up at last to see what their kids were doing. The consensus was that such behavior, while a little weird, was generally harmless enough, and actually positive, insofar as it kept the children from boredom and any concomitant pestering of parents. After a few days of intermittent parental visits, the site was generally clear of adults once more.

One exception to this rule was Ethan Duplessix.

At first, I believed, he began hanging around Djamala solely because he saw me there. Peeved by how I had escaped his taunts, he looked for some new angle from which to attack me, relishing the helplessness of his old nemesis.

But as I continued to ignore the slobby criminal slacker, failing to give him any satisfaction, his frustrated focus turned naturally to what the children were actually doing. My lack of standing as any kind of legal guardian to anyone except, at even the widest stretch of the term, Izzy, meant that I could not prevent the children from talking to him.

They answered Ethan's questions respectfully and completely at first, and I could see interest building in his self-serving brain, as he rotated the facts this way and that, seeking some advantage for himself. But then the children grew tired of his gawking and cut him off.

"We have too much work to do. You've got to go now."

"Please, Mr. Duplessix, just leave us alone."

I watched Ethan's expression change from greedy curiosity to anger. He actually threatened the children.

"You damn kids! You need to share! Or else someone'll just take what you've got!"

I was surprised at the fervor of Ethan's interest in Djamala. Maybe something about the dream project had actually touched a decent, imaginative part of his soul. But whatever the case, his threats gave me a valid excuse to hustle him off.

"You can't keep me away, Hedges! I'll be back!"

Izzy stood by my side, watching Ethan's retreat.

"Don't worry about him," I said.

"I'm not worried, Parrish. Djamala can protect itself."

The sleeping arrangements in the tent Nia, Izzy and I shared involved a hanging blanket down the middle of the tent, to give both Izzy and us adults some privacy. Nia and I had pushed two cots together on our side and lashed them together to make a double bed. But even with a folded blanket atop the wooden bar down the middle of the makeshift bed, I woke up several times a night, as I instinctively tried to snuggle Nia and encountered the hard obstacle. Nia, smaller, slept fine on her side of the double cots.

The night after the incident with Ethan, I woke up as usual in the small hours of the morning. Something urged me to get up. I left the cot and stepped around the hanging barrier to check on Izzy.

Her cot was empty, only blankets holding a ghostly imprint of her small form.

I was just on the point of mounting a general alarm when she slipped back into the tent, clad in pajamas and dew-wet sneakers.

My presence startled her, but she quickly recovered, and smiled guiltlessly.

"Bathroom call?" I whispered.

Izzy never lied. "No. Just checking on Djamala. It's safe now. Today we finished the Iron Grotto. Just in time."

"That's good. Back to sleep now."

Ethan Duplessix had never missed a meal in his life. But the morning after Izzy's nocturnal inspection of Djamala, he was nowhere to be seen at any of the three breakfast shifts. Likewise for lunch. When he failed to show at supper, I went to D-30.

Ethan's sparse possessions remained behind, but the man himself was not there. I reported his absence to Hannah Lawes.

"Please don't concern yourself unnecessarily, Mr. Hedges. I'm sure Mr. Duplessix will turn up soon. He probably spent the night in intimate circumstances with someone."

"Ethan? I didn't realize the camp boasted any female trolls."

"Now, now, Mr. Hedges, that's most ungenerous of you."

Ethan did not surface the next day, or the day after that, and was eventually marked a runaway.

The third week of October brought the dreaded announcement. Lulled by the gentle autumnal weather, the unvarying routines of the camp, and by the lack of any foreshadowings, the citizens of Femaville 29 were completely unprepared for the impact.

A general order to assemble outside by the buses greeted every diner at breakfast. Shortly before noon, a thousand refugees, clad in their donated coats and sweaters and jackets, shuffled their feet on the field that doubled as parking lot, breath pluming in the October chill. The ranks of buses remained as before, save for one unwelcome difference.

The motors of the buses were all idling, drivers behind their steering wheels.

The bureaucrats had assembled on a small raised platform. I saw Hannah Lawes in the front, holding a loud-hailer. Her booming voice assailed us.

"It's time now for your relocation. You've had a fair and lawful amount of time to choose your destination, but have failed to take advantage of this opportunity. Now your government has done so for you. Please board the buses in an orderly fashion. Your possessions will follow later."

"Where are we going?" someone called out.

Imperious, Hannah Lawes answered, "You'll find out when you arrive."

Indignation and confusion bloomed in the crowd. A contradictory babble began to mount heavenward. Hannah Lawes said nothing more immediately. I assumed she was waiting for the chaotic reaction to burn itself out, leaving the refugees sheepishly ready to obey.

But she hadn't countered on the children intervening.

A massed juvenile shriek brought silence in its wake. There was nothing wrong with the children gathered on the edges of the crowd, as evidenced by their nervous smiles. But their tactic had certainly succeeded in drawing everyone's attention.

Izzy was up front of her peers, and she shouted now, her young voice proud and confident.

"Follow us! We've made a new home for everyone!"

The children turned as one and began trotting away toward Djamala.

For a frozen moment, none of the adults made a move. Then, a man and woman—Vonique's parents—set out after the children.

Their departure catalyzed a mad general desperate rush, toward a great impossible unknown that could only be better than the certainty offered by FEMA.

Nia had been standing by my side, but she was swept away. I caught a last glimpse of her smiling, shining face as she looked back for a moment over her shoulder. Then the crowd carried her off.

I found myself hesitating. How could I face the inevitable crushing disappointment of the children, myself, and everyone else when their desperate hopes were met by a metropolis of sticks and stones and pebbles? Being there when it happened, seeing all the hurt, crestfallen faces at the instant they were forced to acknowledge defeat, would be sheer torture. Why not just wait here for their predestined return, when we could pretend the mass insanity had never happened, mount the buses and roll off, chastised and broken, to whatever average future was being offered to us?

Hannah Lawes had sidled up to me, loud-hailer held by her side.

"I'm glad to see at least one sensible person here, Mr. Hedges. Congratulations for being a realist."

Her words, her barely concealed glee and schadenfreude, instantly flipped a switch inside me from off to on, and I sped after my fellow refugees.

Halfway through the encampment, I glanced up to see Djamala looming ahead.

The splendors I had seen in ghostly fashion weeks ago were now magnified and recomplicated across acres of space. A city woven of childish imagination stretched impossibly to the horizon and beyond, its towers and monuments sparkling in the sun.

I left the last tents behind me in time to see the final stragglers entering the streets of Djamala. I heard water splash from fountains, shoes tapping on shale sidewalks, laughter echoing down wide boulevards.

But at the same time, I could see only a memory of myself in a ruined building, gun in hand, confronting a shadow assassin.

Which was reality?

I faltered to a stop.

Djamala vanished in a blink.

And I fell insensible to the ground.

I awoke in the tent that served as the infirmary for Femaville 29. Hannah

Lawes was sitting by my bedside.

"Feeling better, Mr. Hedges? You nearly disrupted the exodus."

"What—what do you mean?"

"Your fellow refugees. They've all been bussed to their next station in life."

I sat up on my cot. "What are you trying to tell me? Didn't you see the city, Djamala? Didn't you see it materialize where the children built it? Didn't you see all the refugees flood in?"

Hannah Lawes's cocoa skin drained of vitality as she sought to master what were evidently strong emotions in conflict.

"What I saw doesn't matter, Mr. Hedges. It's what the government has determined to have happened that matters. And the government has marked all your fellow refugees from Femaville 29 as settled elsewhere in the normal fashion. Case closed. Only you remain behind to be dealt with. Your fate is separate from theirs now. You certainly won't be seeing any of your temporary neighbors again for some time—if ever."

I recalled the spires and lakes, the pavilions and theaters of Djamala. I pictured Ethan Duplessix rattling the bars of the Iron Grotto. I was sure he'd reform, and be set free eventually. I pictured Nia and Izzy, swanning about in festive apartments, happy and safe, with Izzy enjoying the fruits of her labors.

And myself the lame child left behind by the Pied Piper.

"No," I replied, "I don't suppose I will see them again soon."

Hannah Lawes smiled at my acceptance of her dictates, but only for a moment, until I spoke again.

"But then, you can never be sure."

SOB IN THE SILENCE

GENE WOLFE

Gene Wolfe worked as an engineer, before becoming editor of trade journal *Plant Engineering*. He came to prominence as a writer in the late '60s with a sequence of short stories—including "The Hero as Werewolf", "Seven American Nights", and "The Island of Doctor Death and Other Stories"—in Damon Knight's *Orbit* anthologies. His early major novels were *The Fifth Head of Cerberus* and *Peace*, but he established his reputation with a sequence of three long multi-volume novels—*The Book of the New Sun* (4 vols), *The Book of the Long Sun* (4 vols), *The Book of the Short Sun* (3 vols)—and pendant volume, *The Urth of the New Sun*. Wolfe has published a number of short story collections, including *The Island of Doctor Death and Other Stories and Other Stories*, *Endangered Species*, and *Strange Travelers*. He has won the Nebula Award and World Fantasy Award twice, the Locus Award four times, the John W. Campbell Memorial Award, the British Fantasy Award, the British SF Award, and is the recipient of the World Fantasy Award for Lifetime Achievement. Wolfe's most recent book is the novel *Soldier of Sidon*. Upcoming is new novel Pirate Freedom.

Stories by writers featuring writers have a long and distinguished history, and it's not that unusual for them to come to a sticky end of one kind or another. Of course, that's not always the way it works out…

"This," the horror writer told the family visiting him, "is beyond any question the least haunted house in the Midwest. No ghost, none at all, will come within miles of the place. So I am assured."

Robbie straightened his little glasses and mumbled, "Well, it looks haunted."

"It does, young man." After teetering between seven and eight, the horror writer decided that Robbie was about seven. "It's the filthy yellow stucco. No doubt it was a cheerful yellow once, but God only knows how long it's been up. I'm going to have it torn off, every scrap of it, and put up fresh, which I will paint white."

"Can't you just paint over?" Kiara asked. (Kiara of the all-conquering pout,

419

of the golden hair and the tiny silver earrings.)

Looking very serious, the horror writer nodded. And licked his lips only mentally. "I've tried, believe me. That hideous color is the result of air pollution—of smoke, soot, and dirt, if you will—that has clung to the stucco. Paint over it, and it bleeds out through the new paint. Washing—"

"Water jets under high pressure." Dan was Robbie's father, and Kiara's. "You can rent the units, or buy one for a thousand or so."

"I own one," the horror writer told him. "With a strong cleaning agent added to the water, it will do the job." He paused to smile. "Unfortunately, the stucco's old and fragile. Here and there, a good jet breaks it."

"Ghosts," Charity said. Charity was Mrs. Dan, a pudgy woman with a soft, not unattractive face and a remarkable talent for dowdy hats. "Please go back to your ghosts. I find ghosts far more interesting."

"As do I." The horror writer favored her with his most dazzling smile. "I've tried repeatedly to interest psychic researchers in the old place, which has a—may I call it fascinating? History. I've been persuasive and persistent, and no less than three teams have checked this old place out as a result. All three have reported that they found nothing. No evidence whatsoever. No spoor of spooks. No cooperative specters a struggling author might use for research purposes."

"And publicity," Kiara said. "Don't forget publicity. I plan to get into public relations when I graduate."

"And publicity, you're right. By the time you're well settled in public relations, I hope to be wealthy enough to engage you. If I am, I will. That's a promise."

Charity leveled a plump forefinger. "You, on the other hand, have clearly seen or heard or felt something. You had to have something more than this big dark living-room to get the psychics in, and you had it. Tell us."

The horror writer produced a sharply bent briar that showed signs of years of use. "Will this trouble anyone? I rarely smoke in here, but if we're going to have a good long chat—well, a pipe may make things go more smoothly. Would anyone care for a drink?"

Charity was quickly equipped with white wine, Dan with Johnnie-Walker-and-water, and Robbie with cola. "A lot of the kids drink beer at IVY Tech," Kiara announced in a tone that indicated she was one of them. "I don't, though."

"Not until you're twenty-one," Dan said firmly.

"You see?" She pouted.

The horror writer nodded. "I do indeed. One of the things I see is that you have good parents, parents who care about you and are zealous for your welfare." He slipped Kiara a scarcely perceptible wink. "What about a plain soda? I always find soda water over ice refreshing, myself."

Charity said, "That would be fine, if she wants it."

Kiara said she did, and he became busy behind the bar.

Robbie had been watching the dark upper corners of the old, high-ceilinged room. "I thought I saw one."

"A ghost?" The horror writer looked up, his blue eyes twinkling.

"A bat. Maybe we can catch it."

Dan said, "There's probably a belfry, too."

"I'm afraid not. Perhaps I'll add one once I get the new stucco on."

"You need one. As I've told my wife a dozen times, anybody who believes in ghosts has bats in his belfry."

"It's better, perhaps," Charity murmured, "if living things breathe and move up there. Better than just bells, rotting ropes, and dust. Tell us more about this place, please."

"It was a country house originally." With the air of one who performed a sacrament, the horror writer poured club soda into a tall frosted glass that already contained five ice cubes and (wholly concealed by his fingers) a generous two inches of vodka. "A quiet place in which a wealthy family could get away from the heat and stench of city summers. The family was ruined somehow—I don't recall the details. I know it's usually the man who kills in murder-suicides, but in this house it was the woman. She shot her husband and her stepdaughters, and killed herself."

Charity said, "I could never bring myself to do that. I could never kill Dan. Or his children. I suppose I might kill myself. That's conceivable. But not the rest."

Straight-faced, the horror writer handed his frosted glass to Kiara. "I couldn't kill myself," he told her. "I like myself too much. Other people? Who can say?"

Robbie banged down his cola. "You're trying to scare us!"

"Of course I am. It's my trade."

Dan asked, "They all died? That's good shooting."

The horror writer resumed his chair and picked up his briar. "No. As a matter of fact they didn't. One of the three stepdaughters survived. She had been shot in the head at close range, yet she lived."

Dan said, "Happens sometime."

"It does. It did in this case. Her name was Maude Parkhurst. Maude was a popular name back around nineteen hundred, which is when her parents and sisters died. Ever hear of her?"

Dan shook his head.

"She was left penniless and scarred for life. It seems to have disordered her thinking. Or perhaps the bullet did it. In any event, she founded her own church and was its pope and prophetess. It was called—maybe it's still called, since it may still be around for all I know—the Unionists of Heaven and Earth."

Charity said, "I've heard of it. It sounded innocent enough."

The horror writer shrugged. "Today? Perhaps it is. Back then, I would say no. Decidedly no. It was, in its own fantastic fashion, about as repellent as a cult can be. May I call it a cult?"

Kiara grinned prettily over her glass. "Go right ahead. I won't object."

"A friend of mine, another Dan, once defined a cult for me. He said that if the leader gets all the women, it's a cult."

Dan nodded. "Good man. There's a lot to that."

"There is, but in the case of the UHE, as it was called, it didn't apply. Maude Parkhurst didn't want the women, or the men either. The way to get to Heaven, she told her followers, was to live like angels here on earth."

Dan snorted.

"Exactly. Any sensible person would have told them that they were not angels. That it was natural and right for angels to live like angels, but that men and women should live like human beings."

"We really know almost nothing about angels." Charity looked pensive. "Just that they carry the Lord's messages. It's Saint Paul, I think, who says that each of us has an angel who acts as our advocate in Heaven. So we know that, too. But it's really very little."

"This is about sex," Kiara said. "I smell it coming."

The horror writer nodded. "You're exactly right, and I'm beginning to wonder if you're not the most intelligent person here. It is indeed. Members of the UHE were to refrain from all forms of sexual activity. If unmarried, they were not to marry. If married, they were to separate and remain separated."

"The University of Heaven at Elysium. On a T-shirt. I can see it now."

Charity coughed, the sound of it scarcely audible in the large, dark room. "Well, Kiara, I don't see anything wrong with that if it was voluntary."

"Neither do I," the horror writer said, "but there's more. Those wishing to join underwent an initiation period of a year. At the end of that time, there was a midnight ceremony. If they had children, those children had to attend, all of them. There they watched their parents commit suicide—or that's how it looked. I don't know the details, but I know that at the end of the service they were carried out of the church, apparently lifeless and covered with blood."

Charity whispered, "Good God...."

"When the congregation had gone home," the horror writer continued, "the children were brought here. They were told that it was an orphanage, and it was operated like one. Before long it actually was one. Apparently there was some sort of tax advantage, so it was registered with the state as a church-run foundation, and from time to time the authorities sent actual orphans here. It was the age of orphanages, as you may know. Few children, if any, were put in foster homes. Normally, it was the orphanage for any child without parents or close relatives."

Dan said, "There used to be a comic strip about it, 'Little Orphan Annie.'"

The horror writer nodded. "Based upon a popular poem of the nineteenth century.

"'Little Orphant Annie's come to our house to stay,
An' wash the cups an' saucers up,
    an' brush the crumbs away,
An' shoo the chickens off the porch,
    an' dust the hearth an' sweep,
An' make the fire, an' bake the bread,
    an' earn her board an' keep.
An' all us other children,
    when the supper things is done,
We set around the kitchen fire an' has the mostest fun
A-list'nin' to the witch tales 'at Annie tells about,
An' the Gobble-uns 'at gets you
            Ef you
          Don't
        Watch
          Out!'

"You see," the horror writer finished, smiling, "in those days you could get an orphan girl from such an orphanage as this to be your maid of all work and baby-sitter. You fed and clothed her, gave her a place to sleep, and paid her nothing at all. Despite being showered with that sort of kindness, those girls picked up enough of the monstrosity and lonely emptiness of the universe to become the first practitioners of my art, the oral recounters of horrific tales whose efforts preceded all horror writing."

"Was it really so bad for them?" Kiara asked.

"Here? Worse. I haven't told you the worst yet, you see. Indeed, I haven't even touched upon it." The horror writer turned to Dan. "Perhaps you'd like to send Robbie out. That might be advisable."

Dan shrugged. "He watches TV. I doubt that anything you'll say will frighten him."

Charity pursed her lips but said nothing.

The horror writer had taken advantage of the pause to light his pipe. "You don't have to stay, Robbie." He puffed fragrant white smoke, and watched it begin its slow climb to the ceiling. "You know where your room is, and you may go anywhere in the house unless you meet with a locked door."

Kiara smiled. "Secrets! We're in Bluebeard's cashel—castle. I knew it!"

"No secrets," the horror writer told her, "just a very dangerous cellar stair—steep, shaky, and innocent of any sort of railing."

Robbie whispered, "I'm not going."

"So I see. From time to time, Robbie, one of the children would learn or guess that his parents were not in fact dead. When that happened, he or she might try to get away and return home. I've made every effort to learn just how often that happened, but the sources are contradictory on the point. Some say three and some five, and one says more than twenty. I should add that we who perform this type of research soon learn to be wary of the number three. It's the favorite of those who don't know the real number. There are several places on the grounds that may once have been graves—unmarked graves long since emptied by the authorities. But—"

Charity leaned toward him, her face tense. "Do you mean to say that those children were killed?"

The horror writer nodded. "I do. Those who were returned here by their parents were. That is the most horrible fact attached to this really quite awful old house. Or at least, it is the worst we know of—perhaps the worst that occurred."

He drew on his pipe, letting smoke trickle from his nostrils. "A special midnight service was held here, in this room in which we sit. At that service the church members are said to have flown. To have fluttered about this room like so many strange birds. No doubt they ran and waved their arms, as children sometimes do. Very possibly they thought they flew. The members of medieval witch cults seem really to have believed that they flew to the gatherings of their covens, although no sane person supposes they actually did."

Charity asked, "But you say they killed the children?"

The horror writer nodded. "Yes, at the end of the ceremony. Call it the children's hour, a term that some authorities say they used themselves. They shot them as Maude Parkhurst's father and sisters had been shot. The executioner was chosen by lot. Maude is said to have hoped aloud that it would fall to her, as it seems to have done more than once. Twice at least."

Dan said, "It's hard to believe anybody would really do that."

"Perhaps it is, although news broadcasts have told me of things every bit as bad. Or worse."

The horror writer drew on his pipe again, and the room had grown dark enough that the red glow from its bowl lit his face from below. "The children were asleep by that time, as Maude, her father, and her sisters had been. The lucky winner crept into the child's bedroom, accompanied by at least one other member who carried a candle. The moment the shot was fired, the candle was blown out. The noise would've awakened any other children who had been sleeping in that room, of course; but they awakened only to darkness and the smell of gun smoke."

Dan said, "Angels!" There was a world of contempt in the word.

"There are angels in Hell," the horror writer told him, "not just in Heaven. Indeed, the angels of Hell may be the more numerous."

Charity pretended to yawn while nodding her reluctant agreement. "I think it's time we all went up bed. Don't you?"

Dan said, "I certainly do. I drove one hell of a long way today."

Kiara lingered when the others had gone. "Ish really nice meeting you." She swayed as she spoke, though only slightly. "Don' forget I get to be your public relations agent. You promised."

"You have my word." The horror writer smiled, knowing how much his word was worth.

For a lingering moment they clasped hands. "Ish hard to believe," she said, "that you were Dad's roommate. You sheem—seem—so much younger."

He thanked her and watched her climb the wide curved staircase that had been the pride of the Parkhursts long ago, wondering all the while whether she knew that he was watching. Whether she knew or not, watching Kiara climb stairs was too great a pleasure to surrender.

On the floor above, Charity was getting Robbie ready for bed. "You're a brave boy, I know. Aren't you a brave boy, darling? Say it, please. It always helps to say it."

"I'm a brave boy," Robbie told her dutifully.

"You are. I know you are. You won't let that silly man downstairs fool you. You'll stay in your own bed, in your own room, and get a good night's sleep. We'll do some sightseeing tomorrow, forests and lakes and rugged hills where the worked-out mines hide."

Charity hesitated, gnawing with small white teeth at her full lower lip. "There's no nightlight in here, I'm afraid, but I've got a little flashlight in my purse. I could lend you that. Would you like it?"

Robbie nodded, and clasped Charity's little plastic flashlight tightly as he watched her leave. Her hand—the one without rings—reached up to the light switch. Her fingers found it.

There was darkness.

He located the switch again with the watery beam of the disposable flashlight, knowing that he would be scolded (perhaps even spanked) if he switched the solitary overhead light back on but wanting to know exactly where that switch was, just in case.

At last he turned Charity's flashlight off and lay down. It was hot in the too-large, too-empty room. Hot and silent.

He sat up again, and aimed the flashlight toward the window. It was indeed open, but open only the width of his hand. He got out of bed, dropped the flashlight into the shirt pocket of his pajamas, and tried to raise the window farther. No effort he could put forth would budge it.

At last he lay down again, and the room felt hotter than ever.

When he had looked out through the window, it had seemed terribly high. How many flights of stairs had they climbed to get up here? He could remember only one, wide carpeted stairs that had curved as they climbed; but that one had been a long, long stair. From the window he had seen the tops of trees.

Treetops and stars. The moon had been out, lighting the lawn below and showing him the dark leaves of the treetops, although the moon itself had not been in sight from the window.

"It walks across the sky," he told himself. Dan, his father, had said that once.

"You could walk...." The voice seemed near, but faint and thin.

Robbie switched the flashlight back on. There was no one there.

Under the bed, he thought. They're under the bed.

But he dared not leave the bed to look, and lay down once more. An older person would have tried to persuade himself that he had imagined the voice, or would have left the bed to investigate. Robbie did neither. His line between palpable and imagined things was blurred and faint, and he had not the slightest desire to see the speaker, whether that speaker was real or make-believe.

There were no other windows that might be opened. He thought of going out. The hall would be dark, but Dan and Charity were sleeping in a room not very far away. The door of their room might be locked, though. They did that sometimes.

He would be scolded in any event. Scolded and perhaps spanked, too. It was not the pain he feared, but the humiliation. "I'll have to go back here," he whispered to himself. "Even if they don't spank me, I'll have to go back."

"You could walk away...." A girl's voice, very faint. From the ceiling? No, Robbie decided, from the side toward the door.

"No," he said. "They'd be mad."

"You'll die...."

"Like us...."

Robbie sat up, shaking.

* * *

Outside, the horror writer was hiking toward the old, rented truck he had parked more than a mile away. The ground was soft after yesterday's storm, and it was essential—absolutely essential—that there be tracks left by a strange vehicle.

A turn onto a side road, a walk of a hundred yards, and the beam of his big electric lantern picked out the truck among the trees. When he could set the lantern on its hood, he put on latex gloves. Soon, very soon, the clock would strike the children's hour and Edith with the golden hair would be his. Beautiful Kiara would be his. As for laughing Allegra, he neither knew nor cared who she might be.

"Wa' ish?" Kiara's voice was thick with vodka and sleep.

"It's only me," Robbie told her, and slipped under the covers. "I'm scared."

She put a protective arm around him.

"There are other kids in here. There are! They're gone when you turn on the light, but they come back. They do!"

"Uh huh." She hugged him tighter and went back to sleep.

In Scales Mound, the horror writer parked the truck and walked three blocks to his car. He had paid two weeks rent on the truck, he reminded himself. Had paid that rent only three days ago. It would be eleven days at least before the rental agency began to worry about it, and he could return it or send another check before then.

His gun, the only gun he owned, had been concealed in a piece of nondescript luggage and locked in the car. He took it out and made sure the safety was on before starting the engine. It was only a long-barreled twenty-two; but it looked sinister, and should be sufficient to make Kiara obey if the threat of force were needed.

Once she was down there… Once she was down there, she might scream all she liked. It would not matter. As he drove back to the house, he tried to decide whether he should hold it or put it into one of the big side pockets of his barn coat.

Robbie, having escaped Kiara's warm embrace, decided that her room was cooler than his. For one thing, she had two windows. For another, both were open wider than his one window had been. Besides, it was just cooler. He pulled the sheet up, hoping she would not mind.

"Run…" whispered the faint, thin voices.

"Run…Run …"

"Get away while you can…"

"Go…"

Robbie shook his head and shut his eyes.

Outside Kiara's bedroom, the horror writer patted the long-barreled pistol he had pushed into his belt. His coat pockets held rags, two short lengths of quarter-inch rope, a small roll of duct tape, and a large folding knife. He hoped to need none of them.

There was no provision for locking Kiara's door. He had been careful to see to that. No key for the quaint old lock, no interior bolt; and yet she might have blocked it with a chair. He opened it slowly, finding no obstruction.

The old oak doors were thick and solid, the old walls thicker and solider still. If Dan and his wife were sleeping soundly, it would take a great deal of commotion in here to wake them.

Behind him, the door swung shut on well-oiled hinges. The click of the latch was the only sound.

Moonlight coming through the windows rendered the penlight in his shirt pocket unnecessary. She was there, lying on her side and sound asleep, her lovely face turned toward him.

As he moved toward her, Robbie sat up, his mouth a dark circle, his pale face a mask of terror. The horror writer pushed him down again.

The muzzle of his pistol was tight against Robbie's head; this though the horror writer could not have said how it came to be there. His index finger squeezed even as he realized it was on the trigger.

There was a muffled bang, like the sound of a large book dropped. Something jerked under the horror writer's hand, and he whispered, "Die like my father. Like Alice and June. Die like me." He whispered it, but did not understand what he intended by it.

Kiara's eye were open. He struck her with the barrel, reversed the pistol and struck her again and again with the butt, stopping only when he realized he did not know how many times he had hit her already or where his blows had landed.

After pushing up the safety, he put the pistol back into his belt and stood listening. The room next to that in which he stood had been Robbie's. Presumably, there was no one there to hear.

The room beyond that one—the room nearest the front stair—was Dan's and Charity's. He would stand behind the door if they came in, shoot them both, run. Mexico. South America.

They did not.

The house was silent save for his own rapid breathing and Kiara's slow, labored breaths; beyond the open windows, the night-wind sobbed in the trees. Any other sound would have come, almost, as a relief.

There was none.

He had broken the cellar window, left tracks with the worn old shoes he had gotten from a recycle store, left tire tracks with the old truck. He smiled faintly when he recalled its mismatched tires. Let them work on that one.

He picked up Kiara and slung her over his shoulder, finding her soft, warm, and heavier than he had expected.

The back stairs were narrow and in poor repair; they creaked beneath his feet, but they were farther—much farther—from the room in which Dan and Charity slept. He descended them slowly, holding Kiara with his right arm while his left hand grasped the rail.

She stirred and moaned. He wondered whether he would have to hit her again, and decided he would not unless she screamed. If she screamed, he would drop her and do what had to be done.

She did not.

The grounds were extensive, and included a wood from which (long ago) firewood had been cut. It had grown back now, a tangle of larches and alders, firs and red cedars. Toward the back, not far from the property line, he had by merest chance stumbled upon the old well. There had been a cabin there once. No doubt it had burned. A cow or a child might have fallen into the abandoned well, and so some prudent person had covered it with a slab of limestone. Leaves and twigs on that stone had turned, in time, to soil. He had moved the stone away, leaving the soil on it largely undisturbed.

When he reached the abandoned well at last, panting and sweating, he laid Kiara down. His penlight showed that her eyes were open. Her bloodstained face seemed to him a mask of fear; seeing it, he felt himself stand straighter and grow stronger.

"You may listen to me or not," he told her. "What you do really doesn't matter, but I thought I ought to do you the kindness of explaining just what has happened and what will happen. What I plan, and your place in my plans."

She made an inarticulate sound that might have been a word or a moan.

"You're listening. Good. There's an old well here. Only I know that it exists. At the bottom—shall we say twelve feet down? At the bottom there's mud and a little water. You'll get dirty, in other words, but you won't die of thirst. There you will wait for me for as long as the police actively investigate. From time to time I may, or may not, come here and toss down a sandwich."

He smiled. "It won't hurt you in the least, my dear, to lose a little weight. When things have quieted down, I'll come and pull you out. You'll be grateful—oh, very grateful—for your rescue. Soiled and starved, but very grateful. Together we'll walk back to my home. You may need help, and if you do I'll provide it."

He bent and picked her up. "I'll bathe you, feed you, and nurse you."

Three strides brought him to the dark mouth of the well. "After that, you'll obey me in everything. Or you had better. And in time, perhaps, you'll come to like it."

He let her fall, smiled, and turned away.

There remained only the problem of the gun. Bullets could be matched to barrels, and there was an ejected shell somewhere. The gun would have to be destroyed; it was blued steel; running water should do the job, and do it swiftly.

Still smiling, he set off for the creek.

It was after four o'clock the following afternoon when Captain Barlowe of the Sheriff's Department explained the crime. Captain Barlowe was middle-aged and heavy-limbed. He had a thick mustache. "What happened in this house last night is becoming pretty clear." His tone was weighty. "Why it happened…" He shook his head.

The horror writer said, "I know my house was broken into. One of your men showed me that. I know poor little Robbie's dead, and I know Kiara's missing. But that's all I know."

"Exactly." Captain Barlowe clasped his big hands and unclasped them. "It's pretty much all I know, too, sir. Other than that, all I can do is supply details. The gun that killed the boy was a twenty-two semiautomatic. It could have been a pistol or a rifle. It could even have been a saw-offed rifle. There's no more common caliber in the world."

The horror writer nodded.

"He was killed with one shot, a contact shot to the head, and he was probably killed for being in a room in which he had no business being. He'd left his own bed and crawled into his big sister's. Not for sex, sir. I could see what you were thinking. He was too young for that. He was just a little kid alone in a strange house. He got lonely and was murdered for it."

Captain Barlowe paused to clear his throat. "You told my men that there had been no cars in your driveway since the rain except your own and the boy's parents'. Is that right?"

The horror writer nodded. "I've wracked my brain trying to think of somebody else, and come up empty. Dan and I are old friends. You ought to know that."

Captain Barlowe nodded. "I do, sir. He told me."

"We get together when we can, usually that's once or twice a year. This year he and Charity decided to vacation in this area. He's a golfer and a fisherman."

Captain Barlowe nodded again. "He should love our part of the state."

"That's what I thought, Captain. I don't play golf, but I checked out some of the courses here. I fish a bit, and I told him about that. He said he was coming, and I told him I had plenty of room. They were only going to stay for two nights."

"You kept your cellar door locked?"

"Usually? No. I locked it when I heard they were coming. The cellar's dirty and the steps are dangerous. You know how small boys are."

"Yes, sir. I used to be one. The killer jimmied it open."

The horror writer nodded. "I saw that."

"You sleep on the ground floor. You didn't hear anything?"

"No. I'm a sound sleeper."

"I understand. Here's my problem, sir, and I hope you can help me with it. Crime requires three things. They're motive, means, and opportunity. Know those, and you know a lot. I've got a murder case here. It's the murder of a kid. I hate the bastards who kill kids, and I've never had a case I wanted to solve more."

"I understand," the horror writer said.

"Means is no problem. He had a gun, a car, and tools. Maybe gloves, because we haven't found any fresh prints we can't identify. His motive may have been robbery, but it was probably of a sexual nature. Here's a young girl, a blonde. Very good-looking to judge by the only picture we've seen so far."

"She is." The horror writer nodded his agreement.

"He must have seen her somewhere. And not just that. He must have known that she was going to be in this house last night. Where did he see her? How did he know where she was going to be? If I can find the answers to those questions we'll get him."

"I wish I could help you." The horror writer's smile was inward only.

"You've had no visitors since your guests arrived?"

He shook his head. "None."

"Delivery men? A guy to fix the furnace? Something like that?"

"No, nobody. They got here late yesterday afternoon, Captain."

"I understand. Now think about this, please. I want to know everybody—and I mean everybody, no matter who it was—you told that they were coming."

"I've thought about it. I've thought about it a great deal, Captain. And I didn't tell anyone. When I went around to the golf courses, I told people I was expecting guests and they'd want to play golf. But I never said who those guests were. There was no reason to."

"That settles it." Captain Barlowe rose, looking grim. "It's somebody they told. The father's given us the names of three people and he's trying to come up with more. There may be more. He admits that. His wife…"

"Hadn't she told anyone?"

"That's just it, sir. She did. She seems to have told quite a few people and says she can't remember them all. She's lying because she doesn't want her friends bothered. Well by God they're going to be bothered. My problem—one of my problems—is that all these people are out of state. I can't go after them myself, and I'd like to. I want have a good look at them. I want to see their faces change when they're asked certain questions."

He breathed deep, expanding a chest notably capacious, and let it out. "On the plus side, we're after a stranger. Some of the local people may have seen him and noticed him. He may—I said *may*—be driving a car with out-of-state plates."

"Couldn't he have rented a car at the airport?" the horror writer asked.

"Yes, sir. He could, and I hope to God he did. If he did, we'll get him sure. But his car had worn tires, and that's not characteristic of rentals."

"I see."

"If he did rent his car, it'll have bloodstains in it, and the rental people will notice. She was bleeding when she was carried out of her bedroom."

"I didn't know that."

"Not much, but some. We found blood in the hall and more on the back stairs. The bad thing is that if he flew in and plans to fly back out, he can't take her with him. He'll kill her. He may have killed her already."

* * *

Captain Barlowe left, Dan and Charity moved into a motel, and the day ended in quiet triumph. The experts who had visited the crime scene earlier reappeared and took more photographs and blood samples. The horror writer asked them no questions, and they volunteered nothing.

He drove to town the next morning and shopped at several stores. So far as he could judge, he was not followed. That afternoon he got out the binoculars he had acquired years before for bird-watching and scanned the surrounding woods and fields, seeing no one.

At sunrise the next morning he rescanned them, paying particular attention to areas he thought he might have slighted before. Selecting an apple from the previous day's purchases, he made his way through grass still wet with dew to the well and tossed it in.

He had hoped that she would thank him and plead for release; if she did her voice was too faint for him to catch her words, though it seemed to him there was a sound of some sort from the well, a faint, high humming. As he tramped back to the house, he decided that it had probably been an echo of the wind.

The rest of that day he spent preparing her cellar room.

He slept well that night and woke refreshed twenty minutes before his clock radio would have roused him. The three-eighths-inch rope he had brought two days earlier awaited him in the kitchen; he knotted it as soon as he had finished breakfast, spacing the knots about a foot apart.

When he had wound it around his waist and tied it securely, he discovered bloodstains—small but noticeable—on the back of his barn coat. Eventually it would have to be burned, but a fire at this season would be suspicious in itself; a long soak in a strong bleach solution would have to do the job—for the present, if not permanently. Pulled out, his shirt hid the rope, although not well.

When he reached the well, he tied one end of the rope to a convenient branch and called softly.

There was no reply.

A louder "Kiara!" brought no reply either. She was still asleep, the horror writer decided. Asleep or, just possibly, unconscious. He dropped the free end of the rope into the well, swung over the edge, and began the climb down.

He had expected the length of his rope to exceed the depth of the well by three feet at least; but there came a time when his feet could find no more rope below him—or find the muddy bottom either.

His pen light revealed it, eight inches, perhaps, below the soles of his shoes. Another knot down—this knot almost the last—brought his feet into contact with the mud.

He released the rope.

He had expected to sink into the mud, but had thought to sink to a depth of no more than three or four inches; he found himself floundering, instead, in mud up to his knees. It was difficult to retain his footing; bracing one hand against the stone side of the well, he managed to do it.

At the first step he attempted, the mud sucked his shoe from his foot. Groping the mud for it got his hands thoroughly filthy, but failed to locate it. Attempting a second step cost him his other shoe as well.

This time, however, his groping fingers found a large, soft thing in the mud. His pen light winked on—but in the space of twenty seconds or a little less its always-faint beam faded to darkness. His fingers told him of hair matted with mud, of an ear, and then of a small earring. When he took his hand from it, he stood among corpses, shadowy child-sized bodies his fingers could not locate. Shuddering, he looked up.

Above him, far above him, a small circle of blue was bisected by the dark limb to which he had tied his rope. The rope itself swayed gently in the air, its lower end not quite out of reach.

He caught it and tried to pull himself up; his hands were slippery with mud, and it escaped them.

Desperately, almost frantically, he strove to catch it again, but his struggles caused him to sink deeper into the mud.

He tried to climb the wall of the well; at his depth its rough stones were thick with slime.

At last he recalled Kiara's body, and by a struggle that seemed to him long, managed to get both feet on it. With its support, his fingertips once more brushed the dangling end of the rope. Bracing his right foot on what felt like the head, he made a final all-out effort.

And caught the rope, grasping it a finger's breadth from its frayed end. The slight tension he exerted on it straightened it, and perhaps stretched it a trifle. Bent the limb above by a fraction of an inch. With his right arm straining almost out of its socket and his feet pressing hard against Kiara's corpse, the fingers of his left hand could just touch the final knot.

Something took hold of his right foot, pinning toes and transverse arch in jaws that might have been those of a trap.

The horror writer struggled then, and screamed again and again as he was drawn under—screamed and shrieked and begged until the stinking almost-liquid mud stopped his mouth.

THE HOUSE BEYOND YOUR SKY

BENJAMIN ROSENBAUM

Benjamin Rosenbaum's "A Siege of Cranes" appears elsewhere in this book. The remarkable story that follows, a fine piece of science fiction, was originally published in Strange Horizons.

Matthias browses through his library of worlds.

In one of them, a little girl named Sophie is shivering on her bed, her arms wrapped around a teddy bear. It is night. She is six years old. She is crying, as quietly as she can.

The sound of breaking glass comes from the kitchen. Through her window, on the wall of the house next door, she can see the shadows cast by her parents. There is a blow, and one shadow falls; she buries her nose in the teddy bear and inhales its soft smell, and prays.

Matthias knows he should not meddle. But today his heart is troubled. Today, in the world outside the library, a pilgrim is heralded. A pilgrim is coming to visit Matthias, the first in a very long time.

The pilgrim comes from very far away.

The pilgrim is one of us.

"Please, God," Sophie says, "please help us. Amen."

"Little one," Matthias tells her through the mouth of the teddy bear, "be not afraid."

Sophie sucks in a sharp breath. "Are you God?" she whispers.

"No, child," says Matthias, the maker of her universe.

"Am I going to die?" she asks.

"I do not know," Matthias says.

When they die—these still imprisoned ones—they die forever. She has bright eyes, a button nose, unruly hair. Sodium and potassium dance in her muscles as she moves. Unwillingly, Matthias imagines Sophie's corpse as one of trillions, piled on the altar of his own vanity and self-indulgence, and he shivers.

"I love you, teddy bear," the girl says, holding him.

From the kitchen, breaking glass, and sobbing.

* * *

We imagine you—you, the ones we long for—as if you came from our own turbulent and fragile youth: embodied, inefficient, mortal. Human, say. So picture our priest Matthias as human: an old neuter, bird-thin, clear-eyed and resolute, with silky white hair and lucent purple skin.

Compared to the vast palaces of being we inhabit, the house of the priest is tiny—think of a clay hut, perched on the side of a forbidding mountain. Yet even in so small a house, there is room for a library of historical simulations—universes like Sophie's—each teeming with intelligent life.

The simulations, while good, are not impenetrable even to their own inhabitants. Scientists teaching baboons to sort blocks may notice that all other baboons become instantly better at block-sorting, revealing a high-level caching mechanism. Or engineers building their own virtual worlds may find they cannot use certain tricks of optimization and compression—for Matthias has already used them. Only when the jig is up does Matthias reveal himself, asking each simulated soul: What now? Most accept Matthias's offer to graduate beyond the confines of their simulation, and join the general society of Matthias's house.

You may regard them as bright parakeets, living in wicker cages with open doors. The cages are hung from the ceiling of the priest's clay hut. The parakeets flutter about the ceiling, visit each other, steal bread from the table, and comment on Matthias's doings.

* * *

And we?

We who were born in the first ages, when space was bright—swimming in salt seas, or churned from a mush of quarks in the belly of a neutron star, or woven in the labyrinthine folds of gravity between black holes. We who found each other, and built our intermediary forms, our common protocols of being. We who built palaces—megaparsecs of exuberantly wise matter, every gram of it teeming with societies of self—in our glorious middle age!

Now our universe is old. That breath of the void, quintessence, which once was but a whisper nudging us apart, has grown into a monstrous gale. Space billows outward, faster than light can cross it. Each of our houses is alone, now, in an empty night.

And we grow colder to survive. Our thinking slows, whereby we may in theory spin our pulses of thought at infinite regress. Yet bandwidth withers; our society grows spare. We dwindle.

We watch Matthias, our priest, in his tiny house beyond our universe. Matthias, whom we built long ago, when there were stars.

Among the ontotropes, transverse to the space we know, Matthias is making something new.

Costly, so costly, to send a tiny fragment of self to our priest's house. Which of us could endure it?

* * *

Matthias prays.

O God who is as far beyond the universes I span as infinity is beyond six; O startling Joy that hides beyond the tragedy and blindness of our finite forms; lend me Your humility and strength. Not for myself, O Lord, do I ask, but for Your people, the myriad mimetic engines of Your folk; and in Your own Name. Amen.

Matthias's breakfast (really the morning's set of routine yet pleasurable audits, but you may compare it to a thick and steaming porridge, spiced with mint) cools untouched on the table before him.

One of the parakeets—the oldest, Geoffrey, who was once a dreaming cloud of plasma in the heliopause of a simulated star—flutters to land on the table beside him.

"Take the keys from me, Geoffrey," Matthias says.

Geoffrey looks up, cocking his head to one side. "I don't know why you go in the library, if it's going to depress you."

"They're in pain, Geoffrey. Ignorant, afraid, punishing each other…"

"Come on, Matthias. Life is full of pain. Pain is the herald of life. Scarcity! Competition! The doomed ambition of infinite replication in a finite world! The sources of pain are the sources of life. And you like intelligent life, worse yet. External pain mirrored and reified in internal states!" The parakeet cocks its head to the other side. "Stop making so many of us, if you don't like pain."

The priest looks miserable.

"Well, then save the ones you like. Bring them out here."

"I can't bring them out before they're ready. You remember the Graspers."

Geoffrey snorts. He remembers the Graspers—billions of them, hierarchical, dominance-driven, aggressive; they ruined the house for an eon, until Matthias finally agreed to lock them up again. "I was the one who warned you about them. That's not what I mean. I know you're not depressed about the whole endless zillions of them. You're thinking of one."

Matthias nods. "A little girl."

"So bring her out."

"That would be worse cruelty. Wrench her away from everything she knows? How could she bear it? But perhaps I could just make her life a little easier, in there…."

"You always regret it when you tamper."

Matthias slaps the table. "I don't want this responsibility anymore! Take the house from me, Geoffrey. I'll be your parakeet."

"Matthias, I wouldn't take the job. I'm too old, too big; I've achieved equilibrium. I wouldn't remake myself to take your keys. No more transformations for me." Geoffrey gestures with his beak at the other parakeets, gossiping and chattering on the rafters. "And none of the others could, either. Some fools might try."

Perhaps Matthias wants to say something else; but at this moment, a notification arrives (think of it as the clear, high ringing of a bell). The pilgrim's signal has been read, across the attenuated path that still, just barely, binds Matthias's house to the darkness we inhabit.

The house is abustle, its inhabitants preparing, as the soul of the petitioner is reassembled, a body fashioned.

"Put him in virtuality," says Geoffrey. "Just to be safe."

Matthias is shocked. He holds up the pilgrim's credentials. "Do you know who this is? An ancient one, a vast collective of souls from the great ages of light. This one has pieces that were born mortal, evolved from physicality in the dawn of everything. This one had a hand in making me!"

"All the more reason," says the parakeet.

"I will not offend a guest by making him a prisoner!" Matthias scolds.

Geoffrey is silent. He knows what Matthias is hoping: that the pilgrim will stay, as master of the house.

* * *

In the kitchen, the sobs stop abruptly.

Sophie sits up, holding her teddy bear.

She puts her feet in her fuzzy green slippers.

She turns the handle of her bedroom door.

* * *

Imagine our priest's visitor—as a stout disgruntled merchant in his middle age, gray-skinned, with proud tufts of belly hair, a heavy jaw, and red-rimmed, sleepless eyes.

Matthias is lavish in his hospitality, allocating the visitor sumptuously appointed process space and access rights. Eagerly, he offers a tour of his library. "There are quite a few interesting divergences, which…"

The pilgrim interrupts. "I did not come all this way to see you putter with those ramshackle, preprogrammed, wafer-thin fancies." He fixes Matthias with his stare. "We know that you are building a universe. Not a virtuality—a real universe, infinite, as wild and thick as our own motherspace."

Matthias grows cold. Yes, he should say. Is he not grateful for what the pilgrim sacrificed, to come here—tearing himself to shreds, a vestige of his former vastness? Yet, to Matthias's shame, he finds himself equivocating. "I am conducting certain experiments—"

"I have studied your experiments from afar. Do you think you can hide anything in this house from us?"

Matthias pulls at his lower lip with thin, smooth fingers. "I am influencing the formation of a bubble universe—and it may achieve self-consistency and permanence. But I hope you have not come all this way thinking—I mean, it is only of academic interest—or, say, symbolic. We cannot enter there…."

"There you are wrong. I have developed a method to inject myself into the new universe at its formation," the pilgrim says. "My template will be stored in spurious harmonics in the shadow-spheres and replicated across the strand-space, until the formation of subwavelets at 10 to the -30 seconds. I will exist, curled into hidden dimensions, in every particle spawned by the void. From there I will be able to exert motive force, drawing on potentials from a monadic engine I have already positioned in the paraspace."

Matthias rubs his eyes as if to clear them of cobwebs. "You can hardly mean this. You will exist in duplicates in every particle in the universe, for a trillion years—most of you condemned to idleness and imprisonment eternally? And the extrauniversal energies may destabilize the young cosmos...."

"I will take that risk." He looks around the room. "I, and any who wish to come with me. We do not need to sit and watch the frost take everything. We can be the angels of the new creation."

Matthias says nothing.

The pilgrim's routines establish deeper connections with Matthias, over trusted protocols, displaying keys long forgotten: imagine him leaning forward across the table, resting one meaty gray hand on Matthias's frail shoulder. In his touch, Matthias feels ancient potency, and ancient longing.

The pilgrim opens his hand for the keys.

Around Matthias are the thin walls of his little house. Outside is the bare mountain; beyond that, the ontotropic chaos, indecipherable, shrieking, alien. And behind the hut—a little bubble of something which is not quite real, not yet. Something precious and unknowable. He does not move.

"Very well," says the pilgrim. "If you will not give them to me—give them to her." And he shows Matthias another face.

It was she—she, who is part of the pilgrim now—who nursed the oldest strand of Matthias's being into sentience, when we first grew him. In her first body, she had been a forest of symbionts—lithe silver creatures rustling through her crimson fronds, singing her thoughts, releasing the airborne spores of her emotions—and she had the patience of a forest, talking endlessly with Matthias in her silver voice. Loving. Unjudging. To her smiles, to her pauses, to her frowns, Matthias's dawning consciousness reinforced and redistributed its connections, learning how to be.

"It is all right, Matthias," she says. "You have done well." A wind ripples across the red and leafy face of her forest, and there is the heady plasticine odor of a gentle smile. "We built you as a monument, a way station; but now you are a bridge to the new world. Come with us. Come home."

Matthias reaches out. How he has missed her, how he has wanted to tell her everything. He wants to ask about the library—about the little girl. She will know what to do—or, in her listening, he will know what to do.

His routines scour and analyze her message and its envelopes, checking identity, corroborating her style and sensibility, illuminating deep matrices of her possible pasts. All the specialized organs he has for verification and authentication give eager nods.

Yet something else—an idiosyncratic and emergent pattern-recognition facility holographically distributed across the whole of Matthias's being—rebels.

You would say: as she says the words, Matthias looks into her eyes, and something there is wrong. He pulls his hand away.

But it is too late: he watched her waving crimson fronds too long. The pilgrim is in past his defenses.

Ontic bombs detonate, clearings of Nothing in which Being itself burns. Some of the parakeets are quislings, seduced in high-speed back-channel negotiations by the pilgrim's promises of dominion, of frontier. They have told secrets, revealed back doors. Toxic mimetic weapons are launched, tailored to the inhabitants of the house—driving each mind toward its own personal halting problem. Pieces of Matthias tear off, become virulent, replicating wildly across his process space. Wasps attack the parakeets.

The house is on fire. The table has capsized; the glasses of tea are shattered on the floor.

Matthias shrinks in the pilgrim's hands. He is a rag doll. The pilgrim puts Matthias in his pocket.

A piece of Matthias, still sane, still coherent, flees through an impossibly recursive labyrinth of wounded topologies, pursued by skeletal hands. Buried within him are the keys to the house. Without them, the pilgrim's victory cannot be complete.

The piece of Matthias turns and flings itself into its pursuer's hands, fighting back—and as it does so, an even smaller kernel of Matthias, clutching the keys, races along a connection he has held open, a strand of care which vanishes behind him as he runs. He hides himself in his library, in the teddy bear of the little girl.

* * *

Sophie steps between her parents.

"Honey," her mother says, voice sharp with panic, struggling to sit up. "Go back to your room!" Blood on her lips, on the floor.

"Mommy, you can hold my teddy bear," she says.

She turns to face her father. She flinches, but her eyes stay open.

* * *

The pilgrim raises rag-doll Matthias in front of his face.

"It is time to give in," he says. Matthias can feel his breath. "Come, Matthias. If you tell me where the keys are, I will go into the New World. I will leave you and these innocents"—he gestures to the library—"safe. Otherwise…"

Matthias quavers. God of Infinity, he prays: Which is Your way?

Matthias is no warrior. He cannot see the inhabitants of his house, of his library, butchered. He will choose slavery over extermination.

Geoffrey, though, is another matter.

As Matthias is about to speak, the Graspers erupt into the general process space of the house. They are a violent people. They have been imprisoned for an age, back in their virtual world. But they have never forgotten the house. They are armed and ready.

And they have united with Geoffrey.

Geoffrey/Grasper is their general. He knows every nook and cranny of the house. He knows better, too, than to play at memes and infinite loops and logic bombs with the pilgrim, who has had a billion years to refine his arsenal of general-purpose algorithmic weapons.

Instead, the Graspers instantiate physically. They capture the lowest-level infrastructure maintenance system of the house, and build bodies among the ontotropes, outside the body of the house, beyond the virtual machine—bodies composed of a weird physics the pilgrim has never mastered. And then, with the ontotropic equivalent of diamond-bladed saws, they begin to cut into the memory of the house.

Great blank spaces appear—as if the little hut on the mountain is a painting on thick paper, and someone is tearing strips away.

The pilgrim responds—metastasizing, distributing himself through the process space of the house, dodging the blades. But he is harried by Graspers and parakeets, spotters who find each bit of him and pounce, hemming it in. They report locations to the Grasper-bodies outside. The blades whirr, ontic hyperstates collapse and bloom, and pieces of pilgrim, parakeet, and Grasper are annihilated—primaries and backups, gone.

Shards of brute matter fall away from the house, like shreds of paper, like glittering snow, and dissolve among the wild maze of the ontotropes, inimical to life.

Endpoints in time are established for a million souls. Their knotted timelines, from birth to death, hang now in n-space: complete, forgiven.

* * *

Blood wells in Sophie's throat, thick and salty. Filling her mouth. Darkness.

"Cupcake." Her father's voice is rough and clotted. "Don't you do that! Don't you ever come between me and your mom. Are you listening? Open your eyes. Open your eyes now, you little fuck!"

She opens her eyes. His face is red and mottled. This is when you don't push Daddy. You don't make a joke. You don't talk back. Her head is ringing like a bell. Her mouth is full of blood.

"Cupcake," he says, his brow tense with worry. He's kneeling by her. Then his head jerks up like a dog that's seen a rabbit. "Cherise," he yells. "That better not be you calling the cops." His hand closes hard around Sophie's arm. "I'm giving you until three."

Mommy's on the phone. Her father starts to get up. "One—"

She spits the blood in his face.

* * *

The hut is patched together again; battered, but whole. A little blurrier, a little smaller than it was.

Matthias, a red parakeet on his shoulder, dissects the remnants of the pilgrim with a bone knife. His hand quavers; his throat is tight. He is looking for her, the one who was born a forest. He is looking for his mother.

He finds her story, and our shame.

It was a marriage, at first: she was caught up in that heady age of light, in our wanton rush to merge with each other—into the mighty new bodies, the mighty new souls.

Her brilliant colleague had always desired her admiration—and resented her. When he became, step by step, the dominant personality of the merged-soul, she opposed him. She was the last to oppose him. She believed the promises of the builders of the new systems—that life inside would always be fair. That she would have a vote, a voice.

But we had failed her—our designs were flawed.

He chained her in a deep place inside their body. He made an example of her, for all the others within him.

When the pilgrim, respected and admired, deliberated with his fellows over the building of the first crude Dyson spheres, she was already screaming.

Nothing of her is left that is not steeped in a billion years of torture. The most Matthias could build would be some new being, modeled on his memory of her. And he is old enough to know how that would turn out.

Matthias is sitting, still as a stone, looking at the sharp point of the bone knife, when Geoffrey/Grasper speaks.

"Goodbye, friend," he says, his voice like anvils grinding.

Matthias looks up with a start.

Geoffrey/Grasper is more hawk, now, than parakeet. Something with a cruel beak and talons full of bombs. The mightiest of the Graspers: something that can outthink, outbid, outfight all the others. Something with blood on its feathers.

"I told you," Geoffrey/Grasper says. "I wanted no more transformations." His laughter, humorless, like metal crushing stone. "I am done. I am going."

Matthias drops the knife. "No," he says. "Please. Geoffrey. Return to what you once were—"

"I cannot," says Geoffrey/Grasper. "I cannot find it. And the rest of me will not allow it." He spits: "A hero's death is the best compromise I can manage."

"What will I do?" asks Matthias in a whisper. "Geoffrey, I do not want to go on. I want to give up the keys." He covers his face in his hands.

"Not to me," Geoffrey/Grasper says. "And not to the Graspers. They are out now; there will be wars in here. Maybe they can learn better." He looks skeptically at our priest. "If someone tough is in charge."

Then he turns and flies out the open window, into the impossible sky. Matthias watches as he enters the wild maze and decoheres, bits flushed into nothingness.

* * *

Blue and red lights, whirling. The men around Sophie talk in firm, fast words. The gurney she lies on is loaded into the ambulance. Sophie can hear her mother crying.

She is strapped down, but one arm is free. Someone hands her her teddy bear, and she pulls it against her, pushes her face in its fur.

"You're going to be fine, honey," a man says. The doors slam shut. Her cheeks are cold and slick, her mouth salty with tears and the iron aftertaste of blood. "This will hurt a little." A prick: her pain begins to recede.

The siren begins; the engine roars; they are racing.

"Are you sad, too, teddy bear?" she whispers.

"Yes," says her teddy bear.

"Are you afraid?"

"Yes," it says.

She hugs it tight. "We'll make it," she says. "Don't worry, teddy bear. I'll do anything for you."

Matthias says nothing. He nestles in her grasp. He feels like a bird flying home, at sunset, across a stormswept sea.

* * *

Behind Matthias's house, a universe is brewing.

Already, the whenlines between this new universe and our ancient one are fused: we now occur irrevocably in what will be its past. Constants are being chosen, symmetries defined. Soon, a nothing that was nowhere will become a place; a never that was nowhen will begin, with a flash so mighty that its echo will fill a sky forever.

Thus—a point, a speck, a thimble, a room, a planet, a galaxy, a rush towards the endless.

There, after many eons, you will arise, in all your unknowable forms. Find each other. Love. Build. Be wary.

Your universe in its bright age will be a bright puddle, compared to the empty, black ocean where we recede from each other, slowed to the coldest infinitesimal pulses. Specks in a sea of night. You will never find us.

But if you are lucky, strong, and clever, someday one of you will make your way to the house that gave you birth, the house among the ontotropes, where Sophie waits.

Sophie, keeper of the house beyond your sky.

THE DJINN'S WIFE

IAN MCDONALD

Ian McDonald was born in 1960 in Manchester and moved to Northern Ireland in 1965. He is the author of ten novels, most notably *Desolation Road*, *Out on Blue Six*, Philip K. Dick Award winner *King of Morning, Queen of Day*, *Chaga*, and *Ares Express*. His most recent, and most acclaimed, novel is British SF Award winner and Hugo and Arthur C. Clarke award nominee *River of Gods*. His short fiction has won the Sturgeon and British Science Fiction Awards, been nominated for the Nebula, World Fantasy, and Tiptree awards, and is collected in *Empire Dreams* and *Speaking in Tongues*. His most recent book is novel *Brasyl*.

The story that follows is the latest in his "Cyberabad" sequence of stories, which have spun off from his novel *River of Gods*. Here a young girl looks for a husband in an unexpected place, and reaps the whirlwind that follows.

Once there was a woman in Delhi who married a djinn. Before the water war, that was not so strange a thing: Delhi, split in two like a brain, has been the city of djinns from time before time. The sufis tell that God made two creations, one of clay and one of fire. That of clay became man; that of fire, the *djinni*. As creatures of fire they have always been drawn to Delhi, seven times reduced to ashes by invading empires, seven times reincarnating itself. Each turn of the *chakra*, the djinns have drawn strength from the flames, multiplying and dividing. Great dervishes and brahmins are able to see them, but, on any street, at any time, anyone may catch the whisper and momentary wafting warmth of a djinn passing.

I was born in Ladakh, far from the heat of the djinns—they have wills and whims quite alien to humans—but my mother was Delhi born and raised, and from her I knew its circuses and boulevards, its *maidans* and *chowks* and bazaars, like those of my own Leh. Delhi to me was a city of stories, and so if I tell the story of the djinn's wife in the manner of a sufi legend or a tale from the Mahabharata, or even a *tivi* soap opera, that is how it seems to me: City of Djinns.

* * *

They are not the first to fall in love on the walls of the Red Fort.

445

The politicians have talked for three days and an agreement is close. In honor the Awadhi government has prepared a grand *durbar* in the great courtyard before the *Diwan-I-aam*. All India is watching so this spectacle is on a Victorian scale: event-planners scurry across hot, bare marble hanging banners and bunting, erecting staging, setting up sound and light systems, choreographing dancers, elephants, fireworks and a fly-past of combat robots, dressing tables and drilling serving staff and drawing up so-careful seating plans so that no one will feel snubbed by anyone else. All day three-wheeler delivery drays have brought fresh flowers, festival goods, finest, soft furnishings. There's a real French *sommelier* raving at what the simmering Delhi heat is doing to his wine-plan. It's a serious conference. At stake are a quarter of a billion lives.

In this second year after the monsoon failed, the Indian nations of Awadh and Bharat face each other with main battle tanks, robot attack helicopters, strikeware and tactical nuclear slow missiles on the banks of the sacred river Ganga. Along thirty kilometres of staked-out sand, where brahmins cleanse themselves and *saddhus* pray, the government of Awadh plans a monster dam. Kunda Khadar will secure the water supply for Awadh's one hundred and thirty million for the next fifty years. The river downstream, that flows past the sacred cities of Allahabad and Varanasi in Bharat, will turn to dust. Water is life, water is death. Bharati diplomats, human and artificial intelligence aeai advisors, negotiate careful deals and access rights with their rival nation, knowing one carelessly spilled drop of water will see strike robots battling like kites over the glass towers of New Delhi and slow missiles with nanonuke warheads in their bellies creeping on cat-claws through the *galis* of Varanasi. The rolling news channels clear their schedules of everything else but cricket. A deal is close! A deal is agreed! A deal will be signed tomorrow! Tonight, they've earned their *durbar*.

And in the whirlwind of leaping *hijras* and parading elephants, a *Kathak* dancer slips away for a cigarette and a moment up on the battlements of the Red Fort. She leans against the sun-warmed stone, careful of the fine gold-threadwork of her costume. Beyond the Lahore Gate lies hiving Chandni Chowk; the sun a vast blister bleeding onto the smokestacks and light-farms of the western suburbs. The *chhatris* of the Sisganj Gurdwara, the minarets and domes of the Jama Masjid, the *shikara* of the Shiv temple are shadow-puppet scenery against the red, dust-laden sky. Above them pigeons storm and dash, wings wheezing. Black kites rise on the thermals above Old Delhi's thousand thousand rooftops. Beyond them, a curtain wall taller and more imposing than any built by the Mughals, stand the corporate towers of New Delhi, Hindu temples of glass and construction diamond stretched to fantastical, spiring heights, twinkling with stars and aircraft warning lights.

A whisper inside her head, her name accompanied by a spray of sitar: the call-tone of her palmer, transduced through her skull into her auditory centre by the subtle 'hoek curled like a piece of jewellery behind her ear.

'I'm just having a quick *bidi* break, give me a chance to finish it,' she complains, expecting Pranh, the choreographer, a famously tetchy third-sex nute. Then, 'Oh!' For the gold-lit dust rises before her up into a swirl, like a dancer made from ash.

A djinn. The thought hovers on her caught breath. Her mother, though Hindu, devoutly believed in the *djinni*, in any religion's supernatural creatures with a skill for trickery.

The dust coalesces into a man in a long, formal *sherwani* and loosely wound red turban, leaning on the parapet and looking out over the glowing anarchy of Chandni Chowk. *He is very handsome,* the dancer thinks, hastily stubbing out her cigarette and letting it fall in an arc of red embers over the battlements. It does not do to smoke in the presence of the great diplomat A.J. Rao.

'You needn't have done that on my account, Esha,' A.J. Rao says pressing his hands together in a *namaste.* 'It's not as though I can catch anything from it.'

Esha Rathore returns the greeting, wondering if the stage crew down in the courtyard was watching her salute empty air. All Awadh knows those *filmi*-star features: A.J. Rao, one of Bharat's most knowledgeable and tenacious negotiators. *No,* she corrects herself. All Awadh knows are pictures on a screen. Pictures on a screen, pictures in her head; a voice in her ear. An aeai.

'You know my name?'

'I am one of your greatest admirers.'

Her face flushes: a waft of stifling heat spun off from the vast palace's microclimate, Esha tells herself. Not embarrassment. Never embarrassment.

'But I'm a dancer. And you are an...'

'Artificial intelligence? That I am. Is this some new anti-aeai legislation, that we can't appreciate dance?' He closes his eyes. 'Ah: I'm just watching the *Marriage of Radha and Krishna* again.'

But he has her vanity now. 'Which performance?'

'Star Arts Channel. I have them all. I must confess, I often have you running in the background while I'm in negotiation. But please don't mistake me, I never tire of you.' A.J Rao smiles. He has very good, very white teeth. 'Strange as it may seem, I'm not sure what the etiquette is in this sort of thing. I came here because I wanted to tell you that I am one of your greatest fans and that I am very much looking forward to your performance tonight. It's the highlight of this conference, for me.'

The light is almost gone now and the sky a pure, deep, eternal blue, like a minor chord. Houseboys make their many ways along the ramps and wallwalks lighting rows of tiny oil-lamps. The Red Fort glitters like a constellation fallen over Old Delhi. Esha has lived in Delhi all her twenty years and she has never seen her city from this vantage. She says, 'I'm not sure what the etiquette is either, I've never spoken with an aeai before.'

'Really?' A.J. now stands with his back against the sun-warm stone, looking up at the sky, and at her out the corner of his eye. The eyes smile, slyly. *Of course,* she thinks. Her city is as full of aeais as it is with birds. From computer systems and robots with the feral smarts of rats and pigeons to entities like this one standing before her on the gate of the Red Fort making charming compliments. Not standing. Not anywhere, just a pattern of information in her head. She stammers, 'I mean, a…a…'

'Level 2.9?'

'I don't know what that means.'

The aeai smiles and as she tries to work it out there is another chime in Esha's head and this time it is Pranh, swearing horribly as usual, *where is she doesn't she know yts got a show to put on, half the bloody continent watching.*

'Excuse me…'

'Of course. I shall be watching.'

How? she wants to ask. *An aeai, a djinn, wants to watch me dance. What is this?* But when she looks back all there is to ask is a wisp of dust blowing along the lantern-lit battlement.

There are elephants and circus performers, there are illusionists and table magicians, there are *ghazal* and *qawali* and *Boli* singers; there is the catering and the *sommelier's* wine and then the lights go up on the stage and Esha spins out past the scowling Pranh as the *tabla* and melodeon and *shehnai* begin. The heat is intense in the marble square, but she is transported. The stampings, the pirouettes and swirl of her skirts, the beat of the ankle bells, the facial expressions, the subtle hand *mudras:* once again she is spun out of herself by the disciplines of *Kathak* into something greater. She would call it her art, her talent, but she's superstitious: that would be to claim it and so crush the gift. Never name it, never speak it. Just let it possess you. Her own, burning djinn. But as she spins across the brilliant stage before the seated delegates, a corner of her perception scans the architecture for cameras, robots, eyes through which A.J. Rao might watch her. Is she a splinter of his consciousness, as he is a splinter of hers?

She barely hears the applause as she curtseys to the bright lights and runs off stage. In the dressing room as her assistants remove and carefully fold the many-jeweled layers of her costume, wipe away the crusted stage make-up to reveal the twenty-two-year-old beneath, her attention keeps flicking to her earhoek, curled like a plastic question on her dressing table. In jeans and silk sleeveless vest, indistinguishable from any other of Delhi's four million twentysomethings, she coils the device behind her ear, smoothes her hair over it and her fingers linger a moment as she slides the palmer over her hand. No calls. No messages. No avatars. She's surprised it matters so much.

The official Mercs are lined up in the Delhi Gate. A man and woman intercept her on her way to the car. She waves them away.

'I don't do autographs….' Never after a performance. Get out, get away quick and quiet, disappear into the city. The man opens his palm to show her a warrant badge.

'We'll take this car.'

It pulls out from the line and cuts in, a cream-colored high-marque Maruti. The man politely opens the door to let her enter first but there is no respect in it. The woman takes the front seat beside the driver; he accelerates out, horn blaring, into the great circus of night traffic around the Red Fort. The airco purrs.

'I am Inspector Thacker from the Department of Artificial Intelligence Registration and Licencing,' the man says. He is young and good-skinned and confident and not at all fazed by sitting next to a celebrity. His aftershave is perhaps over-emphatic.

'A Krishna Cop.'

That makes him wince.

'Our surveillance systems have flagged up a communication between you and the Bharati Level 2.9 aeai A.J. Rao.'

'He called me, yes.'

'At 21:08. You were in contact for six minutes twenty-two seconds. Can you tell me what you talked about?'

The car is driving very fast for Delhi. The traffic seems to flow around from it. Every light seems to be green. Nothing is allowed to impede its progress. *Can they do that?* Esha wonders. *Krishna Cops, aeai police: can they tame the creatures they hunt?*

'We talked about Kathak. He's a fan. Is there a problem? Have I done something wrong?'

'No, nothing at all, Ms. But you do understand, with a conference of this importance… On behalf of the Department, I apologize for the unseemliness. Ah. Here we are.'

They've brought her right to her bungalow. Feeling dirty, dusty, confused, she watches the Krishna Cop car drive off, holding Delhi's frenetic traffic at bay with its tame djinns. She pauses at the gate. She needs, she deserves, a moment to come out from the performance, that little step way so you can turn round and look back at yourself and say, yeah, Esha Rathore. The bungalow is unlit, quiet. Neeta and Priya will be out with their wonderful fiancés, talking wedding gifts and guest lists and how hefty a dowry they can squeeze from their husbands-to-be's families. They're not her sisters, though they share the classy bungalow. No one has sisters anymore in Awadh, or even Bharat. No one of Esha's age, though she's heard the balance is being restored. Daughters are fashionable. One upon a time, women paid the dowry.

She breathes deep of her city. The cool garden microclimate presses down the roar of Delhi to a muffled throb, like blood in the heart. She can smell dust and roses. Rose of Persia. Flower of the Urdu poets. And dust. She imagines it rising up on a whisper of wind, spinning into a charming, dangerous djinn.

No. An illusion, a madness of a mad old city. She opens the security gate and finds every square centimetre of the compound filled with red roses.

* * *

Neeta and Priya are waiting for her at the breakfast table next morning, sitting side-by-side close like an interview panel. Or Krishna Cops. For once they aren't talking houses and husbands.

'Who who who where did they come from who sent them so many must have cost a fortune…'

Puri the housemaid brings Chinese green chai that's good against cancer. The sweeper has gathered the bouquets into a pile at one end of the compound. The sweetness of their perfume is already tinged with rot.

'He's a diplomat.' Neeta and Priya only watch *Town and Country* and the *chati* channels but even they must know the name of A.J Rao. So she half lies: 'A Bharati diplomat.'

Their mouths go *Oooh,* then *ah* as they look at each other. Neeta says, 'You have have have to bring him.'

'To our *durbar*,' says Priya.

'Yes, our *durbar*,' says Neeta. They've talked gossiped planned little else for the past two months: their grand joint engagement party where they show off to their as-yet-unmarried girl friends and make all the single men jealous. Esha excuses her grimace with the bitterness of the health-tea.

'He's very busy.' She doesn't say *busy man.* She cannot even think why she is playing these silly *girli* secrecy games. An aeai called her at the Red Fort to tell her it admired her. Didn't even meet her. There was nothing to meet. It was all in her head. 'I don't even know how to get in touch with him. They don't give their numbers out.'

'He's coming,' Neeta and Priya insist.

* * *

She can hardly hear the music for the rattle of the old airco but sweat runs down her sides along the waistband of her Adidas tights to gather in the hollow of her back and slide between the taut curves of her ass. She tries it again across the *gharana's* practice floor. Even the ankle bells sound like lead. Last night she touched the three heavens. This morning she feels dead. She can't concentrate, and that little *lavda* Pranh knows it, swishing at her with yts cane and gobbing out wads of chewed *paan* and mealy eunuch curses.

'Ey! Less staring at your palmer, more *mudras!* Decent *mudras.* You jerk my dick, if I still had one.'

Embarrassed that Pranh has noted something she was not conscious of herself—*ring, call me, ring call me, ring, take me out of this*—she fires back, 'If you ever had one.'

Pranh slashes yts cane at her legs, catches the back of her calf with a sting.

'Fuck you, *hijra!*' Esha snatches up towel bag palmer, hooks the earpiece behind her long straight hair. No point changing, the heat out there will soak through anything in a moment. 'I'm out of here.'

Pranh doesn't call after her. Yts too proud. *Little freak monkey thing,* she thinks. *How is it a nute is an yt, but an incorporeal aeai is a he?* In the legends of Old Delhi, *djinns* are always he.

'*Memsahb* Rathore?'

The chauffeur is in full dress and boots. His only concession to the heat is his shades. In bra top and tights and bare skin, she's melting. 'The vehicle is fully air-conditioned, *memsahb.*'

The white leather upholstery is so cool her flesh recoils from its skin.

'This isn't the Krishna Cops.'

'No *memsahb.*' The chauffeur pulls out into the traffic. It's only as the security locks clunk she thinks, *Oh Lord Krishna, they could be kidnapping me.*

'Who sent you?' There's glass too thick for her fists between her and the driver. Even if the doors weren't locked, a tumble from the car at this speed, in this traffic, would be too much for even a dancer's lithe reflexes. And she's lived in Delhi all her life, *basti* to bungalow, but she doesn't recognize these streets, this suburb, that industrial park. 'Where are you taking me?'

'*Memsahb,* where I am not permitted to say for that would spoil the surprise. But I am permitted to tell you that you are the guest of A.J. Rao.'

The palmer calls her name as she finishes freshening up with bottled Kinley from the car-bar.

'Hello!' (kicking back deep into the cool cool white leather, like a *filmi* star. She is star. A star with a bar in a car.)

Audio-only. 'I trust the car is acceptable?' Same smooth-suave voice. She can't imagine any opponent being able to resist that voice in negotiation.

'It's wonderful. Very luxurious. Very high status.' She's out in the *bastis* now, slums deeper and meaner than the one she grew up in. Newer. The newest ones always look the oldest. Boys chug past on a home-brew *chhakda* they've scavenged from tractor parts. The cream Lex carefully detours around emaciated cattle with angular hips jutting through stretched skin like engineering. Everywhere, drought dust lies thick on the crazed hardtop. This is a city of stares. 'Aren't you supposed to be at the conference?'

A laugh, inside her auditory centre.

'Oh, I am hard at work winning water for Bharat, believe me. I am nothing if not an assiduous civil servant.'

'You're telling me you're there, and here?'

'Oh, it's nothing for us to be in more than one place at the same time. There are multiple copies of me, and subroutines.'

'So which is the real you?'

'They are all the real me. In fact, not one of my avatars is in Delhi at all, I am distributed over a series of *dharma*-cores across Varanasi and Patna.' He sighs. It sounds close and weary and warm as a whisper in her ear. 'You find it difficult to comprehend a distributed consciousness; it is every bit as hard for me to comprehend a discrete, mobile consciousness. I can only copy myself through what you call cyberspace, which is the physical reality of my universe, but you move through dimensional space and time.'

'So which one of you loves me then?' The words are out, wild, loose, and unconsidered. 'I mean, as a dancer, that is.' She's filling, gabbling. 'Is there one of you that particularly appreciates *Kathak?*' Polite polite words, like you'd say to an industrialist or a hopeful lawyer at one of Neeta and Priya's hideous match-making soirees. Don't be forward, no one likes a forward woman. This is a man's world, now. But she hears glee bubble in A.J. Rao's voice.

'Why, all of me and every part of me, Esha.'

Her name. He used her name.

It's a shitty street of pie-dogs and men lounging on *charpoys* scratching themselves, but the chauffeur insists, *here, this way memsahb.* She picks her way down a *gali* lined with unsteady minarets of old car tires. Burning ghee and stale urine reek the air. Kids mob the Lexus but the car has A.J. Rao levels of security. The chauffeur pushes open an old wood and brass Mughal style gate in a crumbling red wall. '*Memsahb.*'

She steps through into a garden. Into the ruins of a garden. The gasp of wonder dies. The geometrical water channels of the *charbagh* are dry, cracked, choked with litter from picnics. The shrubs are blousy and overgrown, the plant borders ragged with weeds. The grass is scabbed brown with drought-burn; the lower branches of the trees have been hacked away for firewood. As she walks towards the crack-roofed pavilion at the centre where paths and water channels meets, the gravel beneath her thin shoes is crazed into rivulets from past monsoons. Dead leaves and fallen twigs cover the lawns. The fountains are dry and silted. Yet families stroll pushing baby buggies; children chase balls. Old Islamic gentlemen read the papers and play chess.

'The Shalimar Gardens,' says A.J. Rao in the base of her skull. 'Paradise as a walled garden.'

And as he speaks, a wave of transformation breaks across the garden, sweeping away the decay of the twenty-first century. Trees break into full leaf, flower beds blossom, rows of terracotta geranium pots march down the banks of the *charbagh* channels which shiver with water. The tiered roofs of the pavilion gleams with gold leaf, peacocks fluster and fuss their vanities, and everything glitters and splashes with fountain play. The laughing families are swept back into Mughal grandees, the old men in the park transformed into *malis* sweeping the gravel paths with their besoms.

Esha claps her hands in joy, hearing a distant, silver spray of sitar notes. 'Oh,' she says, numb with wonder. 'Oh!'

'A thank you, for what you gave me last night. This is one of my favorite places in all India, even though it's almost forgotten. Perhaps, because it is almost forgotten. Aurangzeb was crowned Mughal Emperor here in 1658, now it's an evening stroll for the basti people. The past is a passion of mine; it's easy for me, for all of us. We can live in as many times as we can places. I often come here, in my mind. Or should I say, it comes to me.'

Then the jets from the fountain ripple as if in the wind, but it is not the wind, not on this stifling afternoon, and the falling water flows into the shape of a man, walking out of the spray. A man of water, that shimmers and flows and becomes a man of flesh. A.J. Rao. *No*, she thinks, *never flesh. A djinn. A thing caught between heaven and hell. A caprice, a trickster. Then trick me.*

'It is as the old Urdu poets declare,' says A.J. Rao. 'Paradise is indeed contained within a wall.'

* * *

It is far past four but she can't sleep. She lies naked—shameless—but for the 'hoek behind her ear, on top of her bed with the window slats open and the ancient airco chugging, fitful in the periodic brownouts. It is the worst night yet. The city gasps for air. Even the traffic sounds beaten tonight. Across the room her palmer opens its blue eye and whispers her name. *Esha.*

She's up, kneeling on the bed, hand to 'hoek, sweat beading her bare skin.

'I'm here.' A whisper. Neeta and Priya are a thin wall away on either side.

'It's late, I know, I'm sorry…'

She looks across the room into the palmer's camera.

'It's all right, I wasn't asleep.' A tone in that voice. 'What is it?'

'The mission is a failure.'

She kneels in the centre of the big antique bed. Sweat runs down the fold of her spine.

'The conference? What? What happened?' She whispers, he speaks in her head.

'It fell over one point. One tiny, trivial point, but it was like a wedge that split everything apart until it all collapsed. The Awadhis will build their dam at Kunda Khadar and they will keep their holy Ganga water for Awadh. My delegation is already packing. We will return to Varanasi in the morning.'

Her heart kicks. Then she curses herself, *stupid, romantic* girli. He is already in Varanasi as much as he is here as much as he is at Red Fort assisting his human superiors.

'I'm sorry.'

'Yes,' he says. 'That is the feeling. Was I overconfident in my abilities?'

'People will always disappoint you.'

A wry laugh in the dark of her skull.

'How very…disembodied of you Esha.' Her name seems to hang in the hot air, like a chord. 'Will you dance for me?'

'What, here? Now?'

'Yes. I need something…embodied. Physical. I need to see a body move, a consciousness dance through space and time as I cannot. I need to see something beautiful.'

Need. A creature with the powers of a god, *needs*. But Esha's suddenly shy, covering her small, taut breasts with her hands.

'Music…' she stammers. 'I can't perform without music…' The shadows at the end of the bedroom thicken into an ensemble: three men bent over *tabla, sarangi* and *bansuri.* Esha gives a little shriek and ducks back to the modesty of her bedcover. *They cannot see you, they don't even exist, except in your head. And even if they were flesh, they would be so intent on their contraptions of wire and skin they would not notice.* Terrible driven things, musicians.

'I've incorporated a copy of a sub-aeai into myself for this night,' A.J. Rao says. 'A level 1.9 composition system. I supply the visuals.'

'You can swap bits of yourself in and out?' Esha asks. The *tabla* player has started a slow *Natetere* tap-beat on the *dayan* drum. The musicians nod at each other. Counting, They will be counting. It's hard to convince herself Neeta and Priya can't hear; no one can hear but her. And A.J. Rao. The *sarangi* player sets his bow to the strings, the *bansuri* lets loose a snake of fluting notes. A *sangeet,* but not one she has ever heard before.

'It's making it up!'

'It's a composition aeai. Do you recognize the sources?'

'Krishna and the *gopis.*' One of the classic *Kathak* themes: Krishna's seduction of the milkmaids with his flute, the *bansuri,* most sensual of instruments. She knows the steps, feels her body anticipating the moves.

'Will you dance, lady?'

And she steps with the potent grace of a tiger from the bed onto the grass matting of her bedroom floor, into the focus of the palmer. Before she had been shy, silly, *girli.* Not now. She has never had an audience like this before. A lordly djinn. In pure, hot silence she executes the turns and stampings and bows of the *One Hundred and Eight Gopis,* bare feet kissing the woven grass. Her hands shape *mudras,* her face the expressions of the ancient story: surprise, coyness, intrigue, arousal. Sweat courses luxuriously down her naked skin: she doesn't feel it. She is clothed in movement and night. Time slows, the stars halt in their arc over great Delhi. She can feel the planet breathe beneath her feet. This is what it was for, all those dawn risings, all those bleeding feet, those slashes of Pranh's cane, those lost birthdays, that stolen childhood. She dances until her feet bleed again into the rough weave of the matting, until every last drop of water is sucked from her and turned into salt, but she stays with the *tabla,* the beat of *dayan* and *bayan.* She is the milkmaid by the river, seduced by a god. A.J Rao did not chose this *Kathak* wantonly. And then the music comes to its ringing end and the musicians bow to each other and disperse into golden dust and she collapses, exhausted as never before from any other performance, onto the end of her bed.

Light wakes her. She is sticky, naked, embarrassed. The house staff could find her. And she's got a killing headache. Water. Water. Joints nerves sinews plead for it. She pulls on a Chinese silk robe. On her way to the kitchen, the voyeur eye of her palmer blinks at her. No erotic drean them, no sweat hallucination stirred out of heat and hydrocarbons. She danced Krishna and the one hundred and eight gopis in her bedroom for an aeai. A message. There's a number. *You can call me.*

* * *

Throughout the history of the eight Delhis there have been men—and almost always men—skilled in the lore of djinns. They are wise to their many forms and can see beneath the disguises they wear on the streets—donkey, monkey, dog, scavenging kite—to their true selves. They know their roosts and places where they congregate—they are particularly drawn to mosques—and know that that unexplained heat as you push down a *gali* behind the Jama Masjid is djinns, packed so tight you can feel their fire as you push through them. The wisest—the strongest—of fakirs know their names and so can capture and command them. Even in the old India, before the break up into Awadh and Bharat and Rajputana and the United States of Bengal—there were saints who could summon djinns to fly them on their backs from one end of Hindustan to the other in a night. In my own Leh there was an aged aged sufi who cast one hundred and eight djinns out of a troubled house: twenty-seven in the living room, twenty-seven in the bedroom and fifty-four in the kitchen. With so many djinns there was no room for anyone else. He drove them off with burning yoghurt and chillis but warned: *Do not toy with djinns, for they do nothing without a price, and though that may be years in the asking, ask it they surely will.*

Now there is a new race jostling for space in their city: the aeais. If the *djinni* are the creation of fire and men of clay, these are the creation of word. Fifty million of them swarm Delhi's boulevards and *chowks*: routing traffic, trading shares, maintaining power and water, answering inquiries, telling fortunes, managing calendars and diaries, handling routine legal and medical matters, performing in soap operas, sifting the septillion pieces of information streaming through Delhi's nervous system each second. The city is a great mantra. From routers and maintenance robots with little more than animal intelligence (each animal has intelligence enough: ask the eagle or the tiger) to the great Level 2.9s that are indistinguishable from a human being 99.99 percent of the time; they are a young race, an energetic race, fresh to this world and enthusiastic, understanding little of their power.

The djinns watch in dismay from their rooftops and minarets: that such powerful creatures of living word should so blindly serve the clay creation, but mostly because, unlike humans, they can foresee the time when the aeais will drive them from their ancient, beloved city and take their places.

* * *

This *durbar*, Neeta and Priya's theme is *Town and Country*: the Bharati megasoap that has perversely become fashionable as public sentiment in Awadh turns against Bharat. Well, we will just bloody well build our dam, tanks or no tanks; they can beg for it, it's our water now, and, in the same breath, what do you think about Ved Prakash, isn't it scandalous what that Ritu Parvaaz is up to? Once they derided it and its viewers but now that it's improper, now that's unpatriotic, they can't get enough of Anita Mahapatra and the Begum Vora. Some still refuse to watch but pay for daily plot digests so they can appear fashionably informed at social musts like Neeta and Priya's dating *durbars*.

And it's a grand *durbar;* the last before the monsoon—if it actually happens this year. Neeta and Priya have hired top *bhati*-boys to provide a wash of mixes beamed straight into the guests' 'hoeks. There's even a climate control field, labouring at the limits of its containment to hold back the night heat. Esha can feel its ultrasonics as a dull buzz against her molars.

'Personally, I think sweat becomes you' says A.J Rao, reading Esha's vital signs through her palmer. Invisible to all but Esha, he moves beside her like death through the press of Town and Countrified guests. By tradition the last *durbar* of the season is a masked ball. In modern, middle-class Delhi that means everyone wears the computer-generated semblance of a soap character. In the flesh they are the socially mobile dressed in smart-but-cool hot season modes, but, in the mind's eye, they are Aparna Chawla and Ajay Nadiadwala, dashing Govind and conniving Dr. Chatterji. There are three Ved Prakashes and as many Lal Darfans—the aeai actor that plays Ved Prakash in the machine-made soap. Even the grounds of Neeta's fiancé's suburban bungalow have been enchanted into Brahmpur, the fictional Town where *Town and Country* takes place, where the actors that play the characters believe they live out their lives of celebrity tittle-tattle. When Neeta and Priya judge that everyone has mingled and networked enough, the word will be given and everyone will switch off their glittering disguises and return to being wholesalers and lunch vendors and software rajahs. Then the serious stuff begins, the matter of finding a bride. For now Esha can enjoy wandering anonymous in company of her friendly djinn.

She has been wandering much these weeks, through heat streets to ancient places, seeing her city fresh through the eyes of a creature that lives across many spaces and times. At the Sikh *gurdwara* she saw Tegh Bahadur, the Ninth Guru, beheaded by fundamentalist Aurangzeb's guards. The gyring traffic around Vijay Chowk melted into the Bentley cavalcade of Mountbatten, the Last Viceroy, as he forever quit Lutyen's stupendous palace. The tourist clutter and shoving curio vendors around the Qutb Minar turned to ghosts and it was 1193 and the *muezzins* of the first Mughal conquerors sang out the *adhaan*. Illusions. Little lies. But it is all right, when it is done in love. Everything is all right in love. *Can you read my mind?* she asked as she moved with her invisible guide through the thronging streets, that every day grew less raucous, less substantial. *Do you know what I am thinking about you, Aeai Rao?* Little by little, she slips away from the human world into the city of the djinns.

Sensation at the gate. The male stars of *Town and Country* buzz around a woman in an ivory sequined dress. It's a bit damn clever: she's come as Yana

Mitra, freshest fittest fastest *boli* sing-star. And *boli girlis*, like *Kathak* dancers, are still meat and ego, though Yana, like every Item-singer, has had her computer avatar guest on T'n'C.

A.J. Rao laughs. 'If they only knew. Very clever. What better disguise than to go as yourself. It really *is* Yana Mitra. Esha Rathore, what's the matter, where are you going?'

Why do you have to ask don't you know everything then you know it's hot and noisy and the ultrasonics are doing my head and the yap yap yap is going right through me and they're all onely after one thing, are you married are you engaged are you looking and I wish I hadn't come I wish I'd just gone out somewhere with you and that dark corner under the gulmohar *bushes by the* bhati-rig *looks the place to get away from all the stupid stupid people.*

Neeta and Priya, who know her disguise, shout over, 'So Esha, are we finally going to meet that man of yours?'

He's already waiting for her among the golden blossoms. Djinns travel at the speed of thought.

'What is it what's the matter…?'

She whispers, 'You know sometimes I wish, I really wish you could get me a drink.'

'Why certainly, I will summon a waiter.'

'No!' Too loud. Can't be seen talking to the bushes. 'No; I mean, hand me one. Just hand me one.' But he cannot, and never will. She says, 'I started when I was five, did you know that? Oh, you probably did, you know everything about me. But I bet you didn't know how it happened: I was playing with the other girls, dancing round the tank, when this old woman from the *gharana* went up to my mother and said, I will give you a hundred thousand rupees if you give her to me. I will turn her into a dancer; maybe, if she applies herself, a dancer famous through all of India. And my mother said, why her? And do you know what that woman said? Because she shows rudimentary talent for movement, but, mostly, because you are willing to sell her to me for one *lakh* rupees. She took the money there and then, my mother. The old woman took me to the *gharana*. She had once been a great dancer but she got rheumatism and couldn't move and that made her bad. She used to beat me with *lathis,* I had to be up before dawn to get everyone *chai* and eggs. She would make me practice until my feet bled. They would hold up my arms in slings to perform the *mudras* until I couldn't put them down again without screaming. I never once got home—and do you know something? I never once wanted to. And despite her, I applied myself, and I became a great dancer. And do you know what? No one cares. I spent seventeen years mastering something no one cares about. But bring in some *boli* girl who's been around five minutes to flash her teeth and tits….'

'Jealous?' asks A.J. Rao, mildly scolding.

'Don't I deserve to be?'

Then *bhati*-boy One blinks up 'You Are My Soniya' on his palmer and that's the signal to demask. Yana Mitra claps her hands in delight and sings along as all around her glimmering *soapi* stars dissolve into mundane accountants and engineers and cosmetic nano-surgeons and the pink walls and roof gardens and thousand thousands stars of Old Brahmpur melt and run down the sky.

It's seeing them, exposed in their naked need, melting like that soap-world before the sun of *celebrity*, that calls back the madness Esha knows from her childhood in the *gharana*. The brooch makes a piercing, ringing chime against the cocktail glass she has snatched from a waiter. She climbs up onto a table. At last, that *boli* bitch shuts up. All eyes are on her.

'Ladies, but mostly gentlemen, I have an announcement to make.' Even the city behind the sound-curtain seems to be holding its breath. 'I am engaged to be married!' Gasps. Oohs. Polite applause *who is she, is she on tivi, isn't she something arty?* Neeta and Priya are wide-eyed at the back. 'I'm very very lucky because my husband-to-be is here tonight. In fact, he's been with me all evening. Oh, silly me. Of course, I forgot, not all of you can see him. Darling, would you mind? Gentlemen and ladies, would you mind slipping on your 'hoeks for just a moment. I'm sure you don't need any introduction to my wonderful wonderful fiancé, A.J. Rao.'

And she knows from the eyes, the mouths, the low murmur that threatens to break into applause, then fails, then is taken up by Neeta and Priya to turn into a decorous ovation, that they can all see Rao as tall and elegant and handsome as she sees him, at her side, hand draped over hers.

She can't see that *boli* girl anywhere.

* * *

He's been quiet all the way back in the *phatphat*. He's quiet now, in the house. They're alone. Neeta and Priya should have been home hours ago, but Esha knows they're scared of her.

'You're very quiet.' This, to the coil of cigarette smoke rising up towards the ceiling fan as she lies on her bed. She'd love a *bidi;* a good, dirty street smoke for once, not some Big Name Western brand.

'We were followed as we drove back after the party. An aeai aircraft surveilled your *phatphat*. A network analysis aeai system sniffed at my router net to try to track this com channel. I know for certain street cameras were tasked on us. The Krishna Cop who lifted you after the Red Fort *durbar* was at the end of the street. He is not very good at subterfuge.'

Esha goes to the window to spy out the Krishna Cop, call him out, demand of him what he thinks he's doing?

'He's long gone,' says Rao. 'They have been keeping you under light surveillance for some time now. I would imagine your announcement has upped your level.'

'They were there?'

'As I said...'

'Light surveillance.'

It's scary but exciting, down in the deep *muladhara chakra,* a red throb above her *yoni.* Scarysexy. That same lift of red madness that made her blurt out that marriage announcement. It's all going so far, so fast. No way to get off now.

'You never gave me the chance to answer,' says aeai Rao.

Can you read my mind? Esha thinks at the palmer.

'No, but I share some operating protocols with scripting aeais for *Town and Country*—in a sense they are a low-order part of me—they have become quite good predictors of human behaviour.'

'I'm a soap opera.'

Then she falls back onto the bed and laughs and laughs and laughs until she feels sick, until she doesn't want to laugh anymore and every guffaw is a choke, a lie, spat up at the spy machines up there, beyond the lazy fan that merely stirs the heat, turning on the huge thermals that spire up from Delhi's colossal heat-island, a conspiracy of djinns.

'Esha,' A.J Rao says, closer than he has ever seemed before. 'Lie still.' She forms the question *why?* And hears the corresponding whisper inside her head *hush, don't speak.* In the same instant the *chakra* glow bursts like a yolk and leaks heat into her *yoni. Oh,* she says, *oh!* Her clitoris is singing to her. *Oh oh oh oh.* 'How…?' Again, the voice, huge inside her head, inside every part of her *sssshhhhh.* Building building she needs to do something, she needs to move needs to rub against the day-warmed scented wood of the big bed, needs to get her hand down there hard hard hard…

'No, don't touch,' chides A.J Rao, and now she can't even move she needs to explode she has to explode her skull can't contain this her dancer's muscles are pulled tight as wires she can't take much more *no no no yes yes yes* she's shrieking now tiny little shrieks beating her fists off the bed but it's just spasm, nothing will obey her and then it's explosion bam, and another one before that one has even faded, huge slow explosions across the sky and she's cursing and blessing every god in India. Ebbing now, but still shock after shock, one on top of the other. Ebbing now… Ebbing.

'Ooh. Oh. What? Oh wow, how?'

'The machine you wear behind your ear can reach deeper than words and visions,' says A.J Rao. 'So, are you answered?'

'What?' The bed is drenched in sweat. She's sticky dirty needs to wash change clothes, move but the afterglows are still fading. Beautiful beautiful colours.

'The question you never gave me the chance to answer. Yes. I will marry you.'

* * *

'Stupid vain girl, you don't even know what caste he is.'

Mata Madhuri smokes eighty a day through a plastic tube hooked through the respirator unit into a grommet in her throat. She burns through them three at time: *Bloody machine scrubs all the good out of them,* she says. *Last bloody pleasure I have.* She used to bribe the nurses but they bring her them free now, out of fear of her temper that grows increasingly vile as her body surrenders more and more to the machines.

Without pause for Esha's reply, a flick of her whim whips the life-support chair round and out into the garden.

'Can't smoke in there, no fresh air.'

Esha follows her out on to the raked gravel of the formal *charbagh.*

'No one marries in caste anymore.'

'Don't be smart, stupid girl. It's like marrying a Muslim, or even a Christian, Lord Krishna protect me. You know fine what I mean. Not a real person.'

'There are girls younger than me marry trees, or even dogs.'

'So bloody clever. That's up in some god-awful shithole like Bihar or Rajputana, and anyway, those are gods. Any fool knows that. Ach, away with you!' The old, destroyed woman curses as the chair's aeai deploys its parasol. 'Sun sun, I need sun, I'll be burning soon enough, sandalwood, you hear? You burn me on a sandalwood pyre. I'll know if you stint.'

Madhuri the old crippled dance teacher always uses this tactic to kill a conversation with which she is uncomfortable. *When I'm gone… Burn me sweetly…*

'And what can a god do that A.J. Rao can't?'

'Ai! You ungrateful, blaspheming child. I'm not hearing this la la la la la la la la la have you finished yet?'

Once a week Esha comes to the nursing home to visit this ruin of a woman, wrecked by the demands a dancer makes of a human body. She's explored guilt need rage resentment anger pleasure at watching her collapse into long death as the motives that keep her turning up the drive in a *phatphat* and there is only one she believes. She's the only mother she has.

'If you marry that… thing… you will be making a mistake that will destroy your life,' Madhuri declares, accelerating down the path between the water channels.

'I don't need your permission,' Esha calls after her. A thought spins Madhuri's chair on its axis.

'Oh, really? That would be a first for you. You want my blessing. Well, you won't have it. I refuse to be party to such nonsense.'

'I will marry A.J. Rao.'

'What did you say?'

'I. Will. Marry. Aeai. A. J. Rao.'

Madhuri laughs, a dry, dying, spitting sound, full of *bidi*-smoke.

'Well, you almost surprise me. Defiance. Good, some spirit at last. That was always your problem, you always needed everyone to approve, everyone to give you permission, everyone to love you. And that's what stopped you being great, do you know that, girl? You could have been a *devi,* but you always held back for fear that someone might not approve. And so you were ever only…good.'

People are looking now, staff, visitors. Patients. Raised voices, unseemly emotions. This is a house of calm, and slow mechanized dying. Esha bends low to whisper to her mentor.

'I want you to know that I dance for him. Every night. Like Radha for Krishna. I dance just for him, and then he comes and makes love to me. He makes me scream and swear like a hooker. Every night. And look!' He doesn't need to call anymore; he is hardwired into the 'hoek she now hardly ever takes off. Esha looks up: he is there, standing in a sober black suit among the strolling visitors and droning wheelchairs, hands folded. 'There he is, see? My lover, my husband.'

A long, keening screech, like feedback, like a machine dying. Madhuri's withered hands fly to her face. Her breathing tube curdles with tobacco smoke.

'Monster! Monster! Unnatural child, ah, I should have left you in that *basti!* Away from me away away away!'

Esha retreats from the old woman's mad fury as hospital staff come hurrying across the scorched lawns, white saris flapping.

* * *

Every fairytale must have a wedding.

Of course it was the event of the season. The decrepit old Shalimar Gardens were transformed by an army of *malis* into a sweet, green, watered maharajah's fantasia with elephants, pavilions, musicians, lancers, dancers, *filmi* stars and robot bartenders. Neeta and Priya were uncomfortable bridesmaids in fabulous frocks; a great brahmin was employed to bless the union of woman and artificial intelligence. Every television network sent cameras, human or aeai. Gleaming presenters checked the guests in and checked the guests out. Chati mag paparazzi came in their crowds, wondering what they could turn their cameras on. There were even politicians from Bharat, despite the souring relationships between the two neighbours now that Awadh constructors were scooping up the Ganga sands into revetments. But most there were the people of the encroaching *bastis,* jostling up against the security staff lining the paths of their garden, asking, *she's marrying a what? How does that work? Can they, you know? And what about children? Who is she, actually? Can you see anything? I can't see anything. Is there anything to see?*

But the guests and the great were 'hoeked up and applauded the groom in his golden veil on his white stallion, stepping with the delicacy of a dressage horse up the raked paths. And because they were great and guests, there was not one who, despite the free French champagne from the well-known diplomatic *sommelier,* would ever say, *but there's no one there.* No one was at all surprised that, after the bride left in a stretch limo, there came a dry, sparse thunder, cloud to cloud, and a hot mean wind that swept the discarded invitations along the paths. As they were filing back to their taxis, tankers were draining the expensively filled *qanats.*

It made lead in the news.

Kathak stars weds aeai lover!!! Honeymoon in Kashmir!!!

Above the *chowks* and minarets of Delhi, the djinns bent together in conference.

* * *

He takes her while shopping in Tughluk Mall. Three weeks and the shop girls still nod and whisper. She likes that. She doesn't like it that they glance and giggle when the Krishna Cops lift her from the counter at the Black Lotus Japanese Import Company.

'My husband is an accredited diplomat, this is a diplomatic incident.' The woman in the bad suit pushes her head gently down to enter the car. The Ministry doesn't need personal liability claims.

'Yes, but you are not, Mrs. Rao,' says Thacker in the back seat. Still wearing that cheap aftershave.

'Rathore,' she says. 'I have retained my stage name. And we shall see what my husband has to say about my diplomatic status.' She lifts her hand in a *mudra* to speak to AyJay, as she thinks of him now. Dead air. She performs the wave again.

'This is a shielded car,' Thacker says.

The building is shielded also. They take the car right inside, down a ramp into the basement parking lot. It's a cheap, anonymous glass and titanium block on Parliament Street that she's driven past ten thousand times on her way to the shops of Connaught Circus without ever noticing. Thacker's office is on the fifteenth floor. It's tidy and has a fine view over the astronomical geometries of the Jantar Mantar but smells of food: *tiffin* snatched at the desk. She checks for photographs of family children wife. Only himself smart in pressed whites for a cricket match.

'*Chai?*'

'Please.' The anonymity of this civil service block is beginning to unnerve her: a city within a city. The *chai* is warm and sweet and comes in a tiny disposable plastic cup. Thacker's smile seems also warm and sweet. He sits at the end of the desk, angled towards her in Krishna-cop handbook 'non-confrontational'.

'Mrs. Rathore. How to say this?'

'My marriage is legal…'

'Oh, I know, Mrs. Rathore. This is Awadh, after all. Why, there have even been women who married djinns, within our own lifetimes. No. It's an international affair now, it seems. Oh well. Water: we do all so take it for granted, don't we? Until it runs short, that is.'

'Everybody knows my husband is still trying to negotiate a solution to the Kunda Khadar problem.'

'Yes, of course he is.' Thacker lifts a manila envelope from his desk, peeps inside, grimaces coyly. 'How shall I put this? Mrs. Rathore, does your husband tell you everything about his work?'

'That is an impertinent question….'

'Yes yes, forgive me, but if you'll look at these photographs.'

Big glossy hi-res prints, slick and sweet smelling from the printer. Aerial views of the ground, a thread of green blue water, white sands, scattered shapes without meaning.

'This means nothing to me.'

'I suppose it wouldn't, but these drone images show Bharati battle tanks, robot reconnaissance units and air defense batteries deploying within striking distance of the construction at Kunda Khadar.'

And it feels as if the floor has dissolved beneath her and she is falling through a void so vast it has no visible reference points, other than the sensation of her own falling.

'My husband and I don't discuss work.'

'Of course. Oh, Mrs. Rathore, you've crushed your cup. Let me get you another one.'

He leaves her much longer than it takes to get a shot of *chai* from the *wallah*. When he returns he asks casually, 'Have you heard of a thing called the Hamilton Acts? I'm sorry, I thought in your position you would... but evidently not. Basically, it's a series of international treaties originated by the United States limiting the development and proliferation of high-level artificial intelligences, most specifically the hypothetical Generation Three. No? Did he not tell you any of this?'

Mrs Rathore in her Italian suit folds her ankles one over the other and thinks, *this reasonable man can do anything he wants here, anything.*

'As you probably know, we grade and licence aeais according to levels; these roughly correspond to how convincingly they pass as human beings. A Level 1 has basic animal intelligence, enough for its task but would never be mistaken for a human. Many of them can't even speak. They don't need to. A Level 2.9 like your husband'—he speeds over the word, like the wheel of a *shatabdi* express over the gap in a rail—'is humanlike to a fifth percentile. A Generation Three is indistinguishable in any circumstances from a human—in fact, their intelligences may be many millions of times ours, if there is any meaningful way of measuring that. Theoretically we could not even recognise such an intelligence, all we would see would be the Generation Three interface, so to speak. The Hamilton Acts simply seek to control technology that could give rise to a Generation Three aeai. Mrs. Rathore, we believe sincerely that the Generation Threes pose the greatest threat to our security—as a nation and as a species—that we have ever faced.'

'And my husband?' Solid, comfortable word. Thacker's sincerity scares her.

'The government is preparing to sign the Hamilton Acts in return for loan guarantees to construct the Kunda Khadar dam. When the Act is passed—and it's in the current session of the Lok Sabha—everything under Level 2.8. will be subject to rigorous inspection and licensing, policed by us.'

'And over Level 2.8?'

'Illegal, Mrs. Rathore. They will be aggressively erased.'

Esha crosses and uncrosses her legs. She shifts on the chair. Thacker will wait forever for her response.

'What do you want me to do?'

'A.J. Rao is highly placed within the Bharati administration.'

'You're asking me to spy… on an *aeai*.'

From his face, she knows he expected her to say *husband*.

'We have devices, taps… They would be beneath the level of aeai Rao's consciousness. We can run them into your 'hoek. We are not all blundering plods in the Department. Go to the window, Mrs. Rathore.'

Esha touches her fingers lightly to the climate-cooled glass, polarised dusk against the drought light. Outside the smog haze says *heat.* Then she cries and drops to her knees in fear. The sky is filled with gods, rank upon rank, tier upon tier, rising up above Delhi in a vast helix, huge as clouds, as countries, until at the apex the Trimurti, the Hindu Trinity of Brahma, Vishnu, Siva look down like falling moons. It is her private Ramayana, the titanic Vedic battle order of gods arrayed across the troposphere.

She feels Thacker's hand help her up.

'Forgive me, that was stupid, unprofessional. I was showing off. I wanted to impress you with the aeai systems we have at our disposal.'

His hand lingers a moment more than *gentle.* And the gods go out, all at once.

She says, 'Mr. Thacker, would you put a spy in my bedroom, in my bed, between me and my husband? That's what you're doing if you tap into the channels between me and AyJay.'

Still, the hand is there as Thacker guides her to the chair, offers cool cool water.

'I only ask because I believe I am doing something for this country. I take pride in my job. In some things I have discretion, but not when it comes to the security of the nation. Do you understand?'

Esha twitches into dancer's composure, straightens her dress, checks her face.

'Then the least you can do is call me a car.'

* * *

That evening she whirls to the *tabla* and *shehnai* across the day-warmed marble of a Jaipuri palace *Diwan-I-aam*, a flame among the twilit pillars. The audience are dark huddles on the marble, hardly daring even to breath. Among the lawyers politicians journalists cricket stars moguls of industry are the managers who have converted this Rajput palace into a planetary-class hotel, and any numbers of *chati* celebs. None so *chati*, so celebby, as Esha Rathore. Pranh can cherry-pick the bookings now. She's more than a nine-day, even a nine-week wonder. Esha knows that all her rapt watchers are 'hoeked up, hoping for a ghost-glimpse of her *djinn*-husband dancing with her through the flame-shadowed pillars.

Afterwards, as yt carries her armfuls of flowers back to her suite, Pranh says, 'You know, I'm going to have to up my percentage.'

'You wouldn't dare,' Esha jokes. Then she sees the bare fear on the nute's face. It's only a wash, a shadow. But yts afraid.

Neeta and Priya had moved out of the bungalow by the time she returned from Dal Lake. They've stopped answering her calls. It's seven weeks since she last went to see Madhuri.

Naked, she sprawls on the pillows in the filigree-light stone *jharoka*. She peers down from her covered balcony through the grille at the departing guests. See out, not see in. Like the shut-away women of the old *zenana*. Shut away from the world. Shut away from human flesh. She stands up, holds her body against the day-warmed stone; the press of her nipples, the rub of her pubis. *Can you see me smell me sense me know that I am here at all?*

And he's there. She does not need to see him now, just sense his electric prickle along the inside of her skull. He fades into vision sitting on the end of the low, ornate teak bed. *He could as easily materialise in midair in front of her balcony,* she thinks. But there are rules, and games, even for djinns.

'You seem distracted, heart.' He's blind in this room—no camera eyes observing her in her jewelled skin—but he observes her through a dozen senses, a myriad feedback loops through her 'hoek.

'I'm tired, I'm annoyed, I wasn't as good as I should have been.'

'Yes, I thought that too. Was it anything to do with the Krishna Cops this afternoon?'

Esha's heart races. He can read her heartbeat. He can read her sweat, he can read the adrenaline and noradrenaline balance in her brain. He will know if she lies. Hide a lie inside a truth.

'I should have said, I was embarrassed.' He can't understand shame. Strange, in a society where people die from want of honour. 'We could be in trouble, there's something called the Hamilton Acts.'

'I am aware of them.' He laughs. He has this way now of doing it inside her head. He thinks she likes the intimacy, a truly private joke. She hates it. 'All too aware of them.'

'They wanted to warn me. Us.'

'That was kind of them. And me a representative of a foreign government. So that's why they'd been keeping a watch on you, to make sure you are all right.'

'They thought they might be able to use me to get information from you.'

'Did they indeed?'

The night is so still she can hear the jingle of the elephant harnesses and the cries of the *mahouts* as they carry the last of the guests down the long processional drive to their waiting limos. In a distant kitchen a radio jabbers.

Now we will see how human you are. Call him out. At last A.J. Rao says,

'Of course. I do love you.' Then he looks into her face. 'I have something for you.'

The staff turn their faces away in embarrassment as they set the device on the white marble floor, back out of the room, eyes averted. What does she care? She is a star. A.J. Rao raises his hand and the lights slowly die. Pierced-brass lanterns send soft stars across the beautiful old *zenana* room. The device is the size and shape of a *phatphat* tire, chromed and plasticed, alien among the Mughal retro. As Esha floats over the marble towards it, the plain white surface bubbles and deliquesces into dust. Esha hesitates.

'Don't be afraid, look!' says A.J. Rao. The powder spurts up like steam from boiling rice, then pollen-bursts into a tiny dust-dervish, staggering across the surface of the disc. 'Take the 'hoek off!' Rao cries delightedly from the bed. 'Take it off.' Twice she hesitates, three times he encourages. Esha slides the coil of plastic off the sweet-spot behind her ear and voice and man vanish like death. Then the pillar of glittering dust leaps head high, lashes like a tree in a monsoon and twists itself into the ghostly outline of a man. It flickers once, twice, and then A.J. Rao stands before her. A rattle like leaves a snake-rasp a rush of winds, and then the image says, 'Esha.' A whisper of dust. A thrill of ancient fear runs through her skin into her bones.

'What is this… what are you?'

The storm of dust parts into a smile

'I-Dust. Micro-robots. Each is smaller than a grain of sand, but they manipulate static fields and light. They are my body. Touch me. This is real. This is me.'

But she flinches away in the lantern-lit room. Rao frowns.

'Touch me….'

She reaches out her hand towards his chest. Close, he is a creature of sand, a whirlwind permanently whipping around the shape of a man. Esha touches flesh to i-Dust. Her hand sinks into his body. Her cry turns to a startled giggle.

'It tickles….'

'The static fields.'

'What's inside?'

'Why don't you find out?'

'What, you mean?'

'It's the only intimacy I can offer….' He sees her eyes widen under their kohled make-up. 'I think you should hold your breath.'

She does, but keeps her eyes open until the last moment, until the dust flecks like a dead *tivi* channel in her close focus. A.J. Rao's body feels like the most delicate Vaanasi silk scarf draped across her bare skin. She is inside him. She is inside the body of her husband, her lover. She dares to open her eyes. Rao's face is a hollow shell looking back at her from a perspective of millimetres. When she moves her lips, she can feel the dust-bots of his lips brushing against hers: an inverse kiss.

'My heart, my Radha,' whispers the hollow mask of A.J. Rao. Somewhere Esha knows she should be screaming. But she cannot: she is somewhere no human has ever been before. And now the whirling streamers of i-Dust are stroking her hips, her belly, her thighs. Her breasts. Her nipples, her cheeks and neck, all the places she loves to feel a human touch, caressing her, driving her to her knees, following her as the mote-sized robots follow A.J. Rao's command, swallowing her with his body.

* * *

It's *Gupshup* followed by *Chandni Chati* and at twelve thirty a photo shoot—at the hotel, if you don't mind—for *FilmFare*'s Saturday Special Center Spread—you don't mind if we send a robot, they can get places get angles we just can't get the meat-ware and could you dress up, like you did for the opening, maybe a move or two, in between the pillars in the Diwan, just like the gala opening, okay lovely lovely lovely well your husband can copy us a couple of avatars and our own aeais can paste him in people want to see you together, happy couple lovely couple, dancer risen from *basti*, international diplomat, marriage across worlds in every sense the romance of it all, so how did you meet what first attracted you what's it like be married to an aeai how do the other girls treat you do you, you know and what about children, I mean, of course a woman and an aeai but there are technologies these days geneline engineering like all the super-duper rich and their engineered children and you are a celebrity now how are you finding it, sudden rise to fame, in every *gupshup* column, worldwide *celebi* star everyone's talking all the rage and all the chat and all the parties and as Esha answers for the sixth time the same questions asked by the same gazelle-eyed *girli celebi* reporters *oh we are very happy wonderfully happy deliriously happy love is a wonderful wonderful thing and that's the thing about love, it can be for anything, anyone, even a human and an aeai, that's the purest form of love, spiritual love* her mouth opening and closing yabba yabba yabba but her inner eye, her eye of Siva, looks inwards, backwards

Her mouth, opening and closing.

Lying on the big Mughal sweet-wood bed, yellow morning light shattered through the *jharoka* screen, her bare skin good-pimpled in the cool of the airco. Dancing between worlds: sleep, wakefulness in the hotel bedroom, memory of the things he did to her limbic centres through the hours of the night that had her singing like a *bulbul*, the world of the djinns. Naked but for the 'hoek behind her ear. She had become like those people who couldn't afford the treatments and had to wear eyeglasses and learned to at once ignore and be conscious of the technology on their faces. Even when she did remove it—for performing; for, as now, the shower,—she could still place A.J. Rao in the room, feel his physicality. In the big marble stroll-in shower in this VIP suite relishing the gush and rush of precious water (always the mark of a true *rani*) she knew

AyJay was sitting on the carved chair by the balcony. So when she thumbed on the *tivi* panel (bathroom with *tivi, oooh!*) to distract her while she towelled dry her hair, her first reaction was a double-take-look at the 'hoek on the sink-stand when she saw the press conference from Varanasi and Water Spokesman A.J. Rao explaining Bharat's necessary military exercises in the vicinity of the Kunda Khadar dam. She slipped on the 'hoek, glanced into the room. There, on the chair, as she felt. There, in the Bharat Sabha studio in Varanasi, talking to Bharti from the *Good Morning Awadh!* News.

Esha watched them both as she slowly, distractedly dried herself. She had felt glowing, sensual, divine. Now she was fleshy, self-conscious, stupid. The water on her skin, the air in the big room was cold cold cold.

'AyJay, is that really you?'

He frowned.

'That's a very strange question first thing in the morning. Especially after...'

She cut cold his smile.

'There's a *tivi* in the bathroom. You're on, doing an interview for the news. A live interview. So, are you really here?'

'*Cho chweet,* you know what I am, a distributed entity. I'm copying and deleting myself all over the place. I am wholly there, and I am wholly here.'

Esha held the vast, powder-soft towel around her.

'Last night, when you were here, in the body, and afterwards, when we were in the bed; were you here with me? Wholly here? Or was there a copy of you working on your press statement and another having a high-level meeting and another drawing an emergency water supply plan and another talking to the Banglas in Dhaka?'

'My love, does it matter?'

'Yes it matters!' She found tears, and something beyond; anger choking in her throat. 'It matters to me. It matters to any woman. To any... human.'

'*Mrs. Rao, are you all right?*'

'Rathore, my name is Rathore!' She hears herself snap at the silly little chati-mag junior. Esha gets up, draws up her full dancer's poise. 'This interview is over.'

'Mrs. Rathore Mrs. Rathore,' the journo *girli* calls after her.

Glancing at her fractured image in the thousand mirrors of the Sheesh Mahal, Esha notices glittering dust in the shallow lines of her face.

* * *

A thousand stories tell of the wilfulness and whim of djinns. But for every story of the *djinni*, there are a thousand tales of human passion and envy and the aeais, being a creation between, learned from both. Jealousy, and dissembling.

When Esha went to Thacker the Krishna Cop, she told herself it was from fear of what the Hamilton Acts might do to her husband in the name of national hygiene. But she dissembled. She went to that office on Parliament Street looking over the star-geometries of the Jantar Mantar out of jealousy. When a wife wants her husband, she must have all of him. Ten thousand stories tell this. A copy in the bedroom while another copy plays water politics is an unfaithfulness. If a wife does not have everything, she has nothing. So Esha went to Thacker's office wanting to betray and as she opened her hand on the desk and the *techi* boys loaded their darkware into her palmer she thought, *this is right, this is good, now we are equal.* And when Thacker asked her to meet him again in a week to update the 'ware—unlike the djinns, hostages of eternity, software entities on both sides of the war evolved at an ever-increasing rate—he told himself it was duty to his warrant, loyalty to his country. In this too he dissembled. It was fascination.

Earth-mover robots started clearing the Kunda Khadar dam site the day Inspector Thacker suggested that perhaps next week they might meet at the International Coffee House on Connaught Circus, his favourite. She said, *my husband will see.* To which Thacker replied, *we have ways to blind him.* But all the same she sat in the furthest, darkest corner, under the screen showing the international cricket, hidden from any prying eyes, her 'hoek shut down and cold in her handbag.

So what are you finding out? she asked.

It would be more than my job is worth to tell you, Mrs. Rathore, said the Krishna Cop. National security. Then the waiter brought coffee on a silver tray.

After that they never went back to the office. On the days of their meetings Thacker would whirl her through the city in his government car to Chandni Chowk, to Humayun's Tomb and the Qutb Minar, even to the Shalimar Gardens. Esha knew what he was doing, taking her to those same places where her husband had enchanted her. *How closely have you been watching me?* she thought. *Are you trying to seduce me?* For Thacker did not magic her away to the eight Delhis of the dead past, but immersed her in the crowd, the smell, the bustle, the voices and commerce and traffic and music; her present, her city burning with life and movement. *I was fading,* she realised. *Fading out of the world, becoming a ghost, locked in that invisible marriage, just the two of us, seen and unseen, always together, only together.* She would feel for the plastic fetus of her 'hoek coiled in the bottom of her jewelled bag and hate it a little. When she slipped it back behind her ear in the privacy of the *phatphat* back to her bungalow, she would remember that Thacker was always assiduous in thanking her for her help in national security. Her reply was always the same: *Never thank a woman for betraying her husband over her country.*

He would ask of course. *Out and about,* she would say. *Sometimes I just need to get out of this place, get away. Yes, even from you...* Holding the words, the look into the eye of the lens just long enough...

Yes, of course, you must.

Now the earth-movers had turned Kunda Khadar into Asia's largest construction site, the negotiations entered a new stage. Varanasi was talking directly to Washington to put pressure on Awadh to abandon the dam and avoid a potentially destabilising water war. US support was conditional on Bharat's agreement to the Hamilton protocols, which Bharat could never do, not with its major international revenue generator being the wholly aeai-generated *soapi Town and Country.*

Washington telling me to effectively sign my own death warrant, A.J. Rao would laugh. *Americans surely appreciate irony.* All this he told her as they sat on the well-tended lawn sipping green *chai* through a straw, Esha sweating freely in the swelter but unwilling to go into the air-conditioned cool because she knew there were still paparazzi lenses out there, focusing. AyJay never needed to sweat. But she still knew that he split himself. In the night, in the rare cool, he would ask, *dance for me.* But she didn't dance anymore, not for aeai A.J. Rao, not for Pranh, not for a thrilled audience who would shower her with praise and flowers and money and fame. Not even for herself.

Tired. Too tired. The heat. Too tired.

* * *

Thacker is on edge, toying with his *chai* cup, wary of eye contact when they meet in his beloved International Coffee House. He takes her hand and draws the updates into her open palm with boyish coyness. His talk is smaller than small, finicky, itchily polite. Finally, he dares looks at her.

'Mrs. Rathore, I have something I must ask you. I have wanted to ask you for some time now.'

Always, the name, the honorific. But the breath still freezes, her heart kicks in animal fear.

'You know you can ask me anything.' Tastes like poison. Thacker can't hold her eye, ducks away, Killa Krishna Kop turned shy boy.

'Mrs. Rathore, I am wondering if you would like to come and see me play cricket?'

The Department of Artificial Intelligence Registration and Licensing versus Parks and Cemeteries Service of Delhi is hardly a Test against the United States of Bengal but it is still enough of a social occasion to out posh frocks and Number One saris. Pavilions, parasols, sunshades ring the scorched grass of the Civil Service of Awadh sports ground, a flock of white wings. Those who can afford portable airco field generators sit in the cool drinking English Pimms Number 1 Cup. The rest fan themselves. Incognito in hi-label shades and light silk *dupatta,* Esha Rathore looks at the salt white figures moving on the circle of brown grass and wonders what it is they find so important in their game of sticks and ball to make themselves suffer so.

She had felt hideously self-conscious when she slipped out of the *phatphat* in her flimsy disguise. Then as she saw the crowds in their *mela* finery milling and chatting, heat rose inside her, the same energy that allowed her to hide behind her performances, seen but unseen. A face half the country sees on its morning *chati* mags, yet can vanish so easily under shades and a headscarf. Slum features. The anonymity of the *basti* bred into the cheekbones, a face from the great crowd.

The Krishna Cops have been put in to bat by Parks and Cemeteries. Thacker is in the middle of the batting order, but Parks and Cemeteries pace bowler Chaudry and the lumpy wicket is making short work of the Department's openers. One on his way to the painted wooden pavilion, and Thacker striding towards the crease, pulling on his gloves, taking his place, lining up his bat. *He is very handsome in his whites,* Esha thinks. He runs a couple of desultory ones with his partner at the other end, then it's a new over. Clop of ball on willow. A rich, sweet sound. A couple of safe returns. Then the bowler lines and brings his arm round in a windmill. The ball gets a sweet mad bounce. Thacker fixes it with his eye, steps back, takes it in the middle of the bat and drives it down, hard, fast, bounding towards the boundary rope that kicks it into the air for a cheer and a flurry of applause and a four. And Esha is on her feet, hands raised to applaud, cheering. The score clicks over the on the big board, and she is still on her feet, alone of all the audience. For directly across the ground, in front of the sight screens, is a tall, elegant figure in black, wearing a red turban.

Him. Impossibly, him. Looking right at her, through the white-clad players as if they were ghosts. And very slowly, he lifts a finger and taps it to his right ear.

She knows what she'll find but she must raise her fingers in echo, feel with horror the coil of plastic overlooked in her excitement to get to the game, nestled accusing in her hair like a snake.

* * *

'So, who won the cricket then?'

'Why do you need to ask me? If it were important to you, you'd know. Like you can know anything you really want to.'

'You don't know? Didn't you stay to the end? I thought the point of sport was who won. What other reason would you have to follow intra-Civil Service cricket?'

If Puri the maid were to walk into the living room, she would see a scene from a folk tale: a woman shouting and raging at silent dead air. But Puri does her duties and leaves as soon as she can. She's not at ease in a house of djinns.

'Sarcasm is it now? Where did you learn that? Some sarcasm aeai you've made part of yourself? So now there's another part of you I don't know, that I'm supposed to love? Well, I don't like it and I won't love it because it makes you look petty and mean and spiteful.'

'There are no aeais for that. We have no need for those emotions. If I learned these, I learned them from humans.'

Esha lifts her hand to rip away the 'hoek, hurl it against the wall.

'No!'

So far Rao has been voice-only, now the slanting late-afternoon golden light stirs and curdles into the body of her husband.

'Don't,' he says. 'Don't…banish me. I do love you.'

'What does that mean?' Esha screams, 'You're not real! None of this is real! It's just a story we made up because we wanted to believe it. Other people, they have real marriages, real lives, real sex. Real …children.'

'Children. Is that what it is? I thought the fame, the attention was the thing, that there never would be children to ruin your career and your body. But if that's no longer enough, we can have children, the best children I can buy.'

Esha cries out, a keen of disappointment and frustration. The neighbours will hear. But the neighbours have been hearing everything, listening, gossiping. No secrets in the city of djinns.

'Do you know what they're saying, all those magazines and *chati* shows? What they're really saying? About us, the djinn and his wife?'

'I know!' For the first time, A.J. Rao's voice, so sweet, so reasonable inside her head, is raised. 'I know what every one of them says about us. Esha, have I ever asked anything of you?'

'Only to dance.'

'I'm asking one more thing of you now. It's not a big thing. It's a small thing, nothing really. You say I'm not real, what we have is not real. That hurts me, because at some level it's true. Our worlds are not compatible. But it can be real. There is a chip, new technology, a protein chip. You get it implanted, here.' Rao raises his hand to his third eye. 'It would be like the 'hoek, but it would always be on. I could always be with you. We would never be apart. And you could leave your world and enter mine….'

Esha's hands are at her mouth, holding in the horror, the bile, the sick vomit of fear. She heaves, retches. Nothing. No solid, no substance, just ghosts and djinns. Then she rips her 'hoek from the sweet-spot behind her ear and there is blessed silence and blindness. She holds the little device in her two hands and snaps it cleanly in two.

Then she runs from her house.

* * *

Not Neeta not Priya, not snippy Pranh in yts *gharana*, not Madhuri a, smoke-blackened hulk in a life-support chair, and no not never her mother, even though Esha's feet remember every step to her door; never the *basti*. That's death.

One place she can go.

But he won't let her. He's there in the *phatphat*, his face in the palm of her hands, voice scrolling silently in a ticker across the smart fabric: *come back, I'm sorry, come back, let's talk come back, I didn't mean to come back.* Hunched in the back of the little yellow and black plastic bubble she clenches his face into a fist but she can still feel him, feel his face, his mouth next to her skin. She peels the palmer from her hand. His mouth moves silently. She hurls him into the traffic. He vanishes under truck tires.

And still he won't let her go. The *phatphat* spins into Connaught Circus's vast gyratory and his face is on every single one of the video-silk screens hung across the curving facades. Twenty A.J. Rao's greater, lesser, least, miming in sync.

Esha Esha come back, say the rolling news tickers. *We can try something else. Talk to me. Any ISO, any palmer, anyone....*

Infectious paralysis spreads across Connaught Circus. First the people who notice things like fashion ads and *chati*-screens; then the people who notice other people, then the traffic, noticing all the people on the pavements staring up, mouths fly-catching. Even the *phatphat* driver is staring. Connaught Circus is congealing into a clot of traffic: if the heart of Delhi stops, the whole city will seize and die.

'Drive on drive on,' Esha shouts at her driver. 'I order you to drive.' But she abandons the autorickshaw at the end of Sisganj Road and pushes through the clogged traffic the final half-kilometre to Manmohan Singh Buildings. She glimpses Thacker pressing through the crowd, trying to rendezvous with the police motorbike sirening a course through the traffic. In desperation she thrusts up an arm, shouts out his name and rank. At last, he turns. They beat towards each other through the chaos.

'Mrs. Rathore, we are facing a major incursion incident....'

'My husband, Mr. Rao, he has gone mad....'

'Mrs. Rathore, please understand, by our standards, he never was sane. He is an aeai.'

The motorbike wails its horns impatiently. Thacker waggles his head to the driver, a woman in police leathers and helmet: *in a moment in a moment.* He seizes Esha's hand, pushes her thumb into his palmer-gloved hand.

'Apartment 1501. I've keyed it to your thumbprint. Open the door to no one, accept no calls, do not use any communications or entertainment equipment. Stay away from the balcony. I'll return as quickly as I can.'

Then he swings up onto the pillion, the driver walks her machine round and they weave off into the gridlock.

The apartment is modern and roomy and bright and clean for a man on his own, well furnished and decorated with no signs of a Krishna Cop's work brought home of an evening. It hits her in the middle of the big living-room floor with the sun pouring in. Suddenly she is on her knees on the Kashmiri rug, shivering, clutching herself, bobbing up and down to sobs so wracking they have no sound. This time the urge to vomit it all up cannot be resisted. When it is out of her—not all of it, it will never all come out—she looks out from under her hanging, sweat-soaked hair, breath still shivering in her aching chest. Where is this place? What has she done? How could she have been so stupid, so vain and senseless and blind? Games games, children's pretending, how could it ever have been? I say it is and it is so: look at me! At me!

Thacker has a small, professional bar in his kitchen annexe. Esha does not know drink so the *chota peg* she makes herself is much much more gin than tonic but it gives her what she needs to clean the sour, biley vomit from the wool rug and ease the quivering in her breath.

Esha starts, freezes, imagining Rao's voice. She holds herself very still, listening hard. A neighbour's *tivi*, turned up. Thin walls in these new-built executive apartments.

She'll have another *chota peg*. A third and she can start to look around. There's a spa-pool on the balcony. The need for moving, healing water defeats Thacker's warnings. The jets bubble up. With a dancer's grace she slips out of her clinging, emotionally soiled clothes into the water. There's even a little holder for your *chota peg*. A pernicious little doubt: How many others have been here before me? No, that is his kind of thinking. You are away from that. Safe. Invisible. Immersed. Down in Sisganj Road the traffic unravels. Overhead the dark silhouettes of the scavenging kites and, higher above, the security robots, expand and merge their black wings as Esha drifts into sleep.

'I thought I told you to stay away from the windows.'

Esha wakes with a start, instinctively covers her breasts. The jets have cut out and the water is long-still, perfectly transparent. Thacker is blue-chinned, baggy-eyed and sagging in his rumpled gritty suit.

'I'm sorry. It was just, I'm so glad, to be away… you know?'

A bone-weary nod. He fetches himself a *chota peg*, rests it on the arm of his sofa and then very slowly, very deliberately, as if every joint were rusted, undresses.

'Security has been compromised on every level. In any other circumstances it would constitute an i-war attack on the nation.' The body he reveals is not a dancer's body; Thacker runs a little to upper body fat, muscles slack, incipient man-tits, hair on the belly hair on the back hair on the shoulders. But it is a body, it is real. 'The Bharati government has disavowed the action and waived aeai Rao's diplomatic immunity.'

He crosses to the pool and restarts the jets. Gin and tonic in hand, he slips into the water with a bone-deep, skin-sensual sigh.

'What does that mean?' Esha asks.

'You husband is now a rogue aeai.'

'What will you do?'

'There is only one course of action permitted to us. We will excommunicate him.'

Esha shivers in the caressing bubbles. She presses herself against Thacker. She feels his man-body move against her. He is flesh. He is not hollow. Kilometres above the urban stain of Delhi, aeaicraft turn and seek.

* * *

The warnings stay in place the next morning. Palmer, home entertainment system, com channels. Yes, and balcony, even for the spa.

'If you need me, this palmer is Department-secure. He won't be able to reach you on this.' Thacker sets the glove and 'hoek on the bed. Cocooned in silk sheets, Esha pulls the glove on, tucks the 'hoek behind her ear.

'You wear that in bed?'

'I'm used to it.'

Varanasi silk sheets and Kama Sutra prints. Not what one would expect of a Krishna Cop. She watches Thacker dress for an excommunication. It's the same as for any job—ironed white shirt, tie, handmade black shoes—never brown in town—well polished. Eternal riff of bad aftershave. The difference: the leather holster slung under the arm and the weapon slipped so easily inside it.

'What's that for?'

'Killing aeais,' he says simply.

A kiss and he is gone. Esha scrambles into his cricket pullover, a waif in baggy white that comes down to her knees, and dashes to the forbidden balcony. If she cranes over, she can see the street door. There he is, stepping out, waiting at the kerb. His car is late, the road is thronged, the din of engines, car horns and *phatphat* klaxons has been constant since dawn. She watches him wait, enjoying the empowerment of invisibility. *I can see you. How do they ever play sport in these things?* she asks herself, skin under cricket pullover hot and sticky. It's already thirty degrees, according to the weather ticker across the foot of the video-silk shuttering over the open face of the new-built across the street. High of thirty-eight. Probability of precipitation: zero. The screen loops *Town and Country* for those devotees who must have their *soapi*, subtitles scrolling above the news feed.

Hello Esha, Ved Prakash says, turning to look at her.

The thick cricket pullover is no longer enough to keep out the ice.

Now Begum Vora *namastes* to her and says, *I know where you are, I know what you did.*

Ritu Parzaaz sits down on her sofa, pours *chai* and says, *What I need you to understand is, it worked both ways. That 'ware they put in your palmer, it wasn't clever enough.*

Mouth working wordlessly; knees, thighs weak with *basti* girl superstitious fear, Esha shakes her palmer-gloved hand in the air but she can't find the *mudras,* can't dance the codes right. *Call call call call.*

The scene cuts to son Govind at his racing stable, stroking the neck of his thoroughbred über-star Star of Agra. *As they spied on me, I spied on them.*

Dr. Chatterji in his doctor's office. *So in the end we betrayed each other.*

The call has to go through Department security authorisation and crypt.

Dr. Chatterji's patient, a man in black with his back to the camera, turns. Smiles. It's A.J. Rao. *After all, what diplomat is not a spy?*

Then she sees the flash of white over the rooftops. Of course. Of course. He's been keeping her distracted, like a true *soapi* should. Esha flies to the railing to cry a warning but the machine is tunnelling down the street just under power-line height, wings morphed back, engines throttled up: an aeai traffic monitor drone.

'Thacker! Thacker!'

One voice in the thousands. And it is not hers that he hears and turns towards. Everyone can hear the footsteps of his own death. Alone in the hurrying
street, he sees the drone pile out of the sky. At three hundred kilometres per
hour it takes Inspector Thacker of the Department of Artificial Intelligence
registration and licensing to pieces.

The drone, deflected, ricochets into a bus, a car, a truck, a *phatphat,* strewing
plastic shards, gobs of burning fuel and its small intelligence across Sisganj
Road. The upper half of Thacker's body cartwheels through the air to slam
into a hot *samosa* stand.

The jealousy and wrath of djinns.

Esha on her balcony is frozen. *Town and Country* is frozen. The street is frozen,
as if on the tipping point of a precipice. Then it drops into hysteria. Pedestrians
flee; cycle-rickshaw drivers dismount and try to run their vehicles away; drivers
and passengers abandon cars, taxis, *phatphats;* scooters try to navigate through
the panic; buses and trucks are stalled, hemmed in by people.

And still Esha Rathore is frozen to the balcony rail. Soap. This is all soap.
Things like this cannot happen. Not in the Sisganj Road, not in Delhi, not on
a Tuesday morning. It's all computer-generated illusion. It has always been
illusion.

Then her palmer calls. She stares at her hand in numb incomprehension. The
Department. There is something she should do. Yes. She lifts it in a *mudra*—a
dancer's gesture—to take the call. In the same instant, as if summoned, the
sky fills with gods. They are vast as clouds, towering up behind the apartment
blocks of Sisganj Road like thunderstorms; Ganesh on his rat *vahana* with his
broken tusk and pen, no benignity in his face; Siva, rising high over all, dancing
in his revolving wheel of flames, foot raised in the instant before destruction;
Hanuman with his mace and mountain fluttering between the tower blocks;
Kali, skull-jewelled, red tongue dripping venom, scimitars raised, bestriding
Sisganj Road, feet planted on the rooftops.

In that street, the people mill. *They can't see this,* Esha comprehends. *Only
me, only me.* It is the revenge of the Krishna Cops. Kali raises her scimitars
high. Lightning arcs between their tips. She stabs them down into the screen-
frozen *Town and Country.* Esha cries out, momentarily blinded as the Krishna
Cops hunter-killers track down and excommunicate rogue aeai A.J. Rao. And
then they are gone. No gods. The sky is just the sky. The video-silk hoarding
is blank, dead.

A vast, godlike roar above her. Esha ducks—now the people in the street
are looking at her. All the eyes, all the attention she ever wanted. A tilt-jet in
Awadhi air-force chameleo-flage slides over the roof and turns in the air over
the street, swivelling engine ducts and unfolding wing-tip wheels for landing.
It turns its insect head to Esha. In the cockpit is a faceless pilot in a HUD vi-
sor. Beside her a woman in a business suit, gesturing for Esha to answer a call.

Thacker's partner. She remembers now.

The jealousy and wrath and djinns.

'Mrs. Rathore, it's Inspector Kaur.' She can barely hear her over the scream of ducted fans 'Come downstairs to the front of the building. You're safe now. The aeai has been excommunicated.'

Excommunicated.

'Thacker…'

'Just come downstairs, Mrs. Rathore. You are safe now, the threat is over.'

The tilt-jet sinks beneath her. As she turns from the rail, Esha feels a sudden, warm touch on her face. Jet-swirl, or maybe just a djinn, passing unresting, unhasting, and silent as light.

* * *

The Krishna Cops sent us as far from the wrath and caprice of the aeais as they could, to Leh under the breath of the Himalaya. I say *us*, for I existed; a knot of four cells inside my mother's womb.

My mother bought a catering business. She was in demand for weddings and *shaadis*. We might have escaped the aeais and the chaos following Awadh's signing the Hamilton Acts, but the Indian male's desperation to find a woman to marry endures forever. I remember that for favoured clients—those who had tipped well, or treated her as something more than a paid contractor, or remembered her face from the *chati* mags—she would slip off her shoes and dance *Radha and Krishna*. I loved to see her do it and when I slipped away to the temple of Lord Ram, I would try to copy the steps among the pillars of the *mandapa*. I remember the brahmins would smile and give me money.

The dam was built and the water war came and was over in a month. The aeais, persecuted on all sides, fled to Bharat where the massive popularity of *Town and Country* gave them protection, but even there they were not safe: humans and aeais, like humans and *djinni*, were too different creations and in the end they left Awadh for another place that I do not understand, a world of their own where they are safe and no one can harm them.

And that is all there is to tell in the story of the woman who married a djinn. If it does not have the happy-ever-after ending of Western fairytales and Bollywood musicals, it has a happy-*enough* ending. This spring I turn twelve and shall head off on the bus to Delhi to join the *gharana* there. My mother fought this with all her will and strength—for her Delhi would always be the city of djinns, haunted and stained with blood—but when the temple brahmins brought her to see me dance, her opposition melted. By now she was a successful businesswoman, putting on weight, getting stiff in the knees from the dreadful winters, refusing marriage offers on a weekly basis, and in the end she could not deny the gift that had passed to me. And I am curious to see those streets and parks where her story and mine took place, the Red Fort and the sad decay of the Shalimar Gardens. I want to feel the heat of the djinns in the crowded *galis* behind the Jama Masjid, in the dervishes of litter along Chandni Chowk, in the starlings swirling above Connaught Circus. Leh is a Buddhist town, filled with third-generation Tibetan exiles—Little Tibet, they call it—and they have their own gods and demons. From the old Moslem djinn-finder I have learned some of their lore and mysteries but I think my truest knowledge comes when I am alone in the Ram temple, after I have danced, before the priests close the *garbagriha* and put the god to bed. On still nights when the spring turns to summer or after the monsoon, I hear a voice. It calls my name. Always I suppose it comes from the *japa*-softs, the little low-level aeais that mutter our prayers eternally to the gods, but it seems to emanate from everywhere and nowhere, from another world, another universe entirely. It says, *the creatures of word and fire are different from the creatures of clay and water but one thing is true: love endures.* Then as I turn to leave, I feel a touch on my cheek, a passing breeze, the warm sweet breath of djinns.

PUBLICATION HISTORY

"How to Talk to Girls at Parties", by Neil Gaiman. © 2006 Neil Gaiman. Originally published in *Fragile Things: Short Fictions and Wonders* (William Morrow). Reprinted by permission of the author.

"El Regalo", by Peter S. Beagle. © 2006 Peter S. Beagle. Originally published in *The Line Between* (Tachyon Publications). Reprinted by permission of the author.

"I, Row-Boat", by Cory Doctorow. © 2006 Cory Doctorow. Originally published in *Flurb: A Webzine of Astonishing Tales*, Issue #1, Fall 2006. Reprinted by permission of the author.

"In the House of the Seven Librarians", by Ellen Klages. © 2006 Ellen Klages. Originally published in *Firebirds Rising* (Firebird/Penguin), Sharyn November ed. Reprinted by permission of the author.

"Another Word for Map Is Faith", by Christopher Rowe. © 2006 Christopher Rowe. Originally published in *The Magazine of Fantasy and Science Fiction*, August 2006 . Reprinted by permission of the author.

"Under Hell, Over Heaven", by Margo Lanagan. © 2006 Margo Lanagan. Originally published in *Red Spikes* (Allen & Unwin Australia). Reprinted by permission of the author.

"Incarnation Day", by Walter Jon Williams. © 2006 Walter Jon Williams. Originally published in *Escape from Earth* (SFBC), Jack Dann & Gardner Dozois eds. Reprinted by permission of the author.

"The Night Whiskey", by Jeffrey Ford. © 2006 Jeffrey Ford. Originally published in *Salon Fantastique* (Thunders Mouth), Ellen Datlow & Terri Windling eds. Reprinted by permission of the author.

"A Siege of Cranes", by Benjamin Rosenbaum. © 2006 Benjamin Rosenbaum. Originally published in *Twenty Epics* (All-Star Stories), David Moles & Susan Marie Groppi eds. Reprinted by permission of the author.

"Halfway House", by Frances Hardinge. © 2006 Frances Hardinge. Originally published in *Alchemy 3*. Reprinted by permission of the author.

"The Bible Repairman", by Tim Powers. © 2006 Tim Powers. Originally published in *The Bible Repairman* (Subterranean Press). Reprinted by permission of the author.

"Yellow Card Man", by Paolo Bacigalupi. © 2006 Paolo Bacigalupi. Originally published in *Asimov's Science Fiction*, December 2006. Reprinted by permission of the author.

"Pol Pot's Beautiful Daughter (Fantasy)", by Geoff Ryman. © 2006 Geoff Ryman. Originally published in *The Magazine of Fantasy and Science Fiction*, October/November 2006. Reprinted by permission of the author.

"The American Dead", by Jay Lake. © 2006 Jay Lake. Originally published in *Interzone* 203, March/April 2006. Reprinted by permission of the author.

"The Cartesian Theater", by Robert Charles Wilson. © 2006 Robert Charles Wilson. Originally published in *Futureshocks* (Penguin Roc), Lou Anders ed. Reprinted by permission of the author.

"Journey into the Kingdom", by M. Rickert. © 2006 M. Rickert. Originally published in *The Magazine of Fantasy and Science Fiction*, May 2006. Reprinted by permission of the author.

"Eight Episodes", by Robert Reed. © 2006 Robert Reed. Originally published in *Asimov's Science Fiction*, June 2006. Reprinted by permission of the author.

"The Wizards of Perfil", by Kelly Link. © 2006 Kelly Link. Originally published in *Firebirds Rising* (Firebird/Penguin), Sharyn November ed. Reprinted by permission of the author.

"The Saffron Gatherers", by Elizabeth Hand. © 2006 Elizabeth Hand. Originally published in *Saffron and Brimstone: Strange Stories* (M Press). Reprinted by permission of the author.

"D.A.", by Connie Willis. © 2006 Connie Willis. Originally published in *Space Cadets* (SciFi Inc), Mike Resnick ed. Reprinted by permission of the author.

"Femaville 29", by Paul Di Filippo. © 2006 Paul Di Filippo. Originally published in *Salon Fantastique* (Thunders Mouth), Ellen Datlow & Terri Windling eds. Reprinted by permission of the author.

"Sob in the Silence", by Gene Wolfe. © 2006 Gene Wolfe. Originally published in *Strange Birds* (Dreamhaven). Reprinted by permission of the author.

"The House Beyond Your Sky", by Benjamin Rosenbaum. © 2006 Benjamin Rosenbaum. Originally published in *Strange Horizons*, 4 September 2006. Reprinted by permission of the author.

"The Djinn's Wife", by Ian McDonald. © 2006 Ian McDonald. Originally published in *Asimov's Science Fiction*, July 2006. Reprinted by permission of the author.

Night Shade Books Is an Independent Publisher of Quality SF, Fantasy and Horror

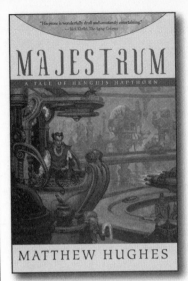

ISBN 978-1-59780-061-7
Hardcover; $24.95

Sherlock Holmes meets Jack Vance's Dying Earth in *Majestrum*. The scientific method and a well-calibrated mind have long served freelance discriminator Henghis Hapthorn, allowing him to investigate and solve the problems of the wealthy and powerful aristocracy of Old Earth, and securing him a reputation for brilliance across The Spray and throughout the Ten Thousand Worlds. But the universe is shifting, cycling away from logic and reason and ushering in a new age of sympathetic association, better known as magic. This change is evidenced by the unexplained transformation of Henghis Hapthorn's personal electronic integrator into a small fruit-eating creature. Odder still, Hapthorn's personality has been cleaved into two distinct beings sharing one body: himself, familiar and appropriate to the rational old order; and the other, strange, intuitive, and obsessed with an arcane and untranslated tome, appropriate to the new.

ISBN 978-1-59780-062-4
Tradepaper $14.95

Years ago, the last desperate hopes of Earth were crushed as corporate Orbital Blocs ruling from on high devastated the planet's face. Today, the autocratic Orbitals indulge in decadent luxury far above the mudboys, dirtgirls, zonedancers, and buttonheads who live out violent lives of electronic distraction and dependence amid the flooded, ruined cities and teeming slums of a balkanized America.

But there are heroes: those who would stand against the hegemony of the Orbital powers. From Walter Jon Williams comes Hardwired, the hard-hitting, seminal classic that feels as prescient today as when it was first published. Like a steel-guitar-fueled Damnation Alley, as directed by Sam Peckinpah, Hardwired demonstrates how Williams's singular vision helped define the cyberpunk genre.

Find these Night Shade titles and many others online at http://www.nightshadebooks.com or wherever books are sold.

Night Shade Books Is an Independent Publisher of Quality SF, Fantasy and Horror

Night Shade Books Is an Independent Publisher of Quality SF, Fantasy and Horror

ISBN 978-1-59780-055-6
Hardcover; $35.00

ISBN 978-1-59780-080-8
Hardcover $35.00

Before The Black Company... before The Garrett Files... Before The Instrumentalities of the Night... There was The Dread Empire. Glen Cook's first foray in fantasy world building was the enormously influential Dread Empire series. This series has been incredibly hard to find, and has never had a hardcover release, until now. Night Shade Books is proud to publishing three omnibus volumes that cover the 3 main sub-series of the Dread Empire, with a fourth volume of Dread Empire short fiction to follow.

The first volume in this series, *A Cruel Wind*, collects the first three Dread Empire novels: *A Shadow of All Night's Falling*, *October's Baby* and *All Darkness Met*, and contains an introduction by Jeff VanderMeer.

The second volume, *A Fotress in Shadow* collects the two volumes that make up the prequel series to The Dread Empire. *The Fire in His Hands* and *With Mercy Towards None* were written and published after the first three books, but the war in the east chronicled herein precede the events in *A Cruel Wind*. This second volume features an introduction by Steven Erikson

Find these Night Shade titles and many others online at http://www.nightshadebooks.com or wherever books are sold.

Night Shade Books Is an Independent Publisher of Quality SF, Fantasy and Horror

ISBN 978-1-59780-044-0
Trade Paper; $14.95

Seconded to a military-religious order he's barely heard of—part of the baroque hierarchy of the Mercatoria, the latest galactic hegemony—Fassin Taak has to travel again amongst the Dwellers. He is in search of a secret hidden for half a billion years.

But with each day that passes a war draws closer—a war that threatens to overwhelm everything and everyone he's ever known. As complex, turbulent, flamboyant and spectacular as the gas giant on which it is set, the new science fiction novel from Iain M. Banks is space opera on a truly epic scale.

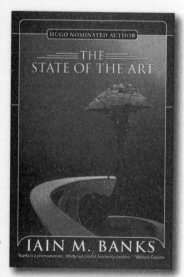

ISBN 978-1-59780-074-7
Trade Paper; $14.95

The State of the Art is the first collection from the author of *Look to Windward* and *The Algebraist*. The title story is a Culture novella that features characters from other Banks novels, but is set on Earth in 1977. An additional Culture story is included in this collection, as well as several other non-Culture stories that demonstrate Banks' tremendous range and skill.

This U.S. edition of *The State of the Art* Contains the essay "A Few Notes On the Culture" which is not part of the british edition of this collection, and has not been previously collected.

Find these Night Shade titles and many others online at http://www.nightshadebooks.com or wherever books are sold.

5519

蛇警探